Praise for *As Fierce as Steel*:

"*As Fierce as Steel* is quite an admirable work of writing for a first-time novelist, and it is with great eagerness I anticipate its sequel, *The Worth of Gold*. Highly recommended for fans of the genre." – **James M. Fisher,** *The Miramichi Reader*

"If you're a fan of epic stories with mythology, politics, interesting characters, and an imaginative world, then the Gold and Steel Saga should be on your reading list." – **Ali House, author of** *The Six Elemental*

Advance praise for *The Worth of Gold*:

"A beautiful body of intricate world-building full of political intrigue and valour. The twists and turns keep you on the edge and wondering what will happen next. The imagery in this sequel is just as vivid as the first book. Author Chris Walsh skillfully paints his vast world in not just imagination, but also intellectually, as he dives into the bowels of politics. Chris Walsh brings his characters to life, making you catch all the feels! – **S.S. Yasumi, author of** *Game. Set. Match!*

Works by Christopher Walsh

The Gold & Steel Saga
Vol. I: *As Fierce as Steel* (2016)
Vol. II: *The Worth of Gold* (2020)
Vol. III: *The Strength of Steel* (TBA)

Short Works from the world of Gold & Steel
Stealing Back Freedom (2016)
In Defense of Our Home Pt. 1 (2017)
The City That Hid From Time Itself (2017)
In Defense of Our Home Pt. 2 (2018)
In Dangerous Company Pt. 1 (2019)

THE WORTH OF GOLD

THE GOLD & STEEL SAGA
VOL. II

BY
CHRISTOPHER WALSH

This is for my father, Brendan, and my stepmother, Mary-Alice
Your support, patience, and generosity
allowed me to grow to my fullest potential

Frozen Wastes
Northern Kingdom of Gildriad
Kingdom City
Tropuri
Prepince
Karmourd Gates
Beris
Berisport
Midlands Republic of Gildriad
Gallick Isles
Cabathos
Wallis
Barkis Island
The Crescent Isles
Southern Knightdom of Gildriad
Paladel
Garja
Doba
Vellick
Azarai
Johnah
Manobius
Tower of Viktor

Gondarrius
Snowy Lands
Elven Forest
Drake
Kushika City
Mount Graelin
Calimfaire
Shatoya
Tusker's Cove
Fuwachita City
Axel's Islands
Portsward
Atrebell
Daol Bay
Hercalest
Biddenhurst
Daol Forest
Western Realm
Eastern Realm
Pelican Harbour
Illiastra
Weicaster Bay
Farmourd
Fort Layn
Aquas Bay
Southlands
Phaleàyna
The Warrens
The Storming Sea

PROLOGUE
THE KNIFE

You best beware,
The man who dare
To harm his own wife
For when she comes
And her work is done
Your blood be upon the Knife

She did not know who had written the macabre little poem that had so encapsulated her recent activities, but in truth, it likely did not matter too much.

Regardless of the identity of the author, the poem had spread throughout Hercalest, moving from person to person like a plague that jumped from mouth to ear faster than could be contained. It made her job far more difficult than it had ever been, putting focus and attention into the shadows from whence she worked. No longer was she an unknown entity, spoken of in whispers without a name or identifying traits. Instead, she had crossed into the tangible, a poltergeist that had suddenly taken on a visible form, left exposed to the naked eye. All of that on account of the viral nature of a little rhyme. Granted, that catchy verse had propelled what were only modestly newsworthy events into a dramatic narrative unfolding on the stage of real life.

At first, she had thought about moving on to another location, or retiring from the cause altogether. After all, people across the city were gossiping about the actions of a woman known as the Knife and debated, and even bet coin, on when and where she would next strike. All of this had served only to put those who would be her targets on edge. The city watch, in their own turn, had further taken to shining lanterns into the darkness from which she once worked without disturbance. That poem, and the infamy it brought with it, had made her role as a liberator for the Women's Road Network difficult and it was a job fraught with danger enough as it was.

The primary task of a liberator was, as the name suggested, to liberate, and what she liberated were people. Specifically, she extracted women and children directly from the abusers they lived with. Despite the peril, it was one of the most sought after positions among the members of the Women's Road, and one that she earned through studious dedication to her craft.

The management of the Women's Road had assigned her to be the Liberator of the Nemeth District, the common name on what was formally known as the Southwest District of Hercalest. The area was cluttered with factories and warehouses and as a result, it was one of the dirtier locales within city limits. The population living in the shadows of these businesses consisted mostly of the poor, underpaid employees that worked within. After dark, things typically grew worse again, as the dimly lit streets attracted the denizens of the city's scummy underbelly. That seedy atmosphere, and the people that walked through the sooty streets, made the Nemeth District a frightening place to be for the faint of heart at night.

Yet, after a year of living and operating out of the district, she considered Nemeth to be almost a home.

A home I might soon be driven from, she thought almost sadly.

To add to her woes, the shadowy figure she presented herself as was now labelled a murderess. The unwanted title had been foisted upon her due to three deaths of similar nature that had occurred in close chronological and geographical proximity to one another. To that end, she was in truth responsible for only two of those kills. The third was a sloppy facsimile, albeit one that borrowed just enough detail from her actual deeds to pass for it in the opinion of the people's court.

The two she had slain were both men, and they were not her first. She was not proud of that fact, as it was an avoided practice amongst her fellow liberators. Yet, there were instances when there was no other recourse. If her own life or the lives of people she was extracting were in immediate danger, at the hands of the abuser or anyone else, it fell to the liberator to be their last defence.

During her training upon the island refuge of Phaleayna, she had been told by an old warrior named Bansam that any battle, no matter how many were involved or how many sides there was, always came down to a series of variables and invariables. Identifying those variables and learning to do so quickly, he posited, was tantamount to any fighter. Whether they went on to become members of the Thieves, the Women's Road, Guardians of the Island, or members of Bansam's own unit, the trainees of Phaleayna were always taught to steer the variables toward the preservation of life. Despite her diligent efforts to follow this training, she had learned from both Bansam and personal experience that the invariables could at times make even the best of intentions turn to dust in her hands.

The house where the extraction was taking place this night was uphill from her hideaway, which made the travelling difficult for one who primarily got about by rooftop. The one redeeming quality of her route was that the homes here were all connected to one another, and most had ladders in place for use by the chimney sweeps. Starting with the lowest point, each ladder was built into the wall of the house that sat further up the incline from the one adjoining it. In her previous ventures in this particular neighbourhood, she knew some ladders were either missing or were in such a state of disrepair that using them was a safety risk.

It's still preferable to walking through the streets, she reminded herself.

The patrolling guards alone made that dangerous for an unescorted woman at night. Being approached by the patrols without a man, or a signed and dated letter from a guardian male meant an immediate arrest and a night in the district's jail. With no guardian to claim her, the next stop would almost certainly be Biddenhurst, the prison city. From there, it would either be the auction block to be sold as a slave, a life of imprisonment, or execution. The unclaimed women of Illiastra were afforded little mercy in their own country.

Then there were the usual ne'er-do-wells that emerged after dark and the Triarchy religion's own police force comprised of lumbering brutes known as the Burgundy Order roaming the roads as well. Given all of that, she was far more willing to take her chances with broken and rickety ladders.

I also have to contend with what waits for me at my destination.

From the information she had been given by the Women's Road contractor for Hercalest's southern regions, the extraction target for this particular job was a woman in a childless marriage. As usual, the husband was the abuser. According to the wife, her husband was short in stature, but thick in the arms and chest with muscle from spending long hours shovelling coal into a furnace for the factory that employed him. His height had long been a point of contention and he had endured taunting and teasing for it from all who knew him. His wife, who was even shorter than he, had become the victim of the rage he bore for his tormentors. The wife stated that the outbursts were solely verbal at first, and she had endured in silence. However, with enough time and rye whiskey, his verbal tirades had manifested into physical violence. To add to the wife's testament to those facts, the contractor's own attestation stated that the woman's eyes showed bruising and she was missing several teeth. Furthermore, she was timid and terrified, and the contractor was certain she would ultimately refuse rescue at the last possible moment, which was common to both a saddening and frustrating degree.

The grade of the hill began to taper off as the Knife climbed, and the roofs here required only a short jump to clear from lower to higher. After five houses, the Liberator came to a stop and lowered herself to a sitting position, turning her attention to the house situated directly across the back alley. It had two storeys and a sloping roof, with a pair of windows poking out in separate dormers. Both were closed, as per the instructions given to the target, though one would soon be the Liberator's means of egress into the home.

While she waited for the signal from the target, she went through her inventory with as little detectable motion as possible. Cotton trousers, soft-soled boots, and a silk fencing shirt were her attire, all of it dyed black and worn beneath a matching cloak of plain wool. Her hands were gloved in a mixture of cotton and leather that was worn so close to the skin that it felt like a second layer. Over her mouth and nose was a bandanna tied tightly to help conceal her identity. To her right hip, she could feel her small satchel of supplies hanging from a thin belt and on the left was the weapon to which her recently earned sobriquet derived. It was composed of good quality steel, but unremarkable in its make, with a simple hilt wrapped in dark brown leather and a short, narrow crossguard. It mattered not to her that it was far from the prettiest knife ever made. Rather, it was of more importance that the knife was sharp enough to do the job and on that account, she kept the blade in superb condition.

From the upper floor window of the house across the alley, the Liberator espied a tiny candle being lit. She took to counting seconds until three minutes went by, letting the numbers roll over slowly in her head. With no disturbance of either the candle or its flame in that time, she stood up, ensured that the alley below was clear, took a deep breath, and leapt across the gap toward the little light.

The landing was graceful and she felt certain that it would be nearly inaudible to the human ear, whether those ears were inside the home or out. In spite of her feelings on the matter, she remained perfectly still for what she felt was a full minute, listening for any sudden movements that might be attributed to someone reacting to her landing. Upon hearing nothing in that span of time, she stepped to the side of the illuminated window and flattened against the dormer wall. Her cloak was undone and stuffed into the corner behind her, as such loose clothing always proved to be a hindrance in close quarters. With one more deep breath, she was ready for what lay within and extended a hand outward to the window, tapping on the pane of glass with a single finger just twice.

Seconds passed, at least thirty by her count, before the candle disappeared and the window slid upward slowly, until a wooden prop was pushed into place by a small, bare hand from within.

"Where is he?" the Liberator asked the owner of the hand in a whisper.

There was a delay before a small voice stammered back. "Asleep in the next room... He's drunk... As I was told to make him."

"Well done, madam," she stated while sliding closer, so that she could see into the room for herself. "Stand back, I'm coming in."

A few gingerly taken steps later and the Liberator was inside the house and crouched just to the side of the window. The target was standing near, breathing rapidly, and from what she could tell with the limited light, dressed for the outdoor weather.

"You are ready to leave?" she asked the target, "Where are your things?"

"I... I don't have much to take, truth be told," the target responded. "Just a few coppers and articles of clothing, not counting what I am already wearing. I was told to travel lightly by the last man I spoke to."

The Liberator's first instinct was to nod, which was a wasted gesture in the darkness, and instead she gave a verbal answer. "Good. Take them to hand and climb out onto the roof. I shall keep watch while you do."

"Out there? What if I fall? Can we not use the door?" the target asked fretfully, her voice creeping just above a whisper.

"Yes, I assure you that you will not, and no," she responded quickly for all three questions in order of how they were asked, inflecting her own voice with a measure of urgency.

Without further queries, the target took a deep breath and approached the window, stopping to hike up a skirt, and revealing a pair of heeled boots worn beneath.

"Heels and a skirt?" the Liberator asked the target rhetorically with exasperation. "You were instructed to wear flat boots or shoes with trousers."

"My flat shoes are worn out so badly that my toes poke through," the woman explained fretfully. "Atop that, I don't own any trousers of my own. If my husband caught me taking his, we would not be talking right now. What choice do I have?"

There was no time to argue further and the target was talking louder by the sentence. "Fine," the Liberator said in relenting. "Hurry on and climb out there. We will deal with it when we are on the roof."

"Hullo? Who's here?" a new voice shouted in a drunken slur. "Opal, where are you? Who are you talking to at this ungodly hour?"

"That's my husband," the target stated with panic, still having not climbed onto the roof. "You're not going to kill him, are you?"

The Liberator pulled her knife from its sheath and fell further back into the shadows. "Not if I don't have to. Distract him for a moment."

The steps from Opal's husband sounded loudly on the creaking floorboards, increasing in volume until the door of the room swung open with a clatter and a bang on the opposite wall from the window.

There he stood, swaying in the doorframe. From the little she could see, he seemed as short as he was made out to be, and every bit as broad too. From the dim light that shone from the hallway, she could see that he was shirtless and shoeless and clad in naught but a pair of tan trousers.

"Opal, what are you doing in here?" he asked with a belch while sauntering toward his wife. "You're all dressed to go somewhere... What is going on?"

Even in near total darkness, the Liberator could see the target freeze with fear, her mouth open and no answer coming forth.

While the couple stared one another down, the Liberator slid behind the man, wrapping the arm with her empty hand around his head while laying the knife against his throat.

The drunk staggered and nearly lost his balance, staying aloft only by virtue of tripping forward into a tall bureau of drawers. The weight of him pulled her along for the ride, but her own stance was sure and her grip firm. She followed his momentum into the furniture and used it to carry him back into the middle of the room. She turned and extended a foot, tripping the man enough to send him down onto his knees.

"Get off me! Who are you?" he bellowed in bewilderment while swinging his arms backward in an effort to grab at her.

"Stay perfectly still, mate," she said in a low voice directly into his ear while avoiding his flailing. "You feel that knife against your neck, don't you? It's deathly sharp and will slice through flesh with the lightest touch. As long as you don't move, I won't have cause to use it."

At first, he groaned and resisted and she pressed the flat of the blade against his throat to give him a better feel for the steel. He gasped and went stiff, relinquishing control to her at last.

"Who are you?" the husband demanded to know, which the Liberator found ironic given that she held his life in her hands.

"Now why would I tell you that?" she gave back. "What I will tell you though, is what is going to happen here: if you do as you are told, you will take a little nap on the floor, and your wife and I will leave. When you wake up, you will not come looking for her ever again. This is inarguable and should you violate this order, you will almost certainly die. Do you understand?"

He grumbled and squirmed a little, but did not make any sudden moves apart from replying. "You're a woman. I can tell from your voice. I wager you're the Knife and you're gonna kill me like you did the other three. You sent for her Opal, didn't you? You bloody bitch, I put a roof over your stupid head, and this is how you repay me!"

"I don't want her to kill you, I just need to leave," Opal declared, the waver in her voice indicating that she was crying while doing so. "We can't keep doing this Vander, *I* can't keep doing this. I've begged you to stop, I gave my all to make this work but it's not enough and nothing ever seems to be. So yes, I did the last thing I could think of: I asked for help to get me out of here. I'm going Vander, and you're not stopping me."

"No!" Vander roared, trying to push back against the Liberator fruitlessly in the process. "You're not going anywhere, Opal! I'm your husband and I forbid it!"

The Liberator pressed the tip of the blade into the tender skin around the throat, pressing just enough that she drew a bead of blood, giving Vander pause long enough for her to speak. "If you move against my orders once more, you die. There will be no more warnings. Your wife is leaving and that's not a debate, that's a matter of fact. The only choice you have remaining to you is whether you live to see the sunrise."

There came a loud series of banging noises from the lower level of the house and before the Liberator could process what it was, a voice from without roared. "City Guards, open this door at once!"

"It sounds like someone heard all the shouting you two were doing and reported it to the guards," the Liberator said to the shattered spouses, before speaking solely to the wife. "Come over here and reach into the satchel hanging on my hip. You're looking for a balled handkerchief that will have a small vial inside."

The husband tensed up in her grip. "You're going to poison me!" he shouted in a panic.

"Just putting you to sleep, mate," she corrected him. "So long as you don't resist me, you'll live through this."

While the Liberator had been speaking to Vander, Opal had switched on a light and did as she was commanded, producing a purple swatch of linen within a few seconds. "I got it!" she declared, over the sound of more banging from the city guards outside. "What do I do with it?"

The Liberator forced Vander to the floor on his side, pinning one arm beneath his body while leaning a knee into the other. His head was held to the floorboards with one of her hands and the other kept the knife firmly to his neck. "The vial is filled with concentrated oil from dreamshade flowers. You're going to pour all of it onto the middle of the handkerchief and tie it around his mouth and nose."

"No!" Vander declared beneath her, trying drunkenly attempting to squirm his way from his position and failing to do so. "You're not going to do this to me!"

"Do it now, Opal we don't have any time to waste," the Liberator instructed sternly, making sure to use the target's name to establish some measure of trust and reassurance.

After a few precious seconds of further delay, which saw Opal staring wordlessly at the cloth and vial, she did as asked. The cork was popped off the glass tube, and its contents poured out onto the handkerchief.

The cheek of the husband that was pressed to the floor was lifted by the hair just high enough to allow Opal the chance to slide the handkerchief beneath, where it was tied tightly in place.

He stopped moving immediately and Opal looked to the Liberator hopefully, "that worked rather quickly, didn't it?"

"It didn't work yet. He's merely holding his breath and hoping we think as much," the Liberator explained while sheathing her knife and sliding her now empty hand over Vander's mouth and nose, where she clamped down tightly. "He seems to think he's clever, but every moron that has necessitated the use of dreamshade on them inevitably attempts the same ruse."

For a scant few seconds, the quarry stayed motionless, likely hoping that the Liberator might fall for the act. With the option to breathe suddenly taken away from him though, he grew panicked and began writhing beneath her. She felt his resistance intensify, his unpinned arm and both legs thrashing uselessly, and when it reached a fever pitch, the Liberator pulled her hand away from his lips and nostrils. The sound of the husband sucking air through the wet handkerchief was the Liberator's reward and she looked down just in time to see his eyes roll backward.

"Now he's unconscious," she explained to Opal. "Normally, on a sober person in a regular breathing pattern, the dreamshade can take ten to fifteen minutes to work properly. Alcohol works wonders to speed the process up, but so does the rapid breaths of say, a person who believed they were suffocating. As I said before, they all try to fool me by pretending to be out like a snuffed candle, but it is they who fool themselves."

The banging and shouting of the guards had not ceased while the Liberator was putting Vander to sleep, rather she had ignored it as background noise. Suspiciously enough, it stopped as she and Opal got to their feet and left the man to his impromptu nap.

The Liberator knew what was to come next and turned to Opal to tell her as much. "The guards are about to warn us that they are going to knock down your door, then there will be a loud crash. Close the door to the room, get the light, and then climb out the window and onto the roof."

"Where will you be? You're not going to try to fight the guards, are you?" Opal asked concernedly while following through with the Liberator's orders.

"You need not worry, I'll be right behind you," she said calmly, laying her hands gently on Opal's shoulders as she did. "As the door falls in, I'll shut the window so the noise of it will be unheard beneath their ruckus. That should give us all the cover we need so that we can get away without them being any the wiser of where we went."

The warning was shouted by the guards as Opal scrambled her way out through the window and the Liberator followed quickly after. Once safely outside, the Liberator removed the prop from the window and held it until she heard the main door being smashed from its frame on the first floor.

She gathered her black cloak from where it had been left and held it out to Opal. "Here, put this on, it will help you to blend in with the darkness."

"Won't you be cold without it?" Opal queried while accepting and donning the garment.

The Liberator shook her head assuredly. "I spent my youth in constant view of the North Casparian Sea. Your eastern autumns chill me not."

With the cloak wrapped about her, the woman named Opal attempted to make her first step, but the Liberator laid a hand gently on her shoulder to stop her. "What are you doing?"

"We're leaving, are we not?" Opal asked, nonplussed.

"Not in those boots," the Liberator stated, before explaining further. "We're going to be walking the rooftops for quite a span and those high heels are begging to twist your ankle or worse. Take them off, please."

Opal's face was one of utter incredulity in that moment and she protested. "It's freezing cold out here and you expect me to walk in stocking feet on the cold tiles?"

The Liberator was stern in her demand but tried in earnest to keep her tone soft. "Aye, we have little other choice. I could carry you, but it would make the going slow and we don't exactly have time to spare. Remove those boots so we can get out of here before the guards think to look on the roof for us."

There was grumbling from Opal but no further protest and soon they got underway, sock footed though Opal was. The journey was not without its perils, but the Liberator guided Opal through each obstacle that presented itself. There was no commotion behind them and things were quiet below, indicating that there were no guards in pursuit.

We might have eluded them, at least for now, the Liberator said to herself with cautious optimism.

The two kept moving without rest, making their way in the same direction that the Liberator had arrived by slowly climbing down each roof in turn, taking Opal's boots to hand as they did. They came to a stop as the buildings gave way to a main thoroughfare street. At this hour, it was usually empty and that night did not disappoint. Regardless, the Liberator looked as long and as far as the darkness would allow, checking for any signs of life that she might find. When she was content that there were no patrols, of either guards or the Burgundy Order, she turned to Opal. "We will climb down into the alley and you can put your boots back on your feet. From there we walk on flat ground, but I do hope you can keep up in those, for we must move quickly."

"You have no worries, ma'am. I will keep up just fine," Opal answered affirmatively.

The concern for the Liberator was not whether Opal could keep up, but whether they might be seen. City guardsmen and Triarchist brute squads were not the only dangers lurking in Hercalest after dark. "Keep the hood of that cloak raised, your head down, and follow my lead. We need to be nearly invisible at best and if all else fails, at least be inconspicuous. Do you understand?"

"All too well," Opal nodded in agreement. "I'm ready to go when you are."

The Liberator found them a ladder to use and they descended into a cluttered, damp alleyway. Once on the streets they strode casually, and the Liberator took on a gait that might pass for that of a man. Opal stuck close to her side with her head down and covered. As far as could be discerned, the pair seemed to be unnoticed, but the Liberator had done this far too many times to allow herself to be lulled into any sense of certainty.

Residential gave way to commercial and they were soon walking before the large, unlit windows of the shops and businesses of the middle-class area just inside the Galdweir District. The Liberator led them into the nearest alley and kept them walking through it until the shops were all behind them. Ahead there lay the looming smoke stacks and tall brick buildings of what could only be the Nemeth district. Specifically, they were walking through the industrial corridor, home to the factories, warehouses, and the coal plant that powered the whole city and the nearby outskirts.

"I know this area. This is near to where my husband works. What are we doing here?" Opal inquired in a whisper, her steps slowing to a shuffle.

"He's not working right now, dearie," the Liberator reminded her. "Besides, what better place to hide if not right under his nose?"

That drew a shocked response from Opal. "You mean to stash me away around here?"

"For a few days, aye," the Liberator confirmed in a soft voice. "But don't worry, for the accommodations are both cosy and safe. You will be more than fine. Until we are ready to take you to Phaleayna, my people will be checking in with you every day and will make sure you want for nothing."

"But my husband-"

"Won't find you," the Liberator cut her off with a voice that was as calm as it was certain.

Opal said nothing further and the two continued on, their walk coming to a stop just outside of a particular factory emblazoned with a painted logo that read *Helmsley Steel* in big, bold lettering.

"In here?" Opal queried in an unsure tone.

"Aye, but we're not going through the front door. Follow me," the Liberator both affirmed and instructed.

She ushered Opal around the corner of the building and onto a narrow avenue shared by Helmsley's and the business next door. There, the Liberator found a sewer grate and slid it off to one side until the way below was passable. "We go this way."

A glance to Opal's face saw her taking deep breaths and though the Liberator expected an argument, she instead was pleasantly surprised to hear Opal say, "I can do this. I can do this."

"I believe you can too, Opal," she added confidently. "It's not far and there is enough space to stand up the whole way throughout. You have come a long way, and I promise that you are almost there."

The sewer shaft had a short ladder that ended on a landing above the stone canals that ferried the wastewater of Hercalest. At the bottom and behind the ladder was a lantern hidden just out of sight, left there so that the way through could be lit. As was the nature of sewers, it smelled abhorrent, but as promised it was only a short walk through the tunnels to what was the sub-basement of Helmsley's factory.

Once within, the Liberator led Opal to an old stairway built into the exterior walls, which was entirely hidden from the workspaces and offices of the factory. The flights were long and winding, leading all the way from the sub-basement to the top floor of the building. The Liberator was given to understand that the original building plan called for the staircase to be a means for the maintenance staff to go from the lowest floor to the top floor without interruption. There had been an exit on every level, but as the stairs fell out of use, they were bricked over until there was only access from the sub-basement and their destination, the attic.

All but forgotten, the attic floor made for the ideal hideaway for the Women's Road. Given its geographical convenience, it was the prime choice for the Liberator to house those from her district while they waited to leave the city. It had been furnished sparsely, with only a small bed with a straw mattress, a greying wooden table and chair combination, and further essentials to see an emergency guest through the night.

Given the narrow parameters of the stairs and the sheer number of flights, it was the best that the Liberator could do. The Helmsley family, for their own part, were aware of the attic's usage and had been the ones to offer it up for such. She understood from her contractors that the family had personal reasons for doing so, and the agreement was held on the basis that if the illegal activity were discovered, the Helmsleys would deny all knowledge of it.

It was far from an ideal arrangement, but when working with the Women's Road, nothing ever was.

"This is where you will stay until we can relocate you to Phaleayna," the Liberator explained once they reached the attic. "I advise you not to leave unless in the escort of one of our people, as there will be a warrant for your arrest issued come morning and it will no longer be safe for you outside. Do you have any questions?"

While she had been briefing Opal, the Liberator had struck a match and lit an oil lamp on the table, casting the visible parts of her face in a glow as she did. As she raised her gaze from the light source they fell on Opal, who was staring directly back at her.

"So you really are a woman?" Opal asked in awe.

"Aye, but you knew that the moment you heard me outside your window," the Liberator confirmed. "However, I get the feeling that it still comes as a surprise to you."

Opal shrugged anxiously while taking in her temporary abode. "Some part of me wanted to believe as much, but in truth, I could not imagine. It's so unheard of for a woman to be doing what you do that it borders on the absurd, at least in civilised Illiastra and in this day and age. How would you even learn the sort of skills you have? Who would train you?"

It was the Liberator's turn to shrug then. "The same people who would train Lady Orangecloak and the Thieves in the wilds of the Southlands. You would be surprised at how many women there are north of the Varras with jobs and duties like mine and with the proper skillset to perform them."

"Do you know Orangecloak?" Opal queried, her eyes going wide at the mention of the name.

"Haven't had the pleasure, I'm afraid," she replied casually. "I arrived in Phaleayna well after Orangecloak last lived there on any permanent basis."

Opal let out a dreamy sigh and undid the black cloak she had borrowed. "I often wonder what it must be like to live as she does. I've been told from the time I was a small girl that men are the superior ones. They are the protectors, the fighters, and the leaders, and we are made only to serve them. *The God's Gift* scriptures seem to support that. The Patriarchs remind us from the pulpit that even among the gods, the goddess Iia was no match for Ios in the Deistic Wars and that is why we are subjugated in the first place.

"Yet, there is Orangecloak, and you too, defying what we were led to believe is the order of things and succeeding at it. How did you find the courage? What made you decide on this way of life?"

"I want you to imagine something for me," the Liberator requested in a gentle voice, directing Opal to the chair before the tiny table. She obliged, sitting down quickly and the Liberator sat on the edge of the table, so as to face her.

"Picture yourself cornered in an alley where a big, swarthy man has chased you," the Liberator began. "He's holding you there, with just a few centimetres between you and a sharp sword in his hand, and the man is promising that he is going to kill you with it. What do you do?"

Judging from the raised eyebrows, Opal seemed confused by the scenario presented to her. "What does this have to do with what I asked?"

"It will become clear momentarily, I assure you," she responded softly. "But to the question: what do you do with those last precious moments if death is all but guaranteed? The dying does not matter, whether slow and drawn out or quick and painless, it is coming and unavoidable. Knowing that, how do you choose to spend those last few seconds?"

"I suppose I would beg for him to spare me," Opal said, still apparently puzzled by it all.

"Sure, pleading with your captor is an option, as is merely accepting your fate and waiting to die," the Liberator said with a ponderous hum. "However, both of those options put control of your life out of your own hands and squarely in his, would you not agree?"

"I suppose so..." Opal granted, dubious though it was.

"What else could you do?" the Liberator put to the other woman.

"I could try to run," Opal suggested, finally sounding at least somewhat confident in an answer. "Maybe if I surprised him from the start and ran fast enough, I could escape and get away."

That was indeed a fair answer and she let Opal know as much. "Aye, running is another way, and it might be a successful means of saving yourself. For many, this might seem like the only means of self-preservation and I do not deny them their choice. For me, though, there is yet another option."

"What might that be?" Opal inquired, now engaged with what the Liberator was saying.

"I stand and I fight back," the Liberator declared with pride inflecting throughout her voice. "You and I and Orangecloak and all the other girls and women of Illiastra, even the highborns, we all have one thing in common: we are all the Cornered Woman, both individually and as a sum of all parts. We were born in those last seconds, with the sword already drawn before we ever came into the Known World. Not all of us are aware of the sword, but once we see it, we must each decide how we will respond to its presence.

"As I said just seconds ago, my choice was to fight," the Liberator continued. "Should I die in the effort, then so be it. At least I will die knowing that though I lost, I took my fate back into mine own hands and fought for my chance at existence beyond the point of the sword. Before me and after me, all women must decide for themselves how they will answer the question. As each of us makes our own choice as the Cornered Woman, we, as a collective, each become one part of the Cornered Woman in the story. Though many of us never realise it, we all play a role in how womankind responds to the captor.

"I find that most are pleading, and many more are lying down and waiting for the sword to be swung. Despite that, the good news is that the woman is not yet dead. For as long as there are those like you who are willing to run, or those like Orangecloak and I who are ready to fight, the Cornered Woman continues to breathe."

There was a deep inhale from Opal as she took in what she was being told. "It took a great deal of courage for me to become a runner. I could argue that it is far easier to surrender and beg or simply do nothing."

"Aye, it certainly is," the Liberator agreed readily. "Yet run you have from the depths of the darkened alley and down a long and often lonely road. I am proud of you, Opal. The more runners and fighters we have the better chance that the Cornered Woman has."

"Perhaps in time, I will return to face the captor and fight back," Opal stated hopefully.

"Oh, that is a great possibility Opal," the Liberator replied while standing and preparing to leave, her cloak in hand. She stopped before the door to wrap it about her shoulders and collect her lantern, turning back to face Opal when she was done. "For the Women's Road is ever long and you have but taken your first steps upon it."

1

MARIGOLD

On the sixty-third day of the autumn season, Marigold Tullivan, the Lady, and heir apparent to Daol Bay, rose from her warm and cosy bed and greeted the morning. At least, she assumed it was the morning. From within her guest chamber at the Parliamentary Manor of Illiastra's capital city of Atrebell, it was difficult to be certain. The lavish apartments given to the lords, ministers, and their families by the Lord Master Grenjin Howland were windowless and reliant on artificial lighting sources. The accommodations on that level of the manor were sandwiched between the servant corridors running along the outside walls, and the central hallway that was reserved for the guests. Should Marigold want to see the outside world, she would have to venture through the servant's door of her room and step into their narrow passageway to find it.

Though she was dressed in naught but a sleeveless, powder blue, silk nightshirt and her underclothes, Marigold was quite warm and comfortable in the bed of her heated guest quarters. Yet, she knew she must rise and so she stretched, yawned, and slid her legs from under the covers. A lamp beside the bed was switched on, giving her enough light to find her way to the lavatory so that she might begin her morning routine.

Marigold had barely slept, and her face showed the evidence of that as she looked upon it in the mirror. Despite her comfortable accommodations, there was a great deal weighing on the mind of Marigold that had prevented slumber from truly finding her. As she washed her face and brushed her hair, she did her utmost to divert her thoughts away from such things. Even if for but a few minutes, Marigold wanted to not dwell on what had been the most dramatic night she had ever witnessed.

Regardless of her intentions, Marigold was still reeling from everything that had happened in the span of just a few short hours over the course of a single night. It had started with a visit to her father, Marscal Tullivan, Warden Lord of the Western Realm of Illiastra, Lord of Fisheries and Oceans, and Minister of the Daol Bay region. His attendance and activity at the autumn Parliamentary Sessions had taken a toll on his already ailing health due to his consumption sickness. As a result, he had decided to skip the usual feast that concluded the events and get his rest for the train ride home the next day.

Delirious with pain, he had spoken to Marigold of events surrounding the deaths of her mother and baby brother over a decade prior. It had shocked both Marigold and their long-serving house steward, Oire Sellars, to hear these things, as Marscal had always been mum on the subject. Whether or not there was any truth to what he had said, there was no denying that her dying father was wracked with guilt over the untimely loss of Farren and Felixander. It was a matter that Marigold intended to look into further, once she was safely behind the walls of the Tullivan's own manor in Daol Bay.

Once her escort for the evening, the dashingly handsome Captain Freyard Archer of Fort Dornett, had arrived at her father's quarters, Marigold had endeavoured to put that out of her mind. As it were, Pyore Palomb, the twisted seventeen-year-old twin son of Eamon Palomb, Warden Lord of the Eastern Realm of Illiastra, forced Marigold to concern herself with more immediate matters. The boy who was arranged to be her husband had tried to embarrass Marigold before the entire Illiastran Parliament and their families at the feast. If not for his own father's ashamedness, Pyore may well have succeeded in that goal.

That was not his last play of the night though, and when Marigold had refused to kowtow to Pyore's will, he had tried to deliver a backhanded blow to her face.

Tryst Reine had intervened on that occasion, though, Marigold reflected. The speed with which his hand shot up and caught Pyore's wrist in mid-swing had been startling, not just to Marigold, but to everyone seated at the dinner table. Lord Eamon, Pyore's twin brother Eldridge, Lord Mackhol Taves, and even Lord Master Grenjin Howland himself had looked dumbstruck at the sight of Tryst's precise, catty reflexes and vice-like grip. Most of all though, was the look of steel in Tryst's bright, Gildraddi-green eyes. *I can only imagine how fierce he would be in a real battle,* Marigold noted to herself.

Imagining it was the only thing Marigold could do now, though. She and Oire had long been piecing together a plan to free Marigold of her marital bonds and the whole thing had revolved around wooing Tryst Reine. The famous mercenary, recognised internationally by the title of Master of Blades, was without doubt one of the most revered swordsman in the Known World. For four years he had served faithfully as the Lord Master's personal bodyguard and protector and during that time, Marigold had attempted to get close to the man.

Above his remarkable skillset, Marigold thought Tryst to be an honourable and attractive man of some thirty years and most importantly, he was a foreigner of modest birth. As a man who could legally hold no lands or political position in Illiastra and had no pre-existing wealth or titles, he could not usurp Marigold as a ruler. However, he could be her husband and the commander of her army. As Pyore's reaction to Tryst had proven, even the richest and boldest men were fearful in the presence of the Master of Blades.

Yet, all her seasons of planning and plotting had been upended inside of a few hours by the appearance of one woman: Lady Orangecloak, Field Commander of the rebel group known simply as the Thieves, who until that moment had been the most wanted woman in Illiastra. Lady Orangecloak had been brought into the lobby of the Atrebell manor in chains by the renowned bounty hunter, Fletchard Miller and two drunken louts he had hired. The Lord Master consigned Lady Orangecloak to the dungeon beneath the manor and that seemed to mark the final, sad chapter of her life.

Marigold was despondent over Lady Orangecloak's fate and had planned to discuss options to help the poor woman with Tryst when next they spoke. However, Lady Orangecloak, Tryst Reine, and an elf who was also incarcerated in the dungeon went missing, having presumably escaped from its confines before any conversation could occur.

It amazed Marigold that Tryst could so easily turn his cloak on the Lord Master at the very sight of Lady Orangecloak. While Marigold had invested a great deal of time in trying to win Tryst over, he readily sprung Lady Orangecloak from capture within hours of her incarceration.

After dabbing her freshly washed face dry with a plush towel and replacing her hairbrush on the stand beside the washbasin, Marigold returned to the main room.

A long, thick, white bathrobe hung on a hook before the lavatory door. As a shiver ran through her, Marigold grabbed it, slid her arms through, and tied it tight with its accompanying belt. As her body began to warm, she began pacing before the bed, planning out her day in her mind. *First and foremost, I shall go see Father. Oire will have news for me as well. It was a late night for everyone, but it will also be an early morning. After that...*

Marigold had little idea what she would do then. Traditionally, the morning after the summations and closing of the Parliamentary Sessions was nothing more than a figurative parade of the ministers and their families. The lords and the vaunted ministers that were given the honour of residence at the manor would gather in the lobby, say their scripted and empty farewells, and take to their carriages. From there, they would begin the journey to the train station, joined along the way by the lesser ministers who had lodged in the opulent hotels of Atrebell's northern districts.

Ever since she was a young girl, Marigold had been a part of that hollow display of vanity. For the first time that she was aware of, the 'Parade of Parliament', as it was informally known, might be cancelled entirely. The Lord Master had always made the trek to see off his lords and to make a protected appearance amongst the commoners. For the last four years, only Tryst Reine had rode before *that* carriage, seated astride his brown courser and scouting for threats in the crowd all the while. With a man as dangerous as he in the wind, with a turned cloak no less, the Lord Master would likely not bestir himself. There would also doubtlessly be emergency meetings to coordinate contingency plans and arrange armed search parties to hunt down the escapees.

Things had changed, and Marigold suspected that those changes would ripple far and wide across Illiastra.

For the time being though, the manor, or at least Marigold's corner of it, was eerily quiet. The ticking clock on the wall told her it was only just past the seventh hour of the morning. Daylight would be breaking, she knew, and with that, her first glance of what the weather might bring for the day. Her feet went into a pair of warm slippers that had been tucked beneath the bed and she slipped into the servant's hallway.

Outside the wide windows, Marigold could already see the blue sky of what promised to be a chilly, albeit sunny day. There seemed to be nary a cloud and the grass of the manicured lawn shimmered as the rays fell upon its frosted visage. Marigold could see the yard between the kitchen and the staff quarters and the single stone pathway that cut through it to connect the buildings. A man walked alone, bearing a heavy burlap sack on one shoulder. She craned her head to the right, following another stone pathway that led along the side of the building to the rear yards. Further down, she saw a pair of guards, walking slowly beside the outer wall, dressed in the standard issue attire of a blue coat and black trousers.

Marigold moved down the hall to a different window so that she might get a better look at them. From there, she discovered that they were actually examining the brick wall, running their gloved hands over every bit of brick and mortar they could reach. *It would seem that a full-blown investigation has broken out after Tryst and the prisoners disappeared.*

At the end of the hallway was a small window that looked on to the grass and garden on the back of the manor and it was there that Marigold went next. The yard beneath the window was teeming with men in uniform. Most were bluecoats, though speckled among them were the indigo jackets of the Honourable Guardsmen, the elite unit comprised of Illiastra's most prized soldiers. Aside from Tryst Reine, they were the Lord Master's most valued protectors. During any festivities at the manor or on the rare occasions that he ventured outside its walls, the Lord Master called the Honourable Guardsmen together. Now, on account of them already being summoned for the Parliamentary Sessions, they were being used to aid the investigation into the escape of the two prisoners.

The front double doors of the large stables situated near the rear outer gate hung open, and guards in both uniform variations could be seen coming and going. More still were looking over the outer walls and searching through shrubbery. Among the gathered uniforms, Marigold saw two tall, shaggy-haired stablehands leaning against a wall of the stables and surrounded by a few guards who seemed intent on keeping them there.

The iron gates leading to a rear service road generally used for supply deliveries were ajar and being guarded by a dozen men. Just beyond it, Marigold could see half a dozen more soldiers forming up on horseback. Heavy packs were fastened to the rear of the saddles and the men all bore musket rifles across their backs.

That's a search party, Marigold realised as she continued to observe the organised chaos going on below her. *I wonder how many have been sent out and in what direction they might all be headed.*

Heavy footsteps began to echo off the walls of the tiny hallway and Marigold spun around to see who might own them. Where she expected a butler or another male servant, Marigold's eyes befell a familiar blonde-haired guardsman in an indigo coat.

"Freyard Archer, what brings you here this morning?" Marigold asked him as he approached. "I was actually expecting to find you outside with the other guards."

He smiled at that, or rather his lips did. Freyard was a handsome man just north of thirty with a cleanly shaven face and a moderately muscular build. Outside of his duties as an Honourable Guardsman, he was the Master-at-arms for Fort Dornett and Captain of a renowned cavalry unit known as the Sun's Rangers. The fort was one of several that lined the south side of the Varras River, the wide, snaking body of water that stretched east to west across Illiastra's southerly realm.

"Until a few moments ago, I was, actually," Freyard answered in a voice that was as weary as it was warm and friendly. "Lieutenant Raspen relieved me for an hour so that I might break my fast. I was coming to see if you were awake, I have news that I think you might want to hear."

When last Marigold had seen Freyard, he was dressed in his Captain's uniform, having briefly served as her escort to the Parliamentary feast the night before. Since then he had changed into his Honourable Guardsman's outfit once more and was put to work in the wake of Tryst Reine's disappearance. As far as he knew, Marigold was completely in the dark on the events that had happened after Lady Orangecloak was consigned to the dungeon. In truth, her steward Oire had dispatched one of the Tullivan's household guards to learn what he could from a member of the Howland household guards that he trusted.

"Tryst is gone. That much I have found out," she answered him sullenly. "Come to my chambers, you can tell me what else you know."

They were quick to enter her room, with her seated upon the edge of the bed and he leaning against the dresser near the servant's entrance.

"So, tell me," Marigold began, leaning back on the bedspread and resting on her hands, "how did Tryst Reine manage to sneak the most wanted person in Illiastra and an elf out of the bowels of the Atrebell manor?"

Freyard shook his head in puzzlement. "That's the strange thing, no one has the foggiest idea how he pulled it off. Neither Lady Orangecloak nor the elf was seen to be leaving the manor. The guard on duty at the stables alleges that he and two stablehands were ordered by Tryst to help him in escorting the bounty hunter off the property. To that end, the hunter's rented jail wagon was hitched up to the two horses that went with it. By the time they finished, they were called to the loft, where they found the drunken louts unconscious."

Having pushed off from the dresser, Freyard started to wander the floor of the chamber. "According to our three witnesses, Fletchard and Tryst both alleged that the sots did not like the deal that Reine was arranging and attempted to turn on both men. A melee ensued and Fletchard and Tryst knocked both attackers unconscious. The lads and the guard helped to load the men into the back of the wagon and the bounty hunter departed through the rear gate shortly after."

Marigold hummed aloud, pondering on what Freyard was telling her. "Did she and the elf somehow find their way into the back of the wagon too?"

"That's what one would think," Freyard said, splaying his arms wide. "However, when Tryst was orchestrating that bit of work, both Lady Orangecloak and the elf, a male named Tyrendil, were under lock and key in the dungeon."

"Alright, so then Tryst sprung the two prisoners after he sent the bounty hunter on his way," Marigold deduced with a shrug. "That seems plain enough."

A shake of the head from Freyard told her that was not as simple as that. "It only gets more complex from there. After he let the bounty hunter go, he made for the dungeon and all the guards he met along the way assumed it was to interrogate Lady Orangecloak. He went into the dungeon, exiled the guards to the top of the stairs, and after a time he returned alone. The guards were given instructions to stay put until he returned once more, so that they would not have to hear the torturer make Orangecloak scream. After that he left through the back door, took his horse from the stable, exited through the rear gate, rode into the forest, and never returned."

While Freyard spoke, Marigold's gaze was on the floor. When he had finished, she met his stare, sharing in the baffled look he wore. "What of the torturer then? What did the guards find when they eventually returned to the dungeon?"

"The torturer had been killed. The guards found him on the cot in his cell, dead of a broken neck," Freyard explained in a tired voice that seemed to beg for sleep. "As for Orangecloak and the elf, they had simply vanished. No guards reported seeing them and there was no trace of where they might have gone. Our first thought was that there was some sort of tunnel or other means of passage, but we could not find a thing. All the cells, the guardroom, and even the bathhouse on the floor above the dungeon show nothing that might allow someone to leave undetected. As it is, though, we still have guards, both from the manor and of the 'Honourable' variety going over every inch of both levels of the basements. There simply must have been a passage down there somewhere for them to fit through. It's just a matter of finding it."

Marigold fell silent as she processed all the information, giving herself a minute to let it all sink in. "Just like that, Tryst Reine is gone," she commented sadly. "The only thing left to wonder now is why he would so wilfully and hastily abandon his post at the sight of Orangecloak."

"Evidently there was more to Tryst Reine than met the eye," Freyard offered in return.

"You knew Tryst Reine better than anyone in the manor, perhaps even more so than the Lord Master himself," Marigold reasoned. "Surely you must have some idea why Tryst would make such a rash decision?"

Freyard exhaled audibly and shook his head slowly at that, taking a few seconds before answering, "I know Tryst passingly well, aye. We were drinking partners and we often spoke at length when I served in the Honourable Guardsmen for one week out of the season. But this..." Freyard's voice trailed off for a moment before he found it again. "I never believed him to be a follower of the policies of the EMP, no more than I suspect you to be. Yet, I had thought he was a man who could be relied on to honour his promises. What are contracts if not promises on paper, after all. That is what he signed when he came into service here. It surprises me as much as it does you that he turned so easily. Perhaps he never valued his contract at all. It might be that he was simply waiting for an opportunity to turn his cloak and the events of last night gave him that. Clearly, if he has a hidden passage within the manor then he has been planning to use it for just that sort of purpose."

That thought sat queerly in Marigold's stomach, but it was hard to deny the logic of what Freyard said. "I knew he had no inclination to support the EMP. I also knew that Tryst Reine was never Grenjin Howland's to control. The man is his own island, independent of a world he was contractually obligated to join. Still, I never expected he could turn on everything so easily. Do you think that either of us ever knew him truly?"

"Tryst Reine is not one to issue his trust easily, that much I can say." Freyard said reassuringly. "I believe that what he showed me and, from what I gather, you as well, was the truth of who he really is. There was just much he left unsaid."

Another thought crept in on Marigold then. "I have to wonder what this will do to the Lord Master. He was paranoid as it was when he thought Tryst was protecting him. Now Tryst Reine has turned his cloak for the other side. The only thing more dangerous than making an enemy of a Master of Blades is making an enemy of one who knows as much about you as Tryst most assuredly knows of Grenjin Howland and his government."

That elicited a hum from Freyard as he considered it for himself. "You raise a fair point. That being said, the old fop will be beside himself over this. I have no doubt that he will send forth everything at his disposal to hunt Tryst down for the rest of his days. Should Tryst emerge at Lady Orangecloak's side, he had best have an army at his back, for Grenjin Howland will most certainly send one to crush him."

He sighed and stepped tiredly toward the servants' entrance of the room. "Anyhow, I have given you all the news I have. I'm quite thoroughly famished and have limited time in which to break my fast. Would you care to join me? We can talk more over a full plate of food."

She was about to stand but caught herself. "Thank you, I am hungry, but it may not be a good idea for us to be seen together for the time being. Pyore was incensed at the sight of you last night and neither he nor his family will take kindly to seeing his bride in the friendly company of another man. I hope you understand."

"But of course. I am sure you have your own duties to attend to this morning as well and I would not keep you. However, once I am relieved of duty, would it be permissible for me to seek you out with further news, should I have any?"

Marigold felt poorly about her choice of words and stood up quickly, giving Freyard's forearm a gentle squeeze. "Yes, of course. We have more in common than a mutual friendship with Tryst Reine. It is important, here and now perhaps more than ever, that we keep in the company of those we can trust. I will learn what I can from the other nobles today and relay it back to you as well. Between us we will have our own little network of information."

"I would not be opposed to that," Freyard nodded with a slight smile while turning towards the door. "Very well then, I shall take my leave of you for now."

After he had gone, Marigold waited until she could no longer hear his footsteps before leaving her room through the guest entrance. The hallway beyond was empty, save for a pair of guards in the black on silver coats of the Palomb household, seated across the hall at the door to Pyore's chamber. Further down were a second pair in the teal of the Tullivan guardsmen, standing watch at the room Marigold's father occupied and it was towards them that she headed.

The two stood up tall at her approach and one tipped his black, beaked hat in greeting. "Good morning, milady. You are awake bright and early, I see."

"I bid a good morning to you, Darrill, and to you as well, Brandyl," Marigold offered in return to the two. "Has Oire arrived from the servant's quarters yet for the morning?"

The second guard, the one named Brandyl answered. "Why yes, my lady, he has been within for the last hour. Unless he ducked out through the servant's door without telling us. Which we all know he is not like to do. Would you like to go in?"

"Yes, thank you," she answered politely.

That request was met by Darrill, a moustachioed man in his early fifties who had been with the Tullivan family guard since Marigold had been but a babe in swaddling clothes. "Please, allow us a moment first to check with Mister Oire and your Lord Father to ensure he is fit to receive, milady."

With a confirmative nod from Marigold, Darrill turned to the door and inserted a key in the hole, knocking with a free hand at the same time. He poked his head within and spoke in a whisper to Oire before retreating again quickly and stepping aside. "You may enter at your leisure, milady."

The door was swung open by Brandyl and Marigold thanked them both and stepped into the room.

Unlike her own guest chambers, Marscal Tullivan's accommodations were located beyond the reach of the servant's hallway and as such, had its own windows. The blue sky quite nearly lit the room of its own accord with a beam of pale light that fell across a wide featherbed, on the end of which sat her father.

The consumption disease had left him sickly thin and gaunt and though he was not quite sixty years old, the disease had aged him at least twenty years more. He was dressed in a tweed overcoat that hung to the floor and a nice, albeit loose, brown suit with a black tie and shoes. Near at hand was his luggage, packed and readied to leave.

"Father and Oire, I bid good morning to you both," Marigold greeted them as she crossed the threshold. She went to Marscal's side and seated herself on the bed. "You are up and about, I see. How are you feeling today?"

"My sweet daughter, a good morning to you as well," he answered in a pain-stricken voice. "I am tired, but I am always tired as of late. However, today I am feeling a little joyous to be putting this forsaken place out of sight and I shan't miss it."

The past week of the Parliamentary Sessions had sapped the strength from her father entirely and the events of last night had taxed him even worse when he heard word.

Marigold had feared for the toll it would take on him, but even still, she was surprised with the haste with which he wanted to vacate Atrebell. "We will be leaving so early, Father," Marigold said concernedly. "Have you spoken with the Lord Master yet? After what happened last night he may want to retain his warden lords for emergency meetings."

"He will," Marscal answered quickly. "That is why I must leave before he has a chance to keep me much longer. I have already dispatched Lewcas to have my cars attached to the next train bound for Obalen. Grenjin knows the state of my health and he won't stop me if I am already in the process of leaving."

"I have not had time to pack, Father," Marigold said as she stood up hurriedly. "I'll have to go at once to my room and even still I shall be rushed. Give me leave to take Brandyl and Darrill to help me and I shall be ready to depart in short order."

A thin hand reached out, gently gripped her wrist, and drew her back down to the bed. "No, Marigold, the only packing you will be doing is to move your things from your current chamber to this one and you will have time enough to do that."

Marigold shot a worried look at Oire, who was busy working mortar and pestle to prepare the Johnahweed her father smoked to lessen his pain. The steward managed to glance at her long enough to give her an assuring wink before putting his attention back into his task.

"You're asking me to stay?" she asked cautiously.

Marscal nodded in reply. "I dictated a letter to Oire and signed it. I have given implicit instructions that you are to substitute for me as my eyes and ears in any further situation that warrants my presence. Furthermore, of our six guards I am only taking three with me back to Daol Bay, the others will stay with you. Do you have any preference of whom you might keep? Lewcas is at the train station as it is and I have already chosen Darrill to come with me. You may have your pick of the other four."

"Very well, Father. If that is your wish then I shall only be happy to obey," Marigold relented to his request. "As for guardsmen, I would like to keep Brandyl, Elden, and Sydnee. They are all larger than Pyore and Eldridge and none less than ten years older than them."

"After what I have heard of last night's events, you shall want two of them about you for the remainder of your time here," Oire added as he joined the father and daughter beside the bed. In his hands was a small envelope he was sealing and tucking into an inside pocket of his jacket. "My lord, we should not delay any further. I will give you and my lady a minute alone, but we can afford no longer. While I wait, I shall issue the guards their instructions and ensure that your carriage is waiting outside. Brandyl and Darrill will escort you out and we will light your Johnahweed when we are safely out of here and within your train car.

Marscal waved at him feebly. "Very well, Oire, that all sounds acceptable. Now please, go on ahead and leave me with my daughter."

The steward nodded and saw himself out without further word, giving them their privacy for a moment.

"Father, are you sure I should stay?" Marigold asked forlornly. "I cannot bear to leave your side like this. I should be at home with you in Daol Bay."

Tenderly he took her hand in his as he answered her. "Daol Bay does not rest when I do. We are the castellans of the west, my darling. It would not do for us to be unrepresented here at such a crucial time for Illiastra."

"We should not worry about that, Father," Marigold reasoned. "Pyore wants to sit in my place so badly, then for today we shall let him. He can think he represents the Tullivans and we will go back to Daol Bay knowing better."

For a brief few seconds it seemed that Marscal was considering what Marigold said, though a sigh heralded the dashing of her hopes. "I have known Eamon Palomb for my entire life. The man is ambitious and greedy and his sons are worse again. You must stay and continue to show your presence. If you run home on my coattails, they will think your courage is only good when I am near at hand. Furthermore, I have a strange suspicion that what is said in the next few days will likely shape the future of our nation. A Tullivan must be present and you are the heir of my legacy now, even if only in name. Serephanie was never suited for this life, but you are your mother through and through. This is a life you were born for and I would not leave you here were I not entirely sure of that."

"If it is your wish, then I promise I shall stay and serve," Marigold declared with a solemn bow of her head.

"I know you will, darling," her father said with as tight a hug as his weakening frame would allow. "It is my promise to you that I shall wait for your return."

As he released her, Marigold met his gaze, furrowing her own brows as she did. "Where else would you go, Father?"

"Nowhere, my dear," he added with a reassuring pat on the shoulder. "Once I am back within the walls of our home I intend to go absolutely nowhere."

Marigold felt a hard pang as she realised exactly what he meant, though she said nothing more of it.

"Will you see me to my carriage?" Marscal asked while feebly making his way to his feet.

She forced a smile and helped him stand. "Yes, Father, of course I shall. Allow me to grab a cloak and shoes to ward off the chill and I will be right with you."

Marigold left him there and went quickly down the hall to her room to garb herself for the cold weather. Inside her room, she found a favourite pair of black, knee-high leather boots and a cloak and donned them both hurriedly. The cloak was her favourite, in a vibrant shade of teal satin, with a white woollen interior and trim, and quilted with goose down. She scarce felt any weather at all when she was wrapped in it.

By the time she had returned to her father, Brandyl and Darrill had been called upon by him and the two stood to either side, waiting on the order to move out. Once she slipped an arm into the crook of her father's elbow, the four began the slow, laboured walk toward the ostentatious staircase that led to the lobby of the manor.

Marscal was weak from sickness, but his pride was too great and he insisted on walking under what was left of his own strength. Even the stairs did not daunt him. With Darrill and Brandyl walking ahead to catch him should he fall, and Marigold beside him to lean on, Marscal Tullivan was able to leave the Atrebell manor for the last time with grace and dignity.

A tight hug, a kiss to both cheeks, and a final farewell were exchanged before Marscal was helped into the carriage and out of sight behind the closed door.

Marigold stood in wait for the carriage to leave, bearing the cold morning while wrapped tightly in her cloak. The third guard to go with Marigold's father, a fellow nearing fifty years of age named Kandell, emerged from the manor beside a pair of servants, all of them carrying luggage. Behind all of them was Oire, carrying a single brown suitcase that Marigold knew to be his lone piece of baggage.

Once all of it was secured away, Kandell climbed aboard the front of the carriage to share a seat with the driver and Darrill slipped inside to sit across from his lord.

Before he could join the two within the carriage, Oire reached inside his coat, produced a brown envelope, and pressed it into

Marigold's hands. "Your letter, my lady," he reminded her. "Your lord father almost forgot, though one can hardly fault him for that."

"Thank you, Oire," Marigold said while drawing him into a quick hug. "Safe travels to you and father. I will join you both in Daol Bay the first moment I can."

Oire held the hug and whispered in her ear. "Keep a guard about you at all times. There is no telling what the Palomb's might do if they can get you alone," he released her then, but kept his hands on her shoulders so that they looked one another in the eyes. "I would stay to counsel if I could, but my duty is to your father first, especially now. Lastly, you should gather as much information as you can, but ruffle no feathers and get home to us as soon as possible. You must not take risks right now, not while you are in such a vulnerable position."

"I understand, Oire. I will do proudly by you and father both. Now go, before anyone can stop you two," Marigold said in a voice full of melancholy.

Any time spent away from her father at this stage of his illness brought those feelings on. His time was so precious now and Marigold felt it her duty to spend as much of it with him as she could. It felt wrong for her to be standing beside the carriage and not within, at his side.

During the time that Oire had spoken with Marigold, Brandyl had positioned himself at her side and she turned to face him. "Thank you for staying with me," she said to him, grateful for the company. "I have no doubt you were looking forward to going home to your wife today and I am sorry for delaying that return. It should not be for long, though."

Brandyl was standing at ease, his hands behind his back, his feet apart, and at the ready for a command. As far as Marigold could remember, he was near thirty and had been serving as a guard of the Tullivan household for some five years. There was a dozen or so centimetres in height difference between him and Marigold, and he had a strong body that he kept in fine form. It made for perfect soldiering material and the handsome features of his angular face and wavy, light brown hair had shortlisted him for consideration to the Honourable Guardsmen.

"You need not apologise to me, my lady," Brandyl assured her. "I am a guardian of the Tullivan household and I go where you and your father command me."

They stood there quietly for a time, waiting for the carriage driver to finish inspecting the carriage and the horses. When the stout little fellow was satisfied, he climbed up beside Kandell, took the reins to hand, and got them rolling with a sharp crack.

Marigold moved not a muscle during the time that it took for the carriage to leave, waiting where she stood until it had gone beyond the gate and out of sight.

"I assume you started your shift only a few hours ago?" she queried while turning to face him again.

"Yes, milady, I drew the morning shift," Brandyl answered obediently.

The cold began to nip at her face and she began walking back toward the manor to escape it. "I am glad you are well rested, for we are going to have a busy day ahead of us," Marigold told him, apprehension creeping into her voice.

Brandyl followed from a step behind her, speaking up when he was directly at her side. "Might I ask what milady has in mind?"

"For starters, I need to get dressed properly for the day. I am still in my nightgown beneath my cloak and bathrobe. After that, I shall pay a visit to the Lord Master's chambers and let him know of my father's arrangements. After which I suspect that I will be in meetings for most of the morning. As for this afternoon, we will be moving my things from my current quarters to my father's."

They were climbing the steps then, with Brandyl taking two at a time to reach the top first so that he might open the door for Marigold. "Would you have me wake Elden and Sydnee? They both worked the night shift, so they're not long abed."

"No, leave them be," Marigold decided as the wave of warmth from within the manor greeted her. "You will more than suffice to be my guard for the day."

2
SEREPHANIE

In her days spent among the elites of Illiastra, Serephanie had spent a great deal of time travelling, and much of that time had been spent between the three major cities. From that experience, Serephanie had come to feel that each of the cities seemed to have its own distinct personality: Atrebell celebrated its own grandeur. It built upon the middle and upper class areas and espoused its colourful architecture and lush greenery growing throughout. There was pride in its vanity, a begging for all eyes to bask in its false sense of artistic vision. Beneath the beautified exterior though, one saw the ugliness with which they treated the poor. The districts to the south were but eyesores to be swept beneath the allegorical rug and were all but forgotten.

Far to the west was Daol Bay, as rugged as the hills and cliffs it was built into. That city was one that had welcomed the perseverant of all lifestyles since the day that Serephanie's ancestor, Ser Davis Tullivan had come ashore on its beaches. The population within its walls were rife with community spirit and neighbourly concern amid an industrious work ethic that carried quite evenly across the income spectrum.

Then there was Hercalest. If ever anyone commissioned a monument to greed, Serephanie believed that one would only need to dedicate a stone marker at the city gates. The Palomb family had built the city on its mining empire and the portion of the workforce that received a paid wage was blindly loyal. Slavery was abundant in Hercalest and the thousands of unpaid and underpaid men and women were what Eamon Palomb and his closest kin depended on for a life of luxury.

Those who earned a sustainable wage were groomed from a young age to believe in the Palomb ideology: wealth before all else. It was never a statement so blatantly sanctified. Rather, Serephanie knew it instead to be an unspoken motto. Furthering their efforts, the Palombs wrapped their beliefs in a veneer of religiosity aided by a corrupt Triarchy who twisted the words of *The God's Gift* and the *Proclamation of Ios* to cast the wealth-hording behaviour of the Elite Merchant's in a favourable light.

From the pulpit of the Tower of Ios, the Patriarchs delivered sermon after sermon ignoring or outright contradicting passages of the Triarchy scriptures that condemned greed and preached of aid for the needy. Instead, they focused on single passages or decontextualised statements that tended to demonise people who were not adherents of the Ios-above-all branch of Triarchy worship.

Elves and dwarves, for instance, were treated as being inferior to humankind and the half-elf/half-human folk known as the Amaroshans were thought of as lesser again. The congregations were instructed to be wary of even non-Illiastran humans, especially those who looked different, such as the ebony-skinned Johnans or the white-haired Drakians. The preachers further spent an inordinate amount of time spewing hatred towards men and women who loved others of their own gender, contending that those of that nature were to be treated as criminals worthy of death. It was a twisted and nauseating creed and Serephanie had found attending services in Hercalest, above anywhere else, to be a grand test of her finite patience.

It came then as no surprise that in a region where prejudicial behaviour was treated like a virtue and greed as divinity, that the Palombs were revered as being almost demi-godly.

Of course, none of that unbridled hatred came without some level of subterfuge. There had to be the appearance of charitable behaviour and that ruse was directed to the sick and the dying, for the Patriarchs claimed that in their suffering, they were one with Ios. Further disingenuous attention was directed at those who were maimed or killed in military service or menial labouring. Those poor souls were spoken of as heroes from one corner of the mouth while the crippled survivors were denied care and compassion from the other.

To Serephanie it seemed that the majority of Hercalestians were blissfully unaware of such a level of duplicity, simply denied that it existed, or had submitted to a state of mass moral delusion. It was a stark contrast to Daol Bay and even Portsward, where Serephanie had found most people to be only too aware of their government's crookedness. The difference she noticed was that while the westerners acknowledged the state of their nation, they focused their energies on making the best of their circumstances.

To blend in here, I must act like a Hercalestian while embodying the spirit of Daol Bayfolk, Serephanie told herself on more than one occasion, calling on that western survival instinct. *As much as it stirs the bile in my stomach, I will praise the Palombs and the Triarchy and act as though they are as righteous as the gods themselves.*

On this particular day in Hercalest, the blending of she and Darrion consisted of keeping their heads down and following the ceaseless rivers of humanity that walked on either side of the streets.

He was Serephanie's love, her joy, and the one who had gotten them both from Daol Bay to Hercalest. Darrion Veskries was a saltwater fisherman by blood and by trade. His father owned a vessel, and as the eldest son, Darrion had worked the skiff from the time he was twelve years old until just mere weeks ago. Fifteen years on the seas had made him into a hardened man with an iron will and a heart as big as all outdoors. When not hauling nets and traps around Twin Bay, Darrion hunted and cut cords of firewood in the forest for his family and for sale, and fished the lakes and rivers with a pole and line for leisure. Beyond all of his regular duties as an eldest son and provider, Darrion pursued his greatest desire: professional hand-to-hand fighting.

Under the guidance of an Aquatican from the archipelago of Tropuri, Darrion trained with every spare minute he could find in the martial arts of the Aquatican folks. When not training, Darrion was pursuing his craft in the fighting pits hidden in basements and cellars of Daol Bay's shadier gambling establishments. He battled the pugilists and drunkards that dared test their mettle against him, and had a spotless record amongst the amateur ranks to be found in Daol Bay's seedy underbelly. Unsurprisingly, Darrion wanted more.

The one who pushed him to take what he wanted in life was Serephanie, the wayward eldest daughter of Marscal Tullivan, the third most powerful man in all of Illiastra.

Serephanie had seen Darrion for the first time on the wharf of her family's fish processing plant, and had taken a liking to him. On subsequent visits, she continued to cross paths with the handsome fisherman, and finally, when she had worked up sufficient courage, Serephanie introduced herself. It turned out that he had noticed her as well, and was as taken with her as she seemed to be with him. Of course, it would not do for a lowborn son of a fishing skipper to be seen addressing a highborn lady, let alone courting one, and so Darrion had wisely stayed away, leaving Serephanie to be the one to initiate the romantic pursuit.

Within weeks of their first meeting, Serephanie was sneaking out at all hours to be with Darrion, bribing and influencing house guards and staff to ignore her dalliances. Attraction grew into infatuation, and infatuation blossomed into love through these nocturnal affairs, but by day, they each returned to distracted lives filled with tasks and obligations. Serephanie was being groomed to be a trophy wife, and Darrion was pulling his weight for his family, and those predestined paths laid out before them seemed certain to pull them apart.

Unwilling to be a silent prize for Eldridge Palomb, Serephanie decided that it was time to leave her life of easement and grandeur, and become her own woman. Darrion's dream of leaving the fighting pits for Illiastra's lone professional fighting league seemed to be the exit from their fates that the pair of lovers needed.

In the wee hours of an early autumn morning the two took what supplies they could, left a note of apology for Darrion's family, and slipped through a hole in the city walls of Daol Bay. From there they struck eastward, making for the Western Plains and the Daol Forest beyond. While they headed for the wilds of Illiastra, their objective was to find a travelling troupe of professional fighters known as the League of the Sacred Fist. The last known whereabouts of that group placed them in the villages of the westerly reaches of the Hercalest region, with the city as their ultimate destination. It was there that the league would be setting up for their yearly open tournament to coincide with the year's-end festival of the Feast of the Winter's King. Darrion hoped that given the open lists of the tournament, he could enter and secure some measure of recognition as a fighter.

The prospect of being in Hercalest, and directly under the nose of the Palomb family terrified Serephanie. Nevertheless, she felt that the massive city and its bursting population offered concealment. To add to that, it occurred to her that the Palombs would not think to look for her so close to their palace and that their search radius would be far from their home city.

The aforementioned overflowing streets were yet another facet that set Hercalest apart from its contemporaries: population density. The main thoroughfares were all but impossible to navigate during daylight hours due to crowd congestion and the easiest way to get about was to know the direction in which the general flow of the people was going.

The issue was further compounded by the structuring of most streets in the city to accommodate the smallest percentage of the populace primarily. Normal folk were restricted to walking on the far side of either street, along narrow, gravel pathways barely wide enough for two to walk side by side. To set foot on the smooth, grey, brick road in the centre, one required a licence issued by the city council. Those passes were typically given only to Hercalest's elite, their essential staff, and vaunted guests. Enforcing that law were city guards on horseback, eager to use corporal punishment for even the slightest trespass onto the roadway.

I had only ever travelled Hercalest in a carriage, witnessing the denizens joined at the shoulder on the sidewalks from a distance, Serephanie noted in recollection. *I remember their slow forward shuffling, their downcast eyes, and the fear of tripping into the street present on their faces. I could not have fathomed then what it would be like to walk among the masses, no more than I can imagine being cooped up in a carriage now.*

She and Darrion had arrived in Hercalest four days prior following an arduous journey across the countryside. Their first stop had been at a lumberjack camp deep in the Daol Forest. Serephanie knew the Ashmond family that operated the camp quite well and reckoned that they would be open to lending them aid. The team of father and son that resided at the camp lived up to expectations, and helped Serephanie and Darrion at a time when they needed it most, giving them clothing, shelter, food and even temporary jobs at the camp to earn them some coin. A second benefit to the employment was that Serephanie got an opportunity to take a refresher in the basic skills that were typically performed by her serving staff until then. Once they were ready to move on, Serephanie and Darrion had turned north and east toward Obalen, booking passage by train under new identities that the Ashmonds had assisted them in establishing.

The locomotive trip from Obalen to Hercalest had eaten up a few days. Having bought passage and a cabin under their falsified names, they managed to keep Serephanie out of sight of all but the conductor for the duration of the ride. In this state of relative comfort, they travelled through Atrebell, along the outer walls of Biddenhurst, and in and about a select few smaller towns before finally arriving at Illiastra's largest city.

Once within Hercalest's walls, Serephanie and Darrion, along with most passengers, were ordered to disembark at what was known as the Vauldner Street Station, yet another Hercalest experience that Serephanie had only experienced from afar before.

Due to the sheer size of Hercalest, the city had three train stations, which was two more than most locales. The most commonly used was the Vauldner Street Station located on the northern side of the city, in close proximity to the downtown core. On the eastern outskirts of town sat the Industrial Yard Station, primarily used for shipping and receiving of goods, and the transporting of workers. It also happened to be the closest station to the poorest city districts, servicing those among the impoverished lot that might be able to afford a ticket. Lastly, there was the Ellison Palomb Station. Much like the centre lane of the city streets, access to what was commonly known as the E.P. Station was prohibited without proper clearance. Named for Eamon Palomb's father, one of the founding members of the EMP, it sat outside the southern city walls. Such a location placed the station only a short distance from Greffold Hills, the guarded and gated community within Hercalest where only the wealthiest resided.

Serephanie knew Greffold Hills better than she knew any other district of Hercalest on account of her previous visits. Based on that knowledge and a great deal of naiveté, she once would have claimed to know her way about the city.

Greffold Hills is but a tiny, sheltered nook in the anthill of Hercalest. I did not know anything about this city, in truth.

"The sign says that this is Wellin Street, Terra," she heard in front of her as she bumped into Darrion's back. The two of them had been walking in single file, with Serephanie holding tight to Darrion's cloak so that they could get through the crowd as quickly as possible without losing one another. "Which way do we turn now?"

Terra was the name Serephanie had taken with her forged identity. In Darrion's case, he was now answering to the name Cole Chere, a moniker he apparently was borrowing from an ancestor in his mother's bloodline who had lived in Galdourn. Serephanie was of course posing as his wife, though she needed a backstory of her own. Eschewing a maiden surname for her character, Serephanie drafted a story about a woman named Terra of Galdourn. This particular woman of Serephanie's creation was the baseborn daughter of an equally baseborn dockworker from the town that the region immediately due south of Daol Bay was named for. It was as close to absolutely no one that Serephanie could think to become: a ragged waif who lived but a single step from the streets.

"If my memory serves me well, turning right here should take us towards Greffold Hills," Serephanie said in response to Darrion's inquiry for direction. "We just have to keep walking toward it until we get to the street that leads to the gates of the hill. You will see a road veering to the left at that point, and Bryten Field should be just around the bend from there."

Shortly after leaving the train station, Serephanie and Darrion had found the cleanest inn within the vicinity and paid for a week of lodging in advance. Their next task was to scout for a roof they could live beneath for an extended period, and to find Darrion temporary work. The first part was proving more difficult to resolve than Serephanie could have imagined, the second practically took care of itself within a day.

The inn they were residing at shared a street with a number of taverns and pubs catering to the working class men of Hercalest. From what Darrion had discovered, there was a dearth of strong, intimidating men willing to supervise the inebriated patrons, considering that it was a precarious job with meagre pay at the best of times. Regardless of the risks, Darrion was desperate to have a steady income of any kind to augment the saved earnings of his and Serephanie's from the lumber camp and he had set out for the watering holes to find work.

Serephanie wiled that particular day away in quietude in the modest room she and Darrion were occupying at the inn. Being an unsupervised woman in the common room would have practically been begging for attention and so she hid herself away. This would have made for a boring afternoon, but Darrion had procured for Serephanie a few books from a tiny shelf of shared literature in the common room before his departure.

Come evening, Darrion returned to the inn with word that he had been hired as the catch-all muscleman of Pencamp's Pub, just four doors down from the inn.

"I see the gates. We are almost there," Darrion stated in a voice filled with anxiousness. "It is hard to believe that this day is here. The ring of the Sacred Fist is just around the bend."

"Not much further now, my love," Serephanie said, echoing his excitement as she stole a glance around his cloaked frame once more.

She could see the gates, made of cold black iron bars lined vertically, their tops spiked to look like a row of spears pointing towards the sky. Before the iron barrier stood half a dozen guards at attention, ready to swing the two sets of bars inward for any approaching carriages. Beyond all of it sat the neighbourhood of Greffold Hills. The gentle slopes were home to rows of leafy trees swaying in the breeze and tall hedges ever so neatly trimmed. Among the foliage stood a small number of businesses that catered solely to the local nobility that lived nearby in their ostentatious homes. The red slate roofs poking above the greenery made the buildings stand out, but almost none stood above the Tower of Ios situated near the top of the hill.

It was the second of two towers in Hercalest and had itself only been built in the last century to serve the residents of Greffold Hills and their vaunted guests exclusively. For everyone beneath that rung of the hierarchal ladder that sought worship, there was a larger, albeit shabbier tower in the city square.

The Greffold Hills Tower of Ios, itself a tangible contradiction to the word of Ios, Serephanie recalled while searching her memory for a certain passage from the Proclamation of Ios. *'For all of those who are of my creation shall find home and sanctuary within all towers that are adorned with my name, this is the will and word of Ios.' That is how the passage goes, if I remember right, yet any not of Greffold Hills or otherwise invited are denied entry at the neighbourhood gates.*

Darrion turned sharply, leading them onto a dusty gravel trail off the stone road and away from the gates just as they had been drawing uncomfortably near to them.

Even from where they now walked, she could see the Palomb Palace, staring out across the city from the flat plateau at the height of Greffold Hills. The exterior was ashen grey brick and the massive outer structure looked as though it occupied the entire hilltop alone. In truth, the outer building was the largest of a small village's worth of buildings. The interior structures were smaller than the exterior and unseen from all but the front gates of the complex, but were several in numbers. Even without them, the Palomb Palace stood thrice as large as the Tullivan manor in Daol Bay and twice as large as the Atrebell manor in the nation's capital.

I always hated that place. I hated even the thought of approaching it and I downright abhorred stepping within.

It was as large a place as one could ever hope to stand and yet it always felt to Serephanie as though she was confined to a tiny cell. Serephanie had come to find that no matter where she found herself in the palace, it managed to maintain an ominous, claustrophobic nature to it.

There was little reason for me to feel that way, in truth. The walls were painted in white and trimmed with actual gold and plenty of light filled the rooms through the tall windows. Servants stood at the ready for my every need and I wanted for nothing as a guest. Yet, for all of that, there was no warmth to the place. Unless I kept to Jorette Palomb's constant company, where her two youngest children usually were to be found as well, one would find no love, either.

It was one thing to be away from the company of Lady Jorette, originally a Morton from Weicaster Bay in the west, and another entirely to share space with Lord Eamon and his twin sons.

Eamon is a cold man whose only love is coin and only pleasure is hoarding as much of it as he can. That he loves so much as that is a far deal more than can be said for Eldridge and Pyore. They were raised to be as cold and cunning as their father, but somewhere along the way a cruel streak that shocked even Eamon ran through them like a poison and of the two, Pyore got the larger dose.

For a few fleeting seconds, it seemed that the only noise Serephanie could hear was the gravel crunching beneath the feet of her and Darrion. The relative silence was short lived, however, and soon the sounds of humanity filled the air ahead of her and Darrion.

Though they remained in the city, Bryten Field felt as though it was a hundred leagues away. The encroaching buildings had fallen away to acres of grass and a smattering of trees in the process of shedding their leaves under open skies. There was a gentle brook emptying into a tiny pond inhabited by prattling ducks. Above that, there were voices and general clamouring, but to Serephanie it sounded less like a city and more like the travelling carnivals she remembered from her youth.

There was a hustle and bustle filling her ears that lent itself to the sight of a spread of pavilion tents and men coming and going between them, hard at their work. In the front of the tarpaulin town was the largest tent that Serephanie had ever seen. It looked to be at least three storeys tall at the trussed peak and Serephanie believed they could fit the entire Tullivan fish processing plant beneath its canvas roof.

The sheer size of it alone gave her pause, but it was the vibrant array of colours in the painted tarping that truly left her awestruck. The entire tent looked to Serephanie as though it had been painted by a giant with a thick brush, painting in brilliant lines of colour that overlaid one another in harmonious nature. From peak and corners there were colourful linen streamers billowing in the breeze and the perimeter was barricaded with matching hempen ropes.

"It is more amazing than I could have possibly imagined," Darrion exclaimed in awe. His approach slowed to little more than a crawl as he took in the splendour that sat before them.

"It is far and above the grey, sailcloth tent I remember, to be sure," Serephanie added.

He turned about to look at her, his face barely restraining his excitement. "Where do you suppose we go to register? None of the tents are marked."

"I suppose a good place to start will be with that big fellow standing at the door of the big tent," Serephanie stated while gesturing her head towards the man in question.

Before the entrance flap of the tent stood an imposing figure with a dark brown complexion and the coarse, curly black hair that was commonplace among most of the island nations in the Crescent. His rugged face was covered with a long beard that was dyed red at the tips and tied off into forks. Though he was taller than Darrion by half a dozen centimetres, it was difficult to tell if they were of a size, given that the man at the door was dressed in warm clothes. Over a thick green doublet and tan trousers, he wore a hooded cloak and padded leather vest, both in dark brown.

Serephanie noted something hanging from the belt on his hip when the wind caught and lifted his cloak. It was only on a second glance that she spotted a sheathed knife of considerable length and width.

The man had been watching them with a look of suspicion from at least the moment that Serephanie saw him. As Darrion turned and looked to the stranger, she saw his nostrils flare visibly.

This is not a man to be trifled with, she surmised.

Darrion appeared to be considering the man for a moment before looking back at Serephanie. "Very well, let us see if he can at least point us in the right direction."

"Excuse me, ser," Darrion said loudly as he strode the few meters of distance between them, Serephanie following close at his side. "I hate to bother you, but I am an applicant for the League of the Sacred Fist and am wondering if you could direct me to the registration area."

The fellow neither answered nor stirred from where he stood, save for his continuing visual study of the two figures before him. Darrion gave Serephanie a confused look and his mouth opened to speak again when the stranger raised a gloved palm to silence him.

"If you were sent here to join the Sacred Fist you would not be bothering me in the first place to find the 'registration area'," he said in the growling dialect of the folk from the Gallick Isles region of the Crescent. The last two words sounded almost mocking in how he phrased them and as Darrion tried to talk, he was cut off again by the surly doorman. "Save your words and I will save mine."

"My apologies, ser, but no one sent me," Darrion explained plainly, in both tone and terms. "I have spent my life in combat training so that I could fight in the League of the Sacred Fist and have come here of my own volition."

For a moment, it seemed that the man was impressed with Darrion as he stroked a prong of his beard with a free hand. "Is that so? You came all the way here on your own with no referral from your trainer or a current member of the Sacred Fist?"

Darrion was quick with an answer. "That's correct, as I said before: no one sent me."

"Aye, just as you said before when I asked," he shot back over Darrion's words, a little more impatient this time around and his earlier interest clearly feigned, as all pretence of such dropped instantly from his tone. "Congratulations, ser, you have done as you have sought and wasted my time and my words. Now that I have given you that much, I trust that our pointless exchange is done?"

A loud thump could be heard from within the tent followed by a wave of laughter and a single, strong, male voice calling above the ruckus, "No! Not like that Cardwin, you bloody fool! Are you trying to cripple Verrit? Run twenty laps around the ring for your carelessness."

"But, ser!" a voice Serephanie guessed to be Cardwin's attempted to argue.

"Fifty push-ups for backtalk," the first voice roared again. "Try me further and more push-ups will come and when they do, they will be added by the hundreds, lad."

"They are training, are they not?" Darrion asked the doorman. "I would like to at least look in on it, if even that would be alright."

Judging from the chuckling that the Gallician was letting out, he found Darrion's statement humorous. "And I would like to have wings so I could fly over the great mountain ranges and see the Endless Ocean. It doesn't matter what you would like to do. No man," he turned to face Serephanie mid-sentence, "or woman, who is not of the League of the Sacred Fist, shall enter this tent outside of the scheduled, public fights."

Both hands of Darrion went skyward with frustration at that. "When is the Tournament of the Winter King, then? How does a layman like me enter that?"

"You're about a week too early, for one thing," the Gallician responded with a lazy shrug. "For another, to enter that sorry show all you have to do is show up on the day of the tournament, pay the fee, and wait your turn to have your pathetic arse thrown out of the ring by one of the champions."

"Would it be permissible for me to at least avail of the facilities so that I might train prior to the tournament, ser?" Darrion asked in a tone that was quite nearly pleading.

The doorman had a snicker remaining in the well for that too. "It would not. I suggest you improvise, and be sure to do so far from here, where I won't see you."

With a last heave, Darrion finally relented. "Very well, ser. I thank you for your time and will see you on the day of the tournament."

Following a grunt from the Gallician, Serephanie and Darrion had no further recourse but to leave the field. She could see the dejection clearly on Darrion's face and he held his tongue until they were nearing the street leading to Greffold Hills once more.

"This turned out to be a great waste of a day," Darrion commented as gravel gave way to stone beneath their feet.

It was Serephanie's turn to be amused at Darrion, though she kept her expression to a reserved grin. "On the contrary, I think the doorman left you with a great advantage."

"Oh?" he asked curiously with a raised eyebrow. "What sort of advantage?"

"Even the man on the door thinks little of the Tournament of the Winter's King," Serephanie explained. "It is as he says: a show. They let in amateur and hopeful fighters in a tournament against handpicked champions from among the professional ranks. Consider also that the format of the fights is a light, barely physical wrestling match instead of the usually violent pugilistic fare of the standard contests. Based on all of that, we can infer that the defending champions expect an easy day of tossing nobodies to the ground one after the other."

"So why would I put myself amongst the nobodies?" he sighed.

She tapped the side of her nose thoughtfully in answer. "Because you are the pupil of Glimlen of the Waves, master of the Tropurian fighting arts and no one will be any the wiser until you step into the ring and challenge a champion. You never told the Gallician at the doorway anything about you and he never asked. Who you are and what you know will be a mystery until the moment that the bell sounds."

A smile crossed Darrion's face as the dejectedness fled and he took her in his arms and kissed her atop the forehead. "By the gods, I do love the way you think, my dear."

3

FREYARD

On duty, we honour Illiastra. Freyard knew these words. He had been repeating them for as long as he had been a soldier. They were spoken by new recruits as often as their own name and a variation of it was uttered in remembrance of fallen brothers. Those words were so ancient that when they were first written, it was Phaleayna, the old kingdom, that was honoured, not Illiastra at all.

The first to say it to Freyard was his own father, himself a highly decorated crossbowman for the Illiastran Armed Forces. Two uncles knew the words and said them often as well, as did their father before them. Every last one had been high-ranking military officers and first class crossbowmen, the breasts of their uniforms adorned with an assortment of colourful medals. Two generations further removed and his family tree was comprised of proud bowmen, a tradition that continued to its roots, and a man named Ser Donious, the first Archer of Collura.

There were a handful of other men and women knighted as the archer of their hometown, and the title eventually became the surname of their houses. After the death of the last king, the knightly names began their descent into extinction. Some, like the Archer family of Collura, continued to produce the best archers of each generation in the armed forces of Illiastra and Phaleayna. They wed sons and daughters to other Archer families so that they might increase the odds of producing naturally gifted offspring so as to continue the tradition.

When Freyard had come into this world, there were still two distinct Archer families in military service to Illiastra: those of southerly Collura and another in Ravenkeep, far to the northwest. Both houses had documented lineage dating back to the time of kings and on account of that, were bestowed a measure of respect and honour, neither of which came without certain expectations. Children born into an Archer family were taught to use a bow practically in tandem with learning to walk. To those who excelled, there was a nearly guaranteed place of military leadership.

Freyard had been no exception, and at twenty-nine years of age, he had already advanced further than most soldiers ten years his senior. As Master-at-Arms for Fort Dornett, Captain of the Sun's Rangers, First Class Rifleman, and senior member of the Honourable Guardsmen, Freyard did not want for titles.

Due to the time Freyard spent in the wilderness of the Southlands, he had never accumulated many friends among the other guardsmen. Granted, his own men in Fort Dornett showed him the utmost respect and his Sun's Rangers were a band of brothers to him. North of the Varras River, though, Freyard always felt as though he was an unwanted visitor who simply did not mesh with fellow men-at-arms.

It was that reason above all that had drawn him to Tryst Reine. Freyard connected with Tryst from the time they had met, their friendship growing from a mutual respect they each had for one another, and from that, they had grown close.

The manor guards were both fearful and envious of Tryst Reine and he had little interest in mingling with the Honourable Guardsmen. Within that fold, the men who should be Freyard's kin were aloof and frigid toward him. The shared exclusion had played a further role in bringing Tryst and Freyard together, and they came to find that any shared free time that was not spent on duty or sleeping was in the company of one another. The two enjoyed a good drink, a few rounds of dice or a board game, and regaling one another with stories of their adventures.

In payment for that friendship, Tryst Reine left me even more alienated than before, Freyard reflected bitterly, bare hands flexing tight on the balustrade that overlooked the opulent lobby of the Atrebell Manor.

No one had been more shocked than Freyard to discover that Tryst had fled into the night with Lady Orangecloak. It was from the exact spot that Freyard now stood that he had last seen Tryst, clutching tight to the signature orange garment that the bounty hunters had taken from the woman.

For all I thought I knew of Tryst Reine, he had never once spoken of Orangecloak with any fondness. Her name had come up, but Tryst never gave me the impression that he desired her. So what does it say that he abandoned everything he had in Atrebell to save her? What did I ever know of him, truly? Freyard pondered to himself, exhaling slowly while glancing upon the faces of the manor guards standing watch before the main entrance.

They never liked me before and now they all look at me with suspicion in their eyes. Every last one of them is well aware that Tryst and I were friends. I too would believe myself to be involved in Tryst's schemes, were I them.

The Captain of the manor guards, Egland Barrid, and his second in command, Lieutenant Brian Raspen, had found Freyard in the dining hall on the morning after the escape and taken him aside for questioning. There was nothing for Freyard to hide and he had told them truthfully that Tryst Reine had never shown any interest in Orangecloak or spoke of any desire to aid her in Freyard's company. Neither man seemed to believe Freyard, but he had a verified alibi for his whereabouts during Tryst's dubious activities: he was guarding the door to Marigold Tullivan's quarters in plain sight of both the guards of the Tullivan and Palomb households.

That Freyard had spent his free time volunteering as a guard for Marigold was cause for questioning in itself. However, with more pressing matters at hand and Freyard's whereabouts accounted for, Barrid and Raspen had dismissed him without further inquiry for the time being.

The pair had yet to reach a decision on what, if anything, they could do with Freyard and ordered him to remain upon the manor premises until further notice. Freyard had come to a decision of his own, though. While the judging eyes of the manor guards continued to peer at him, Freyard had penned his letter of resignation. He was leaving the guards and returning to the Southlands, to be bothered no more by the inane politics of the EMP and their armed protectors.

I won't miss this. As it was, only Tryst had made my time in the Honourable Guardsmen tolerable. Now, with him gone and leaving a chaotic wake that certain people suspect I am entangled with, there is no measure of distance I would not put between this place and I.

His right hand patted the inside breast pocket of his Captain's jacket, feeling for the copy of the letter he had drafted for himself. Another copy had been laid in the hands of Captain Barrid not an hour prior and as far as Freyard was concerned, his time with the Honourable Guardsmen was now only a memory.

"Captain Archer?" he heard a woman's voice call from behind him, and he turned about to find the fair face of Marigold Tullivan. She was dressed in black cotton trousers and a matching corseted, wide-collared vest, worn tightly over a light green, satin blouse with short sleeves that cuffed above the elbow. Long, dark brown hair was tied neatly, with the tail left to fall freely down her back. Standing at ease to her side was a teal-coated guard with short, black curls that Freyard recognised, but had not personally met before.

"Good afternoon, Miss Tullivan. How fares your day?" Freyard greeted her, careful to maintain formality in such public presence.

"It fares as well as it could," she answered, shooting him a curious look before following up with a question of her own. "Should you not be on duty right now?"

"Yes, I should," Freyard answered with a pause, unsure of how much to say where the many ears of guard and servant alike might hear. "However, there have been some extenuating circumstances."

"Oh? That's most unfortunate, Captain. Where will you be for the remainder of the afternoon?"

Freyard took a moment to look about, seeing only the bluecoat guards standing to either side of the stairwell leading to the Lord Master's chambers. Still, they were near enough that Freyard worried about what could well be overheard, and he chose his words carefully. "Staying out of the way of the working guards, I would suppose."

"You and I alike, Captain," Marigold said to that, her voice tinged with resentment. "It would seem that the Lord Master has said all that he thought my father should know and dismissed me for the day. I am returning to my chambers to take my luncheon. Would you care to join me?"

He caught the eye of one of the two guards, a man named Shanen, who Freyard knew to be a paid spy for the Palombs. "I must apologise, for though I am free from duty, I am otherwise engaged for the midday meal. I will have to decline the invitation."

That drew a visible look of dejection from Marigold and Freyard instantly regretted what he said. She was all poise and grace, though and took the declination well. "I understand and I shall not keep you, then. I bid you good day, Captain."

"A good day to you as well, Miss Tullivan," he responded softly, watching her turn away with a feigned smile on her face.

"Come along, Sydnee," Marigold said to the guard beside her. "I will need you to fetch a handmaiden for me so that I might send her to the kitchens. I suspect that there should be two or three still cleaning my former room."

The eyes of the bluecoat guards were still on Freyard, watching and judging him in silence. Freyard gave them his back and descended the wide staircase of the manor, walking around and behind it to the long corridor of the first floor.

Things in the rear of the manor had become a scene of utter disarray since the night before. The exit to the backyards hung open as guardsmen in both bright blue and indigo uniforms came and went hurriedly. Another pair stood shoulder to shoulder before the heavy double doors built into the stairs that led to the basements below. Even the entrance to Tryst's tower had a single guard stationed before the open door. It seemed that whatever staff were within the manor were back here, each one trying to learn what they could of the events that occurred two nights ago.

Freyard kept his head low with his gaze averted to the floor, and stayed near the wall to his left in a careful attempt draw no attention. No one seemed to pay him any mind, and soon he had slipped out of sight into a darkened little alcove that led to an old, wooden, spiralling stairwell. The steps were climbed two at a time and he reached the second floor to come upon a windowless landing with a closed door and a single, bare bulb dangling above.

He lifted the latch and let the door swing out slowly on its hinges, peeking carefully out to ensure the hall was empty. The only sign of life was an open door to Marigold's former chambers, which the maids were cleaning.

Freyard stepped out and carefully closed the door, attempting to make as little noise as possible in the process, and walked lightly, but quickly to the servants' entrance of Marigold's new quarters.

After giving a light knock, Freyard heard movement from within immediately and he could hear Marigold talking as she approached.

"My goodness, I must have the fastest maiden in Illiastra serving the luncheon to..." she had begun to say, although her voice trailed off upon opening the door and realising that it was no maiden before her. "Captain Archer, what brings you here?"

"Miss Tullivan, I beg your apologies for my demeanour moments ago and I ask only for a moment of your time so that I might explain myself," he began hastily in a low voice, hoping there was no one else that might hear.

For a moment she hesitated, lips pursed and eyebrows furrowed, and Freyard was sure she was going to close the door in his face. "I can grant you a few minutes. Do come in quickly though, Captain."

"Thank you, Miss Tullivan, I only desire that much," Freyard replied with a relieved sigh.

She stepped back and allowed him in, closing the door behind him gently, so as not to make a sound. "Now then, what seems to be troubling you, Captain?"

"I- Uh, you may just call me Freyard, if you so like," he started, stumbling a little over his words when he noticed her calling him by his title repeatedly. "I am terribly sorry if I came across as curt earlier. You see, one of the guards near the stairway to the Lord Master's quarters is a spy for Eamon Palomb. I did not think you would want him hearing of us being friendly. Especially not now, given that I am under investigation for my involvement with Tryst's disappearance."

"I was not aware of this. You made no mention of being investigated when last we spoke," Marigold responded in surprise.

"Then, the Lord Master does not yet know either?" Freyard put back with equal shock.

Marigold gave a light shake of her head. "Oh, I do not doubt that he does. I am sure that there is much and more he does not say in my presence. In fact, they are likely speaking of you right now. With that said, I would like to know for myself exactly what you are under investigation for."

"It's foolishness, to be sure," Freyard said with a smirk and a dismissive gesturing of his hand. "I was no more involved with Tryst's doings than you were. Besides, I have both of your own house guards and those of the Palombs' to vouch for the fact that I was right outside your door the entire time."

Her bright green eyes went wide as Freyard spoke the last sentence and he watched her slender fingers flex nervously. "Yes, you were. Not to mention the fact that until those bounty hunters showed up I was inside the room *with* Tryst Reine," she quickly locked eyes with Freyard again as something seemed to come to her. "Was my name mentioned as a possible conspirator in Tryst's activities?"

"No, your name was not spoken in my hearing, other than to say that I was outside your door," Freyard replied, trying his best to sound reassuring.

"That alone may be troublesome," Marigold contemplated aloud. "I had known that the Palomb guards would see him following me into my room. That in itself would barely be worth noting before the escape and I could have explained that I was thanking him for saving me from Pyore's strike. The Palombs themselves were embarrassed by that, they would have said nothing further on the matter. As it is now, though, Pyore's act is all but forgotten and all eyes are squarely on Tryst Reine and anyone remotely associated with him."

Freyard undid the top buttons of his jacket and reached inside, pulling out his copy of the letter and holding it between his middle and index fingers. "Their eyes won't be on me for much longer, I tabled my resignation with the Honourable Guardsmen. There's another copy in the possession of Captain Barrid at this moment."

"Something else that you wanted to tell me where the Palomb's spy could not hear you, no doubt," Marigold commented as she took the letter to hand to read for herself.

"Aye, I would rather let that be heard by everyone else in due time," he told her with a tired sigh and a nod. "As soon as I can be cleared as an accomplice in Tryst's scheme, I am boarding a train for Farmourd and riding south to the Varras River and Fort Dornett."

When Marigold was done with the letter, she carefully folded it and handed it back to Freyard. "You would resign your post so easily? I never took you for the sort."

That remark registered, but Freyard let it slide over him as he put the letter back inside his jacket. "I prefer to think of it as letting the rats have their nest. Besides, my work in the Southlands is far more pressing and I feel it a better use of my time and skills than watching over Parliamentary functions."

"Your 'work' as you have so phrased it, is the efforts of your Sun's Rangers in battling against the raiding gangs, correct?" Marigold asked in a probing manner.

"It is," Freyard answered obligingly. "My men and I are needed in the Southlands and we are respected for our efforts. At times, I feel as though the Sun's Rangers are the only branch of the Illiastran Government not corrupted by the touch of the Elite Merchants. When I am there, I can forget that vile organization."

His back made an audible thud as he let himself lean against the wall beside the servants' door. "It was my duty with the Honourable Guardsmen that reminded me of the grim reality. My mandatory tenure was served to completion years ago and any sense of pride that this role brought my family is no longer worth the hassle. I will not miss this manor or the people within its walls, present company excluded, of course, my lady."

While he had spoken, Marigold's eyes were downcast to the floor, rising to meet Freyard's only when he had finished. "A problem does not cease to exist simply because you have found a way to ignore it," she said with a voice that was equal parts sullen and stern. "It gladdens me to know that you see the EMP with as much disdain as I do, though. You are a selfless man who dedicates himself to driving out the raiding gangs on behalf of the less fortunate people of the Southlands. Would you be as eager to do the same for all of Illiastra against the EMP?"

He swallowed hard at that and tried quickly to form an answer. "Miss Tullivan, do you realize what you are asking of me, the Captain of the Sun's Rangers, Master-at-Arms for Fort Dornett, and the eldest son of House Archer of Collura?"

"I am asking you if you would as readily fight for all the people of Illiastra as you do for those of the Southlands," she stated clearly. "And please, call me 'Marigold'. The 'Miss Tullivan's tend to get exhausting after a time."

"If you insist, Marigold, but I digress. I swore a vow to protect all people of Illiastra. As does every soldier and guardian on the day he first wears the uniform," Freyard said, telling Marigold what he felt she already knew. "Alongside that vow is another, one which states that I serve those who govern over those people."

Marigold's eyes narrowed on him then. "What happens when those vows conflict with one another, Freyard? Does one oath supersede the other?"

"They conflict all the time," Freyard answered her. "As a captain, even one based in the Southlands, it falls on me to decide between the two on a constant basis."

"In your small corner of the Southlands you *are* the government, Freyard," Marigold told him bluntly. "It is easy to forget, as an armed soldier stationed in a remote outpost, that you are beholden to the EMP. However, as a woman and the daughter of a Warden Lord, I am forever reminded just who it is that rules this country. As uncomfortable as this manor makes you, at least you are safe in the knowledge that you can leave and never return with no one ever so much as batting an eyelash in concern."

Her bright green eyes pierced Freyard then, and seemed to affix him to the wall. "Meanwhile, my sister Serephanie is on the lam like an escaped prisoner, with men in uniforms scouring Illiastra in hopes of returning her to Daol Bay. If I ran, my own fate would be no different. My father was forced to trade us both like property or see our whole family ruined and driven into the streets. That is how the EMP sees women: as objects to be valued and bartered for based on our beauty and station."

"I am sorry that you have to endure that. Truly, it is no way to live," Freyard said sullenly. "In the Southlands I have seen women subjected to much the same at the hands of the raiders. They are taken from their villages, put in chains, treated like inventory, and then..."

That seemed to give Marigold pause and it took her a moment to speak again. "Do you and your rangers not try to save these women yourselves?" she inquired.

"Of course we do. The Sun's Rangers have broken many chains," Freyard answered, his brows wrinkling at the brazen nature of the question.

Marigold seemed to be immediately ready for such an answer and was quick with a reply of her own. "And what if I told you that there was a way for you to help me break the chains binding all the women of Illiastra?"

"I can say that in such a case that I would be interested in hearing this plan," he replied slyly, intrigued to hear of what Marigold might be plotting.

She gestured with an outstretched arm to a small table and two chairs nearby. "Then by all means, Freyard, have a seat and we shall talk over lunch."

Freyard hesitated to do so, looking from Marigold to the table before saying, "Forgive me if I seem impetuous in questioning your judgement, but would that be wise? Are you not worried that the maid delivering your food will see us together?"

"I am, but not nearly so much as I was a moment ago. At any rate, I may well have a solution to that," she said in regards to the issue while going to the entrance that led to the main hallway. A knock drew a tealcoat guard into the room, himself surprised to see Freyard. "Elden, could you step into the servant's hallway and intercept the maiden Sydnee sent for?" Marigold asked the man, who was still warily eying Freyard.

"Very well, my lady," Elden answered obediently and without further comment, stepping through the room and exiting into the outer corridor.

Marigold turned back to Freyard again. "I think that should remedy that issue. The handmaiden might find it suspicious that I have a guard waiting to take my luncheon, but she cannot report on what she does not see," she seemed satisfied with her action on the matter and seated herself at the table, waving a hand towards the other chair in silent invitation to Freyard.

He was curious, if nothing else, to know what sort of scheme she was devising and accepted her invitation. "If you insist, then I shall not argue further. What is it you wish to tell me?"

Her fingers tented above elbows resting on the table as she formed an answer to his query. "Things were spoken of today at the meeting that directly affect you. It would seem that the Lord Master is already planning an offensive manoeuvre against the Thieves in the Southlands. He desires to crush the remaining members before Orangecloak can have a chance to rally them."

"That would be awfully rash of him," Freyard said ponderously in response. "The Thieves are incredibly well hidden. Even my rangers have yet to come across anything outside of Phaleayna that might resemble any sort of home base for them. The roaming nature of Old Bansam even makes his crew difficult to track in the great wilds of the Southlands. Grenjin Howland might as well wage a war with ghosts."

"Lord Eamon has pointed out to him that one does not have to find wherever the Thieves might well be hiding. They need only lay siege to Phaleayna," she said while lowering her sight to the table.

That notion made Freyard most uneasy. "You mean he would suggest that we attack the refuge?" he asked in disbelief. "That is unconscionable. What has the Lord Master said of this plan?"

Marigold met his gaze again, her eyes filled with a look that seemed equal parts disgust and regret. "He wants the Sun's Rangers to lead the assault, Freyard."

"You cannot be serious," he gasped, searching her face for some hint that this might all be a ruse.

"In all my years of knowing the Lord Master I have never seen him as wroth as I did today," Marigold began in a voice as deathly serious as he had ever heard. "He had Orangecloak in his grasp and lost her when he was betrayed by Tryst Reine, his sworn protector. Howland believes that both of them will be going directly to the Southlands and he wants to draw them into a fight at the moment they are sighted crossing the Varras. Attacking the poor people of the ruins will almost certainly lure both of them out in defence of the island. Grenjin Howland wishes Orangecloak and Tryst dead and he is willing to go to any length to see to it that his own wish is granted."

"We have an agreement with Yassira Na-Qoia, though," Freyard protested in exasperation. "Surely that is worth considering?"

She shook her head. "It is already considered moot. As it is, that deal was only drafted to keep Phaleayna submissive to Illiastra. If the Lord Master sends an army to crush it completely, then there will be no Phaleayna and no need for any deal. Furthermore, he claims that Yassira has not been upholding her end of the bargain. From what I learned this morning, Orangecloak severed communications with Phaleayna some time ago and Yassira has been unable to provide any reliable information on the Thieves' movements."

"Yet the EMP was somehow able to ascertain the whereabouts of the Dollen sisters and Lazlo Arbor two nights ago?" Freyard asked her with uncertainty.

"As to that, Lord Taves told everyone gathered at the head table during the Summations feast that he had infiltrated the Thieves with an informant of his own," Marigold replied with a despondent sigh. "That mole has also served to further render Yassira's role redundant. The EMP has nothing to lose by destroying her, but striking at

Phaleayna could well be what delivers Orangecloak back into their hands."

"What if she and Tryst do not go to the Southlands? Knowing Tryst, even if they do go, it will not be a direct route. That would be too obvious. They could be delayed in returning in such case," Freyard queried, partly to Marigold and partly in rhetorical pondering.

"Lord Palomb asked that question," Marigold said in sombre response. "The Lord Master told Lord Taves to raze the island regardless. If Orangecloak and Tryst do not appear, it will look to those who believe she is alive as though she abandoned Phaleayna to a terrible fate. To everyone else, it will be an example to anyone who dares rebel against the EMP."

"Something about all of this is not quite right," Freyard put in cautiously, the details turning in his mind. "If Lord Taves has someone within the Thieves, how does he not know where they are hiding? He could go there directly rather than attack Phaleayna."

Marigold grazed her chin with an index finger ponderously at that as she looked to be trying to make sense of it. "I have not even the foggiest idea. However, last night Taves did say something about a 'little mouse that squeaks from both sides of its mouth'. Perhaps whoever is leaking information to the EMP is trying to balance between both factions."

"That may well be," Freyard admitted wearily. "I find it hard to believe there to be a leak within the Thieves, though. Lady Orangecloak knows her people well and it would take an ingeniously clever person to slip secrets beneath her nose."

"What I see is yet another deceitful spider carelessly spinning a dangerous web," Marigold commented, her face a blank slate save for the slightest upturn in one corner of her mouth. "So many of them try their hand at it, never knowing how delicate the silk strands truly are or how far they have to fall when the web begins to break."

"Some might say that you are spinning webs as well, my lady," Freyard boldly stated. "It is only a tiny little thing right now, both the spider and the web. Yet, it has perched itself high into the tallest tree in the forest and should it fall, it has further to tumble than any other."

She smiled mischievously at that, and her eyes looked beyond him for a moment, as if her mind were somewhere else entirely. "It is even more dangerous than you could possibly realise. However, I weigh every last line of that web with the utmost of care, planning every movement well in advance and layering that with even more strands to break my fall should one of them suddenly snap."

That's what I am to her, a contingency plan she has been forced to resort to, Freyard noted, keeping that thought unsaid. "Tell me, what would a spider want with a lowly fly like me?"

"A fly?" Marigold queried rhetorically with an amused scoff and a look of amazement on her flawless face. "You are the eldest son of a knightly house of old Phaleayna and the Captain of the Sun's Rangers of Fort Dornett. Many things you may be, but a fly is not one of them."

Wearing the most serious face he could muster, Freyard shook his head in reply to her statement. "Being of a knightly house does not mean what it once did. If you find that difficult to believe, feel free to ask any of the ministers of the Elite Merchant Party. The deities know they are quick to remind me of as much on a regular basis."

"The knightly houses are a very rare thing in Illiastra and they are nothing to be trifled with," Marigold said in dispute of his statement. "I happen to know a few things about those who descend from the knights of old."

"Such as?" Freyard asked out of sheer curiosity.

Marigold was not one to disappoint, and wasted no time elucidating. "There's two named Archer: your own in Collura and another in Ravenkeep. Both stem from two different men knighted as the 'Archer of' their hometowns and are of no relation. Or rather, their ancestors are of no relation, at least. I am aware that the Archer houses have wedded to one another in the more recent past."

"That much is true, aye," Freyard admitted, though he felt she was barely scratching at the surface. "It is one thing to know about my name, though, and we Archers are far from the only knightly houses around."

"Of course, I have not forgotten," Marigold acknowledged with a smirk. "There's the Shields family out of Hulting, down in the Galren region and of course the Pennywells, who lost their good standing when you and I were children. To that end, I believe there is a Warbridge family or two with some measure of wealth still to their names, although neither seems to know which Warbridge knight they descend from. Most say Ser Nichelon, the eldest, who served under the Great Hero of old. With that said, I know one Warbridge who swears that both families descended from the younger brother, Ser Kenneth.

"Granted, in today's Illiastra no one wants to claim that their family tree had its roots set by a knight who served a woman knight," Marigold stated with noted bitterness in her voice. "Especially if that woman is Ser Eleanor Price, who had the 'audacity' to reach the level of Knight's Commander."

Freyard offered an audible hum in understanding, and Marigold went on otherwise undisturbed. "I have met them all, you know, including the Pennywells and of course your father, Ser Delward Archer of Collura. I have found the knightly families to be different from both nobles and commoners. They are generally very proud of their storied heritage. To them, carrying that name means they are the living legacy of the last knights of Phaleayna and they are forever trying to ensure that their name is never besmirched. Knightly men are often prickly and defensive, but I have found them to be far more kind and courteous than the majority of the EMP in my experience. The strong, fighting members of each generation carry the house forward to the next, but the whole family usually works in impressive cohesion to ensure that honour is sustained. When the fighters or their supporters fail, then they become like the Pennywell family and the legacy is forever lost."

Marigold finished and Freyard swallowed hard, contemplating a thought that came to mind. Though he felt that it might be something he could well regret saying, he spoke anyway. "These things you learned regarding the knightly houses are not notions you picked up just from meeting my father or Winston Pennywell. You know these things because you are the descendant of Ser Davis Tullivan, one of the Teal Knights that served the Great Hero, Segai."

The corner of Marigold's mouth and a single eyebrow slowly arched as Freyard revealed his knowledge of her familial origins. "Very few recognise the Tullivan family for their knightly beginnings anymore," she said, clearly impressed. "Our roots have been overshadowed by our more recent ventures in Illiastran politics, but without our origin, the family tree would never have grown. What is no less a fact is that the Tullivan name is walking into extinction and along with it our legacy. Another knightly house, a piece of living history, all but eradicated."

"A tragedy, to be sure," Freyard answered carefully, choosing his words with caution. "Though one I do not know how to remedy at this time. With that said, I feel as though I am going to be needed now more than ever in the Southlands, if what you say is true."

"What will you do in the Southlands?" she asked, seemingly ready for just such a response, "You think that you are running home to defend Phaleayna, but your station will put you on the wrong side of that conflict. I wonder if you could obey an order from a lord in military garb if he were to command you to slaughter the very people that you have so vigorously defended until now."

"I could delay their efforts..." he began to say, although Marigold seemed to know just how that would work out for him.

"Could you? How? Have you ever known Mackhol Taves to listen to anyone besides Eamon and Grenjin? Anything short of clever verbal persuasion would be seen as high treason, and then what? Will you trade in your uniform and pistols for leather armour and a longbow and hope that the people on the island embrace you with open arms? No, I think not. Your presence on that battlefield would only bring you heartache and remorse. I have a far better use for your talents than setting you against the innocents you have worked so hard to stand for."

Freyard narrowed his eyes on Marigold curiously at that, "And just what would that use be?" he asked before being interrupted again, this time by a knocking on the door to the servant's hallway.

Marigold raised a single index finger to silence him and rose to answer the door wordlessly.

From without came the same guard that Freyard had seen moments ago. The man was pushing a trolley decorated in a long, white tablecloth and topped with a covered platter and a teapot beside it. When the trolley was beside the table, Marigold thanked the guard and he returned to the main hallway, leaving them alone once more.

A lithe hand lifted the lid of the platter to reveal a toasted sandwich comprised of crisp lettuce, strips of cooked chicken, and thinly sliced tomatoes. The bread had been sliced into four corners and arranged around a squared bowl containing a steaming, hearty soup in a tomato-based broth.

"This smells simply delectable," Marigold commented of her meal, "Might I offer you a half of my sandwich to share?"

He shook his head quickly. "Oh no, I could not dare. I have already eaten and it's not proper of me to do so."

Marigold's head tilted ever so slightly at that. "Depending on whom you ask it might be seen as insulting to refuse the offer of a highborn. Please, I insist, Freyard. I won't be able to eat it all anyhow."

Reluctantly he gave in and took a quarter of the sandwich, taking a small bite and trying to chew as quietly as he could.

"It is quite the conundrum, is it not?" Marigold wondered aloud as she shifted the whole platter from the trolley to the table. "The polite and mannerly thing for a servant or guard to do is to never take anything from a highborn, even when offered. Yet, despite that, it is considered an insult if you refuse. Much like you are sworn to protect the people, yet also sworn to answer to the government who may then order you to harm those same, innocent people. However, unlike that particular rule of mannerisms, you have a third option at your disposal when it comes to your current quandary."

It dawned on him then just what she was aiming for. "You want the Sun's Rangers," he stated bluntly after swallowing his latest bite of sandwich.

"And you to lead them," Marigold added quickly while gently blowing on a spoonful of soup to cool it down.

Freyard had an argument of his own for that. "If I am not in the Southlands, then there is no one who will defend the people of Phaleayna. I cannot abandon them. Not now, when the need for my rangers is most dire."

She was ready with a response again. "Orangecloak will come to their aid. They are her people more than they ever were yours. It is her that the EMP is trying to destroy and it is her that the people will cry out. So I say, let it be her who answers."

"Lady Orangecloak is a known pacifist," Freyard said with unmasked incredulity.

"She is every bit of that, I agree. However, do you think for one moment that she would look upon the besieged island she calls home and stand idly by while it is razed into the lake on which it sits? I admit that I know little of her, but I have every bit of confidence that she will fight for her people in such a case. There is no one else better suited to that task and unlike you, there is no dilemma over which side she serves."

Though he had to admit that Marigold certainly had a point, Freyard remained sceptical. "Should she fight back, the Thieves, even if they marshalled all their numbers, are neither trained nor equipped well enough to deal with even a small portion of Illiastra's army."

"Need I remind you that the Thieves now have Tryst Reine on their side?" Marigold asked without waiting for a response between bites of her food. "If he is aiding Orangecloak, then that is figuratively all she needs. Granted, he is only one man, but he is the Master of Blades. A man that skilled and intelligent in the ways of warfare is an immediate boon to any fighting force. That forgoes touching on the fact that he has been in the close service of the Lord Master. The things that man surely knows of the internal workings of the government could likely fill a library. I think we both know that Tryst and Orangecloak are precisely the people who are best equipped to handle any threats to the people of the Southlands."

"Fort Dornett would be left vulnerable without the rangers," Freyard attempted to say.

"Yes, it would need every remaining man to garrison the fort." Marigold stated in agreement. "None could be spared to answer the call to arms lest the fort possibly fall into the hands of the raiding gangs or the Thieves. That would be a blow to the numbers of the Illiastran armed forces. Not a major one, granted, but a blow nonetheless. What more can you do for the Southlanders than that?"

She speaks sense, Freyard thought to himself, before a separate notion occurred to him. "I would have to put it to my men for a vote. Before they cast a ballot, I can guarantee you that many would be concerned that we would be branded as deserters. That alone might be enough to snuff out your wish to hire my rangers."

Marigold, however, had no shortage of solutions. "I will draft a Lord's order. Or rather, I will have my house steward draft it, as I am still not permitted to do so legally. We shall concoct some story of raiders being spotted north of the Varras and that we requested the assistance of an armed force accustomed to dealing with such to flush them out. It will pass muster, though not by much, but neither does it need to. By the time anyone has an opportunity to look deeply into the matter it will be a moot point."

"That depends entirely on how much time we have before Great Valley Lake is besieged," Freyard pointed out. "Have they made any indication as to when that would happen?"

While he had spoken, Marigold had risen again, gone to the counter beneath the window, and retrieved an extra teacup. "Would you care for tea? I cannot imagine drinking this whole pot to myself," she inquired while filling both cups regardless.

"Very well, if you insist," Freyard acquiesced to the invitation, finding that he was far more concerned with the matters at hand. "What of *my* question?"

"As far as that goes, you will be glad to know that the deployment of soldiers is not to commence until spring arrives," Marigold told him while retaking her seat. "That leaves us with a window of opportunity. If you can bring me your rangers by winter, then your men will be well away before you can be called to action against Phaleayna. They want to allow for enough time for Orangecloak to return to, and be sighted in, the Southlands. Otherwise, they risk launching an expensive boondoggle of an operation to bait a target that might be anywhere else in the Known World."

"Then what?" he asked of her, gesturing with his hands out and splayed wide. "I know of the story you plan to sell to the merchants, but I will need to know the truth if I am to convince the Sun's Rangers to fight for you. Surely you must have some objective in mind that my unit would be most suited for?"

Freyard saw a drop in her mood immediately upon asking the question, noticing even a quivering in her lower lip that she stilled with a gentle bite. "There certainly is a task I have in mind," she began. "My father... I suppose there is no pleasant way to say it, Freyard... He is dying. His doctor and our steward both think that he will not live to see the winter. When the worst comes to pass, my dear father would not be cold before the Palombs will be on my doorstep looking for my house and me to claim as their own. I need men to meet them at the door, men that would not stand down to their orders and plenty of them. I have my house guards, like Elden and Sydnee, few though they are. My worry rests with the city guards. There is a possibility that despite their teal coats, they will not follow me. In the Southlands, you and your men are the law and if you join me, you will be the law again in the west and together we will defy the broken order."

Marigold looked to be fighting through any grief that her father's condition brought upon her, and there seemed to be a fire in her eyes then. "I see bigger things for you then fighting the raiding gangs until age or death shuffles you out, Freyard. Your rangers could be the inspiration that the men-at-arms in the west need to see in order to do what is right. Help me deliver Illiastra from the tyrannical grip of its oppressors."

"Forgive my brashness, but you would go through all of that to avoid a marriage?" Freyard asked next, finding the whole plan to be bordering on madness, albeit a madness he was starting to find tempting.

"It is not just a marriage, though I would be lying if I were to say that the nuptials were not a large part of it. This is about liberation for all women. We are every bit as strong and intelligent as men and we should enjoy all the same rights. Orangecloak has talked at length about it and while I find her words inspiring, I desire to do more than merely speak. I have the wealth and the station, at least temporarily, to lead the charge that ushers in a new Illiastra. It will take men and women alike, but I truly believe it can be done."

"You will bring about a war."

"No, Freyard, I will bring about a revolution."

4
MARIGOLD

or the first time since arriving on its doorstep over a week prior, Marigold found the Atrebell Manor to be eerily quiet. The commotion of the day before had started to ebb and the Parliamentary Sessions were over for another season. A few guards remained in place here and there, mostly Honourable Guardsmen and the standard issuance of bluecoats that regularly occupied the manor. The auxiliary forces called in from the city guards had all been dispersed, though most had not gone home. From what Marigold had learned, the majority of the city guards had been dispatched throughout the countryside in small parties to search for the fugitive Orangecloak and the five males, four humans and one elf, who had aided her in escaping.

Despite the quiet, there was no calm. Tension hung almost tangibly in the air, trailing behind every lord and servant wherever they went. Nowhere did that tension linger more than in the presence of the Lord Master, who admitted in the morning meeting with Marigold, the Palombs, and Lord Taves that sleep was eluding him almost entirely.

The same could not be said of Eamon Palomb or Mackhol Taves. In all her years, Marigold had never seen the two look so energetic and excited. They had been delegated a great deal of authority in handling the government's response to the incident and had taken to the task with a suspicious amount of vigour.

For his part, Grenjin Howland was the last word on their decisions, though he had grown so paranoid for his own safety that he refused to leave his apartments. No less than six Honourable Guardsmen were stationed on the third floor of the manor at all times, with windows and the lone exit being of the highest priority for protection.

Though she hadn't been permitted to ask as much, Marigold had learned that Howland lived with the fear that Tryst might return to end his life. The odds of that seemed slim to Marigold as it was, though the Lord Master was taking no chances with his own safety.

Were it me, I would be more concerned with what Tryst knows and what he might do with that information, Marigold pondered. Since he had arrived in Atrebell four years prior, no one, save for Hossle, the steward of the manor, had been in a better position to come into contact with sensitive information than Tryst. *The knowledge in his head is more of a weapon than the blacksteel sword in his scabbard.*

Yet, that seemed to be but a secondary concern and one Marigold could not comment on at any rate, given that she was not permitted to speak in the meetings unless directly addressed. Not that she had any desire to correct any perceived mistakes the others were making. *It would be poor strategy to help the men that will soon be my enemies. Let Grenjin worry about his own hide first and foremost. The longer he lives, the better it is for me. A greedy, miserable miser he might be, though that pales to the potential tyranny of his successors.*

The twin sons of Eamon were present in all the meetings too and under no gag orders as Marigold was. It aggravated her to no end that two bratty, seventeen-year-old *boys* were given leave to speak largely at will and she was denied even so much as a murmur. The only consolation she derived from it all was that this situation was but temporary.

Soon enough she would be reunited with her father, their steward Oire, and the beautiful port of Daol Bay that she called home. Once there and safely ensconced in her manor, her real plans could begin in earnest.

I will need to draft yet another plan, should Freyard not be able to bring me his rangers, Marigold reminded herself, only too aware of how easily such arrangements might fall apart.

Having been dismissed early from the meeting of the lordly men, Marigold was left to spend the afternoon on her own in the manor, giving her much time to dwell on such matters.

They would never dishonour Father in such a way, yet doing so to me is as easy for them as breathing, she reflected. It was a slight, but one Marigold was not wholly offended by as it left her with ample time to sort out her own strategies and investigations.

One of which she was currently embarking on. With Sydnee at her side, she had decided to take a walk behind the grand staircase, where she found that the purportedly bustling hive of activity from yesterday to be all but deserted at present. A trio of guards remained at the heavy, steel doors that led to the basements, denying access to all but Captain Barrid and his second-in-command, Lieutenant Raspen, and their most trusted guardsmen. It had fallen to them to lead the investigation into Tryst Reine's engineered escape of Orangecloak and the elven prisoner that the Palomb's had arrested.

If one were to pay heed to the rumours of the guards and servants, there was a grisly scene featuring a dead man in the dungeon below. To hear some among those tell it, the body belonged to a prisoner that Tryst Reine was alleged to have brutally slaughtered with his blacksteel sword. In closed hearing, though, Marigold got the true story, one that stated that the corpse in the dungeon belonged to that of a habitual killer. After the murderer's arrest and sentencing of lifetime incarceration in Biddenhurst, he had taken the lone offer presented to him and had become the personal torturer for the Lord Master.

That role had originally been intended for, and was still ascribed, to Tryst Reine, lending to his exaggerated reputation. From these reports, it was said that the man's neck had been broken, which compared to being hacked apart with a sword, was comparatively a clean and painless way to leave the world.

Marigold had known of Tryst's hatred for that particular man. In fact, when the notion of torture had been suggested to Tryst on his arrival, he not only detested the idea, he outright demanded that the act be abolished. When a replacement brutaliser had been found for the job, Tryst had no qualms about voicing his loathing of the man and his duties.

The Lord Master and his cohorts ignored Tryst then and they're now flabbergasted at his flight from this cesspool? Marigold asked herself with an audible scoff while listening to the soft clicks of her high-heeled boots on the hardwood floors. Tucked into those boots was a pair of brown trousers, which she had donned in spite of the objections of some of the more pious men. To complete her outfit she wore a dark blue, short-sleeved blouse.

She stopped suddenly at the door leading to the round tower that was once the domicile of Tryst Reine. There were no guards posted at the threshold and Marigold could hear no commotion from within. For all intents and purposes, the tower appeared to be abandoned by the guards and the three at the dungeon entrance were paying no mind to Marigold and Sydnee. Despite the objection of her nerves, Marigold decided to try the door.

Unaware of the fact that the woman Sydnee was charged with protecting had stopped in her tracks, he kept moving towards the rear exit. "Is something the matter, my lady?" he asked upon taking notice of her approaching the door.

The latch lifted in her hand and the door began to swing inward, evidently left both unlocked and unbarred. She put her finger to her lips to serve as a call for silence and to answer Sydnee before gesturing for him to follow.

Inside the room was coal black darkness and Marigold fumbled about on the wall beside the door until her hand came upon an electrical light switch. The tower, being the old remnants of an even older palace that had burned to the ground in years gone by, was only crudely wired for the fairly recent invention of electricity. A few bare bulbs lit the room, swaying in unison on account of a draft from a source unseen. The lone window in the room, situated behind a raised, cushioned platform, was curtained and shuttered, allowing no natural lighting.

This room, which had been an armoury that Tryst had converted into an exercise area, had been left entirely untouched. Racks of wooden weapons lined the circular wall on one side of the room with exercising equipment arranged neatly on the other. Between it all was a large square, straw mat that Marigold guessed was for fighting practice. There were what she had to guess were practice dummies too, made of wood and stuffed with a padding material, and stacked neatly atop one another.

As quickly as her boots would allow, Marigold strode across the floor towards a stairwell that wrapped around the inside walls of the tower and lead to the upper floor.

"My lady, should we be here?" Sydnee asked worriedly.

Marigold shrugged and turned to face him from the bottom step. "It would seem that no one has any interest in Tryst's tower anymore, what does it matter if we decide to look around?" she put to him, continuing on up the stairs when he made no further arguments.

The narrow staircase was lit with the same basic lighting as the armoury and ended in a small landing. The remnants of a door lay on the floor beyond, battered into splinters and left to lie where it fell, divorced from the frame in which it had once sat. Marigold stepped over it carefully, finding herself in a darkened room once more.

"Sydnee, would you mind finding the light switch?" Marigold asked while trying her best to see through the darkness. She stood aside for him and listened to the sounds of his search, hearing little until there was an audible click of a switch that allowed for a dim glow to encompass the chambers.

While the armoury below had been left untouched, Tryst's quarters were practically destroyed. His bedding had been cut to pieces, with the feathers of his mattress having found their way onto every surface. A beautiful armoire in the corner had been beaten open and was in worse shape than the door beneath her feet. Even a shelf of books had been emptied, its contents left in a haphazard pile before it.

The only piece of furniture left alone was a faded wooden table in the centre of the room, a few items that might have garnered momentary interest from the investigating guards remaining atop it.

Marigold turned back to Sydnee, still standing beside the light switch. "Could you keep watch on the door and let me know if you hear anyone coming?"

"Yes, of course, my lady," he called back, hurriedly stepping out onto the landing on the other side of the threshold.

On a cursory glance, there seemed to be nothing among the items on the table of any value, as Marigold suspected. She sifted through them regardless, finding only household supplies and toiletries that Tryst clearly had no need to take with him.

Nearby was a hearth that had long gone cold, its mantle barren and an empty plaque hanging above it. Marigold wondered for a moment what had been there, guessing it to be some weapon that Tryst likely took with him before leaving. In the armoire, either Tryst, or the guards who ransacked it later, had left nothing. Any clothing that had been inside was heaped on the floor and likely picked through.

Whoever was sent to search Tryst's room certainly was thorough, Marigold surmised, letting out an audible sigh and practically giving up hope of finding anything worthwhile.

Marigold began to turn back towards the door until her eyes caught sight of something peculiar in the corner to the left of the entrance. It was a wooden case bound in black leather, its lid left open and the interior empty. Beside it sat Tryst's guitar and like everything else in the room, it had taken a beating. She knelt and picked it up carefully so that she might examine it.

The strings were cut and a narrow gouge ran through the wood on either side of the sound hole, indicating where the slash of a blade had severed the strings. Upon issuing a closer inspection, Marigold discovered that the instrument had likely been thrown hard to the floor, as one whole edge was quite dented where the body of the guitar was at its widest. Even the back of the guitar had been heavily scratched and Marigold had to wonder if it had been kicked about.

It looks as though someone took out their frustrations on the guitar and no one else bothered with it afterwards, Marigold hypothesised while standing up, still holding the broken instrument that she knew had been one of Tryst's favourite possessions.

As Marigold rose to her feet, the loose strings began sliding and slapping about the body of the guitar, making racket enough to attract the attention of Sydnee. "My lady, what is that noise?" he asked curiously while stepping back into the room.

"Tryst's guitar," Marigold replied. "It was left behind by both him and whoever searched his room later. It is broken now, but I think it can be repaired. Do you recall if there is still a luthier in Daol Bay?"

Sydnee took a moment to think about the answer and sounded unsure when he did. "I'm not a musician myself, so as you can imagine, I've never had a reason to seek one out. I know there was one, back when I was a boy. He was from Amarosha, so I suppose he was driven out with the rest of the half-elves. It might be that a human opened up shop after he left, though I am entirely unsure. I think Lewcas plays a mandolin, my lady. I can ask him when we return to Daol Bay, as he would surely know."

"I am not so sure about that, Sydnee," Marigold questioned ponderously. "As far as I know, the only playing that Lewcas does is the board game *Kings and Knights.*"

"You're one of the only people in the Known World that he enjoys the company of," Sydnee offered in correction of himself. "I would defer to you as the expert on all things Lewcas, my lady."

She nodded thoughtfully at that. "It is of no worry. We shall look into it ourselves when we get home. In the meantime, would you be so kind as to pick up the case and help me take this back to my room? It would be a shame to let it get destroyed further."

The case was collected from the floor, laid upon the table, and the guitar situated snugly inside. Marigold gave the room a final visual inspection and, finding nothing of further interest, she departed. Taking the guitar case by the handle, Sydnee followed close behind.

They were in the armoury again and across the floor in a heartbeat. Marigold opened the door to the hallway a crack and peered out through the slit to look for any others nearby. "The way is clear," she told Sydnee, "Just a few men guarding the basement doors. We shall make for the servant's door just down the hall and take the stairs to their corridor on the second floor."

With Sydnee at the ready to go, Marigold turned toward the exit, took a deep breath, and opened the door in as casual a manner as she could muster. Together they strolled across the floor side by side, with Sydnee holding the guitar case vertical to conceal its shape between their frames.

Only one of the three guards took notice and his curiosity seemed to dissipate as quickly as it arose. Once the bluecoats were out of Marigold's sight, she dared not glance at them again so as not to draw any more attention to herself then she already had.

The dimly lit servant's corridor was empty at the moment and the pair took full advantage, practically running up the stairs to the second floor. Marigold was still leading the duo, and at the top of the stairs, they made a blind turn toward her quarters.

"Hello, Marigold," she heard from somewhere behind her.

"Sakes alive!" Sydnee exclaimed, dropping the guitar case noisily. Amid the clamour, he deftly put one hand to the hilt of his sword, the other to the scabbard on his hip, and placed himself in a defensive stance in front of Marigold.

With a quick pivot on one heel, Marigold turned about to face the owner of the voice, finding Freyard Archer casually leaning on a nearby windowsill. Today, like yesterday, she found him clad in his captain's uniform, with not a hair or a strand of fabric out of place.

"Be at ease, Ser Sydnee, tis only I," Freyard said with a hand raised in surrender. "My apologies if I startled you both. I had come to call on the lady for a moment and when I received no answer to my knock, I thought I might wait for your return. I have urgent news that I think you would most like to hear if you would be so kind as to give me a moment of your time."

Marigold glanced about to ensure there were still no eyes on them and only responded once satisfied. "Sydnee, could you set my new prize on the bed in my chambers please?"

"Yes, my lady," her guardian replied with a nod. He released the grip on his sword, scooped up the guitar case, and turned back toward the chamber door.

Once Sydnee had unlocked the door and disappeared inside, Marigold turned back to Freyard. "Alright, come inside, but we must not be making a habit of this right now. You know as well as I that it would not do for us to be seen cavorting for the time being."

"Of course, my lady, I would not be doing this if I did not think it to be of the utmost urgency," Freyard assured her in a low voice.

They made for the room with haste and Marigold closed the door quickly behind them. Once safely within, Marigold went straight for the case Sydnee had laid atop the bed. "Thank you for doing that, Sydnee. Would you mind checking up on Brandyl? He has been by the main entrance to the chambers all morning and I am thinking that he might like to be relieved for a few minutes."

"Yes, my lady," Sydnee affirmed with a quick nod before showing himself out.

"What do we have here?" Freyard inquired while Marigold undid the clasps on the case and lifted the lid.

Marigold picked up the guitar by the neck tenderly as she explained. "I have claimed Tryst's abandoned guitar for my own. I'm afraid it is in dire need of repair, though. Someone took a blade to the strings and, by my estimation, proceeded to kick it across the room."

Freyard rubbed his jaw and looked over the guitar contemplatively. "I think I might know the culprit."

"Oh? And who might that be?" she said with an eyebrow raised inquisitively.

A gloved hand of Freyard's ran softly over the fretboard of the guitar while he spoke. "I have it from one of my few remaining contacts in the Honourable Guardsmen that it was one of them who cut the strings. It was done so that they could ensure that there was nothing of pertinence to the investigation hidden within the guitar. They were looking for letters or hidden maps or some such thing, not that I could see Tryst Reine being so careless as to leave any sort of trail. Regardless, after they were satisfied that it was empty, Captain Barrid dumped it out of its case and took his anger out on it. You're lucky that it's not dust and splinters."

That struck Marigold as odd and raised a question she had. "Is his station suddenly in danger?" she asked curiously.

"Indeed, our rotund friend stands to lose his comfortable position if Tryst and Orangecloak are not found. Grenjin Howland evidently promised to replace him with one of the city district captains," Freyard explained, not the least bit upset at the lazy officer's misfortune. "He and Tryst always openly disliked one another, but now it's as though Tryst is giving him one last show of contempt from afar. I hear that the whole ordeal is driving Barrid absolutely berserk."

"I cannot say that I fault the Lord Master for his frustration towards Barrid," Marigold admitted with a shrug. "Someone will have to take the blame for this whole mess and the captain of the manor guards seems to be the ideal scapegoat. Who better for such than the lazy sot who could not be bothered to do his own job?"

Freyard's handsome face suddenly turned morose. "The only man to blame for this is Tryst Reine. I do not care for Barrid any more than he does, but I am beginning to think that perhaps Tryst had been preparing for such an event for some time. Does Captain Barrid possess some sort of innate ability to read the mind of mortal men and know their intent? Nay, this is not his doing."

That only worried Marigold, who put the guitar back down and turned her attention solely to Freyard. "Do you think Tryst was in the wrong to free Orangecloak? Could you have sat idly by, knowing that the Lord Master intended to torture and execute her?"

Freyard hesitated for a moment, eyes casting themselves downward before he spoke again. "No," he began, choosing his words carefully. "I also do not fault Tryst for what he did. I am, however, somewhat bitter about him leaving without even as much as a farewell, or at the very least, a forewarning," one gloved hand picked at the leather covering the other idly, his brow pinching together in thought. Marigold could see a quiet anger behind his carefully guarded expression, one whose direction was aimed everywhere and nowhere at once. "I might well have left with them, or at least aided in their escape. Yet, the man I regarded as my lone friend in Atrebell kept me entirely in the dark on his whole plan. It makes me wonder what I truly knew of him."

With a wave of his hand, Freyard swept the topic aside as though it were of no importance. "I suppose it's selfish of me to feel this way. He saved Orangecloak from a horrendous fate and for that I should be glad," he finished, heaving a disheartened sigh.

"You can feel both glad and bitter. I know I do," Marigold reasoned, feeling much the same way as Freyard. "As you well know, I too was fond of him and I was quite taken aback when I heard that he had suddenly vanished from the manor with Orangecloak, though I am elated that she escaped. As it was, I barely slept that night thinking about that poor woman being locked up and tortured in the bowels of the same manor where I lay in comfort. "

She folded her arms and exhaled loudly as the words came to her to continue. "It is frustrating that Tryst left with her, though the more I think about it, the more I am realising that he was her only option to get out of that dungeon alive. Howland, Palomb, and Taves all want her dead and there was no one else who had the power to even get close to her without scrutiny from the guards. Tryst could, and he did, and somehow he walked her right out of here under the noses of every guard, minister, and lord. I could not have done that, nor could you, or any of the other Honourable Guardsmen. It had to be him, Freyard."

He let out a deep sigh, his right hand scratching idly at the back of his head. "The sting will pass, I know it will. It merely hurts for now, is all."

Marigold felt a small pang of pity pierce her heart and she felt her eyes soften as she fixed him with a gaze that she hoped would carry to him sincerely. She too felt the burn left in the wake of fire left behind Tryst, and could not fault Freyard for being hurt so deeply. "I have learned in this life that the people closest to us are the ones capable of leaving the largest wounds," Marigold began, the words coming from somewhere deep within.

Though she wondered if they were appropriate to say to someone that she was just getting to know, she did not stop herself. Her tone went soft, losing some of its formal sound. These words came from some place different, a place built on honesty and sincerity. It was only when his eyes met hers did she continue. "Some people use that as a reason to stay distant from others and they wear their distance like armour. It takes courage to let people in, to let them close enough to make a wound. Some will make us bleed and leave behind a nasty scar, but with each scar comes a lesson on how to prevent the next wound before it ever happens. I can tell you from my own experiences that I would rather have the scars, and the stories and lessons that go with them, than the cold, lifeless armour."

"Poignant words, my lady," Freyard responded with a single nod. "Though I know many who don the armour *because* of the wounds they have taken. We all deal with our hurts differently and what works for one may not work for others."

"Just so," Marigold said in continuance. "I had long suspected that Tryst wore armour of his own too. He let few in during his time here and I have to wonder if perhaps it was so he could leave on a moment's notice as he did. It might well be that this was his plan all along."

"You may well be right about that," Freyard agreed, showing all signs of being done with this particular conversation. "At any rate, as much as I enjoy philosophical debate and speculating on the motives of Tryst Reine, neither are why I came to talk to you today."

"Oh? Perhaps you came to exchange gossip, then?" she said jokingly, in a regretful attempt to lighten the mood.

Freyard chuckled softly and reached behind his back for something hanging from his belt. On the return, Marigold espied a sword in a sheath that Freyard held out for her to take.

Marigold collected it from his hands, feeling the weight of it in her own. It was a light blade, all told, with a beautiful, ornate hilt made of gold and set with sapphires on either end of the crossguard and in the pommel. The sheath itself was tight black leather with a gold tip. Carefully, she drew the blade forth by a few centimetres and took a look upon the steel.

"It's not worth much as a weapon, sadly," Freyard commented on the piece. "The steel of the blade is cheap and the hilt is uncomfortable to the grip. I doubt that a man who owns a blacksteel sword would have any use for it whatsoever. They are given as gifts by the Lord Master to the most distinguished of his soldiers, particularly the Honourable Guardsmen. Though expensive, most who own one merely wear it for its ornamental value, present company included."

He carefully turned the sword over in her open hands, revealing the intricately notched initials of T.R. in the leather of the scabbard. "You now have one as well, albeit one bearing the initials of the Master of Blades. It is as rare a sword as there could be."

She continued to admire the beautiful piece now in her possession, asking the only question that came to mind at the moment: "How did you come to have this, Freyard?"

"It was won in a game of dice this morning. Everything valuable of Tryst's that he left behind was divvied up that way. If I am being completely honest, I only bought into the game at all so that I might win the bottle of *Spiced Night* rum being wagered. It is a twenty-six-year-old vintage imported from Johnah. Tryst secured the bottle on his last visit to Aquas Bay, or so he told me. You will not find a better liquor anywhere in this country. Everything else is swill by contrast. Alas, that went to Jarrell of the Honourable Guards and I played on, eventually coming away with that sword."

Regardless of how he came into possession of the decorative weapon, Marigold was thankful and made sure to express her gratitude. "Thank you very much, Freyard. I appreciate the gift. It is a very kind gesture."

"There is more I came to say," he put in suddenly, his voice turning deathly serious. "I have been cleared of any suspicion by Captain Barrid and Lieutenant Raspen."

Marigold furrowed her brows, giving Freyard the nonplussed stare his comment warranted. "I should think that to be a fortunate turn of events," she commented. "For me to understand your disdain, I think I will require a few more pieces to this puzzle, Freyard."

That drew a telling look from Freyard as he replied, "Coming from a scorned Barrid and an ambitious Raspen, their declaration is most certainly a double edged sword. They both told me plainly enough that they still believe me to be involved in Tryst's plot. In fact, if not for a solid, verified alibi vouched for by Eamon Palomb's own guards, I would be in chains right now."

"My men also verified your whereabouts. Do their voices not count for anything?" she asked.

"Your men are under investigation themselves and it may be you that Barrid and Raspen come to question next," he said worriedly. "It was guarding *your* door that kept me in sight of Eamon's men all night, after all, and for a short time it was yourself and Tryst on the other side. The good news is that I am fairly certain that neither you nor your guards would be arrested, even if they somehow concocted a convincing enough story to sell to the Lord Master. Regardless, I will not be here to intervene on your behalf should anything happen."

A feeling of anger began to rise within Marigold and she fought to stifle it. "Let them try and come for me and mine, let them threaten us with shackles and deep, dark dungeons. It will be their mistake to make, not mine."

"Precisely," Freyard added confirmatively. "You are safe, for now at least. The Lord Master would almost certainly veto any notion of detaining you or even your guards, so long as your father lives. You have immunity in that regard, which is something that someone like Orangecloak, or even I, do not have. If I offer you any counsel it would be to take advantage of that immunity while the window is still open and leave Atrebell with haste."

"I may have to do just that. I will not ask the Lord Master to be excused, but should he make an offer, I shall not hesitate to accept it. What of you, Freyard? You mentioned that you would not be here to save me should the worst come to happen. Are you being dismissed?"

"As for me, on account of my resignation, I have been asked to vacate the manor as soon as possible. As it is, a single ticket to Farmourd has already been reserved in my name for the last train of the day."

"You will be leaving soon, then?" Marigold asked sadly, already having a notion of the answer.

"Immediately, as it were," he said, confirming as much. "Along with everything else I have come to say to you, I must add my farewells also. My belongings have been packed and wait for me at the barracks door and I have arranged transport into town with a delivery wagon that should be here at the top of the hour."

"That's only fifteen minutes from now," Marigold stated while giving a glance to the grandfather clock in the corner of the room. "I hope your rangers will be in agreement with our proposed arrangement."

He bowed in kind and began to make for the door, stopping short to turn back and give a reply. "It shall be tabled as soon as I return, that much I can promise you. I can only hope they will be as enticed by the proposal as I was."

"Let us hope so," Marigold said anxiously before asking a question of her own: "How soon do you think you can be in Daol Bay, should the motion pass?"

She watched his chest rise slowly with a long, deep breath as he contemplated his answer. "Should the other rangers vote in your favour, then I will endeavour to begin the journey west without delay. I would sooner be in Daol Bay before winter sets in and time is not on our side as it is."

Against her better judgement, Marigold walked to where he stood and drew his body down into a hug. "Then I hope to see you in the light of the rising sun before the last of autumn. Until such time, may fortune find you, Freyard Archer."

5
FREYARD

trebell was behind him. It was a thought that always brought with it a feeling of great relief after every Parliamentary Session, but this time, it was much more than that. This time, Atrebell was behind him for good.

Three days prior, Freyard Archer had stepped off the train in Farmourd, stored his uniforms neatly in his rucksack, donned his worn and comfortable riding leathers, and retrieved his horse Soldier from the stables. Once reunited with his steed and comfortably in the saddle, Freyard went south through the gates of Farmourd and continued in much the same direction ever since. It was the same routine he had done at least four times every year for what felt like far too long. Despite all the similarities to his previous journeys from Farmourd to Fort Dornett, none had made him feel as free as he did on this occasion.

The sound of the roaring Varras River found his ears and brought with it a wave of relief and yet another reminder of what had come to pass as of late.

My tenure with the Honourable Guardsmen is over. For the first time since submitting my letter of resignation, it actually feels real. Father will be disappointed if ever he hears about it, but I could not be happier to have what amounted to such a prodigious waste of time behind me.

Freyard found himself snorting aloud as the vision of his father floated before him. *As far as Delward Archer is concerned, I am already a disappointment, regardless of my accomplishments. What's yet another coin tossed on the pile?*

From the day he was brought into the world and declared by the midwife to be a healthy baby boy, Freyard Archer was fated to be a soldier. It was his expected duty as the eldest son of a knightly family, and to that end, the entire Archer clan had rallied around him.

On his fifth birthday, he was given two gifts: the first was a short, curved bow and a quiver of arrows from his father, a traditional gift as old as the family name. The other, from his two uncles, was a wooden sword. Not a toy, but an honest, weighted practice weapon, complete with a scabbard and a tiny belt. The three men began the boy's training from then onward, drilling him in the art of combat for what had seemed like every waking hour that he was not in school.

Freyard had two younger brothers of his own, near enough in age to him that when they were old enough, they began training alongside their eldest sibling. Yet, it was to his shoulders that the expectations went. Sylvus and Viertas became aware at a young age that their training was done as a precautionary measure so that they could take Freyard's place should some unforeseen tragedy prevent him from performing his duties. With that lesson of unfairness in mind, they had lived in Freyard's shadow, knowing that unless Freyard was killed or crippled, the glory and legacy of the Archer Clan of Collura was his and his alone.

Sylvus, Freyard's junior by barely a year, resented the attention paid to his elder brother and channelled that frustration into his efforts to be the better of the two siblings in every fashion. To Sylvus' credit, there was no plausible way for Freyard to deny that the middle brother was the best swordsman among Delward Archer's sons. Sylvus' talent for the blade came so naturally to him that by the time he reached adulthood, Freyard could hardly win a sparring match on Sylvus' worst day.

The youngest Archer brother was an excellent hand at both melee and ranged combat in his own right. Despite his abilities, being third in line had given Viertas the security to know that he was not bound to those skills like his siblings. Once both of his older brothers reached adulthood and their military careers were cemented, Viertas announced his intention to leave the family tradition of soldiering in favour of personal pursuits. When Freyard had last corresponded with his family, the word on Viertas was that he was residing in the

Toyell region and happily serving as a sub officer for the regional fire brigade.

In regards to his own talents, Freyard had lived up to the family reputation and his marksmanship was entirely unrivalled. Whether it was a rifle, pistol, crossbow, or longbow in his hands, there appeared to be no target Freyard could not hit.

By seventeen, Freyard was enrolled in the military and it seemed that he was destined to climb high through the ranks. Before the age of twenty, he was regarded as one of the top marksmen in Illiastra, noted by his peers and commanding officers alike for his discipline and diligence. He was the very definition of a good and honourable soldier and Delward beamed with pride at every mention of his eldest son's name.

It was expected of every soldier in their sophomoric year to be dispatched to one of the many forts along the south side of the Varras River. Their duty there was to partake in a ritual that had come to be known as 'standing the southern post' or more colloquially, *'suffering the southern post'*. Delward had already gone to great lengths to get Freyard exempt from having to serve a year in the ramshackle old forts. No, a firstborn son of the Archer Clan of Collura was destined for far greater service than policing the poor folk and chasing raiders, especially someone of the calibre of Freyard.

Yet, it was Freyard himself who had insisted on it: *"How can I lead these men if I am not willing to endure what they endure?"* Freyard had asked his father. *"They will not respect me as a soldier, much less as a leader, if I don't do this."*

It was with great reluctance that Delward finally relented and dropped his case, giving his eldest son leave to be dispatched to the first available posting, which had taken Freyard to Fort Tesse.

Freyard had arrived to find that the bulk of the fort had washed into the river several years prior. The only inhabitable structure remaining to what was referred to as Tesse the Mess was a single tower, itself hanging over the eroded southern bank of the roaring waterway. The tilted, decrepit old building was still the tallest structure on either side of the river and so it remained garrisoned by three men at a time in alternating shifts throughout the day. Substituting for the fortified amenities that Freyard was expecting were a collection of pavilion tents that had been erected amongst the tiny village on the north bank for which the fort had been named.

Before his standing of the southern post had begun, Freyard had been forewarned by his senior peers that the river forts were unanimously dreary and destitute. He had prepared himself for a terrible time in the remote wilderness, to be surrounded by nothing but trees and a river so loud that it drowned out thought. Even the people, he was told, were either savage raiders or backwoods rubes that were either too poor or too dull to move to safer realms.

It was I who was the dullard, he reflected with a sigh from Soldier's saddle, his gaze falling on the downward sloping path that led toward home.

Though he had gone to the Varras River to prove his worth as a leader, the negative influence of his peers had quite nearly steered him astray. It was not as though the townsfolk were unaccustomed to the pretentious air of superiority of the young soldiers. In fact, it was something they had grown to tolerate and ignore for the sake of the protection that the armed and uniformed men offered against the raiding gangs that roamed the Southlands.

As it turned out, speaking to those villagers and learning of their troubled lives had been the cure for Freyard's obnoxious attitude. Once his youthful arrogance was tempered, the people living in the shadow of Tesse the Mess began to shape Freyard Archer's entire outlook on life far more than anyone might have imagined.

I had to learn hard lessons on humanity and humility in a troubled land from toughened folks eking out an existence at the river's edge. That was how I came to distinguish myself as a leader. I could have gone to any military posting in Illiastra after my time at Fort Tesse. Father was already courting a few different lords for a potential job for me as a captain of the guards in one of their manors.

At the time of his posting to Tesse the Mess, such a position sounded inviting to the young man he had been. Now though, the very thought of such seemed absurd to Freyard.

"Desmond Browerford is the Lord of Agriculture. That is an important Lordship, and serving as the Captain of the Manor Guards for House Browerford would be a position of great distinction. It will bring honour and recognition to House Archer of Collura, the latter of which we have quite nearly been without since the Elite Merchants came to power," his father had argued. *"Do you not want that for your family?"*

The question was one Freyard had fully expected from Delward and he was prepared to answer it. *"I want to captain the battle against the raiding gangs, not waste my time protecting potatoes in Leslington. The people of the Southlands need defending from those brutes. They have suffered for far too long."*

Delward had stared at him incredulously for what felt like hours after that response, finally uttering but four words: *"Have you gone mad?"*

"On the contrary, Father, I think I have come to my senses," Freyard had declared to him.

"The eldest son of House Archer is not going to be swashbuckling in the Southlands against madmen. It is unbecoming of you and your name! We are a knightly house," Delward argued in protest.

"That is all the more reason that I should be in the Southlands," Freyard had countered, quite angrily, as he remembered. *"A major part of the oath our ancestors swore when they were knighted was to defend the innocent. While their general sense of innocence is certainly lost, being poor and living in the Southlands does not make one a criminal.*

"I have seen the carnage of the raiding gangs in the mangled bodies they left behind, heard it in the wails of women and children, and smelled it when we burned the corpses. Poor or wealthy, no one deserves to be left to that fate and I cannot turn my back on those in the Southlands in order to guard over some pampered lord."

The patriarch of House Archer was at a loss for words for once and Freyard recalled how he had sunk into his office chair and seemingly surrendered. *"Who will carry on here in our name?"*

Freyard was ready for that question as well. *"I would think that Sylvus would be delighted to hear of these developments. Let him guard over teatime for the lords and ladies. It's what he's always wanted."*

And so it went, Freyard reflected on the memory. *Father got a son who would eagerly advance the social status of our family name and when my tenure at Tesse the Mess had finished, I remained in the Southlands. I even became a captain of my own band of rangers.*

Shortly after earning his Captain's medal, Freyard was visited at his new home in Fort Dornett and inspected by Lieutenant Brian Raspen of the Atrebell Manor guards. *I suspect that Father had some role to play in that. If I would not go by choice to serve in the north, he had a means of forcing my hand, at least partially, anyhow.*

The lieutenant was there to scout on behalf of Egland Barrid, Captain of the Atrebell Manor Guards and Commander of the

Honourable Guardsmen. Almost immediately upon Raspen's arrival, a place in the Honourable Guardsmen was offered to Freyard, and while it was something that most soldiers in his position would leap at, Freyard had little interest.

To underscore his point, when Freyard sent Lieutenant Raspen away empty-handed with a polite refusal, he included an envelope addressed to Captain Barrid. The lengthy letter within stated to Barrid that Freyard's duties as Ranger Captain and Master-At-Arms of Fort Dornett required all his time. The reasoning did not resonate with Barrid and the letter Freyard got in return included an issuance from the Lord Master himself. In that response he was told that the appointment to the Honourable Guardsmen was not only official, but compulsory, for a period of no less than two years.

It was a victory for Father, I will grant him that, Freyard granted as Soldier turned a corner, bringing the town of Dornett into view at last. *He got his wish for his oldest son to be in a finely pressed uniform in the presence of lords and ministers for all to see. However, it was not without some benefit, considering I told him the decision was mine to make as a compromise. I could appease House Archer without feelings of guilt. It seemed to be the only way to achieve that while spending the majority of my time where I am most needed: leading the Sun's Rangers against the menaces of the Southlands.*

From nearby he heard two men calling and laughing gaily to one another.

Sun's Rangers such as these two.

Freyard's eyes befell the form of two strong lads in their early twenties. They were broad shouldered, with dark hair, light complexions, and identical features save for the fact that one wore a full beard where the other had opted for a moustache. That had been Freyard's idea, as it was the only way for him to distinguish between the Pharsey twins of Falsamere. The two were among his more recent recruits, having arrived less than a year prior from the small city that lay northeast from Atrebell.

As he came upon the duo, Freyard discovered them to be in full armour, meaning that they were on guard duty at the moment. Despite that, they were in the middle of a vegetable plot, pulling large, yellow turnips for an old resident of Dornett Town named Schenn. The bearded brother, Lahn, was digging the bulbous root vegetables out of the ground with a hoe while his twin, Brahn, loaded them into a wheelbarrow. They seemed to be making a game out of how fast they could do the work, laughing as they tried to maintain the quick pace that their coordination allowed them to achieve. Nearby, leaning on the wooden fence around the perimeter of his soil bed was old Schenn, smiling and chuckling along with them.

As their captain, it fell to Freyard to chastise them for being in dereliction of duty. However, he could not even feign anger for their selfless act of service for an elder of the community.

The sound of Soldier's hooves on the ground drew the focus of the three all the same and once they realised it was Freyard approaching them, Brahn and Lahn stood to attention with a salute. "Captain Archer, allow me to be the first to welcome you home, Ser," Brahn said, saluting with his right hand, while still clutching a turnip in the left.

Freyard brought Soldier to a stop just outside the fence and gave them a salute in return. "I bid you good day lads, and to you as well, Mister Schenn. How fares things in Dornett since I left?"

Lahn had set aside the hoe in order to salute and was retrieving it from the ground while he answered. "It's been quiet, Ser. No raiders and no other incidents, so we've been helping with the harvest as much as we can."

"Good on you, lads. You have my permission to continue lending a hand," Freyard stated jovially, before adding a condition. "Provided that it doesn't interfere with your regular duties, of course."

His attention went to the elder beside the fence so as to ask him a question. "How's the harvest, Mister Schenn?"

"Bountiful, Captain Archer," Schenn replied warmly. "Barely any bug or critter damage, even in the potatoes, gods be praised."

"That is most wonderful news," Freyard intoned happily, pointing toward the twins as he went on, "Don't be afraid to put those two to work, even when they are not on duty."

The old man approached and stroked the mane of Soldier. "Why thank you, Captain, these old bones could use all the help they can get."

Brahn spoke up for the both of them while tossing the turnip he had been holding into the wagon. "That won't be a problem, Ser. We're only too glad to offer our assistance."

"They're eager. I like that," Mister Schenn commented to Freyard. "You know how to pick good working men, Young Knight."

That was Freyard's name amongst much of the residents throughout the portion of the Southlands that he frequented. The people there held strong to the tales and fables from the days when Illiastra was divided between kingdoms of men, dwarves, elves, and the Amaroshan half-elves. It was in those times that the knightly names originated and the people who brought fame to those names walked the world. Having supped on those tales for so long, the Southlanders still thought quite highly of the knightly houses. To have the eldest son of one of those houses serving as a Ranger Captain was like having the heroes of old live amongst them once more. The more he and his men fought and protected the people, the more the legend of the Young Knight and his Sun's Rangers grew.

Freyard had rebuffed it at first, reminding everyone that knighthood in Illiastra died with the last king eight hundred years prior, but it mattered little. He had the name and embodied the traits of the heroic men and women of the legends that the Southlanders had passed down for centuries. To them, he was their knight and Freyard had come to accept the informal title, such as it was.

"Thank you, Mister Schenn. I hope that their eagerness doesn't ebb," Freyard replied, before turning back to the Pharsey twins. "Lads, how many more of the rangers are on guard duty today?"

The two took a second to think about it, before Brahn answered for them again. "It's us walking the perimeter of town, Troygard and Mack manning the River Giant, and Clem and Fenton on the roof of the fort tower, Ser. All the rest on patrol are from the regular garrison today."

"Well and good," Freyard replied, injecting his voice with sternness. "I'll be calling a meeting in the hall tonight at the nineteenth hour with all the rangers. Ensure that the both of you are there. I'll tell the others myself when I return to the fort."

A glance was exchanged between the brothers and Freyard saw the curiosity plain enough on their faces, but they thought better of asking questions in front of citizens. "Aye, Captain," Lahn replied for the both of them. "We'll be at the hall by the nineteenth and not a minute later. You can count on us, Ser."

"Right, then, as you were, men," Freyard told his charges, offering the old man a parting nod as well. "Always a pleasure to see you, Mister Schenn. I bid you a good day."

He wheeled Soldier about and headed into the village of Dornett. Though it was a bustling little town at present, when Freyard had started his tenure at Fort Dornett, the hamlet that stood across the river from it barely numbered fifty people. It had been no more than a collection of thatch-roofed houses, a few shacks, a barn, and a forge. Once he instituted the Sun's Rangers and actively began driving the raiding gangs out of the eastern reaches of the Southlands, the population of Dornett had begun to flourish. Now, he rode Soldier by more than a dozen homes and a town center that housed a general store, an inn, a pub, and a clinic operated by the fort's nurse.

At last check, there were almost three hundred living in the village. They came from across the Southlands mostly, fleeing the destruction sown by the raiding gangs. However, Freyard had come to discover that Dornett had become home to a small smattering of people from elsewhere as well. Two among them were miners from the Warrens in the far south. Next door from one of them was a family headed by a retired member of Old Bansam's band of fighters. More again had migrated from the other fort villages along the north side of the river. According to reports and testimonials from the recent settlers, they came to Dornett because of the safety provided by the presence of the Sun's Rangers.

Freyard was proud of the reputation his unit had garnered and the village was as much a home to him as Collura had ever been. Indeed, the progress he had made here weighed against his decision to align with Marigold Tullivan and looking upon all that he would be leaving only weighed it further.

If I should go through with honouring Marigold's offer, the townsfolk will say that the Young Knight abandoned the poor folks of Dornett for a wealthy, highborn lady. My men might well say it too.

It seemed to Freyard that every townsperson he met had a hello and a wave for him, especially the children. The adults he passed closely would even stop him briefly, asking of his journey north, the weather, and other benign topics. Freyard answered all their questions as much as he could without mentioning any sensitive information, especially anything pertaining to the incident with Lady Orangecloak.

As he left the last of them and made the lonely trek to the architectural achievement that was the bridge known as the River Giant, Freyard's mind began to wander. *If there is one thing that is a guarantee upon my every return, it is that the villagers never ask about Parliament. They simply are not concerned with the happenings of the Elite Merchant Party and never have been. They just want to be left alone and I would like to think that I have given them that wish to the best of my abilities. The raiding gangs haven't even so much as sniffed around the bridge since I formed the Sun's Rangers and began to drive the bloody bastards away. Because of that silence, no one from the government has any reason to look at Dornett, either.*

The sound of hammering managed to rise above the river's roar, and Freyard followed the sound to see a team of builders busily framing a new house. The head carpenter was another import from the northerly regions, like Freyard, having migrated for the warmer climate and the peace that the Sun's Rangers granted to Dornett.

That peace will be disrupted if what Marigold said of a siege in Phaleayna rings true. We are close enough to that place as it is, not to mention the plans Taves supposedly has for the Sun's Rangers. How can I order my men to put people like those I already protect to the sword? What would the people of Dornett think of their Young Knight then? What will they think if I abandon them for Marigold? To them, she is just some rich woman living in the far west with a famous surname. It is not as though I can tell them why I would be leaving them for her. If the Sun's Rangers vote in favour of the measure, I will have to hope that the townsfolk come to understand and forgive us in time.

Freyard heard the familiar clangour emanating from the tower sitting on an islet in the middle of the Varras, returning his attention to more immediate matters. The River Giant was a three-storied, steam powered, rotating bridge and lighthouse situated mid-river, the lone one of its kind in Illiastra. The turning bridge itself had existed in some form for over a millennium. It was the lighthouse that was added just a decade before Freyard's arrival that made it an engineering marvel.

The islet the bridge sat upon was surrounded by rocky shallows that could tear the narrow boats that plied the river to splinters, especially if they were struck when heading downriver. As more boats began to run aground or sink to the shallow riverbed, they became a hazard of their own. To alleviate the problem during travel in low visibility or after dark, the lighthouse was built atop the bridge itself, to guide river traffic safely around the rocks. The tower rotated along with the bridge and had two soldiers on duty atop it at all hours, ready to activate the turning mechanisms at a moment's notice.

According to the Pharsey twins, two of the Sun's Rangers were presently on duty in the tower and had likely spotted him coming from well away with their spyglass. As Soldier carried him onward to the bridge, Freyard could see one of the rangers standing in wait within the wide tunnel that allowed traffic to pass beneath the lighthouse.

"Good morning, Captain. How goes the Parliamentary Sessions this time?" the ranger, who Freyard identified as Troygard asked upon approach, standing at attention with a salute.

"They were quite eventful, Troygard," he answered warmly while returning a salute of his own. "There is much to tell and to do so I am calling a meeting tonight at the ranger's hall for our men alone to discuss such matters. Inform Mack when you return to him."

Troygard's eyes widened, but he dare not ask further questions. "Aye, Captain, of course. Have you told the brothers Pharsey? They're patrolling in town today."

Freyard nodded before replying, "As it so happens, I came across them on my way through. They know as well as you do."

"Right, then. I won't keep you any longer, Captain," Troygard stated while stepping aside from Soldier's path. "A pleasant day to you, Ser. I shall see you at the hall tonight."

"Thank you, Troygard, may you enjoy your day as well."

Enjoy every last drop of sunlight it offers you, for the days we knew shall not last, he thought to himself as his eyes befell Fort Dornett, a place that might not be home for much longer.

6

MARIGOLD

For the past several days, Marigold had been trying to put an identity on the particular odour that permeated the apartments of the Lord Master. It was a haughty mixture, tinted with the musk of cologne and body odours that refused to be overshadowed. Amidst it was the smell of pipe tobacco that had been carried in from without on the clothing of Lords Eamon Palomb and Mackhol Taves. That particular facet of the smell came much to the disgust of the Lord Master Grenjin Howland, who allowed no smoking of any kind in his presence. Marigold also detected hints of the stronger cheeses and meats that the Lord Master would serve for him and his guests to nibble on throughout each day. The particular whiff of the steam-pumped heating system chimed in and even Marigold's lilac perfume was becoming part of the cacophony.

Atop it all, and the part that permeated the most, was a sort of stale stink one might expect to find in a barn. It always seemed to linger in the Lord Master's chambers and for a brief time, Marigold could not fathom why. She knew the others were aware of the odour as well. They had to smell it, she reasoned, for it was impossible to escape it. Yet, if her company did catch the scent, they were taking great lengths to ignore it entirely.

Not Marigold, though. The smell had reached her from the first day and she refused to surrender without knowing its origins. At last, the answer arrived to her while waiting for the morning meeting to begin.

She had been focused on the tall, potted plants that Grenjin decorated the room with in all four corners. It was not the foliage itself that the odour originated from, but rather, the manure-heavy soil in which they rested.

Arrogance, Marigold said to herself in sudden realisation. *That smell is pure arrogance. They mask the true odour of their actions with the pleasant perfumes that allow them to feign ignorance. As long as the aroma covers the stench, they can act as though their empire is not built on a foundation of excrement.*

What disturbed Marigold most of all, as she sat at the round table in the Lord Master's sitting room, was that she was becoming accustomed to the smell. She had been joined by the silent company of the Lord's Taves and Palomb and the latter's twin sons Eldridge and Pyore. The Lord Master himself had yet to come out of his bedroom, leaving his guests to sit in wait.

This was far from a typical setting for a meeting, but following the flight of Tryst Reine, Grenjin had dispensed with typicality. He now refused to set foot off the third floor of the Atrebell Manor, taking his meetings, meals, and everything else in the safety he felt it provided. There, he was hidden from sight and protected day and night by a sizable presence of manor guardsmen.

Explanations for his hiding came in one of two forms, with their level of falsification dependent on the intended audience. In the first case, the state press were informed that Grenjin had sequestered himself, his warden lords, and the Lord of Crime and Punishment so that they might focus on the prosecution of Lady Orangecloak. A story that hinged on the equally false tale that said she was still in their custody.

To his ministers and lords, even those gathered in the room, the reason given was that Grenjin sought to focus on the escape and recapture of Orangecloak. The first story was a total fabrication that only the most gullible minds of Illiastra would buy and the second, though meant to be a more believable tale, was no less of a lie. Marigold had seen right through the falsehoods to the truth that emerged in flickers of fear across Grenjin Howland's wrinkled face whenever Tryst's name was spoken.

His fear cripples him as much as his arthritis, Marigold had told herself on more than one occasion over the past week. *If Tryst can escape so easily, the Lord Master knows that he can return much the same way. Although the more pressing concern to Grenjin should not be the idea that Tryst might return to kill him, but the fact that Tryst can destroy the EMP's entire bloody empire with what he knows.*

From across the table Marigold felt eyes on her and it was not the first time that morning that she had. With a sideways glance, she caught Eldridge turning away in haste, pretending as though he had brushed something from the shoulder of the grey suit jacket he wore.

Pyore, by contrast, seemed to be acting as though Marigold was not even in the room. Instead, his eyes were on the bookshelf directly behind her, looking as though he was scanning the titles. He had opted for wearing his family colours of silver on black today, deciding against wearing the teal of the Tullivan clan after the incident at the Parliamentary closing feast. Pyore had acted out against Marigold that night, trying to chastise and humiliate her before the entire parliament and their families. His own father had intervened quickly out of embarrassment at his son's behaviour and had even admonished Pyore.

What should have been the damper on the fire had only stoked Pyore's rage further and the blaze erupted violently in the form of a backhanded blow intended for Marigold's face. The attempt had ended when Tryst had seized Pyore's wrist mid-swing and fixed him with an angry gaze from his bright, Gildraddi-green eyes. Marigold had been sure that if Tryst had held Pyore for a moment longer, that the Palomb boy would have soiled his trousers with fear.

Following that night, Pyore had largely stayed holed up in his quarters and resigned himself to silently brooding during the meetings, and Marigold had been glad for it.

As for Eldridge, the sickeningly charming half of the Palomb twins only seemed to have suddenly grown bolder in the last day. Albeit, with far more tact than his brother was capable of. Marigold could not help but notice a smug smirk constantly smattered on his comely face and his empty niceties came at a steady flow. The disgusting act had only raised Marigold's suspicions and she had to wonder what had led to his sudden shift in disposition.

The wondering had to be put aside for the time being, as the door to the Lord Master's bedroom had finally creaked open. Standing in the threshold was Steward Hossle, clad in his usual, spotless attire of a black tailed jacket, grey slacks, starched white shirt, black bowtie, and white gloves. The receding grey hair upon his head was slicked back neatly and his face was so cleanly shaven that one might almost believe him to be an elf. The mere sight of him was enough to prompt Marigold and the other four to stand up for the incipient entrance of their Lord Master.

"A good morning, lady and gentlemen," Grenjin began, shuffling into the room behind the steward. Today, the old man was clad in a three-piece black suit and bowtie with a light blue, buttoned shirt. Even with a hobbled gait, it seemed to Marigold that the Lord Master was growing more tired and aged by the day. If she had not known the reason for his stress, she might have even felt bad for him.

"A good morning to you as well, my lord," Eamon said in his drawling Hercalest accent. "How are you faring this day?"

Eamon's greeting had drawn a weary sigh from the Lord Master and for a split second, it looked as though Grenjin was about to retreat back to his room. "Unless you have news that Tryst Reine and that contemptuous, redheaded wench he stole from me are both dead, then I fare as poorly as I did yesterday."

Mackhol Taves, bedecked in a suit of brown tweed, chimed in on that note. "I pray to Ios that I can personally deliver such news to you before the sun sets, my lord."

"I believe you said that to me yesterday too, Lord Taves, and here we are, seemingly no closer to that wish," Grenjin scowled as he slumped into his chair.

"Everyone may be seated," he commanded with a faint waving of a hand, his eyes fixating on Marigold before she could pull her chair in. "Except you, Miss Tullivan. I think it would be best if you stayed standing."

The other four men in the room exchanged glances of surprise with one another, suggesting that they were as much in the dark as she was on whatever matter was at hand.

While the Lord Master seemed content to let the nervous silence stand, Marigold dared to break it. "My lord, is something the matter?"

Old Howland's fingers rapped loudly atop the arm of the varnished mahogany chair he had seated himself in and he turned to his steward. "Hossle, would you give Miss Tullivan the letter, please?"

Her throat went into a tight lump at that, sensing what sort of letter Hossle might have. The footfalls that brought him around the table to where Marigold stood seemed to ring slowly and loudly off the walls, echoing in her ears until he was beside her. She made eye contact, watching as Hossle produced a brown envelope from the inside pocket of his jacket and held it out for her to take. Not a word was spoken by him, but Marigold saw sympathy in his eyes for the brief moment that he dared look upon her in the exchange.

The first thing she looked upon was the broken seal of the letter. The glob of teal wax that had secured the contents of the envelope was stamped with a leaping swordfish above a letter T. *Father's seal,* she said to herself while trying to mask the dread she felt coming over her.

The entire letter was scribed and signed by Oire, which was evident from the handwriting alone. That it was written by Oire at all told Marigold as much as the black ink on the paper did and she read through it quickly, fighting to maintain poise and grace.

"My lord, might I ask when you received this?" Marigold asked softly while carefully refolding the parchment.

"It came by courier this morning, having been urgently delivered by train," Grenjin explained in a frank tone of voice. "We screen all the mail coming and going from the manor now, in the event that Tryst Reine still has rats lurking within my walls. This arrived ahead of it all and Hossle brought it to me directly, though it was addressed to you."

"I see..." Marigold uttered, her gaze falling to the floor briefly before returning to meet the Lord Master's eyes. "My lord, I beg for your leave to return to Daol Bay at once."

He nodded solemnly in answer and for the first time in her life, Marigold even saw what might be called empathy on his face. "Of course, Miss Tullivan, I would not keep you here under such circumstances. Your steward took the liberty of sending your father's personal train cars as well and I took the further liberty of having them attached to the next westbound train out of Atrebell. You leave by midmorning and I wish you Godspeed for your trip to Daol Bay."

The other four looked continually baffled throughout the exchange and it was Taves that spoke the question they all seemed to share. "My lord, what seems to be amiss in Daol Bay that requires Miss Tullivan's immediate attendance?"

Grenjin looked to Marigold alone as he replied to the group. "That is for Miss Tullivan to explain first and foremost, if she so chooses."

Marigold swallowed hard, thinking about what to say to them and fighting her desire to walk away without any response at all. Despite that urge, she gave them an answer. "My father is on his deathbed and

I have been summoned home in the hopes that I will reach him before he passes," the words fell from her lips with great reluctance, the weight of each one hitting her like a boxer's jabs.

"I am most sorry to hear this news, Miss Tullivan," Eamon stated, in a tone that to most ears would sound sympathetic. "I agree with the Lord Master that you should be at Lord Marscal's side now. We will attend to matters here in his stead."

You are not sorry, Eamon. There is no one in Illiastra with more reason to want my father gone, Marigold thought, keeping that notion to herself while outwardly feigning a polite nod. "Thank you for your sympathies, Lord Eamon. They are much appreciated at such a troubling time."

The remaining three, even Pyore, chimed in with condolences of their own, not that Marigold bought any of them as more than obligatory remarks. She knew that outside of the Lord Master himself, there were no friends of Marscal Tullivan in that room. Marigold thanked them all in turn, even Pyore, once again, as much as it pained her, before turning to face Grenjin. "If the Lord Master may permit it, I would like to be excused at once so that I may prepare for my departure to Daol Bay."

"Consider that permission granted, Miss Tullivan," he answered in an exhausted and uncharacteristically soft voice. "Daol Bay and Illiastra as a whole thanks you for your service in this most trying time and I thank you personally for attending these meetings in your father's stead. May you go with the grace of Ios."

Marigold offered a curtsey at that and offered the expected and customary response. "I thank you for your kindness, my lord and I bid a good day to you all."

She had gotten only as far as the door when she heard the voice of Eldridge speak up. "My lord, with your leave I would be honoured to escort Miss Tullivan to her room."

The very idea of such repulsed Marigold, but from the moment she had read the dire words of Oire's letter, she had resolved herself to broker no arguments that might delay her leaving. While her back was still to the men, she grimaced, before turning to face them while waiting upon the Lord Master's decision.

"Very well," Grenjin answered without raising his eyes from the table before him. "That is a thoughtful gesture, Eldridge. I am sure the lady appreciates it."

"Thank you, my lord," she offered in return, just eager to put everything behind her. "Eldridge is too kind."

Eldridge stood quickly once she answered, with a polite smile on his face as he smoothed out his suit. It only took a few strides to put him beside her and he had the door held open before she could blink. "After you, Miss Tullivan."

Marigold thanked him again and stepped out into the well-lit stairwell, descending the steps ahead of him. At the bottom stood a pair of guards at full attention who, from above, looked to be joined at the shoulder. They parted upon hearing the footsteps and bowed politely as the two nobles reached the second floor.

"Mister Palomb and Miss Tullivan," one of the guards began in an inquisitive tone. "To where are you going while the meeting is in session and shall I expect a return?"

Just as Marigold was about to speak for herself, Eldridge stepped forward. "The lady is departing for Daol Bay and is on her way to prepare for such. I am escorting her and will be back shortly. Now, if you'll excuse us, Sers..."

The same guard answered again, bowing and stepping aside in the same motion. "Yes, Mister Palomb, we will be expecting you back momentarily. Thank you for your cooperation."

He nodded at them and gestured for Marigold to pass, even going so far as to offer his arm for her to take. It was only with reluctance that she accepted, still determined to cause no any further disturbances before she could vacate the manor.

"Marigold, I am most sorry to hear of your father's condition, and I sincerely mean that," Eldridge began once they were out of earshot of the two men guarding the Lord Master's chambers. Marigold harboured no belief in his claim of sincerity, but let him go on unabated regardless. "I always thought him to be quite the resounding example of what it meant to be a gentleman. He shall be missed, both here and in Daol Bay, I assure you. His shoes are not ones that will be easily filled."

Just get to your point, you pompous jackass, Marigold said to herself, hoping her thoughts didn't reflect outwardly on her facial expression. *You never thought anything of my father, other than how quickly you could take what is his, and in this case, that includes my sister and me.*

There was a silence for but a moment, as if Eldridge was waiting for Marigold to add a comment, but she held her tongue and he continued. "I know this is an extraordinarily difficult time for you, but there is something I should tell you before you leave. What I am about to say is not meant to serve as some form of consolation, yet it is something I feel you should take back with you to Daol Bay all the same."

Marigold knew that he would not continue until she acknowledged his previous statement, and so she offered a reply. "What might that be, Mister Palomb?"

He gave her what could almost pass for a genuinely warm smile and a wink at that. "Oh please, Marigold, you do not need such formalities before me alone, but I digress. You see my father, Pyore, and I had a long discussion last night that lasted well into the late hours regarding you and I think you will quite like the arrangement we have reached."

"Are you at liberty to tell me of this arrangement?" Marigold asked, hoping to sound indifferent, though she feared her curiosity might bleed through.

"Why certainly, Marigold, it would be rude of me to tell you as much as I have and leave the remainder unsaid," Eldridge confirmed, his amiability sounding forced. "It may be thought of as inopportune to mention this now, given your father's health. Yet, I know of no other time to inform you…"

He seemed to be waiting for her to say something and Marigold obliged as much as she dared. "I understand," she uttered in a low voice. "Do go on."

Eldridge nodded and took the cue. "It is of no mystery that Pyore and yourself are ill suited for one another, even he agrees as much. To be frank, you have a rather bold personality that conflicts with my brother's limited temperament."

I suppose saying that Pyore has a limited temperament is the polite way of saying that he is a barely-contained, violent psychopath, Marigold thought, feeling particularly incensed by what Eldridge had so brazenly stated. She strained to keep herself from showing any reaction, allowing herself only an affirmative sounding hum.

Unabated, Eldridge went on. "When Father and I are near enough to curb his behaviour, then matters usually go no further than you witnessed during the Parliamentary Summations Feast. However, it is when we are not present that there is an issue and it is in such instances that we worry of what damage could possibly be done to both his and the family's reputations. You would only compound that issue further and Ios knows I would not want you to find yourself in harm's way should I or my father not be there to help Pyore manage his anger.

"Then there is the matter of your sister's disappearance," Eldridge continued to say, as Marigold caught a sly smirk crossing his face. "It complicates my own betrothal arrangement, would you not agree? Yes, I could marry her in absentia, but that is rather embarrassing, especially for the man who will be the Lord Master himself one day."

At that moment, Marigold was fairly certain where Eldridge was steering the conversation, but dared not say it herself. Instead, she let him continue to talk.

Ahead stood Elden, guarding over the door of her chambers and her eyes met his, now watching the approaching party with suspicion.

The elder Palomb twin saw Elden as well and gently brought their walk to a stop before they could get any closer. "To that end, the three of us agreed that unless your sister emerges before mine and Pyore's birthday, Pyore will put aside your hand in marriage and I shall take it. In the interim, another, more suitable, match shall be made for Pyore. I think someone more passive would be ideal for him, perhaps a demure woman who would not challenge his authority."

This revelation made no difference to Marigold, given that she had long resolved herself against marrying any Palomb, regardless of whether it was Eldridge or Pyore. Still, she found this development interesting and at least distracting for the moment from her father's plight and she indulged Eldridge a little further. "What would this mean for inheritance? If he is not marrying me or my sister, I can only assume that Pyore would not be taking Daol Bay as his seat."

"A great question, Marigold," Eldridge said with another wink. "Given that I inherit Atrebell at any rate, I have no problem allowing my brother to claim Hercalest as his own. Besides, my father and his most trusted associates will be there to ensure that Pyore does not run the city into the ground. He needs that guidance and we both know he would not receive such in Daol Bay, at least not in a capacity that he would actually heed."

Marigold weighed her words carefully, knowing that though Eldridge himself might talk freely of his brother's misgivings, he might not appreciate such from anyone else. "It is wise of you to have a plan in place should Serephanie not return home. I am sure my father would be most agreeable to these new terms."

"I hope that *you* above all would be agreeable to these new terms," He added, taking her hand in his. "You would be the wife of the Lord Master and you could still call Daol Bay home. After all, until Lord Master Howland steps aside for me, I have no place in Atrebell yet. Even after such, all I would ask of you is to stay in Atrebell during Parliamentary Sessions. Outside of those, you could spend as much time in Daol Bay as you so wanted. I would treat you well, Marigold. I swear that you would not want for anything if you were my bride."

Another trap, she surmised. *He wants me to tell him how much I hate his brother and would do anything to avoid marrying him.*

"I am not opposed to these new terms, Eldridge, if this is what you desire," she chose to say, trying to sound neither enthused nor monotone in her delivery.

"I am most glad to hear it," he said with a smile, before placing a kiss on the back of her hand. "I bid you a safe journey and offer my sympathies once more for your father. I pray to Ios for an end to his suffering."

"And I thank you yet again, Eldridge and a good day to you," she said in return with a polite curtsey.

The act seemed to satisfy Eldridge well enough and he turned and left with a final nod.

"Is everything quite alright, my lady?" Elden queried from over her shoulder, having left his post at the door to join Marigold.

She turned to face him, shaking her head sadly. "It is my father, Elden. I'm afraid he has taken a turn for the worse. We are departing for Daol Bay as soon as we can be readied for such."

"My lady, I am so sorry to hear," Elden gasped. "We will have everything ready for you in no time at all and you need not worry about a thing. The lads and I will be only happy to take care of the arrangements."

A sigh came forth from Marigold just then, and she laid a hand on Elden's shoulder. "Thank you, Elden, for everything. Let's go to my quarters and retrieve Sydnee, shall we?"

"My lady...I-" the guard began, before suddenly drawing her into a tight hug. She reciprocated and for a few seconds they stood there together, until Marigold released her hold on him.

"I needed that, Elden. Thank you," Marigold whispered.

"I have a sense for knowing when someone could use a hug. My mother always said so," he added with a sad smile.

Marigold felt herself laugh, and she welcomed the humour, despite it loosening the tears she had been fighting back. "She was absolutely right about that, Elden."

"And she would be glad to hear that, my lady," he offered warmly in reply.

They moved into her chambers then, and Marigold asked him of Sydnee, knowing that he was the other guard of hers that was on duty this morning.

"The servants were coming and going in their hallway and he and I agreed that he should mind that door for a while, my lady," Elden explained.

She nodded quickly and went to the doorway that opened into the narrow corridor, finding Sydnee staring idly through the nearest window. As with Elden before him, Sydnee was quite surprised to see Marigold so soon after she had left for the meeting and he attended to her without delay.

With both guards in the chambers, she held the letter forth. "Gentlemen, it is high time that we put Atrebell behind us. My father has summoned me home and we shall be on a train by midmorning, bound for Obalen. I have been assured, both in this letter and by the Lord Master himself, that my father's personal train cars are at the station and being attached to the next westbound train as I speak. There is no time to spare and we will need all the help we can get to ensure that we are on that train."

"We are yours to command, my lady, what would you have us do?" Sydnee stated for the both of them.

Marigold centred her attention on Sydnee. "I will have you wake Brandyl first and foremost. Do you think he alone will suffice to gather everything belonging to you three?"

"Yes, my lady, he will serve sufficiently," Elden answered.

That answer satisfied her well enough and she continued. "Very well, then. While he is attending that, Sydnee can look for the butler on duty and have him lend us whatever servants he can spare. I shall take footmen or maids in this instance. I am not particular. After that, I would like for you to head to the stables at the front of the manor. From there, I will need you to arrange for a carriage and driver to be ready to have us at the station in time to catch our scheduled train. Return here once all of that is arranged so that you can help the servants bring my luggage to the carriage. Do either of you have any questions?"

Elden raised a hand to do just that. "What will I be doing during this time?"

"You will be here with me. I still want a guard near at hand and when the servants start arriving, I will have need of someone to help direct them," she responded firmly.

With no further instruction needed, Sydnee departed immediately for the guards' barracks, leaving Marigold and Elden to commence preparations on their own.

Between Marigold and Elden, they managed to pack the better part of two full trunks before further assistance from the manor staff arrived to assist. Tryst's ornamental sword, gifted from Freyard, was carefully hidden amongst Marigold's clothes in the bottom of one trunk. The guitar, and its bulky case, was tagged as property of Elden's, and the servants made no question of it.

Once everything was situated for departure, Marigold commenced with vacating the premises. At Marigold's insistence, the human convoy departed through the main door of the apartment and to no surprise of hers, it turned out to be a rather efficient process. The wide hallway and staircase made the carrying of the luggage easy and the footmen and Tullivan guards made no complaint of the weight in either trunk. As the party reached the first floor of the manor, they were greeted by Sydnee, standing by with bluecoat guards at the ready to open the doors for them.

"Sydnee, would you care to walk with me?" Marigold asked as she came up beside him.

"Absolutely, my lady," he gave in answer, offering his arm to her and giving a nod to the manor guards beside the front door.

The tall, heavy doors swung inward and the chilly outside air rushed in to meet them. It had rained in the early hours of the morning, leaving the ground heavily dampened and the welcoming scent of petrichor in the air. Despite the earlier weather, Marigold felt that the worst of it had already tapered off, with only a light mist falling by the time she emerged. The bits of blue poking through the clouds to the west gave her further hope that their travels would yet be under a sunny sky.

A carriage stood by at the ready, painted in white with a trim of gold, and decorated in blue and white bunting. Before it stood a pair of tall, chestnut horses and beside the door stood the driver in a black suit and top hat.

He gave a deep bow and a tip of his tall hat as Marigold approached with Sydnee, before drawing open the door for her to enter the carriage. "Good morning, Miss Tullivan, are you quite ready to be off? We should make your train with time enough to spare, but only if we leave at once and make no stops along the way."

"I understand, thank you, Driver," Marigold responded casually, her gaze on the other two guards and the servants loading the trunks onto the rear of the carriage. It was only after witnessing the two heaviest pieces being lashed into place that Marigold was satisfied enough to take her attention away, turning to Sydnee at her side. "Sydnee, you and Elden will sit with me inside the carriage and Brandyl can sit up front."

Sydnee acknowledged the command and strode off to tell the other two as much, leaving Marigold beside the driver.

The servants were the next to be thanked and she called out to them, garnering the attention and approach of both. "Yes, Miss Tullivan?" one of them asked.

She opened her purse and drew forth four silver pieces, pressing them into the hand of one of the footmen with her sincere thanks and clear instructions. "Share these equally between yourselves and the two maids that helped in the chambers, please."

"Thank you, Miss Tullivan," the same fellow answered. "Your kindness is boundless. May good fortune find you."

The servants returned to the manor with a last bow to Marigold, leaving her with the hope that they would follow through with her request.

"Gentlemen," Marigold spoke to her trio of guardsmen in their teal jackets. "We should get a move on."

The three silently obliged, with Sydnee stepping into the carriage first and taking the rear-facing seat. Marigold came after him and Elden took his seat beside her. Brandyl left their company so that he might climb up beside the driver, and after both men made a final check, the reigns were cracked by the latter and the carriage rolled to life beneath them.

Marigold peered through the window, watching the manor fall away when a thought occurred to her. "Sydnee, Elden, were either of you updated on where Raspen and Barrid are in their investigation of the Tullivan guards' involvement with the Orangecloak escape?"

Elden was the first to answer. "As a matter of fact, my lady, I made a point of inquiring with Lieutenant Raspen after I had my breakfast this morning."

"What did he say?" she said, turning to face him as she did.

"It would seem that the Atrebell Manor and Palomb guards alike can all account for the six Tullivan guards in the manor at the time," he informed her, shrugging trivially at the whole matter. "They have no interest in any of us, my lady. In fact, from what the other guards are saying, Raspen is convinced that the Master of Blades acted alone, at least within the manor."

The carriage rounded the hill, descending down the road that cut through the lawn and toward the iron gates ahead. Marigold looked back at the expansive home of both Illiastran Parliament and the Lord Master. "That is all well and good, Elden, thank you for getting a resolution on the issue," she commented wearily. "However, if things keep unfolding as they have been, it is not likely to matter all that much."

The building began to slip away then, the grassy, manicured hill obstructing it from view. Marigold refused to pry her eyes away, keeping her gaze affixed until there was only the slate-tiled roof to be seen. *Eldridge and Eamon Palomb can amend the marriage pact to their heart's content, for I will never marry a Palomb and the Atrebell Manor will never be my home.*

7

SEREPHANIE

The big tent seemed to shake with the energy of the people beneath its canvas walls. The stands were packed with an audience of the common folk, waiting patiently for the master of ceremonies, who would begin the long-awaited Tournament of the Winter's King.

In the days of Illiastran royalty, the original tournament for which this one was named had been a yearly display in Phaleayna. The particular monarch in question was a storied part of dwarven and elven lore alike, believed to be the eldest of four children of Aren and Iia, the gods of the dwarves and elves respectively. In honour of their children, who were gods of considerable power in their own right, Aren and Iia made the four seasons and gave one to each of their offspring.

Ios, the god of humankind, was displeased that the other two gods sought to alter the nature of the world itself and resisted their change. However, where Ios was unbending, Iia was a force of infinite patience.

The dwarven scriptures told that Iia called out across the heavens to Ios in a voice so soft and lilting that its timbre alone brought all who heard it to weep. A long and arduous debate raged between the three gods that went for an eon. When at last it concluded, Iia spoke to every intelligent creature of the Known World, her words ringing unambiguously and understood by all. She decreed that as time moves, so must all things move with it. From then on, that time would be measured by spans delineated in years, and each of those was to be further divided into four seasons. Each season would bring with it change in the form of weather and climate. Through this, there would be a time for birth, a time for growth, a time for harvest, and in the winter, a time for rest.

Governing over these seasons would be the four children of Aren and Iia. To the second born and first daughter, Eika, went the spring. Iia and Aren decreed that her compassion and conviction would lend itself to her responsibility to see that new life be nurtured through the period in which it was most vulnerable. Summer went to Liha, the youngest, so that her loving nature would bring warmth to the early harvests and the maturing of the crops. Autumn was for Fero, the third born son with the bold streak, whose strength would lead the farmers through both the last of the harvests and the preparations for the cold days ahead.

Lastly, there was Garit, the eldest, who would guard over winter. It was left to him to oversee the creatures of Aren and Iia through the coldest and darkest of days and the dwarves and elves alike would pray to him for a season without suffering. To further venerate that season's ruler, they dedicated what would become the Feast of the Winter's King to him.

While honoured, Garit asked that the feast be not an event of worship toward him. Rather, he asked for them to reflect on the year that had been, usher in the year to come, and give solemn remembrance to those whose lives had been lost over the previous seasons. That request went heeded and the Feast grew to become an affair that would last through several weeks of events and festivities to be so named for the King of Winter.

Though the traditions had quite nearly died out amongst the elves, the dwarves continued to hold the Feast in the highest regard. The human adherents of the Triarchy faith, by contrast, had little regard for the festivities of dwarves and elves. The children of Aren and Iia were seen as demigods in human lore, but ones who had no authority over the creations of Ios. As such, they fell into a place of obscure mythos in human culture, eventually defaulting to little more than passing names in the *God's Gift* scriptures.

As recently as only a few centuries prior, the concept of the Winter's King was appropriated by the leadership of the human

Triarchy faith. In these revised fables, the depiction of the Winter's King was that of a human blessed by Ios with great, albeit loosely described powers that seemed to vary between storytellers. Generally, he was a jovial fellow, his energy directed toward the spread of joy and cheer. This version of the Winter's King was something of a mage, known to conjure gifts for those who had been morally upstanding throughout the year. In some tales, he was even seen to be a trickster toward the impish, extolling misfortunes upon them to fit their wicked deeds.

Being known in these old Phaleaynan legends as the king of anything led to further encroachment of human customs, with particular focus on how those customs applied to royalty as the humans had known them.

Most notable were tales that saw him elect five Knight Generals, a tradition contained solely to the ancient royalty of the Kingdom of Phaleayna. Neither dwarves nor elves observed such strict rules of knighthood, nor did any other country across the Known World. However, the increasingly humanoid Winter's King did, and his chosen knights in the earliest tales were the most legendary knighted men and women of the old kingdom. The stories stated that these venerated warriors were brought back to life through the powers of the Winter's King so that they might aid in his efforts to spread merriment to those who had been on their best behaviour throughout the year.

Those stories began to evolve on their own, too. Eventually, the tales drifted away from including actual knights of Phaleaynan history and instead saw knighthood bestowed on the honourable dead of more recent times. Even that narrative changed, until it was commonly explained that the Winter's King chose new, living knights every season, who would then be his representatives until spring returned.

As to how those knights would be selected, it was told that the Winter's King would bestow good fortune to the sword of the chosen people and they would win their temporary knighthood in a duelling tournament. Thus, the Tournament of the Winter's King was born. The swords were made of dulled steel, but the written records that Serephanie had read claimed that the fierce competition more than made up for the blunted weaponry. The tourney was always scheduled to fall on either the last week of autumn or the first week of winter, so that it might usher in the season and the other festivities associated with the human's version of the Winter's King.

The winners, each given status as an honorary knight, were nearly treated as kings themselves for the entirety of the season. Upon their victory in the tournament, they would be sent out to tour throughout human Illiastra and serve as hosts of regionalised events that would occur in the smaller towns and holdfasts.

The swordplay tournament and all the festivals of the Winter's King were swiftly banned as blasphemous during the years that the Elite Merchant Party and the Triarchy were solidifying power in Illiastra. It had remained that way until the League of the Sacred Fist revived the tournament in its neutered form just a few decades prior.

Now, the tournament was less about the fabled Winter's King and more about the profits to be made by the Sacred Fist. In the current iteration, a bidding process among the upperclassmen decided a tangible Winter's King. By choosing a living human to be the ceremonial king, the Sacred Fist could circumvent the offending fables of an omnipresent demigod of vague origins and abilities. Oftentimes the chosen king was an unelected nobleman, though city councillors and backbench ministers were known to find their way to the King's Throne on occasion. Among the first tier ministers and especially the lords, such a thing was seen as being beneath them and while they frequently spectated, they would never dare bid on the throne.

For men of lower birth like Darrion, they could never afford to bid with coin against the highborns. They made their wagers with their bodies for the prize of being one of five champions of the Winter's King.

As her love readied himself for the challenge of being named a champion, Serephanie found herself scanning the perimeter of the tent. Her eyes felt as though they were pulled all about the vibrantly coloured tarp ceiling, watching as it billowed with the gentle winds outside, lifting and rolling like a rainbow lake overhead.

Below the framework of the ceiling and encircling almost the entirety of the tent were sections of wooden scaffolding, accessed by stairs and erected to house a collection of covered booths known as 'the Royal Boxes'. Decorated in blue and white bunting, these posh and lofty seating arrangements were paid for and occupied by those of the nobility with an interest in watching the festivities. Alongside her father and sister, Serephanie had been seated up there in the past, enjoying the high view afforded by the booths, the cushioned seating, and what felt like an endless array of snack foods.

Her eyes wandered down through the rows of bleachers for the common folk until they came to be focused on the hive of human activity taking place in the centre of the floor. The event space of the tent was oval in shape, with its area divided three ways.

The first of those, situated directly beneath where Serephanie sat, was the waiting area reserved for the challengers of the tournament. Including Darrion, there stood fierce looking characters that seemed to have come from all corners of the world. Serephanie wondered about the stories that each man could tell of their lives. Undisciplined street fighters and bar brawlers dressed in their usual daily attire stood amongst the ranks. Those sorts, Serephanie knew from watching Darrion in the fighting pits of Daol Bay, were typically of the mind that a tough chin and a strong fist were enough to see them through a given contest.

She saw a few, like Darrion, that looked as though they might have training in one specific fighting style or another. It was the combat gear and mannerisms that marked these fellows as serious practitioners of the combat arts.

Among the trained were men who merely looked the part. Anyone could buy fighting clothes, and some had done just that. Serephanie could tell, by either their nervousness, or their cockiness, that those types were trying to play the part of a fighter, hoping that they could bluff their way through the tournament.

Then there was the downtrodden, clad in rags and lumpy shifts, with poorly kempt hair and beards. If their bedraggled appearance did not state their unfortunate circumstances plainly enough, the iron chains of their hands and feet and the presence of guards surrounding them left no doubt.

These were prisoners of Biddenhurst or sometimes smaller, regional jails. The few whom Serephanie dared to look upon appeared to be the living dead to her, with the last light of hope having long been snuffed out for them. In years past, she had seen their kin taking part in the tournament, and those around Serephanie lead her to believe that they were men with sordid pasts, whose penchant for violence gave them favourable odds in the prisons' fighting pits. They found themselves in the lists of tournaments outside of their confines by way of their wardens, who sought to profit from the brutality through betting and prize fighting. Many in such a situation were also kept as slaves, whose strong bodies alone made them valuable as labourers. Their pugilistic reputations added to their selling price, as a slave with decent fighting prowess could often make a fortune for an owner who knew how to manage them.

Despite what Serephanie would be told about the indentured combatants, she knew that the unjust ways of the EMP practically guaranteed that many of the shackled fighters were not the terrors they were made out to be.

All of these men shared the waiting area together, making for an eclectic group if Serephanie ever saw one.

Beneath the feet of these fighters was no floor, just the grass of Bryten Field. A row of benches sat in the grass and lined the fencing that separated the fighters from the spectators. Opposite of where she stood there was a gate that led to the centre area of the tent. Barrels of water for drinking were dispersed throughout, and narrow tents for changing were provided for the fighters as well.

On the far side of the tent from Serephanie was a tall stage that took up a surprising amount of space. Plush, red carpeting lined the wooden floorboards, exuding a sense of luxuriousness. Seven chairs rested atop, built with such fine craftsmanship that they looked as though they could have been thrones for the kings and queens of ancient times. Five of those chairs sat beside one another and near the front of the stage while the remaining two were placed further back and elevated above the first five. Behind the seating were thick, violet curtains that looked to stretch all the way to the ceiling. Those served to separate what Serephanie knew to be the changing and preparation area for the professional fighters.

The centremost of the three divisions was bridged to the stage by a ramp, done so that the men who would be sitting the thrones could access the fighting area below. Normally, said area was occupied by a wide, square, rope-enclosed, metre-high structure for the fights to occur on. In place of that, there stood five small platforms. Each was about a quarter of the size and approximately a third of a metre off a sand-covered floor, with no ropes to keep the fighters within bounds. The set of hexagons were arranged squarely, with one platform to each corner of the perimeter and the fifth situated in the middle.

The fighting platforms were colloquially known as rings, a term that dated back to a time when organised fighting was done inside a circle delineated with paint or baled straw on grass or sand. The name stuck, and any surface used for hand-to-hand combat came to be called a 'ring', regardless of whether or not it was even remotely circular.

"I'm amongst some strong competition. This has the makings of a fierce tournament," Serephanie heard Darrion comment from directly in front of her.

He was standing on one of a select few straw mats laid throughout the challenger's area while he ran himself through a warmup routine. Like the other fighters, he was shirtless, with his hands and feet wrapped snugly in white linen. On his legs, he wore tight black riding leathers that tapered at the calves. The trousers were bought specifically for the tournament only days prior by Darrion, chosen because he felt that they would make it more difficult for his opponents to grab and hold on to him. Around his waist was a white linen sash, the single garment worn by all challengers.

Serephanie had been studying the other fighters too and had come to a different conclusion. "Most of the combatants are either young lads fighting for fame and glory or slaves and prisoners fighting on behalf of their keepers. That is not to dismiss their abilities of course. I mention it because if you do as I tell you then most of those will be already knocked from the lists by the time you ever step onto a platform."

Darrion had been looking amongst the other men in the challenger's pen and turned to her when she finished. "Who would you have me pay the closest attention to in the preliminary rounds?"

"Any man who is both over the age of twenty-five and not a product of Mackhol Taves' penal system should register in your sights above the others, my love," Serephanie advised him while her gaze went in the direction of a man near Darrion's age.

The young man was wearing tight leather riding pants cut short above the knee and dyed a deep purple with vertical, narrow yellow stripes. His long, light brown hair was tied in a knot atop his head, with a neatly groomed beard to match. Below that, he looked to be entirely shaven, giving his legs and torso a clean, smooth appearance. "There are professional fighters mixed in among the challengers too, such as that man there."

"I find their presence to be surprising," Darrion commented while taking a sideways glance at the same fighter. "I thought the challengers would all be outsiders to the league."

"They make up but a few of the combatants, in truth," Serephanie explained, having attended more than a few tourneys in her years. "First and foremost are those who are registered under the name of a nobleman and are paid to fight in his stead. Secondly, you have the lower ranking members of the Sacred Fist who see the tournament as a way to raise their profile."

The categories on Serephanie's list earned her a slightly puzzled look from Darrion. "I am guessing that the nobles hire some fairly high ranking fighters. Should I be concerned? Or do they give little effort toward staying in the tournament?"

"Only a fool would not be," she said matter-of-factly. "Their payment is usually not guaranteed unless they can win a championship, or at least place high in the rankings."

A hush fell over the gathered audience and Serephanie glanced to the stage to see a particular man saunter forth. It was his attire, namely a black top hat, a double-breasted, vivid yellow-green coat with long tails, and cream coloured trousers that lent him the air of peculiarity. A long speaking cone in one hand certainly added to that, as did the bushy beard topped with a curling moustache on his face.

"Ladies, gentlemen, and children of all ages: I, Impresario Demorton welcome you to the Tournament of the Winter's King!" He declared through the speaking cone now lifted to his lips in a clear and loud voice.

Serephanie leaned forward and gave Darrion a peck on the cheek. "I should take my seat now, darling. I wish you the best of luck."

"Thank you, my dear," he called back over the roar of the crowd after a kiss of his own. "My performance tonight is dedicated to you."

She left him for the upper area of the seating and nestled herself in an alcove beneath one of the booths. It was the darkest place to sit, one that kept her obscured from sight, or at least generally unnoticeable, while affording her a fantastic view of the proceedings.

Above her in the box, she could hear the voices of two men, the cadence of their speech clear and dignified to mark them as noblemen, if their seating did not already do so. Though she could not identify the speakers, the accent of one clearly sounded to be the brogue of the

Hercalest citizenry while the other was a softer sort that almost lilted, which meant he was of the southwest.

Farmourd or Galren, one of those two regions, I am almost certain, she said to herself while unintentionally eavesdropping.

"You mean to tell me that Lord Eamon has still not returned from Atrebell?" the southerner nobleman queried in a tone of great surprise.

"Nay and I shan't be expecting him for at least another week or perhaps longer, according to the latest news," the Hercalestian answered.

The impresario's speaking cone carried his voice with such effectiveness that it overlapped the noblemen's and Serephanie was forced to turn her attention back to the event.

"This evening you shall bear witness to the five champions of the Winter's King defending their honour against all comers in the field of combat," Demorton declared with gusto to all. He turned and pointed to the drapery from which he had walked through not moments ago before continuing on. "So it is without further delay that I introduce to you this year's Winter's King: Councilman Georn Stavern of Farmourd!"

Emerging from behind the curtains was a middle-aged man dressed in a costume to replicate the garb of the ancient kings of Phaleayna. He was wrapped in a silvery velvet robe lined with fur and tied at the waist with a shimmering rope. A long cape in the blue of the Elite Merchant Party flowed from his shoulders and trailed the ground behind him. Atop his head there sat a crown of lacquered wood in a light brown hue that looked almost golden in the right light.

From above her, Serephanie could hear the hearty chuckling and applause of the noblemen, and one among them shouted out to him. "Good show, Stavern, good show!" the southerner stated with a great guffaw.

"Did you not make a bid for king this year?" asked the Hercalestian chidingly of his companion when the noise of the crowd began to subside.

"And make such a gaudy display of myself?" he answered rhetorically. "I think my lady wife would go into fits to see me dressed in that garish getup."

The Hercalestian seemed to find continued amusement in that. "I had been given word that it was one of Farmourd's councillors that had won the bidding process. You can imagine my disappointment when it was not your name I heard, but Georn's. With that much being said, I suppose it is better for it to be him than Councillor Scarlessi."

"Do you honestly believe that he would place a bid?" the Farmourdian scoffed.

"No, but it would have given me much amusement," the Hercalest man japed.

Serephanie lost the words of the nobles beneath the continued introductions of the impresario, who had waited while Councillor Stavern walked the stage and waved to the crowd. He looked only passingly familiar to Serephanie, the 'king' that was. In all likelihood, she had met him somewhere throughout the functions and parties hosted by the Elite Merchant's over the years. With five councillors for each of the sixty regions of Illiastra, remembering the likeness of each one of them was a task that Serephanie did not feel inclined to dedicate much thought to.

It is hard to tell one from the other most days, she mused to herself. *They all seem to be of similar height and build, with but a few exceptions. As for hair, those who can grow it at all are blond or brown and they wear it either short and tight or with perhaps just enough length to have a slight wave. Once Orangecloak came to prominence with her red locks, any of the EMP members who had red hair of their own either dyed it to a new colour or shaved their head bald.*

The visages of a dozen or so noblemen floated through Serephanie's mind, all of them fitting her description. *Their faces are kept in one of three options: clean-shaven, adorned with a neat little moustache, or perhaps a short beard at most. To add to the conformity, they all dress exactly alike in their suits. Every last one of them is as dull as porridge.*

"The rules of the contest, while not complex, bear explanation for the unfamiliar," the impresario stated clearly, getting Serephanie's attention for the moment. "These one-versus-one matches are scheduled for a single fall, and will take place five matches at a time upon the field of platforms before you.

"At the sound of the bell," the impresario stated while cupping his hand to his ear in the direction of where the bell and its keeper were situated. Three quick identical notes sounded, hanging on the air as a grin crossed the impresario's face. "The two men on each platform will engage one another in an attempt to wrestle his opponent to the mat or throw him from the platform."

The impresario knelt down on one knee to demonstrate the next point. "While a fighter may drop to a single knee, if any other part of the body touches the mat or if so much as a toe touches the ground outside the ring, the match is over."

He jumped up then and pointed to the crowd, moving his extended arm slowly from left to right across the tent. "I implore you, my lovely audience, to keep your eyes fixed on these rings at all times, for as you may have already guessed, these bouts usually do not last long. However, they are highly exciting."

With a single, leaping bound, the impresario brought himself to the lip of the stage and dashed out into the fighting area. He came to a stop atop one of the fighting platforms nearest to the waiting area and thrust a hand toward the eager challengers before him. "As you can see before you, all the hopeful contenders are wearing a sash about their waists and they will need that sash should they wish to challenge a champion. In the waiting pen today, we have forty-six eager contenders. For the preliminary rounds, our gallant challengers shall face one another to earn the right to advance to the championship rounds. To do that, these men come forward and wager their sashes against one another. Those who win, keep their sash, those who lose, go home empty-handed. When the field has been whittled down to twenty that still bear a sash, those finalists will advance to the championship gauntlet rounds."

The Impresario was dashing back to the stage again. With all his running about, Serephanie had to marvel at the man's stamina, for he showed no signs of tiring. Upon arrival, he began pacing before the five thrones, a hand held out over the empty seats. "In the championship gauntlet rounds, the champions who will be seated here will take to a platform, and the finalists can choose which champion they face, and wager their sash against him. Should they lose, to the champion goes their sash, and their battle ends. However, for the man who defeats a champion, he will become the champion himself! They will wear that champion's belt, sit his throne, and defend it from the remaining contenders.

"When there are no more contenders," the Impresario excitedly declared once he was back at the front of the stage, an arm thrust into the air. "The five who sit the thrones and wear the championship belts will be declared the Knights of the Winter's King!"

The audience roared and applauded once more, their ruckus lasting until the impresario raised his free hand to gesture the crowd back to silence. "After long deliberation, our Winter's King has chosen the five men who would stand as his champions. Five who he feels certain will be his knights by the end of this tournament. Five who will have their chance to prove before your very eyes today that they are deserving of the king's judgement."

A woman appeared from behind the curtain, dressed from head to toe in a long, black gown that hugged tight to her slender body. Her mouth and nose were veiled and a golden circlet sat upon her head, but her dusky eyes, long ebony hair, and dark skin were plain to see.

With her dark features, I have to wonder if there might be the long, pointed ears of a half-elf beneath that headwear, Serephanie mused curiously.

The Amaroshan people, or as they were commonly called, the 'half-elves', had been driven from human Illiastra during Serephanie's childhood through a violent, bloody effort by the Elite Merchants. Those who were not killed in skirmishes with armed forces, and who did not die while incarcerated in Biddenhurst had fled the country. While some boarded ships and crossed the Casparian Sea to whatever nation might take them, most ran to the Elven Forest, the home of their ancestral cousins. However, a few remained in human Illiastra, refusing to abandon their home country and opting to take their chances on a life spent in either seclusion or disguise.

Whether or not she was of elven blood, the sensuous beauty was garnering the attention of all. Not for her own sake, but for what was draped across her arms: five leather belts, two hanging across her right and three on her left. The collection of leather and metal were buckled and looped over her folded limbs and she carried the load with relative ease across the stage to where the impresario and Councillor Stavern stood in wait.

Once at their side, she unfurled her arms to reveal the faces of the nearly identical championship prizes. Each one held an engraved, heavy plate of metal upon the centre, cut into a rectangular shape that the leather belt had been tailored to suit. Near to either short edge of the plates was a smaller, semicircle plate that looked as though it aligned perfectly with the centrepiece. The belt plates were decorated with filigree and doves sculpted from similar metals and engraved with words that Serephanie was too far away to read.

Each of the five exquisite pieces differed from one another in two ways: the metals used in the plates and the colour of the leather belt on which they were mounted. On the left arm of the woman hung belts in indigo, maroon, and teal, plated in what looked to Serephanie like silver on gold, but was most likely the cheaper alternative of enamelled nickel. The right arm bore belts of black, one in dual-plated gold, the other in silver.

Once the assistant was in position, she offered her left arm to Georn Stavern and he gently picked up the belt closest to her hand and held it aloft with glee.

The Impresario took that as a cue and lifted the speaking cone back to his lips. "Introducing first: hailing from the mysterious Isle of Tavijh of Johnah and weighing in this evening at one hundred and eight kilograms, I give you the Teal Champion: Dahvi Barajah!"

Behind the curtain of the stage, there emerged a man in a shimmering green robe, trimmed and belted with cloth-of-gold. He had the tanned complexion commonly found among the Crescent Islanders and a muscular, defined frame. Short, spiked hair and a close-cut, coarse beard covered a diamond shaped face, and Serephanie thought that he was as handsome as he was intimidating. She recalled seeing the fighter before, and knew he was a favourite of the regular followers of the Sacred Fist. Of course, if she had forgotten, the cheering and applause of the crowd would no doubt remind her. As he crossed the stage, he spoke loudly to his supporters, encouraging their fanfare even further.

The man commonly known only as Barajah was considered one of the premier fighters of the Sacred Fist. Serephanie had witnessed him fight before and could recall more than one occasion when he had been the league's Heavyweight Champion of the Known World.

Once beside the impresario, Barajah raised his arms to chest height and put his back to Georn, who wrapped the teal belt around his champion's waist and buckled it into place. After a handshake was shared between the two, Barajah left the ceremonial king and took his place upon one of the thrones at the front of the stage.

Next to be summoned was a blond haired Illiastran man with a sharp nose and wearing a robe trimmed in white feathers, who was introduced to the audience as 'The Glorious' Gilbare Bauntreaux. His arrival was met with unanimous disapproval from those who regularly took in the fights, but Gilbare strutted across the stage arrogantly all the same. His muscled, albeit doughy frame was fitted with the Indigo Championship belt and he joined Barajah shortly after.

The Maroon Championship was given to a behemoth of a man known only by the mononym Tahru. The impresario stated that the dark fighter, with his tall, wild-looking mane of black hair, frightening gaze, and imposing figure had come to the Sacred Fist from the Crescent Island nation of Doba. From what Serephanie knew of the place, it was located somewhere in the southeast of the archipelago and was one of the more distant nations.

In a region of the Known World that was regularly embroiled in strife and conflict, Doba had the rare distinction of being the only nation besides Cabathos that could boast to never having been successfully invaded by a foreign entity. Cabathos had come by that claim through a legacy of excellent foreign relations and a history of having a large, disciplined, and upstanding military and naval presence. Doba, on the other hand, had an earned, unshakeable reputation for producing what were widely regarded to be the most fearsome warriors to be found anywhere.

The thickset mass of meaty muscle known as Tahru was definitely a prime example of a Doban warrior. He stood before the crowd in tight, tapered leather trousers to the knee that were painted in bright, bold crisscrossing lines of blue, green and orange. There was no robe or jacket, like the two that came before him, rather he wore a necklace of sharp teeth collected from some predatory animal, and a headband made of wildflowers.

Before accepting his belt, he stepped to the front of the stage and began performing a Doban war dance. The ritual consisted of loud chanting, slapping of the chest, arms, and legs with his hands and heavy stomping, all done with precise rhythm. If Serephanie's books on the matter told it true, entire units of their armed forces would perform such a dance in perfect synchronicity for ceremonial purposes and before battle. She had to imagine that the sight of that alone would be enough to make potential invaders think twice about landing on Doba's shores.

Tahru accepted his belt to hand before Councillor Stavern could attempt to wrap it around his midsection, draping it over a bare shoulder with a heavy, audible slap. The gesture did not seem to faze the impresario, but left Councillor Stavern positively nonplussed. He shared his puzzlement with the crowd, but shrugged it off quickly and nonchalantly and proceeded to collect the silver-plated belt from the attendant.

Before the next name could be called, a man in a deep purple robe stepped forth and the crowd erupted in cheers.

"Ladies and gentlemen," declared the Impresario with noted pride in his voice. "I present to you a man who needs no introduction: the pride of Forrenton, 'The Gentleman' Hann Bravado!"

The uproarious adulation showered on Bravado gave truth to the Impresario's statement and the sight of the fighter even brought a smile to Serephanie's face.

The last time I saw Hann was when the Sacred Fist came to Daol Bay during last year's summer tour, Serephanie reflected warmly. *Hann is Father's favourite fighter and he always insisted on hosting him for dinner at the manor when he was in town. Until Father became ill, that is. Seeing Hann is quite like laying eyes on an old friend again. I wish I could speak to him, but he would know me on sight.*

Hann took a sweeping bow to the audience as he neared the front of the stage, earning another round of their adulation. A second bow was offered to the impresario and the ceremonial king and though Stavern feigned ignorance, even the daftest man would not miss the implication of the gesture.

A man of the people, as always, he was, Serephanie said to herself, feeling a smile forming on her lips as she did. *I remember him telling Father, 'You honour me with this dinner, my lord. However, I am but a low man who fought his way, almost literally, from a hovel in Forrenton. I may look and play the part of a nobleman, but it is not a life for me.'*

Even now, you bow to the poor first.

He accepted his silver belt and joined the other three on the thrones at the front of the stage, leaving one seat still unclaimed.

"Lastly, but certainly not least of all," the impresario called out through his cone. "I give you the Golden Champion of the Winter's King: Landrick of House Imorgan!"

In that moment, Serephanie was glad for her ugly cloak. Without it to keep her face obscured, someone might have noticed the look of surprise she undoubtedly wore.

Landrick was the third son of Dermos Imorgan, Minister of Toyell Region, which bordered on the eastern edge of the Daol Forest and directly north of Torrento. Being a border region to the western realm meant that the Imorgan family had frequent dealings with the Tullivan's and Serephanie knew both Landrick and Dermos passingly well.

A young lad who looked to be just beyond his twentieth year made his way into the stage, waving to the audience in a heavy, black robe trimmed in cloth of gold. His hair was dark, touching just below the ears and curling wildly. It looked as though he was attempting a beard, though it still had a long way to go to earning that distinction.

"What do you suppose old Dermos paid Georn for that belt?" the Hercalestian nobleman asked the Farmourdian in the booth above Serephanie. "And do you suppose he paid in gold or in favours?"

The Farmourd noble gave a quiet laugh before responding. "Given that the great oaf is toppling at last and four of the five councillors in my fair city have gone into business for themselves? I should think that it was *Georn* paying *Dermos* with the belt."

Try as she might, Serephanie could not identify the owner of the voices. The Hercalest man had a deep, clear baritone and she believed it possible that the owner might be tall. Based on that assumption, Serephanie could narrow the options down to a few Hercalestian noblemen she had met. His companion's voice sounded gravelly, but his tones were dulcet, almost soothing, in a way, despite the topic of conversation between the two men.

The man with the deep voice considered the Farmourdian's hypothesis with another question. "Georn is putting himself up for consideration to be Farmourd's minister is he?"

"Aye, he is bold, our Georn," the other man answered with continued humour in his voice. "He is running for the seat when he knows full well that Lord Eamon intends to install his cousin Patton."

The Hercalestian scoffed loudly at that notion. "Georn's a damn fool and Dermos Imorgan too, if he supports that nonsense. Georn would need the support of more than half of the parliament and it would take more than giving away berths in a farcical fighting tournament to get any easterners to go against Eamon's wishes."

"It might not take much for the westerners to vote for it, though," the Farmourdian suggested hopefully.

The mention of the ruling men from Serephanie's corner of the country piqued her interest further, and she craned her head to catch more of what was being said.

"At present, the westerners will not care," the Hercalestian said, likely dashing the southerner's hopes before they could manifest at all. "However, that election, such as it were, will not take place until spring and by then I suspect that Pyore Palomb will be the Warden Lord of the West. They will fall in line and vote with Eamon's wishes."

That revelation might as well have been delivered with a punch to the gut to Serephanie. *Father's health must be declining more rapidly than I thought,* she said to herself. *The rest of the nobility are already acting as though he is dead.*

"That soon?" the Farmourdian asked worriedly. "I had no idea that Lord Marscal's consumption had eaten through him so quickly."

"Oh yes, I am given to understand that he looked to be on the doorstep of his tomb during the Parliamentary Sessions," the Hercalestian confirmed before adding to his statement. "Of course, that was when he could even summon the strength to attend at all."

The Farmourd noble sucked air through his teeth and sighed. "My word, I do feel awful about Lord Marscal. What a truly wretched, horrendous disease. Such a terrible way to go, wasting away like that while still at a strong age."

Both men continued on talking about the unfortunate nature of the disease, though their words faded to nothing in Serephanie's ears as the weight of it all came to bear on her shoulders. Leaving her father while knowing he was terminally ill was a guilt that gnawed on Serephanie constantly.

I will never see my father again, Serephanie realised with a sudden, sharp pain in her stomach. *I was selfish to run off when he was so ill. How stupid could I be? We all knew the disease was going to take him before long. I should have stayed by his side to the end and then left. Why am I so selfish?*

Serephanie could feel panic and anxiety seeping in. The Impresario was barking something through his cone but Serephanie could not be bothered to pay attention. Anything said by the men in the booth above had become indiscernible as well, no matter how hard she tried to focus on them. Above the clamour, Serephanie could only see visions of her father and sister in Daol Bay playing over in her mind.

I left them. I left them and now Father is dying, Serephanie said to herself, feeling tears welling in her eyes. *What else could I do?*

If I had stayed, she stopped the thought firmly as it took hold, and tried to reason with herself. *No, I had to go, not just for myself, but also *for Marigold's sake. With me gone, it would throw the marriage contract into disarray and give her time to concoct a way out of it without losing everything in the Tullivan name. This needed to happen. I am no leader, not like Marigold.*

She tried to pull herself back from the brink with a stern reminder. *If I did one thing in this life for the family, it was ensuring that everything went to her. Our house and legacy would have fallen to the Palombs if left to me. Marigold, though, she planned to fight back and if I had stayed, I would just be in the way. So I left when I did, giving everyone time to get accustomed to her and her alone being the head of our house.*

By the Gods, those excuses feel so hollow, she said, wrestling herself back into the corner from which she had almost escaped. *I am such a pathetic coward.*

Somewhere far away she heard a bell ring out three times and the crowd erupted in cheers. Try as she might to see what caused the commotion, the tears blinded her. With the edge of her dingy cloak, she dried her eyes and made a valiant attempt to stifle any heaves and sobs that worked their way out.

Above the cheers and jeers of the spectators, Serephanie heard grunts and thumps for what felt like minutes until a bell sounded for a second time.

Unable to focus on anything, she buried her head in the folds of her cloak, trying to act as though her world was not caving in around her.

People might see me like this, she realised in panic. *If I draw attention, some gallant fellow might rush to my aid at any second. I have to put my worries in the back of the mind and let the fighting be my distraction. There will be time to process what I heard later.*

When Serephanie was able to see again, she saw five men with their hands raised in victory: one wore a pair of short trousers made of fine, dark brown cloth and at first Serephanie assumed him to be a freelance fighter, until he turned his back toward her to reveal a mass of crisscrossing scars.

The referees, dressed in their matching bright, yellow silk robes stood atop the platforms, each one raising the arm of that battle's victor. Aside from the slave, Serephanie noted that two of the victors were hairy, unclean prisoners, dressed only in the ragged remnants of what were once trousers. Another was an excited young lad of sixteen or seventeen and lastly was a professional combatant. In truth, the professional did not look to be much older than the young freelancer was, but his cleanly shaven body and leather shorts painted in neat, wavy shades of blue set him apart from the other entrants.

Once the victors and losers were all ushered back to the waiting pit, the impresario called out for the next group of hopeful fighters. More slaves, prisoners, and youthful combatants came forward, followed lastly by the professional fighter in the purple trousers that Serephanie had identified earlier.

She watched this round as well as she could, for the action across the five rings was as difficult to follow as the impresario claimed. Her attention focused on a particular young lad and a beefy, bald-headed slave. The teenager had wrapped his arms around the bigger man's waist and was attempting to shove him out of the ring, a strategy that resulted in a comical display of futility. When the bigger man was no longer entertained by the hapless struggle he leaned over the young man's back, grabbed him by the waist, and hoisted him in the air until he was upside down and vertical. For a brief, breathless moment, the lad hung there, his eyes wide with panic and uncertainty until the big slave let out a loud grunt and slammed the lad headfirst to the mat.

A synchronous gasp echoed from the spectators who had their attention on that particular match, and the referee was quick to leap onto the platform and between the two fighters. The young man remained where he landed, writhing in what must have been tremendous pain while the panicked referee called for assistance.

Two men bearing a gurney came running from somewhere beside the waiting pit, accompanied by another in a long white coat and cotton gloves. The slave stepped off the ring to make room and strolled about the sand, looking nervously between his opponent and the person who Serephanie could only assume was his master. The man in white examined the lad on the mat closely for what seemed like several tense minutes and when satisfied, commanded the others to place the young fellow carefully onto the gurney. Once done, he was carried beneath the bleachers and out of the tent, leaving the man in white to confer with the referee and the impresario, who had joined them hurriedly in the moments following the match.

The impresario revealed to the audience that while the lad was not seriously harmed, his injuries were enough to force his forfeiture from the tournament. His opponent was ruled the victor, but as a penalty for reckless endangerment, was disqualified and removed from the lists.

There goes two in one match, Serephanie made note while squaring her gaze on her beau. *I only hope Darrion fares better than they did.* He seemed content to remain where he was, watching his fellow competitors with his hands on his hips and his back to her.

"It's a dangerous game they play at, isn't it?" Serephanie heard a voice say.

Serephanie turned to see that the owner of the voice was a woman standing less than a metre away. She looked to be about the same age as Serephanie, with a skinny build and short, spikey, black hair, and dark eyes. The woman exuded an air of pure confidence as she stood there with her arms folded across her chest and a smile upon her face. Her attire was a plain, long grey dress with the sleeves rolled to the elbows and a slit that rose above the knee. A brown leather purse rested on her hip, suspended there from a thong that stretched over one shoulder. Further below, Serephanie could see a pair of loose, low-rising dark brown boots that looked to be a size too big on the woman's feet.

"I beg pardon?" Serephanie replied to the stranger, thoroughly confused, and entirely mistrustful of her.

"My apologies, Miss, I was merely commenting on the fights," the scrappy-looking woman said, elaborating on her first statement. "That young man who was just stretchered out, was he someone to you?"

Serephanie looked to the platform on which he had lain just moments ago. "The injured lad? No, he was no one to me. Why do you ask?"

An eyebrow of the woman shot upward and the rest of her face took on a worried look. "I was climbing the scaffold stairs and you looked as though you had been crying. I assumed the tears were for the lad. Are you feeling alright then?"

"What?" Serephanie replied, suddenly growing flushed and embarrassed. "Oh yes, I'm fine, thank you for your concern. Really, I am perfectly well."

"Of course, my mistake, you were just having your daily random crying session," the woman intoned flatly. "I usually schedule mine for just after dinner, when the dishes are washed and stored away, and I truly have the time for it."

It was Serephanie's turn to give the woman a look and she went with an annoyed expression. "You're being sarcastic."

"And you're looking better already," the odd woman stated, not waiting for a response. "If the lad is not yours, then I would wager that you have a man down there, don't you?" she asked while gesturing with her head towards the waiting area of the challengers.

"What would make you guess that?" Serephanie responded, trying not to give anything away.

The woman opened her arms wide in Serephanie's direction, "Well, for one thing, you're all alone, dearie. Women typically do not have an interest in the fights and would not risk being arrested to sneak away from their guardian on their own to see them."

Her head cocked to the side and she raised a single finger in a contemplative manner. "On the other hand, you are hidden away beneath one of the rich folk's viewing boxes where you are hoping no one will see you, so perhaps you are interested in the fights.

Just as quickly, she tilted her whole body in the other direction, both hands coming into play with her gesturing. "But that still begs to question why you have been crying if you are not invested in one of the fighters somehow. Now, it might be that you are a follower of one fighter and he has been eliminated, and that is why you are crying. However, since we have already ruled out the most obvious fighter that you would be crying over, my experience and intuition tells me that it is likely not the case."

Serephanie felt her face scrunch up and she groaned audibly. "*My* experience and intuition tell me that you want something from me, although for the life of me I have no idea what that might possibly be." Her tone was admittedly curt, though it was not without reason as the woman was wearing her patience thin.

"It is okay, Miss, I'm a fighter's wife too," the woman continued unabated. "My husband is that fellow in the purple, striped leathers who just won his first round. Kohvee is his name, mine's Syrie. He and I are from Weicaster Bay on the west coast. Your accent tells me that you're from somewhere on the west coast too and if I had to guess, I would place you as having come from one of the two cities in Twin Bay."

I'm not going to shake this one, it seems, Serephanie mused while relenting with a sigh. *I might as well indulge her a little.*

"My husband is over there," she said, pointing with a nod of her head and a glance toward him. "Near the front, the one dressed in plain black riding leathers with the long, blond hair and beard. He's no professional, like yours, just a freelancer."

The woman named Syrie followed Serephanie's line of sight and seemed to analyse Darrion for a moment. From the corner of her mouth there even seemed to be what might pass as a smile. "He's not a professional, or I would know the both of you. I will say that he has the appearance of one, though. If he fights as well as he looks, I like his odds in the tournament."

"You think so?" Serephanie asked with a tone that could almost be mistaken for sincere, until she followed it up. "Or are you merely saying that in an attempt to win me over with flattery?"

There was laughter from the dark haired woman then. "There I go running smack dab into your protective wall again. I mean what I say. I travel with the caravan, have covered this country from east to west a dozen times over, and watched lads of all forms try their hand at cracking the ranks of the Sacred Fist. After a time, you come to have a good eye for seeing the ones who have the means and the measure to make it," she told Serephanie before turning her gaze to a short haired, skinny young man who had already lost his sash and was pacing angrily in the waiting pit, having been eliminated. "And those who just won't no matter how many times they enter the lists."

She offered a shrug as she lowered herself into the alcove beside Serephanie, despite not having been invited to do so. "Your man might prove me wrong, as there are always exceptions to the rule and like I mentioned before, I haven't seen him fight. Yet, for all of that I would still be willing to bet a fine bag of coppers on him."

While Serephanie's own sincerity had been feigned, Syrie's seemed oddly genuine and that caught Serephanie's curiosity. "That's encouraging to hear. I've seen him fight in the pits of Daol Bay, but that is a far cry from the League of the Sacred Fist."

"So it's Daol Bay you call home?" Syrie asked slyly, having noticed Serephanie's slip.

"Oh no, we're both from Galdourn," she replied hurriedly, hoping Syrie would believe her. "When Cole's instructor gave him blessing to begin a career as a fighter, we left Galdourn so that he might try his hand at it. Daol Bay was the closest place with competitive fighting pits, so that is where he got his start."

"Cole is his name, is it?" Syrie asked in what was evidently a rhetorical manner. "His name has not been called yet, I don't think. You had better hope that he's chosen soon. The earlier he fights in the preliminaries, the earlier he fights in the gauntlet round. You see, the logic when it comes to a tournament like this is limited respect shown to a fighter who only appears late in the gauntlet round," Syrie said, giving her temple a tap when she said the word 'logic'. "Even if he wins a championship belt and runs the rest of the gauntlet, he'll just be seen as a latecomer by spectators and the fellow fighters alike, and they really won't respect him."

Her eyes made contact with Serephanie's as she kept talking. "Then again, it's also not seen as ideal to be among the first to fight in the gauntlet round, either. You have to face a fresh champion, and even if you beat them, then you have to defend your newly won championship against everyone else in line behind you. By that, you have probably deduced that the ideal placement is somewhere in the middle, and you would be right to think that. So, for the sake of your man, let's hope he's called for his preliminary bout soon."

Though none of that was new information to Serephanie, she hummed and nodded along as though it were. When she looked back to Syrie, she found that her gaze was not on the fight below, but to the bleachers directly opposite of them. Upon inspection, Serephanie noted that the stands there were occupied solely by women. One in particular, a heavyset, broad-shouldered woman with flowing blonde hair sat above all the others with two young women sitting at her feet. It was her that Syrie had locked eyes with for the moment until Serephanie espied what might have passed for a single nod from the blonde-haired woman across the tent.

"Do you see the ladies seated opposite of us?" Syrie asked when she finally looked back to Serephanie.

Her eyes narrowed on the group and the hair on her arms suddenly stood tall. "I had not taken notice of them before, but now that I have, there does seem to be quite a few women there with no male guardians in sight."

"They and I are the Wives of the Ring. Every woman you see there is married to a professional fighter of the Sacred Fist." Syrie explained with a grin splashed across her face. "Nothing happens in this league without our knowledge. That one looking right at us is the leader of our little group. Her name is Cyrelle, the widow of Fezadore the Giant.

She saw you over here hiding away and crying and she sent me to investigate. It seems she would like to meet you, dearie."

8
MARIGOLD

The train station of Daol Bay was abuzz with activity on the morning that Marigold arrived home. With the exception of the commercial docks along the waterfront, Marigold could not think of a busier place within the entire city. This was in spite of the fact that the rail yard was outside of the old city walls. The railway workers were already busying themselves with the detachment of the Tullivan's railcars, even as Marigold was still stepping off them. All about the station Marigold saw travellers hurrying about, looking for their particular train to take them either north to Portsward, east via Obalen, or through the more southerly coastal regions of the Western Realm.

Normally there were onlookers at the very sight of the Tullivan cars and the accompanying guards in their teal jackets. Marigold was well aware of the spectacle that came with being a Tullivan, and she was more than accustomed to the usual attention. Today though, it appeared that everyone was keeping to a respectful distance and averting their gaze. She pulled her teal cloak tight with one hand, covering the black trousers and white, short-sleeved blouse she was wearing beneath, and glanced across the platforms. There was no doubt that her presence was noted and that most of the gathered in the station knew who she was.

After a time, she began to feel eyes upon her and she met them in return, earning a solemn nod each time. Within a few steps away from the train, the bravest among them even came forth to offer her their sympathies for her father's illness and to let her know that he was in both their thoughts and prayers. She thanked them in turn and told each one of them that she too wished for her father's recovery.

How do I tell them that all hope is gone?

Outside the day was cool and crisp, with a blue sky overhead that was dotted with fluffy clouds languidly rolling by. It was as comfortable an autumn day as Marigold could remember and she was glad for the relatively mild weather.

She found Oire waiting from the saddle of a horse, with the reins of Marigold's black mare, Empress, to hand. Atop his typical black and grey suit he wore a black overcoat and matching flat cap, which he lifted slightly with his free hand in greeting. "I bid you a good morning, my lady," he said once she drew close enough to hear. "I trust your journey has been satisfactory?"

"It has been just that, thank you," Marigold answered courteously, taking the reins to hand for herself while she did so. Having placed a leather boot into the nearest stirrup, Marigold swung herself into Empress' saddle and adjusted herself into a place of comfort.

Most ladies, if seen riding at all, were expected to sit sidesaddle, but not Marigold. She found it to be an uncomfortable and limiting experience and could not fathom how any woman could ride like that. Not that many women of noble birth sat in a saddle unless absolutely necessary, at any rate. Most preferred a carriage, once again in contrast to Marigold's preference. When at home in her own city, Marigold rode Empress wherever she had to go and she did so as well as any man.

"Good morning, my lady," Marigold heard from beside her, finding Lewcas to have brought his horse alongside Marigold and Empress.

"And to you as well, Ser Lewcas," Marigold said in return. "How have you been since last we saw one another?"

The typically stone-faced guard looked like he might almost be smiling today as he replied to Marigold. "Given the circumstances, I have been as well as one could expect. Your presence about the manor was missed, my lady. I am glad for your return."

Marigold took that to mean that Lewcas himself had grown lonely without her. Among the guards, Lewcas Hylesly was something of an anomaly as far as social status went, and Marigold was the only person he seemed to regard as a friend. He tended to speak in an honest and frank manner, and Marigold liked that she almost never needed to search between his words for hidden meanings.

"I am glad to see you too," she told him in return as one of the other manor guards approached on foot. "We will have to sit and chat when I get settled in. Remind me later, and we will make time for it."

"Would you like us to hire a wagoner for your things, my lady?" she heard from below, looking down to find that it was Brandyl, standing nearest to her, who had asked the question. Elden and Sydnee stood further back with a pair of rail workers, the four having carried her trunks through the train station.

Marigold looked to Oire, Lewcas, and Darrill, deciding that they alone should be sufficient accompaniment. "That would suit just fine. See if the wagoner has horses to spare and hire them as well for two of you. The other can ride with the wagon. If you would be so kind, wait here for him and I shall ride along with Oire, Lewcas, and Darrill. Once you see my things to my quarters, the three of you shall be given three days leave to rest and be with your families."

The three bowed at that, with Sydnee speaking for them this time. "You are too kind, my lady. We thank you for your generosity."

"I thank you as well for staying with me in Atrebell," Marigold responded cordially. "I will see you all in three days. Until then, I bid you a good rest."

She left the three to their duties and turned Empress onto the cobblestone path that led to the city gates, with Oire and the mounted guardsmen following suit. The steward was quick to position himself at her side, directing Lewcas and Darrill to flank them front and back for protection and with that, they got underway with haste.

They had barely ridden a few metres when Marigold asked the burning question: "How is my father?"

The gaze of Oire went to the high, brick and mortar walls to their left, looking to the crumbling top that Marigold knew was in need of repairs before long. "Lord Marscal clings to life, my lady. The journey to Atrebell and the Parliamentary Sessions drained what little energy he had left. The only thing that has kept him among the living is the thought of seeing you one last time. He has given up on that for Serephanie, but for you he holds on."

"By the gods," Marigold uttered despondently. "Why must the man suffer so?"

Oire shook his head in answer. "That is for the gods alone to know, my lady."

"So they say," she muttered under her breath to no one.

"I beg your pardon, my lady?" Oire replied, his tone a mixture of surprise and curiosity.

There was no desire in her to be given a theological lecture and so she changed the subject. "Judging from the context of her mention just now, I presume that there has been no sighting of my sister."

A shake of his head served for a reply, and he was seemingly content to allow the shift in subject matter. "No, my lady, there has been not as much as a trace of her."

Marigold let out a sigh. "I had expected no less. She will not return willingly and I have no intention of using father's illness to lure her out of hiding."

"That brings me to a problem that I feel we have encountered," Oire put in worriedly. "There has been but few messages coming this way from Atrebell and beyond as of late and nothing of importance has arrived since before the Parliamentary Sessions. It leads me to believe that we have been excluded from the inner circle of the Elite Merchant Party. I would dare say that if your sister is found in the east, we would be the last to know of it, my lady."

She considered what he said and it was something she had suspected as well, yet Marigold was not too worried. "I do not think my sister would go eastward, Oire. If I were to draw any conclusion, I would think that she and her fisherman struck south to Weicaster Bay or Tippard. She may have even gone over the hills to Portsward."

Oire hummed aloud ponderously for a moment, before arriving at the conclusion that Marigold was leaning towards. "I gather that you believe Serephanie to have gone to another port city and took a ship overseas, my lady?"

"Precisely, Oire," Marigold affirmed. "If I were to wager, I would think that she is halfway to Gildriad by now. Knowing Serephanie, she will not go to the Northern Kingdom. It is a fairly big place, but if they went to the Kingdom City, there is a better than good chance that someone there would know her face. As you know, she has never been there, but, as with all of the royal family members, a painted portrait of the two of us hangs in the throne room."

He nodded along with her train of thought. "I recall that painting quite plainly. King Hector even paid for the painter who had done the other portraits to journey all the way here to do the sitting with you and your sister."

"That he did," Marigold agreed with a nod of her head. "While that took place four years ago, we have changed little in that time. Any guard, servant, official, or anyone else that has laid eyes upon that painting at all would likely recognise Serephanie's face. No, she will not go to the Kingdom. If my sister is in Gildriad, she will settle in the Midlands Republic, likely right in Berrisport. There is a possibility that they could go inland, but if they want to make any coin in short order then the fisherman will likely do what he knows best."

"You have given this a lot of thought, my lady," Oire commented when she was done.

"I had plenty of time on the train back to Daol Bay to do such," she replied stoically. "It kept my mind off of my father for a brief spell, although wondering of my sister's safety is hardly less stressful."

By the time Marigold finished that thought, the party had arrived at the portcullis gate of the city. The heavy, iron bar lattice had been raised and a foursome of guards stood beneath it, keeping a watchful eye on people going to and from the city. As the party approached, one of the guards leaned toward another and whispered something in his ear that was enough to send the listener running.

Marigold kept her gaze on the young lad, watching him dart into the gatehouse tower that had been built into the wall itself. A third guard approached the riders, taking her attention away from the matter with a raised hand and a smile. "I bid you a good morning, Miss Tullivan. I trust that your trip home has been comfortable?"

"A good morning to you too, Ser," Marigold called back, gesturing for her entourage to come to a halt. "My trip was quite fine and I thank you for asking."

"I am most glad to hear it, milady," the young, blond haired guard answered in a friendly, albeit slightly nervous tone. "I was asked to hold you for just a moment so that my superior officer might speak with you. I assure you that this won't take long and I apologise for any inconvenience."

Marigold raised a hand of her own and responded in an accommodating tone. "There are no apologies needed, Ser, and I shall be glad to speak to your officer."

The gatehouse door swung open, banging against the brick wall with a great clamour and Marigold turned toward it to see a guardsman hurriedly emerging. This fellow looked to Marigold to be in his late forties, his uniform neatly pressed and spotlessly clean. His short hair had gone nearly grey but was still full and showed some black amid the tight curls and the long moustache that he wore. For the life of her, Marigold could not recall if she had met the man before, though he seemed vaguely familiar to her.

"I bid you good morning, Miss Tullivan," he called out while striding in the direction of the foursome.

"A good morning to you as well, good Ser. To whom do I have the pleasure of speaking with?" she replied back in as friendly a voice as she could muster.

He was beside her by then, extending a gloved hand. "I am Cleofold Ashe, First Lieutenant to the Southeast district of Daol Bay. My men and I are at your service."

It was expected courtesy for Marigold to offer her hand in return with bent fingers, so that Lieutenant Ashe could kiss it, a ritual Marigold had little care for. Instead, she took Cleofold's hand firmly and shook it, leaving him with a flabbergasted look in the moment.

"It is a pleasure, to be sure, Lieutenant Ashe," Marigold gave in answer before a silence could fall between them. "Do you have anything to report to me, Ser?"

Ashe stared at his now empty hand for a few seconds, looking unsure of how to react. "Uh, yes, my lady, as a matter of fact I do."

"Then I would hear it, Lieutenant."

"Yes, of course, Miss Tullivan," he said, clearing his throat and adjusting his uniform jacket as a means of composing himself. "Our Captain of the District, Captain Dermot Carran, has designated the office in the gatehouse as my official station and as such, I consider this gate and the men guarding it to be my full responsibility. To that end, when your sister had been kidnapped, I wasted no time in doubling my number of guards on staff and ensuring that everyone among them knew what she looked like. Adding to our efforts, I established a thrice-a-day exchange of information with the men at the northern gate. On account of these efforts, I can say with full confidence that your sister never left this city through either passage."

This was not a conversation Marigold was interested in maintaining, not now, when her father was so deathly ill. Yet, she realised that Lieutenant Ashe was eager to discuss his hard work with her and Marigold was not about to discourage such behaviour. "Your dedication to the task is nothing short of admirable, Lieutenant, and I am grateful for your efforts," she commended the man. "Do you know of any other way that she might have slipped out of the city on foot?"

"Yes, well, as to that..." Lieutenant Ashe began, a hand idly twirling a bar of his moustache. "There are...gaps in the wall. As I am sure you are aware, they are crumbling in many areas due to their age. With that said, I know of at least two places that are close to the ground and that a person could squeeze through. I routinely send guards to patrol those areas and they did not report any sightings. However, I cannot speak for areas outside of my jurisdiction."

"I agree that our walls are in poor condition, Lieutenant, and it is a matter that must be addressed," Marigold replied in earnest to his concerns. "I may call on you in the future to aid me in that, as a consultant. Would you be interested in this task?"

The lieutenant's eyes went wide and he dropped to a knee. "You honour me, Miss Tullivan. Of course, I would be glad to help you in any way that I can. You may call on me anytime you so wish."

"Then I shall do just that at a later time, Lieutenant. Is there anything else to report?" she put back to him kindly, though allowing a little urgency to bleed through in her voice.

"I have nothing further and I shall keep you waiting no longer," he said while standing once more. "On behalf of myself and my men here, we extend our best wishes and prayers to you and your father at this time. May Ios strike down his illness."

Marigold closed her eyes and lowered her head toward Cleofold Ashe with a single nod. "I thank you for that, Lieutenant, and bid a good day to you and your men."

A gentle squeeze of her thighs got Empress back to a trot and the rest of her retinue followed suit behind her.

The city sprawled out before them beyond the gates and even there, as far from the ocean as one could be in the city, the salt air found its way to her. The salt air was an intoxicating smell to Marigold, as it was for many who lived in the coastal regions, especially having been away from it for some time.

I am home, Father, and I'll be beside you before you know it. Marigold thought to herself while taking in the sight of her seaside hometown.

The city itself had been founded in the Hero's Era nearly a thousand years prior by Marigold's ancestor Ser Davis Tullivan, one of the Teal Knights who served beneath the hero Knight General Segai himself. Ser Davis had been born in the even older city of Portsward, just barely north of Daol Bay, in a secluded part of the larger Twin Bay that encompassed both cities. After returning from the final war with the third Valdarrow menace, Ser Davis had been granted what was now Daol Bay for his service, and so he had built a home there. The area was named for his youngest child, a boy named Daol, and the massive swath of land was carved up into plots and offered to willing migrants at a pittance. Within a year of his arrival on the beach with only his family, a few adventurous friends, and a royal decree, Ser Davis had established the village of Daol Bay.

In but a short span of time, his reputation as a benevolent and fair leader grew and spread. That good standing worked in tandem with his legend as a Teal Knight and he successfully drew a steady stream of people to the bay from all across Illiastra. Under the steady leadership of Ser Davis, Daol Bay continued to prosper and grow and the retired knight established himself as a highly respected mayor well into his old age. The history books that Marigold had read all told the tale of how Ser Davis tried to encourage a healthy democracy in his town. Meetings were held in order to draw forth others who might want to be mayor, but so beloved was Ser Davis that no one dared challenge him. Therefore, it went that Ser Davis Tullivan ruled as mayor without opposition until he passed away peacefully in his bed in his eighty-fifth year. In that relatively short time, the old knight had raised Daol Bay from a tiny village to a blossoming city.

After Ser Davis was laid to rest, the Tullivan family continued on as the ruling family, becoming something of a monarchy in their own right. They upheld the will of Ser Davis and held candidacy nominations and elections to name mayors and later sealords of Daol Bay. On twelve occasions, the Tullivans even lost those elections. Those few exceptions aside, the Tullivan family had been the steadfast rulers of Daol Bay for nearly a thousand years. Their name carried respect throughout the city, Twin Bay, and the rest of the west coast from Tusker's Cove in the north to Aquas Bay in the Southlands.

All those mayors and sealords, even the twelve who were not Tullivans, were all men, Marigold reminded herself. *The people of Daol Bay and the west coast, for that matter, have never been ruled by a woman. It may take more than my surname for people to accept me as their leader, especially if my leadership is contested by the rest of Illiastra.*

As the entourage moved their mounts into the wide road before them, Oire brought himself up beside Marigold yet again, pacing his horse to match hers. "I see that you have taken a keen interest in the city's infrastructure," he remarked, his voice monotone, but inflicted ever so slightly with curiosity. "What do you suppose other people will make of that when this bit of information makes the rounds?"

Marigold was quick with a nonchalant shrug. "Let them make what they so want of it, Oire. The walls are crumbling and they need to be repaired. I merely want to know where that need is most dire."

It was a flimsy cover and Oire knew as much. "Everyone with a care in the matter knows full well that the responsibility of such would fall to your father first, who delegated those responsibilities to Councillor Marswell Caveth. The man even carries the added title of City Planner to reflect as much. The only persons who can alter that arrangement after your father's passing are the executor of his estate and his inheritor. An inheritor, as you may recall, that is not you, but your husband-to-be, Pyore Palomb. It casts unnecessary suspicion for you to be sending guards and engineers on expeditions to inspect walls that do not fall under your responsibilities. That is not even touching upon how Councillor Caveth will react to such news."

"I am not worried, Oire, and you should not be either," Marigold said lightly in dismissal of his concern. "Lieutenant Ashe was eager to express his concerns to me. I can count on one hand the number of times I have been shown such respect and I am not going to overlook it. He could well prove to be a loyal officer to me, and you and I both know that I will need every bit of loyalty that can be mustered."

"Are you sure that his loyalty is absolute?" Oire queried further. "How can you be sure that he will be so quick to seek your approval when it is you alone to carry the Tullivan name?" he added in a slow, deliberate method that Marigold recognised from him whenever he was making an effort to choose his words carefully.

"I suppose I cannot be certain," she acquiesced, following up with a counterpoint. "However, I would rather take the risk of losing his loyalty later over dashing his enthusiasm now. I see the former as a slight risk and the latter as a guaranteed loss."

"Perhaps so, my lady," Oire relented. "I hope for everyone's sake that you are right."

For a moment, he was silent and Marigold took the opportunity to focus her attention on the city that splayed out before her view.

Being an old settlement, there were structures of varying ages, differentiated most prominently by their architecture. The oldest buildings, of which there were the fewest, were the large stone structures of historic significance. Most significantly among them were the original Daol Bay courthouse, a single tower of an otherwise eroded fort, and the Arameida Amphitheatre, all dating to Ser Davis' lifetime.

The ground beneath the hooves of Empress had begun to incline while Marigold was speaking with Oire. From this increasing elevation, Marigold could see numerous commercial buildings, two factories complete with tall smoking chimneys, and the Tullivan family fish processing plant, all of which were made of matching red brick. These were the newer establishments, though some were as old as a century in age, give or take a decade. As far as the red brick buildings went, most were actually constructed during Marscal Tullivan's lifetime. The remainder of the city, built amid steep hills that protected it from weather and intruder alike, was comprised of more homes and small businesses than Marigold dared to count.

Further on sat a wide bay dotted with fishing boats, merchant ships, and naval vessels, including the massive ship-of-the-line known as *The Sting*. It and its sister ship, *The Chase*, were the only two of their kind in Illiastra, and both of them called Twin Bay home. The former belonged to the Tullivan fleet, while the latter was in service to House Simillon in nearby Portsward.

With even a brief scan of the sheltered waters, Marigold spotted the Tullivan flagship, the clipper known as *The Princess of Daol*. Beyond her in the next three berths at the Tullivan Family's quays sat the pair of sloops-of-war named *The Marigold* and *The Serephanie*, and a frigate named *Felixander's Dream*. The vessels looked pristine and proud where they rested, pronounced in their majesty in contrast to the other ships of the harbour. The three vessels named for Marscal's daughters and son had been built using much of the scrapped remains of the aging three-mast former flagship, *The King of Tides*. In its lifetime, that ship had been tasked to carry Marigold's mother and baby brother to Gildriad and was sent later to provide escort for a return that never came. It was for Marigold's mother, Princess Farren

Aurorais, daughter of King Hector the Fourth of Northern Gildriad that the new flagship, *The Princess of Daol* was named in tribute.

Before Serephanie and Marigold were promised to Eamon Palomb's sons, there was a precursor arrangement between the three families that controlled Illiastra. The agreement stated that if both Palomb and Tullivan could produce male heirs, then it would be the eldest of them who would be given to inherit the Lord Mastership from the childless widower that Grenjin Howland had allowed himself to become. Included in that was the entire Howland dynasty, including the ministership of Atrebell, the manor located within and all its holdings. While it was undisputed that Eamon Palomb's twins won that race, one added dynasty was not enough for him. From that greed was born the marriage pact that had come to shape the life of Marigold and Serephanie Tullivan.

When Farren became pregnant, there was even a brief moment when Marigold had thought that she and Serephanie might be free of the paper shackles. The family doctor and a midwife had both given their opinion that the baby was a boy and while the family was in their glee, concern quickly set in amongst the adults. Marscal had never underestimated Eamon Palomb's eagerness to engage in skulduggery, and now an infant was poised to stand between him and control of all three houses of Illiastra. There was no doubt in the mind of either of Marigold's parents that an attempt would be made on the lives of both the mother and her child.

"It is not safe for you to stay, Farren, for the sake of your health or the baby's," Marscal had declared with nothing less than utter sadness. *"As much as it pains me to admit as much, your father can protect the two of you far better than I can for the time being."*

They had debated back and forth on the matter, with Oire and Marscal's brother and city councillor, Rory, both weighing in with opinions of their own. When the matter was finally put to rest, caution had won and Farren agreed to go back to her childhood home in the Northern Kingdom of Gildriad.

Marigold had only faint memories of that time and most of what she knew was from Oire's recollection rather than her own. However, there was one memory that still stood out to her: the moment her mother said goodbye.

How could I have known it would be forever?

The King of Tides had carried her and a retinue of guardsmen, servants, and handmaidens across the Casparian Sea to the far reaches of the known world. From the moment that Farren had arrived in Kingdom City, she had begun to send letters back to Daol Bay. Among the first of those correspondences came the announcement of the birth of the youngest Tullivan child and as predicted, they had been gifted with a boy. In the child's honour, a great feast was held, one that saw western ministers and city councillors rubbing shoulders with the common men and women of Daol Bay. For that lone glorious night, the city celebrated as one and even Marscal himself joined in the merriment. Marigold could not think of a single time since that her father had ever been as happy.

As time went on, it was decided through the letters that Marigold's parents wrote between them that baby Felixander would stay in Northern Gildriad until his fifth birthday. The reason given to those who would ask was that it was to ensure that the boy was at a hardy age to make the trip across the sea. In reality, Marscal Tullivan felt that it would take that much time to let the Palomb house come to terms with everything and allow for both sides to reconcile.

A letter came on a calm, sunny autumn day that was much the same as the one Marigold was currently experiencing. It was signed and sealed by Farren Tullivan and within it stated that she and Felixander were readying to leave Northern Gildriad for the Midlands Republic. From there, King Hector had already prepared two of the fastest warships in his fleet to carry the two all the way to Daol Bay. It would be aboard *The Stormbreaker* that they would travel, with *Wild Rider* following alongside as an escort. Marscal decided that he would send *The King of Tides* to meet them along the northern shipping route and act as a second escort for the remainder of the journey.

The days went by so slowly after that, Marigold reflected. *I simply could not wait for Mother and Brother to return home and Serephanie was no less excited.*

At last, the lighthouse keeper living on the Southern Point of Twin Bay spotted *The King of Tides* upon the sea through his powerful telescope. A horse and rider arrived at the Tullivan Manor at a gallop bearing the news and the entire household erupted in joy. The girls donned their finest dresses and had their hair tied with ribbons for the occasion. The three remaining members of the family and Oire rode out in a great carriage that needed four strong horses to pull it, with full fanfare and commotion given to them. At the docks, they were met by Rory and his family and together the entirety of the Tullivans waited with baited breath for the arrival of *The King of Tides* and the Gildraddi warships.

There came a moment when Marigold saw her father's joy turn to dread and it was a sight that had never left her. As *The King of Tides* manoeuvred into Daol Bay, it became apparent that it was the lone warship amongst a flotilla of fishing vessels. Marscal's smile faded into a look of worry and was never to return again.

The King of Tides docked and the first mate came running to the waiting party with word that Captain Tuff sought an immediate meeting in his cabin with Lord Marscal. Rory and Oire both joined him on the ship and the house guards that had attended the family escorted the girls back to the manor in a hurry.

That night their father returned, the most morose that Marigold had ever seen him and with the worst news possible: there was no trace of either *The Stormbreaker* or *Wild Rider*. *The King of Tides* had crossed paths with neither one and continued on to Berrisport, capital city and chief port-of-call for the Midlands Republic. Once there, the harbourmaster had met with Captain Tuff and told him that the two ships had already left port. They had trusted the harbourmaster with the details of their route, and he relayed to Tuff that the ships were to take a slightly altered course than what might have been expected. The journey was to take the two ships through Tropuri, a small nest of islands that were home to the Aquaticans, a water breathing, elven race also known as Water Elves.

In response, Captain Tuff sent word to King Hector of the unfolding emergency and turned his sails back toward Tropuri, where the search ultimately ended. Neither ship had docked anywhere in Aquatican's islands nor did anyone there lay eyes on Farren, Felixander, or any other who might have been on those ships. *The King of Tides* doubled back toward Daol Bay, finding not even as much as flotsam or lifeboat of either ship.

Both Marscal and King Hector spared no expense in launching an extensive search for the two ships. A fleet from either nation plied the seas and sailed into ports around Drake, Johnah, and the Crescent Islands Archipelago, looking for anyone who might have seen the ships. Not so much as a clue was found, and *The Stormbreaker* and *Wild Rider* were eventually declared lost at sea with all hands.

It seemed to Marigold back then that every minister on the west coast made the trip to the Tullivan manor to offer condolences. The greater houses of the east arrived as well, and with them, there arrived even the Lord Master Grenjin Howland. The parade of mourners eventually came to an end and the lovely flowers they had left wilted and died. While Marigold and Serephanie tried in earnest to push beyond their own grief in the days and seasons that followed, their father descended further into depression.

Father always blamed himself for Mother and Felixander's deaths, Marigold noted to herself while looking about the city. *No one could tell him it was not his fault, not Oire or Uncle Rory, or even Serephanie and I. The guilt clung to him like a disease in its own right. Oire is certain that the stress of it might have contributed to the consumption that has taken over him.*

The party had climbed high into the hills of Daol Bay's south side while Marigold had been lost in thought. To her right she could see well into the bay itself, the sunlight glistening off the choppy waters below. On her left was a selection of stores that catered to the wealthiest of Daol Bay, who all called the surrounding neighbourhood their home.

"Good morning, Miss Tullivan!" she heard a distinguished male voice greet her. She turned toward the source to discover Mister Redding, her father's banker. He was standing before his business, the Bank of the Seafarers, while an employee worked a key in the door. To one hand, Mister Redding held a long, light grey coat closed tightly against the cold and in the other, he tipped a matching top hat in her direction.

"Good morning to you as well, Mister Redding!" she called back, giving as much effort as she could to sound friendly.

He set his hat back atop his greying head of hair and spoke up again to be heard above the breeze. "Thank you, Miss Tullivan. Tell your father that I send my warmest regards."

For that, Marigold thanked him in return, and the party pressed on again. She waited until her entourage was well away from the bank before turning to Oire with a question: "Does he know how close my father is to passing?"

Oire looked almost ashamed at that question, but he met her gaze all the same as he answered. "I am afraid so, my lady. Something like that is nigh impossible to contain when there are so many employed in your home. I do apologise."

"There is no apology needed, Oire," Marigold assured him. "I had no allusions that the word had not spread. I merely wanted to know how far." A thought occurred to her then, spurred by that knowledge, "Oire, I do have another question, though, if I may."

"Of course, my lady, what might that be?"

"How are the people of the city reacting to word of my father's condition? What are they saying of it?"

"My lady…" Oire began with a heavy sigh. "There is no need to worry yourself about such things right now. You should focus your strength and attention on your father."

Instead, she focused on Oire. "We have a time before we are home and I promise you, I will not be leaving his side once I am there. For now, I would like to know how the townsfolk have responded to the news."

"As you wish, my lady," he said, his eyes coming to meet her as he elaborated further. "The people are very much on edge, I must admit. In living memory, there has not been a leader of the city or the west coast in general that was not a Tullivan. The oldest residents of our city were born when your grandfather ruled and they lived beneath your father's leadership even longer. Even those who may not care for your family or the EMP at least begrudge your family a measure of respect. Both Tullivan men spent their lives trying to protect this city and its citizens, and most people recognise that.

"A life beneath the Palomb family is a frightening prospect for those who know what that truly entails, though it should be said that Eamon is not entirely without supporters. For the rest, there is a sense of nervousness for the unknown that lies ahead."

"I never knew my grandfather," Marigold put in when Oire went quiet. "I came into this world after he had already left it. Regardless, from what you and father have told me, he was a good man who tried to be fair to the people, despite the EMP's efforts to enforce their will. My father walked that road as best as he could too."

Oire nodded thoughtfully and went on. "Your grandfather was an honourable man and your father carried that honour well in his own reign. Now, the Tullivan name is on the verge of dying out and being replaced by Pyore Palomb, a teenaged boy with a loathsome reputation. These are uncertain times, my lady."

"I should mention that it is Eldridge now," Marigold stated, remembering what he had told her before she left the Atrebell Manor.

The revelation surprised Oire. "They made an amendment?" he asked almost fearfully.

Marigold confirmed it with a nod, before elaborating, "Aye, given father's rapid decline and Serephanie's continued absence, Eamon and his sons thought it best to make a more suitable arrangement between the two houses. I am to wed Eldridge now, merging both houses here in Daol Bay until the Lord Master abdicates Atrebell," Marigold explained with a roll of her eyes.

"Pyore will be given to rule in Hercalest, where his every decision will be watched closely by Eamon's trusted councillors." Marigold shuddered involuntarily as a wave of disgust swept over her. "As for a wife for him, they felt I was a poor match, given my headstrong nature. Eamon and Eldridge both feel that Pyore needs a less *'challenging mate'*." Marigold punctuated the last two words in derisive fashion, releasing a hand from the reins to bend her index and fore fingers in mock quotation.

It was unknown who the replacement bride for Pyore was, yet Marigold felt sorry for the any woman who might even be considered a prospect for the position. Her previously betrothed had shown his temper to the whole of Parliament not so very long ago, attempting to strike at her despite the fact they were in plain view. Marigold could not even begin to comprehend what he was capable of doing in the privacy of his own home, and the very thought alone broke her heart and sent a shudder of disgust through her.

"They said the same of Eamon too," Oire said with a derisive scoff. "So to the slavering Palomb wolf they sacrificed the innocent fawn that was Jorette Morton. As sweet and gentle a woman as I had ever known. She did it for the good of the Morton house, so she said."

"Oire..." Marigold started to say, her voice trailing off. "You are from Weicaster Bay, I had almost forgotten. The Sellars house is-"

"Aye, we are highborns from the lowest rungs of Weicaster Bay's ladder who are sworn to serve the Mortons," he said, finishing the thought. "Despite our difference in social class, I considered them as close as family, and my blood relatives still do. I could not reconcile with the Mortons for having done that to sweet Jorette. She deserved more from life, my lady, as do you."

Marigold was at a loss for words and Oire was saying no more. She thought better than to press the issue further than he might have liked and instead stepped their conversation back to the previous topic. "Do you think that the people would feel more certain if I were to resist the Palombs?" Marigold asked next, a little afraid of the answer she felt she was going to get.

He paused for a moment and dodged Marigold's gaze, looking across the bay as though he was searching the horizon for the words he sought. "The people would feel more comfortable if they were guaranteed a stable economy and jobs that paid adequately enough for them to feed their families. They want to feel safe in their own homes, secure in their employment, and to live in a world in which their children and grandchildren have a future. Anyone can promise them that, it takes a leader to uphold such a promise. Your father and his father before him did commendably well, I would say."

Marigold watched as Oire's face wrinkled unsettlingly. "Eldridge Palomb is unlikely to follow suit, but there is still a chance that he will continue to give the majority a life similar to what the Tullivans did. You, though, my lady, can guarantee none of that, at least not immediately, anyhow."

Marigold knew that what Oire was saying rang true, but it still made it no less biting to hear. "I would like to think that I would make a more stable leader than a Palomb."

That drew a thin smile from him. "Aye, you would make a far better Warden of the West than either Palomb twin could on their best day and were this country like the Midlands of Gildriad, there would be no issue. Regardless of how people might feel about having you continue the family legacy though, you cannot do so without great disruption. The people, by and large, do not want great disruptions, or even small disruptions, for that matter. Eldridge, for as many questions as his arrival might have, will at least guarantee an almost seamless transition of power and likely, very little tangible aberration from the normalcy that most people have come to know."

"We both know he would not care for the west coast as my father did and the people would be smart enough to know better," Marigold argued in her defence.

"Would they?" Oire poised the question rhetorically, going on before Marigold even had time to consider it. "I have come to find that people tend to frame matters of the nation with how those matters affect themselves first and foremost. In this way, most people will look upon supporting you as an immediate danger to the lives of them and their immediate families. With Eldridge Palomb, that threat would be conditional."

"You are saying that I have to convince the people that mine is a cause worth the potential interruption to their own lives," Marigold deduced in a grim tone as she fully realised the weight of that goal.

"That is one part of it, aye," Oire agreed. "The other half is to prove that Eldridge is poison in the well. They need to understand the danger of letting him assume power. Of course, it goes without saying that none of that would be easy to achieve. However, I believe that you are more than capable of accomplishing that task."

"I appreciate your faith in me. Thank you, Oire," Marigold relented, content to let the conversation taper off there for now. The two lapsed into silence and Marigold's thoughts wandered back to her father again, prompted by a familiar sight that came into view.

The road beneath the hooves of Empress had continued to incline slightly while the two talked, taking the party higher and further west with each step. They had come to what was known as Knight's Knoll, so named for Ser Davis, who had claimed these heights for his own. It was written that the old knight had chosen it for the strategic advantage that the commanding views afforded him and Marigold had found that claim quite easy to believe. From atop Knight's Knoll, Marigold could see the rooftops of nearly every building in the city and well out into the larger Twin Bay in which it sat. If the hills between Daol Bay and Portsward were lower, she would have seen that city in the distance as well.

For as picturesque a sight as it made, Marigold had found Knight's Knoll to be a lonely place at times. Granted, there was always the company of the employees of the manor, but Marigold had still felt distant from the city itself. There was just one other place in relative walking distance up there, and that was the Tullivan Crypt. Beyond that, there was only the desolate, muddy road that led to the Southern Point Lighthouse at the mouth of Twin Bay.

Marigold's eyes fell to the manor, looking specifically to the second floor, where she knew her father would be, abed and at rest in his chambers at the rear of their home.

The party was close enough now to see the employees that were working outside the manor going about their duties. She spotted

Groundskeeper Irvine raking the leaves on the front lawn and he in turn heard the approaching riders, giving a friendly wave as they drew nearer. A maid with her back to the road cleaned the exterior of the windows of the first floor of the manor while standing atop a ladder. Below the maid who Marigold could not identify was a footman by the name of Curt, who was busy holding the ladder steady. He called the maid's attention to the recent arrival and she in turn knocked on the window to alert whoever was on the other side.

Marigold drew Empress to a stop before the stable and took a second to run a hand through her mane. "Thank you, Empress, you did a wonderful job," she told the horse.

With the lift of a leg, she swung out of the saddle and to the ground gracefully. She took the reins in hand and was about to pass them off when Empress nudged her elbow, eager for a pat on the muzzle. Marigold found herself laughing, in spite of everything she was dealing with, and gave Empress what she wanted. "There now, how was that?" Marigold asked as a lad from the stables named Chet approached to take the reins.

While Marigold had been tending to Empress, two guards had opened the front door of her home and a line of maids and footmen emerged from within. They stood to either side of the stone walkway that led to the front stairs in a V formation, waiting for Marigold to approach.

Lewinson, the portly house butler, stood apart from his charges in a black suit, his white gloved hands folded neatly over his abdomen. "Miss Marigold, I bid you good morning and welcome you home once more. I trust that your journey was uneventful?"

"It was indeed, Mister Lewinson, and I bid good morning to you as well," Marigold answered upon approach.

From behind her, Marigold heard the hurried footsteps of Oire as he worked to catch up. She slowed her walk to give him time and looked back and forth between the servants on either side of her. "Good morning to you all. It is good to see everyone again and I hope you have all been well while I was away. Normally, I would love nothing more than to stay and chat. However, just this once, I hope you will all excuse me if I do not delay to go to my father's side."

The maids and footmen stayed silent where they stood and she noticed a few lowering their gaze to the ground.

Oire was exchanging whispered words with Lewinson for a moment but broke off when he heard Marigold excusing herself and jogged to close the gap between them.

"My lady would you like me to come with you?" he asked in a low voice when he was close enough to whisper.

She shook her head slowly in response. "For the time being I think I would like to be alone with my father, but thank you, Oire."

"Of course, my lady," he said while taking a step back, "Do not hesitate to call on me should you need anything."

Marigold turned to the stairs leading to the front entrance, took a deep breath, and ascended alone.

9

SEREPHANIE

hree facts were running through the mind of Serephanie as she and Syrie closed in on the sitting area of the Wives of the Ring: The first, while in the company of her family, Serephanie had met the giant of a man known as Fezadore and with him on that occasion was his wife, Cyrelle. Secondly, though only a teenager at the time, Serephanie was still recognisable, as her body had grown and changed since then, but her face would still be known. The third and final fact was that should Darrion achieve any measure of success in this tournament, Serephanie would not be able to escape the purview of Cyrelle and her Wives of the Ring.

The Giant's Wife sat alone on a chair that would seem downright ostentatious in size if one were to behold it without knowing that it was made for her late behemoth of a husband. Indeed, seated upon that veritable throne, on an isolated platform built into the bleachers, Cyrelle might well have passed for a queen. She was a tall and broadly built woman in her fifties, with hazel eyes and long facial features framed by flowing, white-blonde hair. A deep red dress accented with intricate silver filigree designs fit closely to her frame, its cleavage cut low and the sleeves flared at the forearm. Fingers ornamented in a number of rings held a goblet of wine and a silver necklace bearing a large ruby pendant hung about her neck.

As Serephanie approached, with Syrie leading the way, Cyrelle broke from speaking with another woman and dismissed both her and the two handmaidens at her feet with but a gesture and a few words. Cyrelle's eyes scanned Serephanie from head to toes, and when they were close enough to be heard, she spoke to the two approaching young women. "This must be our new friend that I spotted across the tent, is it Syrie?"

"It is indeed, Ma'am." Syrie answered with newfound manners, her back still to Serephanie.

Cyrelle placed a thumb and index finger on her chin, resting the elbow on the arm of the chair, a smile playing on her face the entire time. "My name is Cyrelle Molissios, my husband was Fezadore Molissios, better known as Fezadore the Giant, but if Syrie did her job, you should know all that already. Now, who might you be?"

"Her name is..." Syrie had begun to say, until turning to face Serephanie with something akin to panic in her eyes. "I'm afraid I didn't get her name, begging your pardons, Ma'am."

"What *did* you get, Syrie?" Cyrelle said with dry amusement.

Syrie scratched her head nervously at the woman's laughter, answering sheepishly, "She is the wife of a freelance fighter named Cole. The two of them are from Galdourn, where he trained. Although, she claims he got his seasoning in Daol Bay's pits."

"This Cole fellow was not the lad that got dropped on his skull by the big-bellied slave," Cyrelle deduced quickly, as the last of Syrie's words left her mouth.

"No, he was not," Syrie confirmed, her head now lowered and her hands behind her back.

"That's an interesting development," Cyrelle noted ponderously with a flex of her fingers. "Syrie, on your way down, inform Minda Safford that she owes me a silver and send Dilla back here with my wine decanter and an extra cup, please."

"Aye, Ma'am. Will that be all?" Syrie said with a nod.

"It will. Thank you, Syrie," Cyrelle affirmed before looking to Serephanie. "Come join me, my new friend, I would like to get to know you."

Serephanie went to the bleacher seating to the right of Cyrelle, her feet propped on the platform so that she sat sideways in order to face the Giant's Widow.

The chair creaked beneath Cyrelle as she shifted in Serephanie's direction. "Do I make you nervous, Miss?" she asked in a voice that suddenly went soft.

It was undeniable that Serephanie was nervous, given how close she was seated to someone who could easily identify her. With her evident failure to hide those feelings, Serephanie decided her best course of action was to play with the most obvious reasoning. "Aye, Ma'am," she started, mimicking Syrie's manner of speaking. "I've never met anyone famous before. I hope you'll forgive me, as this is all a bit much to take in so suddenly."

"Oh, you flatter me, darling," Cyrelle replied with a nonchalant wave of her wrist. "My husband was the celebrity. I'm just the keeper of his legacy and the leader of our little flock of fighting enthusiasts. Once you get to know me, the nervousness will fade, I promise. Now, let's start with your name. Who are you?"

Serephanie lowered her head slowly as Cyrelle spoke, raising her eyes to meet the gaze of her host. "I appreciate the kind words, Ma'am. My name is Terra."

"That's a lovely name, Terra. Is it the only one you have?" Cyrelle inquired, her attention briefly captured by an approaching handmaiden.

"I'm the bastard daughter of a bastard father. I never had any other name before I married Cole, Ma'am. I'm Terra Chere now, though," Serephanie told Cyrelle while the girl she had to assume was named Dilla poured white wine into a silver goblet and handed it to Serephanie. She thanked the maiden for the refreshment and took a polite sip. It was one of the bolder wines she could remember tasting, with an interesting aftertaste that just begged one to drink more. "This is very nice, thank you, Ma'am."

"My Fezadore preferred the red wines, especially anything with blueberries in it," Cyrelle commented of her late husband. "For my money though, there's nothing quite like the white wines of the Bay of Fog. There's something in their soil, I believe. It seems no matter what year is written on the label, the drink within is always quite delectable."

There were a great many things Serephanie Tullivan could say about the vineyards of the Bay of Fog, of vintages of red and white wines, and her preferences for each. However, that knowledge would be altogether foreign to a woman of a sparsely populated region like Galdourn, who was of such low birth that she did not even have a surname. As such, Serephanie played the game with what Terra could.

"Until now, I have only tasted two types of wine before, Ma'am: one is a swill so bitter that every taste makes me think my lips are going to curl into the back of my throat. The other was watered down so much that it didn't seem to have flavour at all."

"I used to know those wines in my younger days," Cyrelle declared with a chuckle. "And believe you me, I do not miss them. The wines, that is. I miss my younger days a great deal." With a hearty drink, Cyrelle pivoted the conversation. "So tell me, Terra, what brings you and your Cole to the Tournament of the Winter's King?"

For that question, Serephanie had a rehearsed answer that was for the better part of it wholly true. "He always wanted to join the League of the Sacred Fist, Ma'am. It's been his dream since he was just a little boy. You see, his father used to bring him to the matches all the time, and he fell in love with the sport. There's nothing else he's wanted quite so much."

"That's a dream shared by boys from Aquas Bay to Ravenkeep," Cyrelle stated pointedly, while adding to that thought. "I am no mathematician or a statistics scholar, yet I have an idea that the percentage of dreamy-eyed lads who make the roster of the league is somewhere in the lower half of the single digits. What about Cole makes you both believe that he can defy such odds?"

From at ringside the impresario announced the start of the penultimate preliminary round, taking attention away from Serephanie as she pondered on an answer for such a question. Impresario Demorton reminded the audience that only ten berths remained for the championship rounds, and only eleven of the forty-six fighters had been eliminated. With two remaining rounds in the preliminaries, any odd contenders out who had not come forward to challenge, or were the last to do so by the next round, would be eliminated by forfeiture.

The Impresario's declaration was done to put the pressure on the remaining vying contenders, and the men in the pits started to move forward to the gates eagerly, their hands in the air to be seen.

"Do you see him?" Cyrelle asked as her eyes looked over the combatants as ten of them were chosen to step onto the five tiny, circular rings in pairs to wait for their cue to commence fighting.

Serephanie indeed spotted him, telling Cyrelle as much. "Aye, he's in the ring in the far left corner from us, in what would have been the ring closest to where I was sitting. He's looking for me."

"That fellow in the black with the mane of hair?" Cyrelle queried rhetorically. "He's paired against a prisoner. A man fighting for the place he desires most in life versus a man fighting to ease the pain of the confines he's bound to for life. What an interesting story their fight could tell. Let's see what your Cole is made of, shall we?"

The Biddenhurst inmate was a meaty looking fellow with a shaved head and a long, scraggly beard that swayed past his bare, hairy chest. Though he was of a height with Darrion, Serephanie worried that the prisoner would prove difficult to be stirred. *The jailers have been feeding this one by the look of it. They must have seen fighting potential in him early on. It seems likely that he was locked up for something violent to begin with, and his new handlers kept him happy so that his penchant for brutality had some sort of use.*

A worrying prospect for Serephanie, but to her surprise, Darrion looked to be unconcerned with his opponent and was instead opting to spend these precious seconds eyeing the stands for her.

Pay attention to your opponent, Darrion. This is your one chance to inspect him, do not waste this. She wanted to scream, keeping the thought to herself instead.

The five refereeing officials in the gold silk robes were assigned to their matches, each one taking a moment to remind the participants of the rules of the contest. During the process, Darrion's opponent made a point of talking over the official at Darrion. The words themselves were lost to the noise of the tent, yet the scowling, snarling expression on the prisoner's face gave Serephanie clear indication that he was taunting Darrion. Though considered unprofessional in nature, such provocations and mind games were far from uncommon in the fighting contests. Furthermore, it was well known that the Sacred Fist, while not outright encouraging such, certainly allowed the behaviour in their efforts to stoke further drama and interest in what was already a spectacle of a sport.

Though Darrion was previously distracted by his search for Serephanie, the jawing of the prisoner served to snap Darrion's focus back to the immediate concern, much to Serephanie's relief. Once the official had control of the situation and got the prisoner to be silent, he finished his explanation and signalled to the bell keeper that all were ready. Those among the other rings, both officials and combatants alike, had been ready for quite some time and all focus was on the ruckus at Darrion's ring.

"I think we can safely say that your husband's match will be the most watched contest of this round," Cyrelle commented with a side-eyed glance.

"Indeed so," Serephanie had begun to respond, her voice no match for the opening bell that rung out at the same moment.

The prisoner closed in on Darrion quickly with an attempt to grab him, but found nothing as Darrion ducked and sidestepped. Darrion moved to the furthest point away from his opponent that the limited space could offer and crouched as low as he dared.

A fighter in the centre ring went down, his referee declaring an end to the contest loudly. While Darrion was able to block out the distraction, the inmate turned his head quickly and Darrion stepped toward him for a grab. The bearded man caught Darrion before he could be taken completely unaware and the two tangled at the arms in a brief stalemate.

In the ring closest to Serephanie, a fighter was flipped high by his opponent all the way out of the ring and to the sand below, drawing a gasp from the crowd. Still, Darrion remained entangled, with he and the prisoner jockeying for an advantageous hold. Another fighter in a corner ring was pushed to the mat and the fourth match followed close behind with one fighter forcing the other to submit to a standing, wrenching front-facelock.

Now, there was but one match to behold, with the attention of even the champions drawn to it.

Above the waist, the two were twisting and shoving one another, but below, Serephanie saw Darrion's gait widening. At first, the strategy seemed odd, but upon further inspection, Serephanie became certain that the convict was trying to step on Darrion's feet. It was a foul tactic that would normally merit disqualification, but the referee had not seemed to notice, and Darrion's stance was widening at an ungainly rate.

While his opponent had been focusing on foot placement, Darrion had been methodically working his hands onto the opponent's left arm. He wrenched it outward, bent it at the elbow, and ensnared it tightly in both of his own arms at head level.

The hold was called a top wristlock and it was one of numerous positions from which the Aquatican fighters would initiate their signature throws.

Please don't do it, Darrion. You can't let the champions know of your secret before you get to fight them.

If desperate enough, she knew Darrion would do just that. Fortunately, his stance had improved with the application of the hold, though the edge of the ring was still dangerously near and the opponent was pushing toward it. Apart from the ring's edge, Darrion now had the free hand of the prisoner's palming at his face, trying to cut off air and vision. Darrion tried to trip him backwards with a leg, but the prisoner resisted, though the shove managed to give Darrion a little ground to work with. A finger of the prisoner seemed to be sliding dangerously close to Darrion's eye. Now with little recourse before he was potentially blinded, Serephanie knew Darrion would resort to his Aquatican repertoire.

Turning his head from side to side managed to get the opponent's hand away for just long enough for Darrion to get his bearings. With a great bellow, Darrion pulled the locked arm towards him, turned his back to the opponent, and used the man's own momentum against him to flip arm and body over shoulder and down to the mat.

The audience roared and applauded at the sight of the tumbling man and as he thudded onto the mat, the referee declared Darrion the victor.

Amid the cheering and the protestations of the defeated opponent, one might have missed the sight of Tahru, the Doban man who was the Maroon Champion, jumping from his throne. He began pacing excitedly on the champions stage, the maroon belt that had been on his shoulder now sent flying forward haphazardly and onto the floor ahead of him. A stagehand standing ahead of the platform had picked up the belt and attempted to pass it back to its owner, only to be ignored.

Tahru looked surprised at what he had seen and was pointing and yelling in Darrion's direction. "That's Water Elf style!" Serephanie finally heard him saying repeatedly as the crowd quietened down. Tahru yanked the title belt from the stagehand's grasp and held it overhead with one hand, pointing at Darrion with the other while shouting, "Look at me, Water Elf-Man!"

Darrion was nearly out of the ringside area and back to the waiting pens when he heard the ruckus from Tahru. Even from where she sat, Serephanie could see the dread plain on Darrion's face when he noticed the Doban fighter staring him down.

Once Tahru had Darrion's attention, he called out to him, "You are mine, Water Elf-Man! When you come to challenge a champion, you challenge me! Water Elf style cannot beat the Doban style. I'll show you myself. Come and see!"

Cyrelle had slid back in her seat, sipping casually from her wine goblet while still watching the Doban man. "My Fezadore stood two full metres and a third of another in height, weighed nearly two hundred and forty kilos, and was every bit as strong as his size would have you believe. A man that large usually fears for nothing, and yet, even he made a point to not draw the ire of Tahru."

"I did not know that Tahru had such disdain for the Aquatican folk." Serephanie commented worriedly. Their home islands of Tropuri were situated far to the northwest of the Crescent Islands and the Aquaticans steered clear of the Crescent's everlasting geopolitical troubles, making Tahru's outburst confusing. Serephanie could not imagine why the Water Elves would have enemies anywhere, even in the Crescent.

That earned her a curious sideways glance from Cyrelle. "Disdain? No, honey, it's not disdain. Tahru thrives off the challenge. He's been expecting to face untrained scrappers and novice freestyle wrestlers in the gauntlet round." Her gaze and an index finger pointed towards Darrion, now nervously taking a drink of water from a barrel in the waiting area. "Your Cole, with his Aquatican martial arts, is something new and exciting for Tahru. We have never had a real Water Elf fight in our lists and it's unheard of for a non-Aquatican to be trained in their style. That means that unless Tahru fought an Aquatican before he came to us, he has never had the pleasure of testing his mettle against them. Your Cole presents just such an opportunity for Tahru. Now with that said, should your Cole refuse his invitation… Well, then you will see disdain."

"I am not certain that Cole can beat Tahru," Serephanie stated worriedly. "Nor do I think that he had any intention of challenging him."

Cyrelle formed a slender smile at the corner of her mouth, cocked her head after a drink from her cup while Serephanie spoke and was ready with a reply when the opportunity arose, "I can count on one hand the number of people that could beat Tahru and none of them are in this tent. Allow me to offer you a little advice: there is no shame in losing to such an opponent. There is, however, a great deal to lose if he refuses the clear and direct invitation of a respected veteran of the ring. There are many important eyes on the young talents in the waiting pit, and they are being judged on every aspect of their behaviour and actions."

"I- I should go tell him this," Serephanie decided while standing up. "Thank you for the company and the wine, Ma'am. I should be going now, though."

"Wait just a moment, Miss Terra," Cyrelle requested of her firmly. "I said that he is being judged on *his* actions, not yours."

Serephanie had begun to shake her head and managed to say, "I do not follow, Ma'am."

"You will be seen and heard telling him what to do," Cyrelle informed her modestly. "If he fights Tahru after that, it will be known in short time that it was because *you* advised him to. Besides, if he is the man and fighter you say he is then he should know well enough to accept the challenge and make sure he is first or second in line to do so. He will give your Cole a little time to rest and catch his breath, that's reasonable, but any more than that and your man will be seen as a hesitant coward."

During Cyrelle's counsel, the last bouts of the preliminary round had been organised and the bell sounded for them to commence. As with the previous matches, things went fairly quickly and by the time that she finished talking, the last two matches ended in near simultaneous fashion.

It appeared from the signal of one of the referees that another fighter had been injured. Another official indicated that both men in the match he had presided over had been disqualified when the contest devolved into fisticuffs. That meant that there was but one fighter who had yet to compete and was without an opponent. Rather than force his forfeiture, the Impresario announced that the remaining fighter would be granted a bye to the championship round and was seated as an alternate, should one of the winning fighters be unable to compete.

The Impresario let the tent grow silent for a moment before raising his cone again. "Ladies and gentlemen, the preliminary round has concluded! Your surviving contenders will now line up to challenge the champion of their choosing, and when the lists have been evenly filled out for each champion, the gauntlet round shall begin!"

The champions handed off their belts and came forward to meet their challengers for the top of the new round. Both the Barajah and 'The Glorious' Gilbare were each challenged by freelancers like Darrion, and a slave offered himself against Hann Bravado. The young professional in the lined, blue leather shorts that Serephanie had noticed earlier was the first in line to face the most obvious target in Landrick Imorgan.

Lastly and timidly, there came Tahru's opponent, who, according to Cyrelle, was a young trainee of the league. The lad approached one of the two platforms that stood just before the fighters' pit, where the hefty Doban fighter stood. Unfortunately for the young man, the mere sight of his lanky, wiry frame seemed to elicit a deep belly laugh from his larger opponent.

Tahru left the platform and walked toward the pit, leaving the lad standing in puzzlement. The Maroon champion began scanning the remaining fighters until his sights fell on Darrion, who was taking yet another gulp of water from a provided barrel.

"You watch me, Water Elf-Man! Watch closely!" Tahru roared while jabbing a finger in Darrion's direction. Back on the platform, Tahru immediately grabbed the skinny fellow by his tall head of light-brown curls. Words were exchanged between the beastly fighter and the terrified neophyte, though Serephanie was too far away to hear them.

The referee wedged himself between the men and sent them to opposite sides of the platform. Once he had the matter under control, he waved a golden sleeve at the officials overseeing the bell, and with that, the champions' portion of the sixth round was ready to begin.

As the tent filled with the familiar trio of notes, the champions and challengers went toe to toe. While the other competitors had engaged one another at the first opportunity, the curly-haired fellow standing across from Tahru had intended on taking a more subtle approach. He kept to the perimeter of their platform, trying to walk the edge and put distance between himself and the colossal Doban man.

Nearby, Bravado and Barajah both ended their matches in near simultaneous fashion, eliciting a cheer from the crowd.

Tahru's opponent ran in and attempted to shove the big man during the ruckus, a gesture that seemed less than useless, as Tahru went entirely unmoved. Reaching for the throat and the trousers, Tahru pressed his wriggling opponent over his head. A short dash across the platform later and Tahru tossed the young man through the air and all the way into the waiting pit, where he crashed down atop a group of spectating grapplers.

A synchronous gasp echoed forth from the audience and the unoccupied referees all rushed toward the pit. Serephanie scanned the faces of the fighters until she found Darrion, who was standing well clear of the tangled pile of humanity that now lay on the ground. The look on his face was one of concern, but he did not seem afraid. There was nothing Serephanie would have liked more than to run to his side, or even wave her arms about to get his attention, but she thought better of it all.

Somewhere among the fighting rings, there came the sound of a body hitting the floor and a referee ruled another match over.

"You think you're a sly lad, don't you Landrick?" Serephanie heard Cyrelle say, turning in her direction to see a look of derision across her face.

"Is something the matter, Ma'am?" Serephanie asked with affected timidity.

Cyrelle inclined her head toward where Landrick Imorgan now stood victoriously above the man in the painted blue leathers. The Sacred Fist's own fighter was pulling himself from a supine position to his knees with one hand while the other checked a nose now spilling blood. "While everyone was looking at Tahru's spectacle, our 'noble' man here slid his elbow into Killian's nose and broke it. I don't know who else saw it, but I did."

"But this is a non-striking tournament," Serephanie exclaimed with feigned shock. "Landrick should be disqualified for hitting Killian."

"He should, but I'm not sure that the referee witnessed it," Cyrelle agreed as her face contorted in disgust. "Even if he did, Landrick covered it up by shoving Killian face first to the mat. He'll blame the broken nose on that and the officials will only gladly accept it. The rules of engagement are always different for highborns. As I'm sure you are more than aware, coming from such a low station yourself."

Serephanie analysed Cyrelle for any tells as she spoke the last sentence, looking for hints of suspicion, but found none of immediate concern. "You are not highborn yourself, I take it?" Serephanie asked cautiously.

That query made Cyrelle laugh, "Goodness no, Child. I'm an innkeeper's daughter from a town called Camble Corner in the southwestern end of the Old Camble region, right on the border of South Camble. The place of my birth is but a sharp bend in the road and nothing else. In fact, my hometown is so tiny that it usually does not even merit a dot of ink on the map. I was born poor, bred poor, and if not for Fezadore, I would still be poor and running an inn that only manages to exist because it's the only shelter in any direction for days."

There was nothing that Serephanie could think to say to that, outside of a meek, "I'm sorry, Ma'am."

"You have nothing to be sorry for, you had no part in my history," Cyrelle stated, not waiting for a response as she turned her attention to one of her handmaids. "Dottie, come here a moment, please."

The girl came forward from where she had been sitting beside the one named Dilla, who had earlier brought the wine. Immediately upon arrival, she was drawn close by Cyrelle, their conversation whispered for what felt like minutes, until Dottie stepped back with a nod and a confirmation of, "Yes Ma'am, it will be done."

"And make sure to bring Syrie with you instead of Dilla," Cyrelle added with a smile and a dismissive gesture from a single hand.

Dottie waved back in understanding and went to where Syrie was seated. The two young women spoke in similarly whispered fashion and in a heartbeat had hastily departed the stands, leaving sight so quickly that Serephanie was wondering if there was some sort of emergency.

"Is everything alright, Ma'am?" Serephanie queried, her eyes going between the Giant's Widow and Darrion, who was pacing in the waiting pit in slow contemplation.

"If those girls do as they are told, everything will be just fine, dearie," Cyrelle told her in a kind tone, the hand bearing her wine cup extending outward. "Dilla, darling, I need more wine, please."

The handmaid came forward to refill the cup and offered more to Serephanie as well, though she declined. During the events in the centre of the tent, she had drank in small sips and was still holding half of the wine she had first been given.

Cyrelle seemed to see as much from the corner of her eye and commented on it, "Not much of a drinker, are we?"

"Not today, Ma'am," Serephanie explained casually. "I'm too tense to want to drink much."

"All the more reason to do so, in my opinion," Cyrelle opined while raising her goblet.

In the background of their conversation, the toppled mess of men in the pit had been sorted out and the opening matches of the seventh round were set to begin. None among the challengers at the front of the line did Serephanie recognise, though the number of slaves and the incarcerated coming forward were beginning to diminish, replaced instead with seasoned freelancers and the more cautious youth.

If anything was a sure sign of the tournament reaching its midway point, it was the exhaustion of the suppressed population of combatants, Serephanie thought to herself. *Illiastra's dependence on a shackled populace is a sickness, and showcases like this are the open sores of the disease, oozing plainly for all to see. Even in the seeing, few care. Far too many are content to let the sickness spread so long as they or their kin do not become part of the infection themselves. Then, and often only then, does the plight of the restrained become a concern.*

As quickly as Serephanie had that notion, the next round was ready to begin, and Cyrelle's marked excitement brought Serephanie's attention back to the battle at hand.

"It's time for the champions to defend their belts again. Let's see what your Cole does, Terra."

The first to come forward from the waiting pit to greet the four veterans of the Sacred Fist and Landrick Imorgan was Kohvee, the professional fighter and husband of Syrie. His strides were full of purpose, his gaze fixated on one person in particular.

"Landrick Imorgan, let us see what you can do against the likes of me. You fancy yourself the Golden Knight of the Winter King, but based on your performance against Killian, I would sooner call you the court jester," Kohvee declared vociferously as he came to a stop just before the corner platform on which Landrick stood.

The audience hollered approvingly at that and though she did not join their cheering, the smirk at the corner of Cyrelle's mouth certainly seemed to be in agreement with the consensus.

On the leftmost platform beside the waiting area, Serephanie saw Tahru standing silently with his hands on his hips and a fierce expression across his face. She followed his line of sight to Darrion, busily stretching and taking deep breaths. More than anything, she wished that she were at Darrion's side, building him up with encouragement for what was about to come.

She saw Darrion wave at the official tending the gate of the waiting pit and her heart began to race in her chest. *He's going to do it.*

"There we go, that's a good man," Cyrelle commented lowly as Darrion walked across the sand toward the waiting Doban man.

Tahru met him at the lip of the platform and looked down at him, "Are you here to accept my invitation, Water elf-man?" he bellowed.

The chest of Darrion rose with a deep breath and he answered clearly for all to hear, "Yes, I have come to challenge Tahru of Doba for the title of Maroon Knight of the Winter King."

"Then come forth and we shall battle, Water elf-man!" Tahru responded with an uproarious laugh, standing back to allow Darrion onto the platform.

The referees took their places, confirming with the participants that they were ready to begin. Each referee signalled in turn, and when the last one called out, the bell sounded. The second set of matches of the gauntlet round had begun.

Gilbare Bauntreaux was the first to win and retain his championship by getting a cry of submission from his opponent with a tight arm-bar hold applied from the standing position. After him, both Hann Bravado and Barajah finished their fights one after the other with a standing belly-to-belly slam and a snapmare take-over hold, respectively.

Landrick and Kohvee had gone into a neutral position called the collar-and-elbow stance, and were shoving one another about. Kohvee seemed to have the momentum, and Landrick looked rightfully and frightfully concerned with his professionally trained opponent.

In the leftmost ring to the waiting pit was a different matter. At the sound of the bell, Darrion had stayed in place, his arms up at the ready to receive his opponent and his breathing calm and collected. The lack of movement, while not directly engaging, was meant to bring Tahru to him. However, the Doban grappler would not be subconsciously goaded and he had stood firm on his own side of the platform.

Tahru slapped his chest with a closed fist and called out to Darrion, "Come on, Water elf-man, here I am!"

Across the platform, Serephanie espied a subtle shake of Darrion's head and he stayed firmly in place.

They both want to start in a defensive position, Serephanie surmised, glancing back and forth between her husband's contest and that of Kohvee and Landrick.

The minister's son had given up the neutral position and had attempted some sort of arm hold on Kohvee. Much to Landrick's frustration, any advantage the offensive manoeuvre might have offered was slipping away due to Kohvee's methodical efforts to work his way free. With the unconventional and substandard knotty hold unravelled, Kohvee adjusted his own grip on Landrick's arm and slipped behind him with startlingly quick precision, wrenching upward sharply on the arm where it bent at the elbow.

"Good lad, Kohvee, clamp down on that hammerlock." Cyrelle offered as commentary.

Landrick cried out in pain and tried to escape the hold by any means necessary. His first instinct was to try to throw his free arm backward in an attempt to wrench Kohvee's hands away. The gesture was met with Kohvee pressing his head into the right shoulder blade, rendering that arm useless for such a countermeasure. Next, Landrick tried to reach between his own legs for one of Kohvee's, but the movement only allowed Kohvee to apply more pressure. While already bent over, Landrick's follow-up movement would almost seem like a desperate accident, but having observed his antics from the previous fight, a trained eye would know better. Landrick lashed backward to an upright position in a flash and whipped his head back violently, his intent likely to slam his skull into Kohvee's face. However, Kohvee leaned to his left and evaded the attack, his eyes wide and mouth agape in disbelief.

That disbelief turned to a calm fury and after looping his left arm firmly around Landrick's, he threw his free right hand to Landrick's face where he wrapped the arm across the chin and wrenched it sharply to the right.

"NOOO!" Landrick whimpered for all to hear, his whole body beginning to writhe in desperation. "Please, nooooo..."

"That there is the standing Crossface hold." Cyrelle explained contentedly. "I'm told that there are few submission manoeuvres as painful as what Landrick is currently enduring."

Despite his wriggling body and the prying of his free hand, Landrick could not escape the clutches of the Crossface. Further efforts to shove Kohvee off the platform backwards were countered with footwork that seemed a step ahead of Landrick at every twist and turn. With little recourse, Landrick furiously began to tap his free hand against Kohvee's arm, giving the universal fighter's signal of surrender.

The spectators rose in thunderous applause at the sight of Landrick's tapping and the cheering only grew as Kohvee released the hold and had his hand risen in victory.

"Our first title change of the evening," Cyrelle noted, a smile working its way across her lips. "I believe that's the first belt Syrie's Kohvee has ever won. Look at how happy she is."

Sure enough, there was Syrie at the barricades edge between their seating area and the sandy grounds surrounding the fighting platforms, jumping up and down and cheering in excitement. Serephanie had not seen her return from the task Cyrelle had set her and Dottie on, but whatever the job, it clearly had not taken much time.

"Your Cole still stands as well, though I cannot say for how much longer," Cyrelle added, inclining her head toward the fighting platform where his match was playing out.

The pair of Darrion and Tahru had scarcely moved since last Serephanie had looked at them. Darrion, in particular, was standing in exactly the same place and with the same pose. Having closed in by a step, Tahru was now swaying back and forth, making lazy, grabbing swipes that Darrion was knocking away with a single hand.

As if by cue, Tahru began to advance on Darrion just as Kohvee stepped off his platform, as though Tahru were waiting for all eyes in the tent to be squarely on him. When the Doban was within easy reach of Darrion, he made a grab for the head with the right hand, and Darrion moved to deflect it with the left.

"He's not watching Tahru's left..." Cyrelle pointed out.

The words were barely spoken when Cyrelle's observation bore fruit. Tahru's left hand was already in motion and snaking its way to Darrion's jaw, much to Serephanie's dismay.

"He's choking him!" Serephanie blurted out as the hand made contact with flesh.

"No, it's not a choke hold, look closer," Cyrelle corrected while pointing a painted fingernail toward the pair. "It's a nerve hold that Tahru likes to call the Doban Dreamcatcher. It's something of a signature manoeuvre of his."

On further inspection, Serephanie could see that Cyrelle was indeed right, as Tahru's hand clutched Darrion's jaw rather than his throat. However, that did nothing to dissipate her concerns.

Darrion had abandoned any defensive pretence and had wrapped both his arms around Tahru's left, trying vainly to break the hold. There appeared to be a wobble in Darrion's legs, leaving Serephanie certain that he was about to lose consciousness, though he seemed fiercely determined to stay upright. In a last bid, Darrion took his own left hand away from Tahru's and coiled it over the arm instead, reaching with all his might to try and twist the elbow of his opponent.

Seeing what Darrion was trying to do, Tahru bent his elbow before Darrion could apply any torque and tried to ensnare Darrion's left arm with his free right hand. The gesture forced Tahru in closer to Darrion, but kept the hold from being broken. A leg of Darrion's twined around Tahru's and he attempted to push Tahru backward. The big man stumbled, but the hold remained locked in. The legs of the two fighters engaged in a sort of clumsy dance then, as Darrion repeated the tactic. His vining trick kept Tahru in the position of having to step backward to avoid being tripped, forcing him closer to the edge of the platform with every use.

Darrion had one foot of Tahru's on the platform's edge and looked poised to force him out when the Doban shifted his grip from Darrion's jaw to his throat. The move caught Darrion by surprise and he lost his momentum, stepping back enough to give Tahru space to operate.

"Now *that* is a choke hold," Cyrelle admitted reluctantly. She seemed on the verge of saying more on the matter, but Tahru was not done.

Tahru pushed Darrion back a step and grabbed the waistband of Darrion's trousers with his right while still holding the throat with the left. With a mighty roar, Tahru lifted Darrion overhead and slammed him down hard on his back to the mat. In as quickly as Cyrelle could identify the chokehold, the match had ended. Darrion had lost.

"And that, darling, was a choke slam," Cyrelle stated with a disappointed sigh. "I was about to say that a chokehold, while frowned upon, is not entirely illegal in the rules of the Sacred Fist. The user has until a count of five from the referee to release the choke before being disqualified. Tahru did not need five seconds, however. In fact, I would say he barely needed two."

On the platform lay Darrion, looking like his pride was wounded more than his body. Tahru strolled about around him, alternating between raising his arms and slapping his chest proudly, shouting menacingly at the jeering audience.

Serephanie watched Darrion intently as he continued to lie on his back, an arm covering his eyes from the bright lights overhead. She so desperately wanted to run to Darrion's side. However, the thought went to the back of her mind when Tahru paused in his victory celebrations and came to stand directly over Darrion.

"What is Tahru doing?" she asked Cyrelle with restrained panic. "The fight is over, Tahru should leave him be."

Cyrelle made a downward gesture with an open hand, "Wait a moment, Terra. Let's just watch and see."

A slow crouch brought Tahru down to Darrion's side, where eye contact was made between the two. A few words were exchanged, unheard above the ruckus of the crowd, and at the conclusion of their exchange, Tahru stood once more. He paused, watching Darrion rise up into a sitting position. To the surprise of the audience and Serephanie alike, Tahru extended a hand to Darrion and once taken, pulled him back to standing. A pat on the back later and Tahru was raising the hand of Darrion and pointing at him, encouraging applause from the audience.

"What in the...?" Serephanie had begun to say while turning to Cyrelle to gage her reaction.

The Giant's Widow was beckoning Dottie to approach and the handmaid was climbing the stands with a sloped writing cabinet that took up both of her arms and looked to be weighing her down.

"Thank you, Dottie," Cyrelle began as the girl approached. "Did Syrie help you as I asked?"

"Oh but she did, Ma'am," Dottie informed Cyrelle while carefully laying the wooden piece of portable furniture in the lap of her superior. "She asked if she could go watch her Kohvee in his championship match once we were back and I did not think you would mind, what with the job being done and all."

Cyrelle patted her arm gently in response, "That's all well and good, Dottie. We would not want Syrie to miss her Kohvee's shining moment. You may return to your seat beside Dilla."

"And you, Terra Chere, you have a great deal to be proud of this day," Cyrelle declared with a grin.

Serephanie certainly was proud of Darrion's performance. However, Cyrelle had made it seem as though he was a champion, when in fact she was watching him vacate the waiting pit for the dressing tent, with neither sash nor championship belt. "I am proud of Cole for getting as far as he did, that's true…"

While they had been talking, Cyrelle had lifted the writing surface of her cabinet and produced an inkwell, quilled pen and a blank piece of paper. "Did you not see what Tahru did after the fight?" she asked after quickly dipping her pen and putting it to paper. "Your Cole gave him a good match and Tahru acknowledged as much with that show of respect. Tahru owed your Cole nothing and gave him a courtesy he did not and likely will not afford any other opponent of his this day. That speaks a great deal, especially when considering that your Cole is but an uninitiated freelance fighter, as far as the League of the Sacred Fist is concerned. Even without taking his relative inexperience with *professional* fighting into consideration, it is no small feat for your Cole to all but break Tahru's Doban Dreamcatcher hold while quite nearly knocking him from the ring."

Content with her scribing, Cyrelle began to wave a hand over the parchment to encourage the ink to dry faster. "Why, I dare say that his performance has more than earned my respect, too. In any case, this here is for you."

Serephanie accepted the paper to hand and quite nearly began to read it, before remembering that as a girl of low birth, she was highly unlikely to be able to do so.

"What is it?" she instead asked.

"Bring that to your Cole and have him return back here to the tent with it tomorrow," Cyrelle instructed Serephanie while signalling to her handmaidens. "Present it to Na'Zohz, he's our chief of security and can usually be found guarding the door. He will know where to send you both."

Of the two, only Dilla came forward. "How can I be of service, Lady Cyrelle?" she inquired with a curtsy.

"Our new friend Terra would like to be with her husband after his eventful run in the tournament. Escort her to Syrie at the bottom of the stands and tell Syrie to take Terra to the dressing tent."

"I would be glad, Lady Cyrelle," the handmaid said before turning to Serephanie, "Please, follow me, Terra."

Though she stood up, Serephanie was not quite done. "Wait, before I go, Lady Cyrelle, I must thank you for your hospitality. It certainly was a pleasure to meet you and I hope we see more of each other."

"I have little doubt that we will be getting to know one another quite well, darling," Cyrelle responded while extending a hand toward Serephanie.

Though apprehensive, Serephanie took the hand and received a firm shake from Cyrelle. "What I just gave you was my personal recommendation for your Cole to receive an audition for the League of the Sacred Fist. I believe he is worth a closer look, and that means you as well, Miss Terra. I will see the both of you in the morning."

10
FREYARD

As promised to Lady Marigold, Freyard Archer was preparing to proffer her plan to his Sun's Rangers. In the meeting hall of Fort Dornett, Freyard silently sat at the head of the long table and watched as they shuffled in. Their eyes all fell upon him, scanning for any sign that might tell them why they had been summoned.

A heavy, iron chandelier hung overhead, crudely wired for electricity in an old fortress that was built in a time when candles and lanterns alone provided light. The glow it cast reached from one end of the table to the other, but the corners of the room remained darkened. To Freyard's left sat an unused hearth that he could not recall being lit, save for the long rains of spring when the dampness threatened to creep into the bones. Behind him and the captain's chair he occupied there was a small alcove furnished with a simple desk. Typically, the spot was left open to sight, but for the purposes of the vote, Freyard had asked the maintenance staff to adorn the walls with a dark, heavy drape for privacy.

Opposite of the hearth was a wall lined with twelve black banners, with every one of them emblazoned with the yellow sun and crossed recurve bows that were the sigil of the Sun's Rangers. Embroidered in an arch above each crest was a name and date, hanging as a solemn reminder of the rangers that had perished.

Eleven died at the hands of the raiders, one from the bite of a snake, Freyard reminded himself as he read each name in what was as close to a silent prayer as he was as likely to have. *I hope that our decision tonight honours your legacies and sacrifices, gentlemen.*

Officers from the other forts and beyond had told Freyard that to be an active battle commander and have only eleven deaths from direct battle was an accomplishment for which could be proud. For its worth, pride was the last thing Freyard felt when the names and faces of his dead charges floated before the mind's eye.

Every name among them serves as a grim reminder of times when I could have done better as a captain. Eleven mistakes and they just scratch the surface of my life's errors. I hope that regardless of what my Sun's Rangers decide in tonight's vote, that I do better by the living than I did for those who paid the final price.

Rarely did Freyard order a meeting of all forty-six of his rangers and even rarer again did he make their attendance mandatory. Yet, such times called for such measures. One of the reasons that he called so few full meetings was that the room itself was simply not meant to accommodate the entirety of the rangers. To house them all on that night, only the most tenured members were given seats at the table. The remainder of the company were standing about or leaning against the walls.

Before they had begun to gather, Freyard had enlisted the Pharsey twins to perform a roll call, and despite the cramped conditions and short notice of the meeting, all were accounted for. With attendance taken and greetings issued, Freyard dove into the matter and informed the Sun's Rangers of the events of the autumn Parliamentary Sessions in Atrebell. Freyard walked them through the details of the capture and escape of Lady Orangecloak, the suspicions cast toward him personally, and ultimately, his own resignation from the Honourable Guardsmen that resulted from it all. The revelation of Orangecloak's capture shocked the youngest members, but as he looked among the elders seated before him, Freyard saw only dismay.

To his left, Freyard heard the oldest among them, a man named Yarohmer Stylford, known as Yarohmer the Graceful, shift in his seat and clear his throat before speaking. "'Even the cleverest of blackbirds that pokes at the raven risks being destroyed by it'. We all know the saying, and no one more than Orangecloak embodied it. I feel sorry for the girl, truly I do, but I will not act as though I am shocked at her capture. Entering Atrebell was a folly, and perhaps it was only one amongst an otherwise spotless career, but it only takes a single mistake to upend a lifetime of achievement."

Across the room came a reply from a younger man named Delliot Claired. "She escaped though, that in itself is good news."

"If anyone north of here heard us speak of the survival of Orangecloak as a positive thing, we would be hung as traitors," Ladd Dorser commented from his seat at the table, with a grim laugh and a shake of his head.

Yarohmer had a response ready for both men. "She escaped, aye, but her misstep came at the cost of the Johnan and the Phaleaynan she keeps in her company. From all accounts, they were good men who would not have been out of place as Sun's Rangers in their own right. As for the rest of Illiastra, they may call the Thieves the enemy, but they are the only group in the Southlands that are on our side."

"What I can't sort out," started Lahn Pharsey in turn, from where he stood beside his brother, "is how the lordly men knew what the Thieves were doing in the first place. How did they know that Orangecloak was going to be in Atrebell?"

Freyard, who had been content to let the men freely debate with little of his input, knew he had to field that question directly and spoke up. "I have it from a highly reliable source within the lordly circle that there is a mole amongst the ranks of the Thieves."

As the revelation fell over the room, Freyard gave it a second or two to settle, looking to find a mixture of shock and wonderment as to who the informant within Orangecloak's ranks might be.

I'm wondering the same myself, Freyard thought, before moving forward with what he had to say.

"Apparently this person spilled Orangecloak's plan, attempted to right their wrong by informing the Thieves of their slip, and was then forced to leak Ellarie Dollen's countermeasures to the EMP as well. To add to Orangecloak's woes, all three of the Sisters, Lazlo Arbour, and a number of their subordinates were captured or killed in Argesse following an ambush orchestrated by Lord Taves. By now, the survivors of that assault are within the bowels of Biddenhurst."

Another audible reaction rippled through the room upon that revelation and Freyard called for order as everyone talked amongst each other, which made hearing anything quite the task.

When the room fell quiet, Freyard opened the floor to individual discussion again and the first to offer an opinion was seated directly to his right: Glendil Archer, third son of the Archer Clan of Ravenkeep and First Lieutenant of the Sun's Rangers. "The loss of so many high ranking members of the Thieves will surely decimate their morale. It might even be enough to splinter them completely. All that remains in terms of leaders are Edwin the Raven, Garlan Vahn, Old Bansam, and Mell the Huntress. The former two haven't the stomach for fighting, Mell and her loyalists are undisciplined, and Bansam is an old man of old ways. Unless Lady Orangecloak herself returns, I feel it will be us alone defending the Southlands henceforth."

"Then our presence in the forests and keeps outside our walls will have to be increased to meet the raiding gangs," Yarohmer put in. "Ios knows they will undoubtedly grow bolder once word reaches them of the Thieves' loss."

Troygard of the Fog, the eldest and bastard son of Gorge Locklier, the minister of Bay of Fog, raised a hand to offer his opinion. "Perhaps we should reach out to Old Bansam? I think it would be wise to coordinate our defences."

It was Ladd that offered a rebuke of that query. "Despite our station, we are still members of the government that recently captured the Field Commander and a host of lieutenants of the Thieves. Old Bansam would not let us get close enough to him and his to see their campfire."

Voices began to climb again and it seemed to Freyard that every man in the room was talking over the other.

As he was about to steer the room back toward proper decorum, Glendil leaned in his direction to talk in his ear. "When are you planning to tell them about the *other* lady?" he asked, having been told in private of the matters pertaining to Marigold Tullivan prior to the meeting.

"In a moment, Good Cousin, I would prefer to issue one redefining piece of information at a time," Freyard told Glendil before raising a voice and a hand in unison. "Gentlemen, I ask for order, please! I reopen the floor to group discussion."

The men resumed talking one at a time at Freyard's request, with Yarohmer taking the lead. "Lads, I propose a motion to heighten our saddled presence in the Southlands until such a time that we can confirm Orangecloak's return. The people of the Southlands need to be protected from the raider scum and we are the only means of doing that for now."

Ladd was rubbing his chin thoughtfully while Yarohmer spoke and raised his own voice when the elder ranger was finished. "Could we send pigeons to Aquas Bay and the Warrens, and men to the other forts to request reinforcements? We are only forty-six strong, after all. It's hard for us to call ourselves a company, and an army we are definitely not. If the Forsaken and the Sons of Valdarrow believe that the Thieves are weakened, there is a better than good chance that one or both of them could centralise their numbers and go on the offensive. The two cities might not be in immediate danger, but besides Fort Layn, are any of the other forts or Phaleayna or the villages prepared for an army of raiders?"

A ranger leaning against the wall stepped forward with a raised hand to speak and Freyard gave him the floor. The hood of his cloak had been raised at that point, but he pulled it back to reveal a handsome, bearded face and long, light-brown mane before speaking. "With all due respect to Ser Dorser, we have no reason to believe that the Warrens would send so much as a rusty musket toward such an effort. Clay Harlowe will hide behind his walls until they are pulled down and even then, he would just climb to higher ground and throw his slaves at the problem. He is no friend of ours and never has been. In my view he is little better than the raiders themselves."

"With all due respect to young Mister Vernet," Ladd replied haughtily to the ranger who had just spoken. "Such speech against an elected official of the Illiastran government is grounds for treason. You would do well to keep mind of that outside of this room."

Glendil calmly rose to his feet to respond to that. "Ser Dorser, Dayden is right about Harlowe, and I am sure he is well aware of the cost of saying that anywhere besides here. Our own rangers have spied on Harlowe in the act of buying slaves from the raiding gangs. He claims his workforce is made solely of former Biddenhurst prisoners, but it is easier and cheaper for him to deal with the gangs that operate outside his own gates."

"I agree with you, Glendil, but the fact remains that our efforts only continue because we keep a careful tongue in regards to government matters," Ladd responded, his voice beginning to border on nervous.

Yarohmer pounded a gloved fist on the table in front of him, sending his braided, grey beard moving. "Are we hearing ourselves as we speak? Even with the origins of Harlowe's workers notwithstanding, the fact remains that they are taken against their will, locked into chains, and forced to toil in the dirt until they return to the dirt themselves. Calling the likes of him scum is an insult to pond scum and I would sooner eat iron nails than ask him for assistance."

Ladd's eyes went wide at that and he pointed a finger back at Yarohmer across the table. "Whatever you may think of Harlowe, the fact remains that he is an elected minister of Illiastra and working with him is the lawful course of action. Lady Orangecloak, who you wish to aid, by contrast, is the number one enemy of the government."

"And she is far and wide the moral and ethical choice between the two, regardless of the legality," Yarohmer shot back unwaveringly. "That alone should tell you all that you need to know about any interest the Elite Merchants have in doing what is right."

"I have served beside you from the day that Captain Archer formed the Sun's Rangers, Yarohmer, and in all of that time, I have never heard you speak so unfavourably of our government," Ladd uttered despondently, his face the very picture of sheer disbelief.

"We have never faced times such as these, Ladd," Yarohmer stated with a deep breath, taking a moment to gain his composure, a hand idly running through his beard. "One has only to think on the matters at hand to see our own hypocrisy. We ride out to defend the innocent against roaming bands of men who would kill and enslave them. On the opposite end of the Southlands is Minister Harlowe, who is supposedly our ally. Not only does the old buzzard refuse to aid us when asked, he is also guilty of exactly the same thing as those raiding gangs. Go north of here to Biddenhurst and you'll find Mackhol Taves doing much the same, but on a larger scale than Harlowe could ever hope to achieve."

Ladd moved to be allowed to speak, but Yarohmer's hand left his beard and slammed down hard on the table, stifling the thought as quickly as it arrived.

"The only difference between Taves and Harlowe, and the Sons of Valdarrow and the Forsaken, is that the former two are members of the ruling government," Yarohmer declared as he pressed onward with his point. "That's it. There is no grand moral dilemma, Ladd. All of them are sadistic, cruel men who delight in harming the innocent and the only person who had the intestinal fortitude to oppose that tyranny in all its forms was Orangecloak. The well-dressed tyrants got to her and the Thieves, which benefits the ragged tyrants that we were fighting. Now, it falls to us to clean up the mess created by the nobles and hope that we aren't slaughtered by the gangs for the effort. If you don't see the issues here, Ladd, then I can't help you."

A silence fell over the room when Yarohmer finished and it seemed that even Ladd was at a loss for words. Freyard scanned the floor to see if anyone else had anything to say and caught sight of a hand slowly rising far to his left, from one of the standing men. "You have something to add, Delliot?" Freyard asked invitingly, and all turned to see what he might say.

"In response to Ser Stylford, the report from Captain Archer said that Lady Orangecloak had escaped from captivity with Tryst Reine, and Captain Archer believes they are headed this way. Would it not be a boon for all of us if she arrives in the Southlands with perhaps the most skilled swordsman in the known world at her side? Especially considering that Captain Archer and the Master of Blades are known to one another?"

All eyes fell to Freyard for an answer and he gave reply. "I cannot deny that Tryst would bring a great wealth of knowledge to the Thieves and that the friendship he and I have would be beneficial to both parties. However, any contact we would potentially make would have to be done with the utmost secrecy."

As Freyard finished his thought, he saw the hands of both Troygard of the Fog and one of the Pharsey twins begin to rise and he gestured for them to lower before going on. "Gentlemen, before we discuss these matters further, there is another issue I must put before the entire group."

Freyard waited patiently until all the murmurs floating through the room came to a halt and all eyes had fallen upon him. He scanned the faces staring back at him, finding uncertainty and anxiousness looking back. "The proposition I am about to table may well render further questions about the Southlands and all who dwell here moot. In spite of everything, it will undoubtedly put us on an irreversible course, no matter how we decide to address it."

A glance towards Glendil earned him a reassuring nod and Freyard focused his thoughts and began. "My informant within the upper ranks of the Illiastran government leaked to me a plan drafted by Lord Mackhol Taves to recapture Orangecloak. Taves' intent is to besiege

Phaleayna and shed enough blood so that she is forced to answer steel with steel."

Whispers began to circulate amongst the men as Freyard let the news sink in amongst them. He quickly silenced them so that he might continue. "My source tells me that Phaleayna is not merely going to be threatened, but utterly wiped out. Orangecloak, Tryst, the Thieves, and the refugees of the island are to be destroyed entirely to prevent further uprisings. Any means of negotiation are meant to be merely a ploy to lure the Thieves to Phaleayna."

"How utterly repugnant!" Yarohmer declared hotly before turning his attention to Ladd Dorser again. "This is the government you fear angering, Ladd? A wealthy raiding gang, that's what the Elite Merchant Party is!"

Ladd Dorser opened his mouth to answer, but Freyard stepped in before their verbal sparring could go any further. "Gentlemen, if I may continue, there is more you should hear. There will be time for debate when I am done."

Both Yarohmer and Ladd held their tongues and the room fell quiet to hear Freyard. "Taves, with permission from Eamon Palomb, will draft his armed force for this mission primarily from the river forts, calling to arms every man that each fort can spare. The planned leaders of that pack will be, as I am sure most of you guessed, the Sun's Rangers."

"By the gods, I won't do it!" Dayden declared first.

Yarohmer jumped to his feet, the chair beneath him tipping over in his haste. "Nor will I! Mackhol Taves can go swallow a sword!"

"What choice do we have if the order is issued with the express backing of Lord Palomb?" Ladd countered in a tone of near panic. "The only people who can refuse that are Lord Marscal Tullivan and the Lord Master himself."

"I'm with Yarohmer!" Troygard of the Fog shouted. "To Aren's Lair with anyone that dares command me to harm the poor souls of Phaleayna!"

"Order gentlemen, order!" Freyard roared above the growing fury. When the command went both unheard and unheeded, he lifted the edge of the table and slammed it down to the floor. The deafening bang silenced all tongues and put the focus squarely on him. With the room paying attention, Freyard began again. "Gentlemen, I called for order!"

Apologies were offered from the entire group in turn and accepted by Freyard. With the collective rancour brought under control once more, he resumed his attempt to add to the conversation. "Ladd is correct to state that to refuse the orders would put us in direct violation of military law. That much is undeniable. However, before we find ourselves contemplating the choice between wanton slaughter and insubordination, there is a third option I should mention."

Silence descended over the room and Freyard heard the sound of Glendil's chair groaning, turning his head to see his distant cousin looking up at him with a confident smile. Freyard cleared his throat and spoke to the rangers. "We were made a direct offer of service from Miss Marigold Tullivan, second daughter of Lord Marscal."

"The *second* daughter?" a seated ranger named Tobald Eskren asked dubiously. "What could the second daughter of the Warden Lord of the West want with us all the way in the eastern half of the Southlands?"

"A fair point and one I will clarify, Tobald." Freyard said while seating himself again. "As to that, two weeks prior to the autumn Parliamentary Sessions, her elder sister disappeared from the Tullivan Manor in Daol Bay. Despite a heavy search effort from Portsward to Tippard, no trace of her was discovered. Marigold suspects that her sister does not want to be found. Instead, she believes it likely that the older Tullivan sister ran off with a lover of low birth to escape the marriage pact with the Palombs twins.

"That same pact affects Marigold, who, because of her sister's disappearance, is now the heir apparent of Daol Bay. Like Serephanie Tullivan, Marigold intends on breaking that pact. The difference between the two women is that while Serephanie walked away from everything, Marigold has designs on inheriting her father's legacy in her own right."

"You mean by force?" Yarohmer queried cautiously.

Freyard nodded toward him, "Aye, if it comes to that."

"Surely her father doesn't approve of any of this," Troygard posited. Though baseborn, Troygard was still the only Sun's Ranger of the western nobility, and as such, he had a particular interest in the matters of the Western Realm that others would not.

"Lord Marscal Tullivan is near death with his consumption illness," Freyard told the room sombrely. "His doctor does not believe he will live through the winter. When he passes, his lands, wealth, and titles would go to Lord Eamon Palomb's sons. Marigold is preparing to take that station for herself and part of those preparations involves recruiting us, as it were."

The look on Ladd's face was one of confusion as he opened his mouth to respond. "Atrebell and Hercalest would never stand for that. If Daol Bay does not yield to their authority and resists diplomatic measures, it could lead Illiastra into a war with itself. Why would she do that to our good country and its people?"

"Don't you see why, Ladd? The answer is staring you in the face: because it's not such a good country." Yarohmer jumped in, his tone calm, but with a hint of anger flowing throughout it. "We just said as much ourselves when we spoke of the practices of Harlowe and Taves. They take innocent people, mostly women I might add, and force them into slavery. The EMP in our lifetime evicted and slaughtered Amaroshans from Illiastra some twenty years ago. Queer folk are executed by Triarchists without as much as a trial. For all of that, they declared Lady Orangecloak to be the primary enemy of the state for simply speaking out against such atrocities. Our nation is sick, and I for one think that the Sun's Rangers need to do more than turn our backs on everything outside of our war with the raiding gangs. If that means joining up with Marscal Tullivan's second-born daughter, I'll saddle my horse and ride for Daol Bay at once."

"You will help her start a war, Yarohmer? How many do you think will die then?" Ladd threw back at him almost pleadingly.

The grey-maned, seasoned soldier seemed to be nothing if not prepared for Ladd to say that. "How many die every day on account of the practices of the EMP? When does it stop? When do honourable men finally stand up and say 'enough'?"

"Gentlemen, please, there is more I have yet to say," Freyard stated loudly enough to be heard over both of the arguing elders and the whispers floating through the room. His chair scraped the floor as he pushed it back and stood so that everyone could see and hear him. "Miss Marigold would like us to not only serve her, but to help her convince her potential army in the west that she is worth serving. I cannot stress enough that if we are to be a shining example on which to follow, we need uniformity amongst our ranks. To that end, I should say that if the votes go in favour of us aiding Marigold, there would be no ill will towards any among you who chooses to remain in Fort Dornett."

Freyard found himself looking to Yarohmer, whose steely gaze was as resolved as it was angered. "As far as the intentions of Taves go, if we leave the Southlands, the limited remaining garrison of Fort Dornett could not be called to action. The fact remains that there must be numbers enough in the fort to keep it operational."

Ladd was next for Freyard to seek out, and the exasperated old soldier looked back dejectedly. "I am sure any who would choose to stay here while still objecting to the coming aggression against Phaleayna could be spared from that horror if the Sun's Rangers were to leave."

The Pharsey twins standing in the back of the room, surrounded by their fellow younger peers all looked back at Freyard with welcome eagerness, and he spoke to them next. "The truth of the matter is that irrespective of how Miss Marigold intends to claim her rights, she will eventually be branded a traitor to the rest of Illiastra by the Elite Merchants. In that regard, so too shall everyone who stands with her. If we vote to join her tonight, that would include us. That fact, and the implications it carries with it, should be taken into consideration when you cast your ballot. I would advise you to also take into account just who would be calling us traitors and weigh the merits of those would-be accusers. Ask yourselves, 'are they men that are worthy of loyalty? Would their accusations be morally just?'

"Think of the vows you took when you were made a soldier of Illiastra," Freyard bid his rangers to recall, his voice as deathly serious as ever it had been. "You were asked to protect both the people of Illiastra and the government of Illiastra, but which of those two means more to you? Which deserves defending when they go against one another? Though we will be serving a Tullivan with a vested self-interest in overthrowing the Elite Merchants, she expresses a strong desire to put an end to all of the EMP's tyrannical measures. Whether or not she will be able to do that remains to be seen, but the fact that she desires such, and has the financial and political means to attempt as much, is worth dwelling on.

"The decision comes down to which vow you value most," Freyard put to the consideration of the gathered. His hands were held before him and pantomiming the plates of a scale. "Do you put more weight on your vow to protect the people or the vow to protect the government? If it's the former, you then have to decide if the current state of Illiastra serves the needs of the people or if it is time for change. Should you value the latter of the aforementioned vows," Freyard began to say, focusing his sights on Ladd as he did. "I advise you to figure out for yourself which of the two governing factions in the potential war you want to protect."

Freyard lowered himself down into his seat again and folded his hands upon the table. "If you have any questions for me, ask them now. Otherwise, the floor is open for debate and discussion before you go to vote."

The hall was silent for a moment, each man looking back and forth at one another, waiting to see who would speak first. After a time, Tobald cleared his throat and raised a hand. "Do you know when Mackhol Taves plans to make his move against Phaleayna?"

"From what I have heard, he intends to wait until springtime. His goal is to give Orangecloak and Tryst time to return and be spotted in the Southlands," Freyard explained plainly.

One of the Pharsey twins had a raised hand, and having not spoken yet, Freyard granted him the next question. "What if Orangecloak and Tryst are not spotted at all? Surely Lord Taves will delay the assault."

Freyard shook his head and lowered his gaze to the table, searching for a way to deliver what Marigold had told him when he asked her the same question.

"Might I answer this one, good cousin?" Glendil asked while standing up. Freyard saw no reason to object and gestured wordlessly for him to go ahead. "For those who may yet think that any of the EMP's lords have a shred of honour and decency, perhaps this will open your eyes: the Lord Master himself has declared that whether or not Orangecloak surfaces, Phaleayna will still be razed to the ground."

"That makes little sense," Ladd gasped in utter bafflement. "Such an act cannot do any favours for the EMP's standing. They only serve to lose by torching an island full of refugees."

Having regained his voice, Freyard looked directly at Dorser in answer. "The Lord Master will have the people believe she is dead and that Tryst is a wanted man for having balked at his duty to execute her. Those who believe that will see a burning Phaleayna as an example of what happens to anyone who supports or aids rebels against this government. To anyone who does not buy the lie of

Orangecloak's death, they will think that she abandoned Phaleayna in its most trying hour.'"

Delliot Claired was next for a question, having had his hand raised for some time already. "Can you do it, Captain?" he began, his voice trembling. "Can you walk into Phaleayna, likely under the guise of good faith, and drive your sword through the heart of Yassira Na-Qoia? Can you pull the trigger on a crying mother as she begs for mercy before the barrel of your pistol? Can you cast a burning torch into a house full of screaming children?"

"No, Delliot, I could not do any of those things, nor would I ask any person, let alone any of you, to do that either," Freyard answered without so much as a moment's hesitation, leaning back in his seat and exhaling heavily when he had finished.

A chair slid outward over hardwood floor, and Freyard glanced up to see Yarohmer getting to his feet. "By next summer I will have served as a soldier of Illiastra for twenty years and most of that time was spent in the Southlands. I never cared for squabbling lords and minsters, or shrivelled old Triarchists in golden robes and coned hats. I thought of duty as a means to give back to my country, but the longer I served, the more I realised that I was only a meaty shield for the oligarchy. As the years went on and my youthfulness fled, I became a jaded and cynical man. Most days, it was all I could do to keep myself from throwing away my uniform, deserting the Illiastran military, and fleeing with my wife for a quiet existence across the sea somewhere."

Yarohmer pivoted in Freyard's direction and held out a hand towards him. "That changed when this young soldier was voted Master-at-Arms for the fort we now stand in. I had served beneath and beside honourable men before, but every officer was ultimately cowed by the top of the chain of command. I voted for Freyard Archer to be Master-at-Arms because he was the first officer I met to do what was right, even if it meant disobeying a superior's orders. When he announced he was forming a ranging unit to combat the Moon Raiders directly, I was among the first to offer him my sword and pistol. Now, I stand before you with pride in what I do, a pride I thought forever lost until Captain Archer took command.

"His answer to Delliot was precisely what I expected and it reminded me of the man I voted for as Master-at-Arms. It brought me back to time spent in the wilds of the Southlands at his side, chasing down madmen that the rest of Illiastra turned a blind eye to. Captain

Archer was the lone officer with the courage to defy the government and take the fight to the raiding gangs. In this moment, he now stands before you with the courage to outright rebel against that very government and offer you the option to do just that by joining him."

A single fist of the old bear of a man slapped against his thick chest and the leather coat he wore. "I cannot speak for the rest of you, but to me, the options are clear: You can vote to stand today, once and for all, for the collective commonwealth of Illiastra with Miss Marigold, or you vote to wait until springtime to fight beside Lady Orangecloak for the Southlands alone. Either way, if you remain with us, you will be fighting with the right side."

"Thank you for your kind words, Yarohmer," Freyard responded when he finished. "I appreciate the sentiment and the gesture. With that said, I want all of you to know that I will not hold it against any of you should you choose to side with the EMP, regardless of how this vote goes."

The elder soldier was not yet done and replied in kind. "I say those things not merely to be complimentary, Captain Archer. I say them so that it might remind the men of who you are and who we are as a company. We have staked our reputations on being guardians of the good folks of the Southlands. That standard has become more of a banner than any white dove on a blue flag. The Southlands and Illiastra as a whole must know that our morals are not cast aside by the whims of some lord."

"Those lords govern this nation, Yarohmer," Ladd countered, having grown outright fearful by then. "Even without the soldiers stationed west of Obalen, there is still an army at their command. Who are we to defy that?"

"Damn it, Ladd, tell me where you left your spine so I can get one of the greenhorns to run and fetch it," Yarohmer replied with unbridled frustration. "I have stood with you against the raiding gangs and I recall a courageous fighter at the forefront of the action. What happened to him?"

Freyard knew that with the banter turning personal he needed to interject before it became a shouting match and cleared his throat audibly as he did so. "In regards to Ladd's reluctance, fighting the raiding gangs never carried the implications that I am proposing. I fully understand why he and anyone else here would have reservations, Yarohmer. We should let those reservations be heard now rather than later."

"I thank you for that, Captain," Ladd added when Freyard was finished before turning to Yarohmer. "We have families, my friend, and most of them are in the Eastern Realm of Illiastra. If we defy the government and side with either Miss Marigold or Orangecloak, those families could well be in danger. Have you not thought about that? What of your wife and your own daughters?"

A glance from Glendil to Freyard gave notice that the former was taking this question and he was on his feet quickly to do as much. "No matter which way we side, the lords will have much greater worries than us, Ladd. Harassing our families likely will not even make the list of things the EMP *want* to do, let alone *will* do."

That seemed to Freyard like another good moment for him to intercede. "To add to my good cousin's statement, if the vote goes west, I will speak to Miss Marigold on behalf of anyone interested in relocating their family to the coast."

"Captain Archer, Ser," a voice from the back of the room spoke up, face unseen by Freyard. "If we voted to go west, how soon after would we be leaving for Daol Bay?"

Freyard stood so that he might see the speaker and laid eyes on the raised hand of Clemence, commonly known as Clem, a young recruit midway into his twenties.

He nodded in Clem's direction to acknowledge the speaker and replied to him. "Should that happen, I would like to leave in no later than two days hence. That should be enough time to make all arrangements and ensure that the remaining garrison can assume all duties without us."

Mack, who had been guarding the revolving bridge earlier that day with Troygard, raised a hand from beside Clem. "Is there a reason you would have us leave so soon? Did you not say that the EMP was waiting until the spring before they made any move against Phaleayna?"

"I did say that, Mack, that is true. Yet, my reason for leaving for Daol Bay so soon has little to do with it," Freyard began in response. "For one, the winter is not far off. We here on the south side of the Varras have become accustomed to not feeling its true touch, but the northernmost areas of the Western Realm will be fully wrapped in its embrace. It would be wise of us to get to Daol Bay before then, for the sake of both our mounts and us. The primary reason for my actions though, is that Lord Tullivan likely will not make it through the season. As soon as he passes away, the Palombs will be at the gates of Daol Bay to stake their claim, and Miss Marigold would like us to be there to help turn them away."

"Why us, Captain?" Tobald asked with a befuddled face to match his voice. "She has enough soldiers of her own to stand at her gates and intimidate a Palomb envoy."

A sweeping gesture was made by Freyard over the worn and scuffed riding leathers he wore as he worded his response, "This is why, Tobald. It is one thing to have a wall lined with guardsmen in neatly pressed teal uniforms. It is entirely another if a Palomb or an ambassador of theirs lays eyes on a seasoned and highly skilled fighting unit from their own side of the map. When they look at Miss Marigold's soldiers, they do not see hardened fighters. No, they see men who have spent their lives policing the poor on the city streets."

Freyard tapped the silver clasp that held his cloak in place for emphasis, pointing at the engraved and enamelled yellow sun crossed with two recurve bows. "They will know this sigil and that we are not unseasoned sentries, but battle-hardened soldiers who have stared death in its ugly face. It tells the Palombs that Miss Marigold not only has armed forces bound to her by being subjects of the west, but soldiers who are loyal to her by principle."

As he had explained his reasoning, Freyard saw many heads nodding and grinning in approval and heard a few positive grunts and whispers among the men. There were still several who shared Ladd Dorser's scepticism and looked to him for rebuttal and even Freyard turned to see if Ladd had any comment, finding him staring forlornly into his neatly folded hands.

After what felt like minutes of only private murmurs between the men and with no further statements from either side of the debate Freyard decided that it had reached its proper conclusion. "If there are no more questions or concerns that anyone would like to raise, I will ask the Pharsey twins to bring the voting urn and its parchments and quills forward."

The identical brothers from Falsamere waited for a cue from Freyard and when no hands or voices were raised in objection, he waved them toward with a flick of his fingers. "Each of you will receive a single piece of parchment paper. One at a time, you will step behind me into the alcove and write either the words East or West on the parchment. I need not remind you that if 'West' prevails, we will be Daol Bay bound, if 'East' is the choice, we stay and wait for whatever is to come to Phaleayna. For obvious reasons, I will abstain from this vote. Though the rest of you have that option as well, I encourage you to take full advantage of a right fought for with blood and sacrifice by our forefathers."

"The vote will be decided when we have at least thirty-three votes for one side or the other, as that will be a majority of seventy percent. Should we not reach that consensus on the first vote, we will reconvene tomorrow to repeat the process and every day henceforth until a decision is reached."

Freyard stepped out from his chair and pushed it into the table to make room for the line of rangers that soon would be forming, continuing with his instructions as he did so. "When you have written your choice, fold the parchment paper and place it in the urn that Lieutenant Archer will be holding. He will be the first to vote, done so in my witnessing, and afterwards he shall witness the remainder of the voting process. While you are all voting, I will step outside to get out of the way. Lieutenant Archer will send one of the Pharsey twins to fetch me when the voting is done, and with you all as witness, I will tally the votes. With all of that out of the way gentlemen, I ask that you form an orderly line."

From the back of the room emerged the twin brothers, Lahn holding a stack of parchment paper held vertically between his hands and Brahn bearing a tall, ceramic urn clutched tightly to his chest. The sound of scraping chairs drowned out all other noise as the seated men rose as one. Freyard's ears picked up a dozen different conversations between the men, all of them involving the referendum they now faced.

The bearded Pharsey came to stand at Freyard's side, resting the ballots on the table corner and offering the first one to Glendil. Behind the black curtain his distant cousin went, where Freyard heard the sound of an inkwell's cap being removed and the dipping of the quill. The room grew so quiet that even the scratching of the quill on the parchment was audible. In what seemed like seconds, Glendil emerged once more, holding a folded ballot aloft for all to see. He dropped it into the urn, accepted the container from Brahn's hands, and the line began to form. In what was entirely unsurprising to Freyard, it was Yarohmer at the front of the line to cast his vote.

As he stepped away from the table, Freyard laid a hand on Lahn Pharsey's shoulder and leaned in close. "You will vote last, when all but one ballot remains. When you are finished, come find me on the roof."

"Aye, it shall be done, Captain," Lahn returned affirmatively.

Beneath the banners of the dead Freyard strode, feeling the eyes of his men upon him all the way. With the door to hand, he turned back to face them once more and spoke to them in a strong voice. "Come what may tonight, I will stand by your decision and serve as your captain. It is in your hands now, gentlemen, and all I ask is that each one of you follows the path that you think is right."

He left them at that and closed the door behind himself. The night air blew gently through the open windows of the corridor, pleasantly warm and smelling of the dampness of the dew, as ever it was in Dornett. A sharp pivot to his right and half a dozen strides delivered him to the stairway and the steps were climbed two at a time. Once atop them and outside, Freyard inhaled deeply of the fresh air, feeling relief wash over his whole body.

A pair of Fort Dornett's regular guardsmen approached at the sound of the door and one spoke with concern in his voice. "Captain Archer, are you alright, ser?"

"Aye, thank you for asking, Jensen," Freyard returned with a sigh. "I merely needed to step outside for a little air. When Lahn Pharsey comes looking for me, direct him to the southwest corner of the parapets, I will be seated atop the crates there."

"As you command, Captain," the same guard answered. The two then departed to resume their patrol as quickly as they had approached.

Left alone to his moment of quietude, Freyard wandered to the place he often found himself when he sought refuge from the world. From there, perched on the storage crates, Freyard had a commanding view of the surrounding area of the Southlands. Over the course of the evening, the clouds had rolled in and blotted out the moons and stars above, limiting Freyard's view to the oil lamps set in intervals around the bailey wall of the fort. The gentle wind made the single flames in the lanterns dance almost in perfect synchronicity and Freyard decided that they alone would be his view for the few moments he was afforded.

A pair of guards could be seen patrolling the yard below, approaching from the southeast side with a lantern held high on a pole between them. *Always patrol in pairs. That had been my idea and it was one that the Fort Commander had taken to like a duck to water. A single guard is naught but an easily navigated obstacle for the enemy, a pair of them is a solid defence.*

The chatter of the patrols both on the roof and in the yard joined the natural symphony of the chirping crickets and the endless roar of the Varras River. It was as close to home as Freyard now knew and for the first time since the night of the Orangecloak incident in Atrebell, he genuinely felt at peace.

It is home for the nonce. It might be home for one more winter, but no more than that.

From the direction of the stairwell came the rattling of the door, disrupting Freyard's brief tranquillity.

That might be the quickest vote I have ever been a part of, he thought with an audible scoff.

The patrolmen could be heard approaching the opener of the door and a voice asked for Captain Archer.

That's not Lahn Pharsey I hear.

The instructions that Freyard had given were relayed and the guards were thanked for it.

"I am over here, Yarohmer," Freyard summoned his old friend, turning to see the veteran soldier already making his way to him.

"I hope I am not disturbing you, Captain," he called back when the distance between them was but a few metres.

"Not at all, old friend. I was just admiring the view," Freyard said, sweeping a hand in the direction of the bailey. "Is something the matter? Surely the voting is not done yet."

Yarohmer shook his head in answer. "No, it's not. Might I take a seat, Captain?"

"You certainly may. What is on your mind?" he answered while sliding over on the crates to make room.

"There are many things on my mind. As I scrawled the word 'West' on my ballot, I saw all the battles in which I fought beside you. There were visions of violent brutes charging us with machetes and morning stars, armoured in rusting mail and boiled leathers like an old army rising from the dead. Nearly every time, whether we fought in field or forest, they had the numbers, but we had the discipline. Where a gambling man would bet on us all to be dead by now, we lost only eleven in all those years."

"We also had enough arrows, bolts, and bullets to compensate for the disadvantage in numbers," Freyard added to Yarohmer's statement.

"Aye, we had that too," Yarohmer admitted, lapsing into silence with a solemn sigh for a moment before continuing. "I remembered our early battles most of all, Freyard. The fights that earned us the moniker of Sun's Rangers and the events that led to you being given a ranging unit and your promotion to Captain."

Freyard's eyes wandered into the yard briefly, before he dropped his head. "I think about those events every day, Yarohmer. She is never far from my mind."

"What was her name?" Yarohmer inquired in a low voice. "All I can remember is that she was the daughter of Councillor Hawksburn of Aquas Bay."

"Her name was Dayanna," Freyard told him.

Yarohmer gave a long exhalation as the name left Freyard's lips. "Ah yes, Dayanna, that is indeed a beautiful name."

"And she was a beautiful woman, Yarohmer, both inside and out," he said, meeting the stare of his old comrade. "I loved her more than anything in this world."

"You did," Yarohmer agreed. "And the Moon Raiders kidnapped Dayanna on her way to you here. When we got the ransom note, I and many of the men you now call the Sun's Rangers rode out with you to save her."

Freyard took a deep breath, "Where are you going with this? We both know the terrible nightmare of what happened, why are you making me relive it?"

"When I gave my speech earlier about the ills of our overlords, I saw a glimmer in your eyes that I had not seen since Miss Hawksburn's handmaiden arrived here on a starving horse, nearly dead and as naked as the day she was born. You bore the same look tonight as you did when that poor girl relayed the ransom message from the Moon Raiders."

"Did I now?" Freyard propositioned bemusedly. "What did you think that look told you tonight?"

A hand of Yarohmer's went to Freyard's shoulder, squeezing firmly on it. "It told me that you see the EMP as I do: a well-dressed, wealthy raiding gang. It told me that you want to get to Marigold Tullivan before the Elite Merchants do to her what the Moon Raiders did to Dayanna Hawksburn."

"By that reasoning I should be equally eager to stay here and aid Lady Orangecloak," Freyard argued.

Yarohmer laughed outright at that in a great guffaw. "Not if Tryst is even half the swordsman your accounts have made him out to be. Besides, despite her claims of being a pacifist, Orangecloak can fight for herself. She is one of the Thieves, and you know as well as I that they have to learn how to swing a sword and loosen arrows before they leave the Phaleaynan ruins. That was especially true when Orangecloak joined under Marros' tenure years ago. The ginger woman doesn't need you and you know it. Marigold, though, she is but one, all alone save for her immediate retinue and standing against a legion of thugs in frilly clothes with an army ready to do their bidding. Much like Dayanna, this woman has reached out to you for help."

"You have always been quite good at reading me," Freyard uttered, relenting any further argument on the matter.

He released his grip and slapped Freyard on the back. "I hope for your sake that we go west. I know you would do what is right by Phaleayna if we stay, but you will be looking towards Daol Bay the entire time."

"I am not doing it solely for Marigold's benefit. It is a part of it, aye, that I will not deny, but the truth is that there is a major shift coming to Illiastra. We may only be forty-seven men, yet I feel that we have a duty to the people of this country to be in position when that time comes. Our war with the raiding gangs is not done, far from it, in fact. Yet, the Forsaken and the Sons of Valdarrow have settled far in the western end of the Southlands and we have slain every last Moon Raider that we could find. There is not much we can do about them from here, and in the grand scheme of things, there is something far bigger than any of them arriving in the spring. It is time we moved on and prepared for that inevitable calamity."

"I don't doubt your intentions for a second, Captain. Apologies if it seemed that I might," Yarohmer offered in an explanatory tone when Freyard had finished. "As you are well aware from my words said in the hall, I agree with you on where we ought to be. A man can fight for many reasons and his beliefs don't have to be limited to a single thread. I suppose I merely felt the need to remark on the fire that burns within you again, and to find out if you were aware of its rekindling."

It was Freyard's turn to laugh and he even gave his friend a gentle jab in the shoulder. "In truth I was not aware, but as you spoke of the similarities between what was and what is, I had to admit to myself that you are right."

"I stood beside you proudly back then and I will again, no matter if it's in Phaleayna or Daol Bay. My life and my sword are yours to command, Captain."

"Thank you for that, Yarohmer. Your loyalty means a great deal to me," Freyard responded with sincerity. "You have been a soldier longer than I and you go back further with several of these men. Do you think I can rely on all their loyalties as I do yours?"

Yarohmer hummed aloud as he pondered the question for a moment, "Ladd has influence over a few of the men, and after you left for the roof he was talking to them in a mad panic. I truly believe that we can no longer count him amongst our ranks, no matter which way the vote goes. He fought with us in every battle and saw the aftermath of the raiding gangs' butchering and yet, none of that has shaken him as much as the idea of opposing the lords of Illiastra. His loyalty is to you only after it hits every other rung on the hierarchal ladder, I am sad to say."

"If you had said that to me before tonight, I would not have believed you," Freyard told him with marked despondence. "Perhaps he will yet surprise us. One can only hope, right?"

"Aye, one can hope, Captain."

A commotion from the doorway caused both men to turn their heads in that direction and the guards were quick to answer. Within a few words shared between them and the cause of the ruckus, Freyard knew who it was.

"It sounds like Lahn is here," Freyard said as he slapped his legs and stood up, offering a hand to Yarohmer to help him to his feet. "Come on, old friend, it is time to count the votes."

11
Marigold

In the past several days, Marigold Tullivan had learned of herself that she had a finite patience for polite dishonesty. From the moment that Marigold had stepped into the Tullivan Manor, she had been contending with such from the servants, her butler, Mister Lewinson, and even Oire, whose frank honesty she typically relied on.

When any of them dared to speak of future events, they prefaced their statements, saying variations of *"Should his condition take a turn for the worse,"*, *"Should the worst come to pass,"*, or something similar and Marigold had come to loathe every new version of the statement that she heard.

Sitting there at her father's side, observing his stricken, suffering form, Marigold fostered no doubts of what his future held. There was no *"should"* or *"if"* anymore. Rather, it was just a matter of 'when' and that 'when' was far from the worst thing that could happen to Marscal Tullivan.

It seemed to Marigold as though sleep was the lone occasion when her father did not look to be in agony. She was tired in her own right, but it was only when her eyelids betrayed her that she herself rested at all. Even then, it was but for short periods at a time on the settee at the foot of the bed. There were always servants at hand and they continually told Marigold that they would watch over Marscal, assuring her that she would be alerted should his condition change.

However, Marigold refused to leave his side for more than minutes at a time, and only then so that she might attend to the most pressing of her personal needs.

At this advanced stage of her father's sickness, Marigold played witness to the curious ways it had of manipulating what had once been a bright and thoughtful mind. Usually, when Marscal woke from slumber, Marigold found a feeble man in the throes of agony. One who had become too sick to smoke his pipe full of Johnahweed. It had been the only medicine that had brought him any measure of relief and without it, the pain made him delirious. When Marscal was in this form, it took what little energy remained to him to stay awake long enough to grow exhausted from the pain. There was little said in those instances beyond how badly he was hurting and how he wished there was something to be done for it.

The family doctor, Raynalf Bannington, would visit twice daily to feed Marscal a syrupy, chalky looking concoction he had devised to combat the pain. Doctor Bannington had told Marigold it was the strongest pain medication known to mortalkind and as a result, was highly potent and terribly addictive. He further explained to her that so strong was the mixture that only a select few doctors could even obtain it. The formula for making the drug was further held in secret between only a trio of apothecaries, and they would dispense it in only the most extreme of circumstances. Pain relief for the terminally ill, who would not be impacted by the long term implications of the ludicrously addictive nature of the drug, fit that criteria.

Marscal had to be woken in these instances and the good doctor would quickly feed him the medication while he had the strength to swallow it. Usually, he would sleep again as soon as the stuff went down, and wake roughly an hour or so later, once it had firmly taken hold. The Marscal that met Marigold in these moments was one of delirium. He would call for deceased relatives and friends to join him and converse, insisting he had seen them passing through his chambers or standing before the foot of the bed, even as Marigold was trying to correct him. It was difficult for Marigold to tell him differently, as he seemed so sure of the presence of the people he saw that Marigold had begun to wonder if perhaps it was she that was wrong.

She would ask Marscal what the dead were telling him when they came to visit and every time he would look at her with bafflement that she was not observing them also. *"Do you not see my mother sitting beside me?"* Marscal had said in one instance. His voice was deathly serious and his hand gestured toward a spot on the bed a few centimetres away from Marigold. *"Dear Marigold, I raised you with better manners than to so rudely interrupt other people when they are talking, let alone your own grandmother."*

"My apologies, Father, I shall stay silent until you two have finished your conversation," Marigold had answered on that occasion while standing up, deciding to choose that moment to refresh herself in the lavatory.

Marscal's mother, Maisera, had passed away of natural causes in Marigold's infancy and she had no memory of her. However, from what Marigold had been told, mother and son had been close in life. Most of what she knew came from Rory's wife, Leonice, and among the things that Marigold learned from her aunt was that Marscal had made a point of obtaining his mother's private counsel regularly. There was but a select few who knew of this, for a man of the Elite Merchant Party accepting advice from a woman would be cause for ridicule. To Marigold, it was yet more affirmation of not only a strong woman in her own lineage, but also one who had played a role in weaving the tapestry of the Western Realm of Illiastra.

It seemed of all the late guests that Marscal believed himself to be hosting, that Maisera was foremost among them. Marigold occasionally heard him speaking to uncles, cousins, and departed friends, and in one instance, a pet dog her father had owned in his youth. Yet bookending all the visits was Maisera.

After Marigold told Oire of Marscal's supposed talks with his dear departed mother, the steward had confided in Marigold that Marscal had mourned Maisera's passing for some time. *"Poor, dear Marscal grieved for so long for his mother. To his credit, he hid it from Rory, Leonice, and me. He even tried to hide it from Farren, but she was never one to be fooled."*

"What did my mother say when she discovered how Father had been coping with the loss of my grandmother?" Marigold had asked Oire in a hushed whisper in return. The two of them had been sitting quietly in the bay window of the bedroom while Marscal slept nearby in his bed when that particular subject had been broached.

"It was less of a discovery and more of a revelation of what she had known all along, if truth be told," Oire sighed in reply. *"She never held it*

against him, if that is what you are wondering. In fact, she felt it showed a human side of him that he had long tried to deny. Farren told Marscal that it was that very humanity she had fallen for in the first place, not the cold shell that he had shown the world. We allowed him his time to grieve privately when he needed it and Farren and I took it as our duty to ensure that the secret stayed between us three."

Somewhere during his conversations with the dearly departed, Marscal would eventually nod off and slip into slumber. This was when he was at his most restful, when he was free of pain and comforted by warm words he believed to have shared with faces he never thought to see again. Even Marigold came as close as she could to earnest sleep in these quiet hours by wrapping herself in a soft quilt from the foot of her father's bed and curling up on the settee.

When the drug began to work its way through her father's system and lose the height of its potency, he would often wake once more. This reduced high, coupled with his pain being held at bay, allowed Marscal to have as coherent a state of mind as Marigold reckoned he could muster.

It was in these moments, elusive and fleeting though they were, that Marigold found the truest reflection of her father. On the first occasion of him entering this state of quiet lucidity, Marigold awoke to hear her father asking why she was asleep on the settee.

"Because I want to be by your side right now, Father," Marigold answered, rubbing sleep from her eyes as she did. *"This is my place."*

Marscal had groaned and closed his eyes long enough that Marigold thought he might be dozing off again, only for them to slowly flutter open and answer her, *"You of all people have a thousand tasks at hand right now. Don't spend all your time watching the last of me wither away. Go and prepare for what is to come when I am gone, my dear."*

She shook her head at the notion of it. *"There will be time enough for me to do all of that. I have left the duty of maintaining the western realm in Oire's capable hands for the time being. Uncle Rory has been given the task of operating everything relating to the office of Fisheries and Oceans and our own business interests. They both understand that my duty is to you right now, Father. This is where I am staying."*

"They will both serve you as well as they did me, in that you can trust," Marscal had said reassuringly. For a moment, he had sat still as a stone, his eyes on the curtained bay window beyond the foot of the

bed. He swallowed, attempted to clear his throat, and turned to her once again. As she met Marscal's gaze, Marigold saw his eyes glistening wetly with tears left unfallen. *"Before you returned I had Oire edit my will and take my last testament. Rory, Lewinson, and Keneth signed as further witnesses to it. When the time comes, Oire will be the executor of my estate."*

Marigold watched a single tear fall from her father's right eye, rolling its way down through the lines in his face until it was absorbed by the pillowcase. *"When the writers of the books of history put pen to paper for my chapter, let them say that 'in the end, Marscal Tullivan finally found his courage'."*

He had sighed and returned to his slumber shortly after and Marigold resumed her vigil at his bedside.

Two days passed before Marigold, returning after a needed bath, found Marscal awake and alert again. "Oh, Marigold, it's you. That means I'm still alive, aren't I?"

"Yes, Father, this is life," she assured him softly, lowering herself beside him on the bed.

"It's so dark in this damnable room and I was having such a pleasant, painless dream before I woke that I had begun to wonder," he uttered longingly. "If there is one thing this illness has taught me, it's that you can't die when you so feel like it."

Marigold reached above the headboard to a pair of electric lamps mounted in the wall and pulled the little brass chain to switch them on. "There we are. Is that better, Father?" she asked as the dim lights fell over the bed, casting it in a low, yellow glow.

The tiny bulbs in the lamps managed to light little more than the bed, leaving much of the room still unlit. They seemed to be strong enough to cast just enough of a glow that Marigold could make out all the silhouettes of the furniture that stood in contrast to light blue paint of the walls. To her left, on the same wall as the headboard, lay the entrance. Adjacent to that she could make out a wardrobe and bureau that bookended a dresser, and beside the furniture sat the door to Marscal's private privy.

The bay window occupied the vast majority of the wall at the foot of the bed, its heavy tan drapes drawn closed tightly, allowing in none of the moonlight beyond. Lastly, to the right of the bed was a wall hung with paintings. In spite of the dim light of the room preventing

Marigold from seeing the images clearly, she knew exactly what was on each piece.

Ser Davis Tullivan Steps Ashore sat in the centre, depicting her ancestor, clad in a black doublet slashed with teal, stepping through the surf of what is now Daol Bay beach. At his back were a fleet of whitewashed rowboats, his followers pushing them onto the sand.

Situated on a pedestal directly beneath the artwork was a marble bust of Ser Davis, the piece chiselled in the prime of the knight's life some eight hundred years ago. The painting above had been commissioned a full century afterwards, and, not knowing what Ser Davis had looked like in life, the painter had to base the depiction on the carved heirloom that now sat beneath it.

All around the artwork that featured the ancient knight were five portrait paintings of more recent members of House Tullivan: Marigold's grandparents in one, Marscal and Rory as young boys in another, and individual portraits of Marigold and Serephanie in their early teenage years. Lastly, above them all was the painting that was simply titled *Lord Marscal Tullivan, Princess Farren, and Daughters.* It had been painted in Marscal's office over the course of a week in the sparse moments when all four could be gathered together for a sitting. Marscal had dressed in his finest suit, standing with a hand on the shoulder of his wife seated ahead of him, with Marigold on her lap, and Serephanie standing to her side.

No matter how much time had passed since her mother had disappeared, Marigold found that painting difficult to look at for more than the briefest of glances.

Once we were happy and whole, now our family is fractured and all but lost. Mother and Felixander have long perished, Father is dying, and Serephanie has fled for her safety. What are we now? Barely a 'we', truth be told.

"I miss them all too," Marigold heard Marscal utter from beside her, himself looking in the direction of the painting depicting their family. "Your mother was my light in the darkness and when we lost her and Felixander, I stopped fighting that darkness and let it engulf me whole. It reached for you and Serephanie as well and I handed you over to it. Yet another entry on the long list of failings of mine."

"What could you have done, Father? There was no way to prove that Eamon Palomb had anything to do with Mother and Felixander's disappearances. He has the numbers in Parliament to change the laws to suit his every whim and he even has the Lord Master bowing to his will. Your back was to the wall."

"I could have fought," he said, choking back tears. "I know if your grandmother had been alive when Grenjin and Eamon arrived at our doorstep, she would have counselled me against signing their pact. Your mother would never have given you up to the Palombs either. Instead, at the advisement of my brother and city councillors, I gave you over to them on a platter.

"Rory argued that if we signed the marriage agreement, we could get Jaysen Rossadore to put together a team of his fellow attorneys to scour the pact for a loophole. If none could be found, it still bought us time to concoct an alternate plan before the Palomb twins came of age. Jaysen and his men could find no feasible way out of the pact, and instead of fighting it further I retreated into the comfort of cowardice."

Marigold took his papery thin hand in both of hers and placed a kiss upon his knuckles. "There is nothing to be done about it now, Father. There's no need to waste this precious time talking about it."

He audibly cleared his throat and shook his head slowly. "There is much I need to say and the time for me to say it is running out. If not now, when?"

There was no answer Marigold could think of for that. Having come to abhor the white lies and denial of the serving staff, Marigold was hardly going to delve into using such language herself. Yet, in the same breath, she also could not bring herself to say the truth of the matter aloud.

Her father, on the other hand, was clearly well beyond such restraint. "Look at me, Marigold," he commanded softly, reaching a hand for her face as high as he could, his index finger grazing her jawline. As her eyes befell his sickly form she saw a tremble in his lips, but he spoke through it plainly. "I'm dying. Not saying it will not change that simple truth and there are things we should speak of while I have the mind and voice to do so."

With a deep breath and an idle smoothing of her nightgown, Marigold relented. "What would you have us talk about?"

"Your mother and brother," Marscal began, his voice sounding stronger than it had in quite some time. Given how frail and hoarse his tones had been since Marigold's return, she understood that this sudden vitality did not come without a considerable expenditure of energy. "I've long felt that their deaths were no mere *accident.*

Felixander stood as a living flaw in Eamon Palomb's designs and in his cold, callous mind, that flaw had to be removed."

This was far from a shocking revelation to Marigold and yet she was indeed surprised, not in the information itself, but rather in hearing her father speak so candidly of it. The notion was one that Marscal, Oire, Rory, and Keneth had tiptoed around and never more than inferred in even private conversation.

In one instance, the topic had quite nearly been approached. Marigold had almost heard Marscal speak of it in the moments before she was to leave for the feast at the conclusion of the autumn Parliamentary sessions. The hazy state that his Johnahweed brought on had caused him to speak of it, but before Marscal could elaborate, he had retreated into silence for fear of being eavesdropped on.

"We don't know that for certain." Marigold reminded him, before adding to the statement with a question: "Even if it were true, what could we do about it?"

"There is nothing to be done. Direct justice for my wife and son are forever out of grasp," he said regretfully, eyes downcast. A deep breath was taken and he returned his gaze to Marigold. "As for what we know and do not know, I uncovered a tiny thread in Eamon Palomb's great web a few years back. It was all I needed for confirmation and though I could not act upon it, I remained convinced of his role in what happened to Farren and Felixander."

"What thread? Whatever are you talking about?" Marigold inquired quickly, scanning Marscal's face for some sign that he might somehow be slipping back into delirium.

"It was about two years after the incident occurred," Marscal began to explain. "Do you recall a summer around that time in which Keneth spent the better part of the season in the Crescent Isles?"

Marigold searched her memory for what he spoke of and found some faint recollection. "He took his family there for an extended vacation. You gave him the keys to our family villa on Cabathos' capital island for some much overdue rest and relaxation."

"That was what most people believed, aye," he confirmed with as much of a nod as his pillow would allow. "The true purpose of the vacation was for him to establish a base of operations in the villa and launch a private investigation around the Crescent Isles into your mother's disappearance."

He took a moment to regain himself again, and it seemed to Marigold every sentence needed an equal rest. "I still had a few military contacts there from the Vellick Island's Civil War and Kandell sought them out. Two of them, both retired military police, agreed to aid my mission. Along with them, I gave Keneth leave to take two of his most trusted men from outside the manor guards with him as well."

During another rest, he groaned with the pain, his hands flexing repeatedly as he waited for the wave to pass. "The five set out in civilian clothing under assumed names, bought a seaworthy Cabathosi ship, and went about investigating.

"Of *The Stormbreaker* and *Wild Rider* they found nothing." Marscal revealed hurriedly, using a deep breath to ready himself for the next sentence. "No one had reported any traceable wreckage and no bodies ever floated ashore. For two ships to disappear so completely like that is beyond strange. Even with the distance between where the ships were believed to have sunk and the Crescent Isles, the currents would have surely blown something their way eventually."

That brought a thoughtful nod from Marigold. "It is as the old rhyme goes: 'If it floats upon the sea, in the Crescent it shall be,'" she said pointedly.

"It was on that very premise that I sent Keneth to the Crescent Isles in the first place," Marscal agreed. "The absence of any sign of the ship only spurred the search party to look further. They started leaving the larger and collected islands of the Crescent to head for the northern fringes. They began sailing to uninhabited islands and atolls, and the tiny, remote islands belonging to one nation or another. That's where they found him."

"Found who?" Marigold asked curiously.

He patted her hand lightly in a manner Marigold interpreted as a gesture to calm her down and when he himself was ready, his explanation went on. "An Illiastran man named Brunick. We don't know if that was his first or last name or perhaps even an assumed name, but either way, I never forgot it. Keneth and his team had sailed to an island controlled by the Gallicians. It was an outpost island that lay so far north that it was quite nearly outside the banks of the Crescent Isles themselves. All that live there are poor fisherfolk."

He began wiggling his fingers and furrowing his brows and Marigold sensed his plight and piped up. "Are you referring to

Pripence, Father?" she asked in an attempt to jog his memory. "That one little island in the Crescent that looks all alone on the maps?"

"Yes, Pripence!" he exclaimed, his face looking relieved between deep breaths. "That's the one! It was sitting on the edge of my tongue. Thank you for saying it. Now, where was I? Right, yes, I was saying that Keneth had sailed there. It was a long trek from the Gallick Isles, but given that it was the closest place to the route the ships disappeared from, he felt it might be worth investigating for wreckage and remains. If nothing else, he hoped that perhaps one of the fisherfolk had seen the ships passing by.

"Keneth himself stayed aboard the ship, on the off chance that if there was anyone on land that might know something, they might also recognise my Captain of the Manor Guards. He sent the other four in his stead and waited in the cabin of the ship.

"Apparently, as soon as Keneth's team touched the docks they were approached by an old fisherman who asked if they were there to visit the Illiastran man. The four of them had the sense to improvise in the moment and say they were, and he pointed them to a house that once belonged to the island's commissioner. According to the locals, it had sat empty and abandoned for some time, given that the commissioner's operations were moved closer to the Gallician capital. They told my men that the Illiastran man arrived there two years before their party arrived. That timeframe puts him in the Crescent Isles at the time of the disappearance of the two ships."

"The townspeople told Keneth's men that the Illiastran stepped off a ship dressed in a nice suit with a deed for the house and a single trunk of possessions. Once he entered the house, they said that he only emerged so that he might go to the general store for a little food and a lot of alcohol. All they knew of him was that he was a well-spoken, middle-aged Illiastran named Brunick who always had more than enough coin to pay for his purchases without issue."

"Keneth's team spoke with him, then? This Brunick fellow, I mean?" Marigold asked ponderously.

"Indeed they did," Marscal answered affirmatively. "The Vellick soldiers went to pay him a visit while Keneth's men went to inform him of their discovery. The idea of the two strangers coming all the way to the island to visit him was enough to spook Brunick, and he slammed and locked the door in their faces. Keneth decided that the five of them would wait for him to step out of the house. For how much drinking he was purported to do, he was bound to visit to the general store for more alcohol and when he did, they would corner him then.

"The next morning a group of children went to play in a field near Brunick's house and discovered him hanging from a tree at the rear of the home."

Marigold shook her head in bafflement, commenting, "That sounds like a man with more to hide than just himself. Did Keneth search his house?"

"It was the first thing they thought to do after they cut his body down," her father replied. "All they found was a recently used fireplace, an overturned trunk, empty rum bottles, and a filthy straw mattress in one room. Keneth's men sifted through the fireplace and found what was left of his possessions: burnt papers, the brass buttons from his clothes, a few coins, and a silver ring. He had tried to destroy every last thing that he had owned before he destroyed himself."

Marigold felt she was still missing a piece of the puzzle that her father was attempting to assemble. "Was there something among his things to lead you to believe he had something to do with the disappearance of Mother and Felixander? None of it seems to mean much to me, Father."

"The coins were Illiastran in origin. Not surprising, given that their previous owner was Illiastran as well," Marscal managed to say in a single breath, having to stop for a moment of recovery before saying much more. "Yet, for him to have a sizeable sum of our currency still on his person indicated that he was not long gone from the country. Also, given how much he was said to have spent on the house, the cost of passage to the island, and his constant supply of liquor, it begs to reason that he was either quite wealthy or had recently come into that large sum of Illiastran coin. Then there's his ring: the setting was empty and the heat of the fire had damaged it, but if I remember right, I believe Keneth said it was a hastily built fire that was enough to burn clothes and papers, but did not have the materials to burn hot enough to melt metals. You will have to speak with him if you want more details than that."

"What about the ring, though, Father?" Marigold asked, attempting to bring him back to his train of thought.

"Ah, yes, the silver ring! I was just getting to that," he suddenly remembered with surprising vigour. "It was onyx!"

That only served to confuse Marigold further. "What was onyx?"

"The stone that should have been in the setting, of course!" he all but shouted. "The thick silver band had a large empty setting. Even without the stone, Keneth and the other Illiastran officers knew what it was as soon as they saw it and so did Rory, Oire, and I when it was presented to us: a Key to the East."

Marigold's gaze went to the paintings as she mulled it over in her head. *A Key to the East is the name given to silver and black onyx rings gifted by Eamon Palomb to distinguished associates of his. A man flashing a ring bearing the colours of the Palomb House in the eastern half of the nation was given privilege above that of all but the lords and ministers. The idea that the owner of one of those rings was in the Crescent when* The Stormbreaker *and* Wild Rider *disappeared certainly seems more than a little suspicious.*

A question came to her then and she thought to ask it: "What do you suppose his role was in what happened to the ships, Father?"

There came no answer and Marigold looked his way in panic for but a second, until she found him snoring softy.

He wore himself out. Just as well, that is probably enough for one day, she said to herself while sliding down the bed slowly to the settee so that she might rest her own eyes.

The next day brought the same cycle of mental awareness for Marscal. The morning was agony, the afternoon was a medically induced euphoria, and after a brief visit with a late great-uncle of Marigold's that she had never known, her father slipped into blissful slumber.

A maid near Marigold's age named Teresa delivered a covered tray bearing dinner for both Tullivans while Marscal slept. Marigold thanked her for the food, though given her father's almost non-existent appetite there was little chance of him so much as touching it.

Upon lifting the cover, Marigold discovered a teapot, milk, honey, empty teacups, a small jug of water, drinking glasses, and two plates bearing her favourite dish: halibut marinated with lemons and served with a side of steamed, green vegetables and potatoes. She took her plate and a cup of honey-sweetened black tea to the bay window to enjoy as the sun set over the harbour. Feeling fairly famished, since having eaten only at breakfast that day, Marigold devoured her own plate of food in short order. It was while picking at her father's plate and refilling her teacup for seconds that she heard Marscal stir in the bed.

"Marigold? What hour is it?" he asked in a slightly raspy voice.

She turned and went to his bedside, telling him, "It is nearly half past the eighteenth, Father."

"I slept the day through yet again," Marscal lamented. "Would you mind bringing me some water? My throat is so dry."

Marigold practically leapt to answer the request, laying her dishes aside so that she might reach for a clean drinking glass and the water pitcher. Once at his bedside, she held the glass to his lips so that he might drink from it.

Marscal gulped the water down audibly until the glass was nearly empty, with a contented sigh serving to indicate his satisfaction. Between breaths, he even managed a thank-you to Marigold.

"You're quite welcome," she responded while laying the empty glass on the nightstand and heading for the tray once more. With a napkin to hand, she returned to Marscal and dabbed his chin and neck where a few loose droplets of water still remained. "There you are."

"You're too kind, my dear," he uttered sadly.

"It is the least I can do for my father," Marigold responded with a nonchalant shrug.

That earned a faint smile from him. "You don't have to sit here all the time, you know. There are far more important tasks for you right now."

"I know of no task that can take me from your side. This is where I shall be until…"

His eyes began to glisten. "The end… You can say it, it's alright."

She shook her head softly. "I do not want to be like everyone else in this house and lie about it and yet I cannot bring myself to say it to you, Father. That is weak of me, I admit."

"Marigold, my dear daughter, you are anything but weak," he said in a tired voice that managed to be a little more than just a whisper. "I wish I had a thimbleful of your courage. Perhaps if I did, I would not be leaving my mess of a life for you to clean up."

"Don't say that. You did everything you could," Marigold stammered, fighting back the tears.

"Not everything. I could have resigned my position and fled to Northern Gildriad with you and Serephanie. It was an option, but I was too proud to take it. When your mother and brother were lost, your grandfather sent me a letter with the offer to protect you both. I had to have my dignity, though and I stayed, hoping to find an alternative way out of that contract.

His breathing became noticeably more laboured then, but Marscal fought to speak. "In his next message... He offered me an army... He wanted to fight back directly against Palomb and Howland. In his letter... He said... 'From one father mourning the death of his child to another, I know you seek punishment as I do for those who have dared strike at ours.' He was right, you know. I did want punishment... I wanted vengeance... But I was too cowardly to act. I wrote back to him and begged him to stand down. I promised him I would resolve everything myself and instead I wasted all of my time hoping for a solution to suddenly appear."

"What were you to do, Father?" Marigold asked rhetorically. "We have nothing but the silver ring of a drunken recluse to offer as evidence for Eamon Palomb's involvement and that may not mean anything. That Brunick fellow might have been in hiding for any number of reasons."

"I mean to say that I did nothing to protect you and Serephanie. However, I feel certain that Brunick was sent west to find and kill Farren and Felixander. Call it a gut feeling, call it a desperate husband and father grasping for answers, but I think it's true. No, I meant earlier that I should have at least taken King Hector's first offer and fled to Northern Gildriad."

"You stayed because Daol Bay is your home and these are your people," she replied confidently. "The Marscal Tullivan I know could never abandon the West to the tyranny of the Palomb family... No more than I can."

For but a moment Marigold saw a sudden flicker in her father that she had not seen in some time. "No, I suppose you can't. You have your mother's spirit and my stubbornness. I want you to promise me two things, Marigold, and I want to hear you say 'I promise'."

"What might that be, Father?" she asked.

He reached for her hand and she gave it to him to hold as he spoke. "Please do not hold Serephanie's decision against her. I am disappointed that she left, but I cannot fault her for seeking her own freedom from the terrible fate that the stroke of my pen fated to her. She is your only sister, the one immediate family member you have left. If she returns, for both my sake and your mother's, welcome her home. It is my fault she felt that she had to leave, she should not suffer for that."

"I... I promise, Father," Marigold responded with a nod that shook loose the first tear. "I want you to know that I hold no grudge with Serephanie for what she did. I wish she had stayed, but I know why she left. Was there a second promise?"

"Yes there is: I want you to live, Marigold. Whether it is here or in Northern Gildriad or someplace else, I want you to live the life I failed to give you. One with love and laughter, with friends and a family of your own that you can count on. Just live. Can you do that, Marigold?"

Marigold looked at her father through the unfallen tears and tried to find her words. "I can try, Father."

"Don't just merely try, promise me, Marigold." On his face she saw what could only be a smile. A real, honest smile, not one brought on by delirium.

It was something Marigold had not seen in what felt like forever and she found the resolve within herself. "I promise," she answered, reaching in as she did to plant a kiss on his cheek. "I might have to start a war to keep that promise."

Marscal quite nearly laughed as he returned the kiss. "Wars have been started for less."

In a matter of seconds, Marscal's face grew ashen and his breathing became shallow. "I love you, Marigold. Thank you for being my daughter."

Her lips began to quiver and when she opened her mouth to speak, the words stammered out. "I love you too. Thank you for being my father."

As she held tightly to his hand, her father's eyes grew wide and a look of peaceful bliss appeared across his face. With a last breath, Marscal Tullivan slipped away.

12
MARIGOLD

he undertaker had arrived before dawn. He had been sent for by Oire, who had issued the word mere minutes after Marigold informed him and the servants that Marscal Tullivan had passed away. Kandell and five of the house guards went in escort of Marscal's body to follow their lord to the mortuary and begin the solemn, ancient tradition of the Knight's Vigil.

Of all the visible traditions of the knightly houses, the vigil was adhered to with unmatched religiosity. Even Marigold's mother and brother were given a modified nine-day Knight's Vigil at a memorial erected near the Tullivan Crypt for both they and those aboard *The Stormbreaker* and her escort ship, *Wild Rider*.

Neither they nor her father had been knighted, of course. He had never seen a battle from the front lines or so much as thrown a punch at another person insofar as Marigold knew. Yet, due to their lineage, Marscal Tullivan and his family were granted the same honour as their anointed ancestor, Ser Davis. That tradition followed that from the moment the body was taken from its deathbed, no less than four honourable guardians were to be protecting Marscal's remains at all hours until his interment.

Marigold had kept a vigil of her own, having remained at her father's side until the moment that the funeral coach departed. Despite being urged to rest by the woken staff, which accounted for most of the manor by the time the news had spread, Marigold was adamant that she stay with Marscal as long as she could.

After her arduous night, and with the sun beginning to peek over the eastern hills, no amount of persuasion from anyone would convince Marigold to sleep.

"It would be in your interest to rest, my lady. The immediate days ahead will offer you few chances," Oire had protested when Marigold emerged from her room dressed in a black blouse and matching, tailored slacks.

She was entirely without proper mourning attire, and settled on that outfit for the nonce. During the course of the day, Marigold planned to visit her and Serephanie's regular dressmaker to purchase appropriate gowns for the unfortunate occasion. *For Father's sake, I shall adhere to the customary apparel expected of me, just this once,* she had decided.

"I cannot, Oire, not now," Marigold said with a shake of her head to dismiss such notions. "It was you who said that the Palombs will not give us any chronological courtesies once Father was gone. Rest is not something either of us can afford at this time."

Marigold had begun walking down the hallway of the second floor of the manor, towards the open balustrade and the split-level staircase that led to the main level.

Oire followed dutifully, all the while offering a counter argument for her reasoning. "You instructed everyone in the household and even the undertaker to say nothing of your father's passing until the mid-morning bell. That effort alone has ensured that the news does not leave on the morning trains. The earliest anyone who knows of his death can leave the city via locomotive will be on the nightfall run to Obalen. It will be a few days before that will reach the Palombs, even longer again if they have already gone home to Hercalest. If they decide to formulate any response at all over the winter months, we have several weeks before anything more tangible than letters will arrive here."

"You state a fair argument, Oire," Marigold admitted while making her way to the bottom of the stairs. "Yet there is much and more that must be done, including an endless wave of arrangements that must be made for Father's wake and funeral. To add to that, we have scores of formal notices to write and send to the other lords and ministers, not to mention practically every man whom Father even spoke of business with. I will need your help to write all those, and they will need to be done sooner rather than later. That goes especially so for those here in the Western Realm, who will want to attend the services. I say now is the time to get a head start on that work, would you not agree?"

For a moment, it had seemed as though Oire was going to argue further, but he relented. "It would be wise for you to write all the letters yourself. I am aware of just how pressing a task that is, but the lords, most of the ministers, and business associates of your father will know my handwriting. Let the upper crust of Illiastra see that you are stepping forward to lead this household in the wake of our loss."

Their conversation had played out during their walk to Marscal's home office, where the two parted briefly, with Oire leaving for the kitchen in search of a pot of tea for the both of them. While alone inside the office, Marigold stood quietly at the side of her father's desk, working up the resolve to sit behind it. Having never seen anyone but Marscal seated there, the thought of someone else doing so, even Marigold herself, felt strange and altogether foreign to her. Even in Marscal's sickest days, when Oire would tend to most matters personally, the steward would not sit at the desk, instead carrying out his work from the nearby sitting room.

The high-backed chair behind the desk, with its carved letter 'T' of House Tullivan complete with a pair of leaping swordfish, was as close to a throne that Marscal had. There were countless decisions and matters relating to the Western Realm and Illiastra as a whole that had been decided by Marigold's father and grandfather while seated upon that fine piece of furniture.

She ran a hand over the oak surface of the desk, a finger idly tracing its way along a dark line that ran through the wood to a familiar knot. The flat shoes on her feet tapped softly on the hardwood floor as she stepped around to the chair and pulled it away from the desk.

From there, one had the most commanding view of the room, and it was one that Marigold knew well. As a young girl, she had enjoyed spending time in the office with her father, when it could be just the two of them. He was a learned man in many respects, and he seemed to have enjoyed the opportunity to pass his knowledge on. Marigold had appreciated the lessons too, and plied him with questions by the bushel. The educational aspect was but the excuse, though, Marigold realised in hindsight.

I just wanted to spend as much time with him as I could. That it was a learning experience was merely a bonus. I think he knew that too.

She took in the room, her eyes falling to the window to her right that looked out into the gardens at the rear of the manse. When Marigold was young, there used to be a cushioned bench that butted into the frame of the window, and she could recall more than once when she napped there while her father attended to quiet work at his desk.

To either side and beneath the window were shelves full to the brim with books of all sizes. They lent the room the distinct smell of old tomes, a particular aroma that made Marigold feel at home. The shelves and the floor were a deeply varnished hardwood that soaked in the light and lent the room a distinguished air of class.

Straight ahead from Marigold sat the hearth, complete with a landscape portrait of the harbour as seen from the steps of the Tullivan crypt in springtime. The painting was as familiar to her as the view itself. Before the crackling fire was where Marscal seemed to spend most of leisurely evenings, his nose deep in a book. Many of those books were read aloud, with both Marigold and Serephanie seated in his lap.

He had a knack for reading stories to us. Every tale seemed to spring to life with his enthusiastic recitations. The characters had their own voices and personalities, and I don't know that any two were alike.

As she stood at the desk, some part of her expected to see Marscal come striding into the room with a warm hello and a hug. On his heels would be her Uncle Rory and Oire, the two making preparations for meetings on matters of business and governance. Marigold herself had sat in silent observation of so many of those meetings that she had long lost count. The affairs themselves were usually dull and tedious, but Marigold thought of each one of them as a unique learning experience. With her father's example, Marigold had gained great insights into the art of social interaction and negotiation, particularly when it came to his skilful balance of multiple levels of governance in tandem with the affairs of the Tullivan fishery empire.

Now we shall see if I learned anything, Father, Marigold said wordlessly as she lowered slowly into his vaunted chair. *I hope I can do proudly by your memory and your legacy.*

"This is a sight that is going to take some getting accustomed to," Marigold heard from the doorway just as Oire stepped inside with one of the serving maids in tow. "I must say that it suits you well though, my lady."

"Thank you, Oire," Marigold replied, trying to keep the sadness from her voice. "It will take me even longer to get used to sitting here, I would say."

The maid had a silver tray to hand, atop which sat a ceramic teapot bearing a flowery design with matching cups, a loaf of fresh bread, and a warm pat of butter.

"Miss Marigold, please allow me to extend condolences from myself and my family on the terrible news of your father's passing," the maid said as she laid the tray upon the desk, bowing politely and folding her hands over her apron once done.

The woman was Edie Murres, one of the elder members of the staff who had been working for the Tullivans before Marigold was even born. No matter what it was that Marigold's family had faced, Edie had dutifully served under Butler Lewinson with pride. A stout woman of sixty with short, reddish curls and a round face, Edie was known among the staff as the Mother Hen.

As Marigold was about to thank Edie, the woman began to cry softly and dab her eyes with her apron. In sight of such, there was only one thing Marigold could think to do. Pushing to her feet, Marigold stood from the chair, walked around the desk, and drew Edie into a long hug.

"He was a good man," Edie began to say when they parted between sniffles. "Your lord father tried his very best to do well by everyone, all things considered. I'd like to think he did just that, Miss Marigold. I just can't imagine him not being here in the manor. I don't know how we will ever get by without him."

It took a great deal for Marigold to hold back her own tears, though she found her resolve while gently rubbing Edie's shoulders. "My father thought highly of you, Edie. He was always earnestly asking how your husband and children were faring and, in the last few years, your grandchildren too. You have been with our home during our best and our worst times, and we have always pulled through together. I will do my utmost to see that House Tullivan carries on once more and to do that, I will need everyone beneath this roof to come together as we always have."

Edie took a pair of deep breaths in an effort to stifle her tears while Marigold had spoken and though her face and eyes were red from crying, she seemed collected in her reply. "We have seen times of trouble before and good Lord Marscal always saw to it that the Tullivans survived, Miss Marigold. You're a smart one in your own right, I'm sure that you'll know what to do."

"Thank you, Edie. Your words and your work in this house are appreciated more than I can say," Marigold offered in response.

After a bow and further condolences, Edie showed herself out and left Marigold and the steward to their work.

Once seated behind the desk again, Marigold looked to Oire, presently pouring tea for both of them. "I should start with Lord Greggard in Portsward."

"He is a good person to begin with, for many reasons, I should say." Oire replied, laying the teacup filled with the hot, dark red drink before her.

"But of course, Oire," Marigold said in return while adding a touch of milk to the tea. "Our grandfathers despised one another and our fathers maintained those icy relations between our houses, but Greggard Simillon has only ever been amicable towards our family."

Oire had gone to the row of bookshelves immediately behind the desk while Marigold spoke and pulled a large, leather-bound book from upon a shelf. "I will give Greggard credit for putting forth a diligent effort towards reconciliation of the two houses of Twin Bay. Your father felt that the young Simillon was no better than his sire and grandsire and gave him little more than cold courtesy. You have a chance to start anew with House Simillon, and you will need to make inroads on that front straight away."

Marigold nodded in return, taking the book he offered her to hand as she did. Despite its overall size, it was a rather small collection, and the pages were tabbed at certain intervals for quick reference. Her finger went to a tab marked 'West' and she flipped the listings open beyond nearly two thirds of the pages. At the top of the page and written in golden ink were the words: 'A Directory of the Lords, Ministers, and Notable Residents of the Western Realm of Illiastra.' Directly beneath the title in black ink and smaller font were the date on which it was last updated and the signature of the lead author: 'Edition one hundred and sixty, released on the sixtieth of spring in the year eighteen hundred and ten.'

The directory is outdated by four years, Marigold noticed. *An updated version will be released next spring by that rate, as they replace them every fifth year. Whom will it list by then in Father's place? The record keepers, under Grenjin Howland's direction, will not name me, as a woman. Furthermore, by the time their records are compiled, the Palombs will not have had time to lay formal claim to the position, either.*

"Since you already have the directory open, my lady, could you turn the page to the Simillon's listing?" Oire asked while unrolling a map of Illiastra across the opposite side of the inordinately large desk.

Marigold read down through the table of contents hurriedly until her gaze fell on the entry that read: 'Simillon, Greggard – Lord of International Trade and Relations, Minister of the Region of Portsward' and she skimmed to the page indicated beside it. Once there, the first thing to catch her eye was an illustration of a large letter 'S' above two joined hands amid the act of shaking. Below that it listed mailing addresses for Greggard's offices and his manor, which in his case, were one in the same. There were further listings for his five city councillors, a steward, and other managers of governmental affairs in the region.

"Am I to write a letter to each person listed here?" Marigold queried concernedly as Oire finally took a seat beside her.

There are at least a dozen men serving beneath Greggard alone, Marigold noted to herself, as she became slightly overwhelmed by the thought of it. *How in the Known World am I to be expected to write to every noble and notable in the Western Realm before Father's funeral?*

"I should hope not, or you will be writing letters for a fortnight," he hastily replied, almost wittily so. "Just title it 'To Lord Greggard Simillon and the Honourable Officials of Portsward'. From there, Greggard can issue the contents of your letter to his cabinet as he then sees fit."

Oire handed Marigold a blank piece of paper and pushed one of the inkwells close to her right hand with his index finger, asking, "Are you ready to begin, my lady?"

"I think so," she told him with uncertainty creeping through in her voice, despite her efforts to hide such. With the paper before her, Marigold unscrewed the cap from the inkwell, dipped her quill, took a deep breath, and began.

As she was penning the letter and came to the point where she was to tell the date of the funeral, she felt unsure of her own memory and turned to Oire. "The undertaker said he could afford us three days for Father's waking, correct?" she asked him plainly, attempting to hide how much it pained her to say such.

"Aye, he will take today to prepare your father for presentation. Tomorrow morning they will return him here, and after our inspection, the wake will commence," Oire replied in similarly monotone fashion. "By that reckoning, the funeral will be five days from now. That should give even Minister Mattersly time to travel here from Tippard."

"That was what I remembered as well," Marigold admitted as she resumed writing. "Amid everything else that has been happening, the numbers got mixed up in my mind and I began to doubt myself."

"No one would ever fault you for that. It can easily happen to the best among us," Oire offered softly in response.

The room went quiet save for Marigold and the scratching of her quill on the paper and the occasional returns to the inkwell. Minutes more passed before she set down the quill and began fanning the wet ink. "I feel this should suffice," she decided.

It was passed to Oire for review and he nodded with approval when done. "That will more than serve, my lady. Now there are only twenty-two more western ministers to write to and the thirty-three from the eastern half of the continent."

"And another to my grandfather in Northern Gildriad," Marigold added with a direct glance to the steward.

He met the stare and seemed to be analysing it for a moment until her meaning became clear. "Your grandfather is a powerful man, my lady. I counsel that you keep in close contact with him and keep him informed, but all to a point. If you invite him and his armed forces here, any victories you achieve, either by word or by sword, will be attributed to him. This is *your* time, my lady and I believe we can do it without King Hector Aurorais."

"As it so happens I agree with you, Oire. However, as far as living relatives in Illiastra go, I am down to Uncle Rory's family and a smattering of cousins whom I could not identify from a crowd. Wherever Serephanie is, she is out of reach to me, so I very well cannot act as though she is in my life."

She found herself looking at the map on the desk, her attention drawn to the Northern Kingdom of Gildriad and the dot that marked Kingdom City nearly in its exact centre. Her mind wandered to the painted visage of her mother's parents, whom she had yet to meet in person, and the aunts, uncles, and cousins that shared in their royal palace with them. "While my surname is Tullivan, merely having that name does not give that side of my lineage precedence over the Aurorais half. I am their blood as much as I am Uncle Rory's, and I intend to foster the relationship with them that I always sought. There is no reason why that desire and my political goals cannot coexist."

"All well and true, my lady," Oire conceded after a thoughtful pause. "For now, though, might I suggest that we continue with writing letters to the leaders residing in closer proximity to us?"

"Of course, we will continue on with Minister Bickerington in Tusker's Cove and I shall send both letters by the morning train to Portsward," Marigold decided while accepting a fresh piece of paper from Oire.

The two continued their work with little spoken between them beyond idle comments and questions pertaining to the task. After the letters addressed to Simillon and Bickerington, the rest were done alphabetically by surname. For every new piece of paper handed to Marigold, Oire would place a marker on the map at that minister's governing region. Once Marigold finished each letter, Oire would then examine it, fan it dry, place it in an envelope, and apply the wax seal stamped with the Tullivan sigil.

By the eighth hour of the morning, Marigold had a small stack of letters accrued. After a short break to stretch her limbs, Marigold was about to begin writing to Minister Jennis of Levelle when a knocking on the door interrupted her and Oire's work.

"You may enter," Marigold called out.

The door was opened by Mister Lewinson, who closed it behind himself and stepped toward the desk. "Lady Marigold," he began with a bow, "Your Uncle Rory and Aunt Leonice have arrived. Would you like me to show them in?"

"Yes, please, Mister Lewinson. I would see them right away," Marigold answered while sharing a glance with Oire.

The butler bowed once more and departed hurriedly before returning with Marigold's aunt and uncle in tow. He cleared his throat and delivered an introduction: "Lady Marigold, I give you Councillor Rory Tullivan and his wife, Lady Leonice."

The Tullivan brothers bore a strong resemblance to one another and as Rory entered the room, Marigold felt she was looking upon a younger, bearded incarnation of her father. Rory was three years Marscal's junior, but time had been gentle to him and even before the consumption disease had consumed Marscal, Rory looked ten years younger than his elder sibling.

To his side was Leonice, who truly was a decade younger than Marscal. She was a shapely woman, with dark hair and hazel eyes who came from the wealthy Dawe family in Portsward. Marigold had always found her to be warm and friendly, especially towards her and Serephanie, whom she treated like daughters of her own.

Today the husband and wife were both dressed primarily in black. Rory had donned a fine suit and shoes with a starched white shirt beneath, while Leonice had opted for a long skirt and blouse combination.

Before the introduction was fully over, Marigold and Oire alike had quickly walked around the table to greet them both.

Leonice embraced Marigold tightly in a hug, "Oh Marigold, my dear niece, I am so sorry for the loss of our beloved Marscal."

"Thank you, Auntie. I appreciate both you and Rory arriving so soon," Marigold responded as they stepped back.

"One of Marscal's guardsmen made a point to deliver the news as they were escorting him to the funeral parlour," Rory said after drawing her in for a hug of his own. "Tell me, Marigold, was my brother's passing peaceful? Were you with him?"

Free from her relatives' grasp, Marigold gestured to the pair of plush chairs before the desk and returned to her own seat as she replied, "I never left his side, Uncle. Father did not die alone, and that little comfort I could give allowed him to pass into the good night."

As he accepted Marigold's offer, Rory let out a long sigh and ran a hand over his face. "The only solace I take from the loss of my brother is that he is no longer suffering."

By this time, Leonice had begun softly weeping and had produced a handkerchief to dab away the tears from her eyes. "Ios knows that our dear Marscal had endured more than his share of pain."

Within a heartbeat, Rory pulled his chair in close to Leonice and took her hand in his tightly. "Have you... Have you made any funeral arrangements yet?" he managed to stammer out to Marigold

"Some, yes, but just the basics for the moment," Marigold gave in return through stifled tears of her own. "Mister Rynam invited me to come to the parlour this afternoon so that he might walk me through the more nuanced details."

Rory nodded thoughtfully as she spoke and looked her in the eyes when she finished. "I would like to go with you."

"You should be with your family, Uncle," she said after a moment's hesitation.

"You *are* my family, Marigold," Rory reminded her quickly.

For the first time since Marigold's uncle and aunt had arrived, Oire found his voice. "And Rory is Marscal's lone brother, my lady, if anyone should assist you, it should be he."

Marigold had taken the dry quill to hand during the conversation, idly rolling it in her fingers while looking from Oire to Rory as they made the case for the latter's inclusion. "Of course, you are both right. Please forgive my hesitance. Uncle Rory, I would be glad to have you accompany me."

"I am most glad to hear that, Niece," Rory said in acceptance of the invitation while exhaling. He seemed to notice the paperwork on the desk for the first time and reached for the pair of letters intended for Lord Greggard and Minister Bickerington, which happened to be nearest to him. "Are these the notices for the lords and ministers?"

"They are indeed, Uncle," Marigold informed him, watching his face closely as he scanned the other letters atop the larger pile. "I have been awake all through the night and sleep continues to elude me. I thought I would make good use of my time rather than sit idle."

"It is to be expected that such notices would come from me, Niece, as the eldest male of the Tullivan family," Rory began to state worriedly, Lord Greggard's letter still between his thumb and index finger. "Most will look upon your handwriting and signature as suspect. It may seem to be but a trivial matter, but many will see this as an insult, not to mention the reactions of the more devout Triarchists amongst the EMP, and the Triarchy themselves. They will force me to write apology letters to even the foot-scrubbing acolytes of the Triarchy order for allowing this to happen."

"Mind your tongue, Rory," Leonice scolded with a wag of her finger. "This is not the time for such. If those men want to get outraged with a daughter mourning the death of her father then the disgrace is on them alone, not on you and certainly not on Marigold. She is only relaying the information of Marscal's passing and the time and date of his funeral services to the other ministers, not ordering them about."

In less familiar company, a man being chastised by any woman, be they his wife or mother or any other, would be cause for embarrassment. If there was one thing Marigold admired about her Aunt Leonice, it was her determination to have her voice heard in spite of such expectations. That in itself was a value that Leonice had learned from another woman of the Tullivan family that Marigold admired even more.

There were still tears in Leonice's eyes as she spoke, but the expression behind them had changed, as though she had departed for a distant memory. "Lest you forget, Rory, Marigold is the daughter of Princess Farren, as headstrong and proud a woman as I have ever known. She was like a sister to me, and I loved her every bit as much as I did those of my blood. I was right by her side for the births of both Serephanie and Marigold and she was with me when our first son was born."

Her focus shifted squarely to Marigold and she felt as though Oire, Rory, and even the room itself fell away, leaving just the two women. "Your mother raised you both to be like her, but when we lost her, I wondered how much of her would still shine through in you two. Your sister is a Tullivan, of that there is no question. You though, Marigold, you are the very spirit of Princess Farren Aurorais. She was resilience and grace defined, and those very qualities carried through to you. There was no tempest she could not face, no storm too strong for her to weather. I know in my heart that you are every bit the woman she was."

"Thank you, Aunt Leonice," Marigold uttered after a momentary silence. "I assure you, it means a tremendous deal for me to hear you speak so kindly of my mother. I hope that I can carry the torch she lit."

A wistful murmur emanated from Rory and as Marigold turned to face him, he was running a hand through his greying hair for a second time. "She was a wilful woman, one I remember quite fondly and I see her in you as Leonice does. The problem we face is that even in your temporary and limited role as caretaker of the Tullivan estate, you will be met with heavy opposition from all fronts. Men of all standings will not take kindly to a woman with any measure of power. Even if you would only have me as a figurehead, for your own safety, I would counsel you to let me be the face of house Tullivan for the time being."

"I cannot do that Uncle, I am sorry," Marigold said, declining the offer without a second of hesitation.

His eyes went wide, but Marigold did not detect a hint of surprise on his face. "Are you aware of whom you are up against here, Niece? Have you seen how both the Elite Merchants and the Triarchy treat Lady Orangecloak? She and her Thieves do not even have political power and yet both aforementioned entities intend to execute her and her entire outfit for protesting against their rule.

"If those same people believe you to be in violation of law and scripture alike, what do you think they will do to you? I will tell you: they will not recognise your authority and depose you, by force if need be. If by some stroke of good fortune you avoid criminal charges, you and everyone who is believed to have abated you in your crimes will be exiled from Illiastra. Of course, that is the best you could hope for. If the Palombs decide to keep you, your days will be spent as their prisoner in your own manor. Furthermore, should you be criminally charged, you would be given a new home in a dark cell in Biddenhurst. I will let your own imagination determine which of those scenarios is worse."

Marigold shrugged in response. "I am aware of all of that and yet, it does not change my answer."

The exasperation of Rory seemed to be growing with every word Marigold said, and though she felt poorly for how he was reacting, she had no regrets. Being forthright with her intentions was the only course Marigold planned to follow when dealing with her uncle. Rory, Leonice, and their children were the only family that Marigold had left in Illiastra, if she could not convince even them to stand with her, the remainder of the West would certainly be out of reach.

After another moment of head scratching and face rubbing, Rory found his voice again. "It will not be long before the Palombs arrive to claim everything your father once owned, at any rate. If you allow me to be the acting head until then, we would avoid a great deal of trouble."

"Therein rests the next detail, Uncle," Marigold declared firmly. "Under my watch, the Palombs will not be permitted to set one foot in

Daol Bay. I will not be marrying Eldridge or Pyore any more than Serephanie will be and they will not own so much as a blade of grass that grows on Tullivan lands."

"You cannot seriously be considering this," Rory gasped in utter shock. "I understand not wanting to marry into the Palomb family, but this..."

It took all of Marigold's willpower to keep from shouting at her uncle, but she found her resolve and maintained her calm. "If you truly understood, you would not be questioning my decision. You should be every bit as concerned as I am. What do you think they will do to you and your family? You and your two sons are males in the immediate Tullivan line and a clear threat to the Palombs' impending reign. If you think you will get to continue calling Illiastra home, you are deluding yourself. Perhaps I am wrong, though and you will get to stay in Illiastra. I just hope that in such a case, you and I will be cellmates in Biddenhurst, as I would much love the company."

"Come now, you surely do not think that Lord Eamon would do such a thing to me or my boys," Rory said with a scoff and a roll of his eyes.

"Would he not?" Marigold asked rhetorically with a tinge of curiosity in her voice. "My parents and the three of you in this room were so concerned that my pregnant mother might be harmed or killed by Eamon that she went across the sea to her home in the Northern Kingdom of Gildriad so that she could safely give birth. A place where she stayed put until my little brother was five years old. If you all believed that Eamon was capable of killing a mother and her infant child, what makes you think he will not dispose of a father and his teenaged sons? Beyond that, for how heinous Lord Eamon is known to be, Eldridge and Pyore are unilaterally worse."

Rory had opened his mouth to speak, but so had Oire and the steward was first to do so. "The lady is not saying that the Palombs would resort to violence immediately. Rather, she is saying that if you and your family could not be pushed out by conventional means, then they would not hesitate to resort to bloodier measures. Once they had gotten their worth from you as an instructor in the ways of the West, you would be removed as a city councillor. After that, you would be left as the President of Tullivan Seafoods, once again, until you had adequately trained a replacement who is more to the Palombs' suiting."

"There would be no need for any of that, Oire," Rory finally interjected, his tone growing increasingly incredulous with every word. "When Marscal, Lord Eamon, and the Lord Master Howland all signed the marriage pact, it was to unite all three of the great families of Illiastra into one, not eradicate all but the Palombs. We would simply be under one banner. Howland, Palomb, or Tullivan, we would all be working together."

"The last Howland bearing any power in Illiastra is the Lord Master himself," Oire stated pointedly. "Grenjin's younger siblings and cousins all signed away any rights they might have to his estate. His wife died before she could bear an heir, under suspicious circumstances, I might add. After Romera Howland's death, the inheritance was the last piece that the Palombs needed to take the Lord Mastership for themselves. Strict adherence to the laws of Ios kept Old Grenjin from remarrying and fathering an heir of his own, so he concocted the marriage pact. It was his last, desperate effort to disallow, or at least delay, the Palombs ascension to the most powerful office in the nation. Much to the consternation of all but the Palombs, Jorette Palomb was the first to begat sons and everything seemed to fall into place for Eamon."

Marigold had been watching as Oire talked of the marriage pact, and as he spoke of Eamon's wife, a hand had come to land on Weicaster Bay's location on the map. It curled into a fist at the mention of Eamon's name, and thudded softly on the cartographical representation of the bay. "Why would the Lord Master, who spent his life clutching tightly to that power for himself, wager the future of Illiastra on such a pact? I will tell you why: Grenjin was astutely aware that he had lost the support of the other lords and ministers of the Eastern Realm to the Palombs. Outright rebuffing Eamon's advances directly would have seen the last shred of power that Grenjin still held plucked from his hands in an instant in favour of a man that even Howland fears. That alone should clearly illustrate that harmony with the Palombs is but a fever dream.

"Do you think that the Honourable Guardsmen were formed to protect Grenjin from anyone else but Eamon?" Oire put to Rory in rhetorical fashion, his tones having growing exaggerated in the asking. "No, they are formed for any event that Eamon will be attending to ensure that the Lord Master has more swords protecting him than Eamon can bring without looking conspicuous. He then hired Tryst

Reine, a man even Eamon would not dare cross. Grenjin did all of that because he knows that the deaths of Farren and Felixander, and his own wife too, were no mere accidents."

Rory was leaning forward by this point, his hands on the desk and his eyes looking between Oire and Marigold. "Eamon is the true power within Illiastra, of course, and no one here will deny that, least of all me. That helps my point, though, for I am but the younger brother of the late Warden Lord of the West who the Palombs will now legally replace, with no further delays. There is no reason for them to worry about Janus, Terrin, or myself standing in their way. After all, what are small fish to the mighty shark?"

"Food," Leonice declared sharply, "And I have no desire to see my children being eaten, Husband."

"By Ios' will Leonice, what would you have me do?" Rory asked exhaustively, his head coming to rest in his hands. "Marscal is not dead but a few hours and we are already talking of who may lay claim to what was still his as of last night."

"With all due respect Uncle, I had no intention of telling you all of this just yet," Marigold told him in straight terms. "You are right to say that it is not the time for this discussion. Yet, I will not lie to you. When you saw the letters and asked what I was doing, I told you truly, and I did that knowing where this conversation would lead. Honesty is integral, especially between family members, and in that spirit, I would not avoid such a conversation with you.

"For all of that being said, you cannot deny the truth in Oire's words: we are facing our own extinction at the hands of the Palombs. The Lord Master tried to prevent it with subtle measures that would both keep the eastern ministers from turning on him and shield the outside world from seeing the chaos raging within the EMP. For his efforts, Howland has so far managed to sustain only his own life. The eastern ministers were not mine to begin with, and I have no reason to conceal the skeletons in the EMP's closets, so I am not bound by the same rules as Howland.

"What I need is a western realm that will support me in secession at best and war at worst. That starts here, in this office, with a unified Tullivan family to hold a familiar banner for the west to rally beneath."

"You will never have that support, Niece," Rory said with great exasperation. "The west, or any other realm of Illiastra for that matter, will not stand behind a woman."

Marigold expected that Rory would say as much and his words only steeled her resolve further. "Indeed, we both agree that I have an extraordinarily difficult path ahead of me in order to gain the support of the western ministers," she said in a voice that was as calm as it was resolute. "If the ministers of the west see that I cannot earn the support of even my uncle, then I will absolutely fail. I need you, Uncle Rory. For the love you bear my father, I ask you to please stand with me in the darkest hour of our house."

"Your father would never want this," Rory stated while keeping his gaze on the floor. He had taken to nervously rubbing his hands together during the discussion, and was presently massaging each of his fingers in turn. "I would remind you that he signed the pact and abided by it for all these years."

"I know you do not believe that with any conviction," Oire said, clearly having reached a breaking point with Rory's bullheadedness. "Do you remember everything that took place after Farren disappeared? Marscal above all explored every option we could find to annul the marriage pact. We spent night after night grasping at every straw with you seated exactly where you are at this moment. No one was more adamant about keeping the Palombs at bay than your brother. The only difference between then and now is who is sitting behind the desk, and instead of you lending your voice to her cause as you did for Marscal, you are searching for every reason not to."

"Yet in the end, Marscal-" Rory had begun to say.

"In the end, Father died with regret in his heart," Marigold interjected, as equally depleted of patience as Oire. "He told me that he wished to have had the courage to do something tangible to stop House Palomb. After shouldering the blame for Serephanie's desertion, he spent the last of his energy giving me his blessing to break the pact and claim his mantle for my own."

"How can I be sure of that?" Rory queried with uncertainty.

Before Marigold could say anything, Oire provided the answer. "Marscal amended his last will. By its word, Marigold is the heir now, in both name and duty."

It was then that Marigold noticed that Rory was quite visibly trembling.

His still-wringing hands were soon joined by another gloved in black silk as Leonice rose from her chair and knelt at his side, her voice as smooth as honey. "You are afraid, Rory, and that is perfectly alright. Marigold is afraid too, as is Oire, and as am I. That is a normal reaction in the face of such uncertainty and danger. Remember, if you will, what your mother Lady Maisera used to say: 'Only when fear takes hold of us can we truly find our own bravery.' I know you can do just that, if not for yourself, then for your niece, for me, and most of all, your children."

"Do you believe that this is the right thing to do, Leonice? Honest and truly?" he asked in a voice that had fallen to little more than a whisper.

"With every fibre of my being, I absolutely do," she told him with certainty.

Rory cupped her left cheek with his hand and placed a kiss on the right. "Then I shall trust your judgement," he said before his gaze turned to Marigold for the first time in what felt like several minutes. "To honour the memory of my brother and for the future of my children and the entire Western Realm, I commit myself to your cause, Marigold. I acknowledge you as the rightful Lady of Daol Bay."

13

SEREPHANIE

For the third time since arriving in Hercalest, Serephanie and Darrion stood upon Bryten Field. On their first visit, they left defeated at the door, the second was met with defeat in combat, but this day, they arrived with a sense of victory. Part of Serephanie felt as though the feeling was premature or wholly misplaced altogether, but the piece of paper in Darrion's hands was the sail that carried their ship across a sea of hope.

It bore a request for inquiry from the widow of fighting legend Fezadore the Giant, Cyrelle Molissios, herself a vaunted figure in the hierarchy of the League of the Sacred Fist. The subject of the inquiry was Darrion, and while it did not formally constitute an admissions trial for him, it was at least asking for such from someone whose opinion allegedly bore weight.

In the distance ahead of the couple sat the ostentatious tent where the Sacred Fist hosted their public fights, a gentle lilt in the wind giving lift to its brightly coloured, canvas walls and ceiling. There, standing directly before the entry way was the same Gallician man that had denied their passage on the first visit. He was bundled warmly against the cold winds of the late autumn, the plaits of his red, forked beard moving in time and direction with the tent.

Where before there was hesitation in Darrion, he now strode proudly toward the gatekeeper, the piece of paper held gently in his right hand.

"The man with the sack of sand returns," the Gallician uttered with a roll of the eyes and a weary sigh upon sight of Darrion and Serephanie.

"I beg your pardon?" Darrion asked, his face clearly showing the confusion that the statement evoked.

The fellow folded his thick arms across his chest before explaining his meaning, "Among the Gallick Isles the timeglass is an important means of knowing what hour of the day it is. Therefore, it goes that when a man has time to waste, we say he has a sack of sand for the timeglass. Now that I've spent time explaining my words, perhaps you'll do me the courtesy of quickly explaining why you are here when the tournament is over."

Darrion took a glance at Serephanie, then to the paper in his hands. "We've come with a letter that we were instructed to give to Na'Zohz."

"I am Na'Zohz and I am not expecting any letters," he informed them with an uncaring shrug. "Who sent it and what do they want?"

"It is from Cyrelle Molissios, Fezadore's Widow," Serephanie spoke up at Darrion's side. "She recommends that Cole Chere here be given a chance to earn his place in the Sacred Fist."

Na'Zohz began to laugh at that. "Cyrelle must want to see you on the receiving end of another choke slam from Tahru. I must say, I enjoyed it as well. Her tastes and mine align on a great many things."

"Do you want to see the letter?" Darrion asked while offering the paper to Na'Zohz, apparently ignoring the barb about his fight with the Doban strongman.

"Yes, if I must. Give it here," Na'Zohz confirmed with another sigh, taking the parchment to hand to read. Almost immediately, he began to hum aloud and Serephanie followed his line of sight as it went back and forth across the page. When finished, Na'Zohz lowered the paper, still holding it tight as he said, "Well, there is no denying what is written."

Serephanie and Darrion exchanged a glance, with Darrion responding, "does that mean you will let us in?"

His eyes rolled for the second time. "It means you will both stay here while I speak with my... What's the common word...? Inferiors?"

"Do you mean *superiors*?" Serephanie attempted to correct him gently.

"Hmmm... That might be right, I usually just say 'boss' but it didn't feel right for the occasion. It doesn't matter." Na'Zohz turned away and snapped his fingers in the direction of the stable tent. "Cardwin, come here, Lad."

A young fellow with short hair the colour of straw came forward. He was above normal height, with a lanky build and a long, bearded face. To one hand was a spade that he had been using to muck the stables, and he carried the smell with him.

"What can I do for you, Mister Na'Zohz?" the young man inquired obediently.

"Stand here and keep watch on these two, that's what you can do," Na'Zohz instructed Cardwin while pointing at Darrion and Serephanie. "I'll be back in a few moments."

"Aye, ser. You can count on me," Cardwin replied with a half-hearted salute, tapping two fingers against the temple.

That earned Cardwin a glare from Na'Zohz. "I absolutely cannot count on you, Cardwin, but you're all I have at the moment. Just try not to screw up."

Waiting until the Gallician was out of sight, Cardwin turned to the couple. "I'm sorry about Na'Zohz, bitter old codger that he is."

"No need to apologise, I'm sure he has his reasons for being so curt," Darrion offered back, his tone friendly.

"Aye, he's bitter and old, just like I already said," Cardwin told them, his eyes wide as he spoke blithely. "His days in the ring are behind him now, but you can't get angry at time, now can you? So instead, he takes it out on the new blood, like me, that are going to take his place."

Serephanie furrowed her brows as a memory came to her then. "Wait, did he say your name is Cardwin?"

Cardwin shrugged at the question. "Aye, he did, so what of it? Do I know you?

"I could swear I heard someone yelling your name from inside the tent a week before the tournament," Serephanie declared as the incident came back to her.

By then, Cardwin was looking at her curiously. "Might have been. I ask again: what of it?"

"Aye, yeah, I remember now too, Love," Darrion exclaimed, voice perking up as he made eye contact with her. "He almost hurt someone and was told to run laps around the ring for doing so."

"And you were whinging about it, as I recall." Serephanie added.

"I wasn't whinging, Missy," Cardwin huffed.

Darrion was having none of it. "You did, and then they made you do push-ups too. I remember it plainly."

"Oh, who cares?" Cardwin asked rhetorically, growing defensive over the whole matter. "It was Verrit's fault anyhow. Ask anyone who was there, they'll tell you. All you did was hear about it. You didn't actually see anything."

A man's voice interjected on Cardwin's ranting. "If I didn't know any better I would think that someone is eager to start doing push-ups until sundown."

The owner of the smooth voice was a middle-aged man walking at the side of the returning Na'Zohz. He looked to be north of fifty years, with brown hair and a matching beard streaked with grey. He was garbed in a dark blue woollen sweater, tan trousers, and calf-height brown boots, all of it tidy and the body they were worn upon looking fit for his age. His eyes caught Serephanie's attention, their hazel irises bearing warmth while his strong facial features carried a confidence that could not be ignored. Try as she might to identify him, Serephanie could not, and though fit and strong, she could not be certain that he was a fighter of the Sacred Fist, past or presently.

"I'm sorry, Mister Lancer," Cardwin stated, his tone sounding mildly ashamed. When Serephanie looked to him, she found the fellow staring at his own footwear.

"No need to apologise to me, Cardwin," the one he called Mister Lancer instructed the younger man. "Apologise to yourself for letting your tongue get you into this mess, perhaps an apology to Na'Zohz too, for failing to follow his directive. As I heard it from Na'Zohz, he told you to keep an eye on the two folks at the entrance to the tent. No part of that was to spout off at our guests. Just stand there, and wait with them. That was all you had to do."

Na'Zohz was already pinching the bridge of his nose and further added to his disappointment with a shake of the head. "I told you that I could not count on you, Cardwin."

"Head back to the stable tent. I know you have more mucking to do. We'll talk later," Lancer told the lad with a dismissive wave and a stern tone.

The two men stopped short of Darrion and Serephanie, waiting until Cardwin was out of earshot before talking again. Once Cardwin was gone, Na'Zohz did not mince words. "You can tell Cyrelle that I upheld my side of things. Here, you may take this back as a keepsake if you wish." In his extended hand was the letter from the Giant's Widow, which Darrion accepted and handed off to Serephanie.

"This here is Everett Lancer, the talent scout of sorts for the Sacred Fist," Na'Zohz said by way of introduction. "The both of you can go with him now, we're done here."

"Ah, Na'Zohz, your eloquence knows no bounds, my friend," Everett Lancer commented with an amiable guffaw. "Alright, new blood, you and your wife can walk with me and we shall see what it was that got Tahru's attention during the tournament."

During the course of a leisurely-paced stroll and a cordial conversation about the weather, Everett Lancer led Serephanie and Darrion around the perimeter of the big tent. Around the back, they found a village of tarps and poles, bustling with activity in the midmorning light. Serephanie spotted fighters and attendants coming and going from pavilion tents, smelled the work of a trio of cooks roasting meats over a spit, and waited while Everett spoke with a painter applying bright colours to expansive lengths of hempen rope. There were groups of men lifting iron weights in turns, rallying and encouraging one another as they pushed through their sets of repetitions. Further away, Serephanie saw a group that seemed to be comprised equally of men and women thoroughly scrubbing one of the large canvas mats that normally topped the surface of the ring.

"It is quite the lively community that the Sacred Fist has here," Serephanie heard herself saying aloud, earning a look of mild surprise from Everett.

He gave the faintest of smiles in response, "Why, yes, we do. We have even been compared to a hive of bees on occasion, by other outsiders." Stopping to point out a small cluster of tents at the rear of the nomadic fighting troupe's camp, he added instruction while looking directly at Darrion. "Alright, you go ahead, find a tent with an open flap, and get changed into something you can spar in. When you're ready, come to the pavilion tent over there with the green and gold pennants. I'll be waiting inside. Don't dawdle, for much like Na'Zohz, I put value in my time and I have little patience for those who would waste it."

Once Darrion gave a nod of confirmation, Everett departed their company, leaving them to walk the rest of the way to the changing tents without him.

The cold, sun-cast autumn day left the air smelling crisp and fresh and Serephanie took it in while standing outside of the tent Darrion chose to occupy. She could hear him rummaging about, getting out of his street clothing for what she knew to be a pair of cotton trousers and a loose tunic.

"Ser-uh, Terra, darling?" Darrion called from within the tent, quite nearly using her real name.

"Yes, what is it, Love?" she answered back, hoping no one had heard the near-slip.

"Could you have a look about and see if you can spot the tent that Mister Lancer was referring to?" he asked over the sound of his clothes hitting the floor. "I wouldn't want to be late on account of getting lost."

"Certainly, Love," Serephanie decided readily, eager to have a look about the encampment. "This should not take long. I'll come back for you in a moment."

Walking away from the changing area, Serephanie found herself among the closely set pavilion tents, her eyes skyward as much as her cloak would allow without the hood slipping off. She insisted on wearing the dingy, faded thing, worried that someone might recognise her. In particular, she was concerned that she might encounter Hann Bravado or any others from among the various famous fighters that her father had hosted at the manor over the years. In which case, it would likely be impossible to maintain the ruse she and Darrion were conveying.

Beneath the cloak, she wore a simple dress and smock combination in blue and white, respectively. As much as she would like to have a wardrobe like Marigold or Orangecloak and the Thieves, it would not be conducive to her plan to hide in plain sight.

In looking at the tops of every tent she passed, Serephanie noticed that each had a combination of two or three pennant flags and no two tents had the same colours.

This must be how they distinguish tents. I wonder if the colours are coded in any way, Serephanie had begun to wonder.

"Are you lost, Miss?" she heard from somewhere beside her. Serephanie turned toward the voice to see a muscular man in a cuirass over a woollen doublet, a dagger much like the one Na'Zohz wore hung in a sheath on his hip.

"No, ser, I don't believe I am," Serephanie answered him confidently, acting as if she indeed belonged there.

The cadence she carried herself with seemed to befuddle the guard momentarily, though he quickly found a response. "Is that so? Then where might I ask are you headed? You don't look familiar to me and I have been here long enough to know who should and should not be back here among the tents, Miss."

Pointing back toward the changing tents, she directed the guard's vision to Darrion, presently walking toward them with a look of concern on his face. "That there is my husband, Cole Chere. I was asked by him to find the tent with the green and gold pennants so that he would not be late to meet with Everett Lancer."

"That is Cole Chere?" the guard queried with a tone that was half wonderment and half amusement. "So that's the man who got Tahru's attention. I'm sad to say that I never witnessed it myself, as I was patrolling out here during the tournament. It was only afterwards that heard all about him. What brings him back here, might I ask?"

It was Serephanie's turn to be briefly confused, as she had no idea that Darrion's performance had generated any amount of lasting interest, especially among the Sacred Fist's employees. "He was invited by Cyrelle. She would like him to be considered for the league."

"Is that so?" the guard said while stroking the rust-coloured beard on his chin idly, still watching Darrion approach. "Well, if Cyrelle is asking for it, perhaps you will become familiar to me after all."

"Hello there!" Darrion greeted the guard when he was close enough to be heard. "How is the day finding you, ser?"

The guard extended a hand toward Darrion and it was taken to shake. "Put it there, Mister Chere. Your wife was just telling me who you are and I'm quite glad to meet you."

"You are? I lost in the tournament, though. What could you possibly want to meet me for?" Darrion asked with a puzzled laugh.

With a quick glance in all directions, the guard leaned in close to Darrion, the level of his voice dropping to barely above a whisper. "To be quite honest Mister Chere, the tournament of the Winter King is not one that the regular members of the Sacred Fist take seriously. In fact, the big timers, like Barajah, Tahru, and the like? Aye, they find it utterly boring. Those fellows only participate in the Winter King's tournament for the money, not for the competition. What do you think it means if one of them suddenly gets excited and starts giving a shit about the whole show? Tahru was out of his seat and jumping around the stage, as I heard it. The sight of that would send most folks running, but not you. No, you leapt right into the fray and faced him. Do you think that wasn't a big deal back here too? You're the talk of the whole camp after that performance. There's few among us that wouldn't want to meet you, I figure, just to get a measure of you, if for no other reason."

"Surely you jest," Darrion said with a humorous snort. "I didn't do anything special beyond what any other fighter would reasonably be expected to do."

The guard's eyes went wide. "On the contrary, Fella: that tournament is a bore at the best of times for the guys in the Sacred Fist, but you made it interesting."

"But so did Kohvee," Darrion countered. "He was the only challenger to unseat a champion for the whole day. None of the other fighters before or after my round did that. That must have been exciting. Probably took the focus right off mine and Tahru's fight."

"Knocking some spoiled noble on his arse? Nah, Fella. That's nothing special. Landrick Imorgan was cheating, as I heard it. Knocking out teeth and breaking noses whenever he could. We can't let that stand, can we? Kohvee was just making sure that Imorgan's ungentlemanly behaviour wasn't rewarded. None of the other fighters cares much about that, at the end of the day. Say some outsider to the League walks in though, starts throwing someone around with a fancy fighting style that most people have only read about. Now, that there is something on its own. Let alone accepting Tahru's challenge. Every man in the tournament goes out of his way to avoid facing Tahru. You were called out directly, and you answered, with no reluctance as I heard it. You just went ahead and did it, as calm as you please. That put all eyes squarely on you, Fella. You didn't even have to win by that point. As long as you didn't cower off the platform or submit, you had earned a lot of respect that day."

Darrion glanced toward Serephanie, his face showing cautious optimism, before turning back to the guard to ask, "You really think so?"

"The way I see it, there's a fire under you. If that were I and I were your age, I would be doing everything I could to get my career cooking before those flames burn out. You catch what I'm saying?"

"I think I do, but I didn't get your name, Guardsman." Darrion returned with a slow nod.

"It's Jay, if you please," he offered Darrion and Serephanie alike. "Oh, and if you want, I will walk you to the tent that your wife here said you were looking for."

They took him up on the offer, following close behind until he brought them to within the shadow of the big top. "This is the place. Tell Everett I said 'hello' and listen to every word he says. The man is a walking encyclopaedia when it comes to hand-to-hand fighting."

Both Darrion and Serephanie took the time to thank Jay and parted ways with him for the inside of the tent. Within, they found three young men chatting to one another on a wide bench at the back of the tent, all dressed for the occasion in tunics and trousers similar to what Darrion wore. Their eyes all fell on the couple and their conversation fell off abruptly.

"Is it me? Am I not allowed to be here?" Serephanie whispered to Darrion.

In response, Darrion shrugged, "I'm not sure. I had heard that the Sacred Fist had a tight set of unspoken rules, but few in the Daol Bay fighting pits knew any of them. This is new territory for me, Love."

"While I can't say I've heard of that personally," Serephanie countered, "common social convention dictates that we should at least introduce ourselves."

"Aye Love, you speak sense," Darrion agreed, while turning to the others. "Good day, gents. My name is Cole Chere and I was instructed to go to this tent by Everett Lancer."

The trio exchanged curious glances until the one seated in the middle called back to him, "Is that the same Cole Chere that Tahru kicked up a fuss about?"

"Uh... Aye, that's me, I suppose," Darrion put back cautiously.

"You from Illiastra, yeah?" the leftmost among them asked.

Darrion replied with a nod first, before adding, "Aye, Galdourn specifically. Any of you ever been?"

The question went ignored, as the middle fellow threw in a question of his own. "If you're from Illiastra, how in the name of Ios did you learn how to fight like them Water Elves from halfway across the sea?"

"He obviously went to Tropuri and learned it there, ya dummy," the young man on the right put in.

The middle one scoffed and turned to the speaker, "You can't just go to Tropuri. Elves are arseholes, all of 'em: water, woods, half-breeds, it doesn't matter, elves are arseholes. Everyone knows that. They won't just let an Illiastran into Tropuri, let alone teach him to fight their way, 'ya dummy'."

While Serephanie and Darrion both knew neither statement to be true and Darrion's mouth had opened in an attempt to respond, he was cut off by the arrival of Everett Lancer.

"Whose job was it to sweep the mat today?" Everett queried with annoyance weighing heavy in his tone.

Both fellows on the left and right side of the bench jabbed index fingers at the man seated between them.

He groaned at his compatriots, before giving answer to Everett Lancer. "I did sweep it, ser. I promise."

"If you call that a sweeping then you're going to be absolutely gobsmacked when you see the real thing, Domas," Everett shot back while making a wide gesture over the ground that the tent covered.

For the first time since entering the tent, Serephanie took notice of the flooring, finding it to be a straw mat woven circularly, extending nearly to the walls of the tent on any side. Though it looked to have been given some sort of rudimentary sweeping, Serephanie would have called the job haphazard at best.

Everett waved a finger at the two seated to either side of Domas, "Lyle or Kellum, could one of you two sweep the mat? Show Domas and our new fellow here what is expected of them."

Both of them mumbled in annoyance, but stood up all the same to do the task.

As the pair picked up a couple of straw brooms from one corner, Darrion raised a hand. "I'll do it, Mister Lancer. I don't mind."

"No, you won't," Lancer informed him. "You'll watch one of them, to see how I want it done. Even something as seemingly simple as sweeping, you will first observe. That's how I teach. You watch those who know better, study their movements, and when I'm satisfied that you've learned the lesson, then you'll get to apply it. Am I understood, Mister Chere?"

"Yes, ser, Mister Lancer, you have my apologies," Darrion offered in contrition.

Lancer shook his head while strolling to the now vacant bench in the back of the tent. "You didn't know, Mister Chere, there is no need for apologies. Now though, you do know, so if you do it again, that's when apologies will be in order. However, if you've learned the lesson, you won't repeat the mistake, thus negating the need for an apology in the first place. Now, tell me: what did you learn?"

"To not apologise?" Darrion answered with uncertainty, earning a few stifled laughs from the other three trainees.

"Is that a question or a statement?" Everett threw back at him.

"A statement?" Darrion responded, again with the propositional tone.

"Well, which is it?" Everett queried with growing, albeit feigned scepticism. "Because your words say *statement* but the way you say them says *question*."

Darrion shrugged, but gave no propositional tone in his final answer. "A statement, then."

"Then you're wrong, Mister Chere. The lessons are twofold: first lesson is that mistakes are fine so long as we learn from them, don't repeat them, and no lasting harm is done. Second lesson is that apologies are only for those who do repeat their mistakes. Therefore, as long as you learn from your rookie mistakes and abstain from repeating them, I should never have to hear the words 'My apologies' from you. Am I understood?"

"Yes ser, absolutely," Darrion gave with a bow.

"With that out of the way and once the mat is swept, go find a place on it and stretch out," Everett instructed Darrion with a clap of his hands, turning to Serephanie when done. "As for you, why don't you join me on the bench in the back? Consider yourself my esteemed guest for the day."

Serephanie accepted his invitation, putting on a level of shyness in the process. Once seated, Everett offered her a cup of water from a nearby barrel and by the time he joined her, Kellum had finished sweeping the mat.

Everett bid the four young men to stretch their limbs, warm up, and prepare for the training to come. As the minutes began to slip away, he called an end to the preparations, "Alright, that's enough. Let's get those hearts pumping. Start with push-ups. I want thirty. Mister Chere, do you know how to do those?"

"Yes, ser, I should say I do," he replied quickly, albeit with an entirely nonplussed expression across his face. After dropping down into position to show Lancer his form, Darrion demonstrated by doing two proper push-ups.

"That's it, alright," Everett stated, apparently content with what he saw. "Very well, you can join in on this exercise. Lyle, you keep count. Begin when ready."

Doing as he was bid, Lyle began to loudly count his push-ups, with the other three keeping time with him.

Once they were well into it, Everett leaned in towards Serephanie. "You should know that I spoke to Cyrelle about you two while your man was changing."

"I see..." Serephanie responded slowly, sorting through the best way to both continue the conversation and gauge which direction it was headed. "Might I ask what she said, ser?"

"That's thirty, Mister Lancer," Lyle announced before anything further could be discussed.

"Squats next, then. Give me thirty again. Kellum's on the count this time," Everett told them quickly. Once Darrion demonstrated that he knew how to perform the exercise, Everett gave them leave to begin.

"One thing I gleaned from speaking with Cyrelle," Everett started in again, once Kellum's counting began carrying throughout the tent. "Is that it's difficult to say if the Lady is more interested in you or your man."

Serephanie could practically feel the redness seeping into her cheeks. "I-I-I have no idea why that would be. I'm just a-a nameless girl from Galdourn."

"Certainly you are, Miss," Everett said with a thoughtful nod. "The Lady is always on the lookout for capable girls, much like Syrie and Cyrelle's two handmaids. You met them, aye?"

She nodded in response and Everett continued. "The Giant's Widow has taken a liking to you. She told me that if I can find a place for your man, then she could find a place for you as one of her girls. Of course, that's if it's something that you would be interested in."

"But... But women aren't allowed to work, Mister Lancer," Serephanie said with timidity and fear creeping into her voice in equal measure. The whole proposition seemed suspect, as though Everett were baiting a trap of some sort.

"Thirty squats, ser, as requested," Kellum informed Lancer, his voice loud and clear, as though he were a soldier talking to a military officer.

"Sit-ups. Sixty," Everett told them flatly. "Mister Chere, if you show me that you can do one, I'll let you lead the count."

Without complaint or comment, Darrion dropped to the straw mat and did a single sit-up, earning an approving nod from Everett. The other three lowered themselves around Darrion, and he began counting their progress.

Everett turned his attention back to Serephanie. "You need not worry about being an employed woman, not among the Sacred Fist. We will protect you from harm."

"From physical harm?" she asked softly.

"If it comes to that, aye," Everett affirmed without hesitation.

A look of suspicion came over Everett and his eyes fell on Darrion while still talking to Serephanie. "Are you afraid that someone will harm you?"

Serephanie shook her head rapidly. "No, no, not at all. I hear stories of what happens to women who are arrested. It's said that being in the custody of the guards, whether in the city or the roaming highway patrolmen, is awful to begin with, and the road only ever leads to Biddenhurst from there."

"Not if you are one of us, I promise you," Everett countered, his tone turning warm and reassuring. "Walk with us and we will show you that there is a road for the women of Illiastra."

"Where does that road lead, Mister Lancer?" Serephanie queried, looking him straight in the eyes as she did.

He smiled then, genuinely, with every part of his face. "It leads to freedom, Miss. If you so want it."

14
MARIGOLD

The wind chilled her to the bone. It came in billowing gusts from the northwest, carrying its currents from the frigid, impassable lands known as the Frozen Wastes. In the early winter's fading strokes of daylight, the icy tendrils of air were practically tangible to Marigold as they rushed across Twin Bay, into Daol Bay, and up and over the stony cliffs to push against her.

Behind Marigold were the Crypts of House Tullivan, the final resting place of her house's founding ancestor, Ser Davis, and the vast majority of his descendants. It was built high above where even the family manor sat on Daol Bay's south side, accessed by a narrow, dusty road that was used by none but the lighthouse keeper and his family. Beyond those few, who lived well away from the crypts out on the tip of the Lower Jaw of Twin Bay, none dared set foot on the trail, save for the Tullivans themselves.

The marble vault, built into the highest feasible point of the hillside, was a place of sacred value to the Tullivans, holding more importance than any home or business that the family had ever owned. There had been other houses before the current Tullivan Manor, and fish processing had not been their first revenue stream, nor was their current plant even the first place of business for that particular venture. The crypts, though, were the one and only. When Marigold was old enough to understand what death was, she knew that the crypts was where her family rested and one day, she too would go to her long slumber.

Moments ago, she had been within its stale, suffocating confines, having led Marscal's bearers of the pall down to the far depths where only her grandparents were yet interred. With a torch in one hand and an iron sword in the other, she gave light at the prepared tomb, allowing the eight men, made up of Rory and seven of the manor guardsmen to focus on the task of sealing her father's body away for eternity.

With their work complete, Marigold now stood outside, breathing deeply of the salty air that had filled the lungs of her family for eons.

"Rory and the guardsmen are prepared to seal the crypt again, my lady. They wait only on you and the iron sword," she heard a voice say in approach from behind.

From over her shoulder she saw Oire closing the distance between them, his arms wrapped tightly around his aging body, itself already covered in a full suit and a long woollen coat. "In just a moment, Oire. This is the first chance I have had all day of allowing myself to feel anything."

"It's freezing cold and I sense that rain is on the way. We should head back to the manor soon, my lady," Oire reasoned with her in gentle protest.

In only a plain cotton gown and cloak, both in mourning black, Marigold did indeed feel the cold, but for the nonce, it did not bother her. "I do not find the weather as harsh as all of that. I think I would like to stay here for another minute or two while I compose myself again. The guests at the manor can wait."

A funeral procession stretching a full kilometre and comprised of mourners on foot, horseback, and in carriages had made the trek from the Tower of Ios near the waterfront of the northern side of the city. Through the rising road along the southern side of Daol Bay, they followed in a slow line behind the hearse until arriving at the Tullivan Manor. Marigold, Rory, and Oire had proceeded on horseback directly behind the hearse, with the remaining bearers of the pall immediately to the rear of them.

From the manor's gate, the procession grounded to a halt, as Rory and the seven guardsmen, all in their finest teal uniforms, took Marscal's casket to bear on their shoulders for the long walk on foot to the crypts. Marigold, Oire, and the funeral director had gone with, but no one else, not even the regional Patriarch of Ios, Orney Therall, or the present lords and ministers were permitted. It was Tullivan tradition, and as much as Marigold enjoyed eschewing traditions, this was one she was intent on keeping.

Patriarch Therall was incensed when Rory denied him leave to join us, Marigold reflected, almost bitterly so, in spite of her sorrow. *It was at my command, but Therall would never have listened had the words come from my mouth. Therall has been involved in enough today.*

Marigold had perceived it to be something of a slight that only he was permitted to speak at the funeral in the Temple of Ios that afternoon. All throughout the sermon, the greying Patriarch elucidated on Marscal Tullivan's life, while the people who had known him, particularly the remaining members of his family, had been forced to sit silently. When it was over, the collected blood and brethren of Marscal stood in line to thank Therall and act as though the sermon was some profound reflection on Marscal's time in the world.

It was nothing of the sort, as far as Marigold was concerned. In fact, she felt it was little more than a cursory read through a table of contents of the book of her father's life. No sooner had the barest of service been paid to Marscal than Therall segued hastily into the alleged virtues of Ios, a topic he dared not stray from for the remainder of the funeral mass.

Raising the sword still held tightly in her right hand, Marigold laid the flat of the blade across her left so that she might look over the simple, largely ornamental weapon. Given that it was a hand-and-a-half longsword made of iron, it was a heavy thing for Marigold to hold with but a single hand for any length of time.

How I wish that Serephanie were here to carry the weight with me.

By the best guesses of the men Marscal had tasked with finding Marigold's sister, she was believed to be leagues away. Even with no trace or sighting to go on, it was assumed that Serephanie was somewhere across the Casparian Sea, or perhaps heading for, or already hidden within, the island ruins of old Phaleayna.

She likely does not even know that father is gone.

"We'll soon be losing the daylight, Mari," a new voice she knew to be belonging to Rory said, sounding to be the same distance away as Oire. "Might I suggest that we get on with closing the crypt and making for the manor while we can still see the path beneath our feet?"

"Very well," Marigold relented, turning about to face both men and finding them to be standing mere metres away. "I suppose I have kept everyone long enough. Thank you all for your patience."

She left the grassy overlook behind and crossed the gravel lighthouse path running between the viewpoint and the crypts. Half a dozen rounded, deteriorating stone steps led to a covered porch landing, itself decorated with stone benches and a tall, bronze plate mounted on the marble exterior wall of the family mausoleum.

To each side of the doublewide, steel door entrance of the crypt were three Tullivan guardsmen who had been her father's pallbearers. Leading the six of them, and standing at ease before the doorway was the proud and distinguished Captain of the Tullivan Manor guards, Ser Keneth Arisborough, looking resplendent in his military uniform. He was of an age with her father, but beyond his white hair and moustache, Keneth was in fine physical shape and would hardly pass for his nearly sixty years. North of two metres tall and broad in the shoulders and chest, he was an imposing figure at any age, and still more than capable in battle with sword or pistol.

"Bearers of the Pall: stand at attention for Miss Marigold, Lady of our House of Tullivan," Keneth addressed the other guardsmen, prompting them to pull into a tight stance with their legs together and arms at their sides.

As Marigold came to stand before Keneth, his right fist crossed to his left shoulder in salute and the others followed suit in unison, his voice booming as he added, "We are yours to command, My Lady."

Marigold looked about at the seven of them, now made whole to eight by the returning Rory, who joined Keneth at the door. "Uncle Rory, Ser Keneth, Rus, Darrill, Kandell, Lewcas, Elden, and Sydnee," Marigold said, ensuring she mentioned each guard by name. "Thank you ever so much for your unwavering service today in carrying my father to his final rest. House Tullivan is in your debt, always."

Keneth had lowered his fist and levelled his gaze directly on Marigold. "The honour is ours, my lady. Thank you for the privilege to do so."

"My father would have been proud of you all today. I know that as sure as I am standing here," Marigold replied, glancing down at the sword still in her hands. "Please now, be at ease, guardsmen and with your help, I will seal the crypts so that my father may go quietly into his eternal rest."

"But of course, my lady. It will be as you so wish," Keneth stated with a nod, before turning to the others. "Guardsmen, stand at ease and be prepared to assist as our lady so desires."

Moving into the eased position together, the guard's feet stamped on the marble foyer in tandem.

The entire display was one steeped in grand tradition, but Marigold had felt she had endured enough of that for one day. "Ser Keneth, there is no need for such formality anymore. Much like Oire, I consider you as much an uncle to me as Rory, and we lose that behind such rigid behaviour. Besides, there's no one here but us, the other guards, Oire, Uncle Rory, and Mister Rynam from the funeral parlour. We do not need the grand display right now, we need family."

"Oh, well, if it is what the lady wishes..." Keneth began to say, his voice showing a lesion in his stern, military-bred demeanour.

"It is, Uncle Ken," Marigold confirmed while using the name she had called him by since she was but a little girl.

Keneth nodded and gestured loosely at the guardsmen. "You heard the lady, lads. Be as you will."

"Let's close the doors, Uncle Ken," Marigold suggested, walking around him and standing off to the side of the steel barriers, coming to stand beside an iron mechanism built into the wall.

Calling on Rus to help him, Keneth brought the two heavy doors together, until the latch within clicked and they went still. "It's all on you now, Marigold." Keneth told her before adding a further question, "Do you need any assistance?"

"I shall try on my own first, if I may," she replied while pointing the blade of the sword at the circular device using both hands.

There was a slot housing the scabbard of the sword and Marigold slid the blade in until it could almost go no further. The crossguard of the sword was angled toward the blade and cut into teeth like that of a key. It was only when lined up properly before the sword that the teeth could be fully inserted. Once all was in place, Marigold began to turn the sword slowly, hearing the gears within the wall slowly revolve with difficulty, their parts likely in need of oil and grease.

The turning came to a stall just short of the needed ninety-degree turn and no amount of Marigold's pushing could make it continue.

From behind her there were footfalls and she heard Rory softly say, "May I, Mari? The lock is terribly old and needs maintenance. It is known to stick right where you have it, so it is of no embarrassment. We will turn it together, if you would like."

"Very well, Uncle. Here, take half of the crossguard with me," Marigold responded, relenting to his aid.

Together they got the sword to complete the revolution, coming to a stop with a loud clank. Marigold moved to draw the sword and scabbard from the slot as one, but only the sword was returning.

"The scabbard tends to stick," Rory explained, while reaching a hand in between the sheath and the iron casing of the device. "I remember that from when we laid my mother to rest. The previous undertaker, old Clysmere, had an ordeal of a time trying to get it loose, but Marscal knew the trick to it and took care of it." Rory pried a piece of the leather casing free from where it seemed to be pinched and bid Marigold to try again. "I paid close attention myself, for just such an occasion."

On the second attempt, the sword and scabbard came free in her hands, and she collected the pair in her arms. "Thank you, Uncle," Marigold said appreciatively.

She turned toward Keneth commencing with what was the last of the traditions she intended to follow through with that day, as it was one of great sentimental importance. "I bid thee to kneel, Ser Keneth, son of House Arisborough and defender of House Tullivan." Marigold began, the sword held out in her hands toward him. "I hereby appoint you, the Captain of our Guard and a distinguished friend of Marscal Tullivan, as Keeper of the Crypts and bestow to your protection the sword of my ancestor, Ser Davis."

From where he knelt, Keneth stretched out his hands and accepted the blade, reciting the responding passage from memory. "I, Keneth, son of House Arisborough and defender of House Tullivan, accept the appointment to the position of Keeper of the Crypts as so offered by Marigold, heir apparent to House Tullivan, and the interim Lady of Daol Bay and the Western Realm of Illiastra. I vow that from this day to my last that I shall serve with the honour and dignity befitting such a vaunted station."

"Then rise, Ser Keneth, and be henceforth known as Keeper of the Crypts of House Tullivan," Marigold uttered in completion of the ritual.

Dating back to the year that the crypt was completed, the title of Keeper of the Crypts was given to the captain of the household guard of the Tullivan family at the time of the master's death. As a new master came into the role, so too would they bring with them a new captain of the guard, and the former would be retired with pension. The watching of the tomb was indeed a privilege, but one that came with little activity beyond the safeguarding of the ceremonial surrogate sword of Ser Davis' that served as a key. Contrary to the rules of old, Marigold did not intend to send Keneth into retirement. However, on the surface, the act of Keneth transitioning out of the captaincy would free him for a leadership position within any military that Marigold might have to carve out of the western portion of Illiastra's armed forces.

His replacement as Captain of the Guards will require a little further thought, not that the transition need happen overnight, anyway. There will be time for that later.

The voice of Rory cut through the sudden silence. "My lady and gentlemen, I move that we bid farewell to the crypts and go embrace our reception guests at the manor."

"I agree, Uncle Rory," Marigold acquiesced. "The sun shall slip beneath the waves in but a few moments. Let us be off while it can still afford us some measure of light."

The guards lined up for a final salute to the crypts and turned toward Marigold, where they formed a line. Each man in their turn approached, shook her hand, and offered their final condolences and thanks to Marigold for the honour of being chosen as a bearer of the pall. After the guardsmen had their say, the funeral director approached, and it was Marigold's turn to offer thanks and gratitude for the services of his parlour and attentive staff. Lastly were Oire and Rory, arriving in front of her together. She hugged both men tightly one after the other, the embrace of each quite nearly drawing tears that Marigold successfully choked back.

When all was settled, Marigold gave leave to the party to get underway for the walk back to the manor. The men obeyed, leaving the porch as Marigold stood back on her own, waiting for their departure so that she might be alone for a moment. She stepped to the long, brass plate and raised a hand to just above her line of sight, feeling for the embossed lettering she knew to be there.

'Erected in Loving Memory of Farren Tullivan, a Princess of the Aurorais Family, and Felixander, the son she shared with Lord Marscal Tullivan.'

The metal marker was as much as could be done, given that Marigold's mother and brother had no graves of which to speak. Above their names was a partial bust of Farren, emerging sadly from the plate, her eyes cast westerly towards her home in the Northern Kingdom of Gildriad. Further below and taking nearly the entirety of the plate were the lyrics of a song written about Marigold's mother by a local musician and songwriter named Shayle the Spirit. Titled *Princess Far Away, it* was a song as melancholy as the bust's expression above and one Marigold had long committed to memory.

I hope that what I am about to do this night will make her and Father proud.

Leaving the plaque and the crypts behind, Marigold joined the men already standing in wait on the path leading to the manor. Outside of their footsteps and the waves rolling against the rocks and cliffs of the bay below, their trek was one of silence for the first half. The path wended away from the sea and wound itself through a grove of maple trees, the winter winds having already robbed their branches of the leaves.

Casually paced steps of nearly two dozen boots crunched their way through the fallen foliage and dusting of snow. During their wordless march, Marigold could only guess at what the others were thinking. Her own thoughts, though, revolved around her father. It felt to her as though a great wound had been inflicted across her entire body, one she might bleed out and die from at any second. When she closed her eyes at all, even to blink, she saw his face. Once opened again, she was reminded, with an almost stabbing jolt of anguish, that Marscal Tullivan was gone forever.

The flame of his life, and with it his presence in the world, was extinguished. Snuffed out callously by a disease that had torn him apart from the inside out in a way no other enemy ever could. It was a cruelty Marigold was still attempting to come to terms with, even days apart from Marscal's passing.

Atop of all the pain she bore for her father, Marigold felt as if she were entirely alone in the world, with no one to see her through. Granted, she had family members and allies, both near and abroad, and even a sister somewhere in the Known World. Regardless of any friends or living relations that Marigold had, her loneliness cried out into the cold evening.

By contrast, when Marigold's mother and brother were lost, Marigold still had Serephanie and their father to rely on. Together, the three had coped with the devastating blow, and in that bond, they found the strength they needed to heal.

Now, my grief must be faced alone. There's no one in need of my shoulder to lean on, and neither is there one for me.

The path ahead opened wide to meet the road that ran in front of the manor, now illuminated by outdoor lamp lighting. The hearse carriage stood before the gates, with the undertaker's assistant sitting in the driver's seat, reins in hand.

"Mister Rynam," Marigold uttered softly to get the director's attention. "I offer my deepest and sincerest thanks once more for all your efforts in arranging my father's funeral services. Even with payment, I assure you that House Tullivan is in your debt. Please, I would be honoured if you and your apprentice joined us for the reception at that manor. You would be my honoured guests."

"You are too kind, my lady," Rynam replied with the gentlest of laughs. "The honour is mine to have served for House Tullivan for all these years. On behalf of Roybal and myself, I must unfortunately decline the invitation, though. We simply must return to the funeral parlour in order to stable our horses and begin tidying everything up. I am, admittedly, a stickler for such, and it would be difficult for me to be at a function knowing what work I have left undone."

With a polite half bow, Marigold gave him leave to go. "If that is your wish, Mister Rynam, then I shall not keep you further. Thank you again for everything, and I bid you and Roybal a good evening."

"You are more than welcome, and I thank you for your understanding," Rynam replied with a tip of his black felt top hat. "I wish you well on the road ahead." He was gone then, departing from their company with surprising haste for a stooped septuagenarian.

The rest of the entourage were looking at Marigold then, waiting on her cue to return to the manor.

"Gentlemen, our company awaits," Marigold declared after a deep breath. "Rory, Oire, and Keneth, you three will be at my side. The remaining six will be expected at your usual posts. While it is guard duty I ask of you, I also expect no behaviour that will warrant action."

She smiled at them as much as could be mustered in her state of exhaustion, wondering if the expression came across as tired as she was. "So please, eat and drink as you would like, but be mindful to keep your wits about you. The order for the night is to be at ease, yet at the ready should the unexpected occur. Are there any questions?"

"Yes, there is one concern that I still have," Rory offered with a hand raised to shoulder height. "Can we not postpone this until tomorrow or perhaps until later in the week? I fear that it will be seen as callous of you to turn a reception for your father's funeral into a political grandstand. We would risk losing the message entirely."

Oire cleared his throat before speaking up, "With all due respect, Rory, there is no other time but now. Word of Lord Marscal's passing is already heading toward Atrebell and Hercalest as we speak. Once Eamon Palomb has that word, he will come, with those sons of his in tow. Right now, we have our city councillors, almost every minister of the western half of Illiastra, and even one from the east in Minister Felton, at the manor.

The two members of her counsel were staring one another down then, Marigold noticed, with Oire's stern gaze being met with a look of disconcertion behind Rory's pursed lips.

Without waiting for Rory to say anything further, Oire went on talking. "Between this moment and the day that the Palombs arrive to seize everything, we will not have the entirety of the western power in one room again. This is our lady's time to stake her claim. It will not be tomorrow, it certainly cannot be later in the week, so it must be now."

Marigold looked then to the Captain of the Manor Guards. "Uncle Ken, what do you think? Care to have your say?"

"It may not be my place to speak, my lady," Keneth offered carefully. "Social pageantry is hardly my area of expertise."

"Perhaps not, but warfare tactics are. What is our strife with the Palombs if not a war of words? You served in your fair share of conflicts in the Crescent Isles, both as a soldier and as an officer, so tell me, what do the scholars of strategy say about first engagement?"

Rory scoffed in disbelief. "We are calling it warfare already, Niece?"

Marigold countered quickly, "The Palombs' attempted grab for power would be considered conquest by most, but since I plan to fight back, then yes, war seems to be the correct term. Uncle Ken, would you care to respond?"

"I believe you are referring to the element of surprise," Keneth surmised with certainty. "Every tactician worth their weight in salt will try to take their enemy off guard in the first encounter, and continually so, for as long as their enemy will fall for it. If our enemy is Eamon Palomb and his brood, then Marigold's acts of both refusing to yield to them and outright resisting their incursion into the Western Realm would definitely catch them unawares."

"My worry is not catching the Palombs off guard rather it is how they will react to *being* caught off guard," Rory stated firmly. "The more immediate concern though, is what those men waiting for us in the manor will do."

Before anyone else could venture to respond, Marigold took the reins, "There will be those who balk at me. I expect that from both the most ardent and cowardly supporters of the eastern houses. However, I think that there will be enough who keep loyalty with the Tullivans. Perhaps there might even be a few whose loyalties are not necessarily sworn to me, but are otherwise ready to embrace a new way. Regardless, it is my hope that I have the numbers enough for it to mean something. In order for me to do that, though, I will need all of you to show them that I have your support. Do I have that, Uncle Rory?"

"You do, Niece, I promise you, but please forgive me for being nervous," Rory stammered out after a long swallow.

"It is alright, Uncle Rory, I too am nervous," Marigold allowed herself to admit aloud. "This has to be done tonight, though. I will give you a few minutes if you need it to compose yourself, and then we press onward. Are you with me?"

Rory let a nod serve as an answer and Marigold turned away from him to Keneth. "Uncle Ken, I'll leave the positioning of the guardsmen to you. I would like their presence felt, but not in a manner that might be seen as threatening. The goal is to show the ministers that I will do no harm, but neither will I give them the opportunity to do so to me."

"I shall see to it at once, Mari," Keneth affirmed without pause. With a motion of his hand, he drew the guardsmen into a circle to give them their orders.

The ushering of the guards left Marigold standing beside Oire and Rory, the latter of whom had taken to doing deep breathing exercises in an effort to calm his nerves. While the three waited, Marigold caught snippets of what Keneth was telling the others. From what

Marigold could discern it seemed that Keneth's plan was to put the youngest and strongest guards at the closest positions to where Marigold would be. That being at the landing of the stairs in the foyer, which was the only room large enough to host everyone simultaneously.

The elder swordsmen, like Darrill and Rus, would be on the primary exit, putting them the farthest away, but also in a position to observe those who might otherwise go unseen. To add to that reasoning, Keneth noted that should anyone leave during Marigold's announcement, the oldest soldiers would be more likely to know the identities of the departing.

A rogue gust of wind rushed through the grove, lifting Marigold's cloak and sending chills down her arms. Unlike earlier at the crypts, Marigold now felt the cold. Regardless, she would not interrupt Keneth's planning just to hurry them all inside. Instead, she pulled her cloak tight with one hand, turned her face to the ground, and braved the gales.

"If there are questions, this is your chance to ask them, lads," Marigold heard Keneth declare in a tone that sounded as though it would indeed hear any inquiries through.

There was one, and it came from Elden, the most recent recruit to the Tullivan guardsmen, and the largest, standing considerably taller and broader than all the rest. "Ser Keneth, is there a plan in place in the event that things get violent tonight?"

"There won't be any violence, Elden," Keneth told him, his voice clear on the matter.

"With all due respect, Ser," Elden began in reply. "How can you be so sure?"

Keneth came back with an answer without pause. "Because these are soft little lordlings, Elden, and most of them would not even know how to grow violent, at least not with anyone or anything capable of hitting back. That's why they hire men like us to do the fighting for them. As it stands, the only men like us in the manor tonight are our own, and as long as we are guarding the lady, not one of those powdered fops will dare lay a finger on her."

"Careful, Keneth," Oire spoke up, having been listening in as well, "Miss Marigold needs those *powdered fops* to side with her. Granted, we are in trusted company at present, but one never knows where enemy ears might be eavesdropping."

There was a flicker of realisation on Keneth's face, before returning to his usual, measured state. "You are correct, Oire, as always. Please, forgive me Mari if I have said too much."

"There's nothing to forgive, Uncle Ken," Marigold told him bluntly. "As Oire mentioned, we are amongst friends here, and I trust each of you with my life. With that said, I must ask if we are ready to depart. Our company will not wait forever."

After double-checking with the other guards, Keneth confirmed their preparedness with Marigold, and the party set out for the manor with haste. They marched to the gates, with Marigold and Oire flanked on all sides by the men in uniforms, Rory included. At the cast-iron entrance, they were met by a pair of city guards, they being two among over a dozen that were assigned to watch over the manor grounds for the day.

Upon the approach of Marigold, Oire, and the pallbearers, the city guards gave greetings and condolences as they swung open the gates for the party. In return, Marigold thanked them for the gesture and their service at the manor, and, to the evident surprise of everyone, dismissed the entirety of the city guards for the evening.

"Are... Are you sure, Miss Marigold?" one among the pair asked, while sharing a puzzled glance with the other.

"I am entirely sure, Ser. Go tell the others and ride for home. Your duty is done," Marigold stated firmly.

The first guard seemed at a loss for words at that moment, so the second spoke for them, "It will be as you wish, Miss Marigold."

She thanked them again and ushered them off to relay the message to the other city guards. When alone, she turned to the others, "There is such a thing as too much of an armed presence. Having more than the manor guards about might be seen as heavy-handed."

"That's... Fair, actually," Rory offered with a head tilt as he considered her words.

The others held their tongues on the matter, with a few, namely Oire, nodding in agreement. Underway once more, the group strode across the walkway, climbed the steps of the porch, and pushed open the doors.

Inside was heat, washing over them as they stepped across the threshold. Men and women dressed in funeral black were mingling about, with most of them sipping brandy and wine from the Tullivan's fine glassware. None had seemed to take notice of Marigold's arrival and she felt it was all for the better, as it gave her time to take in the room before she would have to respond to it.

The under butlers, maids, and footmen of the house were dutifully doting on the guests, running to and fro with decanters of alcoholic beverages and trays of finger foods. Having shed tears with so many of those same servants over the last few days, Marigold could not have been more proud seeing them work through their grief.

I do not deserve their service, truly, Marigold thought to herself warmly. *They deserve as handsome a payment as I can manage when all of this is done, if nothing else.*

The men and women being tended on were familiar faces as well. Over the years, she had come to know all of the lords and ministers of Illiastra to varying degrees, but it was the westerners she knew best, and all but one were accounted for.

Standing near the stairs side by side were Walter and Elda Mattersly, the husband being the minister of the most southerly region of the western realm, Tippard. Their family enterprise was shipbuilding, and their fortunes were made selling fine vessels all around the Known World. The couple speaking with Walter and Elda were of a house that bore large responsibility for the global expansion of Mattersly's veritable empire, the Simillons of Portsward. The current Lord, Greggard, was the second of their family to have been the Lord of International Trade of Illiastra, itself a position of major influence and importance amongst even the lordships. Both families were key components of Marigold's plan, and she could only hope that they would live up to expectations.

Closer at hand Marigold spotted ministers Vensent Rochford II and Lorence Fields, of Ardwyle Harbour and of Gethingston, respectively, two of the more sizeable regions in terms of population figures. On the opposite side of the room was Madore Isles' minister, Leo Daltis, whose son Marigold knew quite well. Daltis' company at present were Norrin Obarrow of Lakespere and Haymard Nothram of Pelican Harbour. Minister Obarrow presided over the west's lone landlocked region, a lushly forested natural wonderland centred on a sizable, pristine lake of breath-taking beauty. Meanwhile, Nothram's region was defined by its large harbour that was sparse in terms of people, but strangely overrun with the seabirds of which it was named.

Out of the three, both Nothram and Daltis were among the ministers that Marigold believed would be the most difficult to sway.

Marigold felt that Daltis was cowardly, an opinion she had formed after spending countless days in Parliament watching Leo bend to whatever whims Eamon Palomb's majority of ministers drafted. When not in a state of constant capitulation in Parliament, Leo Daltis was residing in Galdourn, refusing to sail to the cluster of islands off Illiastra's coast that he was given to rule. A plenipotentiary handled things in Daltis' stead, and Marigold did not know if it was seafaring or leadership that scared Daltis more, or if it was perhaps both in tandem. Regardless, she felt it would be a task to sway Daltis' fearful mind to her risky proposition.

In Nothram's case, the issue was quite the opposite. Nothram being a stubborn mule of a man whose beliefs seemed to align completely with those of Eamon Palomb.

Haymard Nothram would never side with me. I know it will be a fight with him for even the smallest of concessions.

Marigold knew without hyperbole that Nothram was far from alone in that matter. There were others in the room that were not quite as unyielding in their bigotry as Nothram, but nonetheless, they would be of similar difficulty to win over.

Steffard, Jennis, and Slake, those three will almost certainly be in Nothram's camp. As for Slake, I might be able to work with him, given the dependence that Galdourn has on Daol Bay. The other two though...

Then she laid eyes on Samhais Morton, an amiable, soft-spoken man who presided over the Weicaster Bay region. The man with the gentlest nature of the western ministers was also one of the most powerful, as the city of Weicaster was the third largest in the Western Realm.

He would be as unlikely to swing to Marigold's side as Nothram, she knew, but for a different reason than any other minister: his sister, Jorette, was the wife of Eamon Palomb, and the mother of Eamon's four children.

Samhais is a kindly, agreeable man, but he's tied to the Palombs by blood. I am not even sure what sort of deal I could possibly make to persuade his hand. I will try, though, if given the chance.

From her left side, Marigold caught sight of Lewinson, the head butler of the manor, approaching with a hurried stride. She was about to address him until Lewinson went straight for Oire, and upon getting his attention, began whispering in his ear.

She was seconds away from inquiring into what Lewinson and Oire were conversing about when a man's voice spoke to her from the right.

"Good evening, Miss Marigold," he began in a smooth voice tinged ever so slightly with an accent from one of the Crescent Isles' nations.

In turning, Marigold came to lay eyes on Gallin Myakys, Minister of Kylisport. His region was of modest size, but was an economic stronghold owing to rich soil that allowed for a robust crop yield that could be matched only by Lakespere among the westerly regions. Minister Myakys himself was about a decade or so older than Marigold and on the taller side, with a solid frame that was clearly given care and attention. His face was long, with sad, brown eyes, but his smile was warm and genuine. The thing that stood Myakys apart from the rest, though, was a head of long, black braided hair and a dark complexion. There were no other ministers in any part of Illiastra that were of such dark skin, and though his ancestors had emigrated to Illiastra nearly three centuries prior, Gallin Myakys still faced prejudicial treatment from other Illiastran folk as a result.

For their own part, Marigold and her family had always treated Gallin and his family with the utmost respect, and she considered the House of Myakys to be honourable to a fault. Foremost of all, Marigold recalled that the Myakys' were one of the few families that were genuinely liked by their subjects in the era of the Elite Merchants. That alone told Marigold as much as she needed to know.

"I bid a good evening to you as well, Minister Myakys," Marigold replied, trying to offer a smile of her own. "Thank you so much for coming. I trust that your parents made the journey as well. Our fathers were such good friends, after all."

That seemed to bring some light to Gallin's eyes, and he responded in kind, "They did, Miss Marigold, and my wife as well. The four of us were so sorry to hear of your father's passing. My mother was particularly grieved, and my wife and father escorted her back to our hotel room after the truly beautiful service at the Tower of Ios. In turn, I came to the manor alone, to offer my family's sincerest condolences to you and yours. If there is anything my family can do, you need only say the word and I shall see to it personally, Miss Marigold."

Marigold offered him half a bow with her reply, "I may well take you up on that, Minister Myakys, and I thank you for your condolences. It has been a trying time for us all, but we shall persevere. My father would want no less."

Gallin laughed softly. "I agree wholeheartedly, Miss Marigold. You know, when my oldest uncle passed away, your father came to the service in Kylisport. He spent some time with my father, who was trying to mask the intense pain he was feeling. Lord Marscal told my father something that he later passed on to me, and I would return to you in kind: 'Grief is not weakness so much as it is an expression of love for those we have lost'. My father thought that being in a state of bereavement made him look weak to everyone, but your father had words for him then too. He said, 'Never doubt your strength in times of trouble, for though it may seem strained, you are witnessing how strong you actually are'."

"That does indeed sound like something my father would say," Marigold offered back, breathing deeply as she began to feel tears welling in her eyes.

When she looked back at Gallin again, his gaze had gone to her left side. "Perhaps I should not keep you any longer, Miss Marigold. Mister Lewinson looks eager to get your attention, and he is a busy fellow. I do apologise if my words upset you, though. It was not my intention."

"Upset me?" Marigold replied in a voice that she hoped sounded as strong as she thought it might be. "No, on the contrary, Minister Myakys, your words were exactly what I needed to hear. Thank you for telling me such."

With a last farewell, Gallin bowed and left her company. As his back turned, Lewinson gently laid a hand on her left arm. "How do you fare, Miss Marigold? Shall I go ahead and introduce you to everyone or do you still need a moment to compose yourself?"

"I am as ready as ever I will be. You may proceed," Marigold said quickly, regretting it just as fast for not having inquired into what Lewinson and Oire were whispering about.

"Lords, ministers, councillors, and distinguished gentlemen, and ladies, please allow me a moment of your attention," Lewinson called out loudly, waiting until the room fell silent before continuing. "It is my pleasure to introduce you this evening to Marigold Tullivan, daughter and heir-apparent of the late Lord Marscal, her uncle and brother of our late Lord Marscal, Rory Tullivan, and the bearers of the pall."

It seemed to Marigold that everyone turned in unison to face the front of the room to look upon the few gathered in the porch. There was silence for a beat, and Marigold had time to look back at Keneth and give him an affirmative nod, prompting him to step forward so that he might lead the way to the staircase.

Gentle applause broke out as soon as Marigold took her first step and she paused and bowed appreciatively at the threshold of the foyer. Keneth seemed to be in wait for a lapse in the applauding that seemed not to come, and Marigold nudged him onward, following close behind him as he cleared a path through the people.

Keneth slowed further as the crowd struggled to make way, and Marigold felt Oire brush up behind her. She craned her neck back in his direction while they waited momentarily, "What was Lewinson in such a rush to tell you, might I ask?"

"Nothing of immediate importance, I assure you, my lady," Oire replied directly in her ear. "I will tell you later tonight or tomorrow, at the latest."

Marigold thanked him and left the matter aside for the nonce, with a far more pressing task so near at hand. Glancing above the crowd as much as she could, she saw a number of the guardsmen walking beside the walls to her left and right, surrounding everyone seemingly unnoticed.

A number of the gathered spoke to her as she passed with offerings of both greetings and condolences. Nora Cunningsbee, wife of the minister of the same surname from Davring Harbour region, reached a hand out to briefly hold Marigold's, an action nearly repelled by Elden, who had been walking directly behind Oire.

Before Elden could come between him, Marigold pivoted and put her free hand atop his, "Thank you, Elden, but it is quite alright." Her gaze went directly to Nora Cunningsbee, and she gripped the woman's hand a little tighter. "Thank you, Missus Cunningsbee, I appreciate the gesture."

"Be strong, Miss Marigold. We are with you," she said in response, releasing her grip immediately after saying so.

A few steps later and they arrived at the staircase, and Keneth stepped aside to allow Marigold access. "The floor is yours, my lady," he told her in the process, his formality having returned in full force.

Marigold climbed to the landing, laid her hands on the varnished oak bannister railing, and looked out across the foyer as it erupted into applause for her. Almost the entire ministerial body of the west stood below, with most of their wives, and the councillors of Daol Bay and Portsward, and even a scant few of the same title from further away. There was a handful of Triarchy clergy amongst the crowd as well, standing out from the sea of black in their gaudy burgundy robes, and Newell Felton of Obalen, the lone eastern minister.

Felton is the only easterner in close enough proximity to make it in time, but he will more than suffice to tell Grenjin Howland and the Palombs of what he saw.

The lone absentee whose presence was expected at such an event was Harold Bickerington, Minister of the Tusker's Cove region. His dominion was the collection of outport villages situated between Portsward and the region's namesake, itself perched on the northernmost border between human Illiastra and the Snowy Lands, home of the dwarven people. The only roadway connecting the human-inhabited northern coast to the remainder of the west was the remnants of the Dwarven Highway, a wonder of the world from ancient times. What once had been a remarkable sight was reduced to a decrepit pathway that wound perilously around tall cliffs and deep gulches, just waiting to send the unwary to their deaths in the icy sea.

As a result, Minister Bickerington and the citizens of the north typically travelled by ship. The sea travel made for long journeys, especially when compared to the locomotives usually frequented by Bickerington's contemporaries. Atop that, Bickerington was a common man who captained a fishing fleet, and as such, most of his time was spent upon the frigid northern waters, far from contact. He attended parliamentary functions insomuch as he was required to in order to keep from being expelled, but otherwise was not seen in the public eye. It gave the Tusker's Cove region an almost roguish autonomy, as they took care of themselves and usually did not interfere in national matters. Due to his frequent absences, Bickerington gave permission for his parliamentary vote to be cast at the behest of his closest ally, both geographically and politically, Greggard Simillon.

If I can win Greggard's support, I shall not only have the allegiance of the west's lone lord, but I will gain Bickerington's vote in the process. Greggard always seemed eager to bury the grudge that our families bore from our grandfathers' era, so now would be his time to make good on that.

A firm lowering of both hands from Keneth ended the applause. The old soldier craned his head to where Marigold stood, and everyone else followed, putting the focus of the room squarely on her.

With a deep breath, Marigold cast her worries and fears aside and addressed the gathered masses.

"Lords, ministers, councillors, distinguished gentlemen, and ladies of the west," Marigold began, ensuring her voice was at a volume to be carried across the room with authority. "I humbly thank you all for attending the funeral service for my dearly departed father and our Warden Lord of the West, Marscal Tullivan. There is little doubt that he would be deeply honoured to know that so many rushed out of their way to pay their final respects.

"The days ahead will be trying for all who knew him, especially myself, my uncle Rory, our family, and our staff who cared for him so well throughout the years. Their selfless duty in the face of tragedy does not go unnoticed."

Mentioning the staff sent murmurs through the crowd, as their servants work was rarely given public appreciation, unless it was in an act of valour. Paying due regard to the employees gave Marigold a measure of the audience's limit for such breaches of protocol, and their apprehensive response was giving her second thoughts already. Regardless, she steeled her resolve and pressed onward.

"My father was a man of great perseverance, determination, and willpower, and I endeavour to follow bravely in his footsteps myself as I come to terms with the toll his loss is taking on me. It is as though the very heart and soul of the west has been pulled out, and the hole that is left behind seems impossible to fill.

"While Illiastra slept, I witnessed the closing of a chapter that, until then, I could not imagine having an ending. Those few hours after that are moments I will not forget. Everything was quiet, as though the world itself was giving silent respect to my father, and it was though I was in a state of limbo. With the breaking of the dawn, that moment passed and suddenly, I was thrust into the start of an era I was in no way ready for. It was an era where my father no longer existed."

Her voice threatened to break, and Marigold looked downward to the railing while she took a second to pull her sorrows back. Upon clearing her throat, she resumed her speech once more. "The morning after my father passed, I witnessed the rising of the sun over the eastern hills. I sat in the window of my quarters and watched the sunbeams dance their way out across Daol Bay, and in that light, the city slowly woke. Ships slipped their moorings and lowered their sails, horses were hitched to wagons and carriages to go about their deliveries, and the shops opened their doors one after the other.

"These simple daily routines reminded me that time stops for no person and that life is moving on even as we stand here. I realised that regardless of whether or not I am ready I must indeed join this new era, and even in its infancy, there are already decisions of great magnitude at my feet."

The room had been quiet all throughout Marigold's speech, but as she made mention of 'decisions', whispers began to carry from wall to wall like a wave.

Before anyone could raise questions, Marigold carried on, "In the coming days Lord Eamon Palomb, and his sons, Pyore and Eldridge, one of whom I am engaged to marry, will descend on Daol Bay. Until that time, by the laws of Illiastra, I am the heir apparent and interim Lady of Daol Bay. As your Lady, I humbly ask for your assistance and co-operation in handling the immediate matters of the Western Realm."

As she spoke, the whispers had grown into gasps and shocked voices. For a moment, Marigold considered leaving her speech at that, as doubt creeped its way into the back of her mind.

Either I fight for tomorrow at this moment, or I die a slow, agonising death as a prisoner of conscience, wishing all the while that I had tried to change the world. Today, I will show them the unshakeable poise of Maisera Tullivan and the iron will of Princess Farren of Aurorais. It is time that I made them proud.

Marigold raised a hand to gesture for silence, and waited until she had it before segueing into what had to be said. "Ladies and Gentlemen, I would like to give you a moment to consider what the west would be under the reign of House Palomb. Recall, if you will, that Eamon Palomb has spent a great deal of his time and no small expense to stripping the west of its lordships, leaving only House Tullivan and House Simillon with positions in the cabinet. Those were the actions of a man intent on muting the voice of the west. If Eamon and his sons are permitted to go through with the marriage pact, they will not unite the Tullivan and Palomb houses. There will be no grand union of east and west. We will just be swallowed completely and thoroughly."

The words were left to hang over the room for a moment, and Marigold took in the expressions of the ministers, finding puzzlement as often as she found worry. For the briefest of glances, she caught Lord Greggard with his mouth turned upward at one corner, and as their eyes met, his brows flicked, begging her to continue.

What was that just now? Marigold thought to herself for half a second, dismissing it so that she might move on.

"The first to vanish will be House Tullivan. Our name will go to the crypt with my father, and Palomb will replace it. After that, they will come for the last lord in the west: Greggard Simillon, Lord of International Trade and Relations. That position and my father's fisheries portfolio are the only lordships Eamon could not take, due to the facts that they both relied on the seas, and the only port under eastern control is Aquas Bay in the Southlands. If Eamon can install one of his sons here and bide his time until that son can succeed Grenjin Howland in Atrebell too, then there is nothing whatsoever standing between the Palombs and absolute control of this country.

"When my family is gone and Greggard's stripped of their lordship, who among you will have the confidence to say that he will not remove my father's friends too? Nearly all of you here have voted against Eamon's legislation in the past and stood by my father through thick and thin, and I assure you, Eamon Palomb does not forget the loyalty shown to those who would impede his grab for power.

"There is one thing that Eamon Palomb has overlooked though: I do not forget either. The memory of my treatment at the hands of Eldridge and Pyore is fresh in my mind. Pyore's hand that nearly struck me, their cruel jests towards my sister and I for years before, their disgusting treatment of nearly every person who could not oppose them, I remember it all."

For a moment, Marigold paused, taking the brief lapse to look over the gathered and gauge their reactions thus far. There were many a blank expression looking back at her, and here and there, what might be called optimistic smiles, but mostly, Marigold saw fear and uncertainty by then. The clergy were angered, as she knew they all would be, but she could not dwell on their woes. Beyond the religious representatives, Marigold noted that it was the elder ministers who were looking truly worried. Crossing the Palomb family was a terrifying prospect, something Marigold knew better than most in attendance, but she was not done trying to convince the ministers that it was the right decision.

"That is why I would stand against the encroachment of the Palomb family," Marigold declared, causing a tidal wave of shock to roll through the gathered.

"Heresy!" shouted one of the clergy that Marigold did not recognise. "A woman will not lead us, now or ever!"

"Just so!" another called out, and Marigold looked to find Minister Haymard Nothram with a raised hand. "*The Proclamation of Ios* states that, 'women are to defer authority to their husbands, fathers, and the menfolk of their community', in that order. Is that not correct, Patriarch Leville?"

The same Triarchist called back, "Just so, Minister! We will not bow to a woman."

Minster Walter Mattersly stepped forward, climbing a single step of the staircase, giving him a position just above the crowd. "Good fellows, should we not conduct ourselves as gentlemen? Let Miss Marigold speak uninterrupted."

That was unexpected, Marigold noted, trying to cover her surprise and seize on the opportunity granted to her by Minister Mattersly.

"Thank you, Minister Mattersly," Marigold stated sincerely, before capitalising on the momentum. "I admit that what I propose comes with great risk, but so too does the decision to let the Palombs take everything for their own. You look upon me and see a woman and perhaps many of you believe me weak because of it. Yet, were I as pathetic as that, would I even be standing here before you proposing what the Palombs will view as treason?

"I do this knowing that I am practically tying my own noose should I fail. Despite this, I stand before you today with no regret, for I know that this is the right course, not just for Daol Bay and those of us gathered here, but for the entire Western Realm, and every man, woman and child within. All I ask is that you stand with me and show the Palombs that the West shall not surrender to their rule."

For a moment Marigold stopped herself, letting what was said up to that point have the time to be absorbed and discussed amongst the noblemen. Then, she locked eyes with the closest woman, whom she identified as Talara, the wife of Minister Fields of Gethingston, and segued into her next gambit. "Imagine a Western Realm free of eastern influence, one where women have a say."

She moved her focus to a different woman, this time finding her way to Elda Mattersly. "I would make that a reality, not just for myself, but for all of womankind."

"Do we not deserve a voice as much as any man?" Marigold asked rhetorically while meeting eyes with Gloria, wife of Yancey Morren of Filkas.

At the end of each sentence, Marigold continued to find a new woman to speak to directly, trading between the noble's wives and her own staff alike. "We allow ourselves to be tucked away in the shadows by men, but I ask: is it not high time that we take back what was seized from us a century ago? How did we let ourselves lose the rights our ancestors bled and died for in the time of kings? Why, only eight hundred years ago, we could be knights. Eleanor Price was a knighted general to the last king and women served prominently in the ranks of her forces and those of the other generals of her time. Our own history books deny what I am about to tell you, but the records of Drake and the Gildraddi nations say that the third Master of Blades was a woman named Arvelle Seyanne. The deeds of her life suggest she was every bit as fierce and revered as Tryst Reine is now, yet Illiastran law prohibits us from even acknowledging that she existed.

"My grandfather may sit on the throne in Northern Gildriad at present, yet my family tree on my mother's side is as filled with as many ruling queens as it is kings. Those women presided over my mother's homeland as well as any kings or lord masters anywhere else in the world and helped build Northern Gildriad into the prosperous nation that it is today."

Marigold raised and stretched her arms outward toward the women before her. "My friends, I think it is high time that we reclaim our rights, and allow ourselves to live as freely as the Gildraddi women from which I descend. We, the women of Illiastra, deserve no less."

A polite applause began, starting with Wyla, a servant of the manor, of all people, and it grew, with Elda Mattersly joining in, and Greggard Simillon and his wife following suit. From there it spread, until a third of the women and a handful of men had joined in.

Several of the clergymen were all looking about as fast as their heads could turn. Some seemed like they were trying to take note of those who were cheering, while others were in disbelief at the sight before them. Two of them, a patriarch and his acolyte, were staring at

Marigold directly, hatred searing in their eyes. She smirked at the older of the two, holding her own stare until he averted his gaze in disgust.

Once the clapping had ebbed, Marigold gestured a single hand wide over the room. "To the men here standing before me, I would remind you that women regaining the rights we once enjoyed does not infringe upon the rights you already hold. In fact, whether it is women, queer folk, coloured folk, dwarves, elves, or half-elves gaining rights, you still lose nothing. Far too often, that distinction is lost in the debate, but it bears reminding that giving rights to others takes no rights from you."

I might as well give them my whole agenda now. We are too far down the path to turn back, she decided quickly while bracing herself for the reaction that her words would almost certainly have.

"However, there is one segment of society that I would free whose liberation would affect the ruling class: Illiastra's enslaved and indentured workers. One thing I am proud to say though is that such a proclamation would have little impact on the Western Realm, as there are but a few who purchase their workforce from Biddenhurst or elsewhere."

Marigold raised a fist and laid it against her chest as she prepared to put the men before her to the test. "With my intentions and desires laid bare before you all, I ask of councillor, minister, and lord alike, who among you will stand with me?"

It seemed that everyone was looking anywhere but at Marigold at that point, talking in hushed voices among one another. The fear and shock on the faces of everyone gave Marigold a sinking feeling in the pit of her stomach and she could almost feel her plan slipping into nothingness.

The sound of Haymard Nothram's voice cut through the pack, and when Marigold found him in the group, she discovered him to have moved to the front, putting him mere feet away from Elden and Sydnee, who were guarding from upon the third step of the staircase. "Rory, surely you will not abide this nonsense from a distraught and hysterical woman in the throes of grief. Tell me that you still have your wits about you and I will sign as witness to her madness, so that she can be relieved of her duty. We will have her committed to the madhouse if need be."

All eyes, Marigold's included, fell to Rory, and the uncle and niece shared a brief glance before the former gave answer to Nothram. "My allegiance and confidence is with Marigold, whom I recognise as the Lady of House Tullivan. I assure you, Haymard, she is of sound mind and body. Furthermore, I share in her belief that Eamon Palomb will be a detriment to the Western Realm."

"Has madness consumed all you Tullivans?" The hateful patriarch that Marigold espied earlier cried out.

Nothram pressed on, stepping to the same height as Walter Mattersly and two steps below the pair of guards. "Ser Keneth, surely you must have sense then? If not him, then perhaps you, Steward Oire, a nobleman yourself by birth? Tell me that this whole house is not vexed."

Keneth brought his fist into a salute against his chest, "I am sworn to House Tullivan and its overseer. It is my duty to assist in whatever decisions this house so makes, regardless of my own interests or opinions."

"I am glad to hear that you do not agree with Marigold's ramblings, Ser Keneth," Nothram stated presumptuously, earning him a disdainful glare from Keneth.

"On the contrary, Minister Nothram," Keneth countered with unfazed confidence. "In this instance, I am wholly behind Miss Marigold, in body and conscience."

"She has my undying support as well, without any hesitation," Oire added proudly. "The Lady of the House is wise to resist the aggressive advances of House Palomb. Their will is to subjugate all before them, barring none."

Marigold raised both hands to silence the crowd, which had been steadily growing more raucous. "People, please, I beg you for order!" The request was repeated twice more, and still it went unheeded. Keneth stepped up to the bannister and looked about to yell, when Marigold laid a hand against his chest. "Please, allow me, Uncle Ken," she offered before a deep breath was taken.

"SILENCE!"

The room fell quiet as one, with all eyes going directly to Marigold, and she let her gaze wash over them slowly before uttering another word. "Now that you have seen the unyielding support that the men of my own house have for me, I ask you again: who among you is prepared to support me as the Lady of Daol Bay and the Western Realm?"

From below Marigold on the bottom step, Walter Mattersly cleared his throat and declared, "I will stand with Marigold Tullivan."

"Such ridiculousness from a man of your standing, Minister Mattersly!" Nothram exclaimed, while eying down Walter. "You are under no duress to support such lunacy like the other three."

"And yet, I stand with the lady," Mattersly repeated once more. "The west should not go to House Palomb."

Nothram was facing the crowd then. "Do not entertain this nonsense further. This insanity need not go beyond the isolated ravings of a madwoman, her captive household, and a once-respected minister who has clearly descended into senility."

"She has my avouchment!" a man cried out, his hand darting up to be seen.

Restraining her elatedness at the sight of him, Marigold beckoned toward the speaker. "Come forward, Lord Simillon, and be heard."

"Perhaps my endorsement, as the lone lord remaining to the west, will carry some weight," Simillon suggested, as he ascended to a place beside Mattersly and Nothram. "For one, I think she is correct in her prediction that Eamon Palomb's western ambitions include the arrogation of my lordship. Indeed, it is something of an open secret that he has sought for years to give the position of Lord of International Trade to Minister Polliane in Aquas Bay. In fact, it has only been the direct intervention of both Lord Tullivan and Lord Master Howland that has stayed Palomb's intentions. For another, I happen to agree with the lady's intentions to grant rights to the silenced. Let it be known that henceforth, the future of House Simillon is intertwined with the future of House Tullivan, as always the ruling families of Twin Bay should have been."

A hand was raised in the crowd, and Marigold pointed toward its owner. "Yes, Minister Steffard, can I count on your support?"

"You may not, Miss Marigold," Lanly Steffard stated nervously, his eyes wide and fearful. "I would like to ask what you intend to do when the Palombs and Lord Master Howland are rebuffed at your gates. Will you let this come to bloodshed, if need be?"

With her head lowered in grave acknowledgement, Marigold gave response. "There is a chance that this could well lead to an intracontinental war, yes. That I do not deny. However, I stand steadfastly by my conclusion that the path that has the potential to lead to war is also the best way forward for the Western Realm of this country. To that end, with your support, I plan to direct all available resources toward every avenue that could possibly steer us away from such a catastrophe."

Minister Nothram let loose a loud chortle and cut in on the young minister. "There you have it, gentlemen. This woman is content to let us die by the thousands to avoid a wedding. Need we hear any further, or shall we dismiss her outright?"

"Here, here!" Ike Slake joined in, only to be interrupted by Lord Simillon.

"All the more reason to side with House Tullivan, I say," Greggard began in a tone that was almost ponderous in its delivery. "Think about it, my good people, who will Palomb and Howland dispatch against Daol Bay's might? It will not be their eastern armies, I assure you. The east will pit their western allies against Marigold's supporters, and then sit back and laugh at the hubris of the western houses who pledged loyalty to House Palomb. Just as Eamon Palomb was determined to give my lordship to Petor Polliane, he has an easterner in mind to take the place of every one of you too. Were we to go to war with ourselves at his behest, those replacements would be merely waiting to see who remained of us.

"If we show the east a united Western Realm, they will have but two choices: they can treat with us, or meet us on the battlefield directly, with no proxy to fight on their behalf. Should I maintain my allegiance with the Elite Merchants, my forces in Portsward would be the first to be ordered to the slaughter against Daol Bay. I would rather pool my resources with my neighbour and defend Twin Bay together, as I know we can."

Greggard has long wanted a better allegiance with Daol Bay than my father could give him. I did not think he would so readily seize on the chance, though.

A single man wove his way through the crowd, and Marigold could not help but smile at the sight of him. "I will stand behind House Tullivan as well," stated Gallin as he came to stand just below the step occupied by Mattersly, Simillon, and Nothram. "You may count House Myakys among your allies."

"Of course, the foreigners band together," Nothram snorted derisively. "A Vellicanese immigrant and a woman who is half Gildraddi. What a motley crew you two do make."

"My ancestors have been on Illiastran soil for centuries, Minister Nothram," Gallin intoned sternly while locking eyes with Haymard. "At some point you have to stop calling my family and I immigrants and accept that we are citizens of this country every bit as much as you are."

Nothram's nostrils flared and he moved to speak, but Marigold refused to give what she felt would be nothing less than racist remarks any opportunity to breathe. "Two ministers and a lord have come to stand bravely at my side. Are there any more among you? What of my city councillors? Will you join Rory and me?"

Leeman and Nora Cunningsbee came to the front, hand in hand, with Leeman speaking for them both. "House Cunningsbee favours House Tullivan. Davring Harbour is with you, Miss Marigold."

"That is enough of this!" Nothram shouted, and he made for the stairs, pushing by Walter Mattersly and nearly knocking him over into Gallin Myakys.

"You will go no further, Minister Nothram. Turn back at once, and no action will be taken towards you," Sydnee announced, while he and Elden remained firmly affixed to the step they shared.

Ignoring Sydnee's clear directions, Nothram tried to shove his way past, but the two younger, stronger men would not be moved.

"What in Ios' name are you trying to do, Minister?" Oire asked, as he and Keneth moved to where Nothram struggled against the guards.

"Stop your advances this instant or I will personally see you evicted from the manor," Keneth ordered gruffly, his tone suffering no rebuke.

Nothram stepped back and adjusted his jacket at the lapels. "You bunch of whimpering cuckolds. What poor excuse of a man would allow himself to be servile to a woman?"

"You may insult me as you will, Minister Nothram. I can take your barbs and jabs," Marigold stated with gusto. "But you will not insult my friends, family, or employees without repercussion. I hereby rescind your invitation to this manor and remind you that by law, any refusal to vacate the premises places you in the act of trespassing. Take your leave of this place at once, or be escorted out by my house protectors. The choice is yours to make."

"Very well, then. I shall take my leave," Nothram relented before turning around to face the crowd once again. "Those of you with sense to back our rightful rulers, the Lord Master Howland and Lord Palomb, I urge you to follow my lead in abandoning this manor and its insane inhabitants. Our respects to Lord Marscal Tullivan have been paid, and I consider myself to owe his memory nothing further. The Tullivan name, legacy, and all its holdings are yours to desecrate to your heart's content, Marigold. I just pray to Ios that the Palombs stop you before irreparable damage is done to Marscal's good name."

Once on the floor again, Nothram wended his way brusquely through the crowd, elbowing his way rudely by any who did not move quickly enough. As Haymard reached the doors separating the foyer and porch, Rus and Darrill swung them open and stepped in close to Nothram, doing so to prevent the disgruntled minister from returning. Butler Lewinson arrived with the man's outerwear but made no move to assist Nothram.

"Come with me now, or stand with a doomed, maddened woman," Nothram shouted back into the room from the porch. His voice took on a mocking tone as he quoted Marigold directly, "The choice is yours to make."

The outer door was flung open, being slammed shut again just as quickly. With the sound of the wooden doors colliding with their frame, a silence fell upon the foyer.

"Who else among you would stand with me for a unified Western Realm?" Marigold asked to those who remained, before Nothram's words could taint anyone further.

The first response, though wordless, came from Lanly Steffard, who turned away from Marigold and walked toward the exit with his nose held high. Behind him followed the entire delegation of the Triarchy clergymen.

"House Ferros of Robbston declares for House Tullivan," The minister of that name stated, while walking toward the staircase with his wife. Marigold thanked and welcomed them both by name and turned back to watch the others.

Leo Daltis and Ike Slake both quietly went for the exit next, their wives in tow. Marigold had expected they would, but had hoped that at least one would consider her appeal.

The longest serving of the Daol Bay city councillors came forward to stand before Marigold. Elbert Swylen was among the most elderly men in the room, and was undoubtedly the only to have served in the council of Marigold's grandfather, albeit briefly before Marscal was sworn in. Marigold knew she would need council support if she was to have any mandate at all, and Swylen's would be of most importance.

"Come forward and have your say, Councillor Swylen. You are entitled to it as any other," she said invitingly.

"Why did you not come to us first?" he asked sadly, his wrinkled, thin, hunched frame adding to that image of sorrow. "You conspired with your uncle and house staff, but could not brief the other councillors that you would so desperately need for such a plan. I admit that I feel a little betrayed, Miss Marigold."

She bowed while he spoke and gave answer when he finished. "Between my father's passing and now there was little time to do so, Councillor. I decided that with such limited opportunities, that it would be the best course of action to announce my intentions to minister and councillor alike at the same time. I apologise if that decision left you feeling slighted or embarrassed, for it was never my intention."

Elbert nodded in understanding and went on with his concerns. "If I may be so bold, these intentions of yours have dire ramifications, and they are not to be considered and decided on so hastily, Miss Marigold. They need time to be dwelt on properly, so that one can examine and prepare for all possible outcomes on either side of the argument. Perhaps it would be best to adjourn for the night and give all of us, councillor, and minister alike, the chance to consider our options."

"That is certainly a valid request, Councillor Swylen." Marigold said with gentle grace. "If any of you should feel the same as he, declare it so and I will arrange for a private meeting with you to discuss this matter at a later time."

After thanking Marigold, Elbert stepped back into the gathered, collected his wife, and bid a good night to all. Councillor's Caveth and Mansfield opted to follow Swylen, with both of them promising to deliver Marigold their decision as soon as they had it.

One councillor remained, a short fellow with spectacles, greying hair, and a skinny frame. When the others had gone, he raised his hand to be given leave to speak. "Miss Marigold, I need no further time to decide. If Rory believes in you, then that is good enough for me. I have always trusted his and your father's judgement. I see no reason why that should be withheld now."

"Thank you, Councillor Rossadore. Your support is everything," Marigold offered with a smile. "I will have great need of your council in the coming times.

"As for the rest of you, I would be glad to receive your intentions this evening, or you may take me up on my previous offer to meet at a later time and venue. We can convene in person, either here in Daol Bay or perhaps in your home regions, if you would like, or through written correspondence, if that would be preferable."

Several took that as a cue to leave and did so. By the time that the servants had issued everyone their outerwear and ushered them out, all that remained were Marigold's supporters and a handful more. Whether the remnants were curious onlookers or declarants either for or against her, Marigold could not be immediately certain.

"Miss Marigold," one man spoke up, and Marigold looked to find Arturo Jennis staring back. He was a round man in a three-piece suit, his square face shaped by a chinstrap beard and accented with a curling moustache. She gave him leave to speak, and he took it. "I am sorely tempted to side with Nothram and Steffard, but at my core I am a man of prudence. You and I may be capable of coming to some sort of agreement, if you would care to sit and talk with me another day."

Arturo wants to strike some type of heavily skewed bargain, no doubt. Either that or he will attempt to make a fool of me for even trying to meet his demands. It could be one or the other, with him, Marigold realised, and she let herself play a little into his game.

"Why certainly, Minister Jennis, I would be most glad to meet with you. I will have Steward Oire follow up with your party to arrange for a suitable time and place."

Marigold's words appeared to be acceptable to Jennis, and with an exchange of farewells later, the minister and his wife went off into the night.

"I am inclined to pledge my support and that of House Obarrow to you, Miss Marigold," Norrin Obarrow of Lakespere announced. Though north of forty, he was still among the younger members of the parliament, and Marigold was glad to know that he was open to her offer. "However, I cannot do so without significant protections and insurances in place. Surely, you understand, for I am the only minister whose regional capital is actually within the Daol Forest. I am dreadfully close to the eastern reaches, which would place me in a precarious position should I side with you and war were to occur."

"Yes, of course, Minister Obarrow, that is only reasonable of you to ask," Marigold readily agreed.

"Then consider me yours, for the nonce," Obarrow conceded with a bend of his knee. "I will, if nothing else, vote to legitimise your claim in the immediate future. Beyond that, we will need to negotiate on a case-by-case basis."

With Marigold's acceptance of his temporary and loose allegiance, Obarrow opted to remain among her guests, but stepped back to allow the next minister forward.

Nayle Keeves of the Gull Coast, located immediately north of Tippard, was already in the midst of a whispered discussion with the Matterslys while Obarrow was speaking. When the floor opened, he took his cue and immediately threw in with the other supporters. After him came Lorence Fields of Gethingston, prodded forward by his wife, an action that was met with nervous laughter.

Greggard Simillon added more hope, "Were Minister Bickerington here, I assure you that he would give you his support as well, Miss Marigold, or should I say, Lady Marigold? Although now that I think about it, superstition would have us believe that rushing such a title upon you too soon would be seen as inviting malediction."

"I wish I could count his vote, but in his absence I cannot," Marigold admitted regrettably. "When he next ventures south to Portsward, we may have a need to get it in writing and notarised for authenticity."

"I will demand audience with him at the very moment his fleet docks in Portsward," Greggard promised excitedly. "Harold always makes a point of coming ashore in my city on his way to and from the fishing grounds. I shall intercept him one way or the other, I assure you."

Two men with their allegiances unspoken for remained. One could not declare for her at any rate, and the other, pacing slowly, seemed an unlikely prospect at best.

"Minister Morton, I am surprised you are still here," Marigold said to the latter, getting his attention. "I would give a copper for your thoughts."

"Yes, well... I am a man caught between the cliffs and the ocean, as the old saying goes," Samhais began while stuffing his hands into the pockets of his trousers. The head of House Morton was a tall, lanky man in his fifties, complete with a background replete with scholarly accolades. He stood before her in a standard black suit, with a tidy haircut, a cleanly shaven face, and a soft-spoken voice that seemed to weigh each word individually as he said them. "Being the brother of Jorette Palomb makes me the brother-in-law of Eamon Palomb and an uncle to their children. I thought long and hard of what to say to you, but I suppose there is no string of words that can make what I have to do any easier to bear. Given my familial connections to Eamon Palomb, I cannot support your claim at this time, Miss Marigold. You have my best wishes for a resolution in your favour. I further give you my condolences on the loss of your father, and wish you a good evening."

Knowing that such a rejection was to come, Marigold accepted it and bid him and his wife Marla a good night.

The remaining man began to walk slowly toward her while Samhais Morton was still departing, the chin of his long, slender face trembling as he did. "Miss Marigold... There is nothing I can do for you... I am terribly sorry."

She shook her head back at him. "Just as I have nothing to offer you, Minister Felton. Although it is the hub between both realms, Obalen is an eastern region. I cannot ask you to give me aid, largely because such a request would ensure a war were started, but also because Obalen is a Triarchy stronghold and without any defensive perimeters. Having you remain an eastern loyalist is what is best for both you and me, Minister Felton."

"Thank you for understanding, Miss Marigold." Felton said while wiping his weepy eyes. "I wish you all the best, and I will now take my leave of this place."

"Wait, Minister Felton, for there is one thing I might ask you to do when you return to Obalen tomorrow," Marigold offered, before he could turn away.

"Perhaps I might be of help after all, then," Felton shrugged.

Marigold leaned forward on the railing as she tabled her request. "Eamon and his sons will be heading west very soon by train, which means they will be stopped in Obalen. I would like you to meet with them and tell them everything you witnessed here tonight. I want the Palombs to know that I will not stand down to them, just as I did not bend to the indignations of Nothram, Steffard, or the Triarchy clergy. I want you to tell Eamon and his sons that it was my father who was bound to the marriage pact. My sister and I are under no obligation, legal or otherwise, to uphold a contract we did not sign that reduces the both of us to chattel. Will you do that for me?"

"Yes, Miss Marigold, I will do as you so ask. Consider it my final favour to your father," Newell Felton obliged, taking his leave immediately after. He was met in the porch by Samhais Morton, who had remained to hear Marigold's conversation with Minister Felton.

When Marigold met Morton's gaze, he gave her a flicker of a smile and a quick nod while Felton and his wife were being helped into their coats.

With the room now empty of any undecided nobles, Marigold turned to the men and women who had so bravely stepped up to give legitimacy to her claim. "Ladies and Gentlemen, I cannot begin to thank and repay you all for what you have done for me tonight. Whether it was done out of respect for my father or myself, I owe you all an immense debt of gratitude. Please, take your leave and get your rest, for it has been a long, arduous day for all of us and after tomorrow, there will likely be many more to come."

The lot of them responded in kind, and she walked down the stairs to shake hands and exchange hugs with everyone.

Upon escorting them to the door, Marigold stopped the lot of them. "Tomorrow morning I shall send for you all and we will meet at city hall. As you can all imagine, we must see to the fine details before an official declaration of intent can be drafted."

The group all agreed to the measure, and with a final round of farewells, went to the convoy of carriages waiting to take them to their overnight accommodations in Daol Bay.

Within the foyer once more, Marigold was met by Oire, Keneth, and Rory, the latter now joined by his wife Leonice. Behind them, the guards had broken formation and were milling about, waiting on orders from Keneth. Further back near the stairs, Marigold caught sight of the maids and footmen, having already begun the process of tidying up for the night. She thanked the staff and guardsmen in their turn, and joined Oire and the others for a final word.

"I am proud to call you my niece, Mari," Leonice began to say, her eyes red from crying. "I started my day weeping for your father and ended it with tears of joy for you. He would be proud of your performance, make no mistake."

"Thank you, Auntie," Marigold said while pulling her into a hug. "I would hear from my uncles too. What did you three make of it all?"

Keneth was the first to offer an opinion. "Outside of Nothram's belligerence, I would say that everything went about as well as could be expected. We knew that there would be holdouts and those who could not make a choice so quickly. However, I will say that I am delightfully surprised at how many supporters we did earn on such short notice."

"We even swayed a councillor," Rory added. His face marked with relief rolling across him. "Although I sense that in the days ahead I will have to meet with the other three to try and convince at least one more to back our cause. After all, we will only need three to pass a motion for the city council to recognise you as the chosen Lady of Daol Bay, and my vote is guaranteed already."

Marigold followed Rory's cue and allowed herself a long sigh, feeling her body loosen itself down to the bones after her exhaustive day. "That gives me some comfort, Uncle Rory. I know you are up to the task of doing just that. I will leave such matters in your hands. Remember though, if they need to meet with me for further discussions, schedule it for after the ministers all depart. I can parlay with our city councillors at any time, but the ministers will start leaving by tomorrow evening. Priority for private discussions must need be given to them while opportunity for such remains."

"Certainly, Mari, I would have it no other way," Rory replied amiably.

"What of you, Oire?" Marigold inquired while turning to her steward. "You have been quiet all along and I would welcome your counsel. It must be of concern that we could not reach a majority of ministers tonight."

There was a shrug from Oire, and a smile nearly formed on his lips. "It was of mild disappointment, I admit. You needed at least twelve supporters to earn a majority, and only landed eight definite votes, nine if we count on Lord Simillon's assurances of Minister Bickerington's allegiance."

Oire was right, Marigold knew, and she admitted as much. "You are of course correct, as always. So what would you call what happened here tonight, then?"

He met Marigold's eyes, and allowed his smile to roll across his face. "I would call it a promising start, my lady."

15
MARIGOLD

t had been three days since Marigold had laid her father to rest. Sleep, when it came at all, was dealt in short bouts, coming only when her mind had completely exhausted itself on pain. Even in those rare instances of slumber, she saw Marscal in a dream as real as life itself.

In the courtyard behind the manor is where Marigold would find him, in full health and happier than Marigold could remember, for he was reunited with Farren and Felixander. The dream began the same way, with Marigold wandering through the empty Tullivan Manor calling for someone, anyone to answer. She would look in her parents' chambers, Serephanie's bedroom, the bedroom her brother never had a chance to use, the sitting room, the dining room, and lastly her father's solar. Once there, Marigold would feel the calmest of summer breezes through the open window. The sheer curtains that framed it fluttered and danced with the wind, and it seemed as though they were calling to her. Across the room and to the sill she would go, looking out into the side yard to find no one, until the laughter of a little boy at play found its way to her.

In every recurrence of the dream, Marigold would follow the sound of the laughter to the courtyard, where she would catch a glimpse of the boy as he ran away from her. Giving chase at a hurried stride, Marigold would try to keep up with the shoeless child dressed in a grass-stained light blue tunic and grey trousers, his tousled brown hair standing in all directions. As Marigold followed, the boy would giggle and duck around the hedges, leading her through the gardens while staying just out of reach. The aroma of the freshly bloomed assortment of flowers would touch her nose, and it even felt as though the wind was lifting her hair. After a time, Marigold would call out, asking the boy his name, but he never answered with anything more than joyful laughter. In every instance, they would arrive at the quiet, wooded grove far to the rear of the manor. She could so plainly see the tiny pond, the raft of ducks that called it home, and the big sycamore tree that her great-great-grandfather had planted.

Among the ducks were a familiar lot led by a big mallard that Serephanie and Marigold had called Ernest. He was the biggest among the flock, named for an old fisherman client of Marscal's who had gifted the bird as a duckling to the girls. The duck and his friends paddling behind him were long gone in reality, and their appearance was always the first clue to Marigold that something was amiss.

On the other side of the pond is where Marigold would find her mother and father, seated on a varnished wooden bench that no longer existed. The boy would run ahead and into the waiting arms of Farren, his face never to be seen. However, by then, Marigold knew he must be Felixander, the brother she had never met and whose face she would not know. The visages of Farren and Marscal were vivid and unmistakable, and despite what she had already observed to tell her otherwise, she truly believed what she saw to be above fantasy.

Marigold would dart toward her family to greet them, a feeling of elation overwhelming her and bringing her to tears. They always saw her, favouring her with warm smiles and waves in greeting. As she neared the bench, her mother would invariably ask, "Marigold, where has your sister gotten to?"

Before any words had time to form on Marigold's tongue, her eyes would flutter open, she would look around her room, and realise that it really had been but a dream. Nothing she had seen or felt was real, except for the tears.

The lack of rest, combined with the bereavement she was dealing with, was slowly taking its toll on Marigold, and she was painfully aware of it. As much as she tried to focus on the incipient effects of what had been formally titled as *The Declaration of Agency for West Illiastra*, Marigold's exhaustion seemed to keep her from being at a peak level of productivity.

As fortune would have it for Marigold, her newfound supporters were more than willing to spearhead the campaign on her behalf. They had even given themselves a name: the Alliance for Western Agency.

In prior meetings, Marigold's diligent band of ministers, councillors, interested wives, and Oire and Ser Keneth would gather in the private council chambers of Daol Bay's city hall. At a rate of two meetings per day, with one in the morning and a second in the late afternoon, the band of nearly twenty had been busily drafting her policy platform. Marigold could not be more proud of what they had accomplished in such a short time and with such minimal notice. Despite the pressure to have the documents prepared for the printing press before Eastern Illiastra could formulate a response, the group had seen to it that every aspect of existing municipal, regional, and even national law had been scrutinised and refined to a new standard that would see the proposed nation of West Illiastra become a place of pride.

Aside from Marigold herself, the person leading the charge was Lord Greggard Simillon. From his years as both an understudy to his father, and in his own capacity as the Lord of International Trade and Relations, Greggard had amassed a considerable knowledge bank in regards to the operations of the other nations of the Known World. Of particular interest to Marigold's team were countries that had already seen successful implementation of the rights and freedoms that Marigold wanted to bring to Illiastra. Greggard was quite versed in such matters and the team had deferred to him at every turn and sought his input on even the tiniest of details, especially when it came to legalese. There could be no room for loopholes, and Greggard was exactly the expert that Marigold and her party needed to cinch those knots.

Merely a day after *The Declaration of Agency* was finalised, Marigold put it to her colleagues to choose a campaign manager. Almost immediately after the call for nominations was opened, Greggard's name was put forward by Walter Mattersly and met with resounding approval by the remaining caucus.

"It seems that the entire room has practically jumped to second your nomination, Lord Greggard," Marigold commented while smoothing out a wrinkle in the leg of her black trousers. "I would be honoured to have you as the campaign manager and my chief strategist, but the final decision is yours, ser."

"A political tactician I might be, but I am the only lord among us, and already seen as someone that the people struggle to relate to," Greggard decided calmly and without pause. "Besides, I am better suited to working behind the curtain rather than upon the stage. This is a position best suited to not just a capable strategist, but also someone that the people would feel confident having as your second in command. That person, in turn, should be one who is comfortable with the attention that such a position would bring."

Admittedly, Marigold felt slightly dejected by the declination, but the room was yet filled with capable candidates. "I respect your decision, Lord Greggard. I will still have much need of your counsel, as I am sure our campaign manager will too, once they are chosen."

Greggard offered assurances on his part with a wide, open gesture of his hands. "I will offer every milligram of counsel and support that I can, though I prefer to do it from a position where I am free to come and go with a little more leisure. As the soon-to-be-former Lord of International Trade and Relations, you will see that I do my best work when I have as little attention as possible cast my way."

Marigold found it difficult to argue with the man's reasoning, and she polled the group again. The second consensus now pointed to the original nominator, Walter Mattersly, who quite nearly accepted on the spot.

That was, until Elda raised a valid point, "Walter and I come from Tippard, a place so far south that when we look out from our south-facing windows, we can see the Varras River spilling over the Tear. We will be able to serve you best if we can manage campaign matters from our own home region, be that as a liaison or as the first line of defence in the southernmost regions. To that end, it is my belief that your campaign manager should be someone who can reasonably stay in Daol Bay with you, Lady Marigold."

Though not yet official, Elda and the others had begun to call her 'Lady Marigold', a title that carried significantly more weight than 'Miss', even if it was only honorary at this point.

Based on Elda's recommendation, the next logical nominee was Oire, who was already the steward for House Tullivan. Like Simillon and Mattersly before him, Oire too bowed out gracefully. "You have my support until the end of my days, my lady, but I feel that I too am ill-suited to the role. It might be seen as a patronage offering to jump your own house steward into what will no doubt be a vaunted office. Someone from outside of your house would be the better choice."

Oire turned to look at Rory. "My apologies, Councillor, I am afraid that you too would be out of the running if the lady were to follow my advice."

"No, no, Oire, do not apologise, I was about to suggest the same. At any rate, with our family's fishery dynasty to manage, I am more than content with my workload. My counsel is yours at any time though, Niece. You know that Leonice and I are at your beck and call, if needed."

"Well then, perhaps I will make a nomination then, if no one objects," Marigold suggested while looking back and forth to either side of the table to see if there was any opposition. Finding none, she squared her sights on her choice. "I would nominate Minister Myakys to be my chief tactician and campaign manager."

Gallin looked about with surprise, the long, loose mane of black hair on his head swishing about his shoulders. "Please, pardon my shock, my lady. I... I am honoured by the nomination. I admit that I was not expecting to be chosen for such a position."

"The honour is mine, Minister Myakys," Marigold replied with a chuckle. "Will anyone second the nomination?"

"Aye," Minister Norrin Obarrow piped in confidently, his hand raised for added effect.

"The motion is seconded by Minister Obarrow," Marigold said in acknowledgement, looking again to the nominee. "Do you accept your nomination, Minister Myakys?"

"I... Why, yes, my lady, I do accept," Gallin confirmed with almost a stammer. As he cleared his throat, the minister composed himself to add, "If you feel confident that I am up to the task, then I shall endeavour to live up to your expectations."

"I trust that you shall," Marigold replied, putting the motion back to the others. "The nomination of Minister Gallin Myakys to the newly-created position of Chief Strategist and Campaign Manager was tabled by myself and seconded by Minister Norrin Obarrow. The nomination was then accepted by Minister Myakys. Now, we need to go to the floor for a vote. Those in favour, say 'aye'."

The resounding vote in favour of Gallin was unanimous, but Marigold held to protocol. "Those opposed, say 'nay'."

When none spoke, she nodded and turned to Gallin with a smile. "With all in favour and none opposed, the motion carries. I hereby bestow you the title and duties of Chief Strategist and Campaign Manager to the Alliance for Western Agency. Allow me be the first to offer you congratulations, Minister Myakys."

The men and women seated at the long, mahogany table with Marigold broke into applause, and Minister Myakys rose to take a bow in Marigold's direction.

"Thank you, all of you," Gallin offered, looking almost a little overwhelmed by it all. "I will strive to execute the duties of my station to the utmost of my abilities. I promise to conduct myself in such a manner that I bring no shame or embarrassment to my colleagues, my family, and, last but certainly not least, to our esteemed leader, Lady Marigold Tullivan."

As the applause and congratulations had been going on, the door to the council chambers had been opened by Sydnee, who had been guarding the office corridors where the private chambers were situated. Keneth rose to greet him, having been seated nearest to the door and the pair conferred long enough for Keneth to nod affirmatively and send Sydnee to Marigold.

The others took notice of the guard and went silent as they watched him go to Marigold's side and lean in close to speak privately with her.

"Yes, Sydnee?" Marigold queried as he neared.

"It is no emergency or anything, my lady," Sydnee assured her while whispering in her ear. "I am just making you aware that your guest for your eleventh hour appointment is waiting within your office."

Marigold relaxed a little at that. "Oh, is that all? Thank you for informing me, Sydnee. What time is it, pray tell?"

His eyes glanced about nervously before his tongue gave answer. "It is, uh, a quarter past the eleventh hour, my lady."

"Oh, good graciousness, I have kept him waiting," Marigold admitted with a shameful tsk of her tongue. She stood up and adjusted her black blouse at the lower hem and tapered sleeves, and gathered her papers, prompting the others to all rise in tandem. "Ladies and gentlemen, I think this is as fine a time as any to adjourn our morning meeting. Be proud of everything we have achieved to this point. We are doing remarkable work with only the shortest of timeframes in which to do so. With that, I bid you all a good day until we meet again after the luncheon hour."

Having exchanged salutations on her way out the door, Marigold departed with Sydnee at her side. In the past, particularly since reaching the age of adulthood, Marigold and Serephanie had often gone throughout the city without armed accompaniment. However, such carefree living was no longer an option in the wake of Marigold's speech at Marscal's funeral reception.

In the days after, Keneth had been made aware by officers of the city guard that though Marigold did indeed have support among the citizens of Daol Bay, there was definite unrest as well. Those who were the most disturbed by Marigold's intentions were among the strongest adherents of the Triarchy. The same people who believed in strict abidance to the scriptures would not tolerate a woman in a position of authority, and protests against Marigold, typically led by the clergy themselves, had already begun.

From the pulpits came calls for Marigold to resign at once. Should she refuse, the Triarchy encouraged the most pious of its supporters to remove her by force so that the Triarchy themselves could punish her for crimes of blasphemy. One Patriarch even found himself under investigation by city guardsmen for having suggested that Marigold should be killed outright, even going so far as to opine on the heroics of a potential assassin. Said Patriarch only offered to retract the statement when questioned on it by those with the authority to place him under arrest for issuing death threats. The Patriarch argued that simply stating the opinion that Marigold should perish did not constitute a death threat. Regardless, it was concerning to all involved that someone of such influence would suggest as much to a highly suggestable audience and put Marigold's safety at risk.

At any rate, that the Patriarch only apologised for his statement when punitive repercussions were at stake led Marigold to believe that the Patriarch's opinion was unmoved. Granted, he was merely one clergyman calling for such harsh measures, but the damage of his words had already been done by then.

A considerable portion of the menfolk, it seemed, had become incensed and inconsolable at the prospect of being ruled over by a woman. Further joining the men in their outrage was a surprising number of women from a particular subset of the gender who viewed their own subjugation as a status of virtue.

The city guards were on edge themselves as a result, with the leading officers from all four districts of Daol Bay reported increased tensions amongst the populace. The officers even went so far as to say that an estimated full third of the residents of their districts were vocally opposed to Marigold.

That alone had been enough for Keneth to warrant heightened security for both the Tullivan Manor and city hall, along with constant, armed protection of Marigold at all hours. The manor guards were taking no risks, ensuring that Marigold had a full escort of no less than five guardsmen during travel to and from city hall. Their counterparts guarding the city added measures of their own as well, increasing guard patrols on the most popular and direct routes that Marigold and her supporters would be using to go about their business.

While Marigold felt that the increased security was a tad over the top, her new circle of supporters all insisted it to be a necessity. They claimed that there was now a real and tangible threat to theirs and Marigold's lives. The fear was that the Triarchy's response, while not violent in itself, would be encouragement enough for a lone fanatic, or even an indignant mob to attempt to maim or kill Marigold.

That meant that now, even while city hall itself was guarded without by both manor and city guards alike, Marigold could not be left unprotected while within. The increased protection did not come without a toll though, for the manor guardsmen were stretched to the point of near exhaustion in trying to maintain the numbers needed for such a security level. They had no help or substitutions, should one or more be inhibited from attending to their duty, a stressor in itself.

Furthermore, being a separate armed unit from the city guards, the manor guards could not pull individual members from the city ranks on even a short-term basis. If a soldier or guard were chosen for the personal guard of the Tullivan's, they had to be interviewed, like any other job, and then put through further rigours to ensure loyalty and suitability. To remedy the situation, Keneth had been urging Marigold in private to increase the number of manor guards by at least four or five men to alleviate the stress. Keneth had even delayed his own retirement from the manor guard captaincy so that he could assist with the protection efforts, and offered to oversee the hiring process personally. He even went so far as to draft a list of fifty potential candidates comprised of city guards, ranger patrols, and regular army soldiers from Portsward to Tippard and everywhere in between.

Marigold had held off on making extensions, though, as she could not trust in new faces at such a precarious time, even if Keneth gave them scrutiny. As it was, Darrill and Rus were akin to old friends, and she had grown close with Sydnee, Elden, Brandyl, and Lewcas in the relatively peaceful times when her father reigned. They were men she knew would be absolutely loyal to her. It would be a big leap for Marigold to put blind faith in strange men who could overpower her easily if left alone to protect and escort her as Sydnee presently was.

In addition, the men being nominated to the house guards were always of exemplary skill. Taking such a useful asset from any unit when a potential war was brewing would put a sour taste in the mouths of the officers whom Marigold would be expecting to fight for her. Atop that, Marigold was concerned with the image she would cultivate if her first move after so bravely standing up to the Elite Merchants would be to hide behind a growing wall of muscle.

"Is there any word from the city guardsmen regarding the Triarchist protesters today?" Marigold asked Sydnee as they strolled down the hall.

"Indeed there has, and the tidings are not good, my lady," Sydnee replied worriedly.

She looked up at Sydnee to catch his line of sight. "I would still hear those tidings, good or not."

"Very well," Sydnee gave back without argument. "There has been a noted rise in assaults, typically between the Triarchist protesters and clashing counter-protesters. Thus far, we can say that no firearms or legitimate melee weaponry have been sighted amongst the combatants on either side. Rather, it appears that the clashes are hand-to-hand brawls with the occasional blunt object thrown in. If there is one positive note to be taken away from the violence it's that no deaths or debilitating injuries have been reported as of yet.

"Regardless, the city guards have arrested agitators from both sides, my lady. Those detentions have led to family members of the detained counter-protesters organising demonstrations at the offices of their city councillors and at the primary guard station across the street from here. The demonstrators are asking that you release the counter-protesters that, their families argue, were defending your cause."

Marigold had hummed concernedly during Sydnee's report, and spoke on the matter when he finished. "Thank you for bringing that to my attention. We will have to arrange for the non-violent protesters of both sides to be let go. It does no one any good to see peaceful protesters being whisked off the streets in chains. I would like a list of those charged with violent offenses, from either side. As much as I would rather set my supporters free, doing so would condone the violence, and I want to see the bloodshed curbed."

They arrived at her office then, and Lewcas, who had been guarding over it, informed Marigold that her company was already seated within.

"Thank you to the both of you. I shall call for you when we are finished," Marigold told them gratefully.

The interior of city hall was typically a bright and airy place from top to bottom. The floors had been done in light-grey granite that was polished almost daily to a fine sheen and complemented with white walls and ceilings. The combination caused the light, whether through the windows in the day or from electric lighting overhead after dark, to illuminate every corner of the building. The former office of Lord Marscal Tullivan was no exception to that design.

Within the well-lit room sat a modest oak desk with three chairs before it and one with a high, cushioned back behind. Resting upon one of the three chairs ahead of the desk was a short, stubby little fellow in a dark brown suit whose feet barely touched the floor.

He turned in his seat as Marigold entered and slid to a stand to greet her, "Good afternoon, Miss Marigold. It is good to see you again. Thank you ever so much for meeting with me."

"A good day to you as well, Minister Bradling," Marigold extended in reply over a handshake. "However, I feel it is I that should be thanking you for so quickly responding to my invitation. I appreciate that you made the time to do so before heading home to Samspell Bay."

"It is no bother, Miss Marigold, no bother at all," Minister Bradling uttered with a nervous smile. "I am merely glad that you remembered me in the first place."

"Of course I remember you. It would be hard to forget such a gracious person," Marigold smiled back while gesturing to the chair that Lon had vacated seconds ago. "Please, have a seat, Minister and we will discuss a few things of concern to us both."

Lon Bradling was but one of nine remaining holdouts whom Marigold thought that she might have a chance of swaying to her side.

Despite inviting all of them individually, only five had accepted her requests in the days following the funeral reception, and of those, she managed to convince none of the previous four. Having remained in Daol Bay on business long after the other holdout ministers had gone home, Lon was Marigold's last chance to secure an extra vote, and she hoped his kindness could be appealed to.

Having taken their seats, the two first engaged in polite conversation. Marigold began, asking how Lon's wife and only child were faring. In turn, Lon queried as to how Marigold and her household were holding up in the face of their tragic loss. Such banter, while seemingly banal, gave Marigold a few minutes where she felt able to decompress from every other matter, giving her mind a much needed, albeit fleeting distraction. Midway through, Marigold offered him tea, coffee, and food, though Lon respectfully declined, claiming to have had an early lunch that left him full.

With little else in the way of idle chatter to be had, Marigold dove in on the subject at hand. "Minister Bradling, if I may ask, do you know why I invited you here?"

"Why yes, yes I do, Miss Marigold," Lon replied frankly. "You would like for me to sign your declaration and support you as Warden Lady of the West, correct?"

"That is the way of it, yes," Marigold affirmed.

As she was about to ask Lon the question, he blurted out his answer, "Well, you have it, my support, that is, Miss Marigold."

For a few seconds Marigold was left speechless, and she had to figure that her puzzlement was plain on her face. "Oh... Well, I am glad to have it. You are the only one I have met with since my father's funeral reception who has offered their support, and without any bargaining too, I might add. I might be pushing my luck, but can I ask why you were so ready to jump to my side?"

"I had wanted to support you when everything came up at the manor, truly I did, Miss Marigold," Lon explained while fidgeting with a button on his coat. "The Bradlings have always stood with the Tullivans, going back to the days before the Elite Merchants even existed. There is no reason to break with that position now just because the next Tullivan in line is a woman. Besides, you have demonstrated that you possess the courage and tenacity to do as well as any man in the same position. My wife and I both feel that with the right counsel, that you can grow into a leader every bit as worthy of her surname as those who came before you."

Marigold sidestepped her bafflement with a shake of her head when Minister Bradling had finished. "Why, thank you, Minister Bradling, I am flattered by your kind words. I will do my best to make you and my forbearers proud. Is there a reason you did not speak up at the manor, though?"

Almost immediately, Minister Bradling's face turned red, and beads of sweat began to form on his brow. "Oh my, oh no, I could not do that, Miss Marigold. Just the thought of putting myself in front of a crowd makes me break out in a panic. I-I-I am not brave like you, Lord Greggard, Minister Myakys, or Minister Mattersly."

He was wringing his hands then, stopping only long enough to mop his brow with a handkerchief produced from within his jacket. "Good gracious, I am quite certain that I would have fainted right there on the spot had I even thought about it. Now, that would have been quite the sight, would it not, Miss Marigold. My dear wife would have been embarrassed to tears."

Before Marigold could get another word in, Lon began to ramble on further. "I do not even know that I am suited to be a minister in the first place. I only got the role because I am the oldest son of Rolis Bradling, not for my leadership or public speaking abilities. In fact, if I were my father, I would have skipped me for one of my other two brothers. They are both younger, but far better at leading. I just like to read books, you see. Novels and poetry in particular, and I enjoy writing my own poems too. Nevertheless, I am no leader like the other Bradlings, just a bookworm. My father thought I was smart on account of all that reading, but I don't know how true that is."

There was a lapse in the monologue and Marigold leapt on it. "I am glad you did not encumber yourself at the manor, Minister Bradling, just as I am glad to have your support. We all have our strengths and weaknesses, and I do not believe that your public anxiety disqualifies you as a leader. Rather, I see a man who applies a needed level of careful, deliberate measure to his decision making process, and that is just the sort of quality one looks for in a leader."

"Why, thank you for your understanding, Miss Marigold. I promise that if a day should come that House Tullivan calls its banners, House Bradling will answer."

Lon stopped talking abruptly, a sheepish smile crossing his face. "Um... Although it will probably be my brothers doing the fighting, as they both rose to captaincy in the military. One is a rifleman, and the other is with the cavalry."

Marigold stifled a chuckle, "You need not worry about that, Minister Bradling, I understand completely. I would not call on you to lead an army, but I would call on you for your counsel. Regardless, I am delighted to have the houses of Bradling and Tullivan in league with one another again."

Though certain of the answer before even doing so, Marigold then proposed that Bradling further extend his stay in Daol Bay and join her campaign. As expected, Bradling passed on the offer to join the other supporters. It was evident that Lon just wanted to go home, and it showed, and Marigold was not going to deny him that leisure.

"If there is nothing else, then I suppose I shall let you return to your campaign meetings," Lon said with a shrug while leaning forward in his chair to stand. "Before I depart, though, I will sign the *Declaration of Agency*, if it is kept nearby."

"Yes, of course," Marigold granted while getting back on her own feet. "It is kept under lock and key by my house guards at all times. I shall have it brought to us at once, Minister Bradling."

She raised her voice so as to be heard from without, "Lewcas, could you-"

The noise of heavy, hurried boots on the floor beyond her door caused Marigold to pause in mid-sentence. As she craned to listen to what was now the muffled voices of men, there was a shared curious, silent glance with Minister Bradling, who seemed to have heard the sudden ruckus as well.

The door of the office opened just enough for Lewcas to slide in, his face at its usual, resting stoic expression. "My lady, there is a city guard outside the door with Sydnee. He is a lieutenant by the name of Cleofold Ashe and he claims that you would have met him before."

For a split second, the name seemed to hang in Marigold's mind, until the memory of having encountered him at the southern gate of the city on her way home from Atrebell floated before her. "Oh, yes. I recall Lieutenant Ashe. We met at the southern gate a while ago. If I were to guess, I would say that he has completed his report on the integrity of the city walls."

"If that is so, it is not what he told Sydnee or I," Lewcas relayed flatly.

"Then what did he tell you two?" Marigold asked, trying not to sound as nonplussed as she currently felt.

Lewcas stepped all the way into the room and shut the door behind him. "Perhaps it would be best spoken of in private, my lady."

"I shall see myself out, then," Lon Bradling declared.

"Please, wait a moment, Minister Bradling," Marigold told him before he could reach the exit. She looked to Lewcas, "Minister Bradling has agreed to join our cause and sign *The Declaration of Agency*. If the matter is not of private affairs from the manor, or related to my personal security, Minister Bradling may hear it."

"It will be as you desire, my lady," Lewcas relented without question, his cantor unwavering. It always marvelled Marigold how Lewcas held himself to a strict, unyielding code of discipline, regardless of whether he was on duty or not. When Keneth had recruited the twenty-eight year old from Arnell's Cove in the Gethingston region, he came bearing an impossibly impeccable record. To that end, he was regarded by every superior he served under to be a model soldier and reported to Keneth with a letter of recommendation from each officer. Though entirely inexpressive, the man had a sense of duty and honour that was second to none, never had so much as a single hair out of place, and was deathly fierce in combat. Lewcas was, by all accounts, the ideal soldier.

In the seven years that Lewcas had served thus far with House Tullivan, Marigold had yet to see him laugh, or joke about with other staff. She could not even remember seeing him engage in what could be called a friendly conversation with anyone else. Lewcas never drank, smoked, or gambled, and there were no lovers in his life, or even friends, really. His career as a soldier was everything Lewcas had and it was all there was to him, yet it was the only thing he wanted. Marigold often felt sad for him for living such a bland existence, but he seemed fulfilled, at any rate.

"Lieutenant Ashe has come to report that a company of mercenaries have begun to establish a rudimentary camp in the vicinity of the south gates," Lewcas began after a deep breath. "Their leader has thus far declined orders to vacate the area and wishes to speak only with you, and no other. Furthermore, Lieutenant Ashe informed Sydnee and me that officers from all available ranks in that district have allegedly attempted dialogue, but have been rebuffed. It would not have been brought to your concern at all had the officers on duty been able to resolve the matter otherwise. However, they fear that attempting to evict the mercenaries with force would result in bloodshed. Thus, the city guards have come to see if you will speak to the interlopers before having to resort to such measures."

"Oh, dear me," Lon Bradling commented meekly. "That sounds like a difficult situation."

"Yet it is one that I should see to," Marigold decided, turning to a coat hook in the corner by her chair and grabbing the teal, wool-lined cloak hanging upon it. Tucked into an inside pocket were a pair of ermine gloves and Marigold donned both articles in a hurry, giving Lewcas instructions as she did. "Please, go summon Ser Keneth, Oire, and Minister Myakys at once. Inform them all of what is transpiring. Ser Keneth shall gather the rest of my escort and our mounts, and we shall all convene at the exit leading to the stables.

"Minister Bradling, I apologise for having to depart before you could sign *The Declaration of Agency*, but I shall have Steward Oire remain with you so that you can. He and one of the other remaining ministers will sign as your witnesses."

Lon gave a bow and stepped back out of Marigold's path. "No, no, there is no need to apologise, Miss Marigold. I am at your service, after all. Please, be safe out there and keep your wits about you. Sellswords are given to roguishness even at their best moments."

"Thank you, Minister Bradling, I shall do just that," Marigold told him cordially, as the three of them stepped back into the corridor.

Sydnee was standing in wait with a familiar man in the blue coat and black trousers uniform of the city guards topped with a thicker overcoat in the same shade of blue.

"Lieutenant Ashe, it is good to see you again, though I wish our reunion were under better circumstances," Marigold gave by way of greeting, before turning to Sydnee. "Are you ready to go outside?"

From the window in the office, Marigold had noticed that it had begun to softly snow, adding precipitation to what was already a cold morning. Sydnee, Lewcas and the other guardsmen had shed their own overcoats, and were wearing the teal coats and black trousers of the House Tullivan guard uniform.

"I was not aware I was going outside, my lady," Sydnee replied, clearly caught off guard by the suddenness of it all. "Do I have the time to grab my things?"

"Yes, certainly," Marigold informed him quickly. "I shall go with you while Lewcas fetches the others and relays my orders. Lieutenant Ashe, may I ask that you go on ahead of the party now and let the other guards and the men insisting on my company know that I will be there shortly?"

Cleofold bowed to her quickly. "Yes, Miss Marigold, I shall see to that right away."

"Very good, Lieutenant, we shall see you at the South Gate," Marigold said before turning away with Sydnee. "Come, now. There is little time to waste."

It was there that Marigold parted with Cleofold, Lon, and Lewcas, the latter two heading in an opposite direction from her on their quest to find Gallin, Keneth, and Oire. Together, Marigold and Sydnee made for the closets at the stable exit, where the guards, staff, and councillors all stored their outerwear. While waiting, they were joined by Rus and Elden, who had been augmenting the city guards on patrol directly outside city hall. The former's normally greying beard was dotted with melting snow, and the pair had their woollen hats pulled down tight over their heads.

"How is the weather, gentlemen?" Marigold asked while they waited for the others.

"Bloody cold, my lady, if I may be so blunt," Rus told her, running a gloved hand over his dampening beard. "Are we leaving already? Elden and I were just coming inside to switch with Sydnee and Lewcas."

"I am afraid that we are going, Rus. I apologise for dragging you both back into the chilly air again," Marigold relayed to them with a wince.

"All well and good, my lady," Elden replied, his lips pursing. "May we ask where?"

Marigold recounted what Lewcas had told her, sparing no detail. By the time she finished, footfalls began to echo off the corridor walls from the direction that she and Sydnee had just come from.

"My lady, whatever are you planning on doing?" she heard a voice that could only be Oire's having said. "Giving into ruffian demands is most unwise. Who knows what trickery they might be planning?"

"I am going with the Captain of the Manor Guards and four guardsmen to the thoroughly guarded South Gate to break an impending siege by a mercenary company," Marigold informed him stiffly. "To worry for my safety is to doubt our carefully chosen personal guardsmen, and our city watch, Oire."

"Worrying for your safety is what I am paid to do, my lady," Oire reminded her, his voice returning to its usual, grandfatherly tones. "However, you are correct. I trust that Keneth and the others will keep you out of harm's way. Just promise me that you will be careful."

She sighed, and patted him on the shoulder. "Of course I will, Oire. Take care of matters with Lon Bradling in my stead, and let the other ministers know why Keneth, Minister Myakys, and I are absent should we not return before the afternoon meeting. Rest assured though, I shall endeavour to have us all back here as quickly as possible."

Leaving Oire behind, the party went to the stables and had their steads brought forth. Empress, Marigold's black mare, was led out of her stall first, and Marigold took the reins for herself and walked the horse outside. She was sitting in the saddle by the time the others joined her, a pair of city patrolmen having come to stand nearby while she waited. Once the party were mounted and ready to depart, Ser Keneth arranged the guards in a tight, four corners position around Marigold and Gallin Myakys, who had been given Oire's chestnut palfrey, Zygar, to ride.

"It would seem that my service as Chief Strategist is coming into effect before my contract can even be drawn up," Gallin jested once they were underway.

Marigold gave a polite laugh in response, adding with it, "It could not be helped, Minister Myakys. This needs to be dealt with immediately, and I felt you should be party to it, even if your new role has not yet been committed to paper."

"I understand and I am happy to be invited," Gallin said, his voice maintaining its amiable tone. "As tense a situation as it might be, it does sound intriguing though, no? But how odd is it to have a sudden incursion of sellswords. What do you suppose they could want from you? Where might they have come from? Are there further bands of brigands in the northern wilds still?"

"They want what mercenaries always want, I suppose," Marigold reasoned, using a free hand to pull the hood of her cloak up to ward against the cold and snow. "There is a potential for upheaval, and therefore, a potential for mercenary companies to make money playing both sides of the conflict until either war breaks out, or a resolution is reached. As for where they came from, my best guess is that some highwaymen banded together and called the result a 'company'."

Gallin hummed aloud at that in a ponderous manner. "No matter what their origins, I would advise you to give them no custom. There are but a scant few benefits to be found when throwing money at sellswords. They are good for making an army look larger than it is, and practically nothing else. The history of the Vellick Isles is replete with stories of privateer fleets being paid to fight both for and against my ancestral homeland. With few exceptions, they all turn tail as soon as events even hint at unfurling unfavourably for whatever side happens to be their financiers."

As the party marched down the streets, Marigold looked about. The folks out in the weather were mostly walking along the sidewalks, their heads down and minds on their own business. There were but a few who took notice of her, and a scarce number of those with the time to wave or shout 'hello'. Marigold waved and called back, making sure to acknowledge the scattered greeters.

Gallin waved at one as well, turning to Marigold after he had done so. "I see admirers of you aplenty among the citizenry, my lady. That bodes well for you, especially so early into your new mandate."

"My great-grandfather, the last Tullivan to lead before the Elite Merchants seized power, was quoted to say, 'If you do no harm to your people and provide them with shelter, safety, and decent wages, they will give you a peaceful reign in turn.' My grandmother repeated the quote often, and my father tried to live by it. To my own experience, it rings true, to a point. Nevertheless, I fear that by opposing the EMP and the Triarchy, I will not be able to grant my people the peace that my great-grandfather spoke of."

"There are many in Illiastra who have never seen peace," Gallin offered in consideration of the thought. "They live in chains as indentured slaves, or hide in fear of the rattle they make. Think of how much peace you might bring to those poor folk if you could silence the clangour of the steel links."

Marigold considered his words for a moment, before querying further, "Are you saying I cannot emancipate the oppressed without upsetting everyone else? What does it matter to the free if slaves are released from their bonds? Why would a man be distraught if a woman is granted the same rights he already enjoys and benefits from?"

With a calm and careful delivery, Myakys gave answer, "I am saying that many societies, such as ours, that grant numerous freedoms to the majority, are still often built on soil soaked in the blood of the minority. When the majority starts to feel the ground shaking beneath them, they tend not to care that things are being rebalanced. They only worry that it is shaking in the first place and making them uncomfortable.

"Sometimes though, in order to reshape the landscape into a level field for all, one needs to fill in some holes and move a few boulders."

The sky seemed to darken around the party, and Marigold glanced upward to see that they were advancing into the shadow of the city wall. "I had never known you were such an advocate for the underprivileged, Minister Myakys. I cannot say that I am surprised, but I wish I had known sooner."

Gallin had been looking about as well, and he seemed to be focused on the patrolling guards on the bailey over the gate. "How could I not be? You saw yourself how I was treated by Minister Nothram when I stood for you. He referred to me as 'the Vellicanese'. I was not a fellow minister, or his peer as a noble. I was just a foreigner. You may have noticed over the years that Nothram is far from the only one who looks at me in such a light.

"As I said to him then, my earliest relatives landed here centuries ago. My ancestry is made of medical practitioners, military officers and soldiers, fishermen, and lawyers, much the same as you find on the family trees of other nobles, such as yours. I myself was a lieutenant in my infantry squadron, though I never served in actual combat. When my contract was up, I pursued my Mastership in Known World History at the Weicaster University and graduated in the top five percent of my class. However, many people see none of that when they look at me. They just see a man with darker skin than theirs and a slightly different accent. Have you ever spoken to someone who lives on the Vellick Isles? I do not have an accent at all compared to them, just the remnants of one from growing up amongst a family that still have touches of the old dialect.

"With all that said, you can see that I have an understanding of the struggles of the different, because I am one of them. I admit that my wealth shields me from much of it, but I am still judged every day of my life by what makes me different from other Illiastrans."

Marigold lowered her gaze to her hands and the reins of the horse held in them. "I never saw you as different, Minister Myakys. I chose you to be my Chief Strategist and Campaign Manager because I remembered that you were a historian and a military officer. I had to figure that you, of all the people to have joined my campaign, would be best suited for the task."

"I appreciate you saying that, my lady," Gallin replied softly.

The party had been stopped while Marigold and Gallin had been finishing their conversation and once complete, Marigold looked about to see why they were not moving. Between them and the gates were a throng of people, horses, two covered wagons, and one coach, all waiting to leave the city. With the gates closed tight against the sellswords, everything had come to a standstill.

"It's worse than we thought," Gallin commented while surveying things while standing in the stirrups of his saddle. "The closing of the gates has backed up the flow of people to and from the city. I would imagine that the train station is further packed full of desperate folks trying to get in here."

"That is even more motivation for us to resolve this peacefully," Marigold surmised with determination. "If we have civilians in a largely unguarded train station near those sellswords, they may well harm or use them for leverage."

Spurring Empress forward a little, Marigold sidled up beside Keneth. "Are there any city guards we can attract the attention of? We need to get to the front of the line and get this situation sorted out quickly."

Keneth hummed aloud, "I can certainly go ahead and try to find one. Stay in tight with the other manor guards and I will do what I can."

Marigold beckoned the guardsmen and Gallin forward and they closed in tight around her.

Atop Gallin's long dark hair, the snow had begun to accumulate, but he seemed not to notice, with his attention on the crowd all around them. "There are more packing in behind us, Lady Marigold. It must be getting close to the departure time for the next train."

"Make way! Move aside!" called a booming voice from ahead, and when Marigold spotted its owner, she saw a trio of mounted city guards moving toward them with Keneth tailing behind.

"Right this way, Miss Marigold," one beckoned while turning his horse back the way it came.

The other two city guards gently moved the line of people to make room for Marigold's entourage and they rode ahead in single file. Keneth and Lewcas led the way, with Marigold in the middle, Gallin behind her, and the remaining guards behind him.

Beneath the cover of the baily, Marigold dismounted, handing off Empress' reins to a guard who reached out to hold them. She turned and nearly walked straight into Cleofold Ashe, who had returned well ahead of the party. "What is the situation, Lieutenant Ashe?"

Cleofold gave a salute before replying, "I informed the leader of the men outside that you were on your way. However, I must insist that you meet him in the gatehouse, Miss Marigold. My men are already there and at the ready, and the mercenary captain has agreed to disarm himself and be searched. There will be room enough for two of your own men as well, I should think."

"Fine, I shall have Minister Myakys and..." Marigold took a moment to look over the remaining guards, before pointing to one among them. "Lewcas, you will come as well."

"Yes, my lady, at once," he replied while dismounting in a single, fluid motion. "Allow me to stand ahead of you to keep a shield between you and this captain."

"That would be best, thank you, Lewcas." Marigold acquiesced.

Lewcas nodded back and strode through the gatehouse door without further word, and Marigold followed at his heels.

Inside they were hit with the sweltering warmth emanating from the wood stove. Combined with the body heat of the present guards, and with Marigold having grown accustomed to the winter air outside, it made for a stuffy environment.

"I do not think this room is big enough for all parties," Gallin commented gaily from behind Marigold as he tried to step into the gatehouse. "I do hope that this captain is a small fellow, because if we put one more man in here, the walls might burst."

"I agree with Minister Myakys," Marigold spoke up from where she was wedged between him and Lewcas. "Is it necessary to have five guards along with my own and however many are on the other side of the wall disarming the mercenary?"

At the threshold of the door leading to the city stood Lieutenant Ashe, who gave answer to her concerns, "Yes, Miss Marigold, I am afraid I must insist. This is a dangerous rogue whose intent we cannot verify and therefore cannot trust. He might well have been sent by Eamon Palomb to assassinate you, so we have taken every precaution to ensure your safety."

"Surely we can spare one or two," Marigold reasoned in near exasperation. "I have no doubt that Lewcas will suffice to protect me against one unarmed man."

"I am sorry Miss Marigold, but I simply cannot do that," Lieutenant Ashe uttered in resistance.

A knock came on the outer door and the nearest guard opened the shutter of a window to where another guard was waiting, "We have thoroughly searched the captain and found no weapons other than what he already volunteered. We are as ready as we ever will be."

"Very well, bring him in," Marigold relayed back.

Lewcas tensed up and shielded her in full with his body as the door swung open, his tall, broad shoulders blocking Marigold's view entirely. Marigold could only listen to the sound of boots on hardwood and wonder at what was going on.

"Is this all necessary?" the unseen man asked with a scoff. "Lewcas, surely you can confirm my identity to these men and get them to stand down. Look at you all with your pistols drawn and everything. Surely I am not that much of a threat."

"Wait," Marigold said, while trying to look around the guard. "Who is that and how does he know you, Lewcas?"

"It might be best for you to see for yourself, my lady," Lewcas told her while turning sideways.

At first, she was thrown off by the set of muddied black riding leathers with no discernible markings that the man wore. A newly grown, thick beard did him no further favours either, but beneath it was a familiar countenance, and she gasped at the sight of it. "Freyard Archer, is that you?"

"At your service, Marigold," Freyard confirmed, his face breaking into that handsome smile of his. "It is wonderful to see you again."

There was no masking Marigold's joy, and she stepped around Lewcas to grab Freyard into a tight hug. "What are you doing here, Freyard?"

He squeezed her close in return, and brought her to arm's length. "Well, Marigold, should it be no bother to you, I have come to deliver the Sun's Rangers and myself into your service, if you would so have us."

16
SEREPHANIE

The League of the Sacred Fist was quickly proving to Serephanie to be a world of its own. As an initiate into the wandering community, Serephanie found herself frequently overwhelmed with how much work went into maintaining all the moving parts of the metaphorical machine. Often, she wondered if she could keep up with it all, and more importantly, if she even belonged there.

Most impressively, Serephanie was awed by the woman who sat at the controls of the machine, aware of every nut and bolt under her command. From the outside looking in, no one would ever be any the wiser that the Giant's Widow was an authority before which all seemed to bow. Had Serephanie not been taken into Cyrelle's employ one week prior, she would never have thought so herself.

The position had been extended only after several consecutive days of daily trips to Everett Lancer's tent with Darrion. From there, she was permitted to watch as Lancer drilled and exercised with the other three pupils. Thanks in no small part to Darrion's own dedication and tenacity, Everett had decided that he would take Darrion into the fold. Once Everett relayed his intentions to Lady Cyrelle, Serephanie's own offer of employment came shortly thereafter.

Like Darrion's admission into the Sacred Fist, Serephanie was also on a trial basis. Cyrelle had sent her to shadow both Syrie and the two handmaidens as each went about their job, alternating between the two starkly contrasting positions from day to day. On her first day, if asked, Serephanie felt she would be most comfortable as a handmaid. Her reasoning being that in her previous life, Serephanie had two of her own handmaids tending on her through the better part of any given day. Serephanie had witnessed them performing nearly everything that she presumed could be asked of her to do for Lady Cyrelle, leaving her confident that she could perform those tasks ably herself.

After a single morning of apprenticing beneath Syrie, Serephanie discovered to her own surprise that Syrie's line of work was of both greater interest and suitability for her. It was difficult for Serephanie, or even Syrie herself, for that matter, to put a title on her job. If a person were to see Syrie walking about the tent town occupying Bryten Field, they might think her to be a forewoman. It seemed to Serephanie that at nearly every turn there was another worker or two stopping Syrie for consultation, and if they were not seeking her, then it was her searching out specific employees.

The information and instructions that Syrie was passing along all came directly from Cyrelle, for an outsider looking in though, one would never know. Syrie took careful measures to phrase her orders in such a way that they seemed to be originating from either an unnamed boss or Impresario Demorton. Despite that, it occurred to Serephanie that Syrie did indeed bear a level of discretionary authority of her own. To that end, there were instances when Syrie modified the parameters of Cyrelle's instructions to suit the whims of the recipient in a given moment.

Perhaps what interested Serephanie the most though, were Syrie's duties that seemed to have a more clandestine nature to them. In those cases, Serephanie would be asked to remove herself from hearing distance. After just two days of following Syrie about, Serephanie had come to know nearly everyone employed by the League of the Sacred Fist, if not by name, then certainly by appearance.

There was an exception, though. Far to the rear of the big tent and separated from the rest of the tarpaulin town by the parked wagons of the convoy, there sat a plain grey pavilion tent. Serephanie was not permitted near it when Syrie would go calling. Instead, Serephanie was left waiting in the company of other employees beside the wagons that encircled almost the entire area encompassed by the Sacred Fist.

When Serephanie had asked about the tent after the first time she waited for Syrie, she was brusquely told, *"It's nothing you need concern yourself with."*

Naturally, that only furthered Serephanie's curiosity and on her second day tagging along with Syrie, she had made a point to pay close attention to the tent during Syrie's visit. Even the entrance flap was pointed away from the rest of the convoy, and Syrie had to circle the exterior of the tent to get within.

The dark grey fabric offered no hints as to who or what might be dwelling there, and Serephanie was simply too far away to hear anything. Knowing that she had nothing but her own speculations to go on, Serephanie was on the verge of forsaking her curiosity altogether when she spotted Syrie circling the tent on her way back to the encampment. Following the woman at a jog was a shirtless man, his arms and torso bereft of hair and rippling with slender, taught muscle. A white ponytail ran well down his back, quite nearly touching a pair of tight black trousers, and on his hip was a long, sheathed sword with a slight, discernible curve to it. For the briefest of moments, he made eye contact with Serephanie, but as quickly as it came, so too did it go and he turned his back to her before she could make note of any of his facial features. Words were exchanged between Syrie and the man and with a slap on his bare back and a guffaw from Syrie, the two parted.

"He is a friend of yours, I would guess?" Serephanie asked carefully once Syrie had closed the distance between them.

"Who is a friend of mine?" Syrie replied coyly.

The response was uncharacteristic of the Syrie that Serephanie had come to know. However, Serephanie had to admit that she did not know a great deal about Syrie. While the thought occurred to Serephanie to drop the matter in the face of Syrie's attempt to stymie inquiry, she decided to press Syrie further. "That... That man that you were just speaking with, I was asking if he was a friend."

"I was speaking with no man, Terra," Syrie lied flatly and calmly.

Serephanie glanced back toward the tent as they walked away from it. "There was a man there just now. A Drakian, I think. He had a long sword."

Syrie scoffed, "Would you even know a Drakian if you saw one?"

"His hair was white as snow," Serephanie offered in defence of her claim.

"Who was this? I never saw anyone with white hair. Furthermore, a person doesn't need to be Drakian to have white hair," Syrie put back to her without hesitation. "They could be albino or they might just be old. Now that I think of it, you don't even have to be old to have your hair turn white."

"He was bare above the waist while standing outside in near-winter cold," Serephanie suggested next. "Only someone from Drake could withstand that."

Syrie centred on Serephanie then, her eyes narrowing. "How would a waif stuck in Galdourn for most of her life know all this about Drakians? We get few in Illiastra as it is, let alone in a tiny spot like Galdourn. You certainly didn't read about it. I'd have a hard time believing that a woman who is so poor and baseborn that she doesn't even have a last name could find someone to teach her to read."

"No, that's not it... I... I just know some things... My father taught me," Serephanie managed to stammer out, unsure of how to account for what she knew.

"It's no matter, anyhow. There was no one there, Terra," Syrie stated firmly. She put her back to Serephanie and began walking toward the populated area at the rear of the big tent, leaving Serephanie to catch up.

"But I saw him," Serephanie had begun to say.

Syrie wheeled around angrily, and Serephanie had to stop in her tracks to avoid a collision. "It might be that you're not suited for this job, Terra."

"What? I don't understand. I did everything you asked of me," she stammered back.

"I'd give you back to Dottie and Dilla, but they don't much like you as it is," Syrie continued on, ignoring her plea. "So, my advice to you is to just go back to wherever it is you and your man are staying. Wait for him to get home from training, and then the both of you can arrange to make your way back to Galdourn. This is no place for you."

Serephanie felt frustration growing within as she formed her words. "I don't understand. I was just trying to get to know everyone that you deal with around here. You told me that was an important part of the job on the first day I worked with you."

"Everyone that I felt you should know has already been introduced to you," Syrie informed her sternly. "Did you ever stop to think that if I'm keeping you far away from that tent that maybe you don't need to know what's in it?"

Dual waves of shame and embarrassment washed over Serephanie then, and she relayed as much to Syrie, "My apologies. I should not have prodded as much as I did."

"I need an assistant who understands what it is to use… Uh… There's a word for it that Cyrelle likes to say…"

"Discretion?" Serephanie offered back.

"Discretion, that's it," Syrie said with a snap of her fingers, until her brows furrowed suspiciously. "Wait, how do *you* know that? Do you even know what that means?"

"It means to carry on in such a way that you don't spill secrets," Serephanie said, trying to keep her vocabulary from sounding too refined.

"Well, I… 'Spose that's about right, aye," Syrie responded, throwing her arms in the air. "But you don't carry on that way."

"I-I'll try harder, I promise," Serephanie begged. "I won't ask about that tent no more, I swear."

Syrie pinched the bridge of her nose and grunted under her breath for a moment. "Don't *ask* about *anything*, just do as you're told, savvy?"

Serephanie nodded quickly, but Syrie had more to add. "Listen to me: I won't ask you to do anything I haven't prepared you for. If I don't explain something or introduce you to someone, it's because you don't need to know. There are a great number of things going on here and what happens in the fighting ring is the least of it. Now, before you start fretting, I can tell you that none of those things is sinister. It's more so as Cyrelle says, 'we make flirtations with the law for the right reasons', if you catch my meaning. Until we can trust you to tell you more, you will have to accept a little bit of secrecy from us and remember that discretion is your best mate, do you get me?"

"Understood, aye. You'll get no more questions out of me, Syrie," Serephanie relented, her head bowed.

Syrie patted her on the back in a softer fashion than she had done with the unknown white-haired man, "That's good to hear. Now, let's be off to our next task. You'll like this one, I promise."

Without a further word, the two turned toward the more populous region of the tarpaulin town, with Syrie leading the way. It seemed that once they were among the inhabited area again that Syrie could scarcely turn a corner without someone saying hello or stopping her for a brief chat. Syrie indulged every request for conversation, which combined with the shortened days of late autumn, led Serephanie to wonder if they would finish their rounds before nightfall.

At last, they came to a familiar tent, and Syrie lifted the flap, bidding Serephanie to enter just as the sunlight began to turn to evening hues of pink and orange. Within they were greeted by the sight of Darrion quite nearly rolling directly into Syrie.

Regardless of the fact that Darrion managed to stop his forward rolling within a metre of actually colliding with either woman, the surprise caused Syrie to sidestep defensively, gently pushing Serephanie along with her.

"Watch it, Cole!" Syrie cautioned, with all eyes in the tent going to her.

"Cole was nowhere near you, Syrie," Everett Lancer commented from upon the bench in the back of the tent. "You were in no danger."

Darrion stepped forward all the same. "Are you both alright?"

Syrie cleared her throat and tugged at her tunic, looking almost a little embarrassed with herself. "Aye, no harm done."

"I trust there's a reason for your interruption, Syrie?" Everett asked while pushing to his feet.

She nodded at him and held open the flap of the tent. "I need a moment of your time, if you can spare it, Mister Lancer."

"Well, then let's not delay. I simply cannot wait another moment to hear what I assume is a message from Cyrelle that is intended for my ears only," Lancer relented with dry sarcasm. Before exiting, he turned back to his four charges. "Take this break to drink some water and take a few deep breaths. We will pick up exactly where we left off when I return."

As Syrie and Everett went outside, Darrion quickly went to the water barrel near the bench and procured himself a full cup to quench his thirst. "How has your day with Syrie been?" he asked Serephanie upon return to where she stood just inside the tent. "Did you two do anything interesting?"

Serephanie shrugged and was about to respond, but the whispered voice of Everett on the other side of the tarp reached them first.

"Already? Huh, and here I had thought we were still hauling in good coin at the gates..."

"I can't really say much, Love," Serephanie finally replied, putting an index finger up to signal Darrion to talk cautiously.

He craned his head so that one ear was facing the direction that Syrie and Everett were standing in, but took her meaning plainly enough and began talking at a low volume. "We've been working on forward and backward rolling. It's much like how I was already trained, but Mister Lancer's style is tighter than I'm accustomed to, so I've had to adapt to it to keep up."

Everett's voice came through again, "Well, I'm certain I could work with at least three of them, should they be willing to go out on the road with us. I haven't reached a verdict on the fourth one, but I suppose I could let him go for now and invite him back for another trial when we return to Hercalest again."

"Just rolling? I had figured you would be doing some amount of actual fight training by now," Serephanie replied to Darrion, keeping their conversation going.

"If it's who I think you're talking about," Syrie added in a whisper. "Then you might as well just cut him loose and forget about him. I've seen my share of trainees and I'm not seeing the 'it' factor. Then again, you're the trainer, so you have better insight than I on the matter."

Worry began to creep into Serephanie's bones and she relayed that to Darrion with a look.

His own expression was one of concern, but he nodded casually and kept on talking. "Oh, I'm sure we'll get to it soon enough. We can't keep doing exercises and rolls forever."

"Actually, you're not far off in your assessment," Everett confirmed to Syrie. "I had merely hoped that with a little more time I could be absolutely certain about it. I wouldn't want to throw away good talent over an unfounded feeling."

"We're not leaving for another week, so think of this as more of a notification than an immediate order," Syrie whispered with reassurance in her voice.

"It will come, I'm sure," Serephanie said hopefully. "They will see the fighter's spirit within you. I'm certain of it, Love."

Everett hummed aloud while Serephanie spoke, and she finished in time to hear him say, "Aye, that's true. That'll be more than enough time for deliberation. Who knows, perhaps he won't want to come with us anyway."

"Go on back to the rookies for now. You can talk it over with Cyrelle later," Syrie instructed, ending their meeting.

"Aye, we'll pick this chat up in a day or two," Everett relented with a heavy sigh, suddenly returning to the interior of the tent. "Alright lads, let's get back to it. Kellum, you're up next for front rolls, as I recall."

Syrie tapped Serephanie on the shoulder, having followed behind Everett. "Come now and say your farewells, we have more people to see."

"Of course, Syrie, I'll be with you in a moment," Serephanie responded, turning then to Darrion, "I'll see you this evening, dearest. I love you."

"I love you too, Darling," he told her, giving her a quick peck on the lips before they parted.

Once outside, the cold air of the early winter hit Serephanie and she pulled her dingy black cloak tight around her. "Oh my, I think the wind is picking up," she commented idly, getting Syrie's attention.

"Huh? Aye, it seems to be getting colder. Winter is nearing, after all," Syrie began to say, until she pivoted on a heel toward the sound of rapidly approaching footfalls. "Who's there? Oh, it's you, Dilla. What's the matter?"

The handmaiden had approached quickly, wearing neither cloak nor coat and her cheeks rosy from both the chilly temperature and the jogging pace at which she was coming toward them at. "Syrie! There you are!" she said between rapid breaths. "Lady Cyrelle sent me to find you two and bring you to her immediately."

"Whatever for?" Syrie queried with a mixture of puzzlement and concern in her voice. "We were soon going to be returning to her as it is with the daily report."

Dilla had bent over to catch her breath, a quick shake of her head serving as a temporary reply. Upon standing straight and regaining her composure, she elaborated, "I cannot say, other than to tell you that she has urgent business with the two of you and that she's taken to her wheelhouse."

"For warmth or privacy?" Syrie asked warily.

"Both, I should think," Dilla replied hastily.

Syrie glanced Serephanie and she met her analytical gaze for a brief moment, until she turned back to Dilla. "Alright then, we'll come with you straight away. I haven't the foggiest idea what she could want with Terra, though."

The three set out together, with Syrie and Serephanie having to keep a brisk pace to maintain stride with the impatient Dilla. In a matter of minutes, they arrived at the oversized wheelhouse that Lady Cyrelle had decided to occupy. To Serephanie's understanding, the ostentatious carriage was Cyrelle's means of transport when the Sacred Fist convoy rolled over the roads. It was built to be her office, sitting room, and sleeping quarters in one mobile unit, and required a small team of horses to pull. When it had first been pointed out to Serephanie by Syrie, her first question was why the Sacred Fist used horse-drawn convoys to begin with.

"Because the rails don't run where we do," Syrie had explained. *"They hit the major spots, sure, and a few small places in between, but we bring the Sacred Fist all around the country. The folks in the tiny little nooks and crannies in the far corners of Illiastra probably couldn't tell you the difference between Lord Taves and Lord Palomb but they all know who 'The Glorious' Gilbare and Barajah are. Do you know why? Because the Sacred Fist takes the time to go to the small places, meet the people therein, and deliver them some entertainment.*

"We can draw a fine crowd in Hercalest and Daol Bay, aye, but they are big cities, any promotor with even a smidgeon of our reputation and finances could draw a crowd in such places. You know what, though, those big places don't really care. When we are set up like this in Hercalest, we're just another attraction in a city already spoiled for such.

"You want to see something special though, look at what happens when the Sacred Fist rolls our wagons into somewhere like Tusker's Cove way up in the northwest. We show up in them little spots like that, and our fighters are treated like kings. Some of the towns arrange for festivals and feasts in our honour, even."

Syrie beamed spiritedly as she spoke of the League, and the pride she felt radiated across her face with every word. "The best part is when it comes time for our show, because you can be sure that every single able person in town will show up. Though there might be fewer people in the tent than we can draw here, you would swear there was thrice that many from the excitement and energy they give off. That's a special feeling, Terra. That's something we would miss out on if we stuck to the train tracks."

As the wheelhouse came into sight, Serephanie took notice of a man quickly approaching from that direction, and both Syrie and Dilla slowed their pace to greet him.

"Impresario Demorton, to what do we owe the pleasure, ser?" Syrie asked jovially.

He tipped his top hat to them and gave a half bow. "Good day to you, Ladies. I'm just retiring from my daily meeting with Lady Cyrelle, which is where I would hazard to guess that you two are headed."

"It is indeed, Impresario," Syrie replied with a half bow of her own. "Terra and I were summoned urgently."

"Ah, the lovely lass in the black cloak behind you must be Miss Terra then, I presume?" Demorton asked in what seemed like a rhetorical manner.

Dilla and Syrie both stepped aside, with Syrie giving Serephanie a gentle push toward Demorton. "Aye, this is her."

Serephanie felt a nervous wave rush through her as his hand extended in her direction, but she took it all the same. As they shook, she tried her best to reveal no more of her face than the hood of her cloak would betray.

"I must say, Missus Chere, I was impressed with your husband's performance in the Winter King's tournament," Demorton commented after releasing her hand. "It's rare that we have an outside competitor that excites our seasoned professionals, but Mister Chere managed to do just that. You should be proud of him, Madam."

She offered Demorton half a bow with her reply, "Of course, ser. I am always proud of Cole. He is a good man with a pure, selfless heart who gives his all to everything he endeavours to do. I felt certain when he entered the tournament that he would make his mark, and I feel that he has achieved that goal quite admirably."

Demorton's eyebrow flicked upward and his mouth turned at the corner. "If I may say so, that was quite well spoken, Missus Terra."

Her face felt flush as she suddenly realised that her manner of speaking was indeed too grand, especially for a poor nameless bastard girl from Galdourn. "I'm sorry, ser. I was just so surprised that you even knew who I was that I must have tried to sound like the nobles."

"But of course I know who you are, my dear," Demorton stated amiably. "It's my duty to know all of the staff of the Sacred Fist. Each person on the payroll is important to the function of the League and all deserve to be known and recognised for their efforts toward the operation."

"With all due respect, ser, as a woman I cannot be on the payroll, unless you meant my husband, who is only training as of yet," Serephanie corrected him gingerly.

Demorton hummed aloud curiously, the merriment fading from his face. "I must be mistaken, then. You have my apologies for the misunderstanding." Turning away from Serephanie, he patted Syrie on the shoulder. "Well, I won't keep you both. I just came from meeting with Cyrelle in her wheelhouse, so she should be free to see you now. I'll take my leave and bid good day to the both of you."

"Did... Did I say something wrong?" Serephanie asked once the man had gone on his way, genuinely nonplussed by the sudden shift in Demorton's behaviour.

Syrie sighed and answered Serephanie while walking toward the wheelhouse, "Aye, you did, but you couldn't have known, so don't worry about it. If Cyrelle allows, I'll explain later, or it might be that she will do so herself. In any case, we shall find out shortly."

Having gone on ahead while Serephanie and Syrie were talking to Demorton, Dilla was standing in wait for them before the door of the carriage. Once they were within a single stride of the handmaiden, she unlatched the door, swung it open and stood back to allow Syrie and Serephanie entry. The two thanked Dilla in their turn and climbed aboard, with Serephanie going first and Syrie pulling the door closed behind them.

Though it already looked large to begin with, the wheelhouse was astoundingly spacious inside. Directly to their right sat a modest desk with two cushioned chairs before it and a third behind. In the back of this office space, Serephanie espied a door that she could only guess led to the sleeping bunk. On her left, at the forward side of the carriage there was a sitting area containing a small sofa and a low table. The main area seemed to be heated by a caged brazier full of hot coals found near the sofa, and the smell of the burning briquettes fought to be detected over what smelled to Serephanie like lavender. Fastened to the walls were sconces bearing oil lamps, presently alight to augment the fading evening light filtering in through the tiny window that each area was afforded.

The door behind the desk slid open and Cyrelle strode out into the office area. "Good afternoon, Ladies," she offered in greeting, a smile on her face as she lowered herself into the chair behind the desk. "Please, be seated. We have much to discuss and the day is growing late already."

"Aye, ma'am, as you wish," Syrie replied cautiously. Serephanie followed suit, and the two took their places across the desk from Cyrelle.

"Dottie, you may take your leave of me for now so that you and Dilla can go take your dinner," Cyrelle told the handmaiden. "I'll send Syrie to find you two when we are done here. You need not return before then."

Dottie had entered the office space quietly and had been closing the bedroom door when the order was issued. In a flash, she was at Cyrelle's side offering resistance to her dismissal, "Are you sure, Madam? Would you not want one of us to stay behind to keep watch at the door to the wheelhouse?"

"No, thank you. I'll have Syrie latch it from the inside once you're gone," Cyrelle further instructed. "That will be all, Dottie."

The handmaiden was not so easily shooed, however. "Should I serve beverages and food before going, Madam? Will you not be hungry?"

Up to that point, Cyrelle had been looking through papers on her desk. However, when the handmaid continued to ask questions, Cyrelle turned in her chair and looked the girl in the face. "Syrie is more than capable of doing so, should any of us grow peckish. I thank you for offering though, and say, once more, that you are dismissed, Dottie."

There had been a level of annoyance in Cyrelle's tone and Dottie seemed to pick up on as much, offering a bow and a sheepish, "Yes, Madam, as you wish."

She hurried toward the exit, with Syrie close on her heels. The sharp bite of the winter air snuck in through the caravan quickly enough to be felt on the skin, though Syrie stopped it in its tracks once Dottie was gone. Serephanie could hear Syrie locking the door and a pang of nervousness filled the pit of her stomach.

"I often wonder about those two..." Cyrelle commented ponderously, drawing Serephanie's attention. A finger of Cyrelle's had given the slightest lift to the samite drapes covering the window beside her desk.

Serephanie looked for herself, craning her neck so she could see through the curtains, her eyes befalling Dottie and Dilla as they walked away from the wheelhouse.

Cyrelle sighed and turned back toward Serephanie. "Did you know that Dottie is of the nobility?"

"I did not, Ma'am," she replied truthfully, entirely sure that she had never met either handmaiden before.

"She's the second youngest of the eleven children of..." Cyrelle cocked her head to the side, fingers rapping on the desk in quick succession as a quizzical look came over her face. "It seems that I've forgotten his name all of a sudden."

Syrie's chair creaked beneath her as she sat down again, and Cyrelle turned to face her. "Syrie, who is Dottie's father? I can't seem to recall off hand."

"His name isn't coming to me either, but he's a city councillor out of Gazetown, isn't he?" Syrie chimed in, looking a little uncertain herself.

"Ah, yes!" Cyrelle said, her face lighting up in recognition of the name. "He's one of Minister Hawksbury's men. Braxon? Is that his name? In any case, she's of noble stock, even if it is several parts removed from relative influence. That particular councillor, who I am now ninety percent sure is named Braxon, is keen on sticking the youngest half of his brood in service to anyone of even marginal authority. Originally, the councillor thought he was giving Dottie to Impresario Demorton, and was downright indignant when he found out that she was instead assigned to serve me. In the spirit of fairness, Demorton did send a letter of apology and offered to send Dottie back to Gazetown on the next train home.

"Oddly enough, we got another correspondence in far too short a time for him to have received Demorton's reply. What was even more curious was that as suddenly as Braxon's vitriol rose in the first letter, so too did it fall in the second. It was so saccharine in nature that I was wondering if the paper itself was soaked in honey. There was no doubt that it was his handwriting, but he wrote as though the first letter had never even existed. Furthermore, this new letter even ended with Braxon instructing me, personally, to 'take good care of Dottie'.

"You know, I've not been able to prove it outright, but I would still wager a fare sum on Dottie having sent a letter of her own to assuage her father's concerns with serving me."

None of what Cyrelle was saying made much sense to Serephanie, but she decided to follow Syrie's advice from this afternoon and ask no questions. *If I need to know, someone will surely explain.*

A quick glance to the window gave no sign of either handmaiden. Cyrelle herself seemed to be content that they were gone, releasing the curtain to fall back against the wooden window frame, her focus now falling squarely on Serephanie. "That is enough about my handmaids. You are surely wondering why I asked for you to meet with Syrie and I in private, yes?"

She could feel Cyrelle and Syrie's eyes on her, and nodded in answer. "Aye, Ma'am, the thought had crossed my mind."

Cyrelle leaned forward, her elbows on the desk and fingers intertwined. "You might have heard around camp that there is talk of us pulling up stakes and making for the open road soon."

"No, Ma'am, I cannot say that I did," Serephanie stated nervously after giving the quickest of glances in Syrie's direction.

"The winter fast approaches and our ticket sales for the regularly scheduled fights are beginning to drop off here in Hercalest," Cyrelle explained frankly. "There's nothing to be morose about, I assure you. It's merely the signal that our presence has begun to grow stale. The time has come to head for warmer climes and fresh audiences while the snows allow it."

"Is that so?" Serephanie asked, swallowing nervously all the while.

There was a gentle smile forming on Cyrelle's face then, and she opened her hands wide. "Don't fret, Terra, this happens every year."

She shook her head in response. "But why wouldn't I worry? Cole is not a Sacred Fist fighter. We'll be left to our own devices in Hercalest when you leave."

A side-eyed look was shared between Cyrelle and Syrie, with the former looking curious and the latter appearing positively puzzled. "Whatever could make you think that?" Cyrelle queried on behalf of them both.

"Well, I mean, I assumed that the whole point of meeting with me so urgently was to tell Cole and I to be on our way," Serephanie suggested with a shrug, hoping she did not give away what she had overheard.

"You do not think that your Cole has the necessary qualities to be a member of the Sacred Fist?" Cyrelle asked next.

"Oh, no, nothing of the sort, Ma'am," Serephanie proclaimed hastily.

Cyrelle's head tilted ever so slightly as she posed her next query, "Then why do you think we would evict you both?"

"As to that, Ma'am..." Serephanie began, taking a precious few seconds to compose her thoughts. "Cole is only on trial as of now. There's yet to be a decision as to whether or not he will even be accepted as a trainee."

With a preceding click of the tongue, Cyrelle responded, "What a well-crafted response, Terra. I'm impressed."

Serephanie looked between Cyrelle and Syrie. "Is-is what I said not accurate?"

For the first time since Cyrelle tried to remember Dottie's parentage, Syrie had a response, "We still have a week before we plan to leave, there might still be time for him to be granted a berth in the trainee camp."

"Do you think he will?" Serephanie asked with growing concern, her eyes going so rapidly between the other two women that the question could be seen as open to either one.

Cyrelle took the query, offering a nonchalant reply that came with a shrug of her own, "That's for Everett Lancer to decide. He is the head trainer, after all."

That's not what I asked, Serephanie thought to say, keeping the statement to herself. Instead, in the interest of keeping their discussion going, she posed a different question to Cyrelle, "Is there anything that I can do to help in the matter?"

As the words left her mouth, Serephanie felt a trap of her own making spring on her, and panic began to course through her veins.

"What a curious thing to ask," Cyrelle said with a hum. "What can any of us do, really? We are but women in the world of men, after all. Our right to make decisions extends barely to ourselves. One could hardly expect someone of our gender to be in a position to do much about anything. In fact, I am not legally even permitted to pay my own employees."

An almost palpable layer of sarcasm had been spread atop Cyrelle's statement and a look toward Syrie found her sitting back with a sly grin across her face. Serephanie felt that something was indeed afoot between these two, yet despite that, she could not shake the sense that whatever game they were playing was without malevolence.

"You're not permitted to pay your employees, but I get the feeling that you are about to tell me that you do," Serephanie said in a manner that was both slow and cautious.

Cyrelle gave a mischievous wink. "How astute of you to notice, Terra."

"Are you surprised to hear that?" Syrie followed up, speedily throwing in the question to Serephanie.

"Well, no, not really, Syrie," Serephanie put back to her quickly enough. "As you said to me earlier, you 'make flirtations with the law for the right reasons', I just had no idea what either the flirtations or the reasons were."

A chuckle came forth from Cyrelle. "I wonder where you heard that, Syrie."

"I only quote from the best," Syrie replied playfully.

A thought occurred to Serephanie while Cyrelle and Syrie bantered, and she decided on a rather bold course of action. "Your *flirtation* with the law is that you operate as an employer and maintain your own finances, is that it? That's illegal for a woman to do, aye, but there are far worse crimes."

Cyrelle raised her head and scanned Serephanie curiously then. "It's all that detractors of mine would need to know in order to have me locked away in Biddenhurst until the end of my days. I take on a great deal of risk for doing something that would be seen as otherwise banal almost anywhere else in the Known World."

"Well, I assume that the actual paperwork is all in a man's name, Demorton's perhaps?" Serephanie said next, forcing a measure of feigned confidence to her tone.

"I didn't get this far in life without learning to cover my tracks, if that is what you mean," Cyrelle answered, her eyes narrowing.

For the moment, Serephanie felt the confines of her self-imposed trap giving away. "That is all fine by me, Ma'am. Surely, I can do something to aid in all of this. Cole is a magnificent fighter and simply being here is fulfilling his wildest dreams. I'll do anything I can to see that he is not cut from the roster."

"I am most glad to hear that," Cyrelle said while leaning back in her chair. "As a matter of fact, I too would like to see your Cole continue his training with us. However, you seem certain that he will indeed be released from the Sacred Fist. You must have some reason to believe that."

"It's just a hunch that Cole and I share," Serephanie gave in response. "We reckon that since Cole started his trial well after the other three, he's the most likely to get turned away should the league have to leave on short notice."

From beside her, Serephanie could feel Syrie staring intensely. "What would make you think that Mister Lancer would turn any of them away? He could decide that all four will be offered berths."

"But will they?" Serephanie propositioned, hoping it was enough to throw both women from further probing of her knowledge on the matter.

"When it comes to potential trainees, I always defer to Everett's recommendations and I am not one to try and persuade Everett one way or the other," Cyrelle explained, her tone maintaining the casual demeanour it had worn all along. "He's been training recruits almost as long as his respected career as a fighter lasted. I assure you, he knows what he is doing. On that note, I am expecting him for a meeting later tonight to hear his judgement on the matter. Until then, I can give no promises."

Serephanie fetched on something in Cyrelle's statement, and wasted no time putting it back to her. "With all due respect Ma'am, don't you mean that Impresario Demorton would defer to Mister Lancer's decisions? What part would you have in the matters of men?"

There came another wink from Cyrelle. "You're good at this, Terra. It took Dottie weeks as my handmaid to figure out the way of things around here, but you worked it out in no time at all."

The game was up and Serephanie knew it. While such a twist of fate would have usually filled her with dread, she no longer felt the constraints of the trap from minutes ago. Cyrelle had let her own guard down, and Serephanie felt it was done intentionally.

"While I've always been told I was too clever for my own good, I don't think I figured it out by mere chance, Ma'am," Serephanie remarked comfortably. "You wanted me to know that you are the true impresario of the Sacred Fist."

"Now, why would I do that?" Cyrelle asked, the question seeming to be almost rhetorical.

"As an offering of trust, I should say," Serephanie stated after a deep breath, feeling a weight lifting from her shoulders. "You hoped that by giving away your secret that I would give up mine. But I suppose I couldn't have kept that secret around you, could I?"

Judging from her laugh, Cyrelle seemed to find humour in what Serephanie had said. "No, but I wanted to hear it from your lips. It was your secret to tell. Not mine to give away."

Serephanie let the secret free in a wave of words. "If you would so like, then I shall say it outright: my name is not Terra of Galdourn, it is Serephanie. I am the eldest daughter and the former heir of Marscal of House Tullivan, Warden Lord of the Western Realm of Illiastra. My 'husband' is Darrion Veskries, a fisherman of Daol Bay and an aspiring freestyle fighter. We're not truly wed, not yet, anyhow. Now, Ma'am, with all of that out in the open between the three of us, what do you plan to do about it?"

Without a second of delay, Cyrelle leapt at the question. "Everett informed me that when you first met him, he told you that we could protect you and that women have a road forward with the Sacred Fist. Do you recall him saying that?"

"I do, yes," Serephanie confirmed.

"We extend that offer to all women who could use our protection," Cyrelle declared proudly. "No matter if they are a poor waif from Galdourn or the daughter of one of Illiastra's wealthiest men. When we leave in a week, I want you two to join us on the road. There is no safer company for you to have in Illiastra."

Serephanie looked between the two suspiciously. "Are you doing this for my benefit, or did Darrion earn a berth on his own merit? Is there no intention to evict him?"

"The only one of the brand new trainees that Everett is thinking of cutting is Domas," Syrie informed her nonchalantly. "He's got a piss-poor attitude and once he got as far as he did, Everett noted that he had practically no work ethic. Your man, on the other hand, earned his place on his own. In fact, Everett doesn't even know who you really are, but he thinks your man has what we're looking for in a fighter."

"That's fantastic news. I'm so glad to hear it," Serephanie said with relief, exhaling until her lungs were nearly empty. "In the meantime, what would you have me do? I need no special favours. I swear to you, I'm at your service for whatever you need, Ma'am."

"We need you and Darrion to act as though nothing has changed," Cyrelle told her. "You'll work for Syrie and I, doing as you have. Unless you are told otherwise by one of the two of us, assume that everyone still believes you are Cole and Terra Chere. That ruse must persist so that we can best protect you. While Darrion trains, he will be put to work setting up and dismantling our tents, rings, and staging and the both of you will be paid for your labour. You have my word that we will protect you both, by whatever means necessary. The EMP shall not have Serephanie Tullivan. That I promise you."

17

MARIGOLD

package addressed to Marigold had arrived aboard a train from Obalen exactly one day after Freyard had arrived in Daol Bay. It was sent in the care of an official envoy from the Lord Master Grenjin Howland with direct orders to relinquish the package only to Marigold.

The courier was an assistant to one of Atrebell's city councillors, and came unarmed and without a protective escort. He had made no effort to hide himself or his intentions, and had even presented himself at the city gates. From there, Lieutenant Ashe had taken it upon himself to deliver the man and his package directly to Marigold's protectors.

Marigold herself had been hosting a meeting with her supporters in the private council chambers of city hall at that time. When the man's presence was brought to her attention, she called for a brief recess so that she might attend to him. By the time she made her way to the foyer of the building, she found the man seated in an alcove office, having been turned over to Darrill and Elden of the manor guards.

What the man had attempted to hand over to her was a thick, yellow envelope, which was intercepted abruptly by the gloved hands of Darrill in mid-transfer. At first, she was annoyed that her guardsmen would so boldly take the package from her. However, her feeling of annoyance ebbed when Darrill expressed his reasonable concern that the contents of the envelope might well be doused in any number of poisons. When both guardsmen were certain that the papers were safe to handle, they returned the documents to Marigold's possession.

Having thanked the deliveryman, she released him back to the care of Lieutenant Ashe, who was to see that the man was boarded on the next train headed east. Once both men were gone, Marigold returned to her meeting, and began to read the letters aloud to those in attendance. As she aired the words to her audience, Marigold's previous feelings of annoyance morphed into something entirely different.

The package contained three letters: one from Grenjin, and the other two from Eamon and Eldridge Palomb, individually. They also thought to include a full copy of the marriage pact and copied passages from the Illiastran law books, with attention drawn to specific laws that Marigold was allegedly in the act of breaking. Then there was a replication of the Illiastran Constitution as it now stood under the Elite Merchant Party, which Marigold was knowingly and proudly in violation of.

In summary, the point that the three were trying to impress upon Marigold was that as a woman, she was meddling in laws that men decreed that they and they alone be allowed to legislate. Beyond that, the accusations of law breaking revolved around a belief that she would have the western half of Illiastra secede illegally from the nation.

In his own letter, Grenjin said that he would refrain from pressing charges against Marigold if she were to cease any further actions that could be deemed to be, as Grenjin himself wrote, *against the interests of Illiastra*. There was even a promise to seek no punishment for her or her supporters. Marigold had no reason to believe any of it, though. She further reasoned that even if Howland kept his word, that there was no going back for Marigold and her band of resistors now.

Even without legal repercussions, a party that was openly fostering rebellion to the order of things would never be allowed to exist peacefully again. Every remaining person that had stood with Marigold would be whittled away to nothing in terms of both finances and influence, and those would be the luckiest among them. The rest would be charged and sentenced to either death or a life of incarceration in Biddenhurst on whatever charge the EMP could concoct. There was always a legal loophole to be exploited by those who controlled the ropes, and the EMP were careful enough to keep from being entangled in their own lines.

All of that was underscored with the threat of heresy charges that would likely be laid by the Triarchy. In Howland's letter, he claimed that he alone wielded enough sway over the Triarchy to keep their officials in check, but could only reasonably do so for a short time. In fact, he gave her until the New Year to halt her actions. Any longer, Grenjin claimed, and the Triarchy would sidestep his stalling tactics and pursue Marigold and her supporters on their own. Howland claimed in his letter that he was making such offers to Marigold on both her behalf and in memory of her father, with whom Howland legitimately did share a significant level of camaraderie. That note alone gave Marigold a sense that Grenjin was earnestly attempting to show her some meagre measure of mercy.

While a tiny part of Marigold did feel frightened and willing to turn back, her resolve held her firmly to where she was. Marigold had gone too far to return to the old road now. If nothing else, she owed it to her people and the resistance party who were actively risking their own lives and legacies on her behalf.

There can be no turning back, she reminded herself, affirming her resolve.

Besides that, for whatever miniscule mercies Grenjin Howland was willing to grant Marigold, the letters of Eamon and Eldridge Palomb stated that neither one of them would allow her any such thing.

Eamon's was written in a formal manner, much like Grenjin's, but instead of clemencies, the head of House Palomb promised only to keep the hammer of the law from hitting her too harshly. There was no mention of leniency for her followers and no notion that he would withhold the Triarchy from meting out their own punishments on Marigold and her followers for violating their theocratic laws. In what seemed to Marigold like a ludicrous waste at this point, Eamon had also used valuable real estate on the paper to remind her of the marriage pact. Most importantly, Eamon claimed that despite Marigold not having a say in the matter when the contract was drafted, that he and his legal counsel felt that she was still obliged to uphold the agreement.

There was no denying that in Illiastra, women indeed had no rights over their own bodily autonomy. Yet, it was those exact laws that denied half of the country's people the mere right of personhood that Marigold was on a mission to change. It was only by violating those laws at all that Marigold could even broach the subject of their abolishment. Regardless, any legislature that reduced Marigold to an object to be bartered and sold, and denied her any authority in her own fate, were not laws that Marigold was about to recognise.

A far more scathing forecast was found in Eldridge's letter, which was co-signed by Pyore. For the life of her, Marigold could not fathom why either Grenjin or Eamon had allowed such a wretched diatribe to be sent with the rest of the neatly edited contents of the package.

Ultimately, the two lords had written of the judicial and theocratic legal issues that Marigold was potentially facing and the varying levels to which they were willing to absolve her of those problems. Eldridge, on the other hand, had penned the sort of vitriolic response one would expect from a literate, temperamental toddler whose favourite toy had been taken away. The scathing excuse for correspondence stopped short of using profane language, but made up for itself in its vileness with its utter contempt for Marigold's desire to be treated as a whole person.

Eldridge stated clearly, and in defiance of the polite performance of their last crossing in Atrebell, that upon the death of her father, Marigold had become the property of House Palomb. According to the letter, neither of the two brothers had any desire to marry Marigold, which was the lone relief of the entire diatribe. For the sake of the marriage pact, and the rewards that came with it, Eldridge promised that one of the two Palomb twins would be betrothed to her and would do so by force, if required.

You will go to the altar beside either Pyore or I to be married off. We will let you choose how. You can walk there in a fine white dress, or be dragged there shackled hand and foot, Eldridge had scribed in handwriting that was ironically beautiful, given the terrible meaning behind his carefully penned words.

Furthermore, Eldridge went on to state that he and Pyore had no interest in fathering a child with her, but would, if their father so willed it. Once again, they offered her limited choice in how that was to happen.

"I would choose death first!" Marigold yelled out when she had read that part of the letter aloud. "I am not a prize to be won, or a key that opens the Western Realm like a vault. I will not be treated as chattel at best and a prisoner at worst. If the Lord Master and House Palomb thought this package would signify the end of the Western Rebellion, then I would be only glad to tell them that they failed miserably."

Marigold was quite ready to throw the letter into the fireplace at that point, until Greggard Simillon convinced her otherwise. "That document needs to stand as proof of the dishonourable, verminous behaviour of the Western Realm's would-be rulers," he stated with disgust toward the Palomb twins. "The people need to see what their Lady of Daol Bay, and all women of the West for that matter, would potentially be subject to under a Palomb regime."

As her gaze fell in the letter, held in a tensed hand that was fully prepared to crumble the paper, an idea came to her. "Lord Greggard, can you promise to have this letter copied and sent to every reporter and herald from Tusker's Cove to Tippard?"

His eyes narrowed and a smile started to form on his lips. "But of course, my lady. I would be only glad."

"Then I shall relinquish it to your possession," Marigold decided as she laid the letter face down on the table and slid it in his direction. Starting with Gallin, who had been seated next to her, it was passed down the table until it came to a stop before Greggard.

Once he had the document, Marigold revealed to the room that all three writers of the package had given Marigold the same deadline by which she was to yield to their authority, albeit with varying repercussions for surpassing it: the New Year, which occurred at the end of the first trimester of winter.

Such a deadline gave Marigold mere weeks to have her claim to the Western Realm established. In that time, she would first need to get a signature from one of the remaining three city councillors of Daol Bay to solidify her position as regional minister. Secondly, in order for Marigold to be acclaimed as the Warden Lady of the West, she required three signatures from any combination of the nine ministers who had not outright opposed her rule while abstaining from signing *The Declaration of Agency*.

"Does anyone have any suggestion as to how we are to convince at least three out of nine holdout ministers to join our cause with the precious time we have remaining to us?" Marigold asked the attendees, gesturing openly with both palms turned upward.

"I shall fetch some writing materials for the lady," Oire announced without further explanation.

"Whatever for, ser?" asked Freyard Archer from where he sat at the midway point of the long table on Marigold's right side. Having sworn the Sun's Rangers to her service, Marigold saw no reason to disallow Freyard to join in on the meetings, and he had accepted the invitation readily.

"We will need to write letters of our own to request the immediate presence of the nine ministers not openly hostile towards us, of course," Oire gave in reply, as though it was obvious what his intention was.

Gallin chuckled under his breath, though not low enough that it escaped Oire's hearing. "Is something amusing, Minister Myakys?"

"Do you think that these ministers will come when called?" Gallin asked in what seemed to be a rhetorical manner. "In the meantime, we have little else to do but sit around waiting for their responses. If they decline the summonses, then what do you propose we do? We will not get that time back, ser."

"Do you have some other suggestion, Minister?" Oire sent back to Gallin in sceptical fashion.

"As a matter of fact, I do," Gallin told him confidently. "I propose that we indeed write letters, not to invite the ministers to us, but rather, to request that Marigold visit with them."

"You would have the lady leave the security of Daol Bay for some sort of tour of the west coast?" Oire asked in utter bafflement.

Before Oire could formulate much more of a response, Marigold leapt at Gallin's suggestion. "Why Minister Myakys, I think that's a fantastic idea. We can arrange for a private engine to form a train of the family cars, it would be the quickest means to travel."

"You cannot be serious, my lady," Oire suggested to her, his concern worn plainly across his face.

"Well, why not, Oire?" Leonice asked, having been mum on the subject thus far. "It will do her no favours to remain cooped up here all winter long. That's not to mention that her supporters would likely benefit from having her visit their regions too."

Elda Mattersly clapped her hands excitedly. "What a marvellous suggestion, Lady Leonice. I can think of no better way to endear our Marigold to the people along the west coast than to send her among them. She can give speeches to the public in the friendlier regions while she attempts to pursue negotiations with those who are brave enough to treat with her."

"We would love to host you in Mattersly Castle, if you would like to take yourself as far as Tippard, my lady," Walter Mattersly added to his wife's thought.

"Kylisport would welcome you with open arms as well, my lady," Gallin offered in further invitation.

"We have hardly the manor guards to spare to both protect Marigold and the manor," Oire protested in growing frustration.

"I believe that I might have a solution for that, Mister Oire," Freyard stated while pushing back his chair and rising to his feet to be seen. "My Sun's Rangers stand at the ready to step in and supplant the lady's existing bodyguards, if so requested. Who would be more suited to the task than rangers I ask you? A tour is synonymous with a ranging, as far as I am concerned."

"Yes, of course, Freyard," Marigold readily agreed, delighted at the prospect of having him along. "That should free up more than enough of the manor guards. I will still take some along, naturally, but your men will more than suffice to bolster their numbers for the tour."

Oire had slumped back into his chair, having produced a handkerchief with which to mop his brow. "Oh dear... I foresee nothing but trouble coming from this."

"Worry not, Mister Oire, my men and I will do everything in our power to prevent any harm from coming to Lady Marigold," Freyard said assuredly. "You have my word."

"Ser Keneth, will you be going with the lady, at least?" Oire attempted to ask the captain of the manor guards.

"Actually, Uncle Oire, that returns us to a subject that I was about to broach before Lieutenant Ashe arrived with the Howland envoy," Marigold interjected tenderly, hoping to not further disturb his presently fragile disposition.

Oire groaned then, his eyes scrunching shut. "I sense that whatever it is that you are about to say is not going to be pleasant."

Marigold allowed herself a smile and turned to face Keneth. "I am not so sure about that, Uncle Oire. Uncle Keneth, by my authority as interim Lady of the Western Realm, I would like to appoint you as Field Marshal of the Western Armed Forces. It is a new position, but one that has been created out of necessity. Should we officially secede from the rest of Human Illiastra, we will make the title official on a national level."

"My lady, you honour me," Keneth started to say, until Gallin raised his hand.

"As your chief strategist, I feel it is my duty to raise the concern that appointing the captain of your own manor guards might come across as biased, my lady," the Kylisport minister stated with unease in his voice.

"It might be seen that way," Marigold began in defence of her decision. "Yet, this role needed to be filled with urgency even before that Atrebell courier showed up. I would say that need is even greater now. The person in this role must be someone that I can trust explicitly to both serve the Western Realm and to perform to the high standards that this role demands."

She extended a hand in the direction of Ser Keneth. "To those points, I will say first and foremost that there is no man in a uniform that I trust more than Keneth Arisborough. As far as his suitability for the role, I think that given his exemplary wartime records in the various Crescent Islands' conflicts, and his years of impeccable service as Captain of the Tullivan Manor Guardsmen, there is no one more qualified than he is, either."

Though she wondered if perhaps she was overstating her case, Marigold continued on with her review of the man. "Before Ser Keneth made the lateral move from the Illiastran Armed Forces to the Order of Guardsmen, he was a brigadier with a clear path toward the rank of General laid out before him. I can think of no one else who can possibly supersede Ser Keneth for Field Marshal, regardless of whether or not he's been the protector of my household prior to the appointment. As it stands, if Keneth were to be reinstated into the ranks of the Illiastran Armed Forces, there is no one east of Obalen who would outrank him in the military branch."

"You make a compelling case, Niece," Rory said from where he had sat quietly thus far. "Though as your uncle and a friend of Ser Keneth's, I too may appear biased in such matters."

Walter had been staring off at the wall opposite of where he sat in a ponderous manner, and chimed in when Rory was finished. "You know, now that I give it some consideration, we lack even a naval equivalent to Ser Keneth's military rank in the western realm. All our naval might and the officers overseeing it are located primarily in

Aquas Bay, which is part of the Southlands Realm. It is further understood that the three ministers there are firmly in the hands of House Palomb. The Western Realm holds the vast majority of the Illiastran coastline, but we have only the minority of the naval strength. That's positively baffling when given any thought."

"We have two commodores and an admiral on the west coast," Gallin put in after a thoughtful hum. "Granted, one of those commodores and the admiral are stationed in Weicaster Bay. The remaining commodore is in Portsward."

"You can count Commodore Hylen, if nothing else, my lady," Greggard told Marigold with a reassuring tone. "I work quite closely with him, given the security needs of the country's foremost trading port."

"If no one has any further qualms with Keneth's appointment to Field Marshal, I call for a vote to make it an official requisition of my office," Marigold stated as she jumped back into the conversation. With much left to discuss, she feared that the current subject would only further veer off course when time was of the essence. "Of course, it will have to be approved by the governing body of the Western Armed Forces before being ratified, but this would be the first step toward doing so."

The others followed her back to the original discussion, and without further arguments to be heard, Marigold motioned for a vote on the matter. Keneth and Marigold abstained from voting, and left the decision to the others gathered around the table. With only Oire saying 'nay', the motion carried.

Polite applause and congratulations were offered to Ser Keneth, and after a few minutes of such, Marigold pushed the meeting forward.

"If the lady would allow it, I have a question," Greggard requested when the opportunity to speak arose. He waited until Marigold gave him leave, but wasted not a second further. "How soon would you intend to leave for this proposed tour?"

"As to that," Marigold gave further consideration to her emerging plan. "I will commence with writing the letters to the nine ministers as soon as we adjourn this meeting. While I am doing that, those of you not from Daol Bay shall start making arrangements to return to your regions. By the time you are ready to depart on the evening train, I will have a tentative schedule for you all to return home with so that you can prepare for my arrival. The letters to the nine ministers I wish to meet with will go out on the same train. Provided that there are no issues when making arrangements for my train, I think I can be ready to leave by tomorrow evening."

"You would not have those of us who live to the south of here travel with you?" Nayle Keeves asked while gesturing around him to the other southerly ministers and their wives. "Surely you will want at least Minister Myakys in attendance, given that he is your chief strategist."

"On the contrary, Minister Keeves," Marigold countered gently. "I will want to go with none but my security detail and perhaps a member of my house staff and I will explain why: I need to meet with the holdout ministers myself, so that I might be seen as the lone voice driving the negotiations. As men, all of you, even my chief strategist, would be regarded as my superior by most of these holdout ministers."

"She's right, you know," Gallin offered when she finished, his gaze falling on his counterparts. "Besides, if we go home ahead of Lady Marigold, it will give us a chance to gather pertinent information ahead of her arrival. Can any of us say with total certainty what is transpiring south of here since Marigold called for support amongst our ranks? Men like Nothram and Jennis currently have an undue amount of sway over the narrative surrounding the lady's actions while we remain here.

"Furthermore, I would much enjoy a chance to go home and see Leigh, Ranaya, and my parents before that deadline passes. Something tells me that we may have to get accustomed to seeing less of our families until our troubles with the EMP reach a firm resolution."

"I have preparations to make with both my family and my region as well," Greggard said in apprehensive agreement with Myakys. "Being right next door to Daol Bay puts me in a precarious position should the EMP come rolling down our roads, as I am sure you would all understand. Minister Bickerington will need to be met as soon as his fleet reaches Portsward, too."

Sensing the anxiousness that crept into the room at Greggard's mention of a potential invasion, Marigold stood and bowed her head. "My friends, I apologise for hoisting such stressors upon your shoulders so suddenly. With that said, such reflexive and malleable planning is only the beginning of what we will have to get accustomed to going forward. The tactics of the EMP and the Triarchy will leave us with no other option. We will need to steel ourselves to that reality sooner rather than later. On that note, I move to adjourn the meeting so that we all may commence with our individual preparations. May fortune find us in the uncertain days ahead."

Despite the suddenness with which everything came together in the meeting, both Marigold's supporters and staff rose to the occasion without complaint in the days that followed.

The first order of business was her letters to the nine ministers. With Oire and Councillor Rossadore lending a hand, Marigold had them written, prepared for shipment, and sent via courier to the train station to catch the evening southbound run. Sharing space aboard the train with the envoy for the journey were Gallin and the ministers and wives of the houses of Cunningsbee, Ferros, Fields, Keeves, Mattersly, and Obarrow.

While the southerly supporters were leaving, Freyard and his rangers were making arrangements to split their unit until the tour was complete. Most of the Sun's Rangers would be going afield, heading east to the Daol Forest so that they might patrol for potential eastern incursions. Leading that group was the oldest and most experienced ranger, who was an old bear of a man that Freyard introduced to Marigold as Yarohmer the Graceful. A further band of four, led by a seasoned ranger named Mack Doile, would be remaining in Daol Bay as representatives of the Sun's Rangers.

Given the space limitations of the Tullivan staff sleeping car, Freyard was given three spaces for his rangers to travel with Marigold aboard her train. Surprising no one, he chose himself, an idea to which Marigold was receptive, to say the least. Accompanying Freyard would be Glendil Archer, a man of no relation to him from a knightly family out of Ravenkeep, and another ranger named Dayden Vernet.

Of course, it did no good to have Freyard, Glendil, and Dayden escorting her in the tired, scuffed riding leathers that their unit all wore. With that in mind, Marigold sent the three in the company of Leonice to a nearby tailor's shop that next morning. Marigold's aunt was tasked with choosing an appropriate set of clothing that would be suitable for men charged with protecting a nation's leader.

The trio returned to Marigold dressed uniformly in an ankle-length, black leather coat, cotton trousers with reinforced leather patching in the vital areas, leather boots to the shins, and a teal, button-down collared shirt. The rangers looking downright striking to Marigold in their new clothing, and feeling that her regular protectors were in need of a refreshed look, she decided on the spot to make it the new uniform of her manor guardsmen. Despite the offer of a barbershop having been floated to the three rangers as well, Freyard had opted to keep his burgeoning beard and lengthening hair, for now, much to Leonice's disdain. Whereas Marigold had no issues with Freyard's wavy hair and neat beard, her aunt was of the mind that the ranger captain was far more handsome when cleanly shaven and neatly trimmed.

With her protectors prepared, a private engine and crew hired, and the Tullivan cars hitched up and ready to roll, Marigold turned her attention south. The first two days of the trek took her through regions that had either already sided with Marigold, or were held by men who were firmly against her. She stopped along the way to meet with her supporting ministers and visit their regions. Most importantly to Marigold was the opportunity to speak to the public, regaling the townsfolk at each stop with a speech that borrowed from the address she delivered at her father's funeral reception. There were exchanges of information with her supporting ministers as well, and if time permitted, Marigold would even take a meal with them and their families.

Those of the populace who came to hear Marigold speak seemed to be in approval of her, and she took the successes of her speaking appearances as good tidings thus far. Yet, in the back of her mind, Marigold recalled being at her father's side when he met with residents of Daol Bay and beyond. It seemed that no matter how poorly people thought of the EMP and their policies in whispers, they tended to be only flattering when standing before her father. There were outliers of course, those being people who would approach aggressively and shout curses and slurs at her father for injustices they had been served under the EMP's rule. However, the majority showered him in smiles and praise. It felt to Marigold that the older she got, the stranger the behaviour seemed to her.

When Marigold had finally asked Marscal about it, he replied candidly on the subject, *"It certainly is a strange phenomenon, is it not? I like to call it the Folly of the Famous. I was about your age when I first noticed it too, back when I was following your grandfather around. There seems to be an almost complete inability for most people to be honest in anything but a complimentary fashion around those with any level of celebrity. The narcissist and the fool would both easily be caught up in the endless fawning, but the wise person knows to take it with the grain of salt it is generally worth. You have to look beneath their adulation and amiable exteriors and look for the words left unsaid and the expressions that go unseen. That is where you will find the truth that each person wishes they could tell you."*

Drawing on Marscal's advice, Marigold treated the compliments and encouragement as a sideshow and a curiosity. The real measure of her work would be revealed at the ballot boxes and in the reactions that would only be forthcoming after she left.

She intended to revisit these friendlier regions on her return to Daol Bay, but before they could do so, she had to travel all the way south to Tippard. On the third morning of the trip, her party and their train continued toward that ultimate destination. They had left Minster Cunningsbee's region of Davring Harbour before daylight, hoping to pass through the three unfriendly regions of Dillaney's Bay, Levelle, and Pelican Harbour, respectively, before nightfall. By days' end, Marigold hoped to be meeting with Minister Darrin Darickard in his home region of Cale, located not too far to the south of Pelican Harbour.

Though they would be contending with other trains sharing the tracks, the conductor reckoned that their currently scheduled portion of the trek could feasibly be done with daylight to spare.

At present, Marigold knew the train to be in the wilds between Levelle and Pelican Harbour. Outside the window to her immediate right was a marshland of shrubs and stunted trees, and at the end of its reaches was the Casparian Sea. Even from inland where the tracks held the train to its course, Marigold bared witness to the choppy waves rushing madly toward the shores.

She was seated at a small table beside the window, her gaze returning from the natural sights, coming to rest on Lewcas Hylesly seated across from her.

His eyes were downcast and his hands flat on the varnished surface. A slow, rhythmic wave in the fingers of his right hand signalled his intent, and Lewcas carefully reached out and lifted a figurine that sat facing Marigold from upon a square, wooden board.

That's a bold move if ever I saw one, Marigold commented to herself while giving Lewcas a curious glance, her mouth twitching as she fought to hold it still.

He moved the piece, bringing it directly before another that was pointed in his direction, and with the gentlest brush of the second figurine, Lewcas made Marigold flinch.

"It is your move, my lady."

The game was called *Kings and Knights*, and Marigold felt that with Lewcas' gambit, she was finally in a position to win.

It was a simple game in practice, played between two people atop a typically wooden surface delineated into a square grid pattern and laid atop a painted field of grass. Each side had a number of carved playing pieces all centred primarily on a single king, whom the player was charged with defending. Cast in the role of both protecting the king piece and attacking his enemy was a contingent of knights of varying weaponry and abilities. If access to the king was gained by the opposing army, or all his defenders were captured or slain, the game was lost.

The strategy of Marigold's current opponent seemed clear to her now, as Lewcas had used one of his longsword knights against a matching piece belonging to Marigold. The lone advantage to attacking a piece of equal strength was that the attacker could push the defender back a single space. In what seemed to be inadvertently done on Lewcas' part, Marigold now had an opening between the two to push her remaining spearman forward. As a result, Lewcas' longsword knight looked to be in jeopardy, as Marigold could now use her spearman and her longsword knight to capture the aforementioned piece of Lewcas'. All she would need to do was move both units forward by a single space each to pincer Lewcas' longsword knight.

"You make it too easy, Lewcas," Marigold told him while sliding the spearman one space closer, which was as much as she was allowed.

He gave no response, his focus having returned to the board. With a single finger, Lewcas slid a paladin on the other side of the board forward by its allotted three spaces and looked to Marigold. "It is your move, my lady."

"I see you attempting to sneak that paladin around my defences," Marigold noted slyly, moving one of her archers into a place where it could fend off the paladin. "There, that should hold him."

"It will," Lewcas replied casually while pushing the paladin up against the spearman, who was now surrounded by it and the same longsword that Marigold was attempting to capture. "But it will not save your last spear."

She leaned back in her chair and let out a scoff. "There goes the second to last of my melee defences. You have my king wide open now, save for my longsword knight, who will fall quickly to both of your paladins. The next two moves of yours will essentially take the game."

"It was a good match, my lady," Lewcas complimented in his usual flat tone while shuffling the pieces back to their starting positions. "Your opening gambit made for a fine defence of your king. If not for that last, desperate feint on my part, you would have had me."

"I think you are just trying to flatter me," Marigold responded lightly. "I had the opening salvo, but somehow it felt as though I was playing from one move behind for most of the game."

Lewcas lifted a single eyebrow. "I would never deceive a friend, my lady. You played well, and I mean that sincerely."

"I jest, of course," Marigold stated with a soft laugh. "I know you would never lie to me, even with good intention."

"I suppose you would know that, given that you are the only friend I have," Lewcas noted, before gesturing an open palm to the reset playing field. "Would you care for another match? If we were to play to the best of seven, it would mean that I am only up three matches to your one. There is certainly ample opportunity for you to make a rousing comeback."

There was no falsehood in that first statement of Lewcas' either, Marigold was indeed the only person in the known world that Lewcas could call 'friend'. He was a man married to duty, whose rigid code of conduct and sense of discipline had isolated him socially. By his own admission, it had been that way since he was but a child.

"I liked to play games with the other children when I was but a boy," Lewcas had explained to Marigold a long time ago. *"The problem was that I would grow obsessed with whatever game was popular at a given moment. Tag, marbles, jacks, any sport we could come up with, and especially hide-and-go-seek, I wanted to master any and every game I played. As such, winning the games became more important than simply playing, and in my youthful ignorance, I lost the true value and joy of play. With such a driven and focused mind and the fortune of being*

physically above average, I found a way to excel everywhere that I applied myself.

"Despite my successes, my downfall came rather swiftly and I have no one to blame but myself. In retrospect, I felt that it came down to three factors: the first was that I had no social skills and naturally, the other children had not warmed to me. Therefore, when I was initially ostracised from my social circle, I had no one to vouch for me. Secondly, I was just too good at every game. Imagine that you are participating in a contest and you know that your opponent can only be defeated on the rarest of occasions. Most people would lose interest in playing rather quickly, would they not? The last piece of my puzzle, and this was perhaps the deciding factor, was that in my lust for victory I failed to see that I had made everything unsporting for the other children. What I missed, they saw plainly, though. The children collectively began to avoid me, and even when I found them they would cancel their games, sometimes mid-play, so that I could not join in."

"That is just cruel," Marigold had commented sadly.

"I do not blame them, truly," Lewcas said in dismissal of their behaviour with a shake of his head. *"I was a sore loser, an obnoxious winner, and so focused on competing that I built no friendships with the others. In fact, I cannot even recall any of their names, even now. I just saw them all as obstacles to be defeated. I was as daft as I was skilled, and I had no idea until much later in life."*

With no friends to speak of, Lewcas dedicated his free time outside of schooling to working as an assistant to his father. Lewcas' sire had been a career soldier in his working days and in the twilight of his career had settled into a role as the master-at-arms for the tiny barracks in Arnell's Cove. At his father's side, Lewcas' job was to set up and dismantle the equipment used for training exercises, maintain the weapons and armoury, and in general, keep the barracks in tiptop shape. The discipline that Lewcas' father had instilled in the boy in that time, coupled with his own obsessive nature, proved to be a formula for a model cadet. The military life, and soldiering in general, seemed to be what Lewcas was built for, and from then on, he had dedicated all of his mental and physical resources to that endeavour. In the process, Lewcas had ignored his emotions, and they had atrophied until he appeared to be little more than an obedient husk of a person.

Regardless of the image that Lewcas had transformed himself in to, Marigold had discovered that appearances are not everything. Once he was chosen to be a manor guard, Lewcas found himself routinely in Marigold's company, be it during regular duties or when accompanying the family, together or individually, when they left the premises. These particular circumstances put Lewcas into the inevitable environment that allowed him and the Tullivans to be acquainted closely to one another. However, unlike his guardsman peers, Lewcas had his aloof façade that kept him coolly distant, and that reflected in Marscal and Serephanie's opinion of him.

Marscal's own words on the man rang in Marigold's head often: *"If I have a task that crops up with urgency, or a sudden need for my presence outside the manor, I pick Lewcas to escort me, always. The other guards have wives and children, and even grandchildren, in Rus' case, but not Lewcas. There is no one he has to call family or friend, no place to be, and nothing but his duty to keep him warm at night. Even when his shift ends, he is just preparing for the next. I never feel as though I am a bother when I call on Lewcas, and he never complains when I do. The man just arrives exactly when asked to, does his duty, and departs to prepare for his next shift."*

Marigold instead saw Lewcas' walls of reticence as a challenge to be climbed and overcome, and in that endeavour, she considered herself successful. It was a process that had taken both time and patience, as Lewcas was wary and mistrusting of anyone attempting to befriend him, but Marigold had found a way through. *Kings and Knights*, it turned out, was that way.

The game had only been released to the public in Illiastra four years prior and in short order it had taken the country by storm. Both children and adults enjoyed the relatively simple battle game, and sets of boards and pieces had sold faster than the crafters could produce them. Lewcas had taken notice of *Kings and Knights*, and he revealed as much to Marigold in one of their early conversations. However, despite his desire to buy a game set, he lamented that it seemed pointless, as it required two players and Lewcas had no one else with which to play.

With that in mind, Marigold made a point to schedule a visit to the city's shopping streets and ensured that Lewcas would be guarding her for the outing. At the window of *Ausland's Toy and Game Shoppe*, Marigold pointed out *Kings and Knights* to Lewcas, and when he expressed interest, she went inside and immediately purchased a set. She even handed it off to Lewcas so that he might carry it back to the manor for her.

He kept looking down at the wooden box in his hands, Marigold remembered fondly. *Every now and then, when he thought I wasn't paying attention, I'd catch him running a hand over its shining surface.*

When time allotted, Marigold made a point to invite Lewcas for a few rounds of the game, and in between matches, Lewcas slowly began to open up in conversation with her. Not during the matches, of course, for as much as he tried to restrain his competitiveness, it still squirmed free in those moments.

"I think we have time for one last match," Marigold told him, her hand going for a copper coin laid to the side of the table. "Shall I flip to see who goes first?"

"Be my guest, my lady," he replied with an upturned hand.

"Call it in the toss, then," Marigold offered him. With a flick of her thumb, the coin went spinning into the air and came to a land in her palm.

"I choose tails," Lewcas had declared while it was still spinning.

Marigold flipped the coin over onto the back of her free hand and uncurled her fingers to reveal the dove of the Elite Merchants facing up.

"Tails it is. You may begin at your leisure," Marigold invited, laying the coin back where it previously had been as she did.

Lewcas reached out to move a piece, but drew back and stood up as a knock came at the door. "Identify yourself," he commanded while going across the floor to scan through the peephole.

Having let herself become engrossed in the gameplay, Marigold was suddenly pulled back into reality and she let out a sigh as the weariness of it all returned in a flash. "It is probably Freyard. I believe it is his shift now."

"You are correct, my lady," Lewcas admitted while sliding the door open. A gust of air whooshed in from outside the train car as Freyard quickly slipped in. The lower half of the long coat that Marigold had recently bought him flapping noisily as it was lifted by the rushing air.

"Am I early, my lady?" Freyard asked in slight puzzlement, as he looked between her and Lewcas.

"Not at all," Marigold said with a casual wave of her hand. "Lewcas and I are merely going to play an extra match of *Kings and Knights*. You are welcome to watch if you would like."

Freyard glanced at a heavy, wall-mounted clock situated behind Marigold's double sized bunk. "I would love to watch two masters of the game at work, but perhaps that match may have to wait. We are well ahead of schedule and should soon be reaching Pelican Harbour, my lady. I thought it might be prudent to talk about the upcoming stop."

"Already?" Marigold remarked with surprise. "It feels like we just left Levelle. I will not be disembarking in Pelican Harbour, for obvious reasons," she went on to tell Freyard. "But according to the conductor, a short stop will have to be made to allow the regular train ahead of us to remain on time.

Her focus then went to Lewcas. "I am afraid that I will have to postpone our game of *Kings and Knights*. If you would do me a favour though, I would have you round up the other guardsmen and spare none. I will need them all at the ready for when we arrive in Pelican Harbour. It is not as if I suspect any trouble from Nothram, but we should still be ready for any schemes that he might concoct."

Lewcas stood and bowed, "It will be as you command, my lady. Would you like me to dissemble the game before I take my leave?"

"No, no, I will take care of it," Marigold told him softly.

He left her alone with Freyard then, who took the now vacant seat at the tiny table in Marigold's sitting car. Although narrow, the long car was spacious in its own right, with a dining table for two, a lavatory closet, a double bed, and a dresser. Ahead of it were three further personal cars, one being a sleeping car for the guards and servants, a sitting car for eating and relaxation, and foremost of all of that, a mobile office car. A standard dining car and its hired staff provided food, and further cars to accommodate the necessary train attendants, conductor, and engineers had been booked and paid for, along with an engine itself, by Marigold.

Most of the meetings that Marigold had arranged with potential signees took place in the office car. It gave Marigold the security of staying in one, well-guarded place while allowing for more time with each minister during stopovers. The only noted exceptions to this arrangement were the points when the train was required to stop overnight to allow for maintenance on the engine and rest for the engineers. In those cases, Marigold intended to venture into the community to meet with the minister by evening, and deliver a speech to their townsfolk by morning.

As it was, there were only four ministers who had abstained from signing *The Declaration of Agency* located between Daol Bay and Pelican Harbour, and none of them were open to discussions on the matter. Foremost of the foursome were the two ministers residing in Galdourn, located to the immediate south of Daol Day. The first was Ike Slake, who was the actual minister for the region. The other was Leo Daltis, who was merely a resident of Galdourn. His political riding was the region of the Madore Isles, a cluster of islands located due southwest from Galdourn. Daltis could not be bothered to spend more than a week or two during the summer season in his ancestral home among the tiny island chain, and instead delegated most of his ministerial duties to a plenipotentiary. Apart from attending parliamentary functions and sessions, Marigold could not think of any aspect of his ministerial duties that Leo Daltis actually handled.

Marigold had decided to make no treaty with either minister residing in Galdourn yet thanks in no small part to Greggard Simillon's advice. *"They both live within the shadow of Daol Bay, and neither one has the ability to oppose you, either militarily or financially. Whatever they may proffer to buy their votes would not be worth the price, as it will be they who eventually come to you for protection if the Palombs turn westward. Leave those little men be, for now."*

"What about Arturo Jennis and Lanly Steffard?" Marigold had asked openly to her counsel of the third and fourth holdouts. *"Does anyone have any reason why I should not meet with either of them right away?"*

Gallin Myakys had taken that response. *"Minister Jennis will want the world, having said just as much at the reception. More to the point, he will want everything just for his signature on* The Declaration of Agency. *Going forward from that, he will ask for more and more each time you attempt to do anything that requires his vote, knowing that you would be indebted to him the entire time. I would leave him be for now and let him stew. If we can get the signatures elsewhere, then Arturo loses the one thing he has to give. As pressure mounts from both eastern and western forces in the future, he will reach out to you with an offer of his own. If such a time arrives, we will negotiate from there, if it suits you, my lady.*

"As for Steffard, he's but a young man who only recently succeeded his father. He appears to be heavily influenced by Haymard Nothram, who is a close friend and confidant of the elder Steffard. He will not join your cause as long as Nothram opposes you, rendering a visit with Steffard a worthless endeavour at this stage. Granted, the lad is barely twenty, so his heart might not be as hardened as his mentor. If we can succeed in seceding without Nothram, Steffard might be persuaded to join later, if you can show him that there is a place in the new Western Realm for him."

That thorough assessment of the four ministers left Marigold with no potential ears to hear her pleas until Cale, the home of Minister Derin Darickard and the first region south of Pelican Harbour.

"Did the conductor happen to say how long we would need to wait in Pelican Harbour?" Marigold asked Freyard, as she began removing the figurines from the playing field, laying them to the side of the table as she did. Once the chequered surface was vacant, she flipped the box over to reveal the underside to be individual compartments to hold each figurine. With the placement complete, she folded the box in on a pair of hinges hidden in the compartment side, closed it with a pair of latches, and set it aside on the table.

Freyard had tried to help Marigold during the process by attempting to place the figurines in slots where they would likely fit, even getting one or two placements right. "Aye, he estimated no more than half an hour."

"All well and good, then," Marigold responded with a slow exhalation. "We should reach Cale by mid-evening. I'll invite Minister Darickard for dinner aboard the train. I am not anticipating much from him, mind you, given that he's typically in Nothram's camp. Perhaps he will surprise me, and sign the declaration, though."

"That will leave you needing only one signature if Greggard's skipper from up north shows up in Portsward like Greggard claims he will," Freyard added, reminding Marigold of the assurances of the Lord of Trade.

"I welcome Minister Bickerington's support if I can get it," Marigold told him while leaning back in her chair. "His vote is as good as any other minister's, even if Tusker's Cove region has the fewest people by a wide margin. However, it's no guarantee. Bickerington may still say no, and I will know nothing about it until the tour is over. There's also the matter of Greggard not having the treaty for

Bickerington to sign. I have it. As such, Bickerington will have to write a letter of avouchment for me and that will stand in place of his signature on *The Declaration of Agency* until he can be present to do so in Daol Bay. Who knows when that will be, as Bickerington keeps his own schedule on the seas. There is a chance that he may not even arrive in Portsward while Greggard is there, and as a result, they may not even cross paths before my return. In that case, it would likely be a third of a season before Bickerington gets back from the north wing of the Casparian Sea. Then, we are into the New Year and I will be out of time. I cannot rely on it, Freyard. I need names now."

Freyard had stood up in his seat, his focus on the scenery ahead of the slowing train. "What in the..." he had begun to say, as the front door of the car slid open quickly.

"My lady and Captain Freyard, we appear to have an incident at the train station," Lewcas declared abruptly.

Marigold leapt from her seat and leaned into the window as much as she could to see for herself.

Pelican Harbour was one of the few cities in the west to have functioning perimeter walls, and the train station, much like Daol Bay's, was built outside of those walls. Unlike Daol Bay, the rails ran close to Pelican Harbour's fortifications, and the station itself was practically built against the cold, grey stone that ringed the city. In the space between the side of the station and the city gates, there had been erected a section of scaffolding three flights high and at least two span wide, from what Marigold could reckon. Strung from end to end were two banners made of white sailcloth, with black letters painted messily upon them.

House Nothram bows to no woman
House Tullivan is no more

Marigold gasped audibly as she looked above the banners to the top of the scaffolding. Though Pelican Harbour's winters were milder than Daol Bay's, they were still cold, and subjecting someone to the elements was a cruel fate. Yet, that is what Marigold saw.

Two women were bound tightly at the hands and feet to a pair of timber pillars raised amid the scaffolds. One blonde, the other a brunette and both clad in little more than tattered silk dresses.

"Freyard, please tell me that those are not real women atop those scaffolds. Tell me my eyes are playing tricks on me and that they are merely effigies," Marigold said through gritted teeth.

"No, they are indeed real women," he told her while turning away toward Lewcas. "Gather the others. We've got to go put a stop to this."

"Very well, Ser," Lewcas gave in answer. "In the meantime, I will stay and protect Marigold personally."

Marigold was away from the window then, grabbing her warm teal cloak from the hook on the wall on which it hung. "No need for that, Lewcas. I am coming too."

"My lady, I must insist that you stay here," Lewcas sternly intoned while stepping in front of the foremost exit. "It is not safe for you outside in Pelican Harbour. This may well be a trap."

"I have to agree with Lewcas," Freyard chimed in while loosening the sword in the scabbard on his right hip and adjusting the pair of pistols holstered on his left. "You will be walking into danger. He can stay with you-"

"I have heard enough of this, I am going out there and I command you both to stand back out of my way," Marigold sharply interrupted Freyard to declare. "It is one thing to have bodyguards, but it is another thing entirely to be constantly hiding behind barriers while everyone else jeopardises their lives at my behest. I am not some mewling coward and I will not have my own treat me as such."

Both men apologised and Lewcas stepped back from the door to allow Marigold to pass. As she moved between cars to the sleeping quarters, she looked back to catch Lewcas and Freyard have a whispered conversation and in returning to them, heard only the tail end of it.

"And above all else, you stay immediately at her side, understood?" Freyard was telling Lewcas.

Marigold let her voice wander into territory that could be considered a snarl. "Those women out there are lashed to poles high in the air and slowly freezing to death while you two overthink how to best have six armed men protect me alone. There is no time for this."

"Yes, my lady, we are right behind you," Lewcas declared in a tone that was still apologetic in delivery.

Leaving them to follow, Marigold strode into the sitting car where the remaining guards and rangers were standing in wait. "All of you, with me. Let's go show Nothram what we think of his grotesque display."

The conductor was striding toward Marigold's party through the office car, his hand raised to stop them. "Miss Marigold, I recommend you not go out-"

"Please, go lower the gate outside this car at once," Marigold ordered him, not waiting to hear the rest of his warning.

Wyla, the maid who had come along for the journey, was already standing clear of Marigold and the line of guards behind her. "Be careful, my lady. But please, help those girls."

"I am going to try my best, Wyla," Marigold called back as she reached the door.

Marigold stepped outside to get a feel for the weather while waiting on the conductor as he undid the clasps and chains holding the folding steps in place. It was as she stood there in wait that the cold air truly hit her. It was windless, and only a light dusting of snow was on the ground, with here and there a flake falling from the overcast sky.

It is not terribly freezing, but without proper clothing, those women may have already succumbed to the cold. I only hope I am not too late.

The stairs fell outward from the conductor's grasp and he climbed down to the ground to make room for everyone else. "Here you are, my lady. Please, do be careful. The west would be grieved were anything to happen to you."

"What about those two up there on the scaffolds?" Marigold asked him once on the ground. "Will you grieve if something happens to them?"

He had no answer, but neither did Marigold wait for one, and she strode across the flat, gravelly ground to where the women were kept, her guards jogging to catch up and form up protectively.

Freyard and Glendil had both taken the forward points in what looked to Marigold like a walking heptagon surrounding her. A quick glance to the right and left marked Lewcas' and Sydnee's positions respectively, leaving Dayden and Elden to guard the rear.

"There are only two city guards," Freyard noted worriedly.

"Do you suppose the women are bait?" Glendil queried with a quick glance to Freyard.

He nodded in return. "That was my thought. Either that, or Nothram figures that Marigold is too craven to do anything about his depravity."

Marigold looked about, noting just one guard on the ground and another pacing back and forth before the suffering women up on high.

The heads of the captives were hanging down, preventing Marigold from seeing their faces, although the blonde woman began to raise her eyes at the sound of the approaching footfalls.

Their gaze met, and Marigold attempted to give her a reassuring nod.

"Stop right there, fellas," the guard on the ground commanded Marigold's entourage between loud chews of what looked like the unsightly black tar of tobacco. "Where do ya think you're goin'?"

Marigold stepped between the two Archers. "We are here to see that those women are released safely. This madness ends now."

The guard atop the scaffolding began to laugh loudly at that, and the one standing mere metres away smiled through browned teeth at Marigold. "Ol' Stanny thinks that's funny."

"Nothing that I said was for your amusement," Marigold told him, her nostrils flaring angrily.

"Maybe not, but it is rather comical to see a woman tryin' ta order men around," the yet-unnamed guard said while letting out a gob of black spit on the ground. He gave an upward nod toward Freyard. "I dunno how you bunch o' cuckolds can look yourselfs in the mirror everyday knowing some uppity little bitch has you by the balls."

A hand of Freyard's went slowly to his open jacket, where he brushed the leather back to reveal the pistols he wore. The opposing guard had taken a defensive step back, and Marigold saw Freyard's eyes narrow in reaction. "You're awfully brave for a man who is staring down a six-against-two situation. Doubly brave if you consider how long it will take for 'Stanny' up there to get down here so that he can die next to your carcass. Then again, I always found there was a thin line between bravery and stupidity."

"What, you gonna kill me over a couple o' whores?" the guard before them asked with a tinge of fear creeping into his voice.

"You will hardly be the first," Freyard told him succinctly.

The tobacco chewer looked to his cohort above curiously before turning back to Freyard. "Why, who are you to be such a killer? You think you're Master o' Blades 'er somethin?"

"No, I'm something much more frightening to scum like you than Tryst Reine," Freyard informed the two guards. "I'm the man who led fifty to victory against the entire Moon Raiders gang. We went to war against hundreds of the worst men you could imagine and drove their name into extinction. I personally hanged their leader myself, after he watched what was left of his collection of lieutenants die one by one before him. Little shits like you are hardly worth such a show, though. So, if you would be so kind as to cut those women loose and hand them over to us, we'll be on our way, with no harm to you or 'Stanny' up there."

"The Moon Raiders, eh? How do I know that you're tellin' me true?" the guard put back to Freyard, "Who's to say what stories coming out of those savage lands are real? Might be all lies. Might not be any gangs down there at all any more, besides Orangecloak and her twinks, o' course. I mean, when was the last time that any raiders were seen north of the Varras?"

"It's been a long time, because of people like my Sun's Rangers and Orangecloak's friends keeping it that way," Freyard replied as he rolled his shoulders, causing the guard to flinch for a second time. A step forward brought Freyard closer to the guard, with Glendil following close behind. "The real question is: are you willing to risk your life on the off chance that I'm lying to you? After all, you asked if I'm willing to kill for those women, and I demonstrated that I am. So what remains to be known is if you are willing to die to keep us from freeing them."

The guard stepped back until he was up against the stairwell of the scaffolds, his nervousness plain across his face. "Alright, alright, no need for violence. Stanny, go ahead and cut 'em free."

For the first time since she saw the women through the train car window, Marigold began to relax, even if just a little.

"You sure, Zeb?" Stanny called back, and Marigold detected something wretchedly playful about the way he said it.

"Freyard, I want eyes on the one up top, something's not right," Marigold began to instruct him.

"Aye, let's do as they say," Zeb confirmed above Marigold's words. "We don't want no further trouble with this lot."

"Agreed, my lady," Freyard said before he gestured to Zeb to get his attention. "Excuse me, sers, but if it's all the same to you, Glendil and Dayden will gladly go up there and-"

While Freyard and the other guards focused on Zeb, Marigold's gaze was firmly trained on the two bound women. During Freyard's request to Zeb, the guard named Stanny walked behind the brunette woman with his knife drawn. Marigold first assumed the knife was to cut the ropes lashing the pair to the stakes, until the guard had laid it against her throat and ran it across the flesh, spilling her blood in a violent stream.

"Oh gods, no!" Marigold screamed in horror. "Someone stop him!"

As Marigold had cried out there came shrieks of terror from the blonde woman sharing the scaffolds with the brunette. In her horror, she began to thrash against her bindings, trying fruitlessly to get away.

In a flash Freyard's pistol was in his hand. As the man called Stanny dashed toward the second captive to do to her what he did to the first, a deafening chorus of gunshots rang out from beside Marigold. The guard's body jerked as crimson holes formed in his abdomen. He fell backward against the timber scaffolds, and the railings gave way, sending him tumbling into the brick wall of the city. Now hanging sideways and pressed between wall and scaffold, the body of the man began sliding toward the ground until he came to an abrupt stop on a piece of framework near the bottom, where he hung limp and dead.

Marigold looked around at her protectors and found that all three rangers had fired upon the murderer, their spent pistols smoking in their hands.

The one named Zeb had taken off running northward to the wall's edge and had gotten nearly out of sight when Dayden, with his fresh pistol drawn, trained it on Zeb and called out, "The other one is getting away!"

"Let him go, there's no time to chase him!" Freyard replied. As he holstered his own spent pistol, he pivoted on a heel to face Marigold and the other guardsmen. "The city guards definitely heard our gunfire and will be here before long. Dayden and Glendil, go free the women, we'll take the living with us. My lady, I'll wait with my rangers, you and your guards go on ahead to the train. Have someone tell the conductor to relay to the engineering team that we are in a state of emergency and to have us ready to go in a moment's notice."

The two Sun's Rangers darted up the stairs before the words were out of Freyard's mouth and Marigold and her guards began their retreat to the train mere seconds later.

Among her guards, Lewcas took the lead, with Sydnee and Elden keeping close to Marigold on either side. She noted for the first time that all three men had their sabres out and ready, but she could not recall when they had done so.

Lewcas practically leapt aboard the train and extended a hand to help Marigold along, which she grabbed hurriedly. Taking a second to glance back to the scaffolds, Marigold noted that both women had been unbound, but only the blonde woman was being carried down the stairs.

The brown-haired woman bled out, Marigold realised, suddenly feeling sick to her stomach.

Sydnee and Elden bounded up the steps of the train car, forcing Marigold to step inside the office car in order to make room for them.

"Where is the conductor?" Marigold heard Lewcas asking Wyla, who was shaking and sobbing.

"He... He... He's" she sputtered, unable to finish a sentence.

"Elden, go forward in the train and see if you can find the conductor. Tell them exactly what Freyard said," Marigold commanded, her order being obeyed immediately.

Lewcas gently moved Wyla aside, softly telling her, "Wyla, you need to get a hold of yourself. Captain Freyard is incoming with his Sun's Rangers and a woman, help them close the gate if you can, or tend to the woman, if not. We have to get Lady Marigold to her car."

Pushed forward by Sydnee, Marigold had little choice but to leave Wyla there and follow Lewcas. They jogged the rest of the way through the office car, into the sitting car, and through the sleeping car, until they stopped on the bridge leading to Marigold's personal car. It took but a second for Lewcas to produce a key and fit it into the lock, and the door slid open in Lewcas' hand. With Marigold and Sydnee standing in wait, Lewcas took a step within.

As she followed Lewcas inside, Marigold heard him say the words, "Identify yourself!" before the car was filled with a bang that rang out sharply and painfully in Marigold's ears.

"Intruder!" Sydnee bellowed out loudly enough to be heard above Marigold's muffled hearing. He forced her to the ground with a hand on her shoulder, where he threw himself down atop her as a shield.

She looked out beyond Sydnee's frame as much as she could, and saw the rear, caboose door of her car swinging in the wind as a man dove out through it. Lewcas had given chase to him, but stopped himself short at the threshold.

Another shot rang out through the air, this time from outside and Marigold caught sight of the head and shoulders of Freyard through the doorway, a smoking pistol in his raised hand. "The intruder is down!" he declared, while turning toward Lewcas. "Is Marigold safe?"

Marigold saw Lewcas look over his shoulder at her and Sydnee and nod slowly.

Sydnee released his embrace of Marigold and she crawled out from underneath him and began to rise up. Just as Marigold got her feet beneath her, Lewcas' knees buckled and he fell backward, a hand clutching at the bloody mess that his stomach had become.

Somewhere in the distance, she heard the train's whistle blowing.

"Gods dammit!" Freyard shouted while pulling himself aboard the train through the open door. "Dayden, Glendil, over here!"

Marigold dove to where Lewcas lay and took his head and shoulders into her lap. "Lewcas? Lewcas, talk to me!" she looked then to Sydnee. "Quickly, he needs a doctor!"

"We will have to wait until we get to Cale," Freyard told her without argument while monitoring the rear door for his comrades. "Pelican Harbour is no safe stop for any of us now."

"Sydnee, go and ask among the staff for any medical supplies they might have, and inform the conductor of what has transpired. We need to get to Cale as hurriedly as possible," Marigold commanded of the unharmed guard.

"You're safe, Miss Marigold…. That… Makes me glad," Lewcas uttered from within Marigold's arms, between gasps of air and blood.

"Lewcas, please, don't talk. Just stay with me. We'll get you help in Cale," Marigold pleaded with him.

He looked at her then, his gaze growing long as his hazel eyes peered into hers. "Thank you… My friend."

18

MARIGOLD

The darkness was everywhere. No matter which direction Marigold looked, it stared back at her, taunting as much as it courted, trying to pull her further into its grasp while reminding her of the agony of its touch.

As she coped with the loss of her father, the darkness snaked its tendrils in deeper, breaking open the stitching on the bleeding wounds and making new lacerations as it went. These ones, she knew, were for Lewcas Hylesly, who was now lying in a bed at the clinic in Kylisport and fighting valiantly for his life. The doctor told her to expect nothing, for despite Lewcas' strength and endurance, he had lingered long without proper treatment while a lead ball poisoned him from within his stomach and much of his blood had poured out.

But without hope, what else do we have when the darkness floods in?

Marigold had stayed at Lewcas' bedside for hours after the doctors stabilised him, though all he did was sleep. The rescued woman needed treatment too, and Marigold saw that she would have it, with Sydnee assigned to be her personal bodyguard for the process. Given the medical needs of both Lewcas and the woman, and because of the incident and the toll that it had taken on everyone on board the train, the conductor, Marigold, and the engineers had met and come to the joint decision to remain in Cale for as long as they were welcome. Marigold had a minister to meet with in town, and offered for Derin

Darickard to come to the clinic to treat with her, for she had no intentions of leaving Lewcas or the traumatised woman alone.

Minister Darickard humoured Marigold's request, and arrived at the clinic in the dead of night for the meeting. Seated at a small, creaking, and wobbly set of table and chairs just metres away from where Lewcas rested, Marigold and Derin had sat and talked for nearly two hours. At a few points throughout, Marigold thought an understanding could be met, and it seemed like Minister Darickard was willing to sign *The Declaration of Agency*. However, by the end of their meeting, Derin Darickard could not bring himself to support Marigold's resistance.

"I cannot join you while Haymard Nothram is my neighbour," Darickard had explained fretfully, his eyes darting to the suffering Lewcas lying nearby after every few words. *"I can promise no action for or against you, but nothing else at this time. Take your people from my town's clinic in the morning, and be on your way before I can be accused by Nothram of harbouring and abetting you, Miss Marigold."*

While Darickard's cowardice had unnerved Marigold, she had let him go without reproach. Marigold had simply been too exhausted for further discussions, and was far more concerned with Lewcas and the rescued woman at any rate.

By daybreak on the next day, her two remaining guards and Freyard's rangers had carried Lewcas by gurney back to the train, and the awful tour that seemed without end had carried on.

Following Cale, the train made stops in the regions of Filkas, Crayfish Cove, and Holliford, and all three regions yielded much the same result as the meeting with Derin Darickard.

Ministers Morren, Omallick, and Gorrinson in their turn all sat with me, entertained my ideas, and flatly rejected me. Every man among them cited some combination of Howland, Palomb, Nothram, and the Triarchy as the reason why, proving that fear and complacency are motivators of unmeasurable power.

In Gallin Myakys' home of Kylisport, where the train again docked for the night, they found refuge, and care of a more permanent nature for Lewcas. Gallin had met the party at the train station and escorted them with a complement of his own guardsmen to the cottage hospital that operated in Kylisport, and then onward to his manse. Their stop in the first location was to see that Lewcas was admitted for care and observation. The woman, who was still not talking, was to remain there as well, with Sydnee still providing her protection.

"Is she mute?" Gallin had queried concernedly when he, Marigold, and the rest of their party had left the hospital.

"She might be non-verbal, but she is definitely not mute," Marigold told him in reply. *"I will never forget her screams for as long as I shall live."*

Following dinner with Gallin's family and Marigold's remaining retinue, the minister and the lady retreated to his solar so that the two could convene in private to discuss events past and present. With all others out of sight and hearing, Marigold had told Gallin of every horrid minute of the events in Pelican Harbour and the disappointing discussions in the days afterward.

Even in the telling, Gallin grew completely disheartened.

"I never knew that Minister Nothram was capable of such abject cruelty," he offered as comment when the recollection was complete. "Nor was I aware that my fellow ministers could so blithely ignore a call to action. Each of the men you just met with can affect change in greater strokes than most people could ever dream of doing and somehow, all that the four of them could think to do with that power is to turn away and ignore the pleas."

Marigold had an idea why they did that. "Nothram got to them first, I would wager. Perhaps Eamon Palomb and Grenjin Howland as well and maybe even the Triarchists. If they sent correspondence to the others at the same time that they sent the package I received, then the ministers would have had their letters from the easterners prior to my arrival."

"Just so," Gallin agreed while opening a drawer in his desk and producing a pair of papers he passed to Marigold. "This is what I received from the Lord Master. While it is a dire warning from two desperate old men, it is hardly a reason for the ministers to abandon courage entirely."

The content of the document was written in a passive, suggestive manner. In one breath, it called on the receiver to remember all that the Elite Merchants had allegedly accomplished, and even listed those *achievements*, such as they were. It concluded itself with a look toward the future, and how bright it would be should everyone remain unified under the EMP's parasol during Marigold's act of defiance.

"Is that all?" Marigold asked, her voice echoing how little she was impressed as she dropped the piece of paper back to the desk. "You think this letter restrained those ministers? This is a pithy excuse for someone to go craven."

A sad smile rested on the face of Gallin as he gripped the letter on its edge with just his index and middle fingers, the arm holding them perched on its elbow on the desk. "This is an offer for men who suffer no ill effects of the status quo, asking them to maintain their comfortable existence. That right there is the easiest thing to do. Think about it: all this letter requires of them is to remain loyal to the system and the bodies that maintain that system. They can stay in their homes, act like you do not exist, and simply wait for your eventual defeat by attrition."

Her eyes went to the floor while Gallin had talked, and his words rang poignantly, if not painfully. "So you would say that apathy is the enemy of change."

The papers in Gallin's fingers tumbled back to the desk. "Apathy alone is not the enemy, for it works in tandem with selfishness. Unfortunately for us, the two make quite the efficient team," Gallin uttered in a tone that sounded to be near defeat.

"You are my Chief Strategist, what do you suggest I do next?" Marigold queried exasperatingly, feeling completely at her wits end. "I am due in Ardwyle Harbour by mid-morning, Hodd's Harbour just after the lunch hour, and the Bay of Fog before day's end. How do I fight apathy and selfishness when I meet with the ministers of those regions?"

"What we have in our favour going into those sittings is distance," Gallin noted with hope bleeding into his voice. "We are far from Pelican Harbour, and further again from Atrebell and Hercalest. Haymard Nothram is an unusually influential minister among his westerly neighbours, that much is true, but nestled between Holliford and Weicaster Bay are five regions that have always been beholden to House Morton. In fact, my own house is no exception. How well do you know the old heraldry of each house, before the EMP homogenised everything under the white dove flag?"

Marigold took the few seconds that a deep breath offered her to scan her memory, but came up short of anything approaching recollection. "I know the sigils of my own house and the Palombs'. The only reason I know the Palombs' sigil is on account of the fact that our house and theirs, as the Warden Lord houses, are the only ones to still wear their old colours on their guardsmen uniforms."

"Well then, if you would allow me, I shall tell you a brief tale," Gallin began with an open gesture toward Marigold, waiting until she gave permission before going further. "Did you know that the stretch of coast from Kylisport to Weicaster was once called 'The Blue Coast'?"

"I recall my grandmother would refer to the towns in this area as, 'A Blue Coaster town' when any of them were mentioned, but little else," Marigold told him, having searched within for any reference. "I just figured it was an old nickname for the area based on the colour of the seas around here, or something akin to that."

"A patron of the old days, Lady Maisera was," Gallin commented with a chuckle. "Most would probably think that the Blue Coast title was seawater related, and why not? It can be said that we do enjoy a sunny, mild climate here for most of the year, after all. However, so does the Gull Coast, and they have much of the sandy beaches, too, and yet House Keeves' region is not considered part of the Blue Coast. The reason for such is that House Keeves and their predecessor, House Prowell, have always been sworn to their southerly neighbour, House Mattersly of Tippard."

He leaned ahead in his chair, his elbows resting upon its arms and his fingers tenting. "The reason for the Blue Coast is slightly more complex, while being altogether simple in concept. The land encompassed by the four regions from here to Weicaster, and as easterly as what is now the Toyell region, were once an autonomous fiefdom ruled and protected by House Morton. Of course, this was in ancient times, when human Illiastra was known as Phaleayna and the regency ruled from their island city in Great Valley Lake.

"I will not bog you down in details from the beginning," Gallin added with a light wave and half a smile. "I will say though, that settlement of the west coast had been fraught with danger from the outset. The coast was simply too far west for Phaleayna to have effective rule, and the people living along what would become the Blue Coast could not depend on Phaleayna to protect them from threats either outside the continent or within. To give Phaleaynans with western ambitions the means to manage themselves, the settlements were given autonomy by the royal family. All that the citizens of the west coast had to do was reaffirm their fealty to the crown, and in turn, they were rewarded with sufficient finances with which to establish the new dominion. Along with that influx of gold from the east, there arrived a governor who had been personally chosen by the king of the day to rule with full authority in the royal family's stead."

"That governor was a Morton, I take it," Marigold guessed aloud as Gallin had paused for a breath.

"Marwell Morton, to be exact," Gallin confirmed almost gaily while picking up from where he left off. "Marwell was ill-received at first, as the people felt he was foisted upon them over more viable options already present in the west, but he earned their trust in due time. His family continued to rule right through the Era of the Last King, when the Valdarrow family rose to power in what is now Atrebell. Those were the darkest days in the continent's written history, as I am sure you know, but it is also when House Morton established themselves as something akin to crownless monarchs in the west.

"When the first of the Valdarrow name tried to conquer the west coast, he did so with a measure of success in the Twin Bay area. Bolstered by these victories, Valdarrow turned his gaze to the south, and began a bloody rampage from what is now Galdourn all the way to Weicaster Bay. It was there that his challenge was met by Harte, the ruling Morton of the day. It seems that while the rest of the west coast under Phaleayna's rule was waiting on the king and his five Knight Generals to ride out and respond to the violence, Harte Morton took matters into his own hands. He chose six proven soldiers of loyal standing and raised these five men and one woman to title of lords and lady. Each of the six had orders to build their own army from within the Morton's vast territory, and Harte sent them out to do so from the moment that Valdarrow's western campaign began."

Gallin's excitement seemed to grow as he continued with his history lesson, his words becoming tinged with enthusiasm and his body language growing animated. "Every citizen in the territory was brought to Weicaster so that they could hide behind its tall, stone walls. Any provisions to be had were brought along with them as well, leaving nothing for Valdarrow but empty and abandoned settlements. Meanwhile, the armies built small forts all around the exterior of the city and further protected the new fortifications with wooden palisade walls. The forts were connected to the city by hidden tunnels and the grounds between and before them were sewn with death traps. It was a plan laid out with precision and diligence, and it paid off in spades for Harte Morton.

"Valdarrow lost thousands of men in his effort to conquer Weicaster Bay. The sheer numbers at his disposal, and the previous victories he accumulated led Valdarrow to believe that he could simply overwhelm Harte Morton's army as he had done all along the west coast. It is written that Harte Morton was only happy to let Valdarrow try. Those of Valdarrow's forces who were not killed or maimed by the traps on the ground were slaughtered by the arrows and catapults of the forts and city walls. With his army in tatters and on the verge of collapse, Valdarrow withdrew his attack and slinked his way home to what is now Atrebell. The loss of so much of his army forced Valdarrow to pull almost all of his forces from the areas they had taken, as Valdarrow simply did not have the soldiers to hold them for long. Historians from then to now agree with near uniformity that the only other army to repel any Valdarrow before or after with as much success was the Elven Forest.

"In Weicaster Bay, Harte Morton and his six lords were regarded as heroes, and victory celebrations went on for days on end. Harte rewarded his six knights by giving them each their own piece of his realm to rule over as lords and lady, with him as their Liege Lord in Weicaster Bay."

Gallin's face took on a smile, and Marigold had to assume that he was reaching the apex of his story as he pressed forward in the telling. "During the fighting, each soldier had worn a tabard and shield bearing the sigil and colours of House Morton: a golden crayfish on a blue and white field, divided per fess with a line undy. After their decisive victory over Valdarrow, Morton's new houses were all given leave to create banners of their own. Despite all the possibilities at their disposal, the six of them decided as one to honour their liege lord by implementing the colours of blue, white, and gold into their own sigils. Thus, the six houses, waving their similar flags, went out into Morton's region and settled holdfasts of their own."

At once, Gallin's enthusiasm began to wane, but he seemed far from finished. "In the immediate centuries after the fall of Valdarrow and the death of the last king of Phaleayna, the capital was eventually moved to what would become Atrebell. That relocation not only gave the capital a more central location to the whole country, it also provided us with the first incarnation of the intangible line dividing east and west that we know and live under today.

"Originally, the divide incorporated the regions immediately east of the Daol Forest into the Western Realm, which is where one of Morton's lordly houses, House Pike, had settled and ruled. The line shifted under influence from House Palomb, and House Pike, with their western loyalties, proved a problem during that shift nearly a century ago.

"The house was headed at the time by Griffin Pike, who had two trueborn sons by a first wife. When she died in labour with the second son, Lord Pike remarried to a woman whose family were in the good graces of the EMP. With his new bride, Griffin Pike welcomed three more children into the house, and life seemed to go on. Their normalcy came to a halt when House Palomb first attempted to redraw the line between east and west, though. House Pike resisted, and during that time, Griff, as he was known, died in his sleep of what many suspected to be poisoning. Before Griff's body was cold, his two sons from his first wife were banished from their house by the second wife and they were forced to flee in the dead of night in exile to Weicaster Bay. The second wife then temporarily took over the Toyell Region long enough to abdicate the minister's seat to her oldest brother, Wendell of House Imorgan, whose descendants still rule to this day.

"With only five of Morton's blue-and-white lords left, and all them located along the coast to the north of Weicaster Bay, the area took on the name of the Blue Coast. Today, only Rochford, Bradling, and Locklier remain of the original houses, but worry not, for the other two, Houses Mayweather and Greenwell, both came to natural ends that were without strife.

"One thing that came of the shady happenings with House Pike was for the Mortons to ensure that the remaining five regions kept order and peace. That meant that harmony needed to be maintained both internally, among their own families, and externally, with one another. Part of the Mortons' measures was to encourage relations with families and individuals who could be trusted to uphold these standards. Therefore, any new families that the Mortons' promoted to lordships were already of reliable reputation, and were welcomed by being given the right to design their banners using the original blue, white, and gold colours."

"That includes House Myakys, I presume?" Marigold inquired, trying to hurry along what Gallin had moments ago promised to be a short tale.

Gallin stood up then, and went to a bookshelf in the corner of the room. Reaching an arm behind it, he produced a heavy, circular wooden shield and proceeded to lay it on his desk for Marigold to see. The shield was divided per chevron, white on the top half, blue on the lower, with a large golden, spotted cat of some kind standing rampant in the centre.

"House Morton saved my family from certain doom centuries ago," Gallin explained while looking over the shield with Marigold. "One of my ancestors was a Vellicanese senator. As was common among the Crescent Isles in those days, he and the rest of the Vellick Isles governance were overthrown by conquerors, this time from Garja. As part of this Garjan invasion, they began putting the existing rulers and their families to the sword. With nothing but the clothes on their backs, my ancestors fled their home islands by ship. If not for the compassion of Lyman Morton, my bloodline would have died copperless and broken three hundred years ago. Given that my family owe everything to the Mortons, we were only glad to follow their tradition when given the honour of being inducted into the Blue Coast.

"My family chose the Vellicanese jaguar as our heraldic symbol," Gallin added, while giving the roaring beast a tap with a single finger, "and painted it according to the Morton traditions."

A hand of Marigold's reached out to touch the paint, a finger of her own tracing the outline of the predator. "That was a fascinating story, Minister Myakys, but I am not sure I see the point you were trying to make with it."

"My point, my lady," Gallin elaborated with a rhythmic knock on his shield. "Is that Haymard Nothram's influence has not, and never will breach the Blue Coast, for I hold it as the Castellan of the North of the Blue Coast. Haymard has been known as a man with a callous bend and an affinity for the oppressive ideology at the extreme end of the theological and political spectrum. This is nothing new to any of us, Blue Coast or not, but it is my job to see that his beliefs spread no further south than Holliford, on either the tongues of the commoners or the nobility."

"I have only gotten two Blue Coasters as of yet, where are the other three when I need them?" Marigold threw out. It was only when the words were already in the air that she realised that they and her tone could be interpreted as crass.

If he heard anything that could be considered rude, Gallin made no remark on it as he responded to the question. "Forget what you do not have yet and consider what you do: two Blue Coast houses that could open the door to the remaining three."

That only raised further questions for Marigold. "If you all answer to Samhais Morton, how will you or Lon Bradling open the door to him or the other Blue Coast houses? He, above any other minister in the Western Realm, is bound to serve the Palombs by virtue of his sister being married to Lord Eamon."

"You are correct in saying that. However, I am almost entirely sure that Lord Eamon is not aware that the pact of the Blue Coast houses is still in effect. In fact, I would say that most people younger than your grandmother's generation are entirely unaware of it, having been raised in the shadow of the white dove of the Elite Merchants. I assure you, the five families that once called House Morton their liege lords remember our origins, though. In spite of the markers of the alliance being gone, we keep our pact, even if we must do so in secret. The Blue Coast looks out for one another, and ultimately, we all still answer to Samhais Morton."

Marigold quite nearly recoiled in her seat, and was about to call on Elden and Dayden, who were standing guard outside the solar. Instead, she spoke softly, hoping to keep her racing heart still. "Wait, what are you trying to hint at, Minister Myakys?"

"Nothing as sinister as you might be thinking, my lady, I assure you," Gallin answered calmly while returning to his seat, the shield still resting on the desk. "I would have joined your cause either way, I promise you. My intentions were clear from the start, though Minister Morton came to me during your speech and gave me further reason to lend you aid. You would never believe it had I told you before now, but Samhais deserves a sizeable portion of the credit for where we find ourselves currently. Certainly, he gave you a memorable refusal, did he not? I would like to think that Eamon and his sons heard all about it when they met with Minister Felton in Obalen. Surely, that would be enough to assuage any suspicions of betrayal that they could have possibly harboured for Eamon's brother-in-law."

"So what you are saying is that he cannot support me outright, but…" Marigold had begun to say, as the picture became clear in her mind.

"The rest of the Blue Coast can," Gallin said, finishing her thought.

"Lon Bradling was his doing as well, I would imagine?" Marigold put to Gallin, who was already nodding in confirmation.

"Indeed it was, although that discussion happened between both men on the next morning."

"Why… Why did you not tell me this sooner?" Marigold inquired next, her level of concern tapering off quickly. "As my Chief Strategist, this is exactly the thing that would be beneficial for me to know."

Gallin offered her a bow of his head, "You have my apologies for that, my lady, and I do hope you can forgive me. I do fully believe in your goals and mission, and as I said before, I would have supported you either way. However, I only became your Chief Strategist as of late, and at your discretion. To that end, I have been the Northern Castellan of the Blue Coast for much of my adult life. Even if I was to sever the latter connection in favour of the former, there has to be an appropriate process in place to prevent burning those bridges on my way out. Despite that, I felt that if I could secure you an alliance with the Blue Coast, then there would be no need to sever those aforementioned ties."

"That is all understandable, Minister. I forgive you," Marigold uttered hurriedly, satisfied with his response and eager to descend into the depths of significance. "With that said, what do I need to do in order to secure the support of the remaining members of the Blue Coast?"

"That… That truly is more complicated," Gallin stated while sucking air through his teeth. "We need to arrange a meeting with Samhais, and, well, that will not be easy."

"I fail to see why," Marigold uttered with confused a shrug. "I have only to have him meet me aboard the train when we stop in Weicaster."

A chortle from Gallin marked his amusement with that statement, "If only it were that simple. Samhais is under the constant eye of Palomb informants. There was concern in the early days of Eamon's courtship with Jorette over Samhais, who may have been a bit too… I suppose *haughty* would be the right word, in his opposition to the union. That disdain did irreparable damage to Eamon's trust in

Samhais, so Eamon took to paying a few nobles and commoners working in Morton's purview to regularly report on his behaviour to House Palomb. Samhais has a careful line to walk now, as the first sign of recalcitrance from any member of House Morton could have dire consequences."

"I gather that Minister Morton is aware of who the spies are," Marigold said presumptively.

"But of course," Gallin confirmed with noted enthusiasm. "It was deduced in the seasons following the wedding as to which Weicasterians are on Eamon's payroll. Of course, in the nearly twenty years that Eamon and Jorette have been married, there have been changes to the payroll, but nothing escapes our network for long.

"Samhais regrets the level of subterfuge he must routinely engage in to keep ahead of Eamon Palomb. I feel badly for the man for having to keep up his façade for all these years. The Blue Coast's support has been unyielding, though. The five of us work diligently to ensure that his will is carried out, even if it is in secret. It should be said that passing words about between a few conspirators and putting you and Sam in the same room without Palomb ears there to hear it are two different matters entirely, however."

Marigold thought of something then. "The ministers I am to meet with tomorrow will all reject me, will they not?"

"They will at this junction, for certain," Myakys replied both quickly and affirmatively.

In as hurried a manner as she dared, Marigold pivoted to her proposition. "Then we should skip those meetings and go directly to Weicaster Bay. We can come back to them after the fact."

"That would be unwise," Gallin counselled firmly. "It is well known who has joined you and who has not, skipping potential allies will look suspicious, my lady."

There was sense in that, and for once, Marigold was all out of both questions and ideas. "I believe myself to be growing quite tired and I can think of nothing further to discuss. Perhaps on that note, we can draw our meeting to its conclusion for the night. I have somewhere else to be, after all. Shall I meet you at the station in the morning, Minister Myakys?"

"Of course, my lady, I will be there in the morning to see you off. In the meantime, where might you be headed at this hour?" Gallin asked anxiously while suddenly standing up.

"I would much like to go check on Lewcas," Marigold told him after rising from her chair to make for the solar door. "I am all he has in the world anymore, and I would hate for something to happen to him with no one there. As for tomorrow, I was hoping that you would be open to joining me for the remainder of the trip south. Perhaps while I have you back in my company you could return to Daol Bay with me afterwards. If I get the signatures I need to validate my ascension as Warden Lady, my first action after secession will be to pursue Haymard Nothram for his crimes. No matter what else I do in this world, I will see him brought before justice for murdering that innocent woman."

"I would be only delighted to do so, my lady," Gallin concurred while joining her at the door. "I agree that Nothram needs to be dealt with and I am at your service as your chief strategist in that event. In the meantime, I shall do my utmost to draft a plan to arrange for a safe and secure correspondence between you and Minister Morton."

"I trust you," Marigold told him. "Not just in this, but in all things, even taking the Blue Coast into account. I would not have made you my chief strategist if I did not think you were trustworthy. I know you will not let me down."

Gallin bowed deeply when she finished her statement. "Of course not, my lady. I would never dare to do you any such dishonour. Please, accept my apologies a second time for not telling you of the Blue Coast sooner. Withholding of similarly pertinent information will not happen again, I assure you. If Lewcas is awake, please give him my sincerest wishes on a quick recovery."

"I shall do just that, Minister Myakys," Marigold replied with a bow of her own.

"Wait, my lady, there is one more thing," he said suddenly.

Marigold's eyes narrowed. "What is it?"

Myakys smiled and shook his head at her defensiveness. "You continually refer to me as 'Minister Myakys' but please, feel free to just call me Gallin. There is little need of such formality toward me."

"Very well, Gallin, but only if you refer to me as Marigold. The 'my lady's get tiresome," she offered with a grin in return.

"It will be as you wish... Marigold."

19
FREYARD

Marigold was spiralling downward mentally. If there was but one thing in the Known World that Freyard was certain of now, it was that. Lewcas, the wounded manor guard of hers, was clinging to life in the cottage hospital in Kylisport, and Marigold was harbouring a tremendous amount of guilt over the incident that put him there. The women, both the living and the deceased of the assault in Pelican Harbour, were further weighing on her mind, and atop it all was the lingering grief of her father's death in the recent past.

Freyard wanted to comfort Marigold, to tell her that all her woes would be all right eventually, but it was neither his place to do so or something that he could even say with certainty.

It is too soon to say what way the winds will blow, Freyard reminded himself from his empty booth aboard the Tullivan's sitting car of the train. *She is trying to ensure that everything in her control is accounted for, and doing an admirable job at it, granted. It is that which is out of her control that is so concerning to both her and me. Her worry is with trying to turn invariables into variables, and my issue is with the toll that her worries are taking on her.*

The others were either asleep or guarding Marigold at this early morning hour, leaving the sunrise cresting the skyline of the Western Plains for him alone to see. It was quite the daybreak to behold, if Freyard was any judge of such. The rays of purple and pink had begun to shimmer their way through the treeline, flittering across the frosted fields. The tall grass took on the look of brilliant glass blades, rising precariously into the morning air.

Before him on the table sat a leather notebook he kept on him at all times, with an open inkwell and pen near at hand. The pages were open to his written investigation into the recent happenings in Pelican Harbour, as he and the other guardsmen tried to piece everything together for later use, both judicially and otherwise.

Reaching for his teacup, which was the last remnant of his breakfast, Freyard felt the weightlessness of it and remembered that he had already emptied it. He debated the merits of going for a second cup, or if he even had the time for such before he was to oversee the changing of the guards. In this case, it was he who was changing, replacing Elden, who had taken the overnight watch.

He's a good lad who does not seem to have a complaint in his body, even when we are down a man.

Freyard had seen men wounded like Lewcas before, men whose lives were now represented by a black banner in Fort Dornett.

That one won't make it. Stubborn, bull strength keeps him alive, but it will run out, as it always does, and then Marigold's downward spiral will continue.

By the gods, we need some sort of victory, and soon. Here's hoping that Samhais Morton will deliver something of value today.

Freyard's eyes closed and his hands went over his face instinctually, rubbing deep into the walls of the bridge of his nose.

From at the rear of the car there came the sound of the door sliding open quickly, and Freyard had to assume it was one of the other protectors on their way towards breakfast.

"Excuse me, Ser?" a tiny voice asked from Freyard's right, and his eyes opened so hard he thought his eyelids were going to jam into the sockets.

Glancing sideways, his gaze fell on the woman that was rescued in Pelican Harbour. She was dressed in the yellow, silk, short-sleeved, knee length nightgown that Marigold had given from her own wardrobe, her arms folded over a thin, pale frame that Freyard thought might be malnourished. A pair of big, brown eyes that looked as dark as midnight in the dim glow of the early morning, and a squirrely little overbite added to the picture of a diminutive, terrified creature staring back at him.

The genuine surprise on Freyard's face had to be palpable, he knew, as this was the first time the woman had spoken since being rescued. There was even legitimate wonder among Marigold, the guardsmen, and Wyla if she could even talk at all.

"Yes, what can I do for you, ma'am?" Freyard replied gently, not wanting to frighten her further than she already appeared to be.

"You're the leader of the men that saved me, aren't you?"

Freyard nodded slowly. "Aye, that's me."

"I wanted to thank you for that, Ser," she told him meekly. "I thought I was going to die until you and your friends stepped in."

"You are quite welcome. I am sorry we could not save *your* friend, too," Freyard offered back with a swallow in his throat.

Her gaze lowered, her lips parted, and it looked to Freyard like she might say something. He waited, averting his own gaze in hopes that it might help put her at ease. Instead, she shook her head and silently began her return to the sleeping cabin from whence she came.

Freyard shifted in his seat in her direction. "Ma'am, please wait, there is no need to go. Please, stay and talk for a moment."

She stopped, her head turned slightly in his direction. "What would you like to talk about?"

"Whatsoever you might want," Freyard returned hurriedly, trying to keep his voice low so that he did not scare the young woman. "Until now, I did not even know that you could talk. Surely, you must be hungry, at least. I can fetch your breakfast."

Several seconds went by without the woman moving so much as an inch, her face obscured by her thick head of blonde curls. Suddenly, she pivoted on her heels and padded back in borrowed slippers to where Freyard stood. "Is there buttered toast? Perhaps a small bowl of oatmeal and honey, too?"

Freyard shrugged quickly and slid out of the booth so fast that he nearly fell to the floor. "I am not sure, to be honest, but if you would like to take a seat, I can go forward to the kitchen car and find out for you."

As he stood up, Freyard grabbed his leather coat from the seat where it rested beside him. With permission from the lady, he laid it across her shoulders and ushered her into the seat across from where he had been. "Please, just wait right there, and I will be back as quickly as I can," he instructed tepidly, before darting off to the staff cars in the front of the train.

At this hour aboard the train, there was little movement from the staff members, and Freyard was able to go forward without any delay whatsoever. In the kitchen car, Freyard came across the first signs of life, as the head chef and his cooks were already hard at work preparing breakfast foods. The server on duty caught sight of Freyard and came striding down the narrow aisle that the car allowed for, greeting Freyard jovially. "Good morning, Ser. Miss Marigold is looking for her breakfast, I take it?"

"Not quite, Gerry," Freyard returned, having become familiar enough with the man at this point in their trip to be addressing him on a first name basis.

After riddling off the rescued woman's breakfast order to Gerry, the server hummed aloud, but made no issue with any of it. "I will check with the cook to be sure, but it should be no issue."

"You're a good man, Gerry. It's much appreciated," Freyard said with a smile and a pat on the shoulder.

"Wait, Captain Archer," Gerry called after him. "Same protocol as usual, right?"

Freyard pointed back at him from the doorway. "Of course, aye."

With a confirmative thumb held upward, Gerry let Freyard go, and he jogged all the way back to the sitting car. Freyard slowed himself just before the door to the sitting car, and much to his relief, he found that the woman had indeed stayed at the table.

"Oh, good, you are still here," he commented while sliding back into his seat.

"That is what you asked of me, isn't it?" she asked, her face and tone registering a nonplussed expression.

"Of course," Freyard added, trying to calm his heart rate from where the brief race had elevated it. Glancing down at the table, his eyes fell on the notebook still sitting open and he flipped it shut. "Oh, shit, I am sorry about that."

Just as quickly, he repeated himself. "Oh, shit, I am sorry about that too. You probably can't read, can you?"

The woman shook her head, a look of embarrassment making its way across her face.

"That's ah, that's... Well, it's a useful skill to have, uh reading, that is," Freyard said stumblingly, before clearing his throat. "Um, perhaps Lady Marigold will see to it that you are taught to do so, if you would like it."

"What? Why would Miss Marigold want to teach me to read?" the woman queried with growing puzzlement.

Freyard was painfully aware of his increasing awkwardness and tried deftly to bring it under control. "That is just the sort of thing she intends to do in the new Western Realm. Women have a right to education as much as men and Marigold will see to it that you do. Forgive me, though, I am getting far ahead of myself. I will begin again. Hello, my name is Freyard Archer, Captain of the Sun's Rangers, how do you do?"

"I... Do fine, I think?" she answered with uncertainty. "Hold on, the way you say your title makes it sound like you're famous. Should I know who you are? Or what the Sun's Rangers are, for that matter?"

"Probably not, unless you have spent any time in the eastern end of the Southlands in the last few years," Freyard answered earnestly.

Her eyes went wide and her jaw dropped. "You're from the Southlands? That's a savage place, isn't it?"

"Well, no, I'm from Collura, which is a town out in the East Ateles region, which is part of the Eastern Grasslands quadrant of East Illiastra. Which, when I say it like that makes it seem that if I get any more eastern than that then I'll be a sunrise," Freyard attempted to say to set the record straight, before agreeing in part with the assumption of her second question. "But, yes, the Southlands are a dangerous place to be. That is why my rangers and I were there, to make it less dangerous."

He raised an index finger curiously. "We're getting ahead of ourselves again. Let's reverse course to the start. Would you like to tell me your name?"

The woman seemed to begin retreating to her fearful shell again, but managed to answer the query. "Moya... My name is Moya."

"That is a lovely name, Moya. Is it the only name you have?" Freyard tried next.

Moya's eyes went all around the cabin, even over both shoulders, and she leaned ahead to Freyard, dropping her voice to a whisper. "I'm not being arrested, am I? I mean to say, that Miss Marigold is not charging me with any crimes, right?"

"Whatever would anyone be arresting you for?" Freyard answered while mimicking her apprehensiveness. "Are you a fugitive?"

She sat back and eyed Freyard warily. "I might be, but I don't know if Miss Marigold would think so, if she's fighting for women like you say she is."

"Did you kill someone?" Freyard put to her, his head cocked to the side in confusion.

"What? No, never," she replied with a furious shake of her head.

Freyard wrinkled up the one side of his face. "After what we have all gone through over the last two days, I seriously doubt that any crime you might have been charged with prior to that whole mess is going to register with Marigold, then."

"I-I thought... I didn't know..." Moya stammered, her eyes turning away to the rising sun beyond the window. "I still thought I was in trouble, since Marigold is EMP and all. I hoped that by behaving and saying nothing that she might let me go."

"Look, Moya, I am no one to judge the crimes of anyone else here," Freyard offered with another shrug. "By the laws of Illiastra, most would consider me a deserter for joining Marigold in the first place. I've personally killed somewhere north of a hundred raiders and a decent attorney could probably argue to a judge and jury that most of those deaths were extrajudicial in nature, if anyone cared about the raiding gangs, that is."

"You killed hundreds, you say?" Moya exclaimed, her mouth agape.

Freyard scrunched his face up again. "They were gangs of pillaging pricks who put innocents to the sword and the chain. Save your sympathy, for the men I killed would never be worthy of it."

"Well then, I suppose you're not the only deserter here, if you must know," Moya finally relinquished.

As Freyard was about to inquire further, he heard a distant thumping, and slid out of his seat again. "Your breakfast is ready. Just a moment and I will be right back with it."

Just outside of the front of the office car in the freezing, morning air that whipped its way through was Gerry the server. In his hands was the covered tray of food, clutched in a tight grip as he fought off the shivers, leaving Freyard to guess that Gerry had been tapping on the door with a foot to get attention from within.

"I am terribly sorry about that, Gerry. I must have bumped the locking mechanism on the door as I rushed through," Freyard said while holding the door open for him to enter and set the tray down. "Thank you ever so much for waiting."

"Tis no problem at all, Captain Archer," Gerry stated after setting the tray on the desk and shaking off the cold. "Before I go, would you like me to put in Miss Marigold's breakfast order? Surely it is getting past her waking hour."

"Gods dammit," Freyard grimaced. "Aye, you had best get on that, and I had best get to waking Marigold. I'm bloody late. I'll leave the door unlocked so that you're not standing in the cold next time."

Gerry gave half a bow, "That would be much appreciated, Captain."

The two parted again, with Freyard carrying the tray back to Moya and Gerry rushing back to the kitchen car.

"Here you are, Moya, a fresh breakfast with which to start your day properly," Freyard said while setting the tray before her. "If you will excuse me, I would love to continue this conversation, but I have an important matter to attend to."

Freyard dashed off toward the rear of the train before Moya could say another word. While eating breakfast, Freyard had donned only his cotton trousers and undershirt, and had to stop at his bunk to grab his teal button-down and weaponry. His coat, he realised too late, was still on Moya's shoulders, and while belting his sabre and pistols into place, he opted on a black vest as an overcoat, of sorts.

I'm slightly out of uniform, but that should not be of too much issue at this hour, he bargained with himself while moving to the back of the sleeping car.

Sydnee rolled out of his bunk as Freyard passed, sitting on the edge and rubbing his eyes sleepily in pyjama trousers and an undershirt. "Captain Archer? Is it morning already?" he asked after a quick yawn.

"That it is, Sydnee," Freyard confirmed in answer, before raising a question of his own. "Do a favour for me, would you?"

"Uh, Captain, the blonde woman is not in her bunk," Sydnee interrupted, suddenly jarring awake as he inspected the empty sleeping pod directly across the corridor from his, its privacy drape pulled back halfway.

"She's in the sitting car having her breakfast, nothing to worry about, Syd," Freyard explained hurriedly. "About that favour I asked, could you go to the sitting car and wait on the server carrying Marigold's breakfast?"

"Marigold ordered her breakfast already?" Sydnee asked in a tired stupor. "I did not know she was awake yet. Are we late waking up? Tell me we are not in Weicaster Bay yet."

Freyard sucked his teeth ashamedly. "Not quite, Sydnee. It is I who is late to wake Marigold. I sent Gerry to get started on her usual morning meal, though. So please, be a lad and go wait for it to arrive."

"Hold on, who is Gerry?" Sydnee inquired with a yawn.

Without supplying an answer, Freyard left him to complete the favour and went to Marigold's car. Standing outside the door in the morning air, Freyard waited a beat, listening for any noise within and hearing none.

She's probably still asleep. That might be both good and bad.

He gave a soft knock on the door, and stepped back to wait on who he hoped would be Elden answering.

Those hopes were dashed when the door slid sideways and a barefooted, robed Marigold was standing before him. "Good morning, Freyard," she offered with what little enthusiasm she could muster.

"Good morning, my lady," he said in return. "My apologies on being late to wake you and commence with the changing of the guards."

"There is nothing to worry about," she told him flatly. "Once Elden leaves, you may guard the door while I get changed into something presentable."

Freyard gave half a bow without further issue, "Yes, of course, my lady. I ordered your usual breakfast with Gerry, I hope that will suffice."

She shrugged and moved aside to allow Elden egress. "It will do. I barely had any appetite this morning anyhow. But I suppose I must eat something."

"Aye, that would be advisable, my lady," Freyard agreed readily.

Without further comment, Marigold closed and locked the door, leaving the two men alone on the bridge between the two cars.

Freyard looked to Elden. "Please tell me that she slept last night, at least."

"In spurts, aye," he replied during a stretch of his limbs. "It's the most she has slept since Pelican Harbour, going by what the others who have had the night shift since we even started a night shift have said, though."

There was hesitation in the way Elden spoke, and Freyard was not about to let it go by unnoticed. "There's something else though, is there not?"

Elden looked over his shoulder before giving answer, "She woke once in a cold sweat, and she jumped even further when I stirred from where I was sitting, as she believed me to be another assassin. Then, this morning, she asked to see my sword, unsheathed."

"How did you respond to that?" Freyard queried concernedly.

"I turned to show her the scabbard on my hip first, but when that did not satisfy, I drew it," Elden responded with growing bashfulness. "What else was I to do?"

Freyard's head tilted to the side in what was not an entirely conscious act. "You should have asked why she wanted to see it in the first place at the sixth hour in the morning. Did she even explain what her reasoning was?"

"She did explain, albeit after the fact. It had something to do with a dream that had woken her. I was being told the details of that dream just as you knocked on the door, actually," Elden began to tell Freyard, when the door behind him slid open once more.

"We will catch up later, Elden," Freyard said hastily, following it up with a pat on the guard's shoulder. "Go get some rest, my good man, for you have earned it."

Elden caught the meaning of Freyard's abrupt behaviour and said nothing further of the matter. Upon bidding Marigold a further good morning, he left Freyard and her alone on the bridge.

"Did you two have something to talk about?" Marigold asked Freyard with a hint of suspicion. "I had figured that Elden would be eager to get to sleep."

"I was merely asking Ser Elden how *you* had slept, my lady." Freyard explained, not altogether untruthfully. "As my friend Yarohmer the Graceful is fond of saying, '*Nothing prepares a fighter for battle like a good night's rest'.*"

"I suppose I shall be lacking in today's battle, then," she told him in blunt fashion. "For sleep was fleeting, at best. It's no matter now, though. Has anyone seen Gallin this morning? We will want to confirm our plan with him before we reach Weicaster. I will want all involved to be present for that, and I would hazard to guess that we do not have long before arrival."

"Shall I send for him, my lady?" Freyard put to Marigold frankly.

"That would be fine," Marigold granted amiably. "I shall take my breakfast in the sitting car and we will conduct the morning briefing over our food."

Freyard stepped back and pulled open the door to the retinue's sleeping car, allowing Marigold to pass first before following behind her. "I see no issue with that, my lady. In fact, that might give you a chance to get acquainted with Moya, if she is up for it."

The mention of the rescue's name caused Marigold to pause in her tracks and look back into Freyard's eyes. "And just who is this 'Moya'? Freyard, did you happen to find a lady-friend among the train's staff last night?"

"Uh, no, my lady, it is nothing so salacious as that," Freyard stated with mild embarrassment. "It would seem that Moya is the identity of the surviving woman of the Pelican Harbour incident."

Her eyes widened in surprise, "How did you come to find out her name?"

Allowing himself a slight chuckle, Freyard replied, "It would seem that the woman is not mute after all. She awoke while I was having breakfast and came to me to offer her thanks for saving her life. After that, I managed to talk with her a little more, getting as far as her name and that she is apparently a runaway. We got no further once I became aware that I was past the time to wake you. So as you can see, though my tardiness is regrettable, I feel that it was at least for a good cause, my lady."

Marigold had an amused scoff to offer of her own. "That is as decent a reason as I could think of and a charming story to wit. Very well, let us go meet Miss Moya the Runaway."

"Wait, my lady," Freyard said to stop her after a single step. "I should mention that Moya somehow believed herself to be under arrest by us. There is a chance that she might retreat behind her wall of silence again at the sight of you. Please, don't hold it against her. The poor girl is terribly traumatised already."

"Worry yourself not, for I will give our new friend every bit of leeway that one person can grant," Marigold told him reassuringly. "Everyone deserves the chance to blossom at their own pace."

Freyard nodded in both agreement and understanding, and the pair moved onward into the sleeping car. The door to the privy and the drapery of each bunk were wide open, with all but Moya's bed being carefully made, as soldiers and a maid were wont to do. Even

Elden's bed was untouched, with only his guardsman's jacket left behind.

"Everybody is awake at once," Marigold noted as she and Freyard passed through the car. "Yet, no one is here."

Once they crossed into the sitting car, Marigold's wonder was resolved immediately. Right away, they were met by Dayden Vernet, who was in full uniform and standing with his back to them.

"Good morning, Ser Dayden," Marigold greeted the ranger, making him turn about to offer the same.

"Is there a reason that everyone is in here at once, Dayden?" Freyard inquired, although he felt certain of the answer.

Dayden gestured with his head in the direction of the front of the car. "The rescued woman is not hiding in her bunk anymore. In fact, she's even started to talk. I don't know if anyone got a name from her, though. I arrived just ahead of you two."

"As it turns out, her name is Moya," Freyard informed him.

"Oh, well, there you have it, Captain," Dayden began to say, interrupting himself with another thought, "Wait, Captain, might I ask how it is that you know her name?"

In so many words, Freyard explained to Dayden what had transpired with the woman earlier in the morning, ending with Freyard's abrupt departure to wake Marigold.

"Very well, then. Here, let me clear a path for you to the front so that Lady Marigold can meet her," Dayden offered once he was all caught up. He cleared his throat loudly and bellowed, "make way for the Lady and the Captain, lads."

As Dayden stepped aside, Freyard caught sight of Elden and Glendil standing ahead of him, and the two met eyes with Marigold and parted wordlessly to allow passage. At the front of the car was Sydnee, having taken the seat across from Moya, where Freyard had taken his breakfast shortly before. In front of Sydnee was a tray that looked to contain the honeyed oatmeal, boiled eggs, freshly baked biscuits, side of blackberry jam, and pot of tea that Freyard had ordered for Marigold's morning meal as *the usual.*

The guard was chatting and laughing with Moya, though it was hardly a two-person conversation. Just inside the forward doorway to the car and contributing to the chat was Gallin Myakys, dressed in a three-piece, dark blue pinstriped suit.

Marigold was already moving toward the trio, and came to a stop just behind the shoulder of Sydnee.

As Freyard caught up, he saw that Moya had already clammed up at the sight of Marigold, and he moved to break the tension himself. "My Lady Marigold, might I formally introduce you to Moya. Moya, Lady Marigold would like to speak with you, but only if you are willing, of course."

The poor woman's mouth began to quiver and she tried to stammer out an affirmative answer until Marigold herself decided to take the lead, "Good morning, Moya. It is lovely to finally meet you in earnest."

"I... I don't know what to do," Moya finally managed to say, a tremble beginning to appear in her hands that were folded neatly on the table.

"Perhaps you could tell me what it is that you feel you should do, Moya," Marigold gently suggested, "that way, we can figure things out together as we go."

Moya glanced towards Freyard and Sydnee in turn, her uncertainty as plain as the dimple in her chin. Freyard gave her what he hoped was an encouraging nod, and Moya looked toward Marigold again. "Do I bow to you? Or take a knee, maybe?"

"You don't have to do any such thing for my benefit," Marigold said with amusement in her voice. "Could I sit with you and Sydnee and eat my breakfast? Would that be okay?"

Moya nodded briefly, lowering her gaze to the table as she did. "I would be alright with that. It's your train though, Ma'am, it is not up to me what you do on it."

"Strictly speaking, I own but four cars among a longer train of borrowed cars for the staff needed to run such an operation, and all those cars are being pulled by a rented engine that is operated by paid engineers," Marigold corrected gingerly, with evident regret creeping into her voice and words alike. "However, even as I was saying that, I realise that such distinctions might seem semantic to most. It's no matter, though. Regardless of who owns either train or car, you have final say over your own self, and that includes the company you would like to keep this morning."

"Ever the diplomat, our Marigold is," Minister Myakys chimed in while pressing off from the doorway in which he had been leaning. "To whom I bid good morning to, by the way."

"Likewise to you, Gallin," Marigold responded with a polite half-bow.

While it occurred to Freyard that the two had suddenly come to address each other on a first name basis, now was not the place to comment on the peculiarity of it, and he left well enough alone.

"If I may be so bold to say, my lady, we may be running short on time for idle banter," Freyard noted while checking a clock mounted on the wall opposite of the occupied booth. "We are due in Weicaster by the eighth hour, and it is already well past the seventh. Perhaps, if Miss Moya is willing, we will convene with her after our business in the city has concluded."

Marigold had taken the time to glance back at Freyard while he spoke, and visibly winced when he was done. "I suppose Captain Archer is correct on that front," she replied remorsefully. "His idea of meeting later certainly does seem splendid, though. That is, if you would so want to, Miss Moya."

"Perhaps we are being too hasty to leave Moya out, Marigold," Gallin proposed ponderously. "There may be a role for her to play today, if she is so willing to partake in our ruse."

"It might be considered a bit too much to ask her to be involved in today's plan. She has been through a terrible ordeal recently, after all," Marigold countered, a certain firmness working into her tone.

"What can I do?" Moya asked quickly, gaining silence from the room as all eyes went to her.

"I would counsel against it, Miss Moya. It's too dangerous," Freyard advised her calmly, before looking in Myakys's direction. "Minister, I agree with Lady Marigold: it is too much to ask of Moya to be involved. If we are foiled, it could put her at immediate risk."

"If she is caught, Samhais Morton would turn her loose by nightfall when no one is asking questions," Gallin had begun to reply.

Marigold jumped back into the fray hurriedly as Gallin finished, "We should not even be considering putting Moya in such a position where she could be thrown into a jail cell in the first place, Gallin."

"Excuse me, Ma'am, but if it is all the same, I don't mind helping if I can. I would at least like to hear the plan before I make a choice, anyway," Moya interjected again. "You did mention that I had final say over myself, did you not?"

"I did say that, yes," Marigold admitted after a deep breath full of worry. "Very well, Moya, but before I consider it further, I need to have a word with Captain Archer and Gallin in private. Gentlemen, shall we move into the office car briefly?"

Freyard complied with Marigold's request, following her and Minister Myakys into the next car.

Once within the cabin, Marigold wasted no breath. "Gallin, what in Iia's name are you thinking involving Moya in today's plans? We don't know this woman and it's too early to trust her. For all we know, she might be in Haymard Nothram's employ."

"She is awfully willing to join the fray," Freyard added to Marigold's point.

"Do you honestly believe she is a spy?" Myakys asked in dubious nature, a grin working its way across his face.

While pinching the bridge of her nose between thumb and index finger, Marigold gave a response bathed in frustration, "the odds are low, granted, but the fact that the possibility of such cannot be ruled out pleads to my point that we still have nothing on the background of this woman."

"Captain Archer, I overheard Moya telling Sydnee that she spoke to you before anyone else this morning," Myakys noted before directing a query Freyard's way, "what can you tell us of her based on your interaction?"

"About as much as you can," Freyard relayed to him pointedly. "She says that her name is Moya, and she hinted that she might be a runaway of some kind. Beyond that, I could tell you nothing."

"But do you feel she is a spy?" Myakys continued, redirecting the question to a more specific end.

Freyard was not about to yield his uncertainty though. "Truly, I do not know, Minister Myakys. It might be that Nothram knew we would spring to the girl's rescue after they killed the other one, or Nothram might have planned to kill both and we successfully thwarted his objective. Behaviourally speaking, she's been utterly silent until this morning, and completely withdrawn. The doctors in Kylisport believed her to have 'war-shock', as they called it, and they say it almost definitely stemmed from having witnessed the other woman's gruesome death."

"Forgive my ignorance, but I was never told what war-shock even is," Marigold chimed in. "Other than some sort of mental break that can occur in soldiers."

"They say it's a condition commonly found amongst soldiers on the battlefield, typically after witnessing great carnage," Freyard explained cordially. "There's little known about the condition, but I have had a few of my own men come down with it. When war-shock takes hold of a person, it turns them unstable and unpredictable, which made my affected men dangerous for both themselves and their comrades in the heat of conflict. I would have no choice but to have them removed, by force sometimes, to where they could no longer see or hear the fighting. From there, it could be a matter of days, maybe weeks, before they would come around to their old selves again, if they did at all. In one case, I had to discharge a man from the armed forces completely and send him home to his parents. They in turn had him committed to an asylum after he woke up in a mad panic and tried to kill his father, whom he believed to be a raider. In the last letter that the former ranger's parents ever sent me, the father wrote that I would not know him anymore. It read, *the man we had raised died on the battlefield beside you, Captain, without shedding so much as a drop of his own blood.*"

"How does all of this relate to Moya?" Marigold queried, her voice inflected with genuine interest.

Freyard continued onward without pause, "In the case of my men, I knew who they were before the war-shock took them, so we could recognise the differences between who they were and who they had become. When they began to recover, we could identify their old selves emerging. With Moya, we have no idea who she was before the other woman was murdered. There's no basis on which we can judge her current behaviour, is what I mean to say. She might still be war-shocked or she might be over it. Her ability to speak once more would lend credence to her being at least on the road to recovery, but we don't know that with any level of certainty."

It was Myakys' turn for a question, evidently, "how does all of this help us to determine whether or not she is a spy?"

Rounding in his conclusion, Freyard laid it out for the both of them. "After what she witnessed and what that did to her, the question is not '*is* she a spy *now?*', rather it's '*was* she a spy *before* the affair in Pelican Harbour?'. Regardless of whether she was in collusion with Nothram when she ascended those scaffolds, she knew that what happened up there was his doing. If the experience was traumatic enough to trigger a psychotic break, I would have to think that no amount of former allegiance to Nothram would matter at this point."

"You are saying that we can trust her, is that correct?" Marigold asked, seemingly for clarity's sake.

"I am saying that even if Moya was intended to be an informant, she likely will not be interested in continuing relations with Nothram due to the effect that his atrocious actions had on her," Freyard stated unambiguously.

"Thank you, Captain Archer, I think that's quite the thorough explanation and I feel you have the right of it," Marigold said gratefully. When finished, she pointed her gaze toward Myakys. "Gallin, I would like to hear of your intended use for Moya in today's operation."

Now it was Myakys' turn for elucidation, and he took the opportunity eagerly. "I would have her replace Wyla as your decoy."

The plan seemed to take Marigold by surprise, and she relayed as much. "Whatever for, Gallin? Wyla is more than capable of the task, and she's been preparing for it since yesterday."

"Wyla is fifteen years your senior, almost ten centimetres taller and, most importantly, she looks absolutely nothing like you," Myakys stated frankly. "On the other hand we have Moya. Apart from her hair colour, an issue dealt with easily enough by tying the hair back and hiding it beneath the hood of a cloak, she is far more similar to you in every conceivable way."

"He has a point," Freyard admitted with reluctance. "On appearances alone, Moya is a far more suitable candidate for a decoy."

"I still have to wonder if we can rely on Moya, though, if not for her unknown past, then on the basis of her present mental state," Marigold resisted with a protracted and deep breath.

"We could consider it a test in two parts for Moya," Myakys proposed. "On one hand, we will get an immediate idea of her mental faculties. On the other, we can keep an eye on her afterward, to see if she tries to forward information about the operation to anyone. Besides, she will have one of your guards with her at all times until we are back on the train. Should she fail either test today, they will know and can contain the issue."

Marigold gave a great sigh and threw up her hands. "Alright then, Gallin, we shall try it your way. I want to state that you will share in the responsibility should things with Moya go sideways on us."

"That is more than fair, I should say," Gallin replied gaily, while pointing a hand toward the rear doorway. "Shall we go tell Moya the good news?"

Within seconds, the three returned to the sitting car, finding Moya unmoved, Marigold's breakfast untouched, and Sydnee no longer alone on his side of the booth.

"Decided to take a seat I see, Glendil," Freyard noted lightly. "How do you fare, Moya? Was the breakfast to your liking?"

"Oh, aye, thank you for that, Captain. It was much appreciated," Moya told him with a flicker of a smile. "Can... Can I ask again if I can help you all today?"

There was a slow nod from Marigold, who further confirmed the news, "Why yes, Moya, as a matter of fact we would like you to be involved. How well do you think you could be a decoy?"

"A decoy?" Moya said with marked confusion in her voice. "You mean like those wooden ducks laid into the water by a hunter to trick real ducks? I had a great-uncle that used to use a whole burlap bag full of them to help with hunting, before his leg went lame."

"Somewhat like that, yes," Marigold answered with a chuckle. "Instead of fake fowl, though, you would be pretending to be me for a little while. Just long enough to walk from a nearby book repository to the train. Are you interested?"

Though trembling slightly, Moya discernibly nodded with what might have been excitement. "Aye, Ma'am, whatever you want. 'Tis the least I can do to repay everyone for saving my life."

"Alright then, that is settled," Marigold said gladly with a clap of her hands. "Now, Miss Moya, if you would be so kind as to go to the sleeping car with Ser Sydnee here, he can tell Wyla that you will be replacing her, and she can outfit you from my wardrobe as need be. Sydnee, tell Wyla that she will be staying here and keeping watch on the train. Elden can now sleep unless needed in an emergency."

While Marigold spoke, Glendil had slid out of the booth to allow Sydnee out, and the former remained standing long after the latter was clear of the booth.

"Yes, my lady, it will be as you wish," Sydnee told her with a salute, turning to Moya once done. "If you would follow me, we shall go see Wyla."

Moya got to her feet quickly, the act of which caused Freyard's jacket to fall from her shoulders and to the floor. She knelt to pick it up and offered it back to Freyard with her thanks for borrowing it. Before Freyard could even dust the garment off, Moya had departed behind Sydnee, following close on the guard's heels.

Marigold continued with her commands, "Now, I believe that Captain Archer and his rangers all need to go change into something less conspicuous. With that said, I would ask that you all wait until Wyla and Moya are in my cabin before going to the sleeping cabin and disrobing. There is no telling how our new friend feels about nudity, partial or otherwise, and we would not want any of you to disturb the poor woman."

"What will you be doing, my lady?" Freyard queried plainly.

"I shall be eating my breakfast and going over the mission parameters one more time with Gallin," Marigold revealed while already in the process of sliding into the booth and pulling the uneaten tray of food toward herself.

There was little else for Freyard to say, and he left her to the rapidly cooling meal. With the cabin of the sleeping car cleared, Freyard ushered Glendil and Dayden in, and the three quickly undressed to their smallclothes and began donning their casual gear. In Freyard's case, it was a pair of dark brown trousers, a light green tunic, suspenders, and the scuffed, black, jacket of his old riding leathers. The other two were dressed in similarly unremarkable fashion in short order, and Freyard took their swords and pistols for safekeeping in a footlocker beneath the bunks.

"We'll have no swords and pistols today, lads," Freyard told them. "Not that they will do any good in the dark, narrow catacombs we'll be crawling around in anyway. Keep a knife hidden somewhere on your person, in either a boot or the small of your back, for it would be foolish to go into this completely unarmed."

Back in the sitting car, Freyard found Marigold chewing her way through what remained of her breakfast as she talked over plans, with Sydnee having slid into the booth beside her and Minister Myakys sitting across from the both of them. Freyard took a seat beside the minister, giving him the vantage point to see the sleeping car.

"Are we all ready?" Marigold asked Freyard as he joined them.

"My men and I are at your disposal, my lady," he said, taking the time to look at the other two men as well. "I trust that everyone is comfortable with the plan? There will be little time to dawdle once we reach Weicaster."

"Of course, Captain Archer, everyone here is merely waiting for the whistle to blow," Myakys declared with what Freyard felt was unwise assurance.

"There is a new, potentially unpredictable variable in our midst. We should not feel too sure of ourselves today," Freyard reminded them sternly.

Sydnee spoke up in Freyard's defence, "The Captain is correct, my lady and Minister Myakys. We need to be atop of everything, and ready to respond to anything."

"Do all you soldiers carry on like this?" Marigold asked in jest.

"All the good ones, at least," Freyard responded humourlessly. "Begging your pardons, my lady, but we tend not to jape around when our work is to be done and lives are potentially at stake. It is how we tend to be trained, you see."

The rearmost door to the sitting cabin was opened by Wyla, and she and Moya stepped in. For the entire walk up the aisle, Moya moved in an odd, waddling manner, twisting and pulling at her waistband and thigh area the whole time.

"Is something the matter, Moya?" Freyard queried in puzzlement at the sight of her awkward steps.

"It's just that I've never worn trousers before," she said while still fidgeting. "How do you men walk with all this extra material between your legs? It feels all bunched up down there."

Marigold spun around as much as the booth allowed, getting a good look at her temporary doppelganger. "Oh, you look just darling, Moya. Those trousers and the blouse fit you nicely. Don't worry too much about the feel. I thought they were a little odd too the first time I wore them. In due time, you will wonder how you got by with only skirts for all these years."

"Moya is all ready to go, my lady," Wyla said from behind the odd woman. "Is there anything else I can do for you before we arrive?"

"That will be all, Wyla, and thank you for so graciously stepping aside for Moya," Marigold stated with marked gratitude. "The cars are yours to guard over. Keep everything locked, be on the lookout for any of us returning, and if anything more pressing arises, just wake Elden."

Wyla nodded and left the car through the same door she entered, leaving Moya standing before the booth alongside the two rangers.

"Shall we go over the plan once more?" Marigold began to ask, the last of her sentence being lost beneath the sudden tooting of the train's whistle.

"Normally I would suggest as much, but it appears we have run out of time," Freyard commented while standing up. "Alright, everyone get into place. We move out as soon as the train stops."

A hand of Moya's shot up high, and Freyard looked her way. "Yes, Moya?"

"Where do I go? No one told me as of yet," she asked meekly.

"Take this cloak," Marigold told her while laying the blue plaid garment from her own lap into Moya's hands. "It's Wyla's, but you can borrow it for the day. Keep the hood up at all times."

Dayden had stepped forward into Moya's view. "You'll be with me for the first half of the operation. Just stay directly beside me and keep pace. Take a hold of me if you need to. We leave from just forward of the dining car, so we should go and ready ourselves while the train is still pulling into the station."

"Alright then, I'll go with you, Ser," Moya agreed with a nervous swallow.

The pair departed, and Minister Myakys was close behind them. "I shall grab my warm coat and catch the first carriage I can to the Morton Manor. May good fortune find you all this morning."

Marigold glanced to Freyard and Glendil. "I suppose it's you two next. We shall see you in the dark in a little while."

With farewells out of the way, Freyard and Glendil vacated the Tullivan cars together. They walked silently until they were upon the bridge leading to the last borrowed car of the train. Once there, they came to a stop and stood in wait of the steadily slowing train, breathing in the cold morning air and watching as it clouded before their noses.

"You know, I never imagined there could be a day when I was bothered by the cold," Glendil commented as he rubbed his bare hands together for warmth. "I grew up in Ravenkeep, for crying out loud. Our snows start in mid-autumn and don't let up until late into the spring. Who knew that all those years in the Southlands would have had such an effect on me?"

"It's different along the coast, Glen," Freyard reminded him. "They don't even really get a true winter this far south. Yet, for all of that the cold weather they do get is wetter, and therefore feels harsher than what you know from the comparatively dryer northeast foothills."

Glendil seemed to consider that, and let out a grunt after a second or two. "That must be it then, because I'm damn near freezing."

"I would say that it will warm up come lunchtime," Freyard predicted, with an added note, "oh, and try not to mention, you know, the lands-down-yonder too much. People north of the Varras tend to be unfriendly if they think you're from the wilds."

"That's a fair point, Captain," Glendil agreed, going quiet once more as they watched the conductor fast approaching the door.

The two moved aside to allow the man to drop the gate, and once he was done, they hopped down quickly so that they could be the first off. Freyard kept a slower pace than Glendil, allowing the younger Archer to break out ahead of him by a sizeable distance. With a gap of several strides established between the two, Freyard and Glendil continued through the train station until they were outside again. He lost Glendil in the crowd then, and Freyard stood in further wait before the city's outer wall, glancing upward at the old, brick structure for a moment to take it in. The plan was for both rangers to lose one another for now and meet later, and Freyard's stalling allowed for further distance to be put between the two of them.

Two walls had been built to mark the growth of Weicaster Bay's settlement: the crumbling inner wall marked the old town boundary, having been built in the Era of the Last King by a Morton to protect the populace from the warmongering, theocratic Valdarrow nation. Later, they built a new, taller structure to encase the growing city that Weicaster had become in the years of relative peace that followed, Freyard recalled in pieces from the Weicaster entry in the old encyclopaedia set that resided in his father's study.

It was between those two walls that the destination of the displaced party lay, and where Freyard directed himself in a purposefully aimless manner. After a slow, ponderous browse of the windows of a street filled with shops, Freyard made a stop at a business called *The Painted Bean*, which managed to be both a café and a gallery for promising artists. At Minister Myakys' recommendation, Freyard paid a copper coin for a cup of coffee served with foamed milk and shavings of chocolate atop it.

This is a decent enough beverage, Freyard surmised after the third or fourth taste. *Yet, the chocolate seems to add little against the strong flavour of the coffee. I cannot fathom why Myakys so enjoys this particular brew.*

Wiling away the better part of an hour, Freyard walked about the shop with a coffee cup and matching saucer in hand, taking in the utterly boring artwork of the aspiring creatives. The pieces on display featured portraits of present members of high society, still-life paintings of produce, and a whole wall that was nothing but various naval ships.

In the back of the café was a shrine of sorts dedicated to displaying a collection of work from a particular artist whose subjects were all depictions of the supposed daily lives of average Illiastrans. The wall-to-wall paintings displayed scenes of middle and upper class families that were as saccharine as they were sentimentalised. To Freyard's mind, both facets were drawn out to a point of absurdity.

All of the pieces on display were approved by both the Elite Merchants and the Triarchy, as per the censorship laws that both ruling bodies had in place. Any artwork of contrary political themes, nudity, violence, or other taboo subjects were completely forbidden, and artists caught rendering such subjects were often dispatched to Biddenhurst and sold into slavery. Painters made for pricey, skilled slaves, and Mackhol Taves was known to gloat that he could get a heavy fistful of gold coinage in exchange for just one artist of noted talent.

In its own bizarre way, the pieces before him evoked an odd feeling of misplaced nostalgia in him, and Freyard found that he quite nearly fell for their allure and charm. He had to remind himself that the illustrations were but exaggerated representations of lives that but a fortunate few were privileged to experience from years gone by.

While those few had the freedom to frolic and play in such naïve bliss, the vast majority suffered in oppression, poverty, and prejudice. It is stupidly easy to forget that while looking at the jolly smiles and rosy red cheeks in these pieces.

With a glance to the ticking grandfather clock in the corner of the room, Freyard realised it was quite nearly time for the next phase of the plan. He laid his empty cup and saucer upon the counter and cleared his throat to get the attention of the young worker standing behind it.

"Yes, Ser, how can I help you?" the fellow asked in a voice that seemed eager to please.

"Might your manager be around?" Freyard requested calmly, his hands folded neatly behind his back. "If it is no bother, I would like to speak with him for a moment."

The lad's face took on a look of concern. "Is everything alright, Ser?"

"Quite so, young man, but all the same, I would like to borrow him for a moment," Freyard told him, trying to invoke a kindly tone in doing so.

With a nod and a promise to fetch the man, the worker slid out of sight towards what Freyard assumed was a kitchen area. After a moment or two of waiting, a greying and bearded man in a button-down off-white shirt, black trousers, and suspenders appeared. His hands deep in the pockets of a brown, cloth apron around his waist.

"Yes, Ser, I understand you wished to see me," the elder employee stated upon approach.

"As a matter of fact, I would," Freyard confirmed while outstretching his arm in the direction of the rear wall of the business. "I am interested in knowing more about this art back here."

The bearded man walked quickly around the counter and laid a hand against Freyard's back. "Absolutely, Ser, I would be only glad to tell you about the wonderful works of our contributing artists. Is there a particular piece you had your eye on? Certain works are for sale, I should mention. If you are a collector, it might well be your lucky day."

"As fate would have it, there is," Freyard replied with feigned glee.

They reached the back end of the café, where the syrupy paintings of imagined yesteryears decorated the walls. Once there, Freyard leaned in close to where he could whisper, "I have a need for the art of the written word, my good man. I was told by a man made of blue and white that you could provide a means to access such a thing."

The line was one he had rehearsed, as told to him the day before by Minister Myakys. The café manager glanced about with caution and when there were no observers, he produced an object from his apron and pressed it into Freyard's nearest hand.

"Slip into the hallway that leads to the alley door, but take the door on the left just as you reach it," the manager explained carefully. "Find the keyhole in the back of the closet, and let yourself in with what I just gave you. Leave that in the bucket in the basement. You should know the way from there, and if you don't, the catacombs will eat you anyway and all will be forgotten of this conversation."

"Thank you, Ser," Freyard managed to say before the manager raised his voice once more.

"I say, good Ser, I could never sell that particular piece for such a low price. Don't even bother walking back around to the counter, just see yourself out through the back door, and don't come back until you have a better price in mind." With that declared for all to hear, Freyard's company strode quickly to the counter in a feigned huff, and stood behind it with his back to him.

Once Freyard was certain that no eyes were on him, he made for the short, dark hallway and found the closet he was instructed to enter. He pulled a string hanging from the ceiling to light up the tiny space with a dim bulb. Within were brooms, a mop and bucket, and various other cleaning tools. Freyard shuffled around the equipment until he found the back wall, and began running his hands over the painted surface in search of a keyhole. He found it, oddly enough, at chest height and so close to the corner that Freyard wondered if he would even have room to turn the key.

The wall itself jarred loose and fell outward at practically the touch of the key, nearly taking Freyard with it as he clutched the iron piece between finger and thumb. Beyond the doorway were stone steps butting into the frame itself, with no landing to save the user from tumbling downward into the unyielding darkness.

The man gave me no light source, and there seems to be no lighting down there, Freyard noted while still examining the way forward. *No matter, it's not the first time I've stumbled around in the dark.*

Turning off the bulb in the closet, Freyard began the blind descent. Once away from the door, he pushed it closed and reinserted the key on the other side of the lock until it clicked. With his hands on either wall to the left and right of him, he continued downward until the floor became level under his feet.

Behind me and to the left should be a narrow, twisting stairwell, Freyard recalled of Myakys' instructions while feeling around for the aforementioned bucket so that he could deposit the key. When ready to move on, his left foot slid across the dusty floor in search of the lip of a stair. Upon finding only air beneath his foot, Freyard felt sure he was heading in the correct direction, and began the second descent once he found the next step. Freyard leaned into the wall and continued slowly downward, careful to keep himself away from the spiral's edge.

No railing and no light, I'm sure this would not be considered hazardous at all, Freyard noted sarcastically.

As suddenly as the thought entered Freyard's mind, the descent stopped without warning and the suddenness of it sent him stumbling forward sightlessly, his hands the only thing preventing him from colliding with the wall ahead.

I guess I found it. Now, I'm to go left again from the bottom step, and continue until I find the second alcove on my right, and therein should be a set of stairs to take me up exactly one level.

Freyard kept his right hand on the wall he had stumbled toward, spun to the left on his heels, and began walking forward, with his left hand outward to touch the darkness.

With nothing else by which to judge distance, Freyard began counting his paces. By the twenty-third, Freyard's right hand lost the wall, only to recover it seconds later. At the fifty-sixth pace, he lost the wall again and this time turned into the emptiness he discovered, coming to yet another stairwell. From what his feet could discern, the steps spiralled in much the same manner as the stairs that he had used to arrive in the sub-basement. From his misplaced footing, it seemed that it descended as well as climbed.

I was told to go up by a level. By that logic, I suppose the need for a directional instruction on a staircase should be an indication that there would be options.

Upward Freyard went, clinging to a wall without purchase with his hands, letting his feet lead the way all the while. He came to the landing and worked his way into the new hallway.

Immediately there was a light being carried in his direction from a dozen paces away, and Freyard slid back into the pitch black, unsure of who else might be down in the catacombs.

The figure passed, and Freyard noticed it to be a clean-shaven male with a long face and short, auburn hair.

Is that Glendil?

"This must be the third alcove I've passed and still no light... Did I miss something?"

Sounds like him.

The lantern shone into Freyard's eyes suddenly and he recoiled backward. "Gods dammit!"

"Who goes there?" the man cried out, himself stepping back.

"Oh for fuck's sake, Glen, it's me," Freyard called back while rubbing his eyes as they painfully adjusted to the sudden intrusion of light.

"Captain?" Glendil proclaimed while raising the lantern again. "I thought I would be the last to arrive at the meeting point."

Freyard groaned in response to the dulling pain in his retinas. "Not quite so, evidently. How did you get a lantern? I've been stumbling around in the blackness this entire time."

"The shopkeeper who let me down here lent it to me," Glendil told Freyard while lowering the light source out of his captain's vision. "Seemed like a decent fellow to me. He operates a candle shop. Did you know that they could add scents to the candles now?"

"I did not know that, Glen. Though, it hardly seems important at the moment," Freyard replied with mild annoyance.

Glendil gave a shrug back, as indicated by the rise and fall of the lantern's light. "Sometimes you just need to stop and smell the roses, Cap, and if all you have available is a scented candle, you make do."

"It certainly had a positive effect on you," Freyard admitted tiredly. "Anyhow, we should be near to the meeting point. If Myakys' instructions are to be believed, the door forward will be two alcoves to the left from here and the correct entryway will be lit. Remember, from here on out, use no names. Potential eavesdroppers would be listening for anything identifiable. Address your superiors by 'Ser' and 'Madam' only."

"Understood, Ser. Shall I lead the way? Or would you like to take the lamp for yourself?" Glendil asked, his voice still sounding gratingly chipper.

"Just go," Freyard instructed.

The younger Archer went leftward without further comment, with Freyard close on his heels. They arrived at the directed point, and found only closed doors to either side of the corridor. Glendil shone his lantern over each one, and found no identifying markers or illuminations to indicate which one was their destination.

"What do you propose we do, Ser?" Glendil had begun to ask, until footfalls on stone steps rendered him quiet.

Freyard grabbed the ranger by the coat and dragged him away from the doors. "Snuff the light and get down," he whispered to him.

Darkness enveloped them just as the door on their right swung open. From the opposite end of the hallway, another flame of light appeared, and voices began to echo off the walls.

"Good morning again, Ser." the voice of Marigold beckoned to the approaching carrier of the lantern.

"It seems that we are the first to arrive, Madam," Myakys called back. "What perfect timing, too, if I do say so myself."

Freyard stood up and cleared his throat. "There are two more of us here too. Our lantern gave out, I'm afraid."

"That must be the rangers," Sydnee surmised from where he stood at Marigold's side.

From out of the shadows Freyard and Glendil emerged, each of them giving half a bow to Marigold as the former spoke for both of them. "As promised, Madam, we are on time."

"Well met, Ser," Marigold said with a nod. Turning to Sydnee, she gave him a pat on the arm. "Now would be a good time to go and make the switch with the other man and woman. When you are done, give the man instructions on how to get down here."

"Yes, Madam, I shall do so at once," Sydnee confirmed prior to his hurried departure.

Myakys shone his light toward the opposite door. "If you would all follow me, I shall prepare our meeting site. It is just through here."

"Allow me to go first, Madam," Freyard requested without waiting for an answer, stepping in front of both Marigold and the minister to do so.

"Very well, Ser, if you insist," Marigold responded without complaint.

Minister Myakys held his lantern high, allowing light to cascade in Freyard's direction. "My goodness, you don't suspect that something might be afoul, do you?"

"With all due respect, one can never too be sure," Glendil answered quickly, before Freyard could say something similar. "It is best to let the protection clear the room. That's just good sense. Besides, we were told that the way forward would be lit, and as you can see, there is no light to speak of here. That should raise anyone's suspicions."

"It is probably just on account of a burnt out lightbulb, but I see your point, Ser," Myakys conceded in response.

Freyard undid an iron latch on a door made of old, warped wood and let the aged barrier fall inward with a gentle push. Leaning his back against the doorframe, Freyard looked around the corners in both directions as much as he could. Though the lack of illumination denied him much vantage, there seemed to be no one within what Freyard surmised to be a single, small room.

"Is there a light in here?" Freyard asked Myakys.

The minister moved around Freyard wordlessly, went into the centre of the space, and pulled on an overhead cord. "Yes, just this one. I apologise to the lady for providing such an unwelcoming space for her meeting, but it could not be helped under such circumstances."

All around Myakys stood stacks of books from floor to ceiling. There were no shelves to store the tomes properly, and only wooden pallets to keep them off the bare, dirt floor. The spines of each title were all facing inward, giving no indication of what lay on the pages of the mysterious collection.

"This is quite the pile of books," Marigold commented as she entered the room second to last, ahead of only Glendil. "Whatever would they be kept down here for? The stacks look like they may fall over at any second."

"These, my lady, are the entirety of the books banned from publication in Illiastra by the EMP and the Triarchy in duplicate, and even triplicate, when such could be found," Myakys explained with both wonder and pride in his voice. As he did so, he knelt before one of the pallets and produced a leather-bound folder that was hidden beneath. A single table and chair sat in the centre of the room and he laid the folder atop the former and flipped it open. "As you can see, the shopkeeper has kept a meticulous record of where each book is amongst the striking stacks, and he loans them out to only his most trusted friends and fellow literarians. As it so happens, the man we are meeting today is quite the appreciator of literature, and even helped the shopkeeper to bring the collection to completion."

"I would hazard to guess that he faces the books away so that uninvited persons would not know that they are banned titles?" Marigold assumed while approaching the nearest stack carefully.

Myakys went to stand beside her. "Your skills at deduction are quite sharp, Madam. It's no matter to the shopkeeper that things look so haphazardly stored, though, as the hidden records give all the direction one could want."

"Surely the shopkeeper is aware that his very life is in jeopardy should this collection be discovered," Freyard surmised during his own observation of the neat piles.

"Only too aware," Myakys confirmed worrisomely. "The man we are meeting takes great pains to keep the unwelcome from sniffing around here too much, but there is admittedly an ever present danger."

A gloved hand of Marigold gently caressed the pressed pages of a book directly before her during Freyard and Myakys' conversation and she spoke when they finished. "What sorts of books are here, Gallin?"

"What we have here is a mixture of fiction and historical texts. The fictional works span from across all recognised genres and their associated subgenres. Some of the content is considered controversial by the EMP and Triarchist standards, but there is a great deal of otherwise innocuous writings here. In that case, one need only look at who wrote the book. Elven, dwarven, and amaroshan authors are all banished, regardless of the subject matter in which they write. In fact, there is a whole stack of quaint children's books here somewhere that just happened to be written by non-humans," Myakys told the room, having gone back to his open folder on the table.

"Granted, the elves and dwarves are more than capable of keeping their own libraries, and their titles are in no danger of being lost. They are merely impossible to find or own in human Illiastra without persecution. However, as we all know too well, the half-elves were given no time to preserve their written works. With that goal in mind, the shopkeeper built this collection so that it might primarily serve as an archive of half-elf literature. This is a conservation effort in progress, keeping the history and art of an entire culture from being forever erased, as the EMP and the Triarch would so love to do. To their credit, our friend and the shopkeeper have tried their best to save what Amaroshan literature they can, though we expect much has been destroyed, or is at least out of our grasp at the moment.

"Beyond works written by other races, the banned materials include fiction and non-fiction alike that might be remotely construed as offering a negative depiction of the Elite Merchants and the Triarchy, and their ideological and religious beliefs. With that said, it may come as no surprise that most of the human authors with entries among these stacks are long dead."

Freyard looked away from the pallets of books to find Marigold reading over the pages within the file curiously. "Many of these authors are women. How have I never heard of any of these names before? I'm an avid reader myself."

"The women authors on that list have nearly all been dead for at least the better part of a century," Myakys explained sadly. "As you know, women were prohibited from learning to read once the Elite Merchants and Triarchists came to power. Therefore, women who knew how to read from before the practice was outlawed were punished if seen doing so openly. A woman daring to have her own writings published was subject to any number of unfortunate fates."

"These women were executed, then?" Marigold asked with disgust heavy on her voice.

"Some of the authors of either gender were executed, yes," Myakys admitted with melancholy. "Others who were captured were exposed to cruelties that were erroneously labelled as punishments. As for those who were fortunate enough to escape, they fled overseas to any country that would grant them asylum."

"I had never heard of any of this before," Marigold stated in bafflement. "I am amazed that my grandmother said nothing of it. She had been privately taught to read and enjoyed it immensely. I find it difficult to believe that a woman as headstrong and forward as her would allow such atrocities to be forgotten."

Myakys had little more than a shrug to offer in response. "As to that, I cannot comment, Madam. The Illiastran half of your ancestry certainly bears some responsibility for the awfulness. Perhaps Lady Maisera harboured some guilt for events that happened in her lifetime during the rule of her parents' generation."

The door swung open slowly, and both Freyard and Glendil pivoted in the direction of it, their stances going defensive. A man stepped through, garbed in a dark grey, two-piece suit with a long black winter coat draped over his shoulders.

"It is a weight that all of us nobles must carry, my lady," the man said while stepping into the room, stopping short in his approach until he was just outside of arm's reach of the rangers.

Once in the light, Freyard recognised the features of Weicaster Bay's minister, Samhais Morton. Following close behind Morton was a second man who, despite a tall and thick frame, was nearly unseen in the darkness beyond the room.

"Who goes there with you, ser?" Glendil asked Morton clearly.

Morton turned to face the stranger clad in black leathers. "This is my personal bodyguard, Kairese Yul-Koi, a retired member of the Johnan Elite Forces."

"I was not aware that you had hired a bodyguard, Minister Morton." Marigold confessed, evidently having dropped measures to conceal identities in the wake of Morton identifying his follower.

"Kai is a recent acquisition, to be certain," Morton said with a smile. "It pains me to say that such added protection has become a necessity for my family at this juncture. I shall spare you the details, as we have not the time, though I will say that Ser Yul-Koi is but one of the new protectors of House Morton."

During Samhais' speech, Freyard had been looking over the silent Johnan man, and he was indeed impressed with him. Judging from the man's face, Freyard surmised immediately that on at least one occasion, he had fought without a helm. The Johnan bore what was among the most pronounced of facial scars that Freyard had ever seen. The old wound started on the right side of his forehead, ran all the way to the other side, and extended downward through his left eye, ending at the corner of his mouth. The eyeball itself had not been spared from the damage, and all that remained was milky and most definitely blinded.

Further highlighting the scar tissue was the fact that the soldier was entirely bald, with only a spike-shaped goatee hanging to his chest to account for visible hair. The second part of the man that Freyard noticed was the hilt of a broadsword that poked above his right shoulder, the scabbard of it ending just beyond the former soldier's left hip.

"I am sorry to hear that things have grown so dire for your house as to warrant such added protection," Marigold replied sympathetically. "I would love to hear the entire story when time permits. It is quite likely that our tales have many parallels."

"The feeling is mutual, I assure you, Miss Marigold. I have heard that your campaign tour thus far has been not only fruitless, but also fraught with tragedy. Your wounded housecarl has my deepest sympathies," Morton stated both empathetically and morosely. Upon clearing his throat, Morton pressed forward. "Despite all of that, I can lend you only my moral support and heartfelt well-wishes. The reasoning for such passivity on my part goes without saying at this point."

Marigold walked around the table and came to stand at Freyard's side, her cloak brushing against his arm in doing so.

"That much is true," she told Morton. "Yet, I still believed that we should meet all the same, for I feel that even without your signature on the declaration, there are still ways that you and I can support one another. There is little doubt that we are both in need of favours that you and I are uniquely qualified to offer."

Morton broke out into a chuckle. "Why Miss Marigold, I do believe you read my mind. Very well, let us put our coins on the table. Tell me what it is you want, knowing what I cannot give you. Let me spare you an exchange of glances with Gallin, for I already heard it from him. Nevertheless, I would like you to confirm it in your own words, for my own peace of mind, if nothing else."

There was steel in Marigold's eyes then, and she did not balk at the request for even a second. "Minister Morton, I humbly come before you today to ask for enough signatures on *The Declaration of Agency* to give me a majority amongst the western ministers. I was led to believe though you yourself could not sign, that you held sway with enough ministers to make it possible."

"And how many signatures do you need?" Morton queried quickly.

"At least two for now, though I would gladly accept a third," Marigold told him truthfully.

"Two..." Morton muttered contemplatively, a hand going to his breast pocket while he did, where it produced a handkerchief that he then used to clean the round spectacles on his face. "I might be able to give you that many. However, you should know that such a risk, for both myself and the signatories, does not come without immediate recompense."

Marigold lifted her chin curiously. "Just what did you have in mind?"

"Something that I know might be too much for me to expect of you, yet it is all I need," Samhais prefaced his request. "I ask that my sister Jorette, and her youngest children, Nareen and Dorian, be returned home, alive and unharmed, to Weicaster Bay."

Freyard met a bewildered Marigold's stare, himself as nonplussed as she was. For once, he had nothing to offer her.

"How in the name of Iia do you expect me to do that, Minister Morton?" Marigold finally managed to ask in response.

Morton shrugged initially, before his face took on an expression of weariness. "I... I don't know, Miss Marigold. What I do know is that my sister is miserable beyond all consolation in Hercalest. The children, the youngest two, that is, are all that keeps her from the very brink of despair. Eamon sees the three of them as leverage to be used against me, and frequently dangles their safety and wellbeing to keep me in check. As sure as I am standing here, I know he would harm them if I did anything to make his spies and him suspicious of House Morton's loyalties. That is why I cannot support you.

"What I can give you though, are two more members of the old Blue Coast, those being the houses of Rochford and Cheswell, specifically. With them, you will have your majority and Eamon Palomb will be none the wiser that I am behind their change of heart. However, I need you to swear to me that an effort will be made to free my sister and her two youngest children."

"I would not even know where to start, Minister Morton. It is not as though the Palombs will negotiate with me for their release," Marigold reasoned, her voice almost pleading. "For one, as far as the Eastern Realm is concerned, I am likely arranging my own execution for even sowing the seeds of this rebellion as it is. I have nothing to offer them in a bargain. More importantly, we are talking about Eamon's wife and youngest offspring. He would never entertain any negotiations for them."

A shake of the head preceded Morton's response, "No, no, Miss Marigold, I would not expect you to barter for them with Lord Eamon himself. What I am asking is if you have any connections in the east that might be availed of in order to help them literally escape Hercalest."

"Where would I even begin to inquire about orchestrating such a scheme?" Marigold wondered aloud in a tone bordering on exasperation.

Freyard had been looking between the two for some time while scanning his own mind for any solutions. He had no connections, either military or private, within or in proximity to House Palomb that might be useful, and there was nothing he or his rangers could do for her.

I damn well could have had connections, he recalled, and for the first time, he regretted not having made more friends during his time in the Honourable Guardsmen.

"To that, I do not know," Morton admitted reluctantly. "However, what I do know is that you presently have freedoms that I do not. I am guarded by Eamon's Eyes at all times. Even in this, I suspect that some servant of mine is not too far away and looking about the streets to see where I went. Kai and I will have to concoct some sort of cover story to appease my watchers on our way back to the surface, no doubt. However, I digress, for the point is that you are in a position to do what I cannot. Granted, it is a desperate request, Miss Marigold, but I am also a desperate man. The safety of my family is paramount, and my sister, Nareen, and Dorian are as much my family as my wife and our children."

A hand of Marigold's leaned on the table, causing it to groan slightly, a contrived look having spread across her face. "Therein is the problem, Minister Morton: your sister has four children. You are only all too aware that I am currently performing a tightrope routine on the fine line between war and peace with your eldest two nephews and their father. How do you feel about the implications of that? Should I worry that future loyalties from the Blue Coast will be dependent on what may happen to Eldridge and Pyore in any potential conflicts? Their lives, after all, could well find their way into my hands, either in battle, or in judgement. Given their history of atrocious behaviours, it is unlikely that I would be able to show mercy or lenience."

"Yes... I understand that, Miss Marigold, painfully so," Morton uttered sadly while clearing his throat. For a brief moment, his gaze went to the ceiling before returning to meet Marigold. "Though they are my blood, and I would grieve for the loss of their lives, I have come to accept that they are well and truly lost. In their youth, I blamed their father for what they were becoming under his guidance and example. Yet, somewhere along the way, that responsibility shifted from his shoulders to theirs. Eldridge and Pyore are men grown now, and it falls to them to determine whom they will be. Unfortunately, it seems that they are intent on continuing down the morally vacant path that Eamon has set for them."

As Morton spoke, Marigold stood upright again. By the time he finished, she was staring him down. "If that is how you feel, then you would have no issue with promising me that should I liberate Jorette, Nareen, and Dorian that you will offer no aid to Eldridge, Pyore, or any other relative of yours that might be in allegiance with House Palomb."

"Absolutely, Miss Marigold, that goes without saying and without question," Morton responded immediately, his voice becoming as desperate as he claimed he was.

"Then say so, in your own words," Marigold told him bluntly. "We cannot put as much to paper at this point, and I am often reminded that words are but wind, but nonetheless, this will have to do. Furthermore, we have four men here who can stand in witness of your statement, and two of them are loyal to you. That alone should suffice to give merit to your declaration."

"Very well, Miss Marigold, if you so insist," Morton agreed readily. "I, Samhais of House Morton, vow to make no efforts, directly or otherwise, to offer aid, comfort, or shelter to Eamon, Eldridge, or Pyore Palomb, or any known associates of theirs apart from Jorette, Nareen, and Dorian Palomb, and any members of their house that may assist in their escape. I further vow to take no measures to shield Eldridge and Pyore Palomb from any consequences that their foul deeds may warrant."

Freyard felt Marigold's eyes fall on him, and as they met, he offered her reassurance in the form of a nod. She moved on then to Glendil and Minister Myakys, and lastly to Kairese standing over Morton's shoulder.

"Freyard Archer, Glendil Archer, Gallin of House Myakys, and Kairese Yul-Koi," She began once she had the attention of the other three men. "You all stand in witness of the vow uttered in secret to me, Marigold of House Tullivan, by Samhais of House Morton. Do each of you vow to see that the attestation of Samhais of House Morton is upheld?"

"I do so vow it, Lady Marigold," Freyard stated first, his words quickly echoed by Glendil. Myakys followed suit to the letter, down to using 'Lady' when addressing Marigold.

Lastly was Kairese Yul-Koi, who had thus far not spoken so much as a single word. His silence was held until Morton turned to face him. "Go ahead, Kai."

"I promise you this... Lady Marigold," the Johnan said, the words coming forth in a slow and careful manner, as though he was thinking long and hard on the placement of each syllable. His voice was a deep, gravelly bass, thick with the dialect of the Johnan language.

"Ser Yul-Koi is but a student of the Intercontinental language under the careful guidance of the same tutor that instructs my children in the finer points," Minister Morton explained casually. "He came to me speaking only the Johnan tongue and with an interpreter practically glued to his side at all waking hours. I would say that he has made remarkable progress in learning a second language in his season and a half with me, would you not agree?"

A single eyebrow of Marigold's went skyward at that, but she masked any further feelings from her voice. "He does speak it well, for having only begun his learning not long ago," she looked to the big man then. "Do you understand what you swore to uphold?"

"Up...hold? What this word mean?" Yul-Koi began to inquire, before answering for himself, "Is same as 'keep'? Like promise?"

"Yes, that is correct, Ser Yul-Koi," Marigold affirmed.

"Then yes, Lady Marigold, I understand," the Johnan warrior told her with a kneeling bow. "I make sure that Minister Morton keeps promise."

Marigold thanked Yul-Koi and extended a hand toward Morton. "Then that settles it, Minister Morton. I believe we have a deal, though I have not the foggiest idea how I can reach your sister."

"Thank you, Miss Marigold, from the bottom of my heart," Morton told her in a stammer while accepting her hand to shake. His eyes had moistened and looked ready to weep, but the minister held himself firm. "I have laid a great burden at your feet, I fear, but you should know that I do not expect results immediately. This is something that will take time and patience to accomplish, and in the interim I will support you in so much as I possibly can. When the day comes that Eamon can no longer dangle the lives of my sister and her children above my head, I shall cast out his spies and reveal my pledge of fealty to you for the world to see, of this you have my word."

"I genuinely believe that you will, Minister Morton," Marigold returned amiably. "House Tullivan stands ready and willing to help House Morton from this day forth, even if we must do so in secret for the nonce."

The sound of feet shuffling down stairs reached Freyard, and he moved to respond, but was beaten to it.

"Who goes there?" Yul-Koi shouted while pivoting about on a heel. A short length of steel flashed in the Johnan's right hand and the left reached for the old door, swinging it open to find a cloaked man standing without. "Identify yourself at once, Stranger."

"I am Dayden Vernet, Second Class Ranger of the Sun's Rangers, sworn to Lady Marigold," the man declared while drawing back the hood of his cloak. "Who in the name of Aren's beard are you?"

The Johnan sheathed his knife, but did not move to allow Dayden through. "I am Kairese Yul-Koi, protector of House Morton. State your business, Ser."

"I am here as part of Lady Marigold's retinue," Dayden explained, looking past Yul-Koi to Freyard and the others as he did. "It is high time for us to be back to the train. We should depart before we impede the daily commuter train that is due to arrive."

"Dayden is right, my lady," Freyard added, further advising her, "They could move our train out of the way at the station's junction, but we could spare the engineers the trouble of doing that if we left now."

Marigold turned to face Minister Morton from where she stood in front of Freyard. "My guardians are of course, correct, Minister Morton. I am afraid we will have to adjourn at this juncture."

"I understand, Miss Marigold. Thank you for meeting with me and hearing the pleas of a despondent brother and uncle. I apologise that the setting is so dank and unwelcoming. Gallin will arrange everything with Ministers Rochford and Cheswell. You will have their names on your declaration," Morton replied while stepping aside to clear the way for her. Yul-Koi followed in his employer's wake, the space provided by the large man opening a path for Marigold and her party to join Dayden where he stood in wait.

"You are quite welcome and I thank you as well for agreeing to meet with me. It has been a trying journey thus far, and any friendly face is a welcome one now. As for the setting, you need not worry, as I always feel at home amongst books. I bid you a good day, Minister," Marigold offered as a farewell.

As Freyard began to usher Marigold out, Morton spoke up again. "If I may, I would like to offer you a piece of parting advice, Miss Marigold."

"But of course, Minister, I would welcome it," Marigold replied in invitation.

"When Gallin told you of the Blue Coast, did he tell you of the family heraldry?" Morton quizzed Marigold rhetorically. "Were you told of the old flags that were once so proudly flown? Did you hear of the mottos of each of the old houses? He knows all of the histories of the old families, deep and sordid though they all are."

"In bits and pieces, yes," Marigold confirmed with curiosity clear on her face as she said as much.

Morton nodded thoughtfully. "You may see such displays of symbolism as puffery and pageantry now, but the old families hold dear to their colours and sigils. They wrapped their identities in those old flags, Miss Marigold. The Elite Merchants took that little shred of personality on us, and painted all the families, save for the Tullivans and Palombs, under the painfully plain and obnoxiously contradictory banner of the white dove. All of it done in the name of homogeny, I should add, though the two governing bodies have ironically done anything but spread unity."

"You think I should campaign to see a return of all of that," Marigold summarised for Morton. "Do you really think something as relatively trivial as that would spur the holdout ministers to action?"

"Oh, without a shadow of a doubt, Miss Marigold," Morton opined frankly. "It may seem like a meaningless prayer at the altar of aesthetics, and on a certain level, it is just that. However, I have found that such empty gestures can indeed go a long way. Returning a little lost pride to the western families will yield bountiful returns when it comes time to harvest, of this I promise you."

Marigold reached around Freyard and gave her hand to Morton to shake for a second time when he was done. "Then I shall definitely take your counsel under advisement. May good fortune find you, Minister Morton."

20
SEREPHANIE

The long wait had ended and the real fighting ring of the Sacred Fist finally stood within the reach of Darrion Veskries. There was tangible excitement on his face, and his body was tense in anticipation of what it meant for him to be standing just outside of what was colloquially known as the squared circle.

Domas was gone, having gotten his notice of release days before, cutting the four potential trainees to three. Those remaining had all received written offers of employment with the Sacred Fist for the subsequent winter tour that would take them throughout the southerly regions of Illiastra. Along with that employment, would be the potential to train and possibility of receiving a berth on the roster of the League of the Sacred Fist.

Though he was now practically close enough to touch it, Darrion was made to wait outside the ring with Lyle and Kellum. The three stood in silence, their attention focused on Everett Lancer. Their trainer was within the ring, chatting casually with a trio of fighters that were sharing the space with him, each one in the process of stretching out and warming up before the start of the day's exercise.

The ring itself was essentially a platform, sitting a metre and a half from the ground, with a floor roughly five and a half metres square, and not at all round, as the name 'ring' would imply. Everett Lancer's feet seemed to sink into some form of slight padding as he paced. The soft underlay was further layered beneath an old royal blue, sailcloth canvas that appeared to have been patched and sewn in a dozen places. The structure was kept aloft by a system of wooden beams supported between four steel posts that had been painted red. For aesthetic purposes, the underside of the ring was usually obscured by further canvas skirting, coloured identically to the ring surface. During shows, coloured bunting was further draped along the ring apron, but such decoration was removed during the practice sessions, to avoid being dirtied and damaged by the novices.

Three horizontal lengths of hempen rope, spaced evenly apart, surrounded the fighting surface of the ring. The top and bottom ropes had been painted red and the middle one was a contrasting blue. At each post, the ropes were moored and drawn tight to the steel with the same sort of steel turnbuckles that Serephanie had seen among the sail rigging of ships. To protect the fighters who might find themselves cornered near the posts, the steel rings of the turnbuckles that the ropes were threaded through had been covered in further padding. Red and blue padded corners stood opposite to one another, indicating the starting point for the opposing sides, with white padding adjacent to them for the neutral corners.

Newly seated atop the white corner closest to the ringside fighters entrance was Kohvee, husband of Syrie and the lone successful challenger in the Tournament of the Winter King. Unlike when Serephanie had last seen him, Kohvee was dressed rather plainly today, in an old pair of loose, black trousers and a sleeveless tunic in faded grey.

Both Kohvee and Everett waited while the remaining two fighters readied themselves. Further back from the ring and nearly out of sight in the entryway, Darrion and his fellow trainees stood in complete silence.

Of the two unknown combatants, Serephanie could discern little. However, there was one detail that immediately sprung to Serephanie's attention: the fighter stretching their limbs on the ropes nearest to Serephanie was clearly a woman. She was dressed completely in black, in an outfit that included roomy trousers, a sleeveless tunic, wrapped slippers, and a mask that covered her entire head, save for her eyes and nostrils. Standing short and slender, with the tight definition one might find in a competitive runner rather than a professional fighter, she stood out, to say the least. Such a perception, Serephanie had to figure, was intended for Everett Lancer's purposes.

Sharing space with the woman and Kohvee was a man who looked younger than Serephanie, with a shaggy head of dark blond hair and a moon shaped face bearing a stoic, sad expression. Unlike the others, this fighter was barefoot, his feet wrapped at the ankle for some measure of support. He wore off-white trousers that had been tapered roughly at the knee, a grey undershirt, and naught else.

"The training is always such a bore," Dottie groaned from beside Serephanie. "I have no idea why Lady Cyrelle insisted that I accompany you. It is not as though you are a lost child. You have no need of an escort."

The noble girl's whinging had begun as soon as she and Serephanie had left Cyrelle's presence that morning, when the order had initially been given. In the hour or so since then, Serephanie was sure that Dottie had listed every possible reason why a person might not enjoy watching others train to fight.

"I'm sorry, Dottie, it was Cyrelle's request, not mine," Serephanie offered in explanation, for at least the third time over the course of the morning. "I had only asked for permission to watch the training. I didn't ask for an escort. If you would like, I won't say a word should you choose to sneak off for a while."

Dottie took that suggestion with a derisive snort. "Yes, and then our sneaky little friend Syrie will somehow find me all by myself and report to Cyrelle that I abandoned you. No, thank you, Terra, I will stay here and die of boredom rather than die by Cyrelle shouting me into dust."

"Suit yourself, then," Serephanie relented in frustration, turning her attention back to the ringside area and the men therein.

After another minute or so passed silently between the two women, Everett's chosen fighters signalled their readiness.

Everett turned his attention toward the three trainees. "Gentlemen, are we ready to begin today's training?"

The three on the floor all answered in the affirmative, though Everett was already introducing the lesson. "Today, each of you will be given an opponent of my choosing from the three standing in the ring, and I will referee a catch wrestling contest between the two of you. The methods of victory are to force a submission from your opponent or pin their shoulders to the mat for a count of three. Or rather, that is how each of you will lose."

Without exception, the faces of the men outside the ring were of sheer bafflement, and Lyle and Kellum even shared a look with one another.

"Boxers and kickboxers will be at a particular disadvantage, and the pit fighters among you will be practically helpless, as these three beside me are all wrestlers first and foremost," Everett noted while staring directly at Darrion. "Despite all of that, it is not by limiting your repertoires that I anticipate your defeat. Rather, I know you will lose, because as the referee, I will ensure it personally."

Kellum's hand shot up and it was acknowledged by Everett, giving Kellum leave to speak. "Ser, with all due respect, what is the point of this contest if you give us no way to win?"

"That is not for me to say, but for you to discover, Kellum," Everett told him plainly, while turning his attention to the shaggy-haired lad, "Now, with that out of the way, allow me to introduce these three in the ring. First up is Keverick, one of our promising rising fighters. Been with us, oh, it must be a year or more now, right?"

"Two years come mid-spring, Mister Lancer," Keverick said, gently correcting his superior.

Everett nodded thoughtfully, "Where has the time gone, Keverick? Two years seems like nothing, doesn't it?"

"It feels like yesterday that I was standing out where those three are now," Keverick commented while gesturing his head toward Darrion and his peers.

"You, above the other two here should remember this lesson most of all, then, Keverick," Everett said with the corner of his mouth turned up.

"You may well be right, ser," Keverick agreed, clearly trying not to assume anything over the people to which he shared the ring.

A hand of Everett's gave wave to Kellum, "Alright, Kellum, you're the big talker, so you can go first against Keverick."

Though Kellum looked quite surprised, he did not balk and instead approached the ring. As he stepped through the middle and top rope, Kellum glanced at his trainer. "Mister Lancer, do you have any last minute advice for me?"

"Aye, just lose well, young buck," Everett gave back with a tinge of annoyance in his voice.

The two fighters took to the nearest coloured corner, and Everett stationed himself between them, and waved them in to him. "We will start from the collar-and-elbow stance. Come on in and meet."

As asked, the men walked to the centre of the ring and intertwined their arms through Keverick's instruction. When Everett was satisfied, he raised an arm overhead. "Ready ... Begin!"

The words were barely out of Everett's mouth when Kellum immediately broke from the starting position and went for the legs of Keverick. The seasoned grappler was not one to be so easily moved though, and he leaned his weight forward and pressed his forearms into Kellum's prone back.

Kellum groaned while trying to move Keverick, but the racket did little for his efforts.

All throughout the ordeal, Keverick looked to be downright casual, despite the struggling man in his grasp. Keverick turned toward the trainer and the two met eyes briefly. "Any requests, Coach?" Keverick asked Everett.

"Let him down gently, Kev," Everett commanded with a hearty chuckle.

"Alright, then," Keverick said in lazy acknowledgement. Stepping back just enough to allow space between himself and Kellum, Keverick wrapped his left arm around Kellum's neck while his right arm snaked in through Kellum's left. With the hold cinched in, Keverick used Kellum's forward momentum to roll backward, taking Kellum over in a roll until Kellum came to thud onto his back. Keverick had rolled through with Kellum, using the momentum to pull Kellum into a sitting position, with Keverick coming to a rest on one knee while wrenching on both the head and arm.

"Gods no, I won't submit! Not like this!" Kellum cried out in desperation, his free hand trying to find some part of Keverick's to move off him.

Serephanie spotted Everett winking at Keverick, and Kellum leaned back further on the hold.

"Uuaaaaggh!" Kellum roared out, before his free hand began tapping the mat. "I yield, I yield!"

"Match: over!" Everett declared, ending the bout.

With the hold released, Kellum flopped onto his back, as disappointed as he was frustrated. "Dammit, I couldn't even move him... I'm such a fool."

Keverick extended a hand and once taken, he pulled Kellum to his feet. "Nice try, lad."

Everett was before Kellum then. "What are you so upset over? I told you that you were going to lose, didn't I?"

"I wanted to win anyway, to show you I could," Kellum admitted with marked shame plain across both his face and tone.

"Is that the lesson you took from this?" Everett asked in astonishment. "To just disobey my orders and disregard my advice?"

His face partially obscured by his own hand rubbing away sweat, Kellum took a second to sheepishly utter, "No, ser. I'm sorry for not listening to you."

"Jump out of the ring, get a drink of water, and give me a hundred squats as penance, Kellum." Everett instructed, breaking away from the lad to look at the remaining recruits. "Cole, get in here and wipe down the mat, you'll be sparring when you're done."

"It would seem that Everett is quite displeased with Kellum," Serephanie commented to Dottie beside her, looking over to find the serving girl to be resting her head in her chin. "Cole gets to fight next. I can't wait to see what he does."

"Who cares, Terra?" Dottie replied with what was bordering on disgust. "I see applicants like Kellum and Lyle all the time, and they never make the roster. Do you know how many applied here in Hercalest just on this stop alone before you and your man came along? Dozens wanted in, and this is what's left. More often than not, when we pick up stakes in a town, we have no new trainees in tow. Even Keverick barely scraped his way in when he did, and he can actually fight, as you saw. Besides, fighting is as boring as paint drying, anyway. Who actually likes watching this stuff, anyhow?"

"I like watching..." Serephanie muttered under her breath.

Dottie suddenly had some vigour in her eyes as she turned to face Serephanie. "What was that, Terra?"

"Why are you here, Dottie?" Serephanie inquired, her patience having worn thin.

"Because Lady Cyrelle told me to accompany you," Dottie answered back derisively.

Serephanie met Dottie's gaze then, feeling spite practically burning its way through her. "No, I mean why be involved with the League of the Sacred Fist at all? You don't like the fights, so what could there possibly be to attract you to a company that promotes professional fighting?”

“Why do you care what I am doing?” Dottie threw back at Serephanie, her eyes narrowing and nostrils flaring.

Allowing herself a casual shrug, Serephanie turned her attention back to the ring. “It just seems so odd to me, that’s all.”

“I could ask you questions too, Terra,” Dottie sneered at her. “You forget that Lady Cyrelle is not the only one around here capable of digging up dirt. You know, I have wondered how an illiterate, nameless bastard from Galdourn could talk as properly as a highborn. It is downright amazing, when you think of it. Then again, why is it that a supposed no one is so important for Cyrelle to keep around under our protection all the time? Curious things to think about, they are.”

“Maybe you should ask Lady Cyrelle those questions next time they pop into your head,” Serephanie suggested while turning her neck sharply to look right into Dottie’s face. “I wonder what she would think of you poking around into matters that she has already ordered you to leave alone.”

Down below in the centre of the tent, Darrion was removing his tunic and preparing to climb into the ring for the first time. He leapt up the steps and walked along the edge of the ring, a hand running along the top hempen rope as he strode. A leg swung up and over the second rope, and he swayed his torso under the top rope. From there, Darrion sauntered into the middle of the ring and took a sweeping look about the tent, until Serephanie felt his gaze land on her.

There was a smile, and she smiled back, daring to give him the tiniest of waves, her lips forming the words, ‘I love you.’

“It is something else, right?” Kohvee queried from where he stood in the red corner of the ring. “That first time in the ring, it feels like it’s all been worth it, doesn’t it?”

“Aye, it really does,” Darrion replied in wonderment.

Everett gave a chuckle. “Don’t get too awestruck on us yet, Cole. You’re just a guest right now, one on a special invitational trial based on your strong showing in the Tournament of the Winter’s King. Before you can call this ring home, you have to earn your right to leave your blood and sweat on its mat.”

A damp rag was thrown to Darrion by Keverick, and Everett’s voice carried as he eyed the piece of cloth flying over the top rope,

"First though, do be a good lad and wipe down Keverick and Kellum's sweat as much as you can, we can't have the mat getting slippery."

"You know, Terra, Lady Cyrelle taught me that it is unwise to make enemies of those you may need to rely on," Dottie stated while Darrion was readying the ring. "You would do well to stay on mine and Dilla's good side."

Serephanie practically recoiled at that. "Why in the Known World would I concern myself with the good side of either of you two when all you have ever shown me is the bad side?"

Dottie tossed back a stray strand of hair and for once looked a little apologetic. "We could say the same, you know."

The thought had not occurred to Serephanie, but in retrospect, Dottie might well be correct. It could just be that Serephanie and Cyrelle's handmaids had just not gotten off on the right foot. "To be fair, I always felt that you and Dilla hated me. Perhaps I was just overthinking, though."

"Dilla felt you were cold towards the both of us from the start and I certainly could not fault her for feeling that way," Dottie revealed to Serephanie. "We tried to work with you when Lady Cyrelle commanded it, but you were distant, and we thought that you always seemed so happy to be free of us when Syrie or anybody else would call you away."

Serephanie suddenly felt silly. "Oh, Dottie, no, it was not you two. Being a handmaid was just not a good fit for me, I was far more suited to shadowing Syrie."

"Are you telling me true, Terra?" Dottie asked suspiciously. "You did come across to Dilla and me as uptight, you know."

"I had no intention of being perceived that way, and I apologise if I did," Serephanie offered in contrition. "I'm just not cut out for being a handmaid. It's not a job for just anybody, especially when they don't know what they are getting themselves into."

That final remark elicited a giggle from Dottie. "Especially not when you have to serve Lady Cyrelle, she can be a demanding woman when the mood strikes her."

"You might be right about that," Serephanie agreed, giving a tiny smile as she did. A thought occurred to her then. "I know you can't speak for Dilla, but I would like it if at least you and I could start over again."

"I would like that too," Dottie said with cautious optimism. "And don't worry about Dilla, I will talk to her."

A loud thud echoed out of the ring, and Serephanie looked just in time to see Kohvee having jumped from the top rope and into the ring, rolling forward into a somersault as he landed on his feet. He stepped up to Darrion and extended a hand to shake with a grin across his face. "Nice to finally meet you in person, Cole. I'm Kohvee."

Darrion shook back, "It's great to meet you too. I was impressed by your performance at the tournament. Congratulations on winning and defending one of the championship belts."

"Oh, that?" Kohvee said with a chortle. "Knocking around some cheating noble boy isn't a big deal, but thank you all the same. You though, you ought to be proud of yourself. Most fellas would just as soon soil themselves rather than accept a direct challenge from Tahru. Good show in not backing down."

"Thank you, I hope I can live up to the reputation that my actions have lent me," Darrion replied bashfully.

Kohvee stepped back, removed his tunic, and tossed it onto the nearest corner post. "I guess we're about to find out now, aren't we, pal?"

Darrion gave a great guffaw to that. "That's fine by me. I was hoping I would be picked to work with you."

"Likewise, so hold nothing back, you hear?" Kohvee instructed, taking the time for a last stretch as he did.

Everett was in the ring again and standing between the two. "Alright, Cole, remember to not get too excited. It's your first time in the ring, and the whole thing could well go to your head, so I need you to focus, and remember your objective: lose well."

"Yes, ser, I have not forgotten," Darrion replied after a deep breath to regain his composure.

"Do the Aquatican-style fights start in a collar-and-elbow tie-up like we do, or can I take a moment to give you some instruction?" Kohvee inquired earnestly.

Lowering himself down with his arms out, Darrion gave answer, "We start with a left-handed backhand touch. So, aye, there is definitely room for a lesson."

Kohvee obliged, positioning Darrion's arms in the correct manner while giving verbal instruction on the topic. Once Kohvee was sure that Darrion was comfortable, the former gave a signal to Everett that both men were prepared.

Everett gave a nod and lifted his arm. "Ready... Begin!"

Kohvee took off like an arrow leaving the bow, rendering Darrion unable to do anything but react. As soon as Everett's arm had fallen, Darrion's right arm was lifted at the bent elbow by Kohvee, giving him space to slip under the right arm and around the back to wrap his arms about Darrion's waist.

Keverick, Kellum, and Lyle all reacted with an array of impressed cheering for Kohvee's lightning-fast opening salvo.

Even Dottie seemed intrigued for once. "Kohvee moves as quickly as a cat on the chase," she commented to Serephanie with a sly grin. "He thinks even quicker, too. It seems like he's ahead by three or four moves at a time. Truly, he is one of the few fighters I actually enjoy watching just for how exciting his fights can get, especially when he is outsized as he is now. I think he thrives off of fighting the bigger men."

Darrion had spread his feet and leaned his weight into Kohvee while Dottie was talking, his hands going to Kohvee's to try to break his hold. Holding the wrists of the smaller man, Darrion began to pry the hands apart, letting out a roar as they finally separated. With a toss, Darrion threw Kohvee's right arm aside, and wrapped his hands solely around the left. He bent at the waist, and pulled Kohvee over his shoulder and down to the mat by the left arm. Kohvee came to land on his back, the left arm still held firmly in Darrion's grasp. There seemed to be an attempt from Darrion to apply a wristlock, but Kohvee was already rolling to his side and back to his feet, preventing Darrion from getting a solid grip. Once facing Darrion, Kohvee spun underneath Darrion's arms, twisting the wrists in an effort to free himself. When that failed to break the grasp, he attempted a more forceful twist, only for Darrion to pivot on his hip as Kohvee spun, releasing the hold long enough to catch Kohvee under the armpit and toss him over his hip in an attempt to slam Kohvee to the mat again.

"That was fancy," Dottie noted while glancing to Serephanie. "Is that from the Aquatican fighting style?"

"It is hard to say sometimes," Serephanie replied, knowing her voice likely sounded full of childish wonderment. "I don't know all the holds, and he learned from a few Illiastran wrestlers when he frequented the Daol Bay fighting pits. It sure was well done, though."

During their exchange, Kohvee had rolled through the hip toss and had come to land on his feet, turning in time to be clasped into a front-facing headlock, where he found himself being flipped frontwards over Darrion's hip yet again. The ring let out a loud bang as both bodies came down together. Kohvee squirmed beneath Darrion, a single shoulder of his perched just high enough off the mat to prevent a pinning situation from taking place. The free arm of Kohvee's felt around for any point on Darrion's body that he could exploit in order to facilitate his escape.

Serephanie heard Dottie give a tiny clap of her hands and looked in time for the woman to say, "Your man is quick too. I don't think Kohvee expected that someone as muscled as Cole could be so nimble."

Darrion had lowered his head over Kohvee, his long, flowing mane of hair covering the faces of both men. "Gruuunngh!" Darrion suddenly roared out, pulling Kohvee's head upward and off the mat as he did. The move let Kohvee's captured arm get loose, and he propped himself on the elbow to keep Darrion from forcing him back down to the mat. From there, Kohvee bent a leg and rolled to his knee, Darrion pressing on the headlock all the while. Slowly, centimetre by centimetre, Kohvee regained his footing until he was standing, his head still trapped in Darrion's arm and his own arms around Darrion's waist.

Kohvee let out a shout and began running Darrion straight into the ropes. Darrion's chest hit the top rope, and as his body sprang back, Kohvee popped his head loose, and used the momentum of Darrion's body rebounding at him to roll Darrion backward and down onto the mat. Darrion came to land with his shoulders flat on the mat, and legs bent over himself, with Kohvee seated against the back of his knees, pressing all of his own weight, and that of Darrion's own lower body, down atop his torso and head.

Everett dropped to his stomach and slapped his hand on the mat, "One!"

Darrion wriggled his legs and head, trying to get Kohvee off, but it was not enough.

"Two!" Everett counted again. His hand rose and fell for the final number, slapping down loudly on the canvas over his yelled count of, "Three!"

Kohvee fell forward on hands and knees and Darrion rolled to his side, both men lying there and breathing heavily.

"The victory goes to Kohvee," Everett declared over the applause of the men standing at ringside. "A job well done to the both of you."

Dottie hummed aloud. "I cannot argue with Everett there, it really was a job well done. Be proud of your man."

"Oh, I am, more and more by the minute," Serephanie said over her own applause.

Darrion was the first to his feet, and he offered a hand to Kohvee. "Are you alright?"

"Aye, just fine, Cole. How are you?" Kohvee asked in return.

A pat on Kohvee's back preceded Darrion's response between deep breaths, "I'm perfectly well, thank you for a good match."

"Thank you, as well," Kohvee laughed through his own exhaustion. "You took me for a ride a few times there, and I should have expected as much, but I was still surprised. I would love a rematch sometime, without Mister Lancer pressuring you to lose, of course."

"I would be glad to, Kohvee. You name the time and place." Darrion accepted, standing back as he did to allow Everett room to speak.

Everett leaned in close to Darrion and whispered in his ear, a gesture Darrion returned in reply, and the two nodded at one another before Everett spoke loudly enough to be heard by all, "Aquatican style, I take it? I was not aware that their fighting was so similar to Illiastran wrestling."

Darrion tilted his head from side to side. "Well, water elves rely heavily on grappling versus say, the Kav-Do fighting style of the wood elves. It's all based on what works in water as well as on land and striking goes rather slowly underwater. Moreover, I might have been mentored by a few men of the Daol Bay fighting pits, particularly those who happened to be wrestlers first and boxers second."

"Is that so?" Everett declared with a guffaw. "You're what I call an onion, lad. Every time we get you in here, we peel off another layer and discover something new. Alright, go take a breather and a drink of water and come back to watch the final match."

Everett's attention turned to Lyle. "I hope you were paying attention to that. Clean the mat and ready yourself, you've got the last match."

"You know, Terra, I am highborn myself," Dottie stated from beside Serephanie, giving her a mild bout of panic.

"Are you?" Serephanie managed to ask while giving her the faintest glimpse of eye contact. In truth, Serephanie knew that much already, having been told by Cyrelle, though she did not intend to reveal that to Dottie.

She had begun nodding her head lightly, "Yes, as a matter of fact, I am a Braxon of Gazetown, in the Green Gaze Hills region. Do you know where that is?"

Serephanie again feigned ignorance, despite the fact that she had been there with her family, albeit on a stopover on a train.

"Oh, it's a lovely region, in what's called the mid-south quadrant." Dottie continued explaining with her hand gesturing from upon a bent wrist all the while. "We're south enough that we get a mild winter but far north enough that the savages in the Southlands can't get to us, as my father likes to say. His name is Giles, a city councillor to Minister Lyman Hawksbury. If you get to come with us on tour for the winter, you will no doubt get to see it for yourself."

"That would be lovely. Cole promised me that we would get to see all of Illiastra if he got to join the Sacred Fist," Serephanie said in hopes of making some sort of amiable conversation.

Dottie giggled at that. "Oh my goodness, dearie, you will see more of it than you could ever imagine. We go to far-flung places that the trains never reach. In fact, if you can name a place that is not in the Southlands or up north where the elves and dwarves are, chances are we have been there."

"Mister Lancer, surely you jest!" Serephanie heard from within the ring, looking toward the area to find a shirtless Lyle with a hand outstretched and pointing at the masked woman now occupying the space with him.

"Do I look like a jester to you, Lyle?" Everett answered him from where he leaned against the turnbuckle padding in a neutral corner, his tone as flat as a board.

Lyle flailed his limbs in the woman's general direction, "You want me to fight her, ser? I can't do that."

Everett, who had stepped out into the middle of the ring, looked between both people, "And just why not, Lyle?"

"I'm not going to lose to a woman, that's preposterous!" Lyle exclaimed, as if the request was the most ludicrous thing he had ever heard.

"Help me understand, Lyle: is it that you would not fight a woman, or that you would not lose to a woman?" Everett asked next in feigned puzzlement.

Lyle looked about, first to Kellum still doing his squats and then to Darrion, his eyes pleading for either of them to help him, but neither man moved to do so. "I can... I can fight a woman, but I am not going to lose to one."

"Are you sure of that?" Everett asked, his eyebrows shooting upward. "Even if I let it be a fair fight, do you think that you would not lose to this woman in a wrestling match?"

In a flash, Lyle's expression changed from bewilderment to some sort of false confidence. "Aye, yeah, that's right. It just would not be fair. A woman just cannot beat a man. You'd have to rig the match for that to happen."

"Maybe we should ask her if she thinks that's true," Everett said while gesturing to the woman. "Because I am prepared to promise you a fair fight at this point and something tells me that she is more than happy to take us up on that offer."

The unnamed woman's eyes looked steeled and determined, but she opted not to speak aloud. Calling Everett over, she whispered something in his ear once close, and whatever was said, it made him laugh.

"She wants to make it a wager, Lyle. Are you game for that?" Everett told the young man, his expression having returned to its nervous state.

"What does she want to wager?" Lyle asked somewhat timidly.

"What do you got to offer? Let's start with what money you have on you," Everett asked to open the bidding.

Lyle shrugged nervously. "There's a dozen coppers in my knapsack."

Everett shook his head. "No, that's not rich enough. Do you own any livestock? Maybe a horse or two?"

Sweat began to form on Lyle's brow almost immediately. "My father's got a milking cow and a few hogs. We own no horses. I can't wager them, though, ser. Pa will kill me."

"I reckon that the Sacred Fist could well use a cow and a few pigs," Everett put back to Lyle. "I would even wager their worth in coin in return. What do you say?"

"No, ser, I can't do that to my pa, Mister Lancer," Lyle retorted in growing desperation.

Everett splayed his arms wide. "You were so sure that you would win, lad. What happened all of a sudden?"

The young trainee had gone silent and was now standing with his arms folded and eyes downcast on the ring canvas.

With slow, shuffled steps, Everett walked in close to Lyle. "I'll tell you what happened." When he came to within arm's length, Everett reached out a hand toward Lyle's forehead and flicked him with his middle finger, causing Lyle to flinch. "Somewhere in that damn fool head of yours, you know there is a better than good chance that you could lose, and your poor ol' 'pa' will be short of a few barn animals."

"With all respect, that would only be if you cheat, Mister Lancer," Lyle countered weakly.

"No, no, no, Lyle, I won't cheat," Everett uttered with an astonished chortle. "I've given you my word that it will be a fair fight, if you're so prepared to accept it, and you know damn well that my word is good."

Lyle looked to Darrion and Kellum again, then across the ring to the woman, and finally back to Everett. "You won't be mad if I accidentally hurt her, right?"

"You won't hurt that one, lad," Everett proclaimed firmly. "Of that I am certain."

"Alright, then. I'll do it," Lyle reluctantly agreed with a nod of his head.

"Tremendous. It's a deal then," Everett exclaimed with a clap of his hands. "Okay you two, get in here and lock up. Let's get this thing going."

Lyle was already in close to the centre of the ring, but he was joined now by the masked woman. Everett offered to show Lyle a proper collar-and-elbow starting position, but Lyle claimed to know as much already. By her own understanding, Serephanie had to admit that Lyle did not do too terribly at it. With a few minor adjustments to Lyle's foot positioning and the angle of his right elbow, Everett was satisfied and raised his own arm.

"Ready?" Everett said while glancing at both combatants one last time. In a flash, his arm dropped to start the match. "Begin!"

Lyle started by pushing the woman while still in the neutrally positioned collar-and-elbow hold, but found her giving little more than a few steps. She took him back to where they started and gave a grunt in the process that made it almost seem like it was a struggle for her to move the only slightly larger man. The two opponents found themselves positioned in the dead centre of the ring again, and with neither one willing to be the first to break the hold, it looked to Serephanie as though the match might be a stalemate.

"Is that it, Lyle? That all you got?" Everett asked tauntingly from right beside the two fighters.

The taunting was meant to bait Lyle, and it looked to work, as Lyle began to tug on the woman, trying to pull her faster than she could keep up. The woman kept pace, and pushed back until they wound up in Lyle's corner.

"Alright, alright, break the hold and move back to centre," Everett ordered while getting between them.

At the starting lines, Everett resumed the match, and told them to engage in a collar-and-elbow tie-up at their own leisure. The woman held up her arms to allow the hold, and Lyle came in for it, only to deke at the last second and shoot for her legs. The feint failed, as the woman sprawled her weight atop Lyle's back, and clinched him in a front-facing headlock. Lyle tried to rise and got as far as his feet, albeit while still bent at the waist. The woman went with the flow of the movement, but her hold was applied too tightly for Lyle to escape.

"Guuungh!" Lyle roared out while lifting the woman off the ground. His own arms had wrapped around her waist, and he stood there perfectly straight for a few seconds. The woman's legs pedalled in the air, but she refused to let go of the headlock. A tremble appeared in Lyle's legs, and the woman sensed it, kicking out both of her legs to shift her weight as far out from their mass as possible so that she might throw off his failing balance.

The manoeuvre was enough to send Lyle tumbling forward, and she landed on her feet, Lyle's head still wrapped between her left arm and side.

Another grunt from Lyle preceded a second attempt to lift the woman, but his strength was sapped, and her feet never left the ground.

As soon as Lyle ceased his lifting, the woman let out a "Heeeeyuuup!" and pivoted on her left foot and hip, using her own momentum to roll Lyle off his own feet and forward onto the mat. While going into the roll, the woman released the headlock, snatching his left arm into a keylock that used both of her arms to apply pressure. When Lyle landed on his back, he came to realize that his arm was the least of his worries, as his head was newly trapped between the woman's knees in a head-scissors hold.

"Gods dammit!" Lyle cried out, his loose right arm trying vainly to free his head from the woman's grasp.

"What's the plan, Lyle?" Everett asked him chidingly while lowering to his knees. "You ready to surrender?"

"No," he managed to squeak out while struggling.

Everett surveyed the situation, his eyes running up and down the two intertwined combatants. "Really? Because it doesn't look so good for you from where I sit. You're on your back, with your legs kicking all uselessly, and you have one free arm that won't be enough to pry her crossed feet apart. Do you want her to start wrenching on that left arm a little harder?"

Everett slid along the mat, until he was hovering right over Lyle's face, pointing downward with a single finger at the young man's neck. "On the other hand, she can cut off your air and knock you silly, and that is always fun. She can do either one... Or both at the same time, for that matter. It's your call, really. Technically, you have that one arm flailing around that's keeping your right shoulder from being square on the mat, meaning that I can't count it as a pin. So, we're just sort of stuck here, aren't we? Well, you're stuck here, anyway."

Everett looked to be on the verge of pointing out another flaw of Lyle's when the second man managed to untangle the woman's legs where they crossed at the ankle. Lyle's head slipped free and he quite nearly yanked his left arm out as well. The woman, already on her back, was a step ahead, and as Lyle tried to stand, her legs wrapped around Lyle's extended left arm that she now clutched at the wrist with both hands. Try as he might to pull free, the woman would not be moved, and she inched her body up the arm until her feet were in Lyle's face. She stretched herself out in this position while practically hanging upside down from the extended limb of her opponent. Lyle's face turned away from the encroaching feet and the continued pressure forced his body to twist at an odd angle. After a second or two of delay, Lyle again found himself tumbling to the mat on his back.

"Now you're well and truly screwed, lad," Everett commented amusedly while looking upon the supine form of Lyle. "That there is as neat and tidy an armbar hold as I have ever seen. You have precious few seconds to submit before she breaks something. So, if I were you-"

Lyle's shrieks of pain cut Everett off, "I yield, I yield, get her off me!"

"And there we have it," Everett sighed while separating man and woman. "Alright, that's enough, break it apart."

The woman rolled backward from where she lay, coming to land on her feet before her body bounced softly into the ropes of the ring. Still laying on the mat was Lyle, holding his left arm with his right and groaning in pain. As the woman approached, she extended her hand to Lyle to help him stand, an offer Lyle accepted with hesitation.

"Thank you..." Lyle said with his eyes downcast and an ashamed look upon his face.

A slow, deep nod served as an answer from the woman, and before Lyle or Everett could utter a word, she left the ring by sliding out under the bottom rope.

"Hey, wait a moment, please," Everett called out to the woman, causing her to stop in her tracks as she walked down the aisle toward the fighter's entrance. "Lyle, what do you have to say?"

Silence filled the room, so much so that Serephanie could hear the gentle winds blowing at the canvas at the top of the tent. Finally, Lyle gave answer to both Everett and the fighting woman. "Thank you for the match, ma'am. It was well fought."

"Good job, lad," Everett offered him calmly. "Kellum, grab a pair of stools. Cole, we'll need a clean towel and two cups of water. Both of you report to ringside when you have it."

Serephanie looked to Darrion and Kellum, finding that they had both sprang into action hurriedly.

"How is the arm?" Everett asked Lyle while pointing at the limb.

"It'll be fine, ser," Lyle gave in sheepish response.

"Probably, aye," Everett agreed. "Did you hear or feel any pops or snaps?"

Lyle shook his head to that question.

"Aye, that arm will be just fine then," Everett surmised. "If she popped your shoulder out or broke a bone, you would know it. At any rate, give it a rest for the remainder of the day. Nothing strenuous, understood?"

Darrion and Kellum returned to the ringside area almost simultaneously with the requested items. Everett took the stools into the ring, setting one in the blue corner, the other directly before it, and gestured for Lyle to take the former to sit on. The first cup of water and the towel he offered to Lyle as well, taking the other for himself while lowering onto the stool in front of him.

"Cole, Kellum, come gather in close, and we will have a lesson, lads. Kohvee, Keverick, you're both welcome to listen in too," Everett invited them, prompting the two trainees to stand outside the ring on either side of the corner that Lyle was occupying. Kohvee sat in the ring beside Everett, his legs crossed, while Keverick found a spot next to Darrion.

"Lyle tells me his arm is feeling alright, in case any of you were wondering. But I want to talk about another part of the body that needs as much exercise," Everett told the other four. "Lyle, I would like you to tell me, before your fellow trainees and these two members of the Sacred Fist, how you're feeling up here after that fight," Everett said while tapping the side of his own head to illustrate his point. "Do you feel up to that?"

"I just want to know why you picked me to go against the woman," Lyle requested of Everett. "You knew you were going to ask us all to lose, and you knew who you were going to pick for each fighter. Why was it me against her, ser?"

Everett shrugged his shoulders and took a drink of water. "No personal reason, Lyle, if that's what you're wondering. You're the smallest of the three trainees I have left. The woman was the smallest of the three seasoned fighters at my disposal for this exercise. I put together the most suitable pairs based on little more than that. Cole is the biggest of you three, Kohvee is smaller than he is but not by much, and Kohvee makes up for that miniscule disadvantage in agility and experience. Keverick and Kellum are nearly even in size and both land in the middle of their respective groups. Therefore, that leaves you, as the smallest, to fight that woman. That is all there is to it, lad."

"It doesn't feel fair that I'm the only one who got put in that position, ser. That's all," Lyle uttered, clearing trying hard to keep himself composed.

"I can see why that doesn't seem fair, aye," Everett acquiesced casually. "I would venture to guess that this is not the first time you have gotten a bad lot. Probably feels like another bad apple in an already heaping bushel of wormy fruit, am I right?"

Lyle wiped his brow and gave a nod with his reply, "Aye, ser, something like that."

Everett sighed deeply. "I can't speak to all the other shite you've had to deal with until now, and I don't have the time to get into all of it. I am going to tell you something, Lyle, and it is most certainly going to be something that you don't want to hear right now, but it will make sense to you later, I promise. Every time you enter a situation, there are two groups that every component of that situation can fit in to: things you can control, and things you cannot control. Scientists call those things variables and invariables respectively. Is everyone following me so far?"

The trainees all confirmed as much, and Everett continued on unimpeded. "The invariable for you in this case Lyle, was the opponent I had chosen for you and that was less than an ideal scenario for you, I admit. The variable though, was how you chose to handle that situation. In a perfect world, we have time and insight to see all the angles by which we can approach any given choice and can navigate correctly from there. More often than not though, you will have seconds to sort everything out before making a decision and you will almost never have all the information you need.

"From what few invariables I give you in these exercises, I want to see what you do with the variables, for it is in these moments that I get to see the real Lyle, Kellum, and Cole, and I get a measure of each of you. If you possess the self-awareness to grasp what I am telling you, then the three of you should each be learning a good deal about yourselves too.

"You might be wondering why I want to have such an understanding of my trainees and the reason is that it is my job. I train people to fight in the style of the Sacred Fist, aye, but it is more than that. My name and reputation are on the line every time a student of mine ties up their boots and gets in this ring. Based on that, I am not willing to stake that same reputation on a person who displays anything less than the absolute best that this league demands of every single person working under and around this tent."

Everett stopped for a moment, letting his words and the quiet of the tent fall over everyone listening while he emptied his cup.

"That woman..." Lyle uttered in little more than a whisper. "She met your standard, didn't she?"

A serious sort of laugh came forth from Everett. "Oh, and then some. When I told you who you were up against today, you knew nothing about that woman. Not her name, or age, or birthplace, nothing, not even what her face looked like. All you had was your presumption that she was a woman. Based on nothing but her assumed gender, you immediately placed yourself above *her*, and felt that having a wrestling match with her was beneath *you*. How do you think that made her feel? She has been with the Sacred Fist for years, has paid her dues, and learned her craft from the absolute masters. Despite everything she has achieved, she is still being second-guessed by amateurs like you even though they know absolutely nothing about her. How do you think she felt when you were whinging and flailing around the ring after being told that you would have to fight her?"

"Not good, I reckon," Lyle managed to get in.

"Not good, aye, that's one way of putting it," Everett repeated, his tone measured and calm, but full of intensity. "She earned her spot on our roster, and though she's not legally permitted to fight, and promoting professional women's fighting is outlawed, we keep her with us. Because that is what the Sacred Fist does when the right people come our way: we make them family. Earning your way into this family involves showing decency and respect to every single person who makes what we do possible. Be they man or woman, the Continental Champion or the person scrubbing pots, we treat them well, and we look after one another. Am I understood?"

"Yes, ser!" Cole, Kellum, and even Keverick and Kohvee answered him.

Everett reached out and put a hand on Lyle's right shoulder for a reassuring pat. "Now, lad, I don't want you to think that this is just about beating down on you. Think about something: outside of Cole, who came to us near the end, how many lads started this training with you and Kellum?"

Lyle's head shook, and he seemed to be searching for an answer. "I don't know, ser. Three dozen at least, I think."

"That was a fairly close guess," Everett told him, before revealing the actual answer. "It was forty-three that showed up for the open call, to be exact. Now, there are three of you left, two if we omit Cole again. Do you remember Domas and Cardwin? Both of them were well-known boxers around Hercalest. Supposedly, they were top ranked in the city's fighting pits, and I cut them both from the list. I certainly cannot dispute their claims as fighters, as they both box wonderfully from what I saw. Especially Domas, that lad has a talent for punching things. Cardwin we actually brought on tour with us for a season, and we only fired him yesterday without him having ever fought a single match for us during that tour. Yet, I still cut them, and I would do so today, tomorrow, and every other day from now until my death.

"In time, you may learn why I cut them, and why the dozens that arrive at my tent at every stop we make go away empty handed, and why dozens more show up in Na'Zohz's face at the gates and are turned away before I even meet them. All those lads come and gone, and you're still here in the running for a roster spot. Tonight, Lyle, I want you to go home and ask yourself why you think that might be. Just as importantly, take the time to reflect on all the variables that you acted on today and figure out how your choices surrounding those variables resulted in an outcome that benefitted no one."

"What do I tell my pa, Mister Lancer?" Lyle asked sorely.

"You can tell him that you foolishly took a bet without knowing the odds and almost cost him a cow and two hogs," Everett told him calmly.

Lyle raised his head hopefully to eye level with Everett. "You mean it, ser? You're not going to take Pa's livestock?"

"No, lad, I won't do that. You can keep your animals," Everett confirmed while standing up from the stool. "You will have penance, though. Be here bright and early, you're mucking stalls in the morning. Rest that arm until then."

"Aye, ser, I'll be here before dawn," Lyle agreed while shaking Everett's hand. "Thank you for everything. Do you think I will get to make it up to the woman I fought? I feel poorly now, for how I acted."

Everett nodded thoughtfully. "You might, if your training works out. Consider it a goal to aspire to, Lyle: if you earn a place here, you will get to apologise to her for being an arsehole."

"Aye, ser, I will do my best. Thank you again," Lyle told him from outside the ring, once he rolled out carefully.

"Dottie, there you are, I have been looking all over for you," a stern voice commanded from near the two girls. Serephanie looked up to see Dilla looking back, her face expressionless. "Have either of you seen Syrie around?"

The mention of Syrie's name caused Dottie to turn sharply at Dilla and give her an odd look. "No, Syrie isn't here, Dilla," her face changed as quickly as it had in the first place and she patted the empty bench beside her. "Get over here and have a sit with us. Terra and I have just been having a fine time together watching her man train. Haven't we Terra?"

Dilla chose to remain standing and did not wait for Serephanie to answer the question. "We can't sit around, Dottie. Lady Cyrelle is looking for Terra, and she wants Syrie too. I found one, now the two of you need to come help me find the other. The request was urgent and Lady Cyrelle has little patience for dawdling on the best of days."

"Ugh, fine," Dottie relented while standing up and smoothing out her dress. She cupped her hands around her mouth and gave a shout, "Oh, Mister Lancer!"

"Hello Dottie, can I help you with something?" Everett called back from the ringside area where he now stood, having vacated the ring so that Darrion and Kellum could sweep and clean it.

While Everett had been responding, Dottie had been carefully stepping her way to the staircase between the bleachers, bidding Terra and Dilla to follow as she worked her way down toward the guardrails separating the ringside from the spectating area. "Hello to you too, Mister Lancer," she greeted in return once they got close, a playful smile on her lips the whole time. "Have you seen Syrie around here by chance?"

"Uh, no, cannot say that I have," Everett answered in an odd manner that Serephanie found passingly curious. "Kohvee is around, perhaps he might know. If not, he can at least check in the dressing rooms for you, she might be running messages to the fighters."

"Would you be a darling and do that for us, Mister Lancer?" Dottie asked him with a dainty flick of her wrist. "Lady Cyrelle has apparently summoned her and Terra with urgency, I am told."

Everett cocked his head to one side quizzically. "Really? Did she say what it was about?" he looked about for Kohvee with sudden haste and waved him over once found. "Kohvee, come here for a moment!"

Dilla had stepped up beside Dottie, going around Serephanie to do as much. Once there, she took the lead responding to Everett's question. "Lady Cyrelle ordered me to say nothing and simply deliver Syrie and Terra to her at once."

"Yes, Mister Lancer, what do you need?" Kohvee asked gaily upon approach.

"Right then, we won't keep you girls waiting," Everett told Dilla while turning to the fighter. "The handmaidens of Lady Cyrelle have been sent to find your wife. Have you seen her around?"

Kohvee looked to the women and back to Everett. "No, ser, I have not. I suppose there is a chance that she might be in the tent. Let me check in the dressing room areas and see if I can find her."

Without further word or gesture, Kohvee departed, leaving Everett to keep the three women company while they waited. Everett looked toward Serephanie and gave her a wave. "Tell me, Terra, as your first time seeing our training up close, what did you think of what you just saw?"

Caught a little off guard, Serephanie stammered a bit while thinking of something to say. "It was interesting, to say the least. All three men seemed to respond differently to the task at hand, but I think everyone came away having learnt something from each encounter."

"That was well met," Everett complimented, his eyebrows raised in surprise. "I would like to hear what it is that you felt could be gleaned from what each prospect went through," his focus shifted toward the sound of fast approaching footfalls before they could get into, but he gave her a final glance all the same. "Although I suppose it might have to wait until another day. As we all know, Lady Cyrelle will not be kept waiting."

"No," Serephanie concurred. "I suppose she will not, ser." Her attention was briefly taken by Darrion, who paused his sweeping of the ring for just a split second, giving Serephanie a wave and a warm smile, a gesture she returned in kind.

Syrie and Kohvee came to stand beside Everett on the ring's side of the guardrails. The former was dressed in a long, black woollen coat and matching trousers, her hair concealed beneath a blue cap she had pulled tight over her head. "I've been told that Lady Cyrelle needs to see me. Did she say what it was about?"

"That she has not, just that I was to retrieve both Terra and yourself," Dilla informed Syrie, whose face Serephanie noticed was flush and her breathing deep.

"Are you okay, Syrie?" Serephanie queried worriedly.

"Aye, why?" Syrie returned quickly.

Serephanie shook her head in mild puzzlement. "It's nothing, but you just looked like you were a little fatigued, perhaps."

Syrie shot an eyebrow up. "Eh? I have been running all over this damn camp all day in near-freezing weather, of course I am beat out.

Are we going or not? Cyrelle will have our hides for pissing time away like this."

With a hand from Everett and Kohvee, the handmaids and Serephanie were helped over the guardrail to the ringside area. Dilla was the first over, and once at ringside she seemed to be making note of what each of the fighters were all doing.

"Mister Lancer," Dilla began to get Everett's attention. "Has your training concluded for the nonce?"

Everett was in the process of helping Dottie and gave answer while doing so. "Aye, these lads are done for the afternoon. They are free and clear until bell time tonight, and then I'll put them to work as security for the show. Why do you ask?"

"Oh? Well, in that case, Lady Cyrelle wants Cole Chere too," Dilla informed Everett.

"Very well, you may tell Lady Cyrelle that Cole is all hers, then," Everett permitted before looking to the ring. "Cole, you had best get changed quickly and go with the ladies, it sounds important, lad."

"Yes, ser, I'll go straight away," Darrion replied, handing off the broom to Kellum as he did. He stepped through the ropes and out of the ring, jogging down the aisle and out of sight in a flash.

Syrie waved at the three women. "Follow me through the dressing areas. We'll meet Cole outside when he's changed."

Upon exiting the tent, Serephanie discovered that it was indeed as cold as Syrie said. The chill winds of the late autumn blew down harshly at Serephanie and the others as they strolled through Bryten Field in their winter coats.

"It feels like a hard winter is coming," Dottie commented idly to no one in particular.

Dilla grunted, "I'll be happy once we pull up stakes and turn south. I would welcome the roar of the Varras River over the cut of these northern gales."

"Don't worry, girls, we'll be southbound sooner rather than later," Syrie put in from beside them.

Once the party reached Cyrelle's wheelhouse, Darrion opened the door and held it for the four women. Inside, the limitations of the wheelhouse became immediately apparent with five of them jostling to get out of one another's way.

Cyrelle was waiting for them on the short sofa in the sitting room, a tray of tea and scones situated before her on a low table. "Dottie,

Dilla, steer clear of the other three and be on your way, please," she commanded calmly from within, completely unperturbed by the fracas that the five were making in the cramped foyer.

The handmaids stepped into the office at last, clearing space for Serephanie, Syrie, and Darrion so that they might situate themselves in the sitting room.

"Will there be anything else, Lady Cyrelle?" Dilla asked while fixing the mess that the wind had made of her hair.

"No, that will be all," Cyrelle confirmed. "Just be sure to get the door on your way out. Syrie will lock it behind you. Thank you both, girls."

Doing as requested, Syrie followed the handmaids outside, leaving Cyrelle alone with the couple for the first time. "It is a pleasure to meet you, young man. Your wife has told me a great deal about you."

"The pleasure is all mine, Lady Cyrelle," Darrion replied, him and Serephanie still standing by the door. "I cannot begin to thank you for the generosity and hospitality that you have shown-"

"Wait one moment before you say another word," Cyrelle said with a raised hand. Leaning back on the sofa, she gently shifted the curtain on the tiny window and waited a beat. "There now, Dottie and Dilla should be far enough away that they will not hear us. These walls are not totally soundproof after all."

Cyrelle rose from her seat and extended a hand to Darrion's to shake. "As I said before, it is a pleasure to meet you, Darrion Veskries. I trust that Serephanie has informed you of our discussions here?"

"Why yes, of course she has... Uh, my lady," Darrion answered, stumbling when attempting to decide on a title to address her by.

"Come now, just Cyrelle is fine. I am not a lady by formal title, after all. 'Lady Cyrelle' is an honorary bestowment by those of the Sacred Fist. You are under no obligation to call me by it, Mister Veskries."

"If it is all the same to you, Lady Cyrelle, I feel that you have more than earned the title. But please, just call me Darrion," he told her while in mid bow. "I would just like to say that your husband was nothing short of an icon of the sport, and I admired him greatly. You yourself have been a fierce champion of his legacy. Knowing what I do now of your position with the Sacred Fist, you have done tremendous work by making the league into what it is."

Syrie had silently returned to the sitting room while Darrion complimented Cyrelle and her late husband. By the time Serephanie took notice of Syrie, she found her positioned beside a simple wooden chair that sat next to the low table.

Cyrelle allowed herself a sad smile when Darrion had finished, "You are too kind, Darrion. I assure you that Fezadore, though too humble to accept it, would ultimately be glad to hear you say such things. He would have liked you, I am sure of it.

"Syrie, would you pour some tea for Serephanie and Darrion before you sit, please?" Cyrelle asked before gesturing to the now empty sofa. "Please, take a seat together, you two, and make yourselves comfortable."

Cyrelle sat herself upon a cushioned lounge chair to the left of the sofa, taking a cup of tea and a raisin scone from Syrie once she was satisfied.

With a glance between them, Serephanie and Darrion did as asked, and took their seat together, each of them accepting the offer of food and drink as they did.

After a sip and a bite, Serephanie started for the four of them. "Lady Cyrelle, might I ask why you called us here?"

"Yes... Serephanie, dear, I have something to tell you, and for once, I am unsure of how to do so," Cyrelle said with a noticeable quiver in her lips.

Dread ran down Serephanie's spine, and she set aside her tea and scone, her now free hands going to Darrion's knee for comfort. He set his own cup and saucer down and wrapped his thick hands about Serephanie's, looking as confused as she was.

Cyrelle took a drink of her tea and followed it with a deep breath. "I am afraid that we have received terrible news from the west, my dear. Sometime in the last week, your father succumbed to his illness. I cannot begin to tell you how sorry I am for your loss, Serephanie."

"Father is..." Serephanie muttered, the word practically catching in her throat. "Oh, gods no..."

Darrion wrapped his arms about Serephanie and pulled her tight to his chest. "I am so sorry, my love."

"Oh, Serephanie... I am so terribly sorry..." Syrie uttered morosely.

"There is more that you should hear," Cyrelle informed her after clearing her own throat.

"What... What else?" Serephanie asked as she took a napkin offered to her by Syrie for the tears falling freely on her cheeks. "I would hear it, Lady Cyrelle, please."

"It's about your sister, darling," Cyrelle began, before pausing again. "Do you feel up to it at this time?"

"Yes, please," Serephanie managed to stammer out.

Cyrelle looked longingly into her teacup, considering the drink for a moment. "The word we are hearing is that Marigold is making a stand against the Elite Merchant Party and the Triarchy. There was talk of some marriage pact that involved you and her being promised to Eamon Palomb's sons and that Marigold is breaking that pact. She announced all of it after your father's funeral and has already begun campaigning to a similar tune amongst the western ministers. I cannot confirm this, but there is talk that she intends to divide the country between east and west."

Serephanie looked up at Darrion from where she rested on his broad chest. "I can't believe my little sister is really doing it."

Cyrelle shook her head despondently. "The Palombs are not in Hercalest, either. In fact, the latest news is that after some sort of clash in Atrebell during the latest Parliamentary Session, one that involved Orangecloak and her Thieves, of all people, the Palombs stayed in Atrebell for a time. They have apparently gone west from there to deal with your sister. The opinion amongst those with insight into the matter is that if Marigold causes such a fissure between the two realms, it will almost certainly lead to war... And I for one cannot argue with that prediction."

"She... She told me long ago that she had no intention of marrying Pyore Palomb, and that she wanted us both to fight it..." Serephanie said, her tears having dried up for the moment. "I know that as long as the officials in Daol Bay stand behind her, she will resist, and die in the attempt if need be. Marigold is brave, far more than I ever was or could be. I did not want to marry Eldridge any more than she wanted to marry Pyore, but all I could think to do was run away."

"I must say, I do admire your sister's courage," Cyrelle told her, a little hope inflicting into her voice as she did. "However, do not doubt your own fortitude, either. It not only got you halfway across the country, but into the home city of House Palomb. You are bravely living literally in the shadow of Palomb Palace, for the sake of all things. You are far braver than you know."

Serephanie had nothing to say in response, but knew she must say something. "Thank you, Lady Cyrelle."

Darrion's arms continued to hold her, making Serephanie feel comforted in their strong grasp, one of her own hands held tight to his coat, and at that moment she never wanted to let go.

"The reason I brought Syrie here is because I have something important to ask you in relation to everything I have told you," Cyrelle went on after a moment of silence had passed.

"What is that, my lady?" Serephanie queried softly.

Cyrelle waited another beat, exchanging a look with Syrie as she did. "Your sister's actions will make travel to Daol Bay and the west in general quite difficult in the coming seasons. For instance, you can be guaranteed that train service going west of Obalen will be halted. What I am trying to say is that if you want to go home and be with her in your time of mourning, or to join her resistance going forward, now is the time to do so. To that end, the Sacred Fist is prepared to lend any assistance we can. I will assign Syrie to that task and give her full discretion to marshal any necessary resources toward getting you home, should you want it."

"Go home?" Serephanie asked no one in particular.

"It is up to you, my love," Darrion told her, gazing down adoringly. "I will go where you go, from now until the end of time."

She shook her head, having realized what she idly said seconds ago. "No, Darrion, I am not going back to Daol Bay, not any time soon. Forget I said that, please."

"But you said it yourself, darling, it is home," Darrion reminded her.

"My home is wherever you are. There is nothing else I could want in this life," Serephanie told him in as direct a fashion as she could muster. "Daol Bay is Marigold's, as it ought to be. I would only be in her way."

Cyrelle leaned as close to Serephanie as her chair allowed. "There is a place for you here. We will never turn you out. However, I am sure that your little sister misses you dearly. Each of you is the only family that the other has now."

"I miss her too, painfully so at times, but she and I have chosen our own paths in life with no regrets and no turning back," Serephanie stated, releasing herself from Darrion's hug so that she might sit up again. "I thank you for the offer to help me return to Daol Bay, Lady Cyrelle. I am extremely grateful for the generosity of such an act, but I believe that I am where I belong, and I choose to stay."

"If that is your wish, then I am only happy to grant it, Serephanie." Cyrelle affirmed with a gentle pat on the hand.

Cyrelle stood up from her chair, beckoning Syrie to follow, "Come along, Syrie, we will let Serephanie and Darrion have the wheelhouse to themselves."

"Where are you going?" Serephanie asked, entirely nonplussed. "This is your wheelhouse, after all."

"We are taking our leave so that you might grieve as you please, Serephanie. Your tent has such thin walls that it will be near impossible to talk freely without being overheard. My wheelhouse is yours for the evening. I will arrange to sleep elsewhere for the night."

Serephanie sat up straight and motioned for the two women to return. "I would not hear tell of it. Please, won't you stay with us? I would welcome the company."

"Are you quite sure, dear?" Cyrelle queried for confirmation.

Serephanie smiled as much as the pain would allow. "Yes, Lady Cyrelle, I am absolutely sure."

Cyrelle looked over her shoulder to where Syrie stood in the tiny foyer. "There you have it, Syrie. Would you go to the mess tent and have dinner for the four of us brought here? We will be guesting at Miss Tullivan's leisure for the evening."

21
MARIGOLD

Tippard was as beautiful a town as Marigold had ever seen, and her memories of it were sweeter still.

The sandy beaches ran as far as the eye could see on the north and south sides of the harbour, the sun beating down on their pristine, golden shores. Where the south side of the harbour ascended into steep, rocky hills, the houses were built out from the rock and kept aloft by timber supports. The north side was a rolling, forested slope, and the houses there appeared to be nestled into the leafy green forest of trees. At the southernmost reaches of the city's limits and overlooking everything was the castle and lighthouse of the Mattersly family, the tower rising high on a tall peak that seemed already mountainous.

There were but a few inhabitable castles remaining in all of Illiastra, and among them, only one was to be found in the western realm. Beneath the fading light of the evening, Marigold and her entire entourage were riding uphill toward it, driven there by a steam-engine powered trolley that was set on a track that wound its way up the hillside. During her childhood, Marigold and her family had visited Tippard on several occasions, and nearly always for pleasure alone. On each trip, the Matterslys had insisted on hosting the Tullivans, and the sisters had made friends with Walter's oldest daughter, Leanne, who was in between the ages of Marigold and Serephanie.

Marigold recalled Leanne as a skinny girl, freckled from head to toe, with curly brown hair that seemed as long as she was tall. As a child, Leanne had been an avid explorer, eschewing traditional playtime activities designated for girls like tea parties. Instead, it seemed that Leanne's favourite pastime was leading the Tullivan sisters on adventures around the town, much to the consternation of their guards.

Leanne was not afraid to risk getting into trouble, either. I'm almost certain that her favourite phrase was 'All good adventures come with a risk or two.' I hope that time has not tamed her wild spirit.

The cold nipped at Marigold lightly as the trolley ascended above the distant line of the eastern hills, allowing the wind to find her flesh. Instinctively, she reached for the edges of her teal cloak and pulled them tighter. Beneath she wore only a black, silk blouse and cotton trousers in the same shade with white pinstripes to break the darkness. Her boots were flexible leather that went to just below the knee, lined and rimmed with mink fur for added warmth.

As far as the other eight members of Marigold's party went, seated around the perimeter of the rectangular, metal box, their spirits appeared utterly depleted. Only Moya, positioned across from Marigold, seemed capable of mustering any excitement for the trolley ride, and even that was plainly layered in anxiety. To the left of the blonde woman was Gallin, lost deep in thought, his eyes staring at the floor ahead of his feet. On either side of Marigold sat the Archers, Glendil sitting with his arms folded, gaze on the ceiling, and Freyard constantly scanning in all directions.

I would wager a coin or two that he's taking in the sights as much as he is scouting.

Sydnee and Elden, on Moya's right side, looked to be in a contest to see who could stay awake longer, and the competition was either man's to win. Now and then, Marigold would catch one or the other nodding off, or otherwise fighting away sleep. Seated side-by-side on the pair of seats at the front of the trolley were Dayden and Wyla, the both of them looking altogether bored and ready for the whole ordeal to simply end.

I can find no fault in how any of them feel. Part of me wonders if I should have just stayed home.

Her mind wandered off again, to the last time she had seen Lewcas, lying in a hospital bed in Kylisport. When she had most recently laid eyes on him, his breathing was laboured and weary, and his body wracked with pain as it tried to make sense of the ruinous state of his abdomen.

He took a bullet for me, and for that, I abandoned him to what might well be his death. What sort of horrible person would do that? What does that make me? If there are gods above, they would judge me harshly for that, I do not doubt.

What good even came of it all? A few names on the damned Declaration of Agency. *If I had not come south, Lewcas', Moya's, and the brown-haired woman's lives might have been spared from death and destruction. Nothram only went through with his macabre little show because he knew I would see it.*

No, I cannot hold myself accountable for Nothram's actions.

The battle for blame over the Pelican Harbour incident was one that Marigold fought on a near constant basis in her waking hours, with the violence of it all revisited when sleep found her.

"I've never seen a castle before," Moya stated while tugging at the skirt of a teal dress from Marigold's wardrobe that she was borrowing, her voice being the first thing to break the silence since the trolley ride got underway. "Then again, I didn't know that any still existed. I'm a little excited to get a chance to actually go inside of one. That lighthouse tower poking up on the corner looks quite odd, does it not? No lighthouses that I have ever seen looked like that."

Freyard gave a chuckle and turned to look at the tall stone structure as they drew nearer. "You're not wrong there, Moya. That is certainly a strange looking lighthouse. My lady, you have been here before, would you care to shed a little, er, light, on the subject?"

The lighthouse jutted up from the southwest corner of the castle, standing four stories tall on an already lofty cliff. It was the only building in all of Illiastra that stood higher than the town's accompanying Tower of Ios. A feat achieved simply because there was no other point in the community as lofty as the top of Timber Hill, and Mattersly Castle had occupied the entirety of that space for the better part of a millennia.

"I suppose for once I can offer a little insight," Marigold offered, her own interest in the subject piquing just a little. "I was told about it by the Matterslys over the course of several years, so forgive me if I misremember some parts of it. If memory serves, it's the oldest lighthouse in all of Illiastra, or at least the oldest one still in use. I think I recall being told that the lighthouse in the old dwarven city of Dhalla is still mostly there, but that city has been abandoned almost as long as this tower has been standing. Anyhow, I digress. *This* tower, as we can see from the odd-looking additions to it, serves as more than just a lighthouse."

The beacon room, traditionally found at the very top of any given lighthouse, was instead positioned two thirds of the way up from where the tower emerged from the castle. Above the glass-encased room, the brick and mortar of the original construction turned into a wooden balcony, supported by thick timber beams angled back into the stone below the beacon. Atop the balcony was a dome composed of sheet metal, tiny windows cut into it here and there, and through one of the sheets, their poked a curious tube pointed toward the eternal ceiling above.

Marigold pointed to that tube, and the timber web on which it sat as she finished her explanation, "as you can see, the beacon room is not at the top of the tower in this instance, yet you can tell that it was at one point, and everything above was built much later. That structure on the very top is a laboratory, the only one of its kind in Human Illiastra. Up there, a small, secluded team of scientists use that giant telescope to study the skies. By day they sleep, by night they stare at the moons and stars, trying to unravel the mysteries of it all."

"What a fascinating description, Marigold. You truly have a way with words," Gallin commented in a voice that tried earnestly to not appear overly flattering.

"A giant telescope, you say? I've lived my whole life just a few days' train ride up the coast in Cale and I could have gone the rest of it without knowing such a wonder existed so close by," Moya mused aloud. "It makes me wish that I had the courage to escape my old life sooner."

"Might I ask what it was that you escaped from, Moya?" Sydnee asked gently, turning in his seat and leaning forward to be closer.

She turned away, her face losing all expression. "I... I've said too much."

Sydnee's eyes fell to his hands, folded neatly in front of him. "That's alright. You don't have to say anything before you are ready, or even at all, if you don't want to."

Though she had grown more talkative, and seemed to be coping with the trauma from Pelican Harbour better than Marigold would have imagined, Moya was still practically mum about her past. It was not without trying, as both Sydnee and Freyard had attempted to glean further information from Moya. Yet, for as much as they gently prodded, Moya would say no more than what had slipped out in conversation with Freyard on the morning that the party arrived in Weicaster Bay.

At Marigold's urging, the two men left the poor woman alone about it, agreeing that they would only inquire on the off chance that Moya mentioned the subject. In Freyard's case, he was following through on his duty to protect Marigold, and part of that was ensuring that unknown entities, like Moya, were properly audited. Reduced to basing his opinion on the scant information that Moya had made available of herself, Freyard still claimed he was satisfied that Moya was of no danger.

Sydnee though, he seems interested in Moya for different reasons.

The man and woman were of an age, and though Moya had not yet divulged her marital status, Marigold knew that Sydnee was an eligible bachelor. Marigold was not against the idea of Sydnee courting the odd woman, but she was certainly puzzled by it. According to the other guardsmen whom Sydnee socialised with, the handsome, dark haired man was known to have his choice of mating partners, but had never settled into a relationship at any time. That he was suddenly making overtures towards Moya struck Marigold as uncharacteristic behaviour for a man who seemed content with a life of non-committal, casual intimacy with a revolving roster of women.

"All hands be aware that the trolley is incoming!" a man's voice called out. "Minister Mattersly's guests for the evening have arrived!"

Mattersly Castle seemed to come alive all at once at that declaration. Men in uniform could be seen scurrying about the ramparts, and doors could be heard opening and closing from all over. The trolley, having crested the hill, slowed to a crawl as it passed beneath the bailey of the castle. It came to a gradual stop within the yard, jerking into the final halt with an accompanying blast of steam being released.

On either side of the trolley, there was a line of castle guards in the standard blue uniforms of the Elite Merchants, each one standing at full attention. A splendid water fountain lay ahead, and further on Marigold saw the stone walkway leading to the front entrance, itself flanked by what looked to be the full ensemble of the castle's wait staff.

"So many people... Soldiers in blue coats, too," Moya stated worriedly, her hands beginning to run up and down her legs rapidly in nervousness. "I don't know about this... Maybe I could go back to the train and stay there for the night."

With a reach across the aisle, Marigold laid a hand on her knee, "It will be perfectly fine, Moya. The Mattersly family are old friends of mine. We are as safe here as we would be at my manor. As for those guards, they have just not had a chance to be given new uniforms yet."

"I-I don't belong here... What if they start asking me questions, Ma'am? They'll know I don't belong with you all. They will want to know... What happened."

Marigold stood up and knelt directly before Moya, taking a hand in hers. A glance to Sydnee saw him leaning in supportively as well, and he let Marigold take the lead. "Come now, Moya, nothing could be further from the truth. You will be perfectly fine with us. I promise you, no one will ask you questions. I will take care of everything. If it will make you feel better, I can ensure that you are in Sydnee's company or mine for the whole duration of our stay. Should anyone ask you a question that you do not want to answer, either he or I will take up for you. Would that make you feel better?"

"Aye, my lady speaks truly," Sydnee added in a soft, reassuring tone. "She and I will look after you. Just stick with one of us, alright?"

Moya nodded in response to them before turning her head downward, letting her face become obscured by her long blonde hair.

It served well enough as an answer for Marigold, and she was satisfied enough to leave her be for now. As Marigold stood up straight once more, she tapped Sydnee on the shoulder and mouthed for him to stay with Moya, a gesture he seemed to understand, judging from the wink he gave in answer.

A pair of guards approached the trolley's doors, located on the right side of the vehicle, unlatching them from the outside and standing back, door in hand, to allow the people within to disembark. Before anyone could exit, a crier in a shining, black satin suit rushed in and plopped a short wooden step just outside the door so as to assist their passage.

"Elden, would you care to lead the way?" Marigold offered to the only other guardsman in the teal colours of House Tullivan.

"Yes, of course, my lady, it would be my honour," the now awake and alert guard replied dutifully, jumping from his seat to take the point. On the ground, Elden greeted the Mattersly guardsmen and crier and took a moment to answer some questions that the thin, little old man in satin seemed to have. Once done, Elden beckoned the others to follow.

The crier cleared his throat and stood to attention, "Gentlemen and fair ladies of Mattersly Castle, may I introduce you to Marigold Tullivan, Lady and Heir Apparent of Daol Bay, and Interim Lady of the Western Realm, and her retinue."

As the man continued with naming the members of Marigold's party, the entire group stepped out into the mildly cool and crisp air of what Tippard residents called a winter's evening. Having said the names of Gallin, Wyla, the soldiers, and the rangers, the little fellow paused upon glancing at Moya, and for a moment, he looked entirely nonplussed. "Uh, and the lady's esteemed guest..."

"Moya Starboard," Marigold informed the puzzled crier.

"Ah, yes of course, my apologies, Miss Starboard," he said quickly, as though Moya was someone he ought to know. His voice rose to its previous level and he completed the introduction, "and the lady's esteemed guest, Miss Moya Starboard."

Looking about, Marigold found her hosts strolling casually toward her from around the fountain. Side by side were Walter and Elda Mattersly, dressed in a black two-piece suit and a loose-fitting evening gown in green and white respectively. Behind them was their house steward, a hand of his pushing on the back of an adolescent male in riding leathers who looked to want to be anywhere else.

"Good evening! Good evening!" Walter greeted them with a jolly laugh. "I am so glad to see that you have arrived at last, my lady. Everyone here at the castle has been awaiting your arrival since Elda and I returned home."

"Why, Minister Mattersly, you are too kind, ser," Marigold began to say in earnest, until the crier cleared his throat to speak.

"Honoured guests, may I introduce to you-"

Walter raised a hand, his chuckling ebbing slightly. "Now, now, Frederick, Lady Marigold knows who we all are. There is no need for that. Save yourself the trouble, please."

"Minister and Lady Mattersly, I would like to thank you for hosting my party and me in your castle for the night," Marigold said, in a second attempt to begin a conversation with the Matterslys. "We are most gracious for your hospitality."

Elda stepped forward and drew Marigold into a tight hug. "The honour is all ours, my lady. I am so terribly sorry to hear of your ordeal in Pelican Harbour. Haymard Nothram is nothing more than an uncouth brute."

"I echo the sentiments of my wife fully and completely, my lady," Walter said in agreement, coming in for a hug of his own. "We were all grieved to hear of the bloodshed and violence he forced upon you and yours."

A sigh escaped Marigold in her weariness, and she went along with it. "I thank you for your concerns. It was a trying day for us all. Perhaps it can be best discussed in private at a later time, though. My friends are all in need of rest, and I fear that I am too."

The couple stepped aside, with Walter speaking for them both, "Absolutely, my lady, we will make a point to talk in a more comfortable setting before you depart for home on the morrow. In the meantime, allow us to show each of you to your accommodations for the night and give you time to wash up and rest before supper."

"That would be wonderful. I thank you both immensely," Marigold replied with a bow. When she rose, the young lad was standing in sight with his arms folded and the steward standing beside him.

"My lady, perhaps you remember our youngest son, Nathaniel," Walter gave by way of introduction as he brought the lad to stand directly before her. "He recently celebrated his thirteenth birthday and is growing into a fine young man, if I might so boldly say so."

Marigold extended a hand, and after looking to his father for guidance, the adolescent gave it a quick, loose shake.

"It is a pleasure to see you again, Nathaniel," Marigold greeted him. "I believe you were only about four or five years old when last we met."

"I had just turned five, I think. My family was in Daol Bay for the Winter's King festivities," the boy said, struggling beyond that to be conversational.

"Titles, my boy, you must remember to use proper titles," Elda corrected him, while brushing something away from the shoulder of his jacket. "You must say, 'my lady', when you finish speaking to Lady Marigold."

His face contorted in embarrassment for having been corrected. "Sorry, my lady. It's good to see you again too, my lady."

"Well met, young ser," Marigold told him with a smile. "I gather from your clothing that we have taken you away from horseback riding?"

"No, my lady. I was in the training yard, practicing with my bow," Nathaniel corrected her bluntly. "I know it's really only the elves that use a bow anymore, but I like it more than rifles and pistols. I'm getting good at it, according to my instructor, my lady."

"Is that so?" Marigold responded while glancing toward Freyard, "Well, Freyard and Glendil Archer from the Sun's Rangers here might be up for offering you a lesson before we leave. They are both excellent marksmen in their own right, with the records to prove as much."

The boy's eyes lit up. "Really? Sun's Rangers right here in Tippard? Would you two like to come by the training yard right now, then? My instructor is still there. He's good at it, but he's not 'Sun's Ranger' good."

"Nathaniel, you are bothering two exhausted men who have travelled a long ways," Walter chastised with a wag of his finger.

"It is no worry, Minister, I assure you," Freyard intervened, giving the boy a nod and a wink, "But your father is right, we are all tired. As a compromise, how about I show you a thing or two first thing tomorrow morning? Glendil and Dayden might even join us. It has been a while since we loosened any arrows, though. You might have to go easy on us."

Nathaniel's excitement seemed near to bursting at Freyard's offer. "Oh my gods, yes, I'll be there bright and early, ser. Thank you!"

"It is settled then," Marigold said happily.

"Indeed it is, my lady," Walter agreed while ushering everyone toward the castle. "Until then, shall we all adjourn to the castle? We do not get the biting colds of Daol Bay winters, but the nights are quite chilly here all the same."

Behind the Mattersly family did Marigold and her following go, walking in what was almost a straight line. Arriving at the dual lines of attendants standing before the entrance, Marigold found the entirety of them dressed in their black and white uniforms complete with overcoats and any accessories they needed for additional warmth. One at a time, she introduced herself and shook their hands, ensuring she did so with each person, regardless of where they might rank in the serving hierarchy. The expressions from the workers and the Matterslys ranged from surprised to befuddled, but Marigold insisted on showing everyone the same courtesies and respect.

Upon finishing, the castle doors swung open from inside and everyone filed into the ancient abode.

Once within the foyer, and while removing her outerwear, Marigold remarked to Walter and Elda, "I was surprised to see only one of your children in the welcoming party."

"Ah, yes, Leanne does send her regrets that she could not join us to welcome you," Walter answered on behalf of his family, "and Martel, as you know, is abroad in Berrisport in the Gildraddi Midlands, deep in his studies at their university."

"Leanne is here though, is she?" Marigold followed up quickly.

"Indeed she is, my lady," confirmed Walter in direct fashion. "Leanne is at the top of the tower at present. She is apprenticing as a laboratory technician and working to prepare for the scientists' evening activities. Though she is the daughter of those scientists' benefactor, she balks at the idea of shirking her responsibilities, even to welcome you, my lady. Her work ethic and dedication to her studies are nothing short of admirable, would you not say? Elda and I are ever so proud of her, as we are of all our children."

As she stepped within the castle, Marigold was reminded of how cavernous the Mattersly castle was compared to the Tullivan manor. Yet, in what could only be considered an architectural marvel, the castle maintained a sense of size. The foyer was not as tall as was found in the larger manors of Illiastra, but it was expansive, and seemed to have doors leading in all directions. Windowed ceilings allowed in the outside light, and an impressive crystal chandelier filled in the gaps. It was, in the words of Marigold's father, *"Equal parts opulence and efficiency."*

Even the walls, though insulated and studded out from the original brick, were painted in light, pastel colours to enhance the airiness.

"Are all our guests here?" Elda asked while working her way through the gathered until she found her way to Marigold. While slipping a hand around Marigold's arm, Elda raised her voice to be heard. "Alright everyone, we have set quarters for all our guests to stay in and our butler, Mister Habischer, shall see to it that all of you are directed there."

She leaned into Marigold's ear then, "except for you, my dear. I will show you and your handmaids to your quarters personally. Let us take a walk together, shall we?"

Not wanting to sound rude, Marigold accepted and called on Wyla and Moya to follow. Together, the four of them made for the third floor of the castle, starting with a winding staircase found just to the left of the receiving room that lay beyond the foyer.

At the door to the guest chambers, Elda released her hold on Marigold and took the doorknob in hand. "Here we are, my dear. Please, make yourself at home."

The inside of the chambers turned out to be every bit as bright and welcoming as the rest of the castle had been. The walls were a shade of blue that made Marigold think of a robin's egg and adorned with vibrant pieces of landscape art displaying lush green fields and glistening lakes. A large, soft canopy bed stood at the wait for her to climb beneath its covers, and a small shelf of books, a long dressing stand, and a chest of drawers filled the rest of the room. It was the same chambers that Marigold and her family would occupy during visits, and though the layout of the furniture was as she remembered it, everything else felt different and alien to her.

"The guest quarters have been given a brand new look, Lady Elda. I quite fancy it," Marigold commented politely. In truth, she was only mildly interested in interior decorating at the best of times. A trait that Marigold had to figure came from both of her parents.

The lady laughed in answer. "Oh my, Lady Marigold, you do jest. With it being such a long time since your last visit to Mattersly Castle, it is only natural that we would refresh the guest rooms in that span."

Marigold paused in her tracks, giving the matter some thought for a moment. "You are certainly right about that. When I conjured up the memory of my last visit, it came to me so vividly that it seemed like it was but yesterday."

With a humming noise, Elda turned to Wyla and Moya. "Ladies, perhaps you would like to see your own quarters? They are right through the door to the left of you. We recently redid that room as well and I would much like to get your opinions on our decorative stylings."

"Yes, Lady Elda, I think we will do just that," Wyla responded cordially, taking Moya with her as she went.

With a few shuffled steps, Marigold found herself before the large bed that she was given for the night. A hand of hers ran over the soft, satin bedspread, coloured a shade of blue just slightly darker than the walls, with white flowers embroidered across it.

Slowly, Marigold lowered herself onto it. "Lady Elda, might I ask you a question?"

"Why certainly," Elda said concernedly. In wisp of the skirts of her long, green and white dress, she was seated on the bed beside Marigold. "Whatever is on your mind?"

"Do you... Do you miss your parents?" she stammered out with a shuddering heave, entirely unsure where it even came from. "They have been gone a long time, have they not? Does it get easier...? Not having them, I mean?"

Elda wrapped her arms around Marigold and drew her into a tender hug. "Oh, my poor dear, you have been through so much in such a short time. The answer to your first question is 'yes'. Every day I think about my mother and father, without fail. A week, a season, one year, ten, twenty, it made no difference how long they were gone, for I miss them all the same. Yet, I will say that it does get better, darling. It may seem like an eternal struggle, but in bits and pieces your life will come together again."

"Thank you, Lady Elda," Marigold replied, leaning into her shoulder slightly. "I have been finding myself getting overwhelmed at random since Father passed. It seems like the most innocuous of things loosen these feelings, and I'm practically immobile until they pass."

"My parents both went peacefully in old age," Elda told Marigold with a sigh. "My mother was the first to go. Her health had been steadily failing for some time, and then the gods saw fit to mercifully take her while she slept. Not a season later, my father followed her in the same way. I always felt it was a lonely, broken heart that claimed him. It hurt then, and by the gods, it still does. However, my siblings and I sent them into their eternal rest knowing that they had both lived a long, full life and that both of them had left the world as painlessly as possible. That is all one could ask for with what is an inevitability of our existence. Yet, in your case though, you were denied that simple security."

There was a silence then, as though the world had been emptied of all sound, leaving just the two of them. Everything that Marigold had felt in the past few weeks seemed to come forth in a wave as the quietude set in. Elda seemed to sense as much and wrapped her arm across Marigold's shoulders for comfort as she continued talking. "You know that Walter and I have always regarded the Tullivans as family, Marigold. Our whole house wept when your mother and brother disappeared. Walter vowed to stand with Marscal should he want to oppose House Palomb, as did nearly all of the western ministers in their turn, except for Haymard Nothram and his loyal toads, of course. Even Lord Greggard's father joined Walter's petition, and you do not need me to tell you how much of a rivalry that the Simillons and Tullivans used to have in those days. Walter called what happened to Farren and Felixander *the wound that lays bare the rot beneath the skin of Illiastra,* and ever since then, he has been waiting for a day to rise up against House Palomb and their ilk.

"What pain it had been for us, as close friends of your parents, is only a prick of the finger compared to the heartbreak that you and your sister must have felt. I spent many of my days fretting over you two back then, and I still do to this day, albeit for different reasons. As though that were not enough, you have had to grin and bear your way through your sister's disappearance and your father's illness. It is as though the storm you face knows no abatement."

Marigold felt Elda's thumb whisking away a tear on her right cheek, and she let her clear it while raising her own voice. "Now Lewcas is gravely injured too, or possibly dead, for all I know. It is as much as I can do to get out of bed most days."

"I envy your strength," Elda confessed with a shake of her head. "I do not know that I could muster the kind of energy it would take to carry on after what you have been through. You are an inspiration to us all, and I say that as both a woman and the Lady of House Mattersly."

"I believe we have a long fight ahead, us women," Marigold added, a tingling sensation of resolution running through her suddenly. "It will be exhausting, as it is only just begun and I already feel depleted, but I do so strongly feel that our course of action is indeed the right one."

Elda seemed to find amusement in something Marigold said, and relayed as much. "I do hope that when you refer to the collective 'our' that you are including Lady Orangecloak and her Thieves, too. As far as my opinion goes, that poor girl was the lifeblood of the movement until those curs in Atrebell took her down. We would be long to forget that whatever we build from here, it was she who set the foundation.

"You know, it always amazed me to no end how much loathing Lady Orangecloak stoked in Grenjin Howland and his cohorts. All she had to do was inform people of the horrible things that the Merchants and Triarchists were committing, and the lot of them went utterly berserk in their efforts to kill her."

"They fear her as much as they hate her," Marigold added when Elda took a moment to take a deep breath.

"My greatest regret is standing by silently when those savages delivered Orangecloak into Grenjin Howland's hands," Elda stated sadly. "I promised myself that I would not be so cowardly again, and then you rose up to give me the chance to live up to my promise. Now it is up to the rest of us to continue her work. I only hope we can live up to her expectations."

Marigold turned to face Elda. "I feel that our deeds may yet be measured by Orangecloak."

"Has there been a sighting?" Elda put back to Marigold quizzically.

"Not as of yet, although I do not imagine that she would be anywhere but on a path to the Southlands by now," Marigold told Elda regretfully.

"All we know for certain is that she escaped the Atrebell manor. Her captors went missing too, and the Master of Blades, all without a trace," Elda reminded her. "Of all the compass directions that Orangecloak could run in, I would think that south would be the last that such a clever woman would point herself in. At least, I do not think that she would go that way directly, anyhow."

Marigold paused a moment to consider what Elda was suggesting before offering her own observation. "There would be quite the heightened presence of patrolmen and guards between Atrebell and the Varras River, now that you mention it. Regardless, Orangecloak would never make her presence known to highborns like you and I."

Elda seemed to agree with that point, "Not as we presently stand, no. However, I can foresee a day when such a scenario would be plausible. In the meantime, until the day comes that Lady Orangecloak emerges from the darkness and makes her intentions known, we must forge ahead on our own. I will say that if Lady Orangecloak does appear again, you would be wise to seek her out and make an ally of her. There would be no stronger alliance than what you two could make. If you thought that the EMP and the Triarchy feared Orangecloak alone, then the two of you together could petrify them where they stand."

With a ginger pat on Marigold's leg, Elda rose and moved to leave the room. "For now though, I regret to inform you that I must be off. I am expected in the kitchen to give a taste test for this evening's courses. You should take the time to decompress and relax, darling. I will see you at dinner soon."

Alone for the moment, Marigold removed her boots and laid down across the bed on her back, her eyes going to the samite canopy hanging over her head. Through the walls, Marigold could hear Moya and Wyla moving about in their own quarters. For a moment, the thought occurred to her to call out to them. Just as quickly though, it dawned on Marigold that this was the first time she had been truly alone since the tour started. Lying there as she was, with the bed slowly enveloping her, Marigold's eyes began to grow heavy, and she rolled to her side, letting sleep take her for the nonce.

A few hours passed by the time that Wyla came to wake Marigold from her peaceful nap. If she had managed to dream in that time, Marigold had no recollection of it, but she did feel rested, for once. In a matter of minutes, she was out of bed, her clothing and hair freshened up, and her face and hands cleaned for supper with the Matterslys. That evening, the entirety of her retinue was invited to dine on a main course of honey-glazed duck. Over the course of the meal, Marigold, Gallin Myakys, and the elder Matterslys carried the conversation, which was light and small on account of the company of the youngest Mattersly.

For her own part, Moya stayed entirely silent, save for responding to the servants who asked her questions relating to the meal.

During the serving of a dessert of pumpkin pie and hot beverages, Walter struck up a discussion with Freyard and Glendil regarding the history of the various Archer families of Illiastra. The matter veered into the similarities between the Archer families of Collura and Ravenkeep specifically, and Walter remembered that most of the Archer houses had nearly identical arms differentiated usually only by their colourations. After he challenged himself and failed to remember the specific colours of Freyard and Glendil's houses, Marigold took the opportunity to raise a question of her own.

"Minister Mattersly, if you do not mind my asking," Marigold put to him in a manner that was both curious and polite. "What were the heraldic arms of your house before the rise of the Elite Merchants?"

Walter's face lit up. "Ah, and I am so glad you asked that, Lady Marigold. House Mattersly used to have a lovely shield. It bore the first longship that my family had ever built, set astride a chequered field of forest green and gold. We styled our flag differently, with three horizontal bars of green, white, and gold, from top to bottom, with the longship astride the white field. We still have a flag in the storage basements somewhere. I remember when I found it as a boy that I wanted to hang it in my room. My father would not allow it, not with the Elite Merchants bringing everyone under their one flag."

"It delights me to hear you speak so fondly of your house's heritage, Minister," Marigold told Walter while stealing a glance at a smirking Gallin. "I was recently contemplating the return of the arms of the Western houses with Gallin here. I would certainly like to see the green, white, and gold of House Mattersly flying beside the teal and gold of House Tullivan. How would you feel about that?"

The high-backed chair of Walter's creaked at the head of the table as he leaned his weight into the heavy oak. "Why, Lady Marigold, I think that is nothing short of a splendid idea. It would make these old bones proud to see a proper flag flying from the ramparts of Mattersly Castle again. Have you discussed this with other ministers yet?"

"Not beyond Minister Myakys, no," Marigold told Walter, relying on that little, white lie going no further than the dinner table. "You were the first. This idea of mine had the potential to live and die with you, but I am charmed with your exuberance for it."

"I say let the flags of our ancestors fly high on the winds of freedom, Lady Marigold," Walter exclaimed with a wide gesture of his hands. "If you would permit me, I would be glad to float the idea among my neighbouring ministers. Nayle and Norrin would be as excited as I over the notion, I assure you."

Marigold allowed herself a laugh at that. "By all means, Minister Mattersly. You may feel free to be my herald on this matter."

As Marigold had responded, a female servant who had not been part of the dinner staff entered the room from a side door and approached Minister Mattersly. They spoke in whispers for a scant few seconds before Walter pushed his chair back and rose to his feet.

"Lady Marigold, I have wonderful news," he said, the unabated joy having nowhere further to rise in his voice.

"Oh? Please, do tell, ser," Marigold replied gaily.

Walter stepped away from the table with his cloth napkin in hand, dabbing hastily at his mouth. "It seems that Leanne has a break in her work and sent Frieda to ask if you would like to come and speak with her atop the lighthouse tower for a few moments. Come, come, I will take you there myself."

"So suddenly?" Marigold queried hurriedly while standing up herself. "I would hate to leave our company."

Elda waved her away. "Go on, darling. Nathaniel and I will stay here and keep your friends company in the meantime. I am sure that Nathaniel would relish the chance to ask the rangers a few questions of his own."

"If it is alright with everyone else..." Marigold said while looking across the table at the others. The guards and rangers alike looked to her curiously, and Marigold gave a subtle flick of her fingers to let them know to stay put.

Moya, however, was giving her a pleading stare, and Marigold gathered its meaning plainly.

"Minister Mattersly, would it be asking too much if Moya came with us as well? She took a keen interest in the tower on our trolley ride to the castle, and I know that she would be appreciative if she could see the interior of it and the view from there for herself."

Walter waved Moya toward him warmly. "Why, goodness no, it is no bother at all. Come, come, Miss Moya, and be not afraid. Any friend of Marigold is a friend of House Mattersly and is as welcome as the Lady herself to see our castle in all its splendour."

With courtesies and pardons out of the way, the three departed, stopping only briefly to obtain their outerwear with the help of an attending footman. They crossed the inner courtyard, walking along a stone path that was marked and lit with electric lanterns.

At near the halfway point between castle and tower, Walter leaned in close to Marigold's ear. "My lady, I had hoped we might speak a little on strategies and tactics for the near future, but I dare not unless you feel our present company can hear what we might say."

"Of course, I have no reason to not trust Moya. Speak freely, Minister Mattersly," Marigold whispered back, knowing that Moya could see them whispering.

"I trust your judgement, my lady," Walter said before raising his voice. "Your notion to restore the heraldic arms of old is indeed a wise one. Have you given consideration to restoring the old titles too? As you know, before the EMP conquered Illiastra, the ministers were all titled 'lord' and divided into three geographically defined categories: Sealord, Mountainlord, and Greenlord. The Sealord's were all the western ministers and the Aquas Bay minister, the Greenlord's were the elected men located between Lakespere and the foothills of the great mountain chain that binds our continent, and the Mountainlords were in the foothills themselves. I feel that in tandem with the flags and banners, the title would further bolster pride in your supporters, and when it comes to the nobility, a sense of pride goes a long way."

Marigold had been nodding along with what the minister was saying, and replied when he was finished. "That certainly is worth further consideration, ser. We could add that to the legislative bill I was going to draft for the heraldic arms restoration. I think that would pass a vote among my new government, once I officially have the signatures needed to withdraw the Western Realm of Illiastra from the remainder of the country."

"You have the signatures?" Walter asked excitedly. "That is tremendous news, Lady Marigold. I wish you had said so sooner."

"I have the signatures in theory, Minister. I am short of three that would be needed to make the declaration official. I can tell you that Ministers Bickerington, Rochford, and Cheswell are all tentative signees, but until they do, I am inclined to withhold my own enthusiasm. It will soften the blow should one of the three not come through as expected."

"If Lord Greggard says that Harold Bickerington will sign, then that is all I need to know," Walter stated firmly. "Vensent and Ford, though, I am much more sceptical of.... My lady, have you heard of the Blue Coast before?"

"As a matter of fact, I have," Marigold put in. "I had their origins explained to me in great detail in the recent past by Gallin Myakys, our resident historian and a member of the Blue Coast himself."

Minister Mattersly hummed aloud. "Yes, it had slipped my mind that he was of the Blue Coast as well. Then, you have met with their leader, I take it?"

"Indeed I have, Minister."

They had arrived at the base of the tower while still talking. As Marigold was about to begin her ascent of the outer staircase leading to the landing, she was stopped by Walter gingerly tugging on her arm.

"My lady, forgive my doubt and boldness, but I do hope that you have not entwined yourself too deeply with Minister Morton in order to obtain an arrangement for a few signatures," his voice was total concern, with all hints of the usual jolly demeanour having vanished.

"Why Minister Mattersly, what issues do you have with Minister Morton?" Marigold asked in return as worry began to course through her.

"Eamon Palomb is my issue," Walter explained gravely. "It is well known that Eamon has corrupted Samhais' manor from the cellar to the ceiling. I worry that anything said to Sam will be known to Eamon before you can act on it. Even if you were not directly listened to, Eamon's stooges might still squeeze Sam for information if they suspect anything. It is too dangerous to deal with House Morton, not until the infestation there has been dealt with. Tell me, did he ask you to help him with that? Did he ask for soldiers or financial aid to help him hire an army of sellswords?"

Marigold's eyes went to the ground, and then to Moya, who knew nothing of the meeting and could offer little but a puzzled glance and a shrug.

I need only tell him the basics, I suppose.

"We spoke in secret, in a hidden location known only to those in attendance and the people who maintain the hideaway. There was no one from Minister Morton's household, besides a sellsword bodyguard, that could slip what we talked about to the Palombs. Of that I am sure."

"But there was an arrangement, my lady?" Walter put back to her quickly.

"Yes, there was."

"What did he want in return for the signatures of the two ministers?" Walter continued on, rattling off questions faster than Marigold could address them. "We both know he did not merely offer them without some form of compensation. Might I ask what he requested? Was it favours? Power?"

Marigold extended a hand, palm out in a calming gesture. "Minister Mattersly, please contain your excitement. I assured Minister Morton that our arrangement would be confidential at this time, and I will keep my word, make no mistake. What I can tell you is that the arrangement is definitely to our benefit. Samhais was eager to join us, after all, but he could not merely give me the signatures. *Everything has a price*, as my father used to say."

"He was a wise man and a devoted friend, your father," Walter responded with a deep sigh. "Very well, Lady Marigold, I will leave it to you and assure our compatriots that you have everything in hand, should they ask me." With a hand extended in the direction of the door at the top of the stone stairs, Walter beckoned to both of his guests, "Ladies, after you."

Inside the tower, they found a small living space, cosily warm from a crackling fireplace. Oil lamps hung in sconces on the circular stone walls, providing enough dim light to reveal a winding, iron stairwell at the back end of the living area.

Walter removed his black woollen coat and hung it on a rack of hooks bolted into the backside of the heavy outer door. Ever so gently, he helped Marigold and Moya out of their cloaks, and made a point to hang the garments on a separate rack beside the fireplace. With that done, he pointed to where the stairs sat, "We go that way, ladies, and once again, it is at your leisure."

Climbing the stairs was a task in itself, as Marigold and Moya spent as much time stepping as they did waiting for Minister Mattersly. At every dozen steps or so he required a brief pause to catch his breath, and by the third such break, the sweat running from his head was beginning to pool on the white collar of the shirt of his evening suit.

"Go... Go on without me... Ladies..." Walter told them politely while huffing and puffing. "I'll find... You later. I think... I think I need to sit on my own for a moment... Goodness, I believe I have grown old all of a sudden."

After further persuasion from Walter, Marigold and Moya left the company of the winded minister to continue to the top of the tower on their own. Though worried for their host, Marigold suspected that he had grown embarrassed at his struggle and simply wanted to complete the climb at his own pace and without witnesses.

The stairwell ended in the beacon room, and the pair stepped in to find the place dark and empty, save for the large, rotating electric light.

"Here I thought that the lights were all great big oil lamps. How silly of me. It's clearly done with electricity now," Moya said with wonderment while approaching the rotating machine for a further inspection.

"Are you interested in the workings of such things, Moya?" Marigold asked while going to stand at her side.

Moya turned her gaze away, looking to the windows and the darkness of the night sea beyond. "I suppose I never really thought about it before... I'm a woman, so I was raised being told it didn't matter. I'm supposed to be a wife... That's my interest. At least what I am told my interest should be, Ma'am."

"But what are you really interested in, Moya?" Marigold tried again, finding her way back into Moya's line of sight.

"I always wanted to know how to read," she replied with a shrug. "When we were in Weicaster Bay, in that bookstore waiting for you, I felt so stupid looking around at all those books and not having any idea what the names of any of them were or what was in them. Even when I did look, all I saw were squiggly shapes on paper. Dayden told me a few of the titles, and pointed out a few children's books with lots of pictures for me to look at, but that just made me feel like a baby. Learning to read would be like unlocking the secrets of all those books, so that's what I want to do first. Once I master that, I will plan my next goal."

"That's admirable, Moya," Marigold told her with a gentle rub of the back. "You know, we never did discuss what you wanted to do or where you wanted to go from here."

Moya shook her head sadly. "I don't know where I am going myself, Ma'am. I was running away before I wound up in Pelican Harbour. I really did not know where to go, I just knew that I had to leave from where I was, and that's how I wound up there, cold and hungry. A pair of guards arrested me. The two of them were both bigger than me, about the size of Elden probably. One of them could have taken me to jail with one hand. Instead, one threw me onto the sidewalk on my face and then they both climbed on my back and clapped me in those awful irons. My wrists were raw by the time someone finally took them off me. All of that because I was a woman on my own and I was scared by two big men coming at me so quickly..."

Tears came to Moya's eyes and she looked away to wipe them. "I'm sorry, I rambled on again…"

"You do not need to say more, if you do not want," Marigold said softly while offering a handkerchief from the pocket of her trousers. "You can stay with our party and come live in Daol Bay until you know where you want to go, if you like. I have a whole manor just full of empty rooms, you could have one for yourself, and I can hire a tutor to teach you to read."

"You… You would do that just for me, Ma'am? What have I done to deserve such a kindness?"

"I have never been one to feel that acts of kindness need a reason to be given out. Yet, if there is one, I think that it is the least I can do for all the trouble you were put through for being used as a surrogate for my sister," Marigold reasoned. "You would not have wound up lashed to that pole if not for that."

The big, brown eyes of Moya fell on Marigold. "You know, I had no idea who you or your sister was until that minister in Pelican Harbour came to the jail and looked at me. None of that was your fault, anyhow. You never arrested me, tied me to a pole, and made me wear nothing but a dress in the freezing weather. You were not the one planning to kill me and the other woman."

Marigold answered first with a shake of her head. "People should not wait to help someone just to assuage their own guilt, Moya. I believe that we should help people merely because it is the right thing to do, and that alone is all the reason I need to open my home to you."

"I appreciate your kindness," Moya responded while still dabbing at her eyes with her borrowed handkerchief. "If I can think of a way to repay it, I shall do so tenfold, I promise."

"There is no need for all of that, Moya," Marigold assured her gingerly. "However, there is one thing I can think of that you can do for me."

"Anything, Ma'am, just tell me what it is, and I'll do it," Moya stated eagerly.

Marigold reached for Moya's free hand and gave it a squeeze. "You can call me Marigold. That is what my closest friends and family refer to me as."

Apprehension crossed Moya's face, and in the low light, Marigold thought she saw a little fear too. "Oh, no, Ma'am, I cannot do that. You are a proper lady and I have to call you as such. It would be rude and unmannerly not to."

"That may well be what etiquette dictates," Marigold agreed reluctantly. "But the request is coming directly from the person with the title. The rule can be cast aside at my discretion."

"Alright then, if it is what you want," Moya began with an awkward shrug. The nervousness began to ebb into a sort of smile, and she looked toward Marigold. "It sounds so easy, doesn't it? All I have to do is call you by your first name and I get to live in a huge house and take reading lessons."

From in the direction of the stairwell came the sound of plodding, clomping footsteps accompanied by audible huffing and puffing.

"My mother used to say, '*A home full of family and friends is a home full of love and laughter*'," Marigold told Moya. "She read it in a favourite book of hers, though I cannot recall which one."

That made Moya beam. "Well, maybe the two of us can solve the mystery together, once I know how to read. It can be like a treasure hunt, but in a library."

Marigold chuckled in response. "I would like that very much, Moya."

"Goodness, if I did not know better, I would think that the carpenters came in the middle of the night and built the tower higher," Walter Mattersly gasped as he came through the doorway. "I was just up here this past summer and I was not as addled as all of this. My word, I may well need to alter my diet."

"Are you quite alright, Minister Mattersly?" Moya asked, surprising Marigold to no end.

Mattersly's face was a mixture of fatigue and bafflement as it occurred to him that it was Moya who had spoken. "Why, yes I am, young lady. I merely need to catch my breath again. Thank you for asking. Moya is your name, am I correct?"

As quickly as one could snap their fingers, Moya's expression returned to its consistently nervous state. Deigning to offer a verbal response, Moya gave Walter the faintest of nods.

"My apologies if I frightened you again," Walter told Moya as he came to stand beside the two women.

"No, ser, there is no need to apologise," Moya managed to stammer out, her gaze downcast. "I pushed myself further than I was ready to go. I must've gotten caught up in the happy feeling that came over me."

Entirely puzzled at this point, Walter shared a look with Marigold, and pressed on when Moya said nothing further. "Very well, then. I am not going to pry any further into that. Lady Marigold, the stairway to the laboratory is just outside on the balcony. It is quite steep and dark, and leads to a hatch and a vertical ladder so I dare not attempt it in my exhausted state. If you or your handmaid would be so kind as to go and retrieve my daughter, I would be ever so grateful."

"I'll go," Moya blurted out, while already striding hurriedly to the sliding glass door that led to the balcony.

Once Moya had closed the door behind her and begun the careful climb up the steel steps, Marigold turned her attention back to Walter. "The handmaid designation is but a ruse, Minister. I felt you should know that."

He had already begun nodding his head and humming affirmatively. "Yes, I had suspected as much, and Elda did as well. She has a better memory for faces than I do, and she did not recognise the girl as being among your manor's regular staff. I assume her to be the woman you saved from Haymard Nothram's savagery?"

"That she is," Marigold admitted before directing the conversation to a pertinent point. "I was not aware that word had spread of Moya's rescue."

"I assure you that the information was circulated in only the most confidential of company," Walter gave by way of explanation. "Much like the Blue Coast houses, many of the nobility, both elected and otherwise, tend to bandy information about in closely-knit parties. Nayle Keeves and Norrin Obarrow, for instance, are among my personal network. Nayle is a cousin through his mother's side with House Morren out of Filkas, and he heard it from Yancey's younger brother, Lamont."

"Two houses that are presently opposed on the matter of my succession are in secret communication with one another?" Marigold deduced, making her concern clear in her voice during both that question and her follow-up. "Should I be worried that such allegiances might undermine my campaign?"

Walter lifted an eyebrow, his head cocking to the side slightly. "These allegiances date to long before your succession was even spoken of. In fact, many were fostered before you were even born, my lady. You are talking about families who live along the same coast who almost all have centuries of history behind them. There will be friends and foes among your supporters and resistors alike. As I mentioned before, Nayle's mother is a Morren, he has their blood in his veins as much as he does House Keeves. You cannot expect him to shun and expunge half of his family because they lack in support for someone to which he has no familial connection. Nayle put his name to paper for you, at great risk to himself, as we all did, and that alone should be enough to assure his loyalty to the cause."

"It seems that I have struck a nerve, Minister," Marigold noted with cautious cynicism.

"Nayle Keeves is among my oldest friends, Lady Marigold," Walter told her clearly. "He and I are closer than your father and I on our best day. Surely, you understand that I would defend him from your accusatory tone. The man has a good heart and he will serve you loyally because it is the right thing to do, just as I do. His maternal family, though seemingly opposed to you, are largely sympathetic to your cause. You recall Lamont, the Morren brother that I mentioned?"

"Yes, of course. I have met Lamont before myself on a few occasions," Marigold informed him.

After gesturing affirmatively to Marigold, Walter continued, "He advocated for Yancey to join you, as did two of their sisters. On the other side of that, Yancey's councillors voted three against two to oppose you, and so that is the way House Morren ultimately decided to lean. By the way, that valuable piece of information came to you courtesy of Nayle via Lamont."

Walter took a moment to adjust the lapels of his jacket and compose himself. "I apologise if I came across in my delivery as heated, Lady Marigold. Yet, I admit that you have wounded me by believing that I would consort with those who would do harm to you, a woman I regard as fondly as nieces that share my actual blood."

Shame settled deeply into the pit of Marigold's stomach and her eye contact broke away from Walter Mattersly briefly. "I offer my apologies, Minister. As you said, I have caused you grief in my rush to judgement and that was unduly done. I am terribly sorry for that. I hope that you can forgive me."

He sighed heavily and stepped forward to pat Marigold on the shoulder. "You are forgiven, Lady Marigold. Nevertheless, if I might offer you some advice: you would do well to give thorough assessment to all situations before casting judgement, going forward. Among friends, such rash statements are easily amended, yet with strangers and foes, those slights are not easily forgotten. You must learn to walk a tightrope, knowing that each measured step could be the difference between life and death."

"I agree, ser," Marigold uttered repentantly. "I regret my words deeply, I assure you."

"There were many reasons why I so eagerly supported your cause, my lady," Walter continued on, counting said reasons off one by one with his fingers. "First, I wished to honour the legacy of your father and mother. Secondly, the EMP and the Triarchy do far more harm than good, and their reign is in desperate need of an end. Thirdly, or at least in addendum to the previous point, is that Eamon's twin sons are not fit to rule. The penultimate reason is that although you are young and inexperienced, you show an open mind, an eagerness to learn, and seem to be absorbing every bit of advice given to you like a sponge. From what I have seen thus far, I believe that you are growing to be every bit the leader that Marscal was and more besides. Even with all of that said, the primary reason I am behind you so unequivocally is about to walk down that ladder out there."

It was Marigold's turn to be perplexed. "Why, thank you, Minister, for saying as much. I will endeavour with everything in my power to live up to your expectations. Now, if I might ask, why would Leanne above all be your main reason for supporting me?"

A deep chortle emitted from somewhere within the minister and his face lit up in a warm glow. "My dear Leanne is my pride and joy. Everything good I have ever done in this world is reflected in my darling daughter. Illiastra is... If you will pardon my language, it is well and truly fucked up. The Elite Merchants, of which my father freely joined and I willingly maintained allegiance to, is largely responsible for this sorry state of affairs. We have let this country dive into the chamber pot and let it stew there for nearly a century. The EMP gave unchecked power to religious zealots and we allowed our beautiful and pristine lands to be ravaged by the Palombs' lust for oil and minerals. Despite a heavy opposition of western ministers, our government sanctioned the wholesale slaughter and expulsion of the Amaroshan half-elves. Amongst our own, we were no less cruel. For Ios' sake, human women lost the right to be recognised as persons.

"Ponder this: your Gildraddi foremothers were considered persons with their own autonomy, but not your Illiastran grandmother, and certainly not you, your sister, or Leanne. Even sweet Farren, as much as Marscal tried to shield her with the rule of exception and her royal Northern Gildraddi lineage, was barely considered a person here. It is not just women either: even men have less rights and liberties than they did a full century ago. Can you believe all of that?"

"Believe it, ser?" Marigold asked incredulously. "With all due respect, I lived it."

"You have, and no part of it is right," Walter agreed readily. "Think of what the other nations of the world have accomplished since the EMP came to power. The Gildraddi nations all found peace with one another, and through open-border partnership and trading, have collectively become an economic powerhouse union. Prior to the EMP, Illiastra was considered the pride of the human world. The Gildraddi nations now lay claim to that title. In our present state, there is little that Illiastra could do to challenge Gildriad's claim.

"Thanks to extensive mediation efforts by Cabathos, the Crescent Isles are enjoying their first recorded decade without war. Even corsair and pirate activity is on the decline there. The Johnan coastal cities are still at odds with the Manobius interior, but both sides have resisted the urge to descend into bloodshed thanks to further efforts by, whom else, Cabathos. The country of Drake is home to the premier human minds on the front lines of scientific advancement. Every new discovery, invention, and refinement of existing concepts has a Drakian, elven, dwarven, or an Amaroshan name attached to it.

"Speaking of our northern neighbours right here in Illiastra, The elves were the first to harness electricity, and did so exclusively through clean methods alone. Think about that. Even though we have geographically isolated those same elves, and inundated them with thousands of half-elf refugees, they and the Snowy Dwarves both continue to flourish in the harsh northern reaches of the Illiastran continent.

"So what do we have to show for a century of EMP and Triarchy joint leadership? We have receded into a male-dominated, totalitarian, theocratic shadow monarchy. Illiastra, the country, is a failure through no one's fault but our own. We allowed ourselves to be blinded by greed and religion while the rest of the nations of the world work diligently to better themselves and each other.

"With my ignorance and tacit silence, that is the legacy that I almost left behind. I was just another cog in a machine running in reverse."

The lapse in Walter's speech allowed Marigold an opportunity to speak, and she did not let it pass. "How easy is it for us to stand idle while someone else endures cruelties at the hands of our own kin? My grandmother wrote in her diary, *'The Illiastran man can look away today, for it is Amaroshan people hanging from the gibbets. He can justify the Triarchy patriarch putting a woman to the whip, because she broke rules that only women are forced to abide by. The gays are being marched down the road in chains at the stroke of dawn to build the rich man's palace with free labour, but that is no bother to the Illiastran man for he is not queer. It will never be him fastened to that line of iron links. In fact, the Illiastran man can endure any number of atrocities, because it is always someone else's pain and suffering, and he is but a witness to it. Be it his neighbours or people living a thousand leagues away, the white human, Illiastran man can be indifferent to their misery, because it is not him. It is someone else who looks and acts nothing like him that is being tortured, oppressed, and slaughtered.*

"Tell me though, what happens when the different people are gone, and suddenly the powers-that-be decide that the silent Illiastran is the last one they have left to exploit? Whom will the Illiastran man ally with now that everyone else is dead? Who will stand for the Illiastran man, when he could not be bothered to stand for anyone?'

"I committed that piece to memory, Minister," Marigold told him when she finished the recitation. "I hid grandmother's diary away after that, where no one but Serephanie and I would think to look."

Though they made brief eye contact while Marigold spoke, Walter was looking beyond her by the time she finished, his line of sight going off into the darkness over the sea. His throat trembled as he opened his mouth to speak, "Lady Maisera... She was as wise as the summer days are long. Your grandmother was not wrong, Lady Marigold. Many others like me did and do stand idle, right to this very minute, and damn well most of my contemporaries would gladly continue to do so with startling apathy. I was admittedly and regrettably no different for many years. That is, until Leanne came into this cold, cruel world. When I held that tiny, bubbly bundle of joy in my arms, I knew I could not in good conscience allow her life to be lived in as despotic a place as Illiastra had become. On that day I vowed to all present, which was my wife, our steward, the doctor who delivered the child, and the captain of our house guards, that I would strive to make Illiastra a place that Leanne would be proud to call home."

A single tear had begun a lonely descent over Walter's rosy, wrinkled cheek then, and he cleared his throat before going on, "I could not live up to that vow, try as I might. Discussing anything other than strict devotion to the ideology of the EMP and Triarchy is treason, after all. It was in only the most trusted of company could I even broach such subjects, and even then, fear prevailed over all of us, your father included. There was no chink in the armour to stab at, or at least that is what we told ourselves, because we were all too cowardly to look for one."

Walter was looking at Marigold then, his hands shoving in the pockets of his trousers. "Twenty odd years on, and I now have three children, and the oldest one is not entitled to inherit a single copper from me because of her gender. Until this point, the only thing I could hope to do for Leanne was to either arrange for a decent husband or ensure that her brothers would not evict her from the castle after I am gone."

His head shook, and he laughed almost sadly. "The first option is problematic, as no matter which man is chosen to wed Leanne, he would have to do so knowing that she is incapable of loving him in the way he might want. Of course, I have no doubt that my sons would house Leanne, but I cannot say with certainty that any wife that either lad would take would feel the same way.

"The damn truth of it all though, is that whole thought exercise breaks my heart," Mattersly admitted with regret clear in his voice. "Because not only is Leanne my oldest, but she actually has an interest in leading the household in my stead that neither of the other two have."

That revelation surprised Marigold as much as it delighted her. "I had no idea she was so eager to step into the role."

"Oh yes, and she has sought such since she was a teenager, my lady," Walter said with noted enthusiasm. "Traditionally, the duty would fall to the eldest son, who in our case is our second born child, Martel. As you know, he found greater interest in the sciences, and left to study in the Gildriad Midlands. The Weicaster University would have gladly accepted him, but Martel wished to learn at the feet of those whose knowledge came without religious restriction and bias.

In the latest letter that Martel wrote to us, he indicated that he has chosen physics as his leading field. By now, he will be well into his first semester, and I am certain that he is excelling. He has no shortage of smarts, our Martel. Apparently, he even found time to court a young Gildraddi woman. Both of those things tell me that the Midlands have afforded him a life that our country never could. Lady Elda and I both have our doubts that he will ever return home for more than a visit.

"Though only thirteen, Nathaniel seems to be investing himself in a career as a ship's captain. Whether he will pursue that through the navy or private enterprise remains to be seen, but the fact remains that he would rather sail ships than build them."

He smiled then, in a way that carried both pride and sadness. "Both of my lads will be fine, they have the noble birth and finances to see them set into adulthood so that they might pursue whatever they fancy. Poor Leanne though, I can give her nothing but a loveless sham marriage to some other lordling, despite my promises to the contrary. As a woman, she is entitled to less than any man is, but she is different again from most women, Lady Marigold. Leanne has no interest in the traditional womanly pursuits of motherhood and housekeeping, not even in the slightest. She spends much of her time up here in the tower, charting the stars with Professor Glast. If not here, she is working at the offices of my company. For leisure time, Leanne organised a secret little athletics club in the rear courtyard with a few other women. Furthermore, unless we have company that would take umbrage with her attire, Leanne will never wear a skirt of any kind. It is trousers or nothing, for that woman."

"Why did you wait until now to act on your vow, given everything you have just told me?" Marigold asked him gently.

"I amended the vow, at least to myself," Walter revealed woefully. "I promised that if I saw a seedling of opportunity begin to grow into recognisable change in this country, that I would water it and help it blossom. When I saw you standing there at the reception after your father's funeral, speaking so proudly of the Illiastra you wanted to see to fruition, I saw Leanne. I saw my vow come to life, at long last, and with but a glance to Elda to confirm our choice, I leapt to your side."

While exuberant to hear that at least one person was taken with her words that night, Marigold still held doubt. "What about Lady Orangecloak? Would she and the Thieves have not met your criteria for a seedling of change?"

That drew a humoured scoff from Walter, and their eyes locked again. "A highly improbable, if not entirely impossible suggestion, Lady Marigold."

"What makes you say that, Minister?" Marigold posited with an added point. "Who else could have used the support of a wealthy benefactor than the poor and beleaguered Thieves?"

"Have you heard Orangecloak's protests?" Walter asked rhetorically in a flat voice, not waiting for a reply. "Our vigorous friend from the Southlands would never work with the likes of me. On the contrary, she would see every last member of the Elite Merchants ripped out of our homes, separated from our assets, and thrown to the mercy of the citizens she rightfully claims have been oppressed by our authority. That would include me, Gallin Myakys, Greggard Simillon, and all the other ministers you are counting on, and until his passing, it included Marscal too."

Marigold thought about what Walter was saying, and drew the conclusion that he was leading her to. "You needed unrest from within the EMP."

"Indeed so," Walter confirmed without pause. "Please do not mistake me, though. I do think that Lady Orangecloak would be an excellent partner in what is to come, should she surface again and be in a position to want to fight."

The glass door leading to the beacon room balcony slid open while Walter had been talking. A smiling Moya entered the room ahead of a woman in brown suspendered trousers and a white blouse, its sleeves rolled to the elbows. The once unruly head of long brown curls was cut back to a manageable mop, but otherwise, Leanne Mattersly had not changed since Marigold had last seen her.

"I hope you will forgive our tardiness, Mari," Leanne said on approach in a light-hearted manner. "Your new friend was just so taken with the laboratory, and it simply would not do to dampen her enthusiasm, so I gave her a full tour."

Moya was at Marigold's side then, her excitement bursting forth. "Lady Leanne let me look through the telescope. She and the professor were studying a whole other world they found among the stars. Can you believe that? A whole other world, and who knows, it might be just like ours."

A hearty chuckle came forth from Leanne's direction. "We prefer to call them planets rather than worlds, if truth be told. Nevertheless, yes, we did find a new one in recent weeks, and the professor allowed Moya to see it for herself. Although, we are unsure if there is life on it, or even if it can foster life, for that matter. It might be that it can, and certainly, that is fun to imagine."

"Thank you, Lady Leanne, for allowing me to see that," Moya told the other woman appreciatively.

"Oh, you are so very welcome, Moya," Leanne replied gaily. "It is so rare that we get a visitor to the laboratory who is quite so curious about it all. By the way, it is just Leanne. My mother is the lady of the house, and none of that 'Miss' stuff, either. Leanne will do well enough."

Moya took on a look that was almost nervousness, yet it was far from the usual state that Marigold had come to know. "I'm so sorry, Leanne. I did not know. I thought all noblewomen were called 'Lady', like Marigold."

"It is an easy enough mistake to make, Moya," Marigold reasoned. "I would think nothing of it."

In a split second, Marigold was drawn into a hug by Leanne, cutting her off in mid-sentence.

"Oh, Mari, it is so good to see you again. You are as radiant as ever," Leanne said while still holding tight. "It has been such a hard road for you, my old friend. I wish that I could have been there to help you through everything."

Marigold held her out to arm's length. "I missed you too, Leanne. It has been far too long. How has life been treating you?"

"Decently, I should say," Leanne replied, her voice increasing in seriousness. "I suspect it will only get more interesting from here on out."

That struck Marigold oddly, "Oh? Why might that be?"

"Well, on account of you, of course," Leanne offered as an answer. "Father has filled me in on the details of all your latest work. It seems that thanks to you, the Illiastra we were born into is no more. We are into strange and unfamiliar times now, and that will have a direct effect on all of our lives, but especially for the likes of you, Moya, and me."

"I think we are still a considerable distance away from any marked change, if I am being perfectly honest," Marigold countered with melancholy, having let her arms fall back to her side. "I am three names short of a majority of western ministers. Two are slated to sign on my return voyage to Daol Bay, and a third should follow shortly after, so long as he bestirs himself from the north. For all my effort, all I can do with that majority is ask one among the ministers to table a motion to have me declared the Warden of the West. While I wait to be named to that position, I have to convince at least one more of my city councillors to have me acclaimed as the official interim Minister of Daol Bay. It needs to be official, for strictly speaking, I already am the minister. Though, as a woman in waiting of betrothal, the title is purely ceremonial until that husband arrives."

"Yes, I would not want to utter Pyore's name either," Leanne added with bile in her voice.

"Oh no, did you not hear?" Marigold asked in feigned exaggeration. "I am engaged to Eldridge now. The two wretches swapped because my personality is too bold for Pyore's *'limited temperament'* as Eldridge so put it. By now though, they have surely heard of my rebellious intentions, so they might have switched again. It is just much easier for me to use no names, at this point."

Leanne laughed loudly. "What a bloody farce, Mari. *'Bold personality'* he said. What do they think you are a racehorse? Having to marry Eldridge instead of Pyore though, that's like the old adage where you take an arrow to the foot instead of the throat."

"You could not be more right," Marigold responded, chuckling along with her old friend. "Of course, you know that the real work only begins once I am Warden of the West. We have to secede, and begin the process of building a new, autonomous nation, and that will require that we draft entirely new versions of the constitution and bill of rights, then there will need to be a redress of the laws. It is a long, tedious road ahead before we are unbound from the old ways."

"It goes without saying that the east will challenge the legality of the west's secession," Leanne reminded Marigold. "They will never recognise you as Warden of the West, and therefore, any measures you take to remove the west from the nation of Illiastra will be considered null and void as far as they will be concerned."

"And that might well be enough to start a civil war," Marigold sighed, finishing the thought.

Leanne stared briefly out into the night sky beyond the beacon tower. "Why do they call it *civil* war anyway? The two words do not belong in the same room together."

"I digress though," Marigold stated, attempting to bring the conversation back to the original point. "This nightmare of a tour is but an opening salvo, and I am quite nearly exhausted already."

"My lady, that reminds me," Walter jumped in, having wandered off to the windows while the two women were talking. "If it is not untoward of me to ask, have you given any thought to what action you would take against Haymard Nothram for the murder of one woman, the attempted murder of a second, and your attempted assassination?"

Marigold turned her whole body in Walter's direction. "As a matter of fact, I have. Nothram will be stripped of his position, of course. Once we secede, the regional seat of Pelican Harbour will be considered vacant until a proper election can take place. Nothram himself will be charged with murder and attempted murder, and efforts will be extended to bring him and his conspirators to justice. He will resist, and insist that he is not party to the laws of an independent Western Illiastra. If it comes to that, I will send what force is required to drag him out of hiding so that he might answer for his crimes."

At Marigold's side stood a gobsmacked Moya. "You... You would do all of that over what happened to me and the other woman?"

"Haymard Nothram fully intended to kill two people in cold blood just to send some chauvinistic message to me. You and the slain woman are people, your lives have value and meaning, and they are not Nothram's to end without warrant. There must be consequences for such heinousness."

"What of the attempt on your own life, Mari?" Leanne queried when the opportunity arose.

"As to that," Marigold replied ruefully. "Having been unable to investigate the matter of the intruder aboard my train car, I am unable to prove beyond speculation that Nothram was responsible for wounding Lewcas and attempting to assassinate me. Until I can question Nothram regarding the incident, I will be unable to press charges against him for those particular crimes."

"Regardless of that, you should not wait to charge Nothram for the remaining charges any longer than you absolutely have to, Mari." Leanne advised sternly. "As soon as you have the Wardenship, you need to pursue him. Should you delay, Nothram and his brethren will feel emboldened by your lack of response and will continue to engage in repugnant behaviour against you. Both halves of Illiastra must see that those acting in poor faith will not be tolerated. Our country needs to see a leader who is prepared to mete out justice where it is so needed. Only then will Nothram's ilk be persuaded toward peace, and not a second before."

Their eyes locked and within Leanne's gaze, Marigold saw a passionate fire burning. Yet, Marigold felt that her friend was overlooking something, and spoke up on the presence hovering above their intentions. "There is also the issue of the Triarchy, who have a presence in every single city and village from here to Tusker's Cove. They are men who believe themselves to be imbued with the divine will of Ios. I will not sway such bent minds so easily."

"One step at a time," Leanne stated with a confident, sly grin. "We will deal with the Triarchy after the bell tolls for Nothram."

"What do you mean by *'we'*?" Marigold inquired with curious excitement.

Leanne let the grin grow wide as Marigold hit on the use of *'we'*. "I think I would much like to participate in your revolution. My parents and I discussed it at length after they returned from their last visit to Daol Bay, and with your permission, I would go with you, as the representative of both Tippard and House Mattersly."

"My daughter speaks truly," Walter chimed in, now standing at Leanne's side. "There is no one I trust more to speak on behalf of our house. As you saw just now, travel is not for these old bones anymore. I can barely handle a stairwell, let alone the rigorous schedule that someone within your counsel would be expected to endure. I am of best use to you right here in Mattersly Castle. Leanne though, she is exactly the bright, young, mind that would be a boon to your cause. I have never been so sure of anything else in my life."

"I would more than welcome you, Leanne," Marigold declared elatedly. "The Tullivan Manor is yours to call home for as long as you wish."

Without prompt, Leanne knelt before Marigold, her eyes downcast. "Then, I hereby swear to serve you with the utmost devotion and to counsel you to the best of my abilities. With these words, I vow to serve my house, my region, and my country with the dignity befitting the station that you would bestow to me, and to do nothing that would bring dishonour to the aforementioned or yourself, Lady Marigold."

"You knelt before me as Leanne, a daughter of House Mattersly," Marigold said in response, having heard her father recite as much to the western ministers when they would reaffirm their pledge after elections. "Rise now as Leanne, Representative of House Mattersly, and the region of Tippard. House Tullivan accepts your pledge of fealty, and if fates allow, Daol Bay and the Western Realm of Illiastra will accept your pledge too."

22
MARIGOLD

The foliage of the Tullivan Manor gardens had gone into slumber, blanketed into wintery sleep by the pure white snow. The tiny pond was yet to freeze, and the family of ducks that called it home paddled about, unbothered by the cold.

Apart from the occasional quacking of the waterfowl, it was deathly quiet in the grove behind the pond, and Marigold basked in the silence. She was dressed entirely in black, and when she had donned her trousers, blouse, doublet, boots, and cloak earlier in the morning, it occurred to Marigold that the hue was becoming something of a uniform for her.

Behind Marigold and obscured from her sight by the hood of her cloak were soldiers and guardsmen from Daol Bay and Portsward. Each one of them had dressed in their formal military attire and volunteered to be under the command of Ser Keneth for the day, standing tall and straight at full attention by his order. The staff of the manor stood among the men in uniform, from wherever a vantage point of the grove could be found.

Further back, nearest to the manor itself, were the available members of the Sun's Rangers. Most of Freyard's unit were ranging beyond the city walls under the charge of Yarohmer Stylford, patrolling the forests for potential threats from the Eastern Realm. Those who remained at Freyard's direct disposal were the two members that had travelled south with Marigold, and a handful more that had remained in the city to act as representatives of the group in Freyard's absence.

Freyard Archer himself stood near to Marigold in the uniform she had gifted him for the trip south. Compared to the formal uniforms of the Tullivan house guards standing further back, Freyard stood out like a sore thumb. To the side of them was the assembled counsel that Marigold had come to rely on. Oire Sellars stood the closest, practically in arm's reach. Gallin Myakys was further back, at the same distance as Rory and Leonice Tullivan and Councillor Jaysen Rossadore. Leanne Mattersly was practically shoulder-to-shoulder with Moya Starboard, and lastly, having arrived just that morning from Portsward, was Greggard Simillon.

All had gathered for a solemn ceremony, one that Marigold had decided to lead herself, much to the dismay of the Triarchy clergy in the city. As she prepared to address the gathered, Marigold glanced down to her gloved hands, and a fine, varnished wooden box they clutched to her chest.

For you, my old friend. You deserve no less.

"Ladies and gentlemen," Marigold began as she turned about to face those in attendance. "We are gathered here as one, to pay our everlasting respect and thanks to Lewcas Hylesly, who gave his life in selfless defence of mine.

"To most of you, Lewcas was a comrade-in-arms. Over the course of the past day, I have heard your stories of his unwavering dedication to his duty, and his impeccable and unblemished record of service. The men in uniform gathered before me have all attested that Lewcas was the living definition of what it meant to be a soldier and guardsman in service to Western Illiastra. The high standard he set, I am told, was one that many of you sought to imitate.

"From my own witness, Lewcas was indeed the consummate professional in his role as a guardsman to House Tullivan and there was never a moment when I did not feel safe and secure in his presence. The man was dauntless and unflinching no matter the circumstances, with a calm, measured demeanour that evoked great confidence in his abilities.

"There was no doubt, from my perspective, or even that of his superiors', that Lewcas could have climbed high among the ranks of military officers. The shoulders of his uniform should be lined with stars and the sleeves ringed with filigree to nearly the elbow by now."

Marigold paused briefly and swallowing deeply, daring not to blink, lest the tears start streaming, "And he should still be here, sitting at a big desk at the soldiers' barracks where he would be instructing and commanding a battalion's worth of infantry and cadets.

"My father and Ser Keneth both attempted to persuade Lewcas to further his military career beyond the manor walls. Ser Keneth even offered to vouch for Lewcas in person to every officer that needed to hear it, if need be, but Lewcas declined all, and chose to remain a guardsman in service to my family.

"I heard about that particular meeting after the fact, and made a point to ask Lewcas why he decided to spend his days protecting House Tullivan. Lewcas was never one to shy away from a question, and he explained it to me in that candid manner to which he was so known. He said, 'This is as much of a home as ever I had, Miss Marigold, and House Tullivan is as much of a family as I could ever ask for. The only reason I would leave this station is if it was asked of me, if my presence was a threat to the family's safety, or if I made a nuisance of myself.

"I recall feeling quite sad that Lewcas was so bereft of an actual family that the people he was paid to protect would become surrogates. My father and sister felt similarly, and so the three of us decided that if we were all that he had, then we would be all that he needed."

"He was..." the words caught in her throat and Marigold let herself trail off for a moment. She shook her head and continued. "He was a quiet man, and he was often perceived as cold. Yet, I can tell you all that though he was not known for his conversational prowess, Lewcas was gentle and caring toward those who knew him. People often use outward affections and communication as barometers on which to judge a person's level of concern. Lewcas, in his own way, showed that the reserved and quiet among us are just as capable of compassion."

Marigold extended the box in her arms, the weight of it pressing her forearms into a near-strain. "These ashes are what remain of that man, and this grove is where he was at peace, so it is here that they shall be spread. May he guard over it and all of those who visit."

Darrill and Rus stepped forward at the prompt, standing to either side of her so that they might accept the box into their waiting hands. Marigold carefully removed the lid, noting Sydnee approaching her from the left with a brass cup to hand. The two exchanged items, and Marigold carefully scooped a cupful of ashes and raised it high.

"I raise this cup to Lewcas Hylesly, may he be free at last," she said to the crowd. With a quick slash from left to right, Marigold released the ashes into the wintery air. As they settled on the snow, Marigold offered the cup to Ser Keneth, and stepped back to give space for him to follow suit. One after another, each of the guards repeated what Marigold and Keneth had begun, until the snowy ground was mottled with grey. By the end, it was Brandyl and Elden holding the box, having taken over from Rus and Darrill so that they might join their comrades in the ceremony.

Lastly, there came Oire, who spread a pinch of the ashes himself. Nearly a cupful remained in the box, and Oire produced a small, ornate glass urn. Between Oire and the guards holding the box, the remnants were carefully transferred to the glass receptacle and sealed tightly.

"Ladies and gentlemen," Marigold began in addressing the crowd once more, "I thank you again for attending our service, and invite you all to join us for a reception in Lewcas' honour inside the manor. Your company would be most welcome this afternoon."

After a brief and polite applause, crunching footsteps and soft chatter filled the air. An informal line had begun to form ahead of Marigold, and before she could say anything to those milling about, Oire stepped in.

"Ladies and gentlemen, I would like to announce that Lady Marigold will be receiving your regards and wishes once we are within the manor," he addressed the crowd in a clear voice. "We thank you for your understanding in this matter."

I wonder how many times we will say the words 'ladies and gentlemen' this day. Marigold mused idly.

A hand pressed gently to her back then, and she looked up from where her eyes had fallen to the ground to see Freyard Archer at her side. "That was beautiful, Marigold," he uttered in a low voice just barely above a whisper. "How are you feeling?"

"Thank you, Freyard," she responded, before diving into his question. "I feel so very tired, as though I could sleep for a third of a season and not once rise throughout. Yet, I cannot rest. We must keep pressing on with this thing we have created."

"Just so," Freyard said, his tone calmly assuring. His arm had extended to Marigold at the elbow while he spoke. "Might I escort you to the manor?"

"A kind gesture and I thank you for the offer," Marigold acknowledged while moving to his side, unaided. "But I have no need to be carried. I would enjoy your company, though."

With a single nod and a lowering of the arm, Freyard added, "Then you shall have just that, Marigold."

Side by side, the two joined the funeral goers in their procession that was slowly making its way through the snow and into the rear entrance of the manor. Mild warmth greeted Marigold within, and she slipped from her black cloak and hung it in the closet herself.

At Marigold's request, the staff had readied the first floor sitting room to receive those in attendance, and while removing her outerwear, Marigold instructed those same guests and her servants to join her there for quiet conversation. Though Marigold's counsel in attendance understood her meaning clearly enough, the staff, soldiers, and Sun's Rangers under Freyard looked to be positively nonplussed.

"My friends, I assure you that all are invited, both today and henceforth when I call a gathering," Marigold explained with softness in her voice. "This manor, and to be sure all houses of the nobility, were once shuttered to those of lower financial and political status, and such actions were regretfully discriminatory toward nearly all within Illiastra. I cannot begin to apologise for the actions of rulers past. However, what I can do is right that wrong, and make amends for the dishonour we have done to both the citizenry, and the selfless founder of this family, Ser Davis Tullivan. I shudder to think what he, a knight of the Teal Order, would think of the classism mentality that my family upheld as members of the Elite Merchants.

"After all," Marigold added while laying a hand on the arm of Brandyl, who happened to be the guard standing nearest. "You came to pay respects to Lewcas as much as I or any lord, minister, or lady did, and you should be every bit as welcome to the reception as they. So come, one and all, and join me in the sitting room, where food, drink, and camaraderie await us."

Though reluctance and uncertainty were plain among those standing in the rear hallway, they nonetheless followed Marigold's lead into the sitting room. The fireplace within crackled, the heat from the burning logs greeting Marigold and the guests as they passed through the threshold.

A fine layout of cheeses, preserved fruits, breads, crackers, and dried meats were spread upon a centred, relocated dining table. On the wall opposite the fireplace, the orange and yellows of the fire danced off the dozens of glass bottles filled with wines and liquors that were placed on a long hutch for anyone's consumption. Sofas and lounge chairs awaited the tired, and to one corner, sat a small table and two matching seats, and upon the former, was the board and arranged pieces of Marigold's *Kings and Knights* game.

Already waiting in the room was a pair of men in suits of deep red, crushed velvet. On the lap of the nearest sat a shining flute, and his companion beside him was busily turning the tuning keys of a zither that had what Marigold thought to be an ostentatious amount of strings.

Oh good, the entertainment arrived. No one had told me whether they had, and I had almost forgotten about it myself amidst everything else happening this day.

The two men were but a pair among scores of folk musicians that had been forced to hide their talents from the eyes of the old law. Under the rule of the Elite Merchants and the Triarchy, any music that could be even arbitrarily construed as being critical of the government and its ruling religion, or not adhering to the puritanical guidelines of the Triarchy, was forbidden. Those who dared to sing or bear an instrument were under constant scrutiny. If heard giving a rendition of anything outside of the short list of approved works, they did so at the risk of being punished with startling severity. Minstrels were valuable products to Mackhol Taves, and the threat of Biddenhurst, and the horrors within, loomed above the head of every person who dared pluck an outlawed chord.

The musicians that Marigold had hired were among the most famously infamous in that regard. They owed their reputations to a combination of musical aptitude and skill, their captivating performances, and their determination to play their music with complete disregard of censorship.

As Marigold approached the pair, they met her gaze, and rose without prompt to offer a bow.

"Miss Marigold, on behalf of both Jopaire Graceford and I, we cannot begin to tell you how humbled and honoured we are to be invited to play for you and your esteemed guests this evening," the flautist greeted Marigold. A head of golden curls rolled over his shoulders during a sweeping bow that came in tandem with his opening.

Marigold offered a bow of her own in turn. "The pleasure is all mine gentlemen, I assure you. I presume you to be 'The Singing Wind' Heniello Graceford."

"Indeed I am," Heniello offered with a further flourish of his hands. "And together with Jopaire, we are The Cousins Graceford, the greatest duo of musicians ever driven into the Illiastran underground."

The second man had stepped forward by then and repeated his cousin's sweeping gesture, stepping back just as quickly so that he might resume tuning his instrument.

"Gentlemen, what you and your kin have endured for merely singing against your government is nothing short of a travesty," Marigold began with sincerity. "Though I do not know where to begin righting such a wrong, I hope that your performance tonight might usher in a new era for songsmiths and lyricists throughout the Western Realm. May your songs carry on the wind this evening, and reach the ears of those who would join your chorus. Sing and play freely, my friends."

At Marigold's invitation, the pair did as they were bid, politely excusing themselves from Marigold's company so that they might take up a position to the right of the roaring fireplace.

"Esteemed guests of the Lady Marigold," Heniello began so that they might bring the attention of the room to him and his cousin. "My name is Heniello, this is Jopaire, and we are the Cousins Graceford. Tonight we were brought to entertain you at the courtesy of Lady Marigold herself, and it is our hope that we live up to the lofty expectations set by not only such an invitation, but to the memory of Ser Lewcas Hylesly. To begin, we would like to play a particularly somber ballad from our songbook called *Sunrise through the Fog*. We do hope you enjoy."

The quiet cousin had already taken a seat, his zither positioned on his lap and at the ready for playing. As the word 'enjoy' left the lips of Heniello, the slow chording of Jopaire's zither filled the room with a wave of pure melancholy that raised goose pimples on Marigold's arms and quite nearly brought her to tears. Heniello accompanied shortly after Jopaire with his flute, weaving his tones with that of the weeping strings until it seemed that the very air was alive with music.

The flute faded to nothing, Heniello lowered the instrument, and began to sing. The haunting lyrics were almost immediately evident to be about a soldier having survived a terrible war, one that saw copious loss of life. Particularly, the soldier of the song mourned his comrades and asked the gods why he, above any, was spared.

The speaker told of the carnage and madness he had endured, laid bare the callousness of those who would glorify the bloodshed he had seen, and in a rising, final cadence, turned his anger on those in power who had sent the soldier and his friends against strangers to slaughter one another.

No doubt that may well be me that the soldier is shouting at, if it comes to war with the Palombs.

"Beautiful and frightening at the same time, is it not?" a voice asked from beside Marigold during the first verse. From the corner of her eye, she caught sight of Greggard Simillon, and Marigold had to wonder how long he had been standing there without her noticing.

"It is," Marigold softly agreed. "I cannot help but feel that the cousins chose this song to send a message to us."

Greggard seemed to consider Marigold's suggestion for a moment himself. "Well, these two are certainly not known for shying away from controversy. I would not be surprised if what you said were true. Pacifists too, are they not? That would most definitely put them in opposition to your willingness to forcefully oppose Eamon Palomb and his ilk."

"It is not as though I am completely forgoing peace discussions with House Palomb, though," Marigold added as a counterpoint.

"A great many people seem to believe that when it comes to the Palombs, you might as well be doing just that," Greggard stated flatly.

"I do not want war," Marigold reminded Greggard. "That much I have made abundantly clear, and yet, if the Palombs force my hand, I will not cower."

Greggard nodded in agreement with her. "Aye, it is quite the precarious position that you have found yourself in. *'Stuck between the cliffs and the ocean'*, as the old saying goes. My advice, if you will forgive me for giving it unsolicited, is to recognise now that you will have detractors from both sides of just about any decision you might make. You should listen to what each of them has to offer, of course, but ultimately, you must accept that your eventual ruling will surely leave at least one side or the other partially unsatisfied."

The guests offered applause at the conclusion of *Sunrise through the Fog*, and both cousins gave a bow in response.

"Do you suppose that the applause is merely an act of politeness, or is it possible that a room full of career soldiers in mourning for one of their own genuinely enjoyed the song?" Greggard asked of Marigold curiously.

"Most soldiers do not join the armed forces with the intention of being killing tools, just as they do not go in search of an enemy's sword to die on," Marigold explained in answer. "A life of peace, while still maintaining a readiness to combat the ills of the world, is usually the pursuit of a soldier."

Greggard looked impressed with the sentiment, and said as much in comment, "That is quite the observation. May I ask where you learned that from, perchance?"

Their eyes met, and Marigold could not help but wear a smirk as she told Greggard, "It came from the omnipresence of enlisted soldiers and officers in my life. You tend to learn a great deal about a vocation when said vocation is required for your safety."

"I apologise if I came across as condescending, Lady Marigold," Greggard said with sudden contriteness at her almost sarcastic response. "I did not intend to offend."

"And no offense was taken, Lord Greggard, I assure you," Marigold said with a dismissive wave before sashaying the same hand toward the table in the corner. "Perhaps you would care to join me for a game of *Kings and Knights*?"

A slender smile crossed Greggard's face. "Why, yes, I think I would," he told Marigold, continuing to talk only when they had crossed the floor to where the unoccupied table and chairs and the game they were in service to sat in wait. "I bought a copy of *Kings and Knights* solely for my daughters, you know. I had no intentions of trying my hand at the game. *'It came along when I was just too old to enjoy it'* I had said to convince myself. My oldest told me *'Why would anyone stop playing because they are old? Would you not want to play just to break up the boredom of being a grown-up?'* and she was right, you know. It certainly is a tedious existence, after all, might as well enjoy such things while our bodies still afford us the means to do so."

"She sounds like a wise girl you have there, Lord Greggard," Marigold complimented while motioning him toward the nearest chair. Marigold seated herself across from the Portsward Lord and reached for a copper coin situated in the centre of the board. "Call it in the air, Lord Greggard."

"Heads," he chose as the coin twirled away from Marigold's thumb.

She caught it in her palm before flipping it onto her wrist and announcing to him, "We have tails. I shall get us started."

"Correct me if I am wrong, but do the rules not dictate that the person with the blue figurines starts the match?" Greggard queried in puzzlement.

"Why, yes, because the blue figurines, being in the colours of the EMP, are given the advantage of being on home soil," Marigold acquiesced, before explaining her rule change. "However, I always felt poorly for the person playing with the figures in yellow, so I offer a fair chance at the first move with the toss of a coin. Plus, I will never pass up a chance to stick one to the Merchants, even if it is something as petty and unseen as eschewing the rules of a board game."

"Resistance comes in all forms, I suppose," Greggard noted before raising a further question, "I have often wondered who the figurines with the yellow tabards are supposed to represent. Certainly, there is no well-known enemy of the EMP or human Illiastra that ever dressed in bright yellow in any sort of uniformity. Do you have any idea, Lady Marigold?"

"Orangecloak," Marigold replied with calm certainty.

Greggard's left eyebrow twitched, and he reached out and picked up a yellow-clad game piece in his right hand. "Really? That seems... Unlikely," he said with a hum while looking over the paladin he had taken from Marigold's side of the board.

Marigold gave a shrug and made her first move, nudging a spearman forward one space. "It may well be nothing but rumours, but I had heard that initially the yellow pieces were to be painted orange to represent Orangecloak and her Thieves. Considering that the game was released to the public at the same time that she had succeeded the former leader of the Thieves, the rumour has at least a little merit."

"Aye, but she had not reached any level of infamy in the immediate seasons following the Yaelsville Incident," Greggard offered in debate, having replaced Marigold's paladin and made a move with one of his own infantry pieces. "She would be no more recognised to the public than the second-in-command of my household guards would."

"All well and true," Marigold agreed while continuing her spearman's lonely advance. "And as I said, likely only a rumour. There is always much outcry from the governing bodies any time Orangecloak's name is mentioned, let alone if someone dared have her even obliquely referenced in a publically consumable product."

Greggard continued a forward march of his various infantrymen toward the middle of the board while adding, "As the common phrase goes: *'The EMP are as petty as they are greedy'*"

"This coming from a member of the EMP," Marigold gently prodded. Before her on the board and behind her first spearman, she had begun unveiling what was called a mixed tactic, sending forth half of her special units and infantry while placing the others in defensive positions.

Across from her was a classic 'Specialists Forward' tactic, with Greggard's strongest units taking to the field, leading against Marigold's forces, with his weaker infantry and archers remaining behind to defend the king. "I am *'Born and sworn'*, as another saying goes. I assure you though, once I realised what I had pledged myself to, I went to work engineering its implosive demise. The problem I encountered though is that the combined forces of the EMP and Triarchy are terribly stubborn institutions, and I felt that I was entirely alone in my pursuit, both within the upper crust and in Illiastra as a whole."

"There was always resistance to the EMP, Lord Greggard," Marigold pointed out, using her turns in the game to arrange her units into a varied, 'V' shaped formation, a single paladin taking the forward-facing point.

"Pockets of resistance have cropped up here and there in the wilds, such as Orangecloak's Thieves, that much I grant you. Yet, there has never been a successful, unified front," Greggard agreed. His strongest units were now on the verge of contact with Marigold's army. "I realised that if I wanted to see that unification come to a reality, I would have to illustrate to the populace that there are weaknesses in the armoured front that the EMP and Triarchy put forward and that those same weaknesses could be exploited. There were forces outside of the country that shared my vision, and we have been working together for some time on that goal. It has been a slow, tedious process, but we reached a consensus that it could be done. We just needed the right catalyst to put our plans into motion."

"What sort of catalyst were you hoping for?" Marigold asked, now slowly advancing her front line toward Greggard's own.

"Orangecloak," Greggard answered in the same reserved manner that Marigold had used to invoke her name but a moment ago.

Marigold's gaze went to Greggard, and she held his casual expression. "You have met Orangecloak and discussed this with her?"

Greggard gave a shake of his head as an answer while calling his next move. "No. Also, my first spearman attacks your second swordsman."

"My first paladin attacks your first spear in a pincer with my second swordsman," Marigold responded in kind while moving the latter of the aforementioned pieces into place, commenting on the matter at hand secondly, "Then how did you intend to have her be your catalyst?"

"We were in the process of trying to make contact with Lady Orangecloak's Thieves so that we might finance and arm her faction," Greggard explained in carefully delivered terms. "Thus far, we have been unsuccessful. We were stymied by an inability to concoct a means of communication that would not be rejected on the suspicion of being a trap from Orangecloak's perspective. Likewise, we needed this line of contact to be untraceable to my conspirators and me should it be discovered by the wrong parties."

Marigold readied another query, "Do you know anything regarding hers and Tryst Reine's disappearances from the Atrebell Manor?"

"The point of my statement was to say that Orangecloak ultimately became unnecessary to our planning once your intentions became known," Greggard told Marigold with a visible wince. "Should she emerge, my backers and I would still be interested in supporting her cause, but you are now our primary focus, Lady Marigold."

"You would use me as your instrument of change?" Marigold asked rhetorically, in a tone that she hoped was free of indignation.

"Oh no, my lady, we would never dare," Greggard returned apologetically. "Rather, we are a small band of supporters spread across the known world who are ready to invest in your cause as you would see fit."

"Tell me something, Lord Greggard," Marigold began to say once he finished. "Are any of these investors from the Northern Kingdom of Gildriad?"

Greggard had leaned back in his chair by then, his focus squarely on Marigold and away from their game of *Kings and Knights*. "None who would be within proximity of your royal family, if that is what you are wondering."

"That is indeed what I was wondering," Marigold confirmed for Greggard while waving a hand over the game board. "It is also your turn."

His eyes lowering to the board, Greggard surveyed it for a moment before he moved a piece but a single step. "Second spear to flank your second sword. Speaking of your royal relatives..."

"We will not," Marigold said quickly. She used a finger to push one of the two archer units in the rear of her 'V' formation forward one space in a diagonal direction. "My first archer is in range to bolster all my units."

"Well, that's a precarious position I have found myself in," Greggard commented with a hum. "I call a retreat on my first spear. Your grandfather would be most interested in what is transpiring here. He should be informed, if nothing else, so that he can be at the ready to render aid if things grow desperate on our front."

Marigold shook her head in equal parts refusal and frustration. "Apparently, I cannot express often enough that I will not involve the Aurorais' or Northern Gildriad in this. This rebellion lives and dies on my shoulders. Also, I send my first swordsman to flank your first spear, which with my first paladin, second swordsman, and first archer, is enough to defeat your second spear."

Greggard craned his head over the board and examined the pieces. "Wait one moment. My second spear is not within attacking range of either of your swords."

"Our pieces are still in contact diagonally, Lord Greggard," Marigold pointed out gingerly.

"Damn..." Greggard muttered with a groan. "You will pick off the rest of my units on my retreat and my king is guarded by naught but swordsmen."

The chair beneath Marigold creaked as she sat back in it. "You have little odds of winning this match, Lord Greggard, but it would not be entirely futile to continue."

"No, no, I yield to you, Lady Marigold," Greggard relinquished, his hands raised in defeat. "It was shaping up to be a good match too, until I misremembered the rules."

As Greggard was about to push to his feet, he seemed to stop himself. "Lady Marigold, might I ask you something?"

"Absolutely, Lord Greggard," Marigold replied concernedly. "Is there something else you wished to talk about?"

"How are you feeling? I have not had an opportunity to ask you as much candidly since you returned from your campaigning in the south. You went through an awful ordeal in Pelican Harbour, certainly. Has it been affecting you in any way?"

"Of course it has, Lord Greggard," Marigold told him, her tone nearing weariness. "I would not dare act as though I am so cold as to be untouched by the terrible acts that I was witness to."

Marigold felt her veil of strength slipping for a moment, and she let out a despondent sigh. "We are at the reception of a funeral service for a man who gave his life for mine. This room should be filled with the memory of his life, and here I am, the one who should be leading it, discussing strategy. In the incident that saw Lewcas mortally wounded, a woman also died a horribly violent death, and I still do not even know her name. Yet, since the whole thing has happened, I have not been able to stop the infernal train I have found myself on. It feels as though I have been on this ride since my father passed, and I cannot make it stop. Not for him, or Lewcas, or anyone else."

Greggard exhaled and returned to his seat. "I understand, Marigold. It is as you yourself said the last time we all gathered here for a funeral reception: your opposition, well, I should say *our* opposition now, would, and have given us no alternative."

A hand of Marigold's swept over the game board. "You know, it is much like playing *Kings and Knights*. You and I followed the rules in our match, or at least we attempted to as best as each of us could remember. Imagine for a moment though, that you are playing against Eamon Palomb or perhaps one of his sons. What happens if you are playing by the written rules of the game and the Palomb opponent completely throws out the rulebook and plays by their own? Suddenly, your opponent is giving themselves multiple moves in a turn, returning eliminated pieces to the board at will, or even moving your pieces as if they were their own. How does one counter such brazen disregard of all sense of decency and honour?"

"You must first try to convince your opponent to conform to the rules," Greggard answered, seemingly having a sense of the point that Marigold was about to make. "But what if they refuse?" he asked next, his mouth turning up at one corner.

Marigold allowed herself something of a smile as well. "Then we adapt to their new ruleset on the spot, so as to even the playing field."

"In doing so, one must hope to have not lost too much in the interim," Greggard added, with one final note to follow, "Although I posit that one should remember not to race the opponent to the bottom of the well of depravity. Adaptation, not imitation, is the key."

"Oire told me that those same Palombs made it as far west as Obalen," Marigold told Greggard. Although she could not say as much with total certainty, Marigold felt that the information she was relaying to Greggard would be new to him.

"So I have heard," Greggard revealed with concern heavy in his voice. "Might I advise you to convene the others so that we might discuss what transpired? There is much to be discussed, no doubt."

Marigold masked her surprise and nodded in agreement to Greggard's question. "Yes, most certainly. Although, I believe it will be best to wait until the room empties a little further, perhaps when our evening entertainment concludes."

The musical duo attracting all the attention had been performing all while Marigold and Greggard played their *Kings and Knights* match. While Marigold had admittedly blurred on their songs during the course of the game, she gave the Cousins Graceford enough attention to notice that they were presently in the final stanza of a serenade about a long-dead Illiastran king named Malleon the Gentle-Heart.

> *Oh, it is such a fragile thing*
> *The bridge so built by the old king*
> *To cross a river of pure rage*
> *And deliver his people into a new age*
> *Yet above these currents*
> *Where family did drown*
> *Is where our Good King Malleon*
> *Earned his rightful crown*

Yet another tale of caution that the cousins no doubt want me to hear, Marigold thought to herself as she listened in, the lyrics and music ebbing away into nothingness shortly after.

At Marigold's behest, Greggard left her company to inform the needed individuals that an impromptu meeting was to be held. His departure left Marigold alone at the tiny table dedicated for playing *Kings and Knights,* and she put her focus on the musicians so that she could keep her mind distracted.

From the corner of her eye, Marigold saw the door to the sitting room creak open. Brandyl poked his head within and got the attention of Elden and Sydnee, each one presently engaged in separate conversations.

"Thank you, thank you so much, everybody," Heniello Graceford said with a grateful bow. "That was to be the end of our concert, however we have but two more songs that we would like to perform in encore for you, our fine audience, this evening." The singer then rolled his hand in the direction of Marigold, casting all attention toward her. "Of course, that is if our gracious host grants us permit."

While the thought did occur to Marigold to send the Cousins Graceford on their way, she gave the nod to let them continue playing.

Heniello bowed for a second time, and in this instance, the gesture was directed solely to Marigold. "I thank you kindly for the opportunity, my lady. I promise you that these next two songs will be to your liking."

The seated Graceford cousin took the lead on introducing the song, playing his zither at a slow tempo to a tune that Marigold almost instantly recognised.

"This song was not written by my cousin or me," Heniello told the audience above the sound of the repeated chording of Jopaire. "However, it is a song that gets requested of us at nearly all our shows. If there are dancers among us, please, I implore you to find a partner and take to the floor for *Lovers by the Brook.*

It was a favourite song of Marigold's, and indeed, she had to assume much of the Illiastran populace since it was first written and performed by a guitarist minstrel named Bryceton Damos some seven or eight years prior.

Having turned sideways in her chair to observe the performers, Marigold had only barely noticed the trio of guards approaching on her right side. Sydnee was leading the way, with Elden and Brandyl close behind.

"Is something the matter, gentlemen?" Marigold asked casually as they approached, her gaze remaining on the musical cousins ahead.

When at last Marigold glanced toward the three junior members of the manor's guards, she saw them looking between one another with uncertainty.

"Why, no, of course not, my lady," Sydnee stated on behalf of the three men.

"My mistake, I had thought that for the three of you to be before me all at once meant that something was amiss." Marigold then waved a hand toward the open area directly in front of the Cousins Graceford, where half a dozen people had come together for a waltz. "At any rate, I am surprised that you have not yet swept Moya out onto the floor for a dance, Sydnee."

Sydnee shook his head in reply. "Not yet, my lady, perhaps if time allows."

"Well, what are you waiting for?" Marigold asked, her curiosity rising as she looked between Sydnee standing before her, and Moya sitting in the opposite corner of the room on her own.

The timid new friend of Marigold's had taken a lounge chair while the room had been filling earlier. Dressed in a black silk gown from Marigold's wardrobe, Moya was presently nursing a glass of red wine and watching the Cousins Graceford play.

"Actually, my lady, we were waiting so that we might present something to you," Sydnee explained while turning his side to her, allowing Elden to step forward. In his arms there was a case wrapped in leather and roughly shaped like a guitar.

"What is this?" Marigold queried while leaning toward the three men in her seat.

Sydnee undid the clasps of the case while Elden still held it, opening the lid carefully to allow Marigold to see. "My lady, this is Tryst Reine's guitar. We took the liberty of commissioning the repairs, what with you being so occupied with tasks that were more important. It took quite a bit of work for the luthier. We thought it would merely be for him to restring the guitar, yet, as you can see, whatever blade was used to cut through the strings left a deep gouge, and the back of the body had taken a thorough scuffing as well. The luthier had to refinish the entire instrument, more or less."

With her jaw dropped, Marigold reached into the case, removed the guitar, and laid it upon her lap for closer inspection. "My word... I do not know what to say. You are right, Sydnee, I had forgotten all about the guitar, and I thank the three of you tremendously from the bottom of my heart for taking care of the repairs for me. I can only imagine that with the amount of time and effort needed to refinish the damaged areas that the luthier asked for a fair amount of coin in compensation. Please, let me know what it cost you, and I will see to it that the three of you are reimbursed."

"It was four of us, actually," Brandyl spoke up.

"That is fair enough. Who was the fourth, might I ask?" Marigold inquired, the somber faces of the three men answering as much as Elden's words as he set the case aside.

"The fourth was Lewcas, my lady. In fact, the whole thing was almost entirely his doing," Elden continued in explanation. "We were asked if we wanted to contribute to what he was intending to be a gift for you. When he, Sydnee, and I were asked to go south with you, Brandyl was charged with going to the music shop, retrieving the guitar, and paying the luthier. Beyond that, we merely acted as deliverymen for Lewcas' last offering to you, my lady."

Tears came unbidden to Marigold's eyes then as she felt the varnished, albeit still visibly scarred wood where the blade of an Atrebell guard had slashed the instrument. "Lewcas saw to all of this... I had no idea, nor am I even sure of what else to say."

"There is nothing more you *need* say, my lady," Sydnee added warmly. "I speak for all three of us when I say that we are glad that we could fulfil this last act of Ser Lewcas'."

Marigold had been running her hands silently over the strings, daring not to pluck them while Heniello and Jopaire were still entertaining. "Thank you," she managed to stammer. "This means a great deal to me."

As she sat there staring at the guitar, Marigold's mind began to wander, both to Lewcas for the final kindness he had shown her, and to memories of the previous owner of the instrument. The room began to slip away, and it dawned on her in the midst of it that her grief was consuming her. She drew herself back, and her eyes fell on Sydnee, a distractive thought occurring to her in the process. "Sydnee, you should go ask Moya for that dance."

"Oh!" Sydnee exclaimed at the idea, "But my lady, the song is all but over at this point. I fear I am too late."

"We shall have to see what the last song of the evening is, then," Marigold relented with a scrunch of her nose. "Knowing these two, we may be out of luck for dancing songs, though."

The cousins lived up to Marigold's expectations, yet their choice for a final song was one she found more than fitting.

"This song is dedicated to the memory of Ser Lewcas Hylesly," Heniello told the crowd between performances. "For whom we are all gathered here this evening. I am sure most of you know it, but for those that do not, this is *Farewell for Now*."

"There will be other dances with Moya, Sydnee," Marigold told them while setting the guitar back into its case.

Standing as tall as she could, Marigold walked around the three to the liquor cabinet and the nearest wine decanter. "Here, lads, let's raise a full glass for a final toast for Lewcas."

A gentle strumming pattern on the zither filled the room, and as it began to repeat, Heniello began to sing softly.

To all the friends that I have had
To family I have left behind
I thank you for the memories
Keep them near and remembered well
And someday we will drink to them again

To all of those who toiled with me
To friendly folk who passed my way
I thank you for the company
May your lives be well and full of joy
And I hope our paths might cross again

Though my time has come to leave
I ask that none among you grieve
For this is not goodbye
Nor is it the end
It is just farewell and only for now

The final verse was repeated once more, with Heniello singing the last line higher, stretching his voice to the extremes of its range. As it ended, Marigold raised her glass high and led the others in drinking deeply.

It is just farewell, and only for now, Lewcas.

Heniello bid Jopaire to stand and the former addressed the gathered amidst their simultaneous bowing, "Thank you, thank you so much. You have been nothing short of an amazing audience. We hope that this is but the first of many public performances to come under the generous leadership of Marigold Tullivan, our newly titled Lady of Daol Bay. May her reign be ever fruitful."

"I thank you both for a wonderful showing and your kind words," Marigold offered in response, with a newly raised, albeit empty, wine glass.

After a round of applause, the Cousins Graceford began the process of packing their instruments away. During that, most of the staff and city guards took the time to bid Marigold and the others a good evening and final condolences. From there, they saw themselves out of the room and from the manor shortly thereafter.

During the departures, Marigold had positioned herself at the main exit from her home, offering handshakes and hugs as each attendee preferred. Attending to the task with Marigold was Oire and Mister Lewinson. The manor butler had decided to work during the funeral and had attended to nearly every facet of operating the manor on his own unbeknownst to Marigold until then.

Last in line to leave, and presently being helped into his coat by Mister Lewinson was Lieutenant Cleofold Ashe, a Daol Bay guardsman officer of growing acquaintance.

"Lady Marigold, it has been a lovely evening. I am sure Ser Lewcas would have been honoured by all you have done," Cleofold told Marigold when it came time for them to shake hands, a gesture he did in the routine manner and without hesitation on this occasion.

"Why, thank you, Lieutenant, it means a great deal for me to hear that," Marigold relayed in response. "I thank you for attending."

He shook his head with a smile, "It was least I could do, Lady Marigold. Oh, and before I forget, you should know that repairs to the city walls are progressing quite nicely. I have been giving my full attention to all aspects of it. I suspect that within a fortnight we can commence with the construction of new fortifications on the portions of the walls that needed the least amount of work."

"That is excellent news, Lieutenant," Marigold complimented Cleofold. "Clearly, the right person was chosen to undertake this task."

"You are too kind, Lady Marigold," Cleofold blushed. "The engineers we hired have informed me that they will have a detailed, written report drafted for you by the end of this week, if you would so like it."

Marigold smiled as much as she could while answering, "I would indeed like that. Thank you again, Lieutenant Ashe. Have a pleasant night."

"It is my pleasure, Lady Marigold. I bid a pleasant night to you as well," Cleofold returned with a final bow before heading through the door and into the night.

Oire opened his mouth to speak, but quickly closed it again as the sound of footfalls on the foyer floor drew their attention.

"I hope that my cousin and I have not kept you waiting too long for our exit, Lady Marigold," Heniello Graceford stated as the pair strolled quickly toward the door, their cased instruments to hand.

"Not at all, Mister Graceford," Marigold assured him.

"I must say, Lady Marigold," Jopaire began, taking Marigold by surprise. "We asked your three young guards if we might have a look at the guitar that we spotted them presenting to you earlier. You should know that it is a remarkable piece."

It was difficult for Marigold to say if it was the deep bass of Jopaire's voice or that he talked at all that astonished her more. "Why, thank you, Mister Graceford."

"Lady Marigold, my cousin here has an almost encyclopaedic knowledge when it comes to stringed instruments and their histories," Heniello told her while slipping into his coat that Mister Lewinson was holding open for him. "You might be interested to hear of what he discovered from looking at your guitar."

"As it so happens, I would just love to learn more about my guitar," Marigold revealed to the cousins. "How would you both like to come by for brunch someday in the near future to discuss it? Perhaps Jopaire could even play it for me and give me a lesson, if you would be up for such."

The Gracefords looked between one another with glee, and it appeared to be a race to address Marigold's invitation, with Jopaire winning by a syllable. "Yes, my lady, we would gladly accept your invitation. Though the zither is my primary instrument, I am well versed in all stringed instruments that are not played with a bow. I would be honoured to be your guide to the world of musical performance art."

"How eloquently stated, Mister Graceford," Marigold told him before ushering both men towards a conclusion. "I will have Oire schedule you both for a visit sometime between late winter and early spring. Would that be satisfactory?"

"Wonderful, just wonderful, my lady, we look forward to hearing from your steward soon," Heniello stated with marked elation as both men began to make for the exit. "Please, accept our sincerest condolences on the loss of your friend and have yourself a good night. We thank you again from the bottom of our hearts for the opportunity to play for you and your guests."

"The pleasure was all mine, gentlemen," Marigold said in parting as Lewinson opened the door for them. "Farewell for now."

The outer door had just barely closed when Oire turned to Marigold. "My lady, all that remains is the house staff, guardsmen, and our fellow campaigners. It should be said that the lattermost of those are presently waiting on your company."

"Thank you, Oire," Marigold began while making her way back to the foyer with both he and Lewinson walking to either side of her. "Make a note to follow up with the Gracefords before long. I truly do have an interest in learning all about Tryst's guitar and figuring out how to play it."

"It will be as you wish, my lady," Oire granted without hesitation.

She stopped then, and turned to Lewinson with a hand on his arm. "Ser, I never got to thank you for your tireless work today. Please, take the rest of the night and tomorrow off, for you have earned at least that."

"You are quite welcome, Lady Marigold," Lewinson replied with a gentle pat of her hand with his free, gloved hand. He stepped ahead then, making for the door to the sitting room. "I appreciate your concern for my wellbeing, but I shall be perfectly fine, I assure you. Should you need anything, I will be cleaning up in the kitchens."

On her return to the sitting room, Marigold was greeted by Gallin Myakys. "Lady Marigold, Lord Greggard informed me that you wished to call a meeting. As the campaign manager, I took the liberty of gathering your team around the fire for just such a thing."

"Thank you, Minister Myakys, I appreciate your initiative," Marigold complimented while walking into the centre of the encircled chairs, where she remained standing.

"Everyone, if I might have your attention," Marigold began, waiting until the separate conversations quieted before getting events underway. "I thank you all for coming together so quickly for this meeting, and I apologise for hosting this immediately following a solemn remembrance for a fallen guardsman. However, with all in attendance for the reception and with much to discuss, especially with Lord Greggard, who was absent for much of the recent developments, I felt this to be an opportunity that I could not pass up."

"Shall we start with the obvious, Mari?" Leanne Mattersly queried, dressed in a three piece, black suit and lounging comfortably in a deep chair with a tumbler of rum to hand.

"That is as good a place as any," Marigold replied while turning her focus back to Greggard. "You may have noticed that apart from Leanne, everyone has taken to titling me as 'Lady' over 'Miss'. For that, we have Oire and Aunt Leonice to thank. While I was campaigning for parliamentary votes south of Daol Bay, they had been in continuous discussions with our regional councillors in a bid to curry favour at home and legitimise my claim as Lady of Daol Bay. Out of five councillors, I started with the support of two, those being my Uncle Rory, and Councillor Rossadore, both of whom are here with us tonight. On that, I needed but one more vote to obtain that goal, though fate had plans that are more fortuitous.

"After Oire and Elbert Swylen had a long talk, we managed to sway his favour. Lastly, Sybel Mansfield offered his support with only a few, manageable consolations in return. When it came time to vote, the four voted in favour of acknowledging my authority as Lady of Daol Bay, with only Marswell Caveth standing in opposition.

"Immediately after the motion was carried, Councillor Caveth resigned his post and cursed on my name, claiming that I would be the death of us all. Less surprisingly, Elbert Swylen also resigned, fearing that in his old age that his heart could not endure the stressors of the job. At present, we are arranging for elections to fill those vacant positions."

As Marigold took a moment to take a breath, Greggard jumped in with commentary. "What a fascinating turn of events, my lady. Congratulations on your official nomination as Lady of Daol Bay."

"Thank you, Lord Greggard, but you will find that I have just begun to catch you up," Marigold pressed on confidently. "While I was being named the Lady of Daol Bay, Eamon and his twin sons were in Obalen, having a meeting with Newell Felton."

"I should remind you, my lady, that I too had heard that the Palombs had made it that far," Greggard added quickly.

"Yes, I recall you mentioning that over our game of *Kings and Knights*," Marigold noted with just a tinge of astonishment. "May I ask where you heard it from?"

Greggard laughed in a manner that quite nearly sounded nervous to Marigold, a trait she did not know the usually cocksure man to possess. "We're second cousins once removed, Minister Felton and I. At present, I am hosting his children in my manor as they wait for suitable passage to the Barkis Isles, where my own wife and children are wintering. He is in regular communication with his children and me, practically sending letters to my manor daily. Atop that, and I cannot stress this enough, Newell Felton is as cowardly as the winter's night is long. I can tell you that he followed the instructions that you gave to him at your father's funeral reception to the letter, though I can presume that much is not new information to you. However, what might be new information is that Felton was considering aligning himself with our cause, and was interested in exploring his options to do so.

"It was ultimately a trap, one likely set by the Palombs, at it were. Even knowing that he is my cousin, I can say that Felton is not to be trusted. Everyone here knows that plainly enough. Even Felton said as much himself when he was here last. The Triarchy has owned House Felton since his father ruled, and the Palombs are looking over his shoulder as we speak. However, if Eamon Palomb could get you and me inside Obalen with the bulk of our conspirators to discuss Felton turning his coat, then the Palombs could put an end to the whole uprising in an instant. Who better to bait that trap for than Felton's cousin?"

Marigold was finding Greggard's explanation suspicious, and she was not about to let that feeling slip away. "So you think that Eamon was trying to lure us to Obalen?"

"Oh, most definitely," Greggard confirmed. "The play was destined to fail, but they risked nothing in the trying."

"Did Minister Felton happen to relay anything else of importance in all of your correspondences?" Leanne Mattersly inquired, now leaning forward in her chair, her eyebrows furrowed. "Could he give us nothing of usefulness regarding the intentions of the Palombs? Perhaps he might have told you how many men are in their entourage, even?"

"They likely came with but a few guards, Miss Mattersly," Oire piped in respectfully. "Their intention is to monitor our actions from a safe distance, I would say. They will likely go no further west than Minister Felton's manor."

"With all due respect, Mister Sellars," Leanne responded in kind. "I was not worried about them coming to us. Rather, I was thinking that it should be we that go to them. If nothing else, we could bolster the ranks of the Sun's Rangers with as many of our soldiers as we can muster and send them in to root out the Palombs. All we have to do is take the Obalen city guards unawares, contain the Triarchy's burgundy brutes, and force our way past Felton and Palomb guards. The Palomb's would have to surrender or face certain annihilation."

Greggard shook his head to that and spoke when the opportunity presented itself, "Felton might be scared shitless, but he's far from witless. Obalen will be on high alert for any such incursions and every available reserve guardsman has almost certainly been called up to duty. I have known him to activate the reservists for less, I should add."

"I would be remiss if I did not remind everyone that Geddrick Palomb is the captain of their guards, and he is no fool," Gallin pointed out. "The Palombs are almost doubtlessly ready to flee at a moment's notice from any number of viable extraction methods. I would even go as far to say that Geddrick is far more cunning than his cousins are. If you want Eamon and his boys, we have to circumvent Geddrick first."

Freyard, who had been standing outside the encircled chairs with Glendil, Dayden, and the other Rangers, stepped forward to where the firelight fell upon him. "I can vouch for what Myakys says about Geddrick. He was considered a top candidate for the Honourable Guardsmen that the Lord Master employs for added protection. The Palomb cousin has an exemplary military record that he earned largely on his own. From what I understand, he was involved, with increasing responsibility, in several operations in both the Southlands and at sea before Eamon had Geddrick permanently assigned as

Captain of the Palomb Manor guards. From what I had heard, Grenjin Howland and Eamon Palomb fought bitterly over Geddrick's nomination to the Honourable Guardsmen, but Eamon claimed that he simply could not spare his cousin, and the lordly men fought to a stalemate."

"To be fair, Geddrick would be the least of our issues were we to invade Obalen at the moment," Marigold piped in, turning the conversation back to more pressing tidings that she felt Greggard needed to hear. "As would the Triarchy, Obalen guards, and anything else we might find within city limits."

That seemed to capture Greggard's curiosity and he seemed to have paid close heed to Marigold. "What could supersede all of that, Lady Marigold?"

"The fact that we would be crossing the border, Lord Greggard," Marigold told him with what she hoped was enough gravity to level her point.

"The border between the Eastern and Western realms, you mean?" Greggard asked, indicating that the point had indeed been missed. "Since when has that ever mattered?"

Oire carried the message home. "It is an international border now, Lord Greggard."

Turning about in his seat to take in the whole room, Greggard seemed as though he thought that it was all in jest, but the stone faces looking back at him said plainly enough that it was anything but. "You are all serious. When did this happen? I had thought that following your tour we were one signature short of a majority."

"I am sorry that we could not tell you sooner, Lord Greggard... Or rather, perhaps I should say *Sea*lord Greggard," Marigold offered in consolation, allowing herself a slim smile in the process.

"The title of 'Sealord' has not been in use in nearly a century," Greggard said with a nervous laugh. "The EMP discarded it with our family shields and banners when they took power."

"I think it is due for a return, would you not agree, Sealord Greggard?" Gallin Myakys chimed in from where he sat beside Leanne. "I should say that we can bring those aforementioned banners and shields back too."

Greggard shook his head in befuddlement. "I would still like to know how this came to be, if I might be so informed. Did we have another westerner come to his senses?"

"For that, you can thank Eamon Palomb himself, Sealord Greggard," Marigold began her explanation. "While I was travelling, Eamon and his sons, now briefed on the situation by Minister Felton, apparently took it upon themselves to send letters to both their loyalists and my iconoclasts. The letters all stated that since I had not yielded to them since my father's passing that I was now a traitor to Illiastra. They added that though I was now considered a fugitive, that Illiastra would forgive those who had aided me thus far, with exceptions, of course."

"I am aware of that much, Lady Marigold," Greggard revealed flatly. "I got a letter too, and you should know that I am one of those exceptions. You and I and a few others in this room, are regarded as criminals in the eyes of the EMP."

Freyard evidently found that amusing, were Marigold to judge by his humoured scoff. "And what did they charge you with? My Sun's Rangers and I are all charged with desertion. That's a death sentence for sure. We would not even make it to Biddenhurst, I would think. Going forward, it will be a noose and the nearest hanging tree for any one of my men caught on the other side of the Daol Forest."

"I am likewise backed into a corner, with nothing left to do but either fight back or die," Greggard replied to Freyard, though he did not share in the laughter. "Formally, the charges are fomenting insurrection, apostasy, and blasphemy.

"The latter two charges were brought upon me by the Triarchists residing in Portsward, for those wondering. I will not bore everyone with the details, but I recently met with their leadership. During the course of the meeting, I revoked the regional tax exemptions they do so enjoy and ordered them to pay up. They refused, and threatened to set their brutes in the Burgundy Order upon my household and me. There has been no violence towards me and mine, thanks to swift intervention by my personal guardsmen, but the streets of Portsward have become unsafe after dark. The Triarchists hole up in their tower by daylight, and by night, they go out and terrorise anyone breaking their self-imposed curfew and chastity laws. If my city guards are there to intervene, it tends to become a bloody clash, and if not, people end up disappearing into one of a few Triarchist properties. I am working on shutting down the whole Triarchy operation in the city, but it is a burdensome project, as you will all no doubt come to know soon enough."

"Sealord Greggard, if I may say something," Rory said while raising a hand to get attention.

"Yes, you may go ahead, Councillor," Greggard responded.

Rory cleared his throat and leaned in Greggard's direction. "I apologise if what I am about to say brings offence. You always seem so calm and calculated in your communications that I have to wonder, how did you come to vex the Triarchists into such a furore in just one meeting?"

"If only it was just one interaction that led to my current strife with the Triarchists of Portsward, Councillor," Greggard told Rory and the room, his despondence hanging over him. "All while Marigold was touring the southern reaches of the west coast, I have been dealing with obstinate theocrats at home. They despise you, Lady Marigold, and everything you stand for."

"As I expect they would, but go on," Marigold prompted Greggard.

"Having met with my councillors as soon as I could upon return to Portsward, we began drafting and passing new municipal legislations," Greggard went on. "Our intent was that these laws would be as similar as possible at the city level to the sweeping changes you planned to make to the Western Realm. If nothing else, it would give you a controlled experiment to see how these changes would play out."

Jaysen Rossadore hummed audibly and commented, "I had heard of some rumblings coming out of Portsward's most pious folk while Lady Marigold was gone, now that you mention it. I had simply thought it was their reaction to the forthcoming changes, not to changes you had made already, Sealord."

"Practically destabilising the entire neighbouring city sounded like mere 'rumblings' from here, Councillor?" Greggard uttered in sarcastic shock. "My goodness, I must have done better than I thought, then. Truthfully, while I had expected some amount of backlash from Elite Merchant loyalists and Triarchists, I was wholly surprised that both groups were willing to escalate to violence so rapidly."

"Good gracious, Sealord, what laws did you alter, dare I ask?" Marigold put to him with growing bewilderment.

Greggard gave a shrug. "We simply acted upon the items you mentioned in your speech, Lady Marigold. For starters, we gave women the right to be employed, and receive fair compensation for said employment. They would also be permitted to run for, and vote in, regional elections. The ranks of the city guards and rural patrols were to be opened to their recruitment as well."

"That would certainly upset the most puritanical Triarchists, alright," Oire noted concernedly.

"Oh, Mister Sellars, if only that were the lone complaint," Greggard put back to him. "We put those few laws into effect almost immediately, and while most women were delighted with it and the better part of the men were accepting of it, the expected groups railed against the changes. With the Triarchy still enforcing their theocratic laws, it was decided that we needed to take a drastic step. By that, I mean to say that we moved for total abolishment of Triarchist laws and authority. We further decreed, by punishment of arrest, that their Burgundy Order were to cease all operations and commence with a total disbandment immediately."

"Was this before or after the shouting matches with their rank and file?" Marigold queried while mulling over all the information that Greggard was revealing.

"That would have come afterwards," Greggard told her frankly. "My most trusted Councillor, Maurice Kett, and I met with the local Triarchists several times so that we might come to terms on the new way of things, but they flatly refused to even so much as entertain any of it. Our new vision and the Triarchy's old rules are entirely incompatible."

Leanne chuckled under her breath at Greggard's latest notation. "That is the understatement of the season."

Unlike her old friend, Marigold could not even begin to find humour in anything being said. "If nothing else, Sealord Greggard, you have given us a preview of what is to come all across West Illiastra when our new laws are introduced. We should send word to all sealords of what you have encountered, so that they can prepare and be ready to deal with the religious zealots of their own regions."

"West Illiastra, is that what we are calling it now?" Greggard asked, his voice having grown weary.

"For short, yes," Marigold confirmed. "In full, we have decided on the Autonomous Nation of West Illiastra for the interim. I would hear from all interested constituents before settling on a final name."

Leaning back in his chair, the glow of the fire cast a certain light on Greggard's face, and for the first time, Marigold thought he even looked haggard. "I still would like to hear how we reached that status,

Lady Marigold. I apologise for my earlier derailing of the conversation that was leading to that revelation."

"Yes, of course, Sealord, you should know what happened," Marigold admitted, before quickly returning to that story. "To refresh, those letters from Eamon Palomb that I mentioned moments ago, well, they spurred a nearby minister to seek an audience with me."

"Was it Ike Slake or Leo Daltis?" Greggard inquired presumptively.

For once, Marigold allowed herself a chuckle at Greggard's dry delivery, giving him answer seconds later, "It was Leo, with his metaphorical tail tucked between his legs, having arrived in Daol Bay not two days ago."

"That figures. Do go on, my lady," Greggard commented idly.

At Greggard's invitation, Marigold did just that. "The letters that he and Minister Slake received asked both men to provide detailed information on the feasibility of fortifying and defending their respective regions. Daltis jumped to the conclusion that Eamon intends to use Galdourn as his base of operations, and feared for what would happen if war were declared in that case."

"Might I hazard to guess that the Madore Isles never once entered into his list of concerns?" Greggard asked with a groan.

"He is hardly going to start caring about the islands now, having spent his whole adulthood using them as little more than a seasonal residence," Leonice answered, her eyes coming dangerously close to rolling entirely back into her head as she did.

"My aunt is correct, the safety of the Madore Isles never occurred to Daltis. Rather, his primary concern was the wellbeing of him and his family. He knows that Galdourn is indefensible from the sea at the best of times, and Ike Slake has no standing naval assets. With even a hint of Eamon marching that way, we could besiege Galdourn inside a day from both land and water."

Greggard had taken to tenting his fingers right before his face, tapping them off one another in a slow, contemplative rhythm. "He asked for protection and offered you the Madore Isles so that he might guarantee it, I would wager."

"Precisely, Sealord. Rather, he offered me his full, albeit temporary support if I would allow him and his family to flee the continent. Daltis has no stomach for war, and he told me that to avoid such a fate, he tried to talk Ike Slake into siding with us to avoid Galdourn being a potential target of ours. However, Slake is sure that our rebellion will not last long, with or without a war. According to Daltis, Slake does have some level of concern that Galdourn will become a battleground. Yet, that concern is waylaid by his fear of incurring the wrath of House Palomb for even daring to side with us."

"That puts Leo Daltis in a predicament," Greggard deduced from what Marigold was telling him. "Common sense would say to throw in with us for the time being, even if Slake and Daltis think we will ultimately lose to Eamon. For if nothing else, it takes the Eamon's focus away from Galdourn entirely for two reasons, and the first of those is that Galdourn would no longer be a potential base for Eamon to use to attack us. Secondly, if Galdourn is ours, it becomes nearly pointless for Eamon to invest time and resources taking it from us, as he could never hope to hold it. So, if he cannot convince Ike Slake to side with you, and Eamon Palomb is prodding both men for information on battlements, then Leo Daltis' next instinct is to tuck tail and run."

Marigold pointed a finger affirmatively toward Greggard. "You are right again, Sealord."

"Not even the Madore Isles would be safe for Leo to run to if he sides with Eamon Palomb," Gallin observed pointedly. "The Madore Isles sit just outside of the waters of Robbston region, and even Sealord Ferros' small fleet could sail straight to North Madore and take it without much fuss at all. Of course, simply by being off our coast, Madore is probably the one region that the Illiastran navy out of Aquas Bay could feasibly attack without us knowing until too late."

"To that end, I have already dispatched funds, assets, and resources to the Madore Isles to shore up its existing defences," Marigold put in quickly, to allay any issues Greggard might have with the information Gallin had put out to the room. "It should be enough to satisfy the concerns of the islanders for the time being. Once we know the full breadth of our abilities as a unified nation, we can redistribute our defences to best suit the needs of each region."

"I suppose the next question is who will direct the operations of the Madore Isles until a proper election can be held there?" Greggard put to Marigold, looking to her directly as he asked, "Can we trust House Greyling or will they be seeking to flee with House Daltis?"

Marigold winked at Greggard. "The first question I asked Leo was whether or not we could rely on House Greyling, and he assured me that the current plenipotentiary, Alfred Greyling, will do his duty."

"Can we take Leo Daltis at his word, though?" Greggard wondered aloud.

"I should think so, his freedom depends on it," Leonice declared.

Greggard's head turned sharply in her direction, before looking back to Marigold. "What is Lady Leonice referring to?"

"My offer to Leo was that in exchange for his signature on *The Declaration of Agency*, I would allow his family entry into Daol Bay while they booked passage out of the country," Marigold told Greggard while folding her arms. "He readily accepted those terms, but what he failed to note was that I did not grant them the right to depart. While Leo's wife, teenaged daughters, and staff are occupying a suite in the *Daol View Hotel* located just down the road from here, Leo himself surrendered to the custody of Daol Bay's city guards."

"Leo Daltis is in jail?" a flabbergasted Greggard asked.

"He is being held in the Daol Bay Regional Jail, yes," Marigold confirmed with slight apprehension. "There is a tower cell there for high profile prisoners. It has all the amenities one could want and the guards cater to nearly his every whim at my request. I assure you, Mister Daltis wants for nothing."

"Except his freedom, that is," Greggard noted facetiously.

Marigold was ready for that. "Which he will have in due time. I have tasked Sealord Ferros with paying a visit to Alfred Greyling out on North Madore. Once we receive a written notice of cooperation from House Greyling and the Madore Isles, Leo walks free. Knowing that we cannot take Leo at his word and since he was so sure that House Greyling would serve, I told him that he should have no issue if we hold him here, with his own freedom as collateral, while we confirm his claim. No one but Daltis' wife, his jailers, and those of us gathered here even know that he was imprisoned. When all is in place with the Madore Isles, Leo will walk free from his cell, and onto the deck of a waiting ship. Though understandably reluctant to believe me, I did give him my word that so long as my terms are met, I will permit his requested exile from our country. I mean to keep that promise."

"You did specify that he has to leave the continent, correct?" Greggard queried for clarification.

"Of course I did, Sealord," Marigold said with affirmation. "If Daltis is to be believed, he intends to sail for Cabathos temporarily, until he can find suitable accommodations with one of the other Crescent

Island nations that will accept them on a permanent basis. Unfortunately for Daltis, Illiastra's hateful policies have considerably shortened the list of nations willing to offer citizenship to runaway lawmakers who might be responsible for those policies."

Gallin spoke up as Marigold finished, "Vellick or the Barkis Isles would take him readily. Garja would be open to it, but Daltis would require government connections to make it happen with the expediency he needs, given that the Cabathosi government will not allow him to stay long on their island. Outside of the Crescent, Daltis will find no home besides Manobius in the Johnan interior. However, for Daltis to get there, he would have to be smuggled through the coast, and if he is caught in any of the Allied Johnan City-States, he will be sent out to sea on the first ship going anywhere else."

"My worry is that he will simply sail to Aquas Bay and work his way back east," Greggard said, bringing the conversation back to the point he was apparently trying to make. "Not that he is much of a threat to us once deposed, but we do not want him making fools of us, either."

"That would not be easy, Sealord," Marigold responded to him. "Daltis would have to find a ship willing to smuggle him south. He would need connections along the way to house him and his family, and likely further ships to get him all the way to Aquas Bay. Atop all of that, he would have to pray that he is not caught in one of our friendly ports in the process."

Greggard was apparently ready for such a comment and replied as the last word was leaving Marigold's mouth, "Weicaster Bay is close enough to the Southlands that it offers frequent non-stop passage to Aquas Bay. Furthermore, I should remind everyone that it is in Aquas Bay that Leo's adult son Roland currently lives. Ultimately, the point I was trying to get across is that if Weicaster is Daltis' stop, we have to remember that Minister Morton is no friend of ours."

"There is no stopping Leo Daltis from port-hopping his way to Weicaster through ports held by Palomb loyalists, granted, and they would not hold him for me," Marigold said, relenting to Greggard's point, though she too was prepared. "Yet, if Daltis showed up in Weicaster, I would still know of his arrival there."

"You sound certain about that," Greggard uttered while eyeing her suspiciously. "What am I missing here? Do you have a mole in Weicaster Bay?"

While not necessarily the wisest move of Marigold's to relinquish information on her private parley with Samhais Morton, Marigold would need to offer some explanation for the signatures on *The Declaration of Agency*. "I have an understanding with Samhais Morton. Call it a truce, if you will. For the sake of plausible deniability, I will say no more to any of you on the matter."

"Might it be safe for me to assume that the signatures of Ford Cheswell and Vensent Rochford the Younger were products of this truce with Morton, Lady Marigold?" Greggard queried in a tone that was more of a guess than a legitimate question.

Marigold felt the need to hold her position on the matter of the Mortons, even if it potentially wounded Greggard to be denied his request for knowledge pertaining to the arrangement. "As I said not but seconds ago, I will tell you no more of Samhais Morton and I ask that you allow me the confidentiality I need to assure the terms of our mutual understanding. As for the houses of Cheswell and Rochford, they were convinced to join our cause through the diplomatic and persuasive arguments laid out by Sealord Gallin."

For once, Greggard looked contrite in his response. "Of course, my lady, I apologise for prying too far into the matter. I trust your judgement in this and all things, and it is my sincere hope that the truce with House Morton will bear the fruit you so desire."

"It is of utmost importance that any and all mention of Minister Morton be kept to this room and this company specifically," Gallin stated, looking directly at Greggard as he did. "What we have worked for thus far lives and dies by your confidentiality."

"Lady Marigold shall have my discretion, as always she has," Greggard stated reflexively, a look of annoyance flashing quickly on his face as he exhaled audibly. "Lady Marigold, in the interest of moving on from the discussion of Minister Morton, could I ask what you have planned for the next step in the founding of the country of West Illiastra?"

The attempt to change subjects was welcomed by Marigold and she leapt at it readily. "Yes, Sealord Greggard and that is an excellent question. Before we can alter the map of our nation, we must first deal with those of the EMP and the Triarchy in the west that would be an impediment to our progress."

"The all-but-former ministers will be a contentious lot, I can guarantee you," Greggard commented in counsel. "Though, if my own experience is anything to render judgement by, the Triarchists will be the primary issue."

Marigold had been nodding while Greggard spoke, waiting patiently for him to finish so she could delve further into her plan. "The Triarchists' time will come, I assure you, Sealord. We will deal with them together. First though, justice must be meted out to Haymard Nothram." Gesturing with an open hand, Marigold waved to her newest friend. "Moya, could you come here, please?"

With her eyes on the floor and a nervous expression on her face, Moya stood up from her chair and shuffled to Marigold's side.

"Sealord Greggard, it is my pleasure to introduce you to Miss Moya Starboard," Marigold began while taking Moya's hand gently into her own. "Moya, might I introduce you to Greggard Simillon, Sealord of Portsward, and the Lord of Trade and Foreign Relations for West Illiastra."

"How do you do, Sealord Greggard? It is nice to meet you," Moya greeted him with a bow.

"It is indeed a pleasure to make your acquaintance, Miss Starboard," Greggard offered in return. "Now, to what do I owe said pleasure?"

Marigold took the lead. "Moya is the survivor of the heinous act perpetrated by Haymard Nothram. Leaning primarily on her testimony as his prisoner, and bolstered by the eyewitness accounts of myself, my guardsmen, Wyla the maid, and the train conductor, we have compiled enough evidence to satisfy the threshold for having a warrant issued for the arrest of Haymard Nothram. The list of charges includes, but is not limited to: murder in premeditation, attempted murder in premeditation, two counts of unlawful strife and torture, one count of unlawful detainment, and two counts of intent to terrorise."

"What about the assassination attempt on your life and the murder of Lewcas?" Greggard inquired, looking a little puzzled by its omission.

"I cannot charge Nothram with anything that occurred aboard my train car, as I have no evidence that it was his doing," Marigold told Greggard regretfully, her grip on Moya's hand having slipped during such. "The assassin is dead, we know nothing of his motives, or even if my assassination was his intent. For all we know, it might have been a burglary attempt that was botched when we returned to the train. We cannot even uncover the name of Lewcas' murderer, let alone any potential connection he might have had to Nothram."

Greggard seemed impressed by what Marigold was saying to him, and his words echoed that sentiment. "You seem to have given this much thought, my lady. I must say, I applaud your thoroughness. How do you plan to execute that warrant? We know that Haymard Nothram is not going to surrender himself willingly, after all, and any attempts to arrest him through conventional means will be resisted by those guarding both his town and manor."

"Oh, no, Sealord Greggard," Marigold revealed, her voice growing heavy with the gravity of the situation that she was laying out to him. "I have no intention of carrying out anything so pedestrian. The Haymard Nothram that we all know will ensure that nothing short of an armed incursion into Pelican Harbour will bring him to heel. With that knowledge, why would we waste time and resources escalating to such inevitability?"

Greggard swallowed visibly. "You are going to attack Pelican Harbour?"

"You too, Sealord, if you are so willing to be a part of the operation," Marigold added to his statement. "I plan to sail eight of my own ships to the harbour and march a small army to his gates at the same time. I would greatly appreciate it if Portsward could add to that number. Tell me, what is the current number of seaworthy naval vessels at the disposal of Portsward?"

Greggard's eyes went to his shoes for a moment as he looked to be searching his memory for the answer, before lifting back to meet Marigold's gaze. "I can have seven ships readied for departure within a few days. Double that if given a fortnight."

Marigold gave a single, solemn nod. "In that case, I will take your seven, Sealord. I can give you no more time than that, and we should be more than served by fifteen in total."

"The operation is set to commence in but a few days, then," Greggard inferred in a voice that had grown as serious as the stare he levelled at Marigold.

"Indeed, I plan to leave in six days from today," she told him while returning the long gaze.

"Sealord Gallin, Ser Keneth, and Miss Mattersly have all agreed to come along as well, and if you should so decide to join us, that should more than suffice to be a worthy array of counsellors. Moya will also be accompanying us, I should add. Uncle Rory, Aunt Leonice, Oire, and Councillor Rossadore have opted to remain here so that they might manage Daol Bay in my absence."

Greggard looked to Leanne, the mention of her name having garnered a visible reaction from him. "Your father should know about this. If nothing else, we would have need of any ships he can spare to offer us added aid from the south."

Leanne seemed to agree. "We have but two or three that can sail that far. As the first line of defence from Aquas Bay's naval might, we must keep a sizeable flotilla in Tippard to dissuade southern aggressions. But yes, my father should be informed, regardless."

"If it alright with you, Miss Mattersly, I would like to write the letter to him," Greggard optioned to Leanne.

She shrugged casually in response. "You may be my guest, Sealord."

His attention was back on Marigold then. "My lady, I can add to your marching army too, if you will allow it. Due to my own issues, I signed contracts with assets that I would tell you about in private between only us two, with your permission."

"That can be arranged, Sealord," Marigold permitted readily, as Greggard's clandestine contracts certainly garnered her interest. "I would much like to hear about these 'assets'. However, I will request that Ser Keneth be permitted to attend. He is, after all, the new Field Marshal for West Illiastra. Before we adjourn this meeting though, I must ask how soon you would want to return to Portsward so that you might prepare for departure."

"I... I suppose tomorrow morning, so that I have as much time as possible to ensure that my fleet is ready for the open waters," Greggard relayed after brief consideration. "Furthermore, if Lady Marigold insists on Ser Keneth's appearance, it is not my place to deny that."

"Very well then, Sealord Greggard, it will be as you wish," Marigold allowed, knowing that her private conversation with Greggard would need to take place immediately.

She looked across the room at the guards, Sun's Rangers, Moya, and the conspirators in attendance, announcing to them, "You are all dismissed for the night. I thank you again for being here for Lewcas' service and I shall be seeing you all tomorrow morning. Until then, I bid everyone a good evening."

When the room had emptied of all but Marigold, Keneth, and Greggard, she turned to the newly made Sealord. "Now then Greggard, would you so kindly stoke the fire while I go to the kitchens and get something for the three of us to eat? I would imagine that we might be here into the wee hours."

23
FREYARD

Night had fallen upon Daol Bay, veiling the city in a blackness pierced here and there with the light of the street lamps that dotted Freyard's sightline. Acting in tandem with the darkness were the crashing waves on the rocks far below on the south side of the harbour, stifling any other sounds that might be floating on the night air. Daol Bay, Freyard had always been told, was a bustling, lively city that seemed to know no sleep. Between the shipping and fishing industries, and a small naval yard, Daol Bay by day was indeed a hive of activity. Owing to the strong employment rate of those industries, Freyard had been led to believe that the nights were every bit as alive once the pubs and taverns opened their doors.

Yet, all he observed from where he stood on the roadside next to Marigold and Moya were rumbling waves and darkness.

Accursed Triarchists have vexed this place as much as they have Portsward. It's like a plague.

In the days since Lewcas Hylesly's funeral service, Marigold had begun to follow in Greggard Simillon's stead, and had issued her proposal for the grand sweeping changes that she intended to institute, sending word of it out by herald and journalist. The results, unfortunately, were much the same as they had been in nearby Portsward.

The hardest set amongst the Triarchists were pushing back against Marigold's proposals, despite the fact that she had not attempted to make any of them into laws yet. City guards were reporting an increase in violence in the streets, as Triarchists began to orchestrate mob attacks on anyone they remotely perceived as supporting Marigold. Any men with a measurable amount of piety were being pushed to join the Burgundy Brethren, if they had not already, and even a few city guards had abandoned their posts in order to enlist.

Ser Keneth warned Marigold that shipping out a noticeable number of soldiers for her operation in Pelican Harbour might embolden the Triarchists to attempt a coup in both of the cities within Twin Bay. To get out ahead of this, Marigold began having daily meetings at city hall. There, she would invite the citizenry to attend and ask her, the remaining city councillors, and the city guardsmen any questions that the people might deem necessary so that they might achieve peace of mind.

To Marigold's credit, there had been some tangible measure of success to the method, and she sent word to Greggard so that he might attempt a similar measure.

Freyard had attended most of these meetings as one of many protectors to Marigold, and noted that the most common questions were simply seeking to refute the jilted logic being issued forth from the Triarchists. Marigold had handled the most reasonable of these doubts quite well, and dismissed the most absurd statements outright. However, it seemed that as fast as Marigold and her friends could dispel the myths, more were seeping out from the Tower of Ios.

It will be only a matter of time before civilians wind up dead at the hands of Triarchists, either directly through the burgundy brutes or indirectly through incitement of the masses. Freyard concluded, glancing to check on Marigold and Moya as the notion passed through his mind.

Wrapped in woollen warm coats, hats, and mittens, the trio found themselves situated in a tiny park nestled on the sea's side of Ser Davis' Road. From where they sat on the lone bench, Freyard could even see the Tullivan manor, as they were but a ten-minute walk away and downhill from Marigold's home.

Together, the three sat in wait on neutral ground for a woman that would only agree to meet if that condition was met. Marigold's guardsmen, Oire, and even the butler all attempted to counsel her against the clandestine rendezvous, but Marigold would not be deterred. In an effort to assuage the concerns of the men of the manor, Freyard had offered to employ the few Sun's Rangers at his command in the scheme. Placing them in a role deftly suited to the group.

Behind the bench and hidden by trees and shrubbery were Dayden Vernet and Tobald Eskren. Freyard had sent them into hiding to watch over him and the women, and to respond to any threats, if need be. Walking the streets on opposite sides were two further pairs of rangers dressed in civilian clothes. By Freyard's orders, Mack Doile and Clem Sylart were strolling about in one direction, while Glendil Archer and Delliot Claired headed in the other.

During what Freyard estimated to be the half hour wait that he, Moya, and Marigold had endured thus far, the only traffic to pass by that was not a Sun's Ranger had been a single carriage. It left his plan for discreet protection practically null, given that his pairs of increasingly conspicuous walkers were the only people to be seen on the roadsides.

"Our guests are late, my lady," Freyard informed Marigold. "I estimate that we have been here for half an hour or so, which would put us at just past the nineteenth hour."

"Are you sure it has been that long?" Marigold wondered, reaching a gloved hand into an inside pocket of her coat to produce a pocket watch. She tried to look upon it, but the park's single lamp was just too far away to be useful. "Here Freyard, take my father's watch and go look at the time in the light, if you wouldn't mind."

"Certainly, give it here," Freyard accepted while taking the watch to hand. In the light of the lamp he could look upon the two hands clearly, seeing them pointing to ten minutes after the hour. "I stand corrected. It is ten minutes past the nineteenth hour," Freyard told the two while snapping the cover of the watch closed and handing it back to Marigold. "She's just ten minutes late. I suppose it is nothing to worry about yet."

Freyard chose to remain standing, and wandered outside of the range of the lamplight, hoping to let his eyes adjust to the night.

"For a man who says, *'It is nothing to worry about'* you do seem awfully worried about something, Freyard," Marigold said while audibly rubbing her hands together.

He turned back around to where she and Moya were. "No, my lady, not worried, just wondering if perhaps my security scared off our guests."

"It was a bit much, I will admit," Marigold concurred jovially. "There would be little reason for Triarchists or other troublemakers to be in this part of town. The entire south side hill of Daol Bay is the highborn neighbourhood. Moreover, aside from my inner circle and I, the wealthiest are all on the good side of the Triarchy. Therefore, unless they are looking for our band of rebels specifically, it would be a stretch to see the Triarchists straying this far from their blockaded tower on the north side of the city."

"No, it would be no stretch at all to envision a mob of irate, religious zealots marching up this road with torches and pitchforks for you," Freyard responded, hoping he sounded as deathly serious as he intended. "Given the threat to your safety that is present between the Triarchists and the EMP loyalists, there is no such thing as too much security, my lady."

"Oh, honestly now..." Marigold gave with an exaggerated scoff, though she made no further comment or complaint on the matter.

Freyard was glad for the silence, using the opportunity to listen for any noise that might have a chance of being heard above the tumbling waves.

Feet on gravel, getting nearer and headed up the hill toward the manor. That should be Glendil and Delliot, given that it seems to be coming from the other side of the road.

"Alright, Moya, let's go over everything again while we wait," Marigold began from behind Freyard. With a pivot of his hip he glanced at them quickly to find Marigold with the fingers on her left hand splayed open, her right index finger tapping the left pinkie as though she were about to use the hand for counting. "Now, you met with the Pathfinder personally, right? I mean to say that she identified as the Pathfinder and not a surrogate or a gatekeeper."

"I did, yes," Moya told her. "Me and Sydnee sat and met with the woman who identifies herself as the Pathfinder in the basement of a pub called the Brookside Inn. If it were me though, I would call it 'Overbrook Inn' as the brook runs right under the basement floorboards. I found the place quite fascinating."

Marigold counted to her ring finger. "Excellent, Moya. Then you can identify her on sight. Tell me again what she looked like."

"She had a long head of black curls and skin that was nearly as dark," Moya relayed slowly, as if giving the memory some thought. "I remember these beautiful green eyes, a usual green at that, not like the strange colour of your eyes. Her nose turns upwards just a little, and her chin is dimpled. I thought she was very pretty, to be honest. She is taller than I am, but not as tall as Sydnee, and she looked fiercely strong to me. I feel like she could have picked Sydnee up across her shoulders with ease, if she had wanted."

"That's an impressive memory you have, Moya, if you don't mind my saying, that is," Freyard complimented sincerely. "I don't know that I would have been able to remember half of that."

Moya gave a visible shrug. "I don't know what to tell you, Captain Archer. Marigold asked me to commit everything about the Pathfinder to memory. I just wanted to do the best job I could."

"You did wonderfully, Moya," Marigold added in, while moving her count to the middle finger. "There were two men with her, correct? You said that when she agreed to meet with me, she told you that they would be accompanying her, what did they look like?"

"Both were big, tall fellows," Moya told Freyard and Marigold, looking back and forth between the two as she did. "One was light skinned, and he was the taller of the two by quite a bit. His hair was shaved short, and what was left looked reddish in colour. He wore spectacles on his face, and he had a strong looking, cleanly shaven chin. The whole time we were talking, he kept writing with a wooden pencil in a notebook with a brown, leather cover.

"The second man was not as tall, but was as wide as a house, with a high, thick head of curls and a bushy beard. His eyes were dark and his face was round and somewhat jolly looking. I remember that he had these huge hands that looked like they could be used to rip trees in two. I made notice of his hands because he kept cracking his knuckles by pulling on the fingers. Both men wore leather coats that looked padded, and not just for the cold, but for armouring too."

Freyard gave a hum as he considered what Moya had said, and offered commentary when she finished. "They would be her bodyguards, like as not. The man with the spectacles probably also serves as an assistant of some kind."

"Most definitely, yes," Marigold concluded, her index fingers touching for the next count. "That brings us to-"

"Hold up, my lady," Freyard told her as he caught sight of Glendil and Delliot, the rustling of shrubbery branches following them. "We may have company."

Freyard moved back into the lamplight while he talked, positioning himself directly in front of the bench that the women occupied.

"I believe it's just your men," Marigold hazarded to guess.

"If anyone was seen by the patrols on the road, they were to shake the trees branches or the shrubs on either side of the road as a signal." Freyard explained to them. "Glendil brushed the shrubs at the front of the lawn of the house across the road. Be ready, my lady, for we don't know who might be coming. It might just be our guests. Or at least it should be."

Marigold patted the bench. "Freyard, you should sit, your standing around might make our guests nervous."

Freyard disagreed, and explained with a shake of his head for emphasis. "With all due respect, my lady, it would be best if I remained standing. There is not enough seating for all, and while I am sure these large men that Moya described mean us no harm, I am not about to put myself in a vulnerable position."

Marigold looked to Freyard with furrowed brows and seemed about to say something when a woman's voice in the distance beat her to it. "My, what a lovely little park. I have lived in this city for three years and I never knew it existed until now. I wish I had known sooner."

"Good evening to you," Marigold greeted the voice's owner, though still sight unseen. "Might I ask who goes there?"

A woman strolled just short of where the lamplight might fall upon her, the hood of a black cloak drawn down to conceal nearly all of her face. Lumbering further back and blanketed in the darkness were the silhouettes that, as long as Freyard's eyes were not deceiving him, belonged to two behemoths in human form.

"You might, though I can see from here that I would not have to ask the same in return," the woman replied flatly. "You must be Lady Marigold Tullivan, I presume. Let me say that it is nothing short of a pleasure to make your acquaintance."

"The pleasure is all mine, I assure you," Marigold returned to the shadowy figure. "From the very little that I could obtain, I can tell you that I already admire your work. Would you like to step a little closer so that we can talk quietly?"

"I would not, thank you," the woman politely refused.

Marigold stood up and took a single step forward, bringing her abreast of Freyard. "Then I should like to come to you, if that is alright."

"I would like that even less," the woman told Marigold while withdrawing backward into the blackness of the night.

A shared look between Freyard and Marigold underscored the confusion that the woman's statement garnered, and Marigold readily addressed it. "I apologise if I was perhaps too forward. Is there a venue that would be more to your suiting? My manor is just up the road, if you would like, or we can return to the Brookside, if you would rather. It is just that I would prefer not to discuss things at a volume that might be readily overheard by any random person nearby."

The woman stood motionless, her visage nearly enveloped by the frames of the men behind her. "I will not go to your manor, and the security previously offered by the Brookside has been compromised by your friend's visit. We will have no further association with the place."

"Then I am afraid that I do not know how to proceed from here, madam," Marigold returned calmly. "Have I done something to make you mistrust me so?"

"We have no trust in highborns in general," the woman explained in blunt terms, a tinge of the Johnan accent coming through in her voice. "Highborns are the reason that my organisation need exist at all. Men of untold wealth seeking further riches and power made this country the way it is. Your ancestors helped institute the laws that necessitate people like me to circumnavigate those laws. Your relatives and fellow highborns upheld it for all this time, and with respect to the recently deceased, even your father, the most powerful man in the west, did nothing to change any of it."

Marigold had lowered her head while the other woman had spoken, and kept her gaze on the ground until her chance to reply presented itself. "I will not attempt to ignore the history of neglect that the associates of my family, past and present, are responsible for. In that same countenance, I acknowledge the inaction and compliance of my own family, and indeed my father, in perpetuating a growing series of unfortunate circumstances faced by uncountable innocents. The actions of those who came before me are not mine, though, and I would like to think that I have used the limited time and opportunity presented to me in a way that will begin to impact change."

"Yes, I have seen thus far the sweeping reach of your reign, Lady Marigold, and it is quite impressive," the woman commented, her tone bordering between mocking and complimentary. "Triarchists and many highborns alike seem to be in open revolt to your rule. Those that remain undecided amongst those groups seem to be patiently waiting to see how things begin to unfold before attaching themselves to one side or the other. It has made these to be interesting times, to say the least.

"I recall a particular phrase wherein the speaker wishes the subject to be dealt such events as a punishment, and to a point, I see why. These are not peaceful days under your watch, but we both know there was no way that change was going to arrive in Illiastra unless we were willing to upset our oppressors. Frankly, I have to give my respect to someone so capable of sending the EMP and the Triarchy into such a simultaneous rage. That recognition comes in spite of the fact that you and your conspirators have enjoyed the luxuries provided by the blood and toil of the downtrodden under the whip of those same governing bodies."

Freyard glanced toward Marigold to find her looking completely nonplussed. It dawned on him that someone ought to say something, and as he opened his mouth to do so, Marigold cleared her throat and took the lead. "That's... Well, that's quite the statement. What I took away from it is that you and I see eye to eye on at least a few things, and I think that is a good foundation on which to build a friendship. Would you not agree?"

"I will admit that we have a few common ideals, yes," the woman agreed, though it was clear that there were things yet unsaid on the matter. "However, I find the company you keep to be problematic, with few exceptions. While in your case, I understand that you had to wait before you could make a move toward the betterment of Illiastra, the men had time and opportunity to do the same, and all they could think to do was... Nothing. For them, resting on their laurels required no hardship, but for so many more, waiting was not something they could do, and time was not on their side.

"Do you know how many people have suffered while your friends Gallin Myakys and Greggard Simillon merely waited about? The answer is thousands upon thousands, Lady Marigold. They are among the youngest of the former ministers in your retinue too, aren't they? Would you like to know how many have suffered and died under subjugation since Walter Mattersly or Nayle Keeves rose to their positions decades ago?"

Though Freyard noticed discomfort crossing Marigold's face, she offered a response that managed to belie that unease. "I am aware of the past inaction of my campaigners, Madam. I gather that you are concerned that these men are merely sycophantic in their support of me. Would that be accurate?"

"You would not be entirely incorrect in saying that," she granted to Marigold, "It should concern you as much as it does me that they could so easily transmute their belief systems from one solid state to another."

The discomfort appeared to ebb away from what Freyard could see, and Marigold's confidence began to shine through. "Those four men, and the others who have joined me, and even those who refused, are all men that I have known since I was but a babe. When I stood on the landing of the staircase in my foyer and announced my intentions for all of them to hear, I did so with a strong notion of who would answer the call. There were surprises, to be sure, but it still largely went as I had envisioned. Sycophants find a way to bore their way into every governing institution, and it can be difficult to deal with an infestation, but nothing smokes them out like asking them to upend their whole lives.

"You see, having dealt with men just like the ones you loathe over the course of my entire life, I have learned that grovelling, glorified lackeys like Ike Slake are less concerned with ideology, and are more worried about maintaining an environment that allows them to survive parasitically. My grandmother used to say, *'Shake the tree long enough and all the insects will either fall out or fly away.'* I got to see first-hand what that statement meant after my father's funeral."

"Perhaps I was wrong about you," stated the woman after a pause. While Marigold had been talking, it had begun to snow and the flakes had been visibly accumulating atop the hood and shoulders of the strange woman's cloak, though she made no effort to remove it. "There may be more we have in common than I previously might have thought. Allow me to ask you a question though, if I may."

"You may," Marigold tried to say, though the woman had not waited for such and had merely kept on talking.

"How can we, the people of West Illiastra, trust these Sealords, as they are now calling themselves, after all the tragedy they have allowed to happen under their previous collective reigns as ministers?"

"An excellent question, Madam," Marigold complimented, before taking a deep breath and fielding the query. "When I sent Moya and Sydnee on a mission to seek out the Women's Road and yourself, I did so not only to offer a lucrative contract, but to establish a means of tapping into the vein of the public. Yes, I open town hall to questions and I hear the concerns of our people, but meeting them in person at my level of fame does not usually lend itself to honest decorum on their part, as I am sure you can appreciate. I want to know what way the tide of public opinion truly rolls, and to do that, I need people like you, whose work brings them into contact with those who are most in need. It has been said that to know the health of a nation is to know the health of the most vulnerable, after all, and the gods alone know how sick our country is. I would like for us to heal it together."

If the woman in black had any reaction to Marigold's response, her body echoed none of it, as she remained perfectly still and statuesque. "How compelling, Lady Marigold." She offered in a voice that could well be taken sarcastically. "You certainly are a wordsmith. What of your so-called Sealords?"

From what Freyard could discern, it appeared that Marigold was giving herself a second to think about the query, yet she did not balk at it. "As I said before, I know them all quite well, Madam. Did you know that Walter Mattersly's primary reason for joining me was that he saw the qualities of a true leader in his daughter, Leanne? No, how could you know that. Each of them have been born into this world, just as you and I have, and while each one holds more power than all of Daol Bay, Portsward, and Weicaster Bay's citizens combined, they have been just as restrained in their ability to wield it effectively.

"The EMP and the Triarchy have held sway in Illiastra for almost a full century, and as you do not need me to tell you, that power is theirs primarily through fear and manipulation. You may think that those tools have been used only on the common folk, but the truth is that it is employed on the deceptively titled *ruling class* too. The families currently presiding over the regions of Illiastra are not the same families that ruled a century ago, or fifty years ago, or even twenty years ago, for that matter. Any minister who had stepped out of line in the past was dealt with quickly and often brutally, and their family was not spared from the horrors. I would recommend that you ask House Pike of Toyell about that, but they were excised from the Illiastran political landscape for standing up to House Palomb and quickly replaced with House Imorgan."

The mention of the former house brought pause to Marigold, and as Freyard checked to see if she about to speak, she did so of her own accord. "You see, my associates were raised with the expectation that they were going to be thrust into their positions with little say in the matter. During that time, they supped on the knowledge that the fates of dead men like Griff Pike would be theirs to share if they did not walk in lockstep with the EMP and the Triarchy. I gave the western ministers the chance to break away from that morose march, and the men you named earlier all decided to take it. They owed me nothing and the risks of following me were great, but every one of them to cross the floor, whether minister, councillor, or anyone else, bore part of that risk across their shoulders in the crossing. I cannot say with total certainty that their reasons are completely altruistic, but I can say that Eamon Palomb is not a man of forgiveness. Can I trust them? I had damn well better, because they put their lives in my hands."

The wind had picked up during the course of the heated conversation, and Freyard pulled his coat closed to keep the wind from chilling him.

The woman remained unbothered and unmoving by the gusts, but suddenly lifted an arm and pointed past Freyard and Marigold both. They turned in unison to see Moya standing directly behind them.

"What about you?" the woman asked her plainly. "Why do you follow Marigold of House Tullivan?"

Moya's eyes widened and she quite nearly froze in fear.

"She has been through a terrible ordeal recently. I think you should leave her alone," Freyard attempted to explain.

The strange woman though, was having none of it. "I was not speaking to you, soldier," she said, the final word uttered with a sneer as she interrupted Freyard curtly.

"Be that as it may," Freyard tried again, this time being cut off by a different woman.

"No, it is quite alright, Captain Archer, I can talk. I just needed a moment to swallow my fear," Moya told him, stepping forward beside

Marigold before giving the strange woman an answer. "Marigold saved my life. No, she did more than that: she gave me a life to live."

"Just how did Lady Marigold accomplish that?" asked the woman in a tone that was both gentle and inquisitive.

Moya visibly swallowed and looked to both Freyard and Marigold. He attempted to offer her reassurance in his return glance, but she was already talking by then. "Alright, well, I guess I should tell you how I got to where Marigold could save me. You see, I was sold to be a wife when I was not yet a teenager by my father. He needed the coin to pay off his debts to a lender, I was told. I have no education beyond what either he or the man he sold me to have taught me, which wasn't much. I spent my married days locked in a room when my husband worked and my nights as a servant to him.

"The wife of a couple who frequently visited my husband told me in private to run away and look for the Women's Road, for a Pathfinder like you, so that I could be free. I was told to go to Pelican Harbour, look for a bar called *The Diamond Eye*, and speak to a woman named Stella who served drinks. One night, while my husband slept off a bottle of rum, I finally worked up the courage to leave. I didn't know where I was going, I just knew that I had to go north from Snapper's Cove, where we lived in the Cale region, and make my way to Pelican Harbour.

"I had some help along the way, from a few nice ladies I encountered that I dared to talk to, and they helped me get on a freight train going north. I got off in the wrong place. I heard men in the train yard talking about Pelican Harbour and I thought that it meant that I was there, but it turns out that Pelican Harbour was the next town over. I walked the rest of the way north, and by the time I got to Pelican Harbour, I was so tired and hungry that I didn't know what I was doing. The guards caught me trying to sneak through the town gates, and I was thrown in jail for being an unescorted woman.

Moya's words seemed to fail her, and Freyard glanced to see her lip quivering. "I refused to tell them who I was," she revealed to the stranger in the hooded cloak. "I wouldn't tell them who my husband was either. Even when they hurt me, I said nothing. My husband never came looking, but he wouldn't know where I was anyway. With no man to claim me, they said I was going to be sent off to some place called Biddenhurst. They told me I was going to be sold off as a slave.

"Then Nothram came and had a look at me. He said I looked a little bit like Serephanie Tullivan, but I had no idea who that was or what that had to do with anything. I spent that night in a different cell with a woman named Bess, and neither of us knew either why we were there or what was going on. I found out from Bess that she was there on the same charge that I was, and that she was told she looked like Marigold Tullivan. She knew that both Tullivan's were Lord Marscal's daughters, but we still didn't know what looking like them had to do with anything.

"The next morning, we were made to put on old, shabby looking ballroom dresses, had our hands tied behind our backs, and were walked outside into the cold. One of the guards told Bess and me that we were going to be welcoming Lady Marigold to the town. Then they walked us up some stairs against the town wall and lashed us to tall poles to wait for her. The cold nearly killed us both. I don't know how we lasted as long as we did that morning.

"Then the train rolled in, and after a short time, Lady Marigold stepped off with Freyard here and five more men in tow. They came to where Bess and I were with guns and swords, and Marigold ordered the town guards to let us go. Until then, I thought I was going to die that morning. For a moment though, Marigold gave me hope that I was going to live. The guards lied to Marigold, and when we thought that the guard near Bess and I was going to set us free, he instead killed Bess. I was done then, I knew it, but then I wasn't, and suddenly the terrible guard with the bloody knife was gone and Marigold's men had cut away the ropes and were carrying me to the train."

"I am sorry to hear of the lot dealt to you in life, Ma'am," the woman told her with what sounded like genuine sympathy. "I am further sorry that you did not reach my associates in time to be saved sooner."

Moya was not yet done though, "You don't understand, Ma'am. Marigold saved me. She took me into her company, made sure I was fed and clothed, got me a doctor's care, and when her trip was over, she brought me here and took me into her home. Marigold had no reason to do any of that. She could have just cut me loose and turned away from me, or left me there tied to that pole, but she didn't. Marigold saw someone in need, and she showed me more kindness than everyone else in my life combined. I am the reason that Marigold heard about the Women's Road, because I told her when I heard her talking about a job that needed to be done. It was on her behalf that I went looking in the city for you, Ma'am. I would do anything for Marigold, and not just to repay her for saving my life, but because I know that after everything she has so selflessly done for me that she is an amazing person, and she is worth it."

"Moya..." Marigold managed to stammer out. "Thank you so very much, my dear friend. You deserve everything I could give you and more."

Freyard was taken aback by what Moya had said, his own words failing to leave his tongue. "Moya, I-I did not know. I am so sorry to hear about everything you have gone through before we found you."

"Marigold and Sydnee were the only ones that I told about my life before now, Captain Archer," Moya explained to Freyard while looking between both him and the strange woman. "I trusted them enough at the time, and I know I won't be sent back now, so I don't mind telling others when it might be important for them to know."

"You told me none of this when first we met either, young lady," the woman put in. "Am I to believe that what you did tell me at the *Brookside* was the truth too?"

Moya bowed deeply to the woman. "Oh yes, Ma'am, I promise you, I told you no lies today."

Freyard heard Marigold's boots crunching on the snow, and looked to find her facing the hooded woman. "Does that mean you will take the job?"

"No," she put back quickly. "But I would hear it from your lips exactly what it is you hope that the Women's Road can do for you."

"Gladly, Ma'am, but do you have a name I could call you by? This all seems rather impersonal, and it is an important job."

The woman lowered the hood of her cloak, "You may not, but I shall show my face if that puts you at ease. We do not use our names with the clients, for their protection and ours, as you can surely understand. But, if you must call me something, Pathfinder will do."

"That's her alright," Moya declared confidently. "Not that I doubted that it was you, Pathfinder. I knew you by your voice and the way you carry yourself, but it is good to see your face and be completely sure."

Though difficult to discern in the darkness, Freyard certainly had to agree with Moya's earlier assessment of the Pathfinder in that she was quite the treat for the eyes. The Pathfinder's hair was bound up and coiled at the back of her head, but otherwise, everything that

Freyard could see matched the details that Moya had recalled for Marigold and he during their wait.

"I am glad to have your reassurance, Miss Moya," Pathfinder said, sounding amiable for the first time since showing up. "Now, Lady Marigold, let me hear of your plan in your own words, please."

From over the Pathfinder's shoulder a large, gloved hand extended, a notebook in its grasp. "Would you like my notes so that you can compare?"

"Now, just how do you propose that I do that? I cannot read in the dark," Pathfinder queried while looking back at the taller of her two bodyguards.

"Well, it would involve you moving into the light..." The taller guard suggested, his voice trailing off before he could finish the thought.

"You realised by the end of your sentence that I am going to do no such thing, didn't you?" Pathfinder deduced while turning sideways and extending an arm toward the streetlamp. "Go ahead, S, and let me know if your notes are accurate to what Lady Marigold is about to tell me."

"Very well, ma'am," the veritable giant of a man groaned as he walked from the shadows and past Freyard, Marigold, and Moya, taking himself into the lamplight in but a handful of long strides.

Freyard turned back to Pathfinder. "Might I ask why you referred to him as 'S'?"

Pathfinder's gaze fell directly on him, and he felt that while her eyes were indeed as beautiful as Moya said, Pathfinder had an intense stare that would bestir even the hardiest of hearts. "I told you, soldier, we don't use names. A single, randomly assigned letter usually suffices for all members in a given area of operation for the Women's Road. Now, Lady Marigold, without any further delay, I would like to hear this plan of yours from you when you are ready to talk."

"Alright, then," Marigold affirmed while taking a deep breath. "Moya has told me that your group has coverage in almost every corner of Illiastra, correct?"

"This is true," Pathfinder confirmed without hesitation. "We have but a few blind spots, but if a person in need can make their way to a major centre, they can find us."

That seemed to lead into Marigold's next question, given how quickly she asked it, "And you are but one Pathfinder?"

Pathfinder nodded in answer to that before offering further explanation, "We designate areas based on geography and the need of our services and assign a Pathfinder to each area. I am the Pathfinder responsible for overseeing the operations from the north side of Twin Bay all the way south to Galdourn. Strictly speaking, I also answer to any requests that might arise of us in the Tusker's Cove region too, though I have no agents out that way."

"It is through you that I would make a request for a job that takes place outside of my area, though, am I right?" Marigold queried up next. "I would not have to go to another area and seek out their Pathfinder?"

"The request would go through me, primarily," the Pathfinder confirmed. "I would weigh judgement on the merits and if I think the parameters of the job are within our scope, I pass it on to the Pathfinder in the applicable area. From there, it is up to them to determine if the job is something that they have the ability to do. That, of course, would be based on the requirements of the job and their available people and resources, as I would not have such information personally."

Marigold's face took on a look of concern. "Then you can give me no assurances that the job will even take place?"

"I cannot, no," Pathfinder told her unapologetically. "However, I can say with good certainty that if a Pathfinder recommends the job to another Pathfinder, it has an excellent chance of being fulfilled."

"What if the job might take place across multiple areas? Will that need approval of all the Pathfinders? For instance, if it involved transporting a person from say, here to Farmourd, would every Pathfinder between here and there have to be involved in the approval process?"

The Pathfinder had a reply at the ready. "That would depend on the nature of the job. In the case of transportation, a raven would be sent ahead of the travelling party to alert the agents in each area to be on the lookout for the party and offer shelter, sustenance, and guidance on the party's journey through the area. The only Pathfinders that would be needed for approval would be the Pathfinder in what we call the extraction area, and the Pathfinder in the settlement area. If the transported party were leaving the country, the settlement area would be instead referred to as the departure area, and the same approval rules would apply. Does that all make sense?"

"I think so, yes," Marigold relayed, looking quite satisfied. "Do you use ravens for all means of communication? Are they reliable?"

"Yes and yes, to answer those questions," Pathfinder replied hurriedly. "Our ravens are far more reliable than sending humans on trains. They are bound to no schedules and are held by no guards. Our only issue is having them perish on route, and that rarely happens. Am I ever going to hear about this task from you? Or do I have to ask Moya to repeat it to me?"

"I am getting to it, there were merely questions that I had first," Marigold informed the Pathfinder in a tone that begged for calm.

"You do realise that it is you that needs me and not the other way around, correct?" the Pathfinder reminded her in a voice bordering on condescending. "I was under no obligation to answer questions, and I assure you, there are far better things I have to do tonight. Do you think I want to be here in the cold being catechized by some fussy little highborn? There are people in serious need of our services, and this meeting delays me from attending to them."

Marigold seemed unfazed by the insult and refused to bend to it. "And yet you came, and remain to listen to me, why is that?"

"I wonder as much myself," the Pathfinder answered indirectly.

If the Pathfinder was hoping that Marigold was going to leave it at that, she was sorely mistaken. "I think you realise that there is a fortune to be made for the Women's Road in doing this. Serious coin that could go towards helping a great many people in short order. Furthermore, I think this job, on account of being so high profile and different, excites you. As the leader of a group constantly living on the cliff's edge, you are so accustomed to the constant excitement and danger that you thought nothing could stir you emotionally any longer. Until this offer came along, that is. Lastly, I would be remiss if I left out that you were curious, even if just a little bit, to meet the woman who is currently dividing the mighty, unshakable nation of Illiastra into two wholly different countries, if just to see what she wants of you."

A tense silence followed Marigold's statement, and Freyard found himself looking between the Pathfinder and her men, watching the three of them cautiously for any signs of danger.

After what felt like a painfully long time to Freyard, the Pathfinder offered a response, "You think a lot of yourself, Lady Marigold. Then again, in my experience I have found that highborns always do. Get to telling me about this job, or I walk away."

"Pathfinder, please wait. You promised me that you would hear Marigold out," Moya blurted out pleadingly.

"I have heard plenty from your friend," Pathfinder stated impatiently. "In fact, I feel that I have heard enough to satisfy conditions of the promise I made you. Either she talks immediately, or we are through here."

"I need your Women's Road to help me orchestrate the escape of Jorette, Nareen, and Dorian Palomb from Hercalest, and to further see them transported safely to my manor," Marigold declared hurriedly as soon as the Pathfinder had finished.

"There it is, at long last," the Pathfinder uttered in great relief, her voice transcending into the realm of complete sarcasm. "The job of a lifetime for the Women's Road, if money and excitement was our objective, that is."

Marigold shook her head with a smile. "You seek excitement about as readily as you do fame and glory, I should think."

"But we could use the money, though. That much is true," the Pathfinder reminded Marigold. "Speaking of, is the amount that Moya told us at the inn today that you were willing to pay accurate?"

"It is, yes, twenty-five hundred gold pieces in total," Marigold relayed to them, the very mention of the sum making the eyes of the man known as S bulge out of his head. "I will give you five hundred upon signing the contract and the remaining two thousand when Jorette and her children arrive at my doorstep."

The Pathfinder looked to be almost smiling. "Yes, that is a considerable sum of money. Gold has no worth to the dead, though. My people will be risking their lives to extract the wife and youngest offspring of Eamon Palomb, as great a terror as Illiastra has known since the Valdarrow brood, and then we must escort them from there to here. What is the value of their risk? What do you hope to achieve by bringing those three to Daol Bay? Do they even want to leave their opulent lives for a journey fraught with danger?"

"I have been given to understand that the three Palombs in question merely await the chance to flee, and I would like to provide that to them," Marigold told the Pathfinder with measured certainty.

"What are Jorette Palomb and her youngest children to you?" the Pathfinder inquired with befuddlement. "There has to be some reason why they are so valuable."

Marigold looked to Freyard with a look of incredulity on her face, and he noticed it for the signal he felt it was. In return, he scoffed and acting as though Pathfinder's question bore an obvious answer.

"Think about it, Pathfinder," Marigold prompted her. "I am plotting with Eamon's wife to undermine his own household. Imagine what will be made of Jorette defecting to West Illiastra with Eamon's own flesh and blood in tow. The things that woman alone surely knows could well bring him down if it was slipped to his enemies. If your agents of the Women's Road succeed in this, they could well be the catalysts that end House Palomb. Let that thought mull in your head for a moment."

"It will not end the war that you are helping to ferment, Lady Marigold," Pathfinder pointed out in a tone that Freyard thought to be overly brusque.

"Perhaps not, but it will go a long ways towards ending it sooner, possibly before it even becomes a war," Marigold countered hastily.

"You think that Eamon Palomb is the head of the serpent that's constricting Illiastra? No, my dear girl, he is but one of many heads, each one competing for dominance over the others. You seem to forget that Lord Eamon has ministers and lords waiting in the wings for their chance to prove themselves to him and the Lord Master.

"Then there's the Patriarchal Council of the Triarchy sitting in their tower in Hercalest, pulling the strings every bit as much as the EMP, perhaps even more. If one should fall, even if they are as powerful as Palomb, you can be sure that another will quickly rise to fill the void."

For a second, Marigold seemed to be trying to contain a chuckle that came forth, but the effort proved futile. "You have been calling me a highborn since you arrived here, Pathfinder. I am the daughter of the only man whose power came close to that of Eamon and Grenjin. The power structure of Illiastra is as familiar to me as the back of my hand and I do not need a lecture from you on the workings of it."

"The price just went up by five hundred golds for your disrespectful attitude," the Pathfinder told her bluntly.

"I beg your pardon, but you will do no such thing," Marigold shot back in frustration.

The Pathfinder had a laugh then herself. "Won't I? You came to my associates and I to avail of our services, and it is we that set the price for that service. You made the initial offer, granted, but we did not accept it. I merely asked if the amount that Moya told us was correct."

Oh, damn, the Pathfinder is right, Freyard thought to himself while recalling the conversation from minutes ago.

"The whole thing is meaningless anyway unless you take the job," Marigold gave back with a nonchalant shrug. "Until then, you and are I just calling out numbers into the air."

The Pathfinder remained unstirred, though. "I still have not been given a sufficient reason as to why our agents, who have spent their lives undergoing extensive training in the clandestine crafts, should put those lives in jeopardy for this job. The risks to their wellbeing and freedom are extraordinary, and are not to be taken lightly."

"I understand, truly I do, Pathfinder," Marigold pleaded. "I scattered the ashes of one of my good friends a few days ago, who gave his life for mine as my protector. I have harboured feelings of unworthiness for such a sacrifice since the day he was killed and I shall for the rest of my life. What makes me so worthy that Lewcas Hylesly should die to further my life? I don't know that I have an answer, any more than I have an answer for you.

"What I can tell you is that I know Jorette Palomb, and I am painfully aware that behind the veil of extravagance that Eamon presents to the world that Jorette is in pain. Eamon, the father of all four of Jorette's children, uses the lives of the youngest two against her, to keep her bound in paranoia for what he might do to them. We may never see the marks on her flesh, but I have seen it in her eyes at the Parliamentary functions that she has been permitted to attend. It is not only Eamon either, for I have witnessed the disrespect and oftentimes the downright contempt that Jorette's oldest two sons have for her. If for nothing else, the Women's Road should help Jorette, Nareen, and Dorian escape that tortured existence because it is not only the right thing to do, but because they are exactly the people that your organisation was built to assist."

Freyard spoke up while Marigold stopped to catch her breath. "Lady Marigold, I would like to say something to the Pathfinder, if it is alright with you."

He waited until she gestured affirmatively, and went on, "People like your agents, and Marigold's friend Lewcas, and I and my Sun's

Rangers have all spent countless hours honing a set of skills while safe in the knowledge that if those skills are put to use it will be to protect the innocent. This is what we do, and indeed, what many of us feel like we were put in this world to do. No, the vast majority of people like you and me do not intend to die in the line of duty, but it is a risk we accept when we buckle our holsters and scabbards to our hips at the start of our shifts. I might die protecting one of those two women standing next to me tomorrow, who knows? It might be the most random act of violence that you can think of that takes me out, and maybe I will not even see it coming. Yet, if it means that the life of an innocent person, whether they are friend or stranger, was spared because of my actions, then all of my training and knowledge will have been worth the sacrifice. I cannot speak for anyone else but myself, but if that is how I leave the mortal realm, I will go into the ever after in peace."

The Pathfinder was looking at Freyard as he spoke, and while he still felt the intensity of her stare, it held not the weight that it did moments ago. "I must say, soldier, you speak sense."

"I have a name, Madam," Freyard told her in a level voice that was brimming with frustration.

"You will have to forgive me, for we were not properly introduced," the Pathfinder said in return.

Freyard felt it was a convenient excuse, but he was no longer in the mood for such. "You have twice heard Moya address me as 'Captain Archer', and while I really could care less if you use the title, you should at least be aware by now that my surname is Archer."

"Alright then, Mister Archer," the Pathfinder uttered cautiously, "I have but one more concern to table to Lady Marigold, and then I will render my decision."

Marigold had turned her back to both he and the Pathfinder during their terse exchange, but spun around when the Pathfinder said her name. "Can you please make it quick, Madam?" she asked while rubbing Moya's shoulders, which she had evidently been doing until then. "Moya is shivering uncontrollably and I am not far behind her, I fear. It is freezing cold out here, the snow is showing no signs of slowing, and the hour is surely getting late."

"I will be quick about it, I promise," the Pathfinder assured her.

"Oh, for the love of all things, please do keep it brief," Freyard exclaimed while removing his jacket and laying it over the shoulders of Moya for extra warmth.

Pathfinder paid no heed to Freyard's comment, yet thankfully went on with her point anyhow. "After meeting with Moya and her companion today, I sent S on a little fact finding mission. What he was able to uncover in just a few hours of talking to the right people was quite interesting. You know, I had no idea that Jorette's surname at birth was Morton. I have no doubt that you knew, though, just as you knew that her brother is the current Minister of Weicaster Bay, Samhais Morton. I was further unaware that your campaign manager, Gallin Myakys, is among Minister Morton's closest confidants. Am I to believe that your request to rescue the sister of your campaign manager's dear friend is coincidental?"

"The potential for Jorette to soften her brother's heart towards me is certainly a possibility that I have explored," Marigold cleverly told her with what Freyard knew to be a mixed truth. "However, despite a past friendship, Sealord Gallin and Minister Morton have not spoken to one another since my father's funeral reception. They apparently disagreed vehemently when it came to supporting me."

"Very well, Lady Marigold," the Pathfinder said, appearing to be satisfied with the explanation. "I will give you the benefit of the doubt if you will give me the down payment of five hundred golds."

Marigold looked excited for the first time tonight. "You mean you will take the job?"

"S, G, do either of you have any concerns with anything that Lady Marigold or her friends have said?" the Pathfinder asked while looking between her guards. Receiving no answer from either, she focused on Marigold again. "They raise no issue, and while I still have reservations about the entire operation, I am willing to let it advance to the next step. I will send S and another agent to your manor tomorrow afternoon at the top of the fourteenth hour to collect the payment in coin. In that time, I would like you to draft a list of employees and other associates of Jorette's. These need to be trustworthy folks that my associate agents in Hercalest would be safe to contact. Their purpose would be to act as messengers between our agents and Jorette, or perhaps to even assist in the eventual escape."

"Of course, Pathfinder, I can think of a few names for you. Is there anything else I can provide in terms of information?" Marigold asked with cautious optimism. "Would you require me to be a part of planning the escape? I have been to the Palomb Palace, after all."

"You can leave all of that for the Hercalest agents to concoct. There is only so much information a raven can carry, after all," the Pathfinder told her while drawing the hood of her cloak back up. "I should say in warning that this job will require a great deal of human resources to be successful. The Hercalest agents may ultimately be taxed to their limit and unable to fulfil the request."

The agent referred to as S had returned to the Pathfinder's side then, his notebook still open in his hand. "As to that, Pathfinder, unless there has been some variation in the scheduling, our mobile enterprise should be stationed in Hercalest at the moment. Their agents may just give them the needed numbers."

"I had not even thought of that, thank you, S," Pathfinder said to him while giving Marigold a glance. "It may well be your lucky day. For now, I will bid you, Moya, and Archer a good night."

Mere seconds later, the night engulfed the strange trio, leaving no trace of their existence but the sound of footsteps crunching softly in the new snow.

Freyard, Marigold, and Moya stood in near silence, save for the chattering of Moya's teeth. When Freyard was certain that the Pathfinder and her men were out of sight, he called to his own sentries hiding in the shrubbery. "Dayden, Tobald, you can come on out of there. Let's head back to the manor on the double, before we all freeze to death."

The walk to Marigold's manor went as quickly as it did quietly. The party of five encountered Glendil and Delliot part way between the park and the manor, where the two had found a sheltered place to observe the meeting. Delliot was sent down the hill to retrieve Mack and Clem and return with them to the manor for debriefing.

At the gates of the manor, Freyard left his remaining rangers so that they might wait on the return of the others, and proceeded toward the door with Marigold and Moya. The door swung open from within, and Kandell was holding the heavy oak piece as he greeted them at the entrance. "Good evening, Lady Marigold. A fruitful outing, I hope?"

"It was, yes, I thank you for asking, Kandell," Marigold revealed while stepping through the door that he held open for all.

Lewinson came striding through the foyer to the porch, still in full formal attire, despite the late hour. "Welcome home, Lady Marigold. Please, allow me to take everyone's coats and footwear. You must all be so cold and tired. Shall I send to the kitchen to have a late snack prepared and some valerian tea brewed? Or will it be straight off to bed for all?"

Marigold undid the toggles of her coat, slipped it off, handed it to Lewinson, and was in the process of unbuckling her boots as she told him, "Well, I cannot speak for the others, but I think I am headed to bed, Lewinson. I thank you for the offer all the same."

"The tea sounds nice. I think I will take a cup, if it is no trouble," Moya spoke up from where she stood in front of Freyard while he handed his own coat to the butler.

"Why of course it is no trouble, Miss Moya," Lewinson told her cheerfully. "Follow me when I am done here and I will personally set the kettle to boil for you."

Lewinson and Moya had scarcely departed from their company when Kandell announced, "Captain Archer, your rangers are approaching the door."

"Thank you, Ser, I appreciate the notice," Freyard told the senior-level guard as he swung open the door.

After greeting the guard, the entering rangers all looked toward Freyard, Glendil, and Marigold while still dressed in their outerwear, a smile across the face of Mack, who spoke to Freyard on behalf of them all, "Captain and milady, I hear that things went well."

He nodded once in answer, adding with it, "It did, rangers. Come on in, remove your coats and boots and we will have Lewinson seat us in an available room for debriefing."

Marigold had slipped in at Freyard's side then. "If I may, Freyard, perhaps the rangers would be interested in having tea and a late snack with Moya in the kitchen first?"

The few Sun's Rangers that remained in the city were guesting in Marigold's home while Freyard sought suitable accommodations for the entire unit within Daol Bay's walls. The hospitality of Marigold and her staff was unwavering, though he often worried that he and his men might wear out their welcome, particularly amongst the servants.

"If you are sure that they will not be an encumbrance on Mister Lewinson and the kitchen staff, my lady," Freyard said in tentative acceptance.

"Of course not, Freyard. I am sure that Moya would like the company," Marigold assured him with a pat on the arm. "Rangers, please feel free to make your way to the kitchen so that you might eat and warm up when you are ready. We all have a busy schedule tomorrow before departure and I need everyone at their best for the days ahead."

"Very well, my lady, if you insist," Freyard said with a polite half bow. "For now, I shall adjourn with my men to debrief them over our refreshments with Moya."

"Wait, Freyard," Marigold said while laying a hand on his forearm. "If you would not mind, I would much like to have a word with you in private."

Something peculiar went through Freyard from head to toe as Marigold spoke, and a coy smile on her face only increased the feeling. "I should probably get to the debriefing, my lady."

"Can it not wait until tomorrow?" Marigold queried, her voice sounding suggestive. "Surely once you are under sail with a ship full of your rangers and soldiers you can fill some portion of the time that you are not training with a debriefing before we reach Pelican Harbour."

Freyard paused for a second as he considered things, looking about to find that it was but he and Marigold remaining in the porch.

She waited until we were all alone, and I had not even noticed myself. How did I miss the room emptying?

"Well, what do you say?" she asked again, a little more forward in her tone this time. "Shall we adjourn to the second floor to... talk?"

"I... I suppose we shall, my lady," Freyard replied softly.

She reached out and took his hand, intertwined her fingers with his, and led him toward the stairs without another word. Together they climbed the steps, with her taking each one slowly and carefully so as not to draw a single creak that might merit attention.

At the second floor, she brought him deep into the corridor, past the guest quarters he shared with his men, beyond the door to Moya's chambers, and further away until they came to a pair of double oak doors. Their hands parted and Marigold produced a key, turning it in the lock of the rightmost door until it clicked.

"Come on in, Freyard, and make yourself comfortable," Marigold invited, gesturing him toward her with a wave of her index finger.

The room was the master's chamber, once having belonged to Lord Marscal and before that his father, according to Marigold. While she, Freyard, and the others had ventured south, the staff had been tasked with moving Marigold's things from her former room to the master quarters. In the process, they made sure to alter as little as possible from the arrangements of the previous occupants.

As quickly as he could cross the threshold, Marigold was behind him and closing the door.

Within, Freyard found the room to be cast in the glow of a crackling fireplace opposite of the entrance, clearly having been attended to by someone else prior to their arrival. Beyond the glow of the fire, the rest of the room danced in shadow. A large featherbed encroached into the centre of the open space, its headboard touching the wall to the adjacent right of the doorway. Opposite of the bed was a large bay window overlooking the rear yard, cushioned benching surrounding it in semicircle. Bookcases filled with what looked like equal parts tomes and decorations filled the wall sharing the doors, and over the fireplace were wall-to-wall paintings.

Freyard found himself drawn to the artwork, his eyes going between the pieces to observe them as much as the limited light in the room allowed, catching points of interest in each portrait. Finally, he came to examine the large painting situated directly over the fireplace.

"That is the founder of our house, Ser Davis Tullivan," Marigold explained as she walked up to Freyard and wrapped both of her arms around his left. "That painting depicts the day he walked onto the shores of Daol Bay to claim it as his own. Before then, where we now stand was but a part of Portsward's jurisdiction and was little more than a scarcely inhabited collection of fishing stages and huts. Ser Davis was a Teal Knight of Segai, the original Master of Blades, and this harbour was his reward from the Governor of Portsward for his valiant service to Phaleayna during the Valdarrow crisis."

Having nodded along softly with Marigold as she explained, Freyard spoke when she finished, "It is a splendid piece. I never knew it existed. Easy enough to see why teal is the primary colour of the Tullivan's, knowing what you told me."

Marigold hummed affirmatively before adding, "Starting tomorrow, those colours will fly from the mast of all our ships and from the flagpoles here at the manor and at city hall. We are using the flags of old for now, though when time allows I plan to design a new banner to incorporate both the history of the Western Realm, and the new direction of West Illiastra."

"Outside of the teal colour, what is the banner of House Tullivan, anyway?" Freyard asked, taking his gaze away from the painting to look upon Marigold. "The only sigils I know are those of the old knightly houses like mine, which are usually plainly obvious when you consider our surnames."

Leading him by the arm, Marigold pulled Freyard toward the bay window where a neatly folded stack of teal cloth sat. Marigold let go of Freyard and reached for the fabric, lifting it up to let it unfurl, where it rolled all the way to the floor.

"It is a single swordfish rendered in gold," she explained in lacklustre tones while lifting it high enough and on an angle to allow the firelight to illuminate for Freyard's viewing. "I was told that originally it was the helm and sword of Ser Davis, with the sword standing upright behind the helm. Sometime in between Ser Davis' life and the rise of the EMP, it changed to the swordfish to reflect our family legacy shifting from that of being military brass to titans of the fishing industry."

Freyard took the cloth between thumb and forefinger at about midway between where Marigold held it and where it began to bunch on the rug-covered floor, lifting it in this manner so that he might inspect it for himself. "Something tells me that you are none too inspired by our finned friend here."

"I suppose a swordfish is fairly inspiring, given that he's practically wearing a weapon on his face," Marigold admitted while wrinkling up her nose. "As far as fish go, few others can cut such an imposing figure, I have to admit. Still though, I wish there was some surviving example of the old sigil."

He released the banner then, and she took it to fold up once more while he offered response to her statement. "All the more reason to make your own later on and brand things in a manner that inspires not just yourself, but everyone else who serves beneath the banner. A new look for a new era, and dare I say it will be your era, my lady. I think for now, though, the swordfish will do just fine. Let it be a reminder to those who know the old sigils that the Tullivan name can once more be a force to be reckoned with."

Some part of what Freyard said had made Marigold laugh a little, "You have a charming way with words, Freyard. I like the way you think."

"Thank you, my lady," Freyard offered in return. Something caught his eye from upon the benches of the bay window, and he pointed it out to Marigold, "Is that a sword I see there? It looks like the banner was on top of it."

"Hmm?" Marigold said while looking for herself. "Oh, yes, that was my grandfather's rapier, passed down to my father, who meant to pass it down to my brother when he came of age. It instead went to the attic when Felixander never returned. I recently dug it and the banner out with a little help from Moya after we returned from down south. Oh, and please, just call me Marigold, or even Mari, like Leanne does, if you prefer."

Freyard had picked up the sword in the meantime, holding it by the hilt and scabbard in both hands. "Oh, well, sure, I can call you by whatever you would like, Mari... No, that's not right to me. I think that I will stick with Marigold. Do you fence at all?"

"You get into the habit of being formal with me in the presence of outside company, I noticed," Marigold pointed out, the banner long folded and replaced on the bench. "It is a hard spell for you to break, I gather."

"It can be," Freyard admitted with a sigh. "Knightly families tend to raise their children with a rigid code of manners, especially the eldest born son, like I was. We are drafted into the military life from practically the moment we are conceived, and barring physical deformity or mental malady, such is our fate. Breaking the habits instilled by years of such arduous training can be damn near impossible, and I do apologise if I come across as overly formal at every turn."

"You just issued a formal apology for being too formal, Freyard. That's cute," Marigold giggled as she stretched out atop her bed. "To answer your question, I am no fencer. Neither was my father. He wore that sword once when he went overseas to the Crescent Isles as a naval officer, but it was never drawn from the scabbard with malice toward another person."

"I suppose I did," Freyard offered in response with a wistful little smile of his own. "You are planning on wearing the rapier for the Pelican Harbour operation, I take it?"

Marigold gave a confirmative hum. "Aye that is part of the reason I wanted to find it. The other is that after the assassination attempt within the train car, I felt completely and utterly helpless. Without guards, that intruder would have killed me, and there was nothing I could have done to stop him. I do not want to feel that helpless ever again, Freyard. I can learn to fight as well as any other. With that in mind, when we got home from the southbound excursion, I asked Keneth if he would be willing to teach me the art of swordplay. Of course, having propelled him into such a busy role as Field Marshal, with a campaign to manage right from the start, he had little time for mentoring me. He did recommend Rus for the job, though. Not so coincidentally, Rus is also acting as captain of my manor guards until Keneth and I can sit down to choose an actual successor."

"Rus seems like an able man with a sword," Freyard commented, having drawn the blade far enough from the sheath to see the bare steel. "And a rapier is an excellent choice of a weapon for you too, Marigold. It is light enough to handle easily, yet long enough that you can reasonably manage the reach of larger opponents. It lacks for a cutting edge, though. Personally, I prefer a sword to be capable of slashing, as do most others I know that are trained in the matter. Yet, what it lacks in a cutting edge, it more than makes up for as a thrusting weapon. A competent fencer can poke a man with a dozen holes or more before he knows what's hit him.

"This particular sword, despite being fairly old and stored in an attic, is in operable condition. It just needs a little maintenance and it would be ready for battle. Of course, that owes to the fact that the steel is of excellent quality. Will this be your weapon of choice, Marigold?"

When Freyard looked to her for a reply, he found her having pulled herself into a lounging position against the overly abundant pillows atop the bed, fiddling with an undone button on her white, silk blouse. "I wanted to see if it was a good fit for me first. If it is, then yes, I shall get it into working order. If not, I will make a visit to the Hammer Brother's forge."

Freyard had to laugh at that, as he laid the sword atop the banner. "Yes, I had seen their sign when I was out yesterday. I meant to ask if they were legitimate blacksmiths with a name like that." He was at the bedside then, right in range of where one of Marigold's bare feet could reach his leg.

"Oh indeed, their works speaks for itself," Marigold responded as her toes brushed his trousers.

"Marigold, about the operation…" Freyard began carefully, wanting his thoughts to be said before anything else occurred. "There are a few things I would like to speak with you about, if you would give me leave to speak on them. As little more than a mercenary in this situation, I would understand if you felt that I was overstepping my bounds."

She sat up suddenly, concern wiping her seductive smirk away. "Of course, Freyard, whatever is on your mind?"

Gently, he lowered himself to the bed so that he was facing her at level. "Marigold, I have supported you from the first moment that I could, and I continue to. However, I have serious reservations when it comes to your intentions in Pelican Harbour."

"I am seeking justice for Moya and Bess," Marigold told him flatly.

"How many more will die in order for you to achieve that goal?" Freyard asked sadly, unable to veil his emotions on the matter any longer. "How many of his men do we have to kill and how many soldiers of ours will be slain in the effort?"

That gave her pause, and she looked down at the bed, idly tracing the floral pattern on the eiderdown while apparently considering her answer. "Probably quite a few, is that what you want to hear me say?"

"Marigold, I lead hardened soldiers into battle as a lifestyle," Freyard uttered with gentle gravity. "My rangers are trained in the field of dealing death and pain, but I further train them in the art of using discretion. In addition to that, part of my duties is to ensure that my soldiers come back alive, all of them, and I have prided myself on being effective in that role. Do you feel that the tactics that yourself, Ser Keneth, Greggard, and Gallin have lain will do just that?"

"It would be impossible for any pursuits in Pelican Harbour to not result in deaths right now," Marigold told him despondently. "Haymard Nothram will not come peacefully, and he is cowardly enough to send every man at his disposal to the grave before he will be taken. There is no other way, and justice must be served for what he did."

"I have a hard time reconciling with the act of sending hundreds to perish for the sake of one person who is already dead and another that we have since saved," Freyard stated with his voice at little more than a whisper. "What good can come of this? The warrant for his arrest has already been issued. Perhaps we can convince a few of the morally upstanding and understanding of his town guards to execute that warrant for us. Maybe they can take him unawares when his personal guards may not be able to respond quickly enough. We could send a few of my men to scout and spy for such avenues for us to exploit. In the meantime, we can be focusing on the real enemy to the east: Eamon Palomb. It is hard to overlook the threat he poses, and the damage he could do if he knew our forces were not all here and at the ready."

A hand of Marigold's came to rest atop one of Freyard's that he had neatly folded on his lap. "That is all well and good for men at war to do to one another. I know as sure as we are sitting here that Nothram is hoping I will attempt those exact types of shadowy tactics to take him down, and that is precisely why I cannot do that. As a woman trying to stake my claim in the world of men, I simply must resort to a show of strength. Men like Nothram need to see that I will not allow them to shove me around, and that I will exert my authority on those who dare resort to the sort of grotesque transgressions that Moya suffered. I need to send a clear message to Nothram's allies and those in the east who are watching that I will bring the fight to them."

"You are set on this, then?" Freyard asked with a heavy sigh.

Marigold gripped the hand, lifting it into both of her own. "Freyard, you have been privy to all our war councils thus far, you heard on the day of Lewcas' reception just what forces of ours are going to be descending on Pelican Harbour. This battle will likely be over inside a morning. Greggard has the Flying Hawks of all groups going forward of the armed forces that are going overland, for crying out loud. On the waters, we practically have an armada sailing into a harbour equipped with two seaworthy warships, two decrepit lookout towers, and approximately half a dozen cannons perched on either side of the harbour. This will not be an even battle, and I did not intend to make it one."

"Those men guarding Pelican Harbour that you are about to crush are not ruthless brigands like my rangers normally pursue," Freyard said, pleadingly so at that point. "They are average men who might have even been conscripted into the forces against their will. Are you prepared to kill those men, your own westerners, just to get to Nothram?"

"It is not something I relish," Marigold answered stoically. "But my hope is that those Flying Hawks can take Nothram's manor before much blood, if any, has to be shed."

"You put a lot of faith into a group that was corrupted by the EMP and used by them as an arms-length, extrajudicial death squad for the better part of a century." Freyard said, perhaps a little harshly, judging from the feeling of remorse he felt at the exact moment the words left his lips.

If what he said had hurt Marigold, she showed no signs of it, and instead forged on. "The Thieves operated in much the same capacity before Lady Orangecloak's predecessor turned his cloak on the EMP. For that matter, you and your Sun's Rangers served as soldiers to a government wholly dictated by the EMP. Furthermore, what you should know, as an Honourable Guardsman attending to Grenjin Howland at every Parliamentary Session, in many of his private meetings, no less, is that the Flying Hawks had all but gone rogue on the EMP. Their current leader, the one that Greggard convinced to work for him, is the root of that dissention, and Howland even feared that the previous leader of the Flying Hawks was assassinated by the man now answering to Greggard. Lastly, if Greggard vouches for them, how can I second-guess someone who has joined my cause knowing that his own life is forfeit for doing so if we lose?"

"You have raised many good points," Freyard said as he relented in arguing further. "I apologise if I have come across as contentious in this matter. You seem to have, and I say this with no condescension, a good handle on things. I assure you that I will raise no further questions. Despite all of that, I will tell you now that my top priority is the safety of my rangers. Any orders from your ship to mine may ultimately go unheeded if I feel that the risk to their lives is too much. Will you respect that decision if it comes to it?"

Marigold's gaze had gone back to the bedspread, but she raised her eyes as he asked his question. "Of course I can, Freyard, and I promise you that barring the direst of circumstances, I would not ask you or anyone else to put themselves in jeopardy for this mission."

"Thank you, Marigold," Freyard said, looking down to find her still holding his hand.

"When our ships set sail tomorrow, I probably will not see you until things are settled in Pelican Harbour," Marigold pointed out.

"Aye, that thought has crossed my mind too," he replied softly.

He felt the bed shift beneath him and found Marigold having inched closer. "Though my ship will be at a distance from the action, I still cannot help but feel that there is a chance, however small, that these might be the last days of our lives."

"There is no need to worry. You said yourself how much of a force we will be sending to Pelican Harbour," Freyard replied with assurance.

"Things may still happen," she said, sliding nearer again. "Seafaring is no game, as my own family is painfully aware. Not to mention that there may still be traps if we take Pelican Harbour and go ashore. I...I would not want to leave this world with too many regrets, should something happen."

"I would not want that either, Marigold," Freyard told her, feeling her breathe upon his cheek as she spoke so close to his ear.

Her hands went to his tunic, and she fell backwards onto the bed, pulling him down atop her. "Then come here and help me do something about that."

24
SEREPHANIE

The snow was accumulating at an alarming rate in Hercalest. It came in flurries and squalls throughout the passing days that seemed to have slipped by for Serephanie, and the static cold that clung to the air kept it firmly on the ground. There was talk of needing good snow shovels if the snow got any higher, and worries of the city charging the League exorbitant fees for damages to Bryten Field due to the muddy foot trails being worn into the grass. Despite the legitimate financial and mobility concerns being echoed throughout the tented town, the League of the Sacred Fist was curiously staying put.

By now, Serephanie and Darrion had expected to be well away from the city and headed southbound in the shadows of the geese and songbirds fleeing for warmer climes. The League had no discernible reason to stay in the fields behind Greffold Heights. The gatekeepers and coin counters were reporting fewer attendees in the stands and shrinking ticket sales. From what the two of them had been told, that trend always signalled that it was time for the League to move on to a new region and a fresh audience. Regardless, the order to lift the stakes was yet to arrive.

It has to come soon, Serephanie reasoned while walking across the field with Darrion, bundled up with a coat, scarf, gloves, and hat, all of it in knitted wool. *We will be frozen into the field if we stay here for much longer.*

For the life of her, Serephanie could not recall a time when she had been so cold, though admittedly, it had been the most sheltered existence out of everyone within the orbit of the big tent. She kept complaints about it between her and Darrion, and even that she tried to keep to a minimum. However, if her work alongside Syrie was any evidence, she was clearly the only one making such an effort.

Every person that she and Syrie had come across in their daily duties, by either pursuit or happenstance, whinged about the weather and the slowing flow of coin to the League's associated revenue spinoffs. Most of all, people wanted to know if a departure date had been announced. Without hyperbole, it was the most sought after piece of information in the tent town, and fielding that question so often was clearly beginning to grate of Syrie's nerves.

"I know nothing about the move, so don't ask me," Syrie would practically chant as she and Serephanie went between the tents. "Aye, you're cold. Aye, you got family and lovers elsewhere that you want to see. Aye, you're not making enough coin, but there's not a damn thing that I can do about any of it."

Even the Drakian man with the long sword was concerned, or at least Serephanie assumed as much from Syrie's grumbling when she would return from talking with him at his secluded tent. Having learned from her first sighting of the white-haired man, Serephanie made no mention and asked no questions about him, and Syrie offered nothing in return. Yet, what she had seen in that one instance could not be denied.

I will know when and if I need to know, Serephanie had reminded herself.

It seemed that any reason that Cyrelle and Impresario Demorton had for holding the League in Bryten Field was held under the same sort of secrecy. Any meetings held to discuss the matter were reserved for just those two and Syrie, with anyone else being expressly prohibited from even being remotely close to Cyrelle's wheelhouse during said conversations. It had become a running gag between Serephanie, Dottie, and Dilla, with the three of them all ready to drop their tasks and practically flee at the sight of Demorton approaching the wheelhouse.

While the lack of forthcoming information bothered Serephanie to an extent, she did enjoy the chance to wander off with Cyrelle's handmaids without duty or direction. Dottie had warmed up considerably toward Serephanie since the two had verbally sparred during one of Darrion's training sessions, and thanks to Dottie's efforts, Dilla was coming around to Serephanie as well. As a result, Serephanie now frequently found herself invited to join the handmaids for leisurely pursuits when time and duty allowed. In order for Serephanie to be included in their leisurely activities, Dottie and Dilla first proposed to teach Serephanie how to read. To keep them from wasting considerable time and effort to tutor Serephanie in a skill she already possessed, she revealed to the handmaids that she in fact, was literate. To explain why 'Terra' knew how to read, Serephanie came up with a story of Darrion teaching her how to do so. Evidently, Serephanie had spun a convincing enough tale, as both women not only accepted Serephanie's lie, but were thoroughly taken with the apparent sweetness of Darrion's fabricated gesture.

With the need for tutoring gone by the wayside, the handmaids wasted no time in including Serephanie in their favourite pastimes. Notably, Dottie and Dilla enjoyed playing card games, indulging in white wine, and writing fictionalised romance stories starring the various members of the Sacred Fist. The former two activities Serephanie enjoyed quite a bit, even if she privately disagreed with Dottie's claims of expertise when it came to judging wines. It was the romance stories, Serephanie decided, that would be an acquired taste for her, if ever she warmed up to them.

That the tales were tawdry did not upset Serephanie, in fact, while such literature was banned in Illiastra, she had wanted to try reading from the romance genre if books pertaining to such could be obtained. Rather, Serephanie's problem stemmed from how the stories made her feel when in the presence of those chosen by Dottie and Dilla to star in the fictionalised romantics.

If you only knew what Dottie and Dilla were getting you up to in their stories, Serephanie would think as she and Syrie dealt with the people being fantasised. *The things that those two have had you do... And whom they have had you doing those acts with.*

She found that her opinions of the actual people changed as she read about their fictional representations, too, and she had to make a constant effort to keep the real person separate from the handmaid's romanticised versions.

It was enough to make Serephanie wonder if she and Darrion, either together or in separate entries, were written into one of the journals, or Syrie and Cyrelle, for that matter. If there were stories revolving around the people that Dottie and Dilla knew that Serephanie was close with, the handmaids took measures to conceal them from her. Either that or the pair only wrote about those with no greater than an arms-length relationship to themselves.

Despite her feelings on the matter, Serephanie still read what Dottie and Dilla penned, for she welcomed every distraction she could possibly get to help her through her grief. The truth though, was that nothing seemed capable of pulling Serephanie away from the grasp that the pain held on her.

When last Serephanie had seen Marscal, his illness told her plainly that it would be their final shared moments together. In the time since then, she had tried to steel herself for when the consumption disease inevitably took him away. To that end, she felt that having already been through a period of mourning, that she would be able to handle it when the news finally came.

I could not. Just hearing from those nobles of his condition during the Parliamentary Sessions in Atrebell sent me spiralling.

Serephanie knew that a gnawing feeling of regret was playing a large role in everything too. Not a day went by that she did not guilt herself into a headache for having left her sickly father's side when he needed support and family the most.

I could not stay. I had waited too long as it was. Marigold needed the time to be cemented as the heir, to let the idea of her as the natural successor to our father foster in the minds of those whose support she needed for her cause. Iia knows that I would be less than useless were I in her position right now.

Even if she had stayed with her sister, Serephanie knew that whatever Marigold could accomplish, Serephanie's presence would only undermine her work.

They would look at me as the true heir for simply being the older sibling. Detractors would use me as an excuse not to back Marigold, saying that they would only follow Marscal's natural successor, and even then, if I exerted any power, those same people would conveniently label me as Marigold's puppet.

Marigold deserves better than that, and I have to believe that I deserved better than to be thrust into a position I did not want. Of course, those would have been the best outcomes...

Serephanie's mind shuddered at the thought of the rule of the Palomb twins, and apparently, so too did the rest of her.

"Are you quite alright, darling?" she heard Darrion ask from beside her. "Would you like us to go home? If it is too much for you to be out and about, there is no shame in saying so."

Together the two had ventured into the nearest marketplace of Hercalest for a day out. Given that Darrion was permitted so few breaks since being granted a berth in the Sacred Fist as a trainee, Serephanie had proposed that they use the opportunity to leave Bryten Field and appreciate the offerings of Hercalest. She argued that such a chance would likely not present itself again for a year or more once the League removed itself from the city.

Darrion was worried about Serephanie, and how she was coping with the passing of her father, and readily agreed to the outing. While Serephanie appreciated his concern immensely, there were times when it felt as though it were a touch overbearing to her. "I am fine, Love. I was just thinking to myself."

"Alright then, but you will let me know if this gets to be too much, right?" he asked her carefully.

"Yes, of course, love," she replied, looking about at the various stalls to see what wares were being sold. "Quite a selection they have in this particular corner of the market. It appears to be all clothing and accessories."

There was an affirmative hum from Darrion in response to that. "One of these stalls should have stockings and undergarments. I think we should replenish our supplies before we head south. It's hard to say when we will find proper clothiers once we leave."

"An excellent proposition, darling," Serephanie agreed. "Perhaps we could get a few new articles to keep us warm, too. It will be some time before we reach the really warm climates."

"We can certainly see what they have to offer and try our hand at a little haggling, if you would like," Darrion proposed while stepping up to the nearest booth.

A thin, middle-aged man in a fitted, dark blue suit and a matching brimmed hat stood behind the table. He broke out in a smile while tugging at his suspenders and rocking on his heels during Darrion's approach. "Good day, good day, young man, are we perhaps in the market for some of the finest clothing in all of Hercalest?"

"Perhaps, good ser, do you by chance sell socks and undergarments?" Darrion responded with a query of his own.

"Yes, yes, of course we do, my good man, of course we do," the shopkeeper replied gaily while ducking beneath the counter to produce a clean stack of socks. "Will you take them in white or grey, and will you need garters?"

"No garters, ser, just the socks. I will take four pairs in either colour, if you can spare them, please," Darrion requested, while looking to Serephanie and suddenly having his eyes go wide with a sudden realisation. "Oh, and the same for my wife, with the socks all in white, please."

The salesman had retrieved a roll of brown paper and was carefully placing the socks on a sheaf he had spread on the table when Darrion had placed the order for Serephanie. He stopped his activity and considered her for a moment, the moustache on his face wiggling as he clicked his tongue. "I do not think I can do that, ser. You see, she is quite small, and unless her feet are enormous compared to the rest of her, I think that I have nothing that will fit. You see, I do not make women's clothing to begin with, so I tend to not tailor anything to such a small size as hers, not anything that I have amongst my regular stock, at least."

"Uh, alright then, just the socks and underpants for me, then, I suppose," Darrion said with a baffled shrug as he looked between the seller and Serephanie.

"Ask him where he recommends we go for women's clothes, then," Serephanie put to Darrion when she caught his glance.

"Oh, right," he jumped before looking back at the booth. "Ser, where would you advise us to go for women's clothes?"

"Hmm?" the clerk hummed as his attention remained focused on packing Darrion's purchases. "Oh, you should go see my brother-in-law, he runs a branch of my family's store over on Biltner Avenue that sells clothes for men, women, and children. *Lionel's on Biltner*, to be exact. This is the original *Lionel's Fine Clothing for Men*, started by, and named for, my great-grandfather. Why, we're as old as the Elite Merchants. Our motto is, 'Tailor-making the best tailors for four generations and counting'."

His family did not make the brother-in-law, Serephanie noted resentfully. *Something tells me that it is this man's sister who does the work at that store, and the brother-in-law gets all the credit and profits.*

"What is your waist size, young man? You look to be just a little more than ninety centimetres, to me," the salesman asked while plopping down a stack of underpants where the neat pile of socks had just been.

Darrion confirmed the man's guess, picked four choice pairs of the pants, and paid him sixteen coppers for the lot.

At the end of the exchange, the seller wrapped the clothing in the paper in a tidy square, tied it with twine and handed the bundle to Darrion while saying, "Remember now, when you go looking for the lady's clothes, it's *Lionel's on Biltner*, tell them that Bern sent you. Thank you for your custom, and have a great day, ser."

"I'll be sure to do that, thank you, ser," Darrion told him while accepting the package.

"He never even so much as acknowledged that I was even a person," Serephanie pointed out as they walked away.

Darrion's face contorted into an expression of resentment. "Aye, you're probably not used to that, given that people have typically doted on you in your old life for being... Well, you know. The sad reality though, is that this is usually how women are treated."

"It is outrageous, to be honest. I am a person as much as you," Serephanie continued.

"I agree, darling, truly I do," Darrion responded with noted nervousness. "But you may not want to say things like that too loudly, it might draw attention. He's probably been acting like that his whole life. Given the way things are, I would imagine that it is an accepted behaviour."

She stifled herself for the sake of getting by, but the indignation she felt was not so easily tempered. "Anyway, that is enough about that for now. Biltner Avenue is several blocks away, if memory serves me right, though I do not know exactly where on the street this *Lionel's* shop is. With that in mind, we had best get the work component of our adventure out of the way now, and then we can move on."

"Absolutely, darling," Darrion agreed with audible relief at the change of topic. "Do you see the stall that we were told to find?"

"Not in this particular corner of the market," Serephanie said while trying to look around as best as her short frame allowed. "Let's move on to the next row of stalls. This is the correct marketplace. Of that, I am sure. It just so happens to be the largest in the whole city, so there is a lot to sift through."

Hand in hand, they continued up and down the rows of booths and tables, stopping here and there to answer pleas from determined sellers or to examine things that caught the eye of one or the other. They purchased but a few things that they could use on their travels, including new toothbrushes, a crock of toothpowder, a sewing kit, a tin of shortbread biscuits, and a deck of playing cards. The products were stored carefully by Serephanie into Darrion's knapsack, watching it grow tighter as the bag of copper coins hanging on his waist lightened.

Along the last row of booths and tables, and tucked into the corner, Serephanie spotted a simple black on white sign that read, "*The Travelling Tome: Books and Stationary*"

"There it is, Love, look," she said while giving Darrion's hand a squeeze. "Let's hurry up, darling, for daylight is fading."

Together they approached the booth to find a white-haired man of approximately sixty years. At the rear of the store's small square of space on the street, Serephanie saw a person busily working while standing with their back to the counter. At first, Serephanie merely noticed their blue cloak, but beyond the outerwear, she caught sight of a brown, woollen dress and a bonnet. Given that the person was wearing such an outfit in a public space in Hercalest, Serephanie had to figure it was a woman.

The man, in a three-piece suit in grey, complete with a mustard yellow vest, approached the front of the outdoor shop space with his eyes locked on Darrion.

"Aye, what's it ya want, laddy? We're not far from closing hour, so you best make it quick," the man asked gruffly, the words slightly garbled by barely parting lips that held tight to a wooden pipe emitting tufts of smoke.

"I'm looking for a book," Darrion began his request.

"And somehow I knew that," the hard looking fellow replied in jest, a heavy hand running up through one of his bushy muttonchops. "Do you know what book? I got a lot of 'em, as you can see."

The other hand of the man gestured wide across several wooden pallets stacked nearly as tall as he with reading material. "Maybe you will want two or three books, make it easier on me poor ol' donkeys that gotta lug the leftovers home."

Darrion glanced towards Serephanie with uncertainty plain on his face. She told him what to say with a whisper and waved him forward before the salesman could see.

"I was sent by Mister Hunch of Bryten Street for his usual order," Darrion stated in a low voice. "He told me to tell you that he might catch the next train to Farmourd for the winter. Wants you to hold his next few orders until you hear from him again, if you don't mind."

The man's thick eyebrows shot up, and a wrinkled forehead curled with it. "Hey now, you're not one of the usual lads running orders for him."

"The others were too busy, so they sent the new guy. That would be me, ser," Darrion replied in a manner that was as quick as it was anxious.

Serephanie glanced around and saw no one, either guard or civilian, paying the booth any mind, but that did little to put her at ease.

"I see, I see," the man said, falling quiet while he seemed to ponder something for a moment. "Ralla, this lad and lass need Mister Hunch's usual order. Do you know where it is?"

"Aye, Da, it came in with this morning's shipment," the woman answered, raising her head from where it was, the clinking coins in her hand indicating that she was in the act of counting them. "I wrapped it and put it under the counter."

She wore a loose fitting, brown dress and a white smock under a blue cloak, all of it faded and well worn. While the men had been talking, Serephanie had seen nothing of Ralla's face, but upon being spoken to, Serephanie caught sight of a freckled visage of about forty outlined with a head of bouncing red curls that she had been hiding.

The man bent down below the line of sight with a groan, his round belly making the task difficult. "I don't see it, Ralla. Be a lamb and come help your ol' father find it, would ya?"

"I swear you'd lose your head if it wasn't attached to your shoulders, Da," Ralla said with exaggerated frustration. As she reached the front of the booth, she produced the paper-wrapped package with her first reach. "Look, it was right in front of you."

"Hey now, hold your tongue, Ralla," the salesman said worriedly. "If the guards hear you backtalk a man they will expect me to correct the behaviour, even if I am just your tangly ol' da."

The woman groaned at that while handing her father the package, "Aye, Da, sorry about that."

"Hush now, there's no need for saying sorry, just so long as you don't call attention," he told her while taking the parcel and turning it over to Darrion. "Here you go now, lad. Tell Mister Hunch that I might have trouble getting books from the printers out west for a while, but I will hold whatever packages I get for him. Understood?"

"Yes, ser, understood clearly," Darrion told him while giving the package to Serephanie who immediately went to the task of stuffing it into Darrion's pack. "What do I owe?"

Serephanie noticed Ralla looking across the counter at Darrion, studying him intently. She slid sideways towards her father and whispered something in his ear quickly that gave him pause. "Is that so? Ralla says she saw you last time she went to Mister Hunch's and that you are surprisingly good at what you do. You'll have to forgive me lad, my eyes are not what they used to be, and I must not have seen it myself. I'll take Ralla's word, though. Oh, and four coppers is the total."

Darrion thanked them both for the compliment and paid the requested amount, laying the coins directly in Ralla's now outstretched hand. They parted with shared farewells between the four, and left *The Travelling Tome* behind.

"Closing time! Closing time!" a herald called out from atop a house balcony overlooking the market. "Please, complete all sales and exit the market in an orderly fashion. We will reopen again in the morning."

Serephanie intertwined her fingers with Darrion's, his strong grip holding tight as they waded into the throng of people leaving the market with them. Unable to see, Serephanie had to rely on Darrion to navigate, and she hugged in tightly against his shoulder, the hood of her cloak over her head and her eyes on the ground beneath them.

"You, there!" she heard what sounded to be a man's voice call out, daring not to look up for herself to verify.

"Who, me?" Darrion called back to the owner of the voice.

"No, not you, ya lummox, but get out of the way all the same," the voice called back.

Suddenly, Darrion was moving sideways, pulling Serephanie with him.

"There, Chapman, grab that one by the big muscly idiot!" the same voice called out, causing Serephanie to freeze in terror.

She felt Darrion turning, putting Serephanie in a defensive position behind him. "What is going on here?" Darrion asked of someone that Serephanie had to figure was a city guard.

Against her better judgement, Serephanie lifted her head high enough to peek out through her hood, her eyes falling on a man in a blue guardsman's coat standing on a low baily above the gates of the market. Another guard was pushing and shouting for people to stand aside on the ground near them, and as they obeyed, his pace quickened.

"Is he coming for me?" she whispered to Darrion, though it went unheard as he repeated his earlier question to the approaching guard.

Serephanie spotted a rail-thin woman in an old, stained dress who was trying to move away, shuffling between the couple and the guard in a slow, laboured fashion.

"Wait, stop right there!" the guard on the ground called out, grabbing the woman by the arm and yanking her sharply toward him.

The strange woman fell into the guard, and a messy head of long hair went flying toward his face.

"Help! Someone, please help!" she cried out as she was taken to the ground.

"Bind her hands, Chapman!" the guard situated above the crowd ordered loudly above the woman's unheeded pleas. His partner below straddled the woman's back as she hit the ground, and he carried out the order quickly with a pair of handcuffs he produced from his belt.

The woman kicked uselessly from beneath the arresting officer all the while. As she did, a pair of brown slip-on shoes flipped off her feet, revealing that her ankles were linked together with a set of ugly, black irons.

"The woman's a slave," Darrion gasped while continuing to shield Serephanie.

"Stand back or move along, people, there is nothing to see here!" the guard up above commanded of the onlookers.

Darrion took the cue to keep moving, pulling Serephanie with him, much to her dismay.

The guard was pulling the restrained woman to her feet as Serephanie and Darrion continued on hurriedly with their departure.

"Put her in the wagon, Chapman," instructed the overhead guard. "We'll see if we can't find her owner before sundown. If not, she goes to the lockup. Damn runaways."

With the market behind them, and daylight fading, both Serephanie and Darrion agreed to postpone their visit to the second *Lionel's* store. Serephanie reasoned that she might convince Dottie and Dilla to arrange for the three of them to go shopping together for their next activity, if such an opportunity presented itself before the League left Bryten Field. Dottie and Dilla always seemed capable of mustering up men to escort them about in public, and she knew that they enjoyed shopping, so the request would likely be heeded.

Barring that brief discussion, the remainder of their return to Bryten Field derived no further conversation, as Serephanie's mind went to a place of utter sadness for what she had witnessed with the enslaved woman.

When the silence was finally broken, it was Darrion who did so. "The field is ahead, watch your step onto the path, darling."

"We should have done something," she declared remorsefully.

"If only I could have, darling," he replied, his voice as morose as hers.

"It's not right," Serephanie told him bitterly.

Evidently, he agreed with the sentiment. "No, it's not. To be honest, I had never seen an actual slave before. Or at least I don't think I have."

Serephanie shook her head, realising too late that the activity was futile, given that Darrion was not looking at her. "You would not have seen them in either part of Twin Bay. My father..."

The mere mention of Marscal sent a shock through Serephanie, and she had to take a moment to compose herself. "My father could not expressly forbid the practice, but he showed enough disdain toward it that anyone who engaged in buying slaves did so well out of sight. Greggard Simillon felt the same way as my father when he replaced his own sire, and so anyone in Portsward who engaged in slavery also took to doing so in secret."

"The poor woman was in chains, for crying out loud," Darrion uttered through gritted teeth. "How can that be right?"

"That is an eastern practice, as far as I know," Serephanie explained. "You heard the guard. She was accused of being a runaway, and it probably was not her first time. Some slavers put all their workers in leg irons, while others only chain those who pose a risk of fleeing. A select few, like Clay Harlowe down in the Warrens, chain them hand and foot and secure them to the walls of their workplace."

"The sickening part is that all of it is perfectly legal," Darrion commented over the sound of the tarps of the nearing tents responding to the wind pulling and pushing on them. "I wanted to help her so badly, but if I had, we would both be in chains now too. There is not one thing we could have done to help her without damning ourselves."

Serephanie swallowed hard as Darrion spoke, the truth of his words ringing in her ears. "You are right, Love. That does not make me wish any less that we had tried, though."

He was looking at Serephanie then, having stopped in his tracks. "Would your sister put a stop to it if she could?"

"Oh, without a doubt," Serephanie answered proudly. "She just needs the chance to do so."

"I hope she gets that chance, then," Darrion said with anger flaring through in his response. "I hope she makes the slavers suffer as they have made those under their whip suffer."

"Hello, you two!" a voice heavy with the Gallician dialect called to them. She raised her head to lay eyes on Na'Zohz, presently waving to get their attention. "Come over here a moment!"

They parted hands and jogged toward Na'Zohz, whose behaviour seemed urgent, or as urgent as he was like to get, Serephanie reckoned.

"What can we do for you, Na'Zohz, ser?" Darrion asked once they were close enough to converse.

He waved them in until they stood within a few dozen centimetres, where he could speak to them in a whisper. "Go see Lady Cyrelle, immediately. Syrie asked me to flag you down as soon as you came back. Go on, now, on the double."

The two shared a concerned glance, and Serephanie answered for them, "Thank you for telling us, ser. We'll go straight away."

They strode off hastily around the big tent, and in their hurry, almost walked into Kellum and Lyle exiting through the back door.

"Coming through! Heads up!" Kellum called out, as the two exited bearing a long, thick wooden beam that was being carried between them.

Darrion and Serephanie dashed out of the way, with the former speaking up, "Fellas, what's going on?"

"The ring is coming down. We got the order to clear out without delay," Lyle answered hurriedly during their departure with the heavy piece of lumber.

"We better hurry to Cyrelle," Darrion told Serephanie. "Mister Lancer is going to be expecting me to help tear down whatever is left of the ring and the Sportatorium."

The last word puzzled her, "Wait, what is the Sportatorium?"

"That's the official name of the big tent." Darrion explained while getting back up to speed. "Everyone just calls it 'the big tent', though, so the name gets lost. Mister Lancer keeps trying to get Kellum, Lyle, and me to use the proper name like he does, to try and bring it back."

Dilla was the next person they saw, lugging a trunk from the tent she shared with Dottie. "You know that Lady Cyrelle is looking for you, right?" she asked as Serephanie and Darrion passed.

"Yes, thank you Dilla!" Serephanie called back over her shoulder. "Maybe I will see you and Dottie tonight once we get on the road!"

A wave served as Dilla's response, and once Serephanie returned the gesture, she was looking forward once more. Try as she might, Serephanie was having a difficult time keeping up with the strides of Darrion, who was only at a casual jog compared to her near sprint.

"Damn you and your long legs!" she shouted at him half-heartedly.

The door to Cyrelle's wheelhouse appeared to be locked when Darrion tried it, and he began knocking immediately after the failed attempt to open the door.

"Aye now, what's all this racket?" Syrie asked in surprise as she flung open the door. "Oh, it's you two. What perfect timing, I was afraid that Lady Cyrelle was going to send me to search for you again. Na'Zohz told you that we were looking for you, I'm guessing?"

A nod preceded Serephanie's reply. "He did, yes. Shall we come in?"

Syrie stepped down from the wheelhouse and moved aside. "Aye, of course. Lady Cyrelle is getting antsy."

Inside the wheelhouse, Serephanie heard several voices speaking in turn, albeit frantically. The office, where they first looked, was empty, and they turned instead to the sitting room, finding Cyrelle hosting Impresario Demorton and a stranger of a woman dressed head to heel in black leather.

"Terra and Cole, it is good to see you both," Cyrelle greeted them, using their sobriquets as an indicator of the level of secrecy needed in this company. "Allow me to introduce you to N'ailla Sa-Terys, an associate of the League of the Sacred Fist. N'ailla, this is Cole Chere and his wife, Terra. The former is a newly signed trainee, and Terra is a pleasant signing bonus for us."

The woman stood to shake their hands, and offer 'how-do-you-do's in a thick Johnan accent.

Cyrelle gestured an open hand toward the Johnan. "N'ailla here was just delivering us an important piece of news that she was sent all the way from Barnam in the Obalen region to deliver. She tells us that she risked sneaking aboard a military train that took her far as Atrebell, stowed away again from there to Biddenhurst, and then rode a third train from the prison city to here."

"That is quite the journey, Miss Sa-Terys," Serephanie commented impressively. "What could be so important?"

N'ailla was still on her feet and looking back and forth between Cyrelle and Serephanie in an effort to gauge some sort of response from the former.

"Please, N'ailla, feel free to tell our friends here," Cyrelle permitted with a sly grin. "Chances are that they are carrying the same news in written form from our usual messenger. By the way, Terra, I will take that package if you have it."

Without delay and while N'ailla was speaking, Serephanie went to Darrion's backpack and produced the purchase from *The Travelling Tome*. Seconds later, she laid it directly into Cyrelle's waiting hands.

"An associate of mine in Daol Bay sent us a contract for a job that she has already approved of," N'ailla began cautiously. "It needs the final approval from another associate here in Hercalest, but the Hercalest associate needs help from Lady Cyrelle and your group in order to see it to fruition."

The whole thing only served to baffle Serephanie, and a glance to Darrion indicated that he was feeling exactly the same way, and Serephanie answered for the both of them. "I apologise, Miss Sa-Terys, but I don't understand what any of that meant."

Cyrelle pinched the bridge of her nose and let out a laugh. "Your confusion is entirely my fault, I apologise to the three of you for that."

Seated upon the sofa, Cyrelle gave it a gentle pat. "All of you take a seat. I must explain a few things to Cole and Terra. Syrie, go into the office and grab one of the chairs there for yourself to sit on, please."

Serephanie had not even noticed Syrie having come to stand behind her and Darrion, and nearly jumped at the sight of her standing so close.

"Sorry, I'm told I can be as quiet as a shadow sometimes," Syrie offered by way of apology for startling Serephanie.

"No, no, that is alright, I should have known you were there, given that it was you who let us in," Serephanie replied, waving off the need for an apology.

They parted there, leaving Syrie to retrieve a chair while Serephanie and Darrion joined Cyrelle on the sofa.

Cyrelle pointed a hand to the coffee table before them and the food and drink upon it. "Would either of you care for green tea and some lovely saltines with a delicious spinach-based spread?"

Both accepted the offer, and Serephanie took the time to serve tea to not just the recent arrivals, but to both N'ailla and Demorton too, both of whom were seeking refills.

"It is hard to know where to begin explaining things," Cyrelle started while looking to the impresario. "I guess the obvious part is that as you know already, Markus Demorton answers to me, and is the impresario of the League of the Sacred Fist in name only. His actual title, amongst those with knowledge of such matters, is 'Director of Event Operations', and it is I who is the actual Impresario of the League. Demorton takes care of everything relating to the fighting events we produce, leaving me free to handle our actual mission."

"What mission might that be, Lady Cyrelle?" Serephanie asked warily.

"To help the oppressed escape the ties that bind them," Cyrelle said, a proud smile working its way from ear to ear. "Do you remember me and Everett Lancer alike telling you what seems like a long time ago now that there was a road forward for women who come seeking it with the Sacred Fist?"

Serephanie nodded slowly. "Yes, I do, Lady Cyrelle."

Cyrelle's hands went wide to gesture to Syrie and N'ailla seated across from her. "After years of using that phrasing in reference to our operation, it slowly morphed into the name of our nationwide outfit. Perhaps you have heard of the Women's Road?"

The name meant nothing to Serephanie, but invoking it seemed to be a point of pride for Cyrelle, Syrie, and N'ailla, so she dared not dash their enthusiasm. "Oh, yes, the Women's Road, that's a name I had heard around Daol Bay. In hushed whispers, of course."

"You humour me, I can tell," Cyrelle noted before seguing into an explanation. "Our network, extending from Ravenkeep to Tippard, to Daol Bay, and down to Farmourd in the south, can be found in every major holdfast. We seek out women, children, and other oppressed minorities who are in need of escape and protection from their husbands, guardians, and masters. Our goal is to provide them with the services they need to accomplish that. Often, we facilitate their transport to safe havens, be they in Phaleayna in the Southlands, overseas to a country willing to grant asylum, or even just to friends and relatives sometimes located in the same region. Nothing is out of our reach, in that regard."

Cyrelle stopped long enough for an extended sip of tea, and went right back into her teaching. "The League of the Sacred Fist is our primary means of transporting those seeking refuge. Given that it is a travelling show fronted by some highly intimidating men engaging in a largely inconspicuous and highly distracting medium, it more than serves its purpose. Very few investigative city guardsmen or highway patrolmen are going to go poking around where Tahru, 'Glorious' Gilbare, and Barajah call home, or at least not without due cause, search warrants, and heavy backup in tow.

"While our fighters entertain the masses, we women, the ones that Syrie told you were the Wives of the Ring, operate in the shadows," Cyrelle revealed, her delight in her work clear in her voice. "First, we accept contracts from those in need of escape and investigate their case both to verify the claim and to establish mission parameters. Once we have that in place, we then extract the targets to our camp and integrate them into the staff. From there, they simply need to wait until we eventually move out, and then we safely escort the target to wherever it is that they so desire to go. If the camp is not in town, our agents bring them to a safe location and either wait for the camp to arrive, if we are due in town within a reasonable timeframe. If not, an escort is arranged to get the target either to the camp, or to their desired location, if that is the more feasible option."

"All of that is going on behind the scenes in a professional fighting club," Serephanie uttered in awe. "I never would have imagined such an elaborate ruse taking place here."

"Oh, really?" Cyrelle said with a scoff. "You and your man figured out that the winner of the fights is usually determined before the fight even starts."

All eyes went to Darrion then. "I have to admit that I was disappointed to learn that," he told the room with a smirk. "However, I had come this far, so I wanted to know how much further I could go with the League, regardless of that world-shattering revelation. In terms of figuring it out, all I did was pay attention to what Mister Lancer was telling me during the exercise where he told me and the other trainees that we had to lose. I gathered that it was not that we lost that he was concerned with, it was how we handled the request."

"It was astutely done, lad," Demorton chimed in. "Everett told me that he was quite impressed that anyone picked up on it. The other two are still in the dark, and Everett, while unsure of their potential, is taking them on the tour as a trial run. ...You though," Demorton said with a smile in Darrion's direction. "You, he is ready to begin training in earnest."

Darrion looked utterly shocked. "I... I don't know what to say, ser. I am flabbergasted and delighted to hear that. I will do everything I can for the Sacred Fist, I promise. Thank you, to you too, Lady Cyrelle, and to Mister Lancer for this opportunity."

"You are quite welcome, Darrion," Cyrelle told him with a grin. "I have no doubt that you will be a valuable asset to the League."

Cyrelle leaned forward to look at Serephanie then, who tried her best to hide her fear following Cyrelle's use of Darrion's real name. "As for you, I think that as Darrion will be valuable in the ring, you will have a role to play in the Women's Road. For starters, we have an immediate use for your, shall we say, *former connections*."

Serephanie felt an anxious wave roll over her, and looked to the women across the room for assurance, finding some measure of such in the calm, confident expression that Syrie wore.

With Syrie's approving glance, Serephanie gave response to Cyrelle, "I will do what I can to help, Lady Cyrelle. What do you have in mind for me?"

"I will let N'ailla tell you," Cyrelle instructed while opening the package that was received from the bookseller. "I have a feeling that the same tidings are contained in here, and I would like to confirm as much while N'ailla talks. Go ahead, dear."

"Yes, as I said before, we received a highly lucrative contract from a wealthy noble in the west," N'ailla attempted to inform Serephanie for the second time. "This highborn went in search of us, and once found, they requested the extraction of three equally rich people right here in Hercalest with the request that they be brought to safety in Daol Bay. Normally, we ask for nothing in the way of compensation from our contracts, unless they offer it after the fact. However, this noble came with a promise of a fortune in gold, and rightfully so, as this job requires the use of every asset at our present disposal, myself included."

The mention of Daol Bay came at Serephanie like a kick to the chest. *If this noble is from the upper crust of Daol Bay, I almost certainly know them.*

"The Pathfinder representing us in Twin Bay decided to allow the contract to proceed as far as us for deliberation," N'ailla continued on while that Serephanie's mind wandered. "Nothing is confirmed as of yet, though and both the local Pathfinder and Lady Cyrelle will both need to sign off on this job before we can begin with preparations. That level of approval from both parties is needed in this situation on account of our Hercalest agents requiring assistance from the League if we are to succeed at all."

Cyrelle was busy leafing through a stack of papers that had been concealed between the pages of a pair of books, sorting them into different orders, her furrowed gaze indicating that she was trying to make sense of what was in her hands. "Oh, I am more than happy to sign off on this one, N'ailla. What the Pathfinder in Twin Bay did not know is that we have the perfect asset sitting right next to me that can make this particular job work."

N'ailla had ceased talking, and waited until Cyrelle paid her attention. "Lady Cyrelle, shall I tell the girl the names of our targets and their benefactor?"

A smirk and a nod from Cyrelle conveyed her excitement as much as her words. "Yes, N'ailla, please do."

"Very well, Lady Cyrelle," N'ailla confirmed while clearing her throat and turning back to Serephanie. "We were contacted by the current Lady of the Autonomous Nation of West Illiastra, Marigold

Tullivan. Our targets are Jorette Palomb, and her youngest children, Nareen and Dorian."

Serephanie visibly reacted to that revelation, her eyes blinking rapidly and her mouth falling open. "Wait, Marigold Tullivan of where? Extracting Palombs? To what end?"

A hand of Cyrelle's went into the air while holding a single sheaf of the paper. "Yes, it's written here as well. Marigold officially split Illiastra in two. It would seem that our country has shrunk since last we checked. Everything west of Obalen and north of the Varras River is now a separate nation entirely."

Cyrelle's eyes fell directly on Serephanie, and she felt the woman's glee as she said, "How do you like that? She pulled it off. Are you not proud of her?"

N'ailla raised a single eyebrow, confusion etched across her face. "Why would Terra be proud of that, Lady Cyrelle?"

"Terra here knows Lady Marigold quite well, I should say," Cyrelle said with a nudge of her elbow. "Go on, you can tell N'ailla. Besides, she is far too smart to let my earlier error go unnoticed."

"You mean when you referred to Cole as Darrion? I thought that odd, alright..." N'ailla thought out aloud. "So how do you know Lady Marigold, Miss Terra?"

Serephanie exhaled audibly and let go of her secret. "I know Lady Marigold because she is my little sister, Miss Sa-Terys."

It was N'ailla's turn to be shocked, her eyes widening as the revelation struck her. "You are the lost Tullivan daughter?" she said while pointing toward Serephanie, her finger as quickly landing on Darrion. "Then he must be the man accused of kidnapping her."

"I certainly did not kidnap Serephanie," Darrion reacted defensively. "I rescued her in much the same fashion that your organisation seems to operate. Surely you would not believe an accusation levelled by the EMP of all people."

"No, ser, I do not believe a word said by those wealthy vermin," N'ailla said in a candour matching that of Darrion's. "I am merely repeating what they have put out to the people as their version of the truth."

"There are no alternative versions of truth. There is just the truth and fabrications," Cyrelle stated firmly, her own finger holding in N'ailla's direction.

"Forgive me, Lady Cyrelle. You are correct, of course," N'ailla offered contritely.

Cyrelle turned in her place on the sofa until she was facing Serephanie. "You know Jorette Palomb and her children, correct?"

"I do, yes," Serephanie confirmed, looking nervously at her hands gripping tight to the blue, tartan dress she wore.

"Their staff too?" Cyrelle asked next. "Servants and guards that might be sympathetic toward Lady Jorette in particular would be most useful."

"I do know a good many of them. I should also mention that whoever I do not know by name, I can identify by sight, if that is helpful," Serephanie told her.

"You have also been inside the Palomb Palace as well, I take it?" Cyrelle asked next.

Serephanie's heart began to race wildly in her chest, the beating so loud that she was sure everyone else could hear it. "I might have been..."

"Excellent," Cyrelle exclaimed while laying the papers and books on the corner of the low table. "That means that you could draw us a map of the palace layout, give us names of their house staff who might be convinced to aid us, and perhaps... Well, would you be capable of making contact with Lady Jorette herself?"

Serephanie began to shake, and she grabbed for Darrion's nearest hand, grabbing as tight as she could.

"Are you alright, darling?" he asked while looking into her eyes. "You need only tell me if you are not."

"That palace..." Serephanie managed to mutter. "I cannot go back there. None of you know, and I do not want to relive the memory long enough to tell you what I have experienced there. Just please, do not ask me to go back."

"No one is going to make you go anywhere near it, Love," Darrion declared while wrapping his big arms around her. "Do all of you hear me? Sacred Fist or not, I will walk away from all of this if you try to force Serephanie to go to the Palomb Palace. Look at what you are doing to her for just asking."

Serephanie started to take deep breaths, and tried to look anywhere but at the others outside of her and Darrion's sphere. "I can draw you maps, and I will even speak to her staff if you can arrange to meet outside of Greffold Hills, can convince them to help, and are sure of that cooperation. I guarantee that I will trust your judgement in that matter. In fact, bring Jorette, Nareen, and Dorian here and I will show them the same generous hospitality that I have been shown. Nevertheless, I will not set foot near where Eldridge and Pyore might find me."

"We would never ask you to do any such thing, Terra. You have my word," Syrie said from across the small room. "My friends and I will handle matters in the palace. Besides, from the way you make it sound, I would like to introduce those Palomb boys to my knife."

"No, stay away from them, Syrie, they would kill you if you got close," Serephanie pleaded with a shake of her head. "Them or their cousin that protects them, he is quite deadly in his own right."

"Do you think I am afraid of a few fops, Terra?" Syrie said with a derisive scoff. "They would not be the first men I killed. Won't be the last, either, in this line of work."

N'ailla spoke up then, "Speaking of, I was sent to replace you as the liberator in the Nemeth district. The local Pathfinder feels that you have spent time enough here and should move on with the League. From what we are hearing, you have made a reputation and a nickname for yourself. The Nemeth district needs to cool down, and the guards need to believe that you are gone before we can resume our work there unimpeded."

"I figured as much," Syrie said with disappointment. "I was used to that district too, knew it like the back of my hand at this point. Now don't mistake me, N'ailla, I am ready to move on and give you Nemeth district, because you're right to say that I've been there far too long. Besides, this job might take up all my time from here on out, not to mention the fact that it could damn well put our whole operation on high alert in Hercalest. Of course, it goes without saying that high profile targets like Eamon Palomb's own wife and children will need all the protection that we can give them."

Cyrelle had taken to rubbing Serephanie's free hand reassuringly, though her focus was across the room. "I will be glad to have you back in my employ full time again, Syrie. You were missed this last year on the road."

"Aye, it will be good to see the open countryside again..." Syrie mused with cautious optimism. "Although, living long enough to see any of that means having to first steal away into the night from the Palomb Palace with three of their friggin' family members in tow."

"That is where Serephanie can be of great assistance," Cyrelle said with a pat of Serephanie's hand. "Will you help us? I promise that when the operation commences that you will be well away from Hercalest and in the safety of the convoy, which as you have seen, are getting ready to vacate Bryten Field by tomorrow morning."

"Might I ask if that is why the order to leave was finally given, Lady Cyrelle?" Serephanie put to her.

Cyrelle took some humour in that. "Actually, Serephanie, we were merely waiting to see what your sister did. Truthfully, we were expecting her to do something drastic as soon as she had the power to do so, and wanted to make no moves until we knew where the League could safely travel without scrutiny. Seceding entirely from Illiastra caught us off guard, admittedly. Her contractual offer that followed, on the other hand, was entirely unprecedented. That was something that I never would have predicted even if I had the rest of my life to do so."

"I wish I could offer some reason why she wants Eamon's wife and youngest children. Certainly, I can see her worrying for their safety. Eamon and his sons are cruel beasts, and are not above hurting their own. That alone would compel her to action, but there is probably more at play that we do not know about. Jorette herself may not even know what Marigold's motives are."

"Well, while we can certainly sit here all day and ponder your sister's logic, Serephanie," Cyrelle said, with an obvious proposition to follow. "I must ask again, for posterity's sake, will you lend us your knowledge on the Palombs and their household?"

Serephanie looked to Darrion, and found assurance in his eyes. Imbued with his confidence, she gave answer, "With your promise that I not be directly involved, I will help you, Lady Cyrelle. I promise that you will know every detail that I can possibly provide. We will get Jorette and her children out of that wretched palace."

25
MARIGOLD

From the moment that she had put her head down on her pillow in the Tullivan family quarters aboard *The Princess of Daol* that evening, Marigold knew that she would not sleep. She stared at the ceiling, her eyes having long adjusted to the darkness, allowing her to discern every beam and runner on the ceiling above. The ship rocked gently beneath, creaking and groaning with the roll of the Casparian Sea.

Lying next to her was Moya, resting on her side and facing away from Marigold. With limited space on the ship for crew, guards, and Marigold's entourage, most on board, save for the captain, were made to open up their sleeping spaces to others. Marigold had chosen Moya to share her bed with before they had even boarded the ship, and thus far, it had been an enjoyable experience. Her friend was a light sleeper with a gentle, barely audible snore that Marigold found almost soothing. Looking upon Moya lying as she currently was, it reminded Marigold of sharing a bed with her sister.

It is the hair, Marigold told herself while glancing over at Moya. *The differences between their colouring and length would be imperceptible. Otherwise, they look nothing else alike. It seems that she has stopped snoring, that's odd.*

"Moya, are you sleeping?" Marigold asked in a whisper, counting off the seconds while she waited for an answer.

"Did I wake you?" Moya answered while rolling over to face her. "I was trying to be still so as not to disturb you. Our day will begin before you know it. You should make sure to get your rest before then."

Marigold rolled to her side, reached out, and took Moya's hand, "You did not wake me at all. I simply could not sleep. Every possible scenario that might happen in just a few hours has been running through my head simultaneously."

"There has been quite a lot running through my mind as well," Moya revealed, squeezing back on Marigold's hand. "The last time I was in Pelican Harbour it was the worst day of my life. It should be said that it was a pretty miserable existence before I met you, so you can imagine how awful my experience in Pelican Harbour was if it surpassed everything that came before.

"I also can't help but think about poor Bess," Moya said sadly. "All she did was run away from her father who used to beat her, and for having done that, she ended up dying. I keep wondering why the gods allowed her to be killed, and why I was spared."

Marigold reached for a strand of Moya's long hair and let it fall across her friend's face. "That's why, Moya. Bess had brown hair, like mine. The guards killed her first because she was my surrogate on those scaffolds and they wanted me to watch their version of me die. You were standing in for my sister, because of your golden hair, and that spared your life long enough for Freyard and Glendil to save you."

"Bess died because of the colour of her hair?" Moya asked in a voice that was just utterly, heartbreakingly despondent. "I hadn't even thought of that. Why would that Nothram man stoop to that level? Why would those guards carry out his wishes? Why am I even asking? My husband would have done the same if a minister had asked him. My father too, for that matter. Why are so many men so awful, Marigold?"

"To that I have no answer," Marigold sighed. "I just thank whatever powers there are in the universe that we are surrounded by those who recognise their privilege and are willing to use it for the right reasons. You are a praying woman, Moya. Have you said a prayer for all the people who are going to fight for us today?"

"I will, if you would so like it," Moya consented to the request. "I will be saying a lot of prayers before the fighting starts. Here's a secret that I have told no one, not even Sydnee: I don't pray to Ios. My father used to force me and all my little brothers and sisters to go to mass at the Tower of Ios. He would herd us in and watch us like a hawk to make sure we were praying along with the Patriarch. I did as I was told, and taught the others that were old enough to understand to do the same. Yet, from the time that I was about six, I began saying all my prayers to Iia and Aren. I mean, it is the Triarchy, right? That means the three of them are all in it together, but the Triarchists only care about Ios. I have heard the Patriarch of our town talking about the gods, and though the human Triarchists might not like Iia and Aren, by their own teachings, they too are gods every bit as powerful as Ios.

"I have to say, even from the stories I heard from the Patriarchs during mass, Iia and Aren seem like nice, fair gods. They worked together to stop Ios from erasing the elves and dwarves, they care for the weak and the sick, love the beggars and scorn the greedy."

Moya's voice trailed off momentarily, and Marigold looked in her direction to see how she was doing, finding her friend having scrunched up her face in curiosity. Their eyes met, and Moya continued talking. "For all of that, the Triarchists treat Iia and Aren as if they are just there to keep Ios company. There is nothing so good about him, though. It seems like all Ios knows how to do is sow hate and jealousy. He commands men to destroy the creations of Iia and Aren for not worshipping him. What kind of a god would do that? If he cannot convince regular people like us to worship him, can we even say that Ios is much of a god? I mean, it's a god. It should not take much convincing for a god to prove itself. It needs only to show up and say, 'It's me, Ios, worship me.' Then again, why would a god be so desperate for attention that it creates beings just to worship it? Why would a god need to be worshipped? That seems... Needy, doesn't it?"

Moya had pulled the thick blankets to her chin until nothing but her face was visible. "I never could bring myself to ask any adult those questions. My father beat me over the littlest of things as it was, let alone questioning the gods themselves. So, though my father and later my husband never knew it, I began to say all my prayers to the fair gods, Iia and Aren." There was a pause in Moya's soliloquy, and she rolled onto her back, her gaze going to the ceiling overhead. "You know, even though I went through some terrible times to get here, maybe Iia and Aren did answer my prayers by bringing me to you."

"I cannot say for sure, Moya," Marigold admitted, now looking at the ceiling herself. "What I am certain of is that I am glad for every day that you are in my life. I think it was quite cleverly done of you to pray to Iia and Aren instead of Ios, though."

"I say the same about having met you," Moya replied with her charming little laugh. "If you don't mind my asking, do you really not pray? Do you not believe in the gods?"

Marigold considered what she wanted to say, feeling Moya's eyes on her as she did. "I do not know what I believe in, to be honest. Everyone in my immediate family is gone. Ripped from me by disasters at sea, terrible disease, or, in my grandmother's case, she just died in her sleep, with no prior warning that it was coming. When I was but a babe, my parents went to bed one night with grandmother alive and well, and woke to find she was gone, just like that. Apparently, her heart just stopped beating.

"Even my sister, the only option she had was to leave her home and family behind. Nothing father or I could have said or done would have convinced her otherwise, because the Palombs had already forced her into a corner. Why would the gods will into existence a world where that sort of anguish is permitted on any one person?

"Look at what you have been through, Moya. You have been through far too much in your short lifetime. So much hurt and pain, but there are people out there who have suffered even more. That's not to detract from what you have endured, of course.

"A god of any level of mercy would not allow that, I would have to think. Oh sure, they say it is all to teach us lessons and make us worthy of joining them in eternity, but why bother making us suffer for a relative fraction of time just to determine where we spend all the rest of existence that supposedly comes after? It has never made sense to me to let such a tiny piece of eternity be the bar by which to judge whether a person can spend the rest of all time in either complete bliss or constant punishment. What do I know, though? Maybe there are gods, but I have to believe that if there are, they just have no desire to pay us any mind and are indifferent to our suffering. To that end, I simply cannot be bothered to pay any heed to all-powerful creators who would allow or cannot be bothered to prevent the suffering of our world. I shall go on without the gods, and if they want to prove to me that they exist, they need only show their faces and do so."

Moya had nothing to offer in response to that, her eyes remaining fixed on the ceiling above.

Marigold suddenly felt terrible for having been so critical of the faith to which Moya clung. "I apologise if anything I have said has hurt you, Moya. It was not my intention."

"It has given me a lot to think about, that's all. There's nothing to worry about," she muttered back.

They laid there, in the dark, together yet alone for what felt like the better part of an hour. When Marigold finally thought that sleep might visit her, however briefly, there came a knock at the door from an actual visitor.

"Lady Marigold, tis Captain Cayan. I am sorry for waking you, but we have sailed within sight of Pelican Harbour," the ship's captain from without.

"Thank you, Captain. I will be right out," Marigold told him. She turned her attention to Moya and said, "I won't ask you to come above deck, for you might not like what is about to happen. Yet, if you so choose to join me, I would welcome the company, Moya."

While waiting for an answer, Marigold had thrown back the covers and swung her legs over the side of the bed, touching down on a soft rug that her feet barely felt for how quickly she was across the room. Her ashen grey, leather trousers went on quickly, though she fumbled nervously with the laces as she tried to tie them. Her tunic, which had been doubling as a nightshirt for convenience, she left untucked and her boots went on haphazardly, laced in some fashion so they were not outright clumsy for navigation. Atop her outfit was a combination of woollen coat, ermine gloves, and a warm black cloak, the hood of which was pulled up over her head as she headed for the door.

In the hallway outside there were men dressed head to heel in black moving about hurriedly, coming and going in either direction. The captain had remained in wait, directing a few of his crew as they passed.

"Captain Cayan, what is our status?" Marigold asked as she pulled the door closed behind her.

The captain began walking toward the stairway hatch that led to the topside while he gave answer, "All ships are present and accounted for, except for our southern relief from Tippard. We are ready to move into position at your command, Lady Marigold."

"Well and good, Captain," Marigold commented as she climbed the stairs close behind him. "Have my guests been woken yet?"

"Aye, my first mate was sent to rouse them," Captain Cayan told her. "I wanted to be the one to wake you personally. I hope you did not mind, my lady."

Captain Lorne Cayan was a pleasant, if not serious man, of some forty-odd years. A seasoned sailor who had earned his captain's stripes serving in the Illiastran navy as a first mate to two different admirals. In his capacity as the captain of Daol Bay's flagship, *The Princess of Daol*, he had served without a hitch in more than five years. As the fastest of any of the ships calling port in Twin Bay, and the pride of Marscal Tullivan's fleet, it was no small honour for Cayan to be chosen to stand on its quarterdeck.

"No, of course I did not mind, Captain," Marigold assured him once she stepped off the ladder and onto the deck.

The cold hit her quickly, brought to slap against her face rudely in the winter's wind. The darkness of the night was whole and blanketing, and large flakes of snow tumbled down, further obscuring any potential sightlines from the shore.

How does the captain know where our other ships are?

Marigold was about to ask him that question herself when she noticed that he had left her for the ship's wheel. Giving follow, Marigold was intercepted by a crewmember her own size.

"Good morning, Mari," they greeted her, and she turned to look into the bundled face of Leanne.

"Oh, Leanne, it's you. I thought you were one of the crew dressed like that in all black."

"Well, that's not a far cry, I suppose. Are you ready?" Leanne asked excitedly. "There will be no going back once you give the signal to *The Sting* and *The Chase*. But you know that without me having to tell you."

Marigold looked about at the crew busy at their work. "I would be lying if I said I was not nervous. Nevertheless, I suppose I am as ready as everyone else on this ship is. Come with me and we will go tell the captain to signal the other ships into position.

"I would like that. Lead the way," Leanne decided while stepping aside for her to pass.

"Captain Cayan," Marigold addressed him when she reached the quarterdeck where he presently stood at the wheel. "When you are ready, give the signal to slip into position. How far off from sunrise do you wager we are?"

"Aye, Lady Marigold, it shall be done," Captain Cayan told her. He left the wheel briefly, stepped to the rail, and leaned over to talk in a restrained voice. "The Lady has given the order, signal to the other ships that we are ready to begin."

A crewmember dashed off to relay the order, and the captain returned to where he was while answering Marigold's query, "As for your earlier question, we have an hour, perhaps two at the very most before daylight hits. If I may pass counsel, you will want to launch the attack as quickly as you can. Even under the cloak of total darkness and with all our added measures, I cannot say with certainty that we will evade notice until dawn."

Black sails, the crew completely outfitted to match, all ornamentation removed from all ships, and bright colours all painted over as much as possible with the time given to do so. Did we really undergo all of that expense and effort just to buy us a few extra minutes before the first light?

"Understood, Captain," Marigold told him, her voice falling flat as it dawned on her just how close they were to commencing with her plan. "If the lamps are ready to give the signal, then I shall do so as soon as you say that we are in position."

On the starboard bow, Marigold espied one of the crew striking a machete against a piece of flint, causing it to spark. "What is that crewman there doing, Captain?"

Lorne Cayan leaned to his right to see what Marigold was referring to and seemed to find the activity amusing. "He is signalling from ship to ship in code. It's a system that I actually had a hand in devising for just this mission. The sparks would be harder to see from the shore than the lamp, but in closer proximity here on the water, we can see them plainly enough. This snowfall helps us in that matter, as they would be even more difficult for the men in the towers on the cliffs to distinguish through the snow."

Footsteps could be heard climbing the staircase leading to the quarterdeck, and Marigold looked to see Sealords Greggard and Gallin having come to join her.

"My lady, I trust that we are not late," Gallin said for the both of them.

"On the contrary, my good Sealords, your timing could not be better," Marigold stated upon their approach.

Greggard looked about, performing an audible headcount of those in attendance. "We seem to be missing Ser Keneth. It is doubtless that he would want to be here for this."

"He is probably rousing the house guards," Marigold presumed. "It has been a lax few days for them, sailing down the coast like this. Today though, they will need to be on alert."

Gallin had gone to the railing on the starboard side, looking around intently. "I think I see the other ships, but it's hard to tell. On the other end of things, we have to rely on blind faith that Sealord Greggard's unit and the soldiers that they are leading have arrived outside of Pelican Harbour."

"Sealord Leeman Cunningsbee's scouts made contact with our army in the Daol Forest east of Davring Harbour," Greggard reminded him. "They sent back word that not only are things proceeding at the requested pace, but they should be in Pelican Harbour ahead of schedule. My unit knows what they are doing."

"Forgive me, Sealord Greggard, I did not mean to sound critical of your tactics," Gallin offered sincerely. "I am merely concerned. Our detour into Davring Harbour was several days past, and Sealord Cunningsbee's contact with the armed forces was a day stale again. It is hard to say what came of them in that time. If they were discovered by one of Eamon Palomb's loyalist ministers, we may be walking ourselves into a situation."

Marigold had her turn to chime in then, "If my letter reached Minister Morton in time, then there should be no other withholding ministers in their keeps at the moment. As far as they know, Morton is plotting a coup against me and is calling a meeting with the greatest of secrecy. None of the holdouts would want to miss that, as he is the lone minister west of Obalen who they could rally around as an alternative to my rule. Except for Nothram. I requested that his invitation from Morton was to be lost in transit."

Captain Cayan had himself a laugh at that. "I gotta say Lady Marigold, that's quite cunning. Hopefully it all worked."

"I am still amazed that you secured any sort of truce with Minister Morton, my lady," Greggard told her in subdued awe. "If he comes through with this, all that will be left in the regions around Pelican Harbour will be caretakers to the ministers, and they will not send out anyone to respond without permission from their ministers. We have Nothram all alone."

"Sparks off the starboard side," a crewmember relayed to the captain.

"Very good, Sailor," Cayan replied to the man down below. "Signal for *The Sting* and *The Chase* to drop anchor and take aim, tell the others to hold their position, and all hands are to wait on Lady Marigold's signal with the lantern."

The captain turned the wheel over to a crewmember waiting quietly nearby and put a hand on Marigold's back. "It's all up to you now, Lady Marigold. The lamp is on the main deck, come with me and we will get you set to send the signal to the two ships-of-the-line. You remember the code I taught you, right?"

With Leanne in tow, Marigold walked ahead of Captain Cayan to the stairs. "I have it memorised, Captain. Two quick flashes, a third delayed one, and one more quick flash. Is that correct?"

"It is, my lady, you have done well," the captain complimented her. He brought her to a covered, metal box secured to a pedestal that was bolted to the deck. Stepping around her, he laid a hand on the handle that controlled the signalling shutter. "Everything waits on your order, now. Here we are. You remember how to work the lamp?"

"Aye, we practiced it many times on our journey here, Captain," Marigold assured him. "Thank you for getting us this far, we could not have done it without you."

"It is my pleasure to have served you and your family for so long, Lady Marigold. I am proud to be a part of this operation," the captain replied, turning away to return to the quarterdeck as he added, "May fortune find us today."

"Form up here with Lady Marigold and Miss Mattersly, men," Marigold heard from an approaching voice at the port side of the ship. Looking over her shoulder, Marigold found Ser Keneth marching with three guards, all dressed in black coats to conceal their uniforms. "My lady, we stand at the ready for you."

Marigold nodded at the four of them. "Elden, Brandyl, Darrill, and Ser Keneth, thank you all for coming. May fortune find us today."

"We aim to serve you, my lady," Ser Keneth spoke for the group.

Marigold stood beside the lantern, her left hand coming to rest on the handle. *Once I give the signal, there is no looking back.*

As she braced herself to do the deed, she felt someone reach for her right hand, and as she looked to her side, her heart filled with joy.

"Moya, you came!" Marigold exclaimed jubilantly.

"Of course I did. I could not live with myself if I had hid away when you needed me most."

"Thank you, my friend," Marigold replied before taking a deep breath. "Here we go."

She gripped the handle tight, twisting until the shutter opened, flashing a beam of light across the dark waters. The shutters were snapped shut with a clank, and she opened and closed them again just as quickly. Marigold waited a beat on the next beam, and gave one more quick flash before letting the shutters come to a rest.

Voices on the ships-of-the-line could be heard calling back and forth to one another and for a split second, Marigold thought she saw flashes of flames. Just as hurriedly, everything fell silent and black.

Marigold held her breath, feeling Moya's hand holding tight to hers. They shared a glance, and looked to the sky.

The air erupted with the sound of two massive, concussive blasts. Sparks and smoke could be seen flaring out from where Marigold knew the two massive warships sat. For but a second or two, there was nothing but deathly silence and darkness. Out of that void, there came the terrible sound of blasting brick and tumbling stones, the skies on either side of the harbour turning red and orange so brightly that Marigold had to cover her eyes.

"Oh my gods!" Moya cried out. "What was that?"

"Mortar cannons, one firing from each ship-of-the-line and directed at the tower on either side of the cliffs," Leanne calmly told her.

"The towers must have contained a heavy amount of munitions of their own," Ser Keneth mused. "Hopefully they were lightly garrisoned."

Marigold turned to Keneth. "I was told that Greggard was going to arrange someone from the rear guard of the marching unit to harry the tower guards and lure them out to safety. Do we know if that ever came to happen?"

"I have no worldly idea, Lady Marigold. We shall hope so," Keneth replied, his voice sounding doubtful, despite his wishes to the contrary.

"Lady Marigold," Captain Cayan called out from the quarterdeck. "*The Tidebreaker* and *The Morning Light* are on the move toward Pelican Harbour."

With Moya, Leanne, and the guardsmen following close behind, Marigold darted to the quarterdeck again to see for herself. The two were a pair of frigates, the former from Marigold's fleet, and the latter from Greggard's.

The Tidebreaker was given point, with *The Morning Light*, Greggard Simillon's own flagship, in close proximity to offer support. Freyard was given command of the personnel on board of *The Tidebreaker*, and as expected, his forces included all of his available Sun's Rangers, except for Dayden Vernet. Having drawn the short straw, Dayden had remained behind in Daol Bay as the representative of Freyard's company.

"I do not see the ships, Captain," Marigold confessed while straining to see off the starboard side.

"Daylight will hit any second, you should see them then," the captain told her.

Those Flying Hawks better be springing into action at the town gates. Those mortar cannons were supposed to be their cue.

"There, Mari, I see *Tidebreaker* and *Morning Light*," Leanne announced from Marigold's left side, where she had come to stand.

"Oh, yes, I see them now too," Marigold exclaimed, pointing them out to Moya as she did, who still seemed to be having difficulty.

"Make for the harbour, Captain," Marigold called out to him. "We will tail them at a safe distance."

Captain Cayan looked concerned at that, and said as much, "That would put us out of position, Lady Marigold. Are you certain of that decision?"

"Aye, Captain, haul up the anchor, if you do not mind," Marigold confirmed. "I would like to keep both of those ships in sight."

"As you wish, my lady," Cayan acquiesced while cupping his hands around his mouth. "Anchors up, give me some sail, we head for the harbour."

"Lady Marigold, what in the name of Aren's beard are you doing?" Ser Keneth asked in near panic.

"We will accomplish nothing and see less by hiding in the back of the armada with the sloops and support vessels," Marigold reminded him. "We should be inside the harbour, where we can at least see what is going on. Look, two more ships have entered ahead of us. That would make four. Pelican Harbour does not have the firepower to cut through all of that to get at us. The narrow harbour would keep the other ships from spreading out far enough to allow for a clear shot at our ship, that is if they even know that I am aboard *The Princess of Daol*. Chances are that they would think that I am on *The Tidebreaker* out in front."

Ser Keneth remained unconvinced. "I am not so sure of that, Lady Marigold...But I do hope that the battle is over by the time we get close enough to see the shore. Greggard, you have faith in these Flying Hawks of yours, right?"

"Of course I do, Ser Keneth," Greggard answered with certainty. "Completely and totally. The flag of surrender will be raised before long, I just know it."

"Look ahead of us, Mari," Leanne beckoned her while pointing to two frigates situated on the seas between *The Princess of Daol* and *The Morning Light*. "*Felixander's Dream* has moved in ahead of us on the port side, and *Ser Clendon Mooresby* is on position on the starboard. The plan is coming together nicely."

The *Ser Clendon*, as it was typically known, was a sister ship of *Felixander's Dream*, having been built in the Mattersly's shipyard, and sent to serve in Sealord Greggard's fleet. For the battle, it had been reunited with its sibling and the two were to be used to both close off the harbour and support the flagships. The five ships sailed between the cliffs of Pelican Harbour together, the minutes ticking by with every noise that *The Princess of Daol* made beneath Marigold's feet as it cut through the choppy waters.

The dawn had begun to draw back the veil of night, replacing it with the first rays to hit the grey dome of clouds overhead. It was not much in the way of lighting, but it was enough to reveal Marigold's navy completely, removing any mystery behind the destruction of the watchtowers.

"Nothram only has two ships," Captain Cayan noted with cautious relief. "And just one has slipped its moorings. It's a clipper, judging by the look of it. I can't imagine that it will have much in the way of armament."

Ser Keneth was looking over either shoulder at the stern. "Our escort has come to a near stop, we're overtaking them. We should do the same."

"No, Ser Keneth, with all due respect, I want us to keep at our current pace," Marigold ordered firmly. "It does not look like Pelican

Harbour has any defences to threaten us with, besides that one ship trying to get under sail. Captain Cayan, keep steady, please."

With an audible, exasperated sigh, Ser Keneth resigned to his fate. "You heard Lady Marigold, men. Keep your eyes open and scan the hills and the town for cannons. Report anything remotely suspicious. Lady Marigold's life, even if she personally shows disregard toward it, is our highest priority."

The Morning Light veered to the starboard side, heading to the south side of the harbour in the direction of the docked vessel of Haymard Nothram's.

"It would seem that *The Morning Light* is lining up for a broadside," Gallin nervously observed.

"Only if they have to, like as not," Captain Cayan informed the group. "That ship they are lining up to could not even get to sea. That tells me the crew has likely few, if any, of its cannons prepped. Were that ship to open fire, it would only piss off *The Morning Light*. Yet, a broadside from them would sink that Pelican Harbour ship at her moorings. Unless they have cannons on the shore, I should think that we have the south side of the town subdued. Lady Marigold, I would advise you to have *Ser Clendon Mooresby* signalled so that it can bolster the presence of *The Morning Light*. In the meantime, that clipper moving toward *The Tidebreaker* is our main worry."

Marigold spun about to face Greggard, "Sealord Greggard, that ship is from your fleet, the decision is yours."

"I could get in to the technicalities, but ultimately, *Ser Clendon Mooresby* is yours to command at this point," Greggard explained, sending the final decision back to Marigold. "To that end, I would recommend you heed the captain's advice, though."

"Fine then, I will not argue," Marigold relented before giving her attention to Cayan. "Captain, send the signal, please."

"Signal the *Mooresby* to bolster *The Morning Light*!" Captain Cayan called out before Marigold even finished the sentence.

Leanne had grabbed Marigold's arm then, pointing with her free hand toward *The Tidebreaker*. "Look, Nothram's ship is hailing to *The Tidebreaker*!"

"Perhaps to offer surrender?" Gallin posited while looking all about. "Surely they see their burning towers on the hills and the behemoth ships just outside that did it. They would have to know that those mortar cannons alone could reduce their remaining battlements to dust without breaking a sweat. This battle was a complete rout, Lady Marigold."

Captain Cayan had produced a telescope from his jacket pocket and was busily surveying the distant hills of the eastern side of town. "Lady Marigold, come have a look. I think Sealord Gallin might well be on to something."

She stepped up beside him and took the apparatus in hand, looking through in the direction that Cayan indicated. "A white flag!" Marigold shouted out excitedly. "I see a white flag!"

"From where?" Greggard asked hopefully.

"It looks like Nothram manor," Marigold told everyone, offering the telescope to anyone else who might want to see.

To her surprise, Moya stepped up and put the glass to her eye. She observed long enough to observe for herself, and lowered the telescope to her side once satisfied. "You did it, Marigold. You took the beast down."

"May I see, Moya?" Leanne asked next, taking the telescope to hand as Moya wordlessly gave it up. "That's a white flag, alright. Do you suppose that they keep them on hand for just such an occasion?" she joked.

"Our side carried the flags," Keneth stated, having missed the jape entirely. "Knowing that Nothram would not, but that he would have need for them once his walls came crashing down."

"Look, there's another being raised at the town hall!" Leanne shouted with glee. "And another at the barracks! It's over, Mari! It's over!"

"Does that ship of Nothram's know that, do you think?" Gallin asked, pointing to where it sat in the water, its crew tossing lines to *The Tidebreaker*.

Marigold went to the port side railing where Gallin now stood, Leanne close behind with Captain Cayan's telescope still in her possession.

"Leanne, may I have that, please?" Marigold queried with an open hand. The telescope was quickly up to her eye, and things aboard the two lashed vessels became clearer. "I see Freyard, he and Captain Mavril are standing on the port side, talking to a handful of men on the other ship."

"You know that they are looking for you, right?" Marigold heard from beside her, glancing to her left to see Moya standing there in a manner that was frighteningly calm. "Those men on that other ship, I mean."

Ser Keneth was behind them then and asking for the telescope.

Marigold handed it off to him and turned to Moya, "What makes you say that, Moya?"

"They have to see the flags by now, you would think," Moya said while nodding her head in the direction of *The Tidebreaker* and the clipper. "That ship is much closer to the shore than we are, and even I can see the white flags with my bare eyes now. What need do they have to stop *The Tidebreaker* now?"

"They would be discussing terms of surrender, Moya," Marigold told her, attempting to explain away the behaviour.

"What is there to talk about? The flags are up across town. That means that their side has given up, right?" Moya queried worriedly. "They can't set terms once they already give up. Don't they have to do that beforehand?"

Marigold gave a shrug, "The clipper had already hailed before the flags went up. I am sure that they are merely making arrangements for our ships to land."

"I do believe that Miss Starboard might be correct, Lady Marigold," Keneth commented while holding the telescope out to a waiting Leanne, who took it eagerly. "They are still yet talking, and both sides have weapons drawn. You should get below decks before someone on the clipper with a telescope of their own looks our way and sees you."

"We will send *Felixander's Dream* in to lend support to-" Marigold had begun to say, her words lost beneath the rapid, popping sound of a rifle line.

The scene aboard the two ships had descended into battle, with one side having unleashed a volley of gunfire on the other. The decks had become a chaotic mess of smoke and darting bodies moving to a soundtrack of screaming and rifle blasts. Marigold could only watch, desperately trying to discern the identities of the combatants.

The Tidebreaker stood between firing range of *The Princess of Daol*, *Ser Clendon Mooresby*, and *The Morning Light* alike, rendering all three useless to send cannon fire. Marigold looked to *Felixander's Dream*, and saw her sails already unfurling.

"We're heading toward *The Tidebreaker*!" Captain Cayan called to his crew, "Ready the gaffs, rings, and rafts, so that we can start pulling *The Tidebreaker*'s crew and soldiers out of the water. The cold will take them in seconds if they start abandoning ship. Come on, lads, no time to waste!"

Ser Keneth was marching toward the wheel in full objection, "Excuse me, Captain, we have Lady-"

"Uncle Ken, wait, no. I will not let *The Tidebreaker*'s crew perish for the sake of my safety," Marigold told him while darting between him and the captain.

"Lady Marigold, this course of action is unwise," Keneth warned her sternly.

Marigold was not about to yield, though. "I am but one person. Why would my life supersede the lives of the men and women willing to fight for me? I am afraid that I must respectfully overrule you, Uncle Ken, Field Marshal or not."

"I see..." Ser Keneth said while taking a step back. "Is that your final order on the matter?"

"It is, Ser," Marigold told him in a voice that she thought sounded at the same time firm and respectful. "I am sorry that you and the other guards will potentially be put in harm's way by my decision. Yet, I feel that it is the moral thing to do."

Keneth looked between the guardsmen and Marigold, and finally to Captain Cayan, to whom he said, "Steady as she goes, Captain. You have my apologies for interrupting."

"Think nothing of it, Field Marshal," the Captain replied. Given that *The Tidebreaker* had grown closer in the past few minutes, Cayan had paid no mind to the argument that was taking place directly beside him. "We're almost in position, folks. Brace yourselves."

Keneth strode away from Marigold to the nearby manor guards. "Alright, men, you heard Lady Marigold. Watch the sides of the ship for anyone trying to board that's not of our alliance, and keep your eyes trained on *The Tidebreaker* and that clipper for rifles and cannons."

With his orders relayed, he turned back to Marigold. "Lady Marigold, will you at least do me the favour of keeping low and out of sight?"

"I will try, Uncle," Marigold said while grabbing Moya by the hand. "Come with me, I will need your help. Leanne, I will take you too if you can spare yourself."

Together the three of them left the quarterdeck and ventured down to the main deck. Marigold pulled open the hatch and grabbed

Moya. "Could you please go below to our cabin and get my grandfather's sword from the trunk? Leanne and I will be ducked down by the nearest mast with the guardsmen when you return."

"I'm on it!" Moya answered while already descending the ladder.

"Just what in the name of Iia are you planning to do with a sword, Mari?" Leanne asked as they lowered the hatch again and headed for the cover of the tall, wooden mast.

"Hopefully nothing," Marigold answered. "But I want it just the same in the event I might need it. I know that if I go below that deck myself that my guards will forcibly keep me there."

Brandyl, Elden, and Darrill had caught up to the women by then, their pistols brandished and at the ready. "Lady Marigold," Brandyl spoke up concernedly, "Please do not run off like that on us."

She gave Leanne a confirmatory look and received one of acknowledgement in return.

The battling ships had grown close, with *The Princess of Daol* having turned her port side toward the two, putting what Marigold estimated to be twenty to thirty metres of water between itself and *The Tidebreaker*. With every inch they gained on the fighting, the shouting and the igniting gunpowder grew ever louder.

"It is like sailing into a thunderstorm," Leanne observed from where she crouched beside Marigold.

From behind Marigold, she heard someone shout, "I'm back, Marigold!"

She turned and quite nearly collided into Moya, who was clutching the sword in its scabbard to her chest. "Where did you come from, Moya?"

"The hatch near the bow. I couldn't get the one near us to open. I think the crew kept walking on it."

"Lady Marigold, what are your intentions with that rapier?" Elden asked while watching her slip the scabbard's belt around her waist.

"I have no intentions, unless absolutely needed," Marigold told him. "I will not be caught unarmed, though."

Elden nodded, seemingly satisfied with the answer. "As you wish, my lady. In the meantime, what do you intend to do now?"

She pointed to *The Tidebreaker* and the waters between it and *The Princess of Daol*. "Help anyone who leaves that ship. We will need blankets and bandages, at the very least. You heard the captain, that water is enough to freeze a man solid in minutes. Are you all with me?"

Though the women both agreed, the men deigned to answer, instead sharing a glance between the three of them.

"My lady, our duty is to protect you," Brandyl said on behalf of the guards. "If we lend a hand, we risk being caught unawares by someone attempting to harm you."

"Suit yourselves, gentlemen, just stay out of our way," Marigold allowed, instead focusing her attention toward the women. "Moya, Leanne, go below decks and get as many spare blankets and bandages as you can afford. There should be a gurney in the sick bay too, bring it along, as there will no doubt be injuries."

While still crouched, Marigold moved forward from the starboard to the port side of *The Princess of Daol*, making sure to keep low and obscured as much as possible. At the railing, she peeked overboard to find crewmen of *The Princess of Daol* having already lowered two lifeboats, the oarsmen paddling their way into the shadow of *The Tidebreaker*.

On board the two ships, there was no way to tell one man from another, as chaos had fully engulfed both vessels.

That damn Nothram has already surrendered, why are they still fighting?

Black smoke began to rise from somewhere between the two ships, billowing toward the sky and blotting out the overcast sunrise.

"Fire! Fire!" Ser Keneth shouted at *The Tidebreaker* through cupped hands upon the quarterdeck. Marigold began shouting the same, until it seemed that everyone aboard her ship was following suit to warn *The Tidebreaker*'s crew.

"My lady, you should not call attention to yourself like that," Brandyl cautioned while reaching for her arm.

"Get off, Brandyl," Marigold told him angrily. "You are here to protect me, not babysit a toddler. Away!"

A man in a long leather jacket and teal shirt emerged in a tumble through the smoke, coughing and hacking into a free arm while the other hand clutched limply to a sword. His hair looked dark in the dim, overcast lighting and seemed a little longer than Freyard kept his, but she could not be entirely sure that it was not him, given that his mouth was covered.

Where are you, Freyard?

The unidentified ranger reached for the railing to steady himself, giving Marigold a good look at his face.

That's Mack, Marigold had time to say to notice, before his hand slipped and he plunged overboard and into the sea.

"Pull that man out of the water!" Marigold shouted down at the lifeboats. "Come on now, hurry, hurry, hurry!"

"There he is!" one of the sailors called to the others in the boat. "Give me a gaff! I can almost reach him! He's sinking! Quickly now!"

A trio of crewmembers still on board *The Princess of Daol* had begun tossing the mooring lines over the gunwales and into the water. Marigold moved to help them, but found none left to toss, and returned to the railing in time to find the lifeboat crew having pulled Mack into their craft, the oarsmen paddling furiously toward *The Princess Daol.*

"Get him on a line, we'll pull him up!" Marigold cried out to them. She grabbed the nearest rope and began shaking it to get their attention. They looped it around Mack's waist and signalled for Marigold to pull, but she was not enough to budge him.

Damn it all, I can't do it alone.

"Try again, Mari!" Leanne said as she and Moya ran up from behind her and grabbed on to the rope.

"Shit! Brandyl, Elden, come on!" Darrill yelled to the other guards, holstering his pistol and joining in on the rescue effort with the three women and a few of the crew as he did so.

The group hauled on the line hand over hand, until Mack appeared on the other side of the railing.

"Leanne, help me grab him," Marigold ordered. "The rest of you hold the line until we get him in."

Together they went forward, grabbing onto Mack by his arms and the back of his coat in an effort to drag him over the rail and onto the deck.

"We need to get him below deck and out of his wet clothes," Leanne told them. "Cover him in blankets once he's down there."

Two crewmembers that had been holding the line come running and had already begun to sling Mack's arms over their shoulders. "We'll take him, milady," one of them said to her, and she dared not to stall them.

A sickening crash of splintering wood rang loudly in Marigold's ears, and she looked toward the ships to find *Felixander's Dream* having rammed into the bow of Nothram's ship.

"By the three!" Greggard exclaimed from up near the railing of the quarterdeck while jumping backward, though he was in no real danger.

"That's *Felixander's Dream*, the shipbuilders from back home built a ram onto the bow for just that sort of thing!" Leanne shouted out almost gleefully.

The collision of the other two vessels had driven *The Tidebreaker* from where it sat, and its stern began to swing toward *The Princess of Daol*.

"Taking evasive action! Brace for possible impact!" Captain Cayan called out while turning the wheel hard.

Though he tried to swing *The Princess Daol*, there was little to be done to avoid a collision by then.

"Get down!" Marigold yelled as she went sprinting away from the port railing with Moya running behind. She ducked for cover behind a small stack of barrels, pulling Moya down with her as *The Tidebreaker* came at them.

Lumber scraped together furiously, sliding and gnashing along *The Princess Daol* from what seemed to Marigold like its stern to its bow. *The Tidebreaker* kept its swing until it managed to find its way clear of *The Princess of Daol*.

When Marigold looked, she saw that *The Tidebreaker* still appeared to be lashed to the rapidly sinking clipper ship by at least one line.

"*The Tidebreaker* is going to be dragged down!" she said to no one in particular. Sticking her hand in beneath Moya's arm, she helped her up and the two looked around.

What remained of the railing of *The Princess of Daol* was in splinters, and at least one mast sustained damage to the yardarms.

Of Leanne, Elden, Brandyl, and Darrill there was at first no sign, until the door to the captain's quarters flew open and three of the four emerged from within.

Once Marigold and Moya got close, it appeared that while Elden was unscathed, both Leanne and Brandyl were bleeding.

"You're both cut!" she told them.

"Fuck it all!" Leanne said while looking at her hand as it came away bloodied from her forehead. "The damn windows near the stern blew out in the captain's quarters. It must have got us."

"We're heading for the south side wharf!" Captain Cayan called out to his crew. "Tell the rowboats to head for the nearest landing. Our soldiers are all around the shore now, it should be safe!"

Marigold attempted to order Leanne and Brandyl below decks to treat their wounds, but Brandyl refused to leave her side, and Leanne echoed his sentiments immediately after.

"It's just a few cuts, I'll live, my lady," Brandyl protested.

"Likewise, Mari, I am not going anywhere now," Leanne added sternly.

With neither time nor patience to argue with them, she sent Moya to retrieve the bandages that were brought above decks, and issued her further orders to patch up Leanne and Brandyl with them. Leaving the three behind with Elden on her heels, Marigold darted up the starboard side stairs to the quarterdeck. Gallin, Keneth, and Greggard had gone to the starboard side as well, the two Sealords having knelt by the rail, while the Field Marshal had taken to standing to the right of Captain Cayan.

"Captain, how much damage has our ship taken?" Marigold asked him.

"I cannot say with certainty, but I fear we might be taking on water," he told her without taking his eyes off the sea around them. "We need to get you to safety and assess whether or not we need to ground the ship."

"But what of *The Tidebreaker* and our lifeboats," Marigold attempted to counter, only for Cayan to cut her off.

"They are not far from shore," the captain said sharply, his tone refusing to compromise. "Those are good, hearty sailors in those rowboats. They'll pull what they can from the water, get to land quickly, and return half a hundred times more if they need to. *Felixander's Dream* looks unharmed from its charge and is right there with them. They'll pick up *The Tidebreaker*'s men too. Don't you worry, Lady Marigold."

She looked again to see the clipper starting its plunge at the bow, its stern lifting, and *The Tidebreaker* still bound to it at that end. "Will Nothram's ship drag *The Tidebreaker* down with it do you think?"

The Captain looked to where Marigold's gaze was affixed, and seemed to consider it for a moment. "It might, if *The Tidebreaker* is taking on water itself, but that water isn't deep enough for the clipper ship to drag a seaworthy vessel under."

"I am sorry, Marigold," Ser Keneth said from beside her, his voice sounding truly empathetic. "Your intentions were pure, and we tried to support *The Tidebreaker* as best we could. When I saw you pulling that ranger onto the ship with your friends, I could not help but fill with pride. That was selfless, and well done. Captain Cayan and I made the joint decision to pull *The Princess of Daol* away from the fray while time still allows us to get the ship to safety. Again, I apologise if you feel hurt by mine and the captain's choice."

"What fool thought it was such a wise idea to ram that clipper, anyway?" Captain Cayan asked Keneth scornfully.

Keneth engaged both the question and the speaker, allowing Marigold to slip away unnoticed while he did such. "That's Captain Chet Brineholst, if I recall. We will have to hear his reasoning before jumping to anything, but that decision is almost definitely going to send him before a military tribunal."

Having left the two officers to their discussion, Marigold made her way back to where she left Leanne, Moya, and Brandyl. She found her friends right where they had been and now joined by Gallin and Greggard. In joining them, Marigold witnessed the Sealord of Kylisport busily doing his best to wrap Leanne's head in the gauze bandages provided by Moya.

"My lady, are you alright?" Greggard greeted her sombrely.

"I am fine, thank you. At least physically, at any rate," she responded to him, giving her focus to the wounded. "How are you two faring?"

"I took a bad cut on the eyebrow. I got lucky, I suppose, because it could have been the eye itself," Leanne informed her blankly through a face that was now red with her own blood.

Brandyl's right forearm was held to his abdomen and wrapped in bandaging in a manner that seemed odd to Marigold, given that it looked to be coming to a point in the centre.

"What happened to you?" Marigold inquired while gesturing to the wound.

"A piece of glass lodged in my arm, and I've got a good gash along my jaw, and a few other cuts," Brandyl said between wincing breaths.

"I just hope the doctor in town is not as fanatical toward Nothram as those sailors on that clipper were."

The sealords and Elden were all no worse for wear, although Greggard seemed quite shaken. It was then that Marigold made note of one person's absence.

"Where has Darrill gotten himself to? I have not seen him since we were collided with *The Tidebreaker*," Marigold put back to anyone who might care to answer.

No one among her party seemed to know where he was, leaving Marigold to go in search. At his insistence, Elden joined Marigold, issuing his concern with how close the ship was to docking at a wharf where their reception might be less than hospitable.

The crew moved about the pair busily, their minds occupied with surveying damage and preparing to dock. Those who stopped to hear her had not seen the guard, and there was none among the sailors that could be lent to assist in the search.

After looking across the decks, Marigold was about to go below to continue the hunt for her guardsman, when the thought came to her to check near the bow.

As they approached the area, Elden called out, "I see a boot." Following the point of his finger toward the foremast, Marigold saw the black, leather footwear, the toes pointed upward and the leg within sticking out just shy of the forecastle deck.

The two broke out into a short sprint from there, and Elden was first to round the foremast. As Marigold closed the distance, she saw Elden's face drop, followed by the rest of him as he went to his knees.

"He's gone," Elden declared in as morose a voice as Marigold had ever heard.

"What happened to him?" Marigold asked as she joined Elden to look upon Darrill.

Elden felt around Darrill's throat with the index and middle finger of his left hand, placing the fingers of his right on his own throat for comparison. After an achingly long few seconds, Elden's eyes fell on Marigold to tell her, "He has no pulse, my lady."

Seated against the mast, Darrill was grey in the face, but otherwise almost peaceful. There were no visible wounds, and other than his forward slouch, one might have thought he was simply sitting down for a rest.

"It must have been his heart," Marigold managed to utter. "The commotion all around us might have been too much for him to take."

"I...I didn't know, my lady," Elden muttered. "He never said he was in any distress, and I saw no signs. He just disappeared when *The Tidebreaker* slid into us. We should have noticed, at least Brandyl and I. By the gods, how did we not see that Darrill was gone?"

Marigold reached in and took Darrill's hand. "He was only fifty two years old. He planned to stay on as a guard until he was fifty five, then he and his wife were going to buy a cottage on one of the Red Isles and enjoy their retirement."

Upon exhaling whatever air was apparently left in his lungs, Elden stood up and patted her on the shoulder. "Stay here, my lady. I will go fetch the gurney and let the Field Marshal know."

Darrill was one of father's guards. One of the first that he had the opportunity to appoint himself, and not a guard inherited from grandfather. That made Darrill different from those who came both before and after him. Father treated him more like an old friend than a paid subordinate. They drank together from time to time, and Darrill was constantly invited to enjoy brandy and gambling card games with Keneth, Rus, and the businessmen that Father entertained. No, Father did not just treat Darrill like a friend. Darrill was his friend. A close one, at that, and he stayed on to serve me...And this is how I repaid him for that loyalty and friendship.

The voices of sailors shouting to one another across the ship and the stevedores accepting mooring lines with grunts and complaints were all around Marigold by then. Seagulls went flying from the waters by the wharf as the ship slid sideways and took away the space where the cluster of birds had been paddling and feeding. From upon the quarterdeck, Marigold could hear Captain Cayan calling orders above every other local sound.

In the distance, timber cracked and split, and Marigold looked to see it coming from *Felixander's Dream* as it detangled itself from Nothram's destroyed ship. *The Tidebreaker* was drifting rather aimlessly by then, a small flotilla of lifeboats rowing away from it in a line. Fishing skiffs were working toward both the enemy wreck and *The Tidebreaker* alike, valiantly volunteering for rescue efforts. Further out at the mouth of the harbour, the sloops *The Marigold* and *The Serephanie* were wending their way between the cliffs to offer further support.

The lumber beneath Marigold began to pulse with the sound of soles slapping on it in her direction. She reached out to Darrill's face and ran her hand over his cheek. "I am so sorry, Ser Darrill. Please forgive me for having done this to you. It is all my fault."

"Darrill? Darrill, can you hear me?" Marigold heard Ser Keneth ask frantically as he swept in on Darrill's left and dropped to a knee.

"I'm sorry, Uncle Ken, but he's already gone," Marigold told him in little more than a whisper, her gaze diverting to a nondescript spot on the floor.

Keneth went oddly quiet, and Marigold lifted her eyes to find him having pressed his forehead to Darrill's. As she sat there with them, she heard Keneth mutter something under his breath, whether a farewell or a prayer or something else, Marigold could not tell over the ruckus all around them. From the tone, Marigold thought that it sounded oddly sentimental for a man who typically came across as unflinching.

After a few more seconds had passed, Keneth waved to Elden standing nearby, "Ser Elden, come here and help me get Ser Darrill onto the gurney. My lady, you should go back to the main deck. Your friends are all there."

Marigold stepped aside and walked away toward the stern of the ship, unprotected and unconcerned with that status. She sidestepped the handful of crewmembers busily manoeuvring the gangway onto the wharf, and made her way to Moya, Leanne, and the three men, all milling about in exactly the place where she left them.

"What happened?" Leanne asked worriedly, looking entirely unbothered by the drying crimson mask splashed across her face.

Glancing back, Marigold witnessed as Elden and Keneth carefully carried Darrill toward the gangway, having taken the time to cover him with a white sheet that had been strapped to the gurney.

"Ser Darrill Aylen passed away while we were lending aid to *The Tidebreaker*," Marigold informed the group. "It appears that he might have had a problem with his heart, went off by himself, sat down, and died."

Moya immediately ran to Marigold and threw her arms around her. "I'm so sorry, Marigold," she told her as they hugged tightly.

"Gods be damned," she heard Greggard utter into the air.

The others stepped forward and offered condolences as much as they could, and Greggard joined them lastly.

"Sealord Gallin, Miss Mattersly, Brandyl, Miss Starboard, and I were talking while you were searching," Greggard said after a moment of silence. "We all recommend that you stay aboard the ship until such time that we can arrange for a full complement of soldiers to escort you around Pelican Harbour. There is no telling how the townsfolk will react to your presence, given what has occurred since your arrival."

"I understand and agree with that recommendation," Marigold relented, having grown far too tired for much debate. "One thing I will ask is that Leanne, Brandyl, and Mack of the Sun's Rangers, and any other wounded be taken ashore at once and brought to a doctor for treatment. Perhaps one or both of Greggard and Gallin can go ashore and get a report on the surrender and the events that led to it. *The Tidebreaker*'s crew and soldiers are going to need every bit of help we can give them, and the men on the clipper ship too. Belligerents of ours or not, we will give them aid. Lastly, could someone please find out where Freyard Archer is?"

26
SYRIE

Bryten Field was empty again, a feat accomplished in what Syrie had to imagine was record time. The grass billowed in the wind where it poked through the low snow, and even in the near darkness of the night, Syrie could still see where the tents had pressed the green down and kept it free from snowfall. In fact, the air still smelled of the League, pleasant aromas like roasting meats, boiling vegetables, and laundry soap, and even the odorous smells of sweat and horse manure. It clung to the field like the grass itself, keeping a memory, even if just temporary, of the hustle and bustle that recently existed near where Syrie and Fujita knelt beneath the tall maple tree in the field.

"I am beginning to wonder if our groundskeeper grew craven," Fujita whispered to Syrie, his eyes echoing that concern.

"A man can be late, you know," she replied nonchalantly.

Fujita let out a scoff. "He is late for a task that will irreversibly alter the course of Illiastra's future? I'm thinking that might be the sort of thing a person makes sure that they are on time for."

"Any number of things might have held him up," Syrie reminded Fujita chidingly. "His task is of grave importance, but those he might cross in his path would know of no such thing. Give him time."

"If our agent gets caught sneaking into Palomb Palace, it will be her end," Fujita stated without any hint of jest or exaggeration in his voice.

"Whether here or in Biddenhurst, they will hang her, and call her one of the Thieves while they do it. You know this as well as I."

Unlike Fujita, Syrie had some faith in N'ailla. "I don't argue it, but I would like to think that our agent is not so daft as to get detected before she even makes contact with the targets."

"It should have been you that went in," Fujita said in continuance of his grievances with the whole plan. "An agent who has only ever worked in a backwater town like Barnam is entirely inexperienced compared to you. Furthermore, there are few women of Johnan descent around the country. I argue on that fact alone that it would be difficult for her to blend in at the Palomb Palace. I would even go so far to say that if her dark skin is seen, this operation is over."

"Getting in is not the problem," Syrie countered while keeping her eyes trained on where the gateway to Greffold Hills sat. "It's getting out unnoticed with those three targets and having enough time to get away without anyone being aware that they are gone."

"That issue becomes doubly so if that gardener is late," Fujita added, reminding Syrie why it was a bad idea to feed his pessimism. "We have only an hour before our district agents begin setting off my distractions."

"So we do," she noted, refusing to say any more on the matter.

On any other day, Syrie enjoyed Fujita's company. The Drakian swordsman had a great deal to teach about their shared craft, and Syrie was one of the few people he was willing to divulge those secrets to. Atop that, he was usually quite amiable, despite his stoic exterior. Perhaps what Syrie enjoyed the most about Fujita was the wealth of interesting stories that his years of experience provided. To Fujita's credit, he had an unexpected knack for telling those tales that kept the listener hooked from the first word to the last.

When it came to working jobs, though, unless everyone involved was operating flawlessly, Fujita could be a notorious pain to work with. His mind worked in that strange way that would automatically assume the worst, a trait he was actually aware of and made strides to improve. In spite of all his efforts, the bothersome habit still emerged on missions, and it took all of Syrie's patience to deal with it.

"That him?" Fujita asked Syrie as they watched a lone man exit the gates of Greffold Hills, stopping shortly to speak to the two guards on duty.

"Hard to say from here, but one would think so," she surmised while taking a deep breath and preparing herself for the next step in the plan.

Syrie looked toward the gates again and saw no sign of the gardener, which was exactly what was to happen. In turning back, she thought Fujita had left, only to find him seated on the ground, his legs crossed, and hands resting on his bent knees.

"What in the Known World are you doing?" Syrie asked him in bafflement.

"I am clearing my mind of every possible distraction outside of the mission parameters," Fujita told her bluntly. "You would be wise to do the same. Perhaps if you did, you could have avoided killing three men on your own missions over the past year."

"It was two, and no amount of clearing my mind could have spared them from that fate," Syrie explained sharply while scanning the edge of the field for signs of life.

When no snide remark was heard from Fujita, Syrie looked down to where he sat, finding him with his eyes closed and his breathing having slowed to a measured pace.

I envy how easily he can slip into that state, Syrie admitted with frustration. *No matter how many times I follow his instructions, or even try to meditate with him, I just cannot seem to do the same.*

Instead, she decided to use the spare minutes to check her equipment once again. The first things on her list, as always, were her clothes. *Silk fencing tunic, cotton trousers, leather boots, a newly-bought leather vest, gloves made of patched leather atop cotton, and a plain, albeit warm woollen cloak, all of it in black.*

Her hands felt around her face and head, checking the placement of a new mask. The piece had been gifted to her by Fujita when the two were reunited upon the Sacred Fist's return to Hercalest. Like the rest of her outfit, and even his, it too was black. The garment covered the whole head, had a pair of holes for her eyes, a tiny slit for breathing through her nose, and concealed every other part of the face. It laced at the back, and she and Fujita had taken turns making sure that the bindings were as tight as they could possibly be without pain or constriction on each other's mask.

It definitely beats my old bandanna.

On her left hip sat a weathered scabbard concealing a rather plain looking knife made of unassumingly excellent steel. Its edge held quite well, and to that end, she kept it deathly sharp. To the right hip was a cache of necessary supplies contained within a spacious pouch.

Having donned similar gear, the only way to differentiate between Syrie and Fujita was the more masculine features of the latter and a slight height difference in his favour. That was, of course, if the large sword strapped across his back was missed by the viewer.

It was a Drakian-made, single-edged steel sword just north of a metre in length and shaped with just a slight curve. In most of his practice sessions that Syrie had witnessed, she saw him wielding it with both hands wrapped around the black, linen-wrapped hilt. Yet, the sword was light for one of that size, allowing him to be capable of using it with just the one hand with a fair amount of ease. If he did need a weapon of a smaller nature, a near facsimile of the sword sat on his hip.

The second blade matched the first in all but the size and arc, being but half the length of his primary weapon and bearing no curvature whatsoever. As Fujita told her, he had ordered the two swords from one of Drake's foremost smiths as a pair, and waited over a year for the order to be filled. In honour of an older sister that he lost at a young age and the bond the two shared, Fujita named his swords Aita and Ozo. In the Drakian tongue, Syrie was told, the names apparently stood for "big sister" and "little brother" respectively. For all the time that Syrie had spent with Fujita, she had never been told what befell Fujita's beloved sibling, or even her name, and Syrie was not one to pry into such matters.

"Our gardener approaches," Fujita informed her from where he still sat, his eyes trained on the outskirts of the field.

Syrie raised her gaze to see a grey-haired man in bib overalls striding quickly toward them, his head pivoting back and forth as if he were looking for followers.

Fujita was scrambling to his feet, a request at the ready on his tongue, "You do the talking."

"Fine," Syrie acquiesced before the man got within earshot.

The man entered the shadows cast by the light of the two moons on the tree and declared in a clear voice that might have been a touch too loud for Syrie's liking, "I am here to sing you a song."

"And what song might that be, stranger?" Syrie asked in return, affecting a monotone voice that was in a lower octave than normal.

The gardener looked about one more time before offering reply, "The Dirge of the Wounded Boar, if it pleases you."

Syrie gave a glance to Fujita, making sure he recognised the passphrase as well as she did. "I think that song will please us. Tell us how it goes, stranger."

"Your agent is where they need to be and no one was any the wiser," the gardener began in an accent so heavy with the Hercalest brogue that Syrie could hardly understand him.

"Good. Are our packages ready to be shipped?" she queried next, watching his face as closely as the darkness allowed.

"Um...Yes, they are ready to go, but there is a small issue," they were told by the increasingly nervous old-timer.

Syrie and Fujita shared a look, and she took the lead again. "Do tell."

"The uh...smallest packages...it's that the primary package does not want them being transported...down," the gardener explained while pointing at the ground to accentuate his point.

"That complicates things a great deal," Fujita muttered frankly, putting his back to Syrie and the gardener and focusing his gaze on the cliff backing the Palomb Palace and overlooking Bryten Field.

The gardener cleared his throat and scratched his neck as he kept on talking. "The agent said she will still lower the...means of conveyance...and wants you two to enter that way. But, once there, all three of you will have to come up with some new manner of transporting the goods to the post office."

"You know Greffold Hills better than we. So tell us, what you would suggest, ser?" Syrie asked the gardener calmly, ignoring Fujita's annoyance.

"The access to the cliffs from the walled-off rear garden of the palace is through a rusted gate buried in the tall grass," the gardener began to explain. "Your agent will be using it to get to the cliffs to establish your means of entry. However, if you instead walk the narrow perimeter between the wall and the cliffs, it will lead you around the palace and onto Greffold Lane."

Fujita spun about to face the man again. "You would have us exit onto the main street, with all three targets, in a gated and highly guarded hill full of the rich and the paranoid who are each further guarded by their own brute squads. Are you trying to get us killed, old man?"

"No, no, no, mister, you mistake me," he corrected Fujita in a calming tone. "I was trying to say that you should not go so far as the road. Instead, leave the path and head through the shrubbery on the rear end of the other mansions on that same side of the road. It will lead you to the bottom of Greffold Hills with nearly no chance of being noticed. Nearer to the bottom of the hill you just have to cross Greffold Lane, go through the gardens of Winchell Manor, and look for an old cellar door hidden amongst the shrubs outside of their property. The cellar, at one time, went all the way down through Greffold Hills and had an access door on the far eastern side of the cliffs.

Years back, Eamon had wanted to seal all exits to Greffold Hills besides the main gate, so he had the Winchell family close the cellar tunnel. I investigated it last night, at the lady's request, and the Winchell's did in fact seal the old exit outside Greffold Hills as was asked of them. Yet, as luck would have it, they dug deeper into the ground and built a narrow tunnel beneath even that exit. The newer passage leads two streets over from where the old exit was, to the cemetery that serves Greffold Hills' residents, and exits in the Winchell family's mausoleum. Judging from the sheer number of casks and bottles I found stored in the cellar, I would wager that the Winchell's use the tunnels for running contraband liquors. It should be said that there is a risk that you might come across the family themselves or their rumrunners. Despite that, I think it is the best chance you have of getting everyone out."

"Now it is my turn to say 'no, no, no, mister'," Fujita told him with a dismissive scoff. "The ladder was their way out. It was clean, easy, and gave us multiple routes out of Bryten Field to safety. Some tunnel on the far end of Greffold Hills that I have no way of verifying the existence of that might be further filled with ornery bootleggers is out of the question. I am in no mood to cut my way off that damnable bluff tonight."

The gardener interlaced his fingers and dropped to his knees. "Oh, please, ser, please go save the lady and her children. You must, you simply must. You have no idea what I have watched her endure over the years. The violence... So much violence... It is enough to make me weep just thinking about it. I hate myself so much for being too cowardly to stop it. I wanted to, I tried to build up the courage, but I am old and broken up, ser. I would only get myself killed and the lady would be no further ahead."

He pointed his still locked fingers towards Fujita and Syrie in turn. "You two and the one with the ladder, though, are strong and fierce. I can see it by the look that each of you has. Please, I worked up the courage to do this much, please help the lady and her young ones get the rest of the way out. She wants it so badly, she needs it, or I fear she will die. If not for the youngest children, she would have left this world by her own hand long ago, and she still might. Cancelling this job... Oh gods, it would be enough to send her over that edge. Worse yet, the master might kill her himself in his rage if he ever found out that she contemplated escape. I'm begging you, ser. You must go to them, you must!"

"Get up and cease your wailing before someone hears," Fujita ordered the man, lifting him up by the arm as he did. "You told us that the master and his eldest offspring were out west somewhere. Was that a lie?"

"No lie, ser. No lie at all," the gardener said while wiping at his eyes. "They are in Obalen, responding to the trouble that the new Lady of the Western Realm is giving them. Their cousin Geddrick is with them too and a host of their best guards. What remains here at the palace is a small garrison made up of the least of the house protectors. The old and the green, I mean. They have a few city guards who don't know the palace so well that are helping to bolster their numbers, but those fellows are usually only about in the daylight. It is just the house guards here at night, barring an emergency, of course."

Fujita released the old man from his grip with an expletive-filled grumble and returned his gaze to the cliffs, leaving the old man without any sort of answer.

"I cannot speak for my associate, old ser, but I will not leave the lady to suffer any longer," Syrie declared while giving Fujita a hard stare. "My other associate is already there, so we two should be enough to get her and the children out."

"Oh, thank you, thank you so much young lady," the old man exclaimed while reaching for her hand with both of his. "Listen to me, the nanny and I that are helping will be hung if we are caught, of that I have no doubt. The arrangements for she and I are still in place too, right?"

Syrie gently pried her hand loose while giving a response, "Aye, old ser, all is still in place."

"The ladder is rolling down the cliffs," Fujita said to Syrie with a weary sigh. "Our associate will not be kept waiting, so let's be on our way."

"You changed your mind awfully quickly," Syrie commented to Fujita in jest.

"I have changed nothing of the sort," Fujita stated resolutely. "I will go up that ladder, try to convince the lady to see the sense in our plan, and if she does not agree to it, I will climb right back down and be on my way. Now, are you with me, or not?"

Syrie looked between Fujita and the old man, and spoke to the latter directly. "Go to the designated waiting place and make sure our transport out of the city is ready, old ser. We will join you soon."

"Thank you so much, ma'am," the man said during their parting. "Please, be safe."

"What was all of that back there?" Syrie queried Fujita as they crossed Bryten Field. "We have come too far to back out now, and you know it."

Fujita stopped in his tracks and stared her down through the eyeholes of his mask. "Nonsense, we can back out at any time. The life of the agent must always be considered in our actions. We have worth too, you know."

Syrie jabbed a finger toward Palomb Palace looming overhead. "There is a beaten woman, a teenaged girl, and a boy of eleven up there waiting to leave a life of horrors. The lives of a nanny and a gardener who both had the bravery to help them in their escape hang in the balance with theirs as well. That's five people depending directly on you, our fellow agent, and me. I don't go into these jobs looking to die, but I do go in knowing that my responsibility is to protect the innocent, and I am prepared to lay down my life if it means one person has a chance at a better existence. When it comes to three of us weighed against five innocents, you had best believe that their needs far outweigh ours."

"That would be a tragic waste of what I consider to be one of the finest agents that I have had a hand in training and an amazing, strong woman furthermore," Fujita said with what Syrie thought to be genuine affection. His tone softened then, and he seemed to slacken in his frigid approach. "But I do understand the sentiment behind your words, and your compassion is an asset in this line of work, even if my attitude would make you think it to be a detriment. Well, come on, our associate will be upset if we are late."

With nothing further for either of them to say, they completed the jog to the cliff in silence. The ladder clacked softly off the rock wall in the gentle breeze, and Syrie reached for a rung so she could help steady it.

That's a long way to climb on a rattling pile of rope and lumber, she noted, keeping her hesitance contained.

"I'll hold it as steady as I can for you from down here. Go ahead," Fujita told her with reassurance, leaving Syrie to guess that he had somehow sensed her apprehension.

"Thank you," Syrie told him while setting her foot into a rung.

The ascent went without major issue, with Syrie having to stop only twice to steady the ladder on a climb that she counted at fifty-four rungs. At the top, she scrabbled onto a knobby surface covered in light snow and wild grass. It was empty, with no sign of N'ailla or the Palomb family to be found. The light reflecting from the two moons in the clear sky lent white and red hues that allowed for sight in the darkness, but despite this, she could see no sign of any rusted gate.

Her line of sight went out across Bryten Field, soaking in a view she had never before been afforded in all her various stints in Hercalest. The shimmering snows, glowing here and there with the red of the more distant of the two moons lay before her, disturbed only by the indentations of where the Sacred Fist's tents once lay. From where she knelt, Syrie could see clear across the northern skyline of Hercalest, and for the first time in what felt like an eternity, she was truly awed by the scenery before her.

I may never see the like of this again.

"Move, please," she heard from beneath, looking down to see Fujita trying to complete his climb.

Syrie offered him a hand, and helped pull him onto the cliff's edge beside her.

"What were you doing just now?" Fujita asked while adjusting the short sword on his hip. "I had figured that you would have already sussed everything out by the time I joined you."

A sweeping gesture preceded a verbal response from Syrie, "I was taking in the sights. All this time in Hercalest and I had still never quite seen a view quite like it."

"Aye and it just goes to show that even natural sights and beauties can be monopolised by the elite," Fujita commented with tapered frustration as he took a second to have a look at the view for himself. "I think of the walls and gates that went up on this hill to keep the wealthy isolated from the many, and what those expensive boundaries purloined, and it is in the thinking that I am sickened."

Fujita had left behind the view while he spoke, and Syrie jogged a few steps to catch up to him. "Tonight we are going to steal something from those same rich folk, if you stop to consider it."

"People cannot be stolen. They can be taken against their will, but stealing implies that they are someone's property to begin with," Fujita countered correctively while scanning the wall for the rusted, iron entrance they sought.

Syrie had a further point to make, and did as much while walking ahead of Fujita and conducting her own search. "I was not referring to the targets, not in the literal sense, anyhow. What we are stealing is that concept of ownership that the possessor feels he has over the targets. We are helping them exercise the right to self-autonomy. To me, nights like this remind me that even nobodies like us can be responsible for change in this dreary, old world."

"I rather liked that," Fujita complimented in rare fashion. "We will have a hard time doing anything if we cannot find that gate, though."

The shrubbery around the wall seemed to be inching taller as they walked along it to the right of where they climbed the ladder. Their search seemed fruitless until a sudden cropping of dead, frostbitten hanging moss gave Syrie some hope. "The old gardener said it was fairly hidden. I would say that this is the area," she whispered to Fujita.

A few steps later, Syrie's hands felt iron bars, and there, practically at ground level, was a small gate that looked like it was built out of rust. It had been left partially open, which she found was as far as it could be moved in the dense foliage. It was enough to allow Syrie and Fujita to slip through, but anyone even slightly bigger than he would have been helplessly wedged between brick and iron.

The light of the moons seemed incapable of penetrating into the rear yards of the palace, and Syrie found herself emerging into total darkness. Instinctually, she stayed in a crouched position and made her way along the wall and moving to her left, her eyes scanning for any signs of life, friendly or otherwise.

A finger tapped on her shoulder, and a glance over it saw Fujita pointing toward a shed in a corner on the opposite side of the property, unlit and with its door hanging slightly ajar.

The gardener's shed. That makes sense.

She reversed course and kept to the wall, with Fujita now leading the way. Once at the entrance they slipped inside, taking care to leave the door undisturbed, lest they risk the protest of any unoiled hinges.

"You're here at last, I was about to go in search," the voice of N'ailla called through the darkness.

"What of the targets?" Fujita called back, wasting no time on banter.

"All four are here," N'ailla revealed while stepping forward enough to be seen by Syrie and Fujita.

Syrie's eyes could discern but a few shapes in the direction that N'ailla had emerged from and said as much. "The nanny is the fourth? I don't see them, where are they?"

"Squat down low out and shivering in terror, of course," N'ailla explained while peeking through the door. Her face was masked much the same as Syrie's, and her outfit was identical, save for a long leather jacket in place of a cloak. Strapped to N'ailla's back was a crossbow, the only other differentiating feature between the two women. While most agents preferred melee weaponry, N'ailla was keen on the long ranged weapon, and Syrie knew that beneath the coat and resting on N'ailla's hip was a full quiver of bolts just waiting to fly.

"We need to talk about altering the plan," N'ailla conferred with urgency. "Have you spoken to our informant?"

"We have, aye," Syrie told her. "A new plan was mentioned, but our fellow agent has objections to it."

Fujita looked into the corner of the shed. "Where is the mother? Come on out, we need a word."

"Yes?" a frightened squeak of a voice inquired as its owner stepped into where the moonlight might illuminate her.

Having spent years as a liberator for the Women's Road, Syrie was well accustomed to seeing women in battered and terrified states, yet she was still perturbed by the sight of Eamon Palomb's wife. She had to believe it was on account of seeing a woman of wealth, who should want for nothing, looking so desperate and broken. There were no bruises, abrasions, or scars on the parts of the woman's body that Syrie could discern. What Syrie could see though was a noticeable droop in the left eye, and the ear on the same side had been damaged in the cartilage and was both swollen and turned outward. The condition was common among professional fighters, and was typically called *'cauliflower ear'* in such circles. While those same fighters tended to view the destroyed tissue as a point of pride, the wife had no such allusions. Further adding to her sad visage was that even in her layers of fine, warm clothing the woman looked rail-thin and utterly fearful.

I am amazed that she even agreed to be rescued. The gardener was right to say that this is for her children. She would have done away with herself or suffered in silence if not for them.

If Fujita noticed the same, he made no mention of it, verbally or otherwise, and dove straight to the issue. "Ma'am, we heard from the man on the outside that you would like your children to not have to escape via the original mode of transport that we arranged. Is this correct?"

"Yes," the wife stammered out.

"Might I suggest that we reconsider?" Fujita had begun to ask.

Syrie was not about to entertain the old plan any longer, though, "Look at her, she is shaking already. You cannot expect her to climb down a rope ladder in that state. She will beat herself to dust on the rocks."

"I agree," N'ailla sternly intoned. "The children are a little better than the woman, but I have no faith in any of them successfully descending over the cliff."

"What about the nanny, at least?" Fujita asked quickly. "We can send her down, lower the ladder to her, and send her to meet the gardener."

N'ailla peered off into the back corner of the shed. "She might make it, but I would rather keep them all together."

"We cannot leave the ladder hanging there," Fujita argued, annoyance flaring heavily in his tone. "They will discover it come morning."

"No, you are right," N'ailla consented, already appearing to have a plan in mind for that. "You and I will take the extra coil of rope, cut the ladder, and lower it to the ground. When all of you are free and on your way out of the city, I will go retrieve the ladder. I am staying in Hercalest to take the other agent's place, if you haven't forgotten."

Fujita exhaled with a grunt. "Alright then, let's go do that immediately."

"I will stay on watch," Syrie volunteered, though it seemed to be a foregone conclusion.

With N'ailla and Fujita gone, Syrie took a moment to encourage everyone to relax, knowing that the intimidating presence of the fearsome, sullen Drakian tended to put even the stoutest hearts on edge.

The wife had stayed exactly where she stood when speaking with Fujita, her eyes flittering nervously between Syrie and the back corner of the shed.

"You might as well all come on out where I can see you," Syrie told the children and the nanny. "I have a few questions to ask about the amended plan and you are all welcome to have a say."

The three followed her instructions and emerged from where they hid. The daughter led the way, stepping into the light with an unexpected vigour. The nanny brought up the rear, with the boy standing between them. The girl had long dark curly hair tied into a tail, and had dressed herself in both a warm cloak and a coat, with a scarf wrapped around her face and gloves on her hands. The boy was dressed similarly, minus the cloak. It was the nanny that worried Syrie though. Having donned an old, plaid jacket that looked to belong to a man and no further warm garments, she did not look prepared for the elements.

She's going to freeze her hands and ears off once we get riding. We will have to see what we can come up with to prevent that.

The two women and the girl all wore skirts below the waist, and Syrie found herself annoyed at the mere sight of them.

"Those skirts might get in the way," she told the women bluntly. "You were instructed to secure trousers."

"We tried, ma'am, we really did," the nanny answered for both of them. "There were none to fit any of us."

Each person had either a lightly packed knapsack on their back or a satchel over the shoulder, as requested, with what Syrie hoped were only food and the most important of items within. However, she noticed the boy to be clutching a wicker picnic basket in his arms.

"What's in the basket?" Syrie tried to ask them in as gentle a voice as she could muster in such a state of urgency. "A single light satchel or knapsack each that was to be packed with only essentials was what we asked you to bring."

"Please do not be angry, miss," the boy said while laying the basket down and reaching for the latch.

"No don't open it, Dorian," the girl scolded while slapping away his hand. "They'll get away."

"What will get away? What's in the basket?" Syrie queried with increasing apprehensiveness.

The boy looked up at her with big, baleful eyes. "It's a cat and her three kittens, Ma'am."

Fujita is going to be incensed when he hears this.

Syrie took a second to breathe and keep herself calm. "Could someone explain to me why four cats are joining us?"

"The mother gave birth to them in the loft of our stables on the front of the palace," the daughter answered defensively. "Dorian and I have been looking after them all this time. No one but a groom knew about it outside of Dorian and me. The kittens are getting to an age where they might wander outside and we are afraid of what our older brothers will do to them."

Nareen's voice trailed off, and she knelt before the basket and ran a hand over its surface and what came forth from her next was said in a grave whisper that chilled Syrie to the bone, "They have killed and tortured animals before. Well, Pyore usually does the worst of it, and Eldridge goads him on and has a laugh at the suffering. I am going to have to insist that they come along, ma'am. I will not let my older brothers hurt our kittens and their mother any more than I will let them harm my little brother and mother."

It's fortunate for the twins and Eamon that they are not here now, or I would end all three before sunrise.

"What did the other female agent say about them?" Syrie asked next. "I have no doubt she asked the same question I did."

The children looked between one another, and the nanny patted the boy on the shoulder and answered for them, "The agent said she would have to ask you two, but she was sceptical of bringing the cats, ma'am."

"I am afraid to say that I share her concern," Syrie admitted with a nervous swallow. "And the male agent you just met will be downright pissed off about it. I can tell you that now. Let me ask something of you two: between you, can you both carry that basket all night long?

You cannot ask any of us agents to carry it for you, as we have to keep our hands free, and there may be points along the way that your mother and nanny might have to be put to use too."

"We shall do it. You have my word," the girl answered while looking to her brother, "Is that not right, Dorian?"

The lad nodded rapidly, "Yes, ma'am, Nareen tells you the truth."

A pair of shadows encroached on the limited moonlight in rapid fashion and upon verifying their origins, Syrie stepped back to allow Fujita and N'ailla to return.

"It's done," Fujita relayed to Syrie, not that she doubted that the task was complete. "Have you gone over the plan with the four of them?"

Syrie pointed down to the basket at Dorian's feet. "We had a minor complication arise."

"What's this now?" Fujita asked, entirely nonplussed at the sight of the wicker container.

"Three kittens and their mother-"

"No," Fujita answered with instant indignation, before the word 'mother' had even fully left Syrie's lips. "We are not carting around a litter of kittens."

"The children said they will carry the basket," N'ailla offered in their defence.

"No. Animals are unpredictable and capable of being quite loud without warning. In this case, cats can further attract dogs if they start making a ruckus," Fujita said by way of explanation for his stance. "We risk upending everything by bringing them along, especially given the route we have to take now."

Nareen took a step toward Fujita and stood up straight. "They will die if we abandon them, ser."

"Not my concern," Fujita stated in brusque rejection of her plea. He looked toward the mother and the nanny, "The cats stay, or I leave."

"Just what route are you going to take for that exit?" N'ailla asked before Syrie could, the same thought having occurred to her.

Fujita had begun to respond, even making an audible start, though he clammed up before the first word could come out.

"We all have to leave the same way," Syrie sighed while laying a hand on Fujita's shoulder and leaning in to talk a little more intimately with him. "I understand your frustration, but we are stuck here right now with the cats as much as we are with the women and children. If it helps, I have already made the children promise to carry the basket themselves and leave us out of it. The older brothers are sadistic, and the children are terrified of what they will do to their beloved pets. Come now, how can you do that to them?"

"I will not be responsible for the cats. This is fully on you two," Fujita negotiated while pointing at N'ailla and Syrie. "If the cats make noise and draw guards or anyone else who might take umbrage with our presence, you two will take responsibility should I find myself with no alternative but to respond with force to any attackers. Think about that: people's lives could potentially end because of four cats. Weigh the consequences of that action and decide if you are willing to accept such a risk."

Syrie gave the thought a considerate moment to pass through her mind, yet came to the same conclusion that she already had. In her decisive response, she patted Fujita on the shoulder, "I can accept that risk."

"Me as well," Nareen stated, earning a groan from Fujita. "These guards are the only ones around here with the size to stand up to my father and brothers and they never do. What good are they anyway? They take an oath to protect the innocent and then look away when my father strikes my mother. Why even bother to take the oath? I will not fret if you kill any of them."

"It is one thing to say that as a foolish, innocent girl," Fujita countered grimly, "It is another thing entirely to take a life or to see one taken right before your eyes. Everything changes in that instant and your words become wind. All but the most callous break on the first death they witness, and most never get so complacent that they repeat statements like yours again."

"Please do not speak to my daughter like that, ser," the mother uttered so quietly that Syrie barely heard it at all.

Fujita gave a nod to that request, "Very well, so long as she makes no further outlandish statements, I will abstain from lecturing her."

The mother leaned over to Nareen and whispered, "Do not agitate that man, do you understand me? He agreed to allow the kittens to come along and came all this way to help get us out of here. Give him no grief. That goes for the both of you."

"Yes, Mother," they both answered in an identical, contrite tone.

Syrie took the break in tensions to take command of the situation. "Ma'am, did you bring the broom like you were asked?"

"Yes, ma'am, it is right here," the nanny answered while holding out the straw cleaning tool.

"Hand it off to the male agent, please," Syrie instructed while commencing the briefing. "Alright, for our trek across Greffold Hills, we will put me and the other female agent in front. The nanny will follow behind us. The young lady follows her, then the boy, and the mother. That leaves the male agent to guard the rear and cover our tracks with the broom to the best of his abilities. Are there any questions?"

When none made a noise, in either query or protest, she held a finger to her lips and began surveying the outside world for signs of life. Once she was certain that the coast was clear, Syrie waved a hand and began her departure, calling to the other six as she did. "Alright, off we go."

Once all were without, N'ailla slipped to the front with Syrie, and the two led the way through the rear garden, keeping near the outer wall as they went. At the old gate, Syrie went through first, doing a check to ensure that no one was about before allowing the others to follow. At that point, she knew, they were wading into unknown territory for the agents, and she all but crawled forward, slinking along against the opposite side of the wall until it curved away sharply.

With the party having stopped behind her, Syrie scanned the direction toward the road, seeing a streetlight in the distance but no people or movement between her and the road. Across the narrow patch of ground between the Palomb Palace and the considerably more humble neighbouring manor was nothing but snow and grass, though the density of the shrubbery on the other side gave her concern.

"Move carefully," Syrie directed the others while pointing directly to the inherent danger. "We have thick bushes ahead to walk through, with only an iron fence and the cliff's edge between them. Stay close to the fence at all times, try not to make too much rustling, and be careful not to end up hooked on anything, savvy?"

After a handful of seconds without objection, Syrie moved forward, careful of where every new footstep landed her. From behind her, Syrie could hear leaves being moved aside, snow crunching, and twigs snapping, leaving her with nothing but the hope that their noise did not attract attention. At the end of the property line of the second manor, Syrie found a similar situation as before, and the trek continued almost identically to the previous leg.

We just need to keep low, avoid talking, and we should be fine. It is far too late for anyone but guards to be active, and it is too cold for them to want to be outside any more than is absolutely necessary.

At the start of the sixth yard, the first since the Palomb Palace to have a brick and mortar wall, Syrie brought the group to a halt once they were all safely obscured.

"How much further is it to the bottom of the hill?" Syrie asked the wife after making her way close enough to be within whispering range.

"Five or six more houses, at the most," she answered back with equal parts nervousness and uncertainty. "I think that this is the Burchfield's house, but I do not know for sure. As you can likely understand, I have never travelled this way before and I cannot see the house through the wall."

"That's fair enough," Syrie offered in reply while another question came to mind. "Will you know the correct house that is supposedly across from the Winchell residence when we reach it?"

The wife considered the question for a moment before giving a response, "I should, but if I do not know, Darla, Nareen, or Dorian certainly will."

"Who's Darla?" Syrie inquired, the answer coming to her as she did.

"That would be the children's nanny," the wife confirmed.

Syrie looked over to the attendant, who appeared to be a fair woman about Syrie's own age. "I apologise for not giving you the consideration to even ask your name before now. That was not right of me."

"I accept the apology, but it is perfectly alright, ma'am. I am well used to as much," Darla told Syrie quickly.

"Well, you shouldn't have to be," Syrie responded to the nanny before looking back to the mother, "And you, shall I call you Jorette?"

"That would be fine, just make sure to not use my surname," Jorette stated confidently. "I refuse to be called a Palomb anymore."

"Then so shall it be," N'ailla agreed as she gave a gentle tug on Syrie's arm. "We have little time to dawdle. Please, get moving."

The apparent onset of nervousness in N'ailla jarred Syrie back to the task at hand, and she ushered the group back to their normal pace.

The greenery and the various barriers backing each home provided their own challenge, but Syrie navigated each as the party encountered them.

At the second home that the group passed since their last discussion, Syrie began to hear chatter coming from the children, apparently directed at their mother.

"Is something the matter back there?" Syrie asked softly.

It was Jorette who offered a response on behalf of all three. "Nareen and Dorian believe that this is the home that sits directly across from Winchell Manor. For my own part, I am not entirely sure, Ma'am. It does not look familiar to me from here."

"We have been through these old paths before, Miss," Nareen told Syrie in earnest fashion. "This is where the Hallthorpe's live. They have a son who is a little older than I am named Lexington."

"Nareen used to have a crush on Lexington," Dorian blurted out unexpectedly.

"No, I did not. Pay him no mind, please," Nareen shot back bashfully. "This is the Hallthorpe Manor, though."

Even in the direst of circumstances, the young folk can find a way to lighten the mood, Syrie said to herself while looking over the expansive, three-storied home on the other side of a black, wrought iron fence. *Whether rich or poor, some things will never change.*

Syrie looked to Jorette, who still appeared uncertain. "The children seem convinced, and that is really all we have to go on at this point. If I escorted you to the street, could you tell me for certain?"

"Oh yes, I know things from the street quite well," Jorette confirmed for Syrie. "I have been staring down this road from on top of this bloody hill long enough to know that much."

"Then that's what we'll do, dearie," Syrie decided, giving a nod to N'ailla next. "You and our other agent remain here with the children and their nanny. When Jorette is sure of our whereabouts, I will signal to either advance or hold position."

"Understood, Agent," N'ailla answered Syrie before giving a command of her own to the others. "Everyone get as low as you can below the shrubbery line without getting to your bellies and keep your eyes on me."

"Let's me and you get a move on," Syrie told Jorette as N'ailla issued her instructions to the other three rescues.

The path between these houses was not only clear of foliage, but had a stone walkway running from front to back. At the midpoint of the path was a pair of matching arched gates in the iron fences on either side, with each one leading to a doorway illuminated by a single electric bulb.

These ones must be family, or otherwise friendlier to one another than most on this street. This is the only clear path between houses that I have seen thus far. Either way, it makes for easier going, although I hope there is no one else out here at this hour.

At the point where the stone walkway met the sett brick street there was little cover for the two women, apart from the iron fences. Syrie called for Jorette to wait a few steps back from that junction while she went ahead to check for signs of activity. The street was thankfully bare, though troublingly lit up, with lamp posts at what seemed like every seven or eight metres. The houses were further casting light from outdoor fixtures and scattered windows, though at this hour most interiors appeared to be darkened.

"It looks clear, come have a look," Syrie said once she returned to Jorette's position.

Together, they crept out to where the path met the street, with Syrie again taking the lead and giving a last glance before allowing Jorette to look for herself.

"Well?" Syrie asked when Jorette withdrew to safety.

"It should be alright. I was thrown off for a second, because we came out between the Hallthorpe and Yennfeld houses, I recognised them by the archways between them. I mistakenly thought that would put us one house off from the Winchell home, but there it is, right across the way."

"That house with the three dormer windows on the second floor and the big windows in the loft?" Syrie asked for clarification.

Jorette let a nod serve for her answer, and it was enough for Syrie to give a beckoning wave toward the rear of the Hallthorpe property.

"Can I ask a question while we wait for the others?" Jorette posed to Syrie.

"You might as well. We have a moment for it," Syrie gave back with a nonchalant shrug while continuing to monitor the street as best as she could from the obscured space they were occupying beside the Hallthorpe's fence.

When no query came, Syrie gave a glance to find Jorette with a puzzled look on her face. "Is something wrong?"

"No, I am just trying to find the right words," Jorette revealed thoughtfully. "You are all so careful with saying names and such. The only slip we have had so far was the nanny's name. I do not want to compound it any further."

"You have my apologies for that mistake," Syrie relayed back. "I merely responded to the use of the name in general, as I had not heard anyone referred to with that name up until then."

Jorette gave a shrug of her own. "It is alright, the mistake was mine in the first place. My question is: do you know why the benefactor in this mission was willing to pay so much and go to such lengths for me and my children?"

"I'm sorry, but I have no information to offer," Syrie said as she caught sight of N'ailla and the others approaching from a crouched walk. "Perhaps you can ask the benefactor once we deliver you to them."

"I still have not the foggiest idea how you intend to make that happen," Jorette stated to Syrie while her attention went to the children.

"A discussion for a later time," Syrie told Jorette while moving to be closer to N'ailla. She waved in Fujita as well and the three went into a huddle. "She says this is the house. We will go across the street in small groups rather than one long line, with one agent to each group."

Syrie waited a beat for the other two to nod in agreement, and she glanced around defensively before elaborating further. "Alright, I will go first with the mother. I will scour the path on the other side and attempt to locate the cellar door and leave the mother there to keep an eye out. Once that is done, I will come back to the street." She pointed to N'ailla next. "You will go second with the children and bring them to me. While I take them to their mother and guard all three, you wait for the nanny and him. Both of you should be capable of finding your way to me without any help."

With no objections to the plan, Syrie stepped back and took Jorette by the hand. "You, come with me, we're crossing the road."

"What about the children?" Jorette inquired worriedly.

"They'll join us next," Syrie explained calmly. "We have to go in small groups to better avoid detection. Are you ready?"

"As ever I will be," Jorette said with a deep breath.

"Stay low, and don't let go of me," Syrie advised her while edging towards the wide, brick pathway leading to the top of Greffold Hills.

With a last glance to either side of the road, Syrie dashed out into the street, moving as fast as her legs could take her in such a lowered stance. Once on the other side, she allowed herself to breath and looked to Jorette to find her gasping.

"Oh dear, oh dear, that was a rush," Jorette told Syrie in a panicked whisper.

"Hush, we have to move quickly," Syrie said while pressing a finger to her lips. "Come now."

Unlike their neighbours across the street, the Winchell's had no shared walkway with those next door, and instead erected a tall, groomed hedge for privacy. Syrie led Jorette around the outer perimeter of the hedge and around to the rear of the home.

At the back of the property, Syrie began feeling around on the ground for anything that might pass for a hatch. Once it became apparent to Jorette what Syrie was doing, she fell to her knees and joined Syrie in the search. The fallen snow served to chill Syrie's hands and numb them as the melted snow leeched through. It felt to Syrie as though an eternity passed by the time their increasingly painful scramble finally uncovered lumber. Having found an edge of the doorframe, Syrie began clearing away snow until she found a pair of iron rings fastened into the pair of wooden doors. A single chain was woven through the links and held fast together by a thick, rusting padlock.

"Well, fuck," Syrie muttered in frustration.

"That does not bode well," Jorette surmised while joining Syrie to have a look for herself. "Oh dear, Jensen never said that the hatch was locked."

"It does not look like it was a recent installation, either," Syrie pointed out while lifting the rusting links and their fastener carefully. "You stay here and keep low. I will go get the others so that my fellow agents might assess the situation with me."

Syrie darted back around the corner of the Winchell hedge as quickly as caution allowed and arrived at the street in short order. When she caught sight of the others, Syrie waved them over and stood back to allow N'ailla and the children to access the narrow pathway.

"Go with the children," Syrie told N'ailla hurriedly. "I will wait for the nanny and our remaining agent. Have a look at the entry to our escape route while you wait."

"Understood," N'ailla replied, taking off into the night without question.

Once they were gone and Syrie could confirm that the way was still clear, she motioned to Fujita, who led the nanny out onto the street by the hand and crossed in almost too quick of a fashion for Darla to keep up.

"You deviated from your plan already," Fujita noticed as he and Darla met Syrie on the other side.

"And for good reason, as you will soon see," Syrie offered as a temporary explanation. "Quickly, follow me."

Returning to the hatch, Syrie found the family reunited and the children busily checking on the cats in their basket. Beside them were N'ailla and Jorette, inspecting the iron links that were keeping the heavy wooden doors shut.

"This is quite peculiar, I admit," N'ailla said while lifting the lock for Fujita to see.

"That certainly raises a great deal of questions, and coincidentally, the man who can answer them has gone off into hiding," the sarcasm in the second half of Fujita's musings was unmistakable, and Syrie was of a mind with his apparent frustrations.

Jorette was looking between the three agents then with confusion etched on her face. "I do not understand. Can none among you pick a lock? I would think such a skill would be commonplace amongst your vocation."

"Picking the lock is no issue," N'ailla affirmed to Jorette, revealing the shared concern of the agents immediately after. "What the three of us must now determine are the implications of this cellar door being locked when in fact we were warned of no such thing."

The burning issue on Syrie's mind from the moment she saw the lock came out in that moment. "Do you think the gardener lied about having explored the cellar?"

"Either that or he had a key and did not turn it over to us," Fujita posited grimly. "If we unravel that thread, we have to ask if he merely forgot to give us the key or intentionally withheld it."

"Wait now, Jensen is no delinquent," Jorette said in defence of her friend. "I have known that man my entire married life and he is one of the few people in the palace that I have been able to rely on for confidentiality in all this time."

Fujita's gaze went to the runaway wife. "If he told us no lies, then that means he happened upon the door without a lock and one was added after his visit. We have to then wonder if he was somehow detected and whether or not his detection warranted further security than a few links of chain and a lock."

"Or perhaps when he came looking for the door it was by chance left unlocked by carelessness," Darla added to support Jorette's case.

"That might be the case, and I do hope that you are right," Syrie said considerately while reaching for the supply pouch on her hip. She drew out a small kit bound in leather and chose a pair of picks she thought best suited for the task. "However, on the off chance that they are wrong, and I inadvertently lead us into a trap or a dead end, we have to decide on our actions ahead of time. For instance, if this leads nowhere, how then do we get all of us off of this forsaken hill?"

"There is only one other exit..." Fujita reminded everyone, the inevitably dire outcome that waited at the gates for all of them echoing clearly in his voice.

N'ailla was looking all about, her eyes scanning for life in the low light of the two moons. "I just thought of something: the door is locked from above. That means if there is a tunnel to the Winchell's mausoleum, whoever accesses it from there cannot emerge here. Therefore, the only people who can use this hatch as a passage, barring destruction of the door that is, are those who both possess a key and can access the door from this side.

Fujita hummed in amusement at something N'ailla had said. "The bootleggers deliver the liquors to the cellar, but without violence, they have no access to their employer, who can do as they please. Sounds like an apt metaphor for business in Illiastra as a whole, if you ask me."

"More likely it is because the Winchell's know only one or two of the bootleggers, and those few would be the supervising staff to begin with," Jorette countered, in what seemed to be a reflexive manner. "The men doing all the labour would be unknown to Rexford Winchell, and therefore, would not be trusted to have access to a vulnerable entry point that leads directly to his family's home."

Syrie gave that name consideration as she worked on the lock. "Rexford Winchell... I know that name. What is his business? Besides bootlegging, that is."

Jorette chimed in once more, "He is a columnist for *The Illiastran Investigator*, the primary newsprint in the country. You probably remember him from all the opinion pieces he writes favouring the political interests of my husband and his closest friends. He was not always like that, mind you. There was a time when he was critical, albeit tepidly, toward the EMP's eastern half. I still do not know if it was a deteriorating sense of self-awareness in his old age, financial incentive from eastern ministers, or the combination of both that turned him into a curmudgeonly mouthpiece for awfulness. Whatever it was, it afforded him a lovely mansion amongst the elites of Hercalest."

"Sounds like a right prick," Syrie added, the lock having given away during Jorette's discourse on the patriarch of the Winchell family. Careful to prevent the rattling of the chain, Syrie detangled it from the rings on the door in a slow, deliberate manner with one hand while piling it in a neat stack in the other. The pile was laid in the grass softly, and she managed to do it all with barely more than a 'clink'.

"It is because of that Winchell man that we have an escape route at all," Darla reminded Syrie in a tone that just barely sounded reprimanding. "We should be thankful for what he has given us."

"I stand by what I said," Syrie told Darla while stepping off the doors, allowing Fujita and N'ailla to step in and take a door each to open. "And besides, he didn't give us anything with any intention. We made use of what he already had without his knowledge."

Once the doors were opened, Fujita returned to the entryway. He stared down into the black abyss of the cellar with his left hand on the shorter sword on his hip and the right still clutching the straw broom taken with them from the Palomb Palace. "It occurs to me that there is one advantage to this escape plan: if ol' Rexford would like his dalliances with illegal liquors to remain unknown, he will not say a thing about what he might discover here once we are gone."

"That certainly does work to our favour," N'ailla agreed while peering down into the cellar that Fujita quickly disappeared into the confines of. "How does that air smell in there? Will it be safe for firelight, do you think?"

"There is nothing unusual about it," Fujita relayed back to her. "I detect no odours and no weight in my breaths. I think we will be fine."

Syrie began ushering the others wordlessly to the old, wooden steps of the cellar after Fujita's assessment, and gave him leave to produce light.

"One burning broom at your request," he answered Syrie, his voice growing slightly faint as he moved further within the hole.

The nanny went first, with Nareen and Dorian walking side by side, each one holding half of the arching handle on the basket of kittens. Jorette followed lastly, leaving Syrie and N'ailla up above.

"Grab that door," Syrie instructed N'ailla, while taking the door closest to where she stood to hand. The pair walked down the steps while closing the exit above in as quiet a manner as possible.

In the centre of the floor of the cellar stood Fujita, the rapidly burning straw of the broom casting an orange glow over the small, damp room. "We need a more permanent light source," he called out to Syrie and N'ailla while pointing at the dwindling flame.

"Look around, surely there are lanterns somewhere," Syrie commented while feeling around on her own.

"I found a switch of some kind," Darla declared from on the far side of the cellar. Before Syrie or the other agents could investigate, Syrie heard a mechanical grinding noise. Along the top of either wall, starting with the area directly above Darla, single bulbs began to light up in a string, culminating at the edge of the stairs leading to the Greffold Hills exit.

Fujita snuffed out the broom on the floor and went hurriedly to the doors with the handle still in hand. "Cut those lights!" he ordered while dashing past Syrie and N'ailla.

"What the?" Syrie had begun to say, until voices and footsteps from overhead began to resonate. "Everyone to the back exit, hurry now."

N'ailla rushed ahead with Syrie toward a narrow hole in the ground and a ladder that protruded from it. "Come on now, children first," N'ailla ordered them while pushing both Nareen and Dorian towards it.

"What about the kittens?" Dorian exclaimed in a voice that was far too loud for Syrie's liking.

"I'll carry them down," Darla insisted while taking the basket to hand. "Go now, hurry up."

Reluctantly, with his eyes fixed squarely on the basket, Dorian went to the ladder and lowered himself onto the rungs. "Do you promise that you will bring them?"

"I promise I will, now please start going down the ladder so that your sister can join you," Darla said to him frantically.

The doors leading to the surface were pulled on from above, but resisted opening thanks to the broom jammed in the handles on the lower side.

"That stick won't hold long and it looks and sounds like at least two strong people on the other side," Fujita surmised while unsheathing Oto in a single, fluid motion.

From beside Syrie, N'ailla swung her crossbow from where it sat across her back and into her hands. She stuck the nose of it into the dirt and pulled the bowstring back with both hands with a mighty tug. Once it was properly in place, she had it loaded and at the ready. The process went startlingly quick, leaving Syrie to admit that N'ailla definitely knew her way around the weapon.

"We're really doing this, dearies?" Syrie asked them both while drawing her ugly little knife from its sheath.

"If we have to," Fujita shot back in affirmation.

Syrie glanced to the ladder to see Dorian and Nareen having disappeared below, and Jorette setting herself in position to descend.

"The doors are stuck," Syrie heard a voice declare from above them.

"What? Come on then," a second voice replied. "The three of us will pull. If that don't work, we'll break the bloody thing in."

"Why has no one killed the lights?" Fujita queried as he stepped backward toward the three remaining women.

"Those doors are not exactly tightly sealed," Syrie noted. "They should already be seeing the glow flitting through. If we cut the lights now, they'll know for sure that we're down here."

"I'm fairly sure that they know that someone is down here by now," Fujita countered dryly.

"I'm going down now," Darla told the agents, waiting until Syrie gave an approving nod before beginning her descent.

N'ailla had returned to where the light switch was moored to the wall, keeping herself in reach of it while nervously tapping her fingers on her crossbow's wooden frame.

Syrie checked on Darla's progress and found her moving slowly on account of only having one free hand with which to descend. "Damn."

The word had barely left Syrie's mouth when the broomstick snapped and the doors of the cellar flung open.

"Nobody move!" a voice declared, proving to belong to a blue-coated guardsman bearing a raised rifle as he charged down the steps.

Another followed directly, dressed and armed similarly to the first. A third man, who was far more stout than the first two, brought up the rear, but came barrelling forward through his comrades and called to the agents, "Who in the name of Aren's beard are you three? State your business in Mister Winchell's cellar at this ungodly hour."

"I could ask you the same question," Fujita threw back at them.

"What?" the same guard asked incredulously. "We're city guardsmen of Hercalest, that's who. What in the blazes is going on here and why are you all armed to the teeth."

"I don't think that we're going to answer that," Syrie told him bluntly.

The head guard seemed ready for such a retort. "Then I am going to have to place you all under arrest until I can get some answers. As it stands, the three of you are trespassing on Mister Winchell's private property."

"Look around, Guardsman," Fujita bid him. "I think there's fair more going on here than the three of us trespassing.

"Well, would you have a gander at that, Verne," one of the remaining men told the head guard, his own gaze having gone to the wine racks stacked with bottles bearing a translucent substance that looked to Syrie liked moonshine.

"That's a lot of booze, alright," Verne agreed. "What are you three, bootleggers or something? Does Mister Winchell know that you are using his cellar for such nefarious deeds?"

"Mister Winchell is the owner and operator of this illegal liquor dispensary," Syrie told them truthfully. "You should all go have a chat with him and forget you saw us. Savvy?"

Verne guffawed in amazement, "It most certainly is not *'savvy'*. Now drop your weapons and go to your knees."

"Can't do that, sorry," Fujita stated in flat refusal.

"I have three people in the act of trespassing, two of which are women, dressed in black and wearing masks, all of them armed and dangerous, and refusing to follow my commands," Verne summarised in pleading intention for Syrie and her company. "Surely you can understand why I merely cannot let you all go. Something is afoot here, so either I get some convincing answers or all of you are being arrested, by force if need be, and taken to the lockup."

Syrie gave a shake of her head, "And we are in no position to either speak of what we are doing here or heed your commands. I'm afraid that we have come to a stalemate."

"And I'm about to break that stalemate, Missy," Verne said while raising a hand to signal his subordinates.

"Wait just a moment," Fujita called out. "If you fire those rifles in here you could damn well kill us all. Look over your heads and tell me if that ceiling looks sturdy to you. What kind of effect do you think three loud guns are going to have on a pile of clay held back by only a few old wooden beams that don't even have the support of centre posts? Use your common sense, Ser."

"He might be on to something, Verne," the guard who had entered first told his superior. "I should go get some help."

"No, you fool, you'll leave us outnumbered. Stay right where you are," Verne ordered his subordinate. He lowered his rifle and laid it aside against the wine racks that were nearest to him. "Alright, my gun is down. If the lads follow suit, will you surrender to us then?"

All three agents gave a glance between each other, but none dared to speak.

Verne drew his sabre in a flash, issuing orders for the remaining guards to follow suit.

Once the firearms were out of reach, Syrie spoke up. "You might as well go ahead and leave us be, now. You have little chance of beating us in melee combat."

Verne began to laugh, his fellow guardsmen joining in nervously from behind him. "You don't seem to get it, Missy. We're not going anywhere. The only thing that we are discussing is the terms of your surrender."

"Which is something that we are not about to do," Fujita told the guards. "Are you willing to die over this? All you have to do is walk up over those steps, out through that door, forget you saw us, and everyone gets to go on living their lives as normal as you like."

"You seem quite sure that it's my guards and I that will die," Verne replied with a snort.

Fujita's eyes narrowed in his mask, and his voice became quite confident. "I am quite sure that if we clash, some combination of the six of us will die. The thing that you have to ask yourself is if you're willing to take that risk. I know that I am, and my associates here would tell you the same."

"Bugger me, Verne, look at that sword the man has. It's a Drakian style blade. I think he's the Master of Blades," the second guard said in growing panic. "He could kill the three of us all by himself."

"He's not Tryst Reine, you idiot," Verne snapped at the guard. "Tryst's sword is made of blacksteel, and this man has a white ponytail sticking out the back of his mask. He's Drakian to be sure, but he isn't the Master of Blades. For that matter, I saw Tryst Reine once and I can tell you that he is in fact not a Drakian, he merely fights like one."

It was Fujita's turn to laugh then. "I am not Tryst Reine, but I do like my odds against him if he and I were to go sword to sword. I favour the odds of my friends and me against you three even better."

"You ask us what we're willing to do, but why are you so ready to risk being killed, lad?" Verne asked Fujita pointedly.

"There is a difference between your side and mine, Guardsman," Syrie said calmly, jumping in on the question. "You stand here ready to match swords with us because you believe us to be in contravention of laws that you are paid to uphold. Laws some other men set and have neither the ability nor the courage to enforce on their own, so they rely on men like you to do that. Your reward for being enforcers is just enough coin to keep you and your kind barely complacent. The truth is that no one pays a dead man though, and at the end of the day, coin is all there is to hold you to your obligation to die fighting against us.

"You see, it does not matter what your personal ideology is or whether or not you like the laws, your job is to uphold those laws, and if you don't, you lose your job. Once again, dead men can't hold jobs though, and by daybreak, your superiors would already have some other guards ready to fill your spots. Would you go to all the trouble of dying for a pithy wage you won't be able to collect from men who don't know that you even existed?

"Us three though, we are bound by a cause, not coin, and that, my good fellows, can hold a person to where they stand, even if it means death."

Despite the cold of the night, Verne began to sweat profusely, the beads forming on his receding brow and reddening face. "Answer me this: is what you are doing malicious?"

"We are helping some friends leave an abusive situation," Syrie revealed, careful of her phrasing. "The abuser might find it malicious, but that's about all."

"You're those bunch that goes around stealing women and children from their husbands and fathers, aren't you?" the first guard asked.

"We cannot comment on that," Syrie answered quickly, before either N'ailla or Fujita might say anything more direct.

Verne's gaze was on N'ailla and her crossbow, held at the ready and pointed at the guards since they arrived. "That one could kill one of us in a blink, then it's three against two, and one of the three is a Drakian swordsman who might be from their special fighter school. Tell me, what coin do you three have on you? It might be that I can fine you for trespassing and we'll leave you to be on your way."

"I have some copper in my pouch," Syrie informed Verne.

"Verne, what are you doing?" the second guard asked frantically. "If Mister Winchell discovers his cellar broken into and finds out that we let the perpetrators go, we will be in hot water."

Verne stole a glance toward the speaking guard. "What do you want me to do? If we shut the doors and put the lock back on, Mister Winchell might not even know that they were here. If he asks, I'll just say that we were investigating noise but it turned out to be some racoons trying to get into the cellar and we shooed them off. It does not look like these three disturbed anything besides the lock, anyway. Moreover, if Winchell's running booze out of his cellar, he won't want us poking around here. What he's doing is illegal, but he's Lord Eamon's friend, so you can be damn sure that it will be us that's punished if all of this comes out, not Winchell. That's the way it works around here when you dig up dirt. They don't care about the dirt on your shovel. They only want to know who dug it up."

The head guard looked back at Syrie and her friends. "You won't take anything, right? You're just using the tunnel back there behind you?"

"I've got no interest in moonshine, if that's what you're asking," Fujita replied with cautious optimism. "I refuse to indulge in anything that might dull my senses."

"We don't want the stuff either, Ser," Syrie answered on behalf of herself and N'ailla. "We just want to go, and the coppers in my pouch are yours if you will let us do that."

With a hard swallow, Verne looked to his guards and gestured for them to lower their swords. "I accept your terms. Hand over the coin."

"Come on, Verne, you can't do that," pleaded the second guard. "We can't let them get away."

"You'll stand down as I command, Hugo," Verne told him decisively. "I'll hear no more of it."

Syrie shifted her knife from the right to hand to the left and went for her pouch. She undid the toggle deftly with the one hand and slowly reached for the little cloth bag bundled in twine that she knew to be there. To avoid any rash moves, Syrie drew the bag out slowly, pinched at the top by just two fingers, giving the guards a full view of it. "Should be fifteen or sixteen coins here," she told Verne while holding the bag aloft. With a flick of her wrist, the bag went through the air toward him.

Though an attempt to catch the coins was made, Verne's free hand was clearly not his dominant one and the coins fumbled to the ground. He scooped them up quickly and gave them a jingle in his hand. "We'll leave, shut the doors, and put the lock on. You three go your own way, and we'll all pretend that neither party saw the other. Is that a deal?"

A quick check of N'ailla and Fujita earned Syrie a pair of nods and she met the eyes of Verne. "It's a deal."

"Alright then," Verne agreed before turning to his guards. "Lads, get your rifles and let's be out of here."

"It's not right, Verne," Hugo protested again, this time while gesturing with his free hand toward the three dressed in black. "We can't just let them go, or take them at their word. They're up to no good, I can sense it."

Verne reached over to Hugo and slapped him behind the ear. "Bollocks on your senses. I'm not getting you or I killed over a runaway from a wife-beater."

"They might be lying," Hugo reasoned.

"Might be, aye," acknowledged Verne, though he still seemed unmoved. "Nothing else outside is disturbed, no booze appears to be missing, and Mister Winchell is snug in his bed and none of his house look to be in distress. This bunch here, as shady as they look, say that they're leaving, and we're locking the door up top so they can't come back."

"What if they do come back?" Hugo questioned of his superior while rubbing the ear that was just slapped. "It's only an old pair of plank doors. They could bust through."

Verne audibly groaned before giving response, "We're going to guard the doors with our rifles, you imbecile. If they dare disturb the hatch, we'll blow ponytail and his friends back to Drake in pieces."

"You have no worries, Sers. We intend to leave as soon as you do," Syrie assured them.

"There, that settles it," Verne said while pointing toward Syrie. "Grab your gun, Hugo. We're done here."

Begrudgingly, Hugo obeyed, and the three guards departed for the surface. The doors were flung closed, shutting out the encroaching sunrise, and a chain could be heard scraping through the ringed door handles.

As soon as the chains ceased their clanking, Fujita sheathed his sword and turned to the women. "Let's not waste any time."

"I'll stand guard while you two get down that ladder," N'ailla told them while letting her crossbow arm relax at her side.

Allowing N'ailla's suggestion, Syrie sheathed her knife, and went for the ladder first. "Be sure to switch off the lights before you go."

The hole bearing the ladder felt even narrower than it looked and as she descended, Syrie's back kept constantly brushing against rocks, dirt, and what felt like a rope that ran all the way down.

At the bottom, Syrie was greeted by Darla, with neither the basket of kittens nor the Palombs anywhere to be seen. "Watch out, Agent, there's a bucket at the bottom of the ladder, and the rope does not give it enough slack to be moved out of the way."

"That must be how they lift the moonshine up to the cellar," Syrie surmised as she navigated around it.

"That was quite brave and selfless, what you three did up there." Darla commented above the sounds of Fujita's feet on the rungs.

"We did what had to be done," Syrie answered flatly.

"The lady will be moved by such courageousness, I assure you," Darla went on as she and Syrie moved out of Fujita's way. "All of you were willing to risk your lives for her and the children. I...I don't know many who would have done that."

"Any person worth their weight in salt would have," Syrie added, her discomfort with compliments shining through as always. "It is not so big of a deal."

"We're about to lose our light," Fujita warned them as he reached the bottom of the hole. "Why is there a bucket here? Do we all want twisted ankles?"

"It's attached to the rope," Syrie explained while hauling it away from his feet. "We didn't bring another light source with us, did we?"

Fujita moaned and turned his gaze upward, hands cupped around his mouth. "Agent, see if you can find a lantern or a lamp that we can bring with us before you-"

"She shut off the lights, didn't she?" Syrie asked rhetorically.

"Aye..." Fujita offered as a weary response.

Darla was tapping Syrie's shoulder to get her attention. "Actually, it shouldn't be too bad of a trek. The lady and the children went on ahead on their own and I haven't heard any distress calls yet."

"It looks like we will have to do the same," Syrie sighed.

"A shame that no one thought to bring a candle," Fujita said with a click of his tongue.

They waited in the silent darkness, the weight of what quite nearly transpired falling hard onto Syrie's shoulders as they did. Despite the compelling words and confident delivery ushered forth by Syrie and Fujita, it was likely that even the survivors would have been left maimed if that interaction had turned violent.

Those hideous guns scared me the most. I have no doubt that at least one of the guards would have went for them, and then...

If a cave-in had not happened, the ruckus would have woken all of Greffold Hills and brought on an all-out hunt for Syrie and the others. The mere thought of it filled her with immense dread.

I still don't feel like we're clear of it all yet.

"Watch out for the bucket," Fujita called to N'ailla as she neared their position.

"Oh my, I quite nearly stepped in it," N'ailla noted.

Aye, we all quite nearly stepped in it.

"We'll walk single file," Syrie instructed the other three. "Be sure to give the leader a few steps ahead of the rest, as whoever it is will have to find the way forward for all of us blindly. Bumping into them could prove disastrous if there are any pitfalls ahead."

"Very well, allow me to lead, then," N'ailla volunteered, taking the lead despite Syrie planning to do the same.

"I was going to do so myself, but if you want the task, I will not stand in your way," Syrie told her while moving aside as much as the tiny passage allowed.

"It should not be too bad, I would not think. There seems to be no issue from the wife and children," N'ailla observed, beginning the slow, plodding trek as she did. "Ow. Gods damn it all!" she called out after a few steps, letting out a further expletive-filled grumble in the process. "A word of advice: keep your heads low. The low ceiling does not yield in the slightest."

Syrie followed N'ailla after a count of five, with one hand on the ceiling above and the other stretched out into the abyss in front of her. Darla proceeded behind Syrie, as evidenced by the soft hand resting on her shoulder for support.

They walked together without so much as a word spoken between them, save for N'ailla's warnings and cautions. The pathway twisted and turned, and seemed to slope ever downward. In certain places, the ceiling seemed to dip, with sharp, rocky points threatening to claw at the heads of the unwary. As a guide, N'ailla did not falter in her duty, and with each careful step, she led Syrie and the others through the tunnel and its numerous hazards.

"There's a door here, luckily it's not locked," N'ailla told the group after what felt like hours of trekking. The sound of dry hinges creaking overlapped with N'ailla's voice. "The path widens considerably here," the group was told as N'ailla passed the threshold ahead of them. "The ceiling has risen as well. Oh...Oh gods what is that stench?"

As Syrie entered the space, she was blasted in the face by an overwhelming smell of decay, and she audibly and uncontrollably gagged, rendering her temporarily speechless.

"Oh my, that smell is quite pungent," Darla declared in a queasy voice that trailed off as she too became overtaken by it.

"That is the unmistakable smell of death," Fujita remarked through a cough, followed by retching and gagging. "Even for death, I must say that this brew is particularly rancid."

N'ailla's feet could be heard pivoting about in the gravel. "There must be bodies stacked all around. How else could such a smell be born?"

"The entirety of the departed Winchell family must have been moved into here from the mausoleum," Syrie deduced through gasped breaths. "N'ailla, get moving. We can't stay here."

"I'm looking for the exit, but I can't find it," N'ailla panicked. "Oh gods, I think I'm going to die from this smell."

Somewhere through the ruckus they were all making there came a squeak of a voice, though Syrie could not discern what it was saying.

"Everyone, hush, someone is talking to us," Syrie said loud enough to get the attention of the room.

The voice beckoned to them again. It sounded familiar, yet muffled somehow, and Syrie could not quite place it.

"The exit is over here, people. Just listen to my voice and follow it. Come this way and you will find it in no time. Oh, and try not to slip on the vomit near the door."

Syrie outstretched her hands and found N'ailla first. "Go. Follow the voice that's calling."

She went back for Darla, and grabbed the first hand of hers that she could find. "Take the other agent's hand and come with me, we have to follow that voice if we're ever going to get out of this."

Through a few stumbles and the near-loss of the contents of her stomach, Syrie managed to find a brick wall with her free hand. "I found brick. Am I close to the door?"

"You sound near," the owner of the voice relayed. "Walk to your right a little ways, and I will try to grab you."

Syrie did as asked and walked along the wall to the right, her free hand tracing its way through the lines of mortar between the brick. "I found a hand," Syrie announced after a short time.

"That's mine." A voice thick with N'ailla's heavy accent answered through the darkness. "I'm going in the same direction you are. Hold on tight."

As much as light would help in this instance, I am not sure I want to see what lurks all around us, Syrie thought amid the blind crawl and the continued assault on her nostrils.

"I've got someone," the unknown voice said excitedly. "Mind the door frame. It extends a bit too much and you could bump into it."

The four of them stepped out from the wall and one by one, slipped through the exit and into a different sort of blackness.

"I need help closing this door," the voice declared. "The children and I managed to move it, but they're indisposed at the moment now. It should not take much pushing, but it's a little heavy on my own."

"Guide me to it," Fujita volunteered readily.

Seconds later, the sound of stone scraping against stone bounced off the walls and with a soft whooshing noise, the smell began to dissipate to the far less nauseating odour of stale air, general mustiness, and mildew. There were grunts and groans from all parties and muttered, half-hearted pleas to any observing deities for mercy.

"Does anyone know where we are?" Syrie asked the others after a brief moment of respite.

"The Winchell Mausoleum, I should think, or rather, a sublevel of it," the owner of the voice that had guided them said.

"Is that the mother?" Fujita asked from what sounded like the opposite side of the room.

"It is me, yes," Jorette answered back in confirmation. "The children are on the main floor, where there's a bit of a draft of fresh air coming through the door. My poor darlings both lost their dinner, I am afraid."

"I'm right there with them," Fujita said between urges. "Which way to the upper level?"

"Walk until you come to the wall, then turn immediately to the right. Feel for a timber staircase and climb," Jorette informed Fujita with certainty.

Syrie laid a hand on Jorette's shoulder and leaned in close. "You did well getting the children here through the pitch black."

Jorette let out a short laugh. "Compared to what you and the other agents did, my task was nothing. I have not a clue how you three managed to get away from the guards unscathed, but I would gladly hear about it when we are not in a blackened crypt."

"I'm of the same mind, dearie," Syrie said with a pat. "Let's get up the stairs, shall we?"

"Oh, I should tell you that I found a lantern on the main level of the mausoleum," Jorette said with a snap of her fingers. "I was afraid of lighting it down here, I have heard that decaying corpses give off gasses and I worried what a flame might do in that. Also, and you may think less of me for saying this, but I was utterly terrified of what the lantern might have revealed in that pit."

That enticed a nervous chuckle out of Syrie. "Believe you me, I would think no less of you for not wanting to see the undeniable horrors we just passed through."

The four women quickly climbed the steps one after the other, walking into a scene if Syrie ever saw one. The two Palomb children were seated beside one another, the lantern and a mewing basket of kittens situated between them. Their faces had lost all colours, the once neatly tied hair of Nareen was a frizzy mess, and Dorian was slowly rocking back and forth.

"There's my loves, are we doing any better?" Jorette asked cooingly as she went and knelt before them.

"I do not think that I will ever be capable of eating again," Nareen whimpered.

"I was sure I would never eat again either, but you know what? I am downright hungry now," Dorian said in an almost delirious voice. "Do we have any snacks?"

Off to one side of the tiny space there was a hunched mass of black bent over between two crates, and Syrie could only assume the shape to be Fujita.

She went to him and rubbed his back softly. "What about you? How are you feeling?"

"I'm saddened by the loss of my meal," Fujita japed macabrely while raising his head toward Syrie. His mask had been lifted from the neck, revealing his nose and mouth, but practically leaving his eyes blindfolded. "It was a lovely leg of mutton and a garden's variety of vegetables, and now it's all gone."

Syrie left him to clean himself up and let her eyes fall on the children. "No worries, young ones, we'll have food on our escape wagon. In the morning, we should be at our first stop. It's a little inn I know well that's called *The Buttered Fork*. They serve a real nice chicken pie. We'll all have to grab a slice tomorrow."

"For the love of all things, please don't mention food," Fujita whined between heaves.

"Aye, you might have a point. Sorry about that," Syrie apologised with a second, quick pat on his back.

At the door of the crypt stood N'ailla, already studying the locking mechanism and Syrie went to her side to confer with her. "What do you make of this?"

N'ailla hummed aloud and gave Syrie her assessment. "It looks like it does not need a key to open from this side. We just need to lift that latch there, and turn a standard vault wheel. The gardener said it was in frequent use, but the rust spots and lack of grease indicate to me that our bootleggers neglected to give the wheel much maintenance. I would venture to guess that all three of us agents will need to turn it together to get it to open."

"Before we do that, we need to re-evaluate the next phase of the plan," Syrie surmised, leaving N'ailla to go stand before Jorette. "Ma'am, you know this section of the city well, where are we in relation to Ravenell Street?"

"We should currently be in *Brother Lyle's Holy Cemetery*, given that it's the closest to Greffold Hills and the primary place of burial for those that lived there. Based on that, I think we are three or four blocks away. Ravenell Street is on the western side of Greffold Hills, it runs almost parallel to the patch of forest on the western side of Bryten Field."

"That would be correct," Syrie noted while trying to picture the cemetery in her mind's eye so she could get her bearings. "That would be three to four blocks west of here, I assume?"

The sound of distant explosions rocked through the air, and Fujita stood up straight, pulling his mask down over his face in the same motion. "Our distractions are starting. We have to move now or never if we are going to get out of the city."

"What distractions? What's the racket out there?" Darla asked in mild panic.

Fujita took point on that question. "Those are a Drakian machination known as fireworks. I studied under a gunpowder expert and learned to make them as sort of a specialty before I moved here. For this particular outing, I had to make a large quantity in a short time. Unfortunately, that means that they lack the usual showmanship that the craft is known for, yet, they will undoubtedly serve well enough to keep the city guards busy as they attempt to find the sources."

"Agents, I need you both to come help me with this door. The rest of you, stand back out of sight," N'ailla ordered, apparently unwilling to spend any further time in the mausoleum. "We need to get this thing open if we want to even entertain taking advantage of the fireworks distraction."

The latch was lifted up and held in position by a volunteering Darla, and the three agents began to crank on the wheel. It held fast on their first attempt, and required a great deal of strain to get moving, but once the state of inertia was overcome, the wheel gave little other protest. They pulled the door inward to bring it ajar enough to allow them to see the rest of the cemetery.

"It's quiet in the graveyard. Morning is not far off, judging from the sky, but it's still plenty dark," N'ailla informed the others. "The distractions are likely sending the guards in every other direction than here."

"Let's not waste any more time, then," Fujita requested while fixing himself up and giving a last check of his possessions.

Syrie had been helping the children to their feet, placing the basket of kittens into Nareen's hands as a last measure before addressing the others. "The plan from here on out is that we go north around Greffold Hills, staying tight to the cliffs themselves. There's a ring of trees around Bryten Field that extends most of the way around the field, we will walk the edge of those trees, ducking in for cover as needed. Once we cross the little river that feeds the duck pond, there are a few paths that we can take to reach the alley of Ravenell Street. There we will find an old, dilapidated stable, where our wagon awaits. I will relay our next orders before we leave in the wagon. Any questions?"

"How are we going to get out of the city?" Darla inquired concernedly.

"We'll discuss that when we are at the stable. For now, we go while the fireworks last," Fujita answered with mild annoyance in his voice.

"He's right," Syrie had to acknowledge. "We will go with the same order of people that we had on the hill. Find your positions and we'll be off."

The cemetery, as off-putting a place as one could be found after dark, was vacant and eerily tranquil. The moons continued to shine down and provide enough light by which to see with relative ease, and Syrie called for the lantern to be extinguished and replaced. With the mausoleum left as undisturbed as possible, Syrie and her agents led the family of three and their nanny out.

"This is sort of scary, but I am not scared, not one little bit," Dorian observed while the agents closed the door. "We should watch out for ghosts, though. They could pop out of anywhere."

Syrie had to laugh at that, even if just a little. "We'll be sure to do that, young ser."

With the same single file line established again, Syrie ordered the party to a crouch and began to lead them toward Greffold Hills and the moonlit shadows it cast.

"The gate is to the south, Ma'am," Jorette notified Syrie as the party veered west, using the cover of the aboveground tombs to keep them obscured.

"I'm aware of that," Syrie acknowledged flatly. "That way is quite obvious though, and we lose the protection offered by the other mausoleums in favour of old, worn down headstones. That would be unwise. I'm going to take us right over the fence on the west end of the graveyard instead. It's only a low, wrought iron thing anyway."

Once at the fence that Syrie espied, she called a halt and commanded everyone to hunch over against the nearest crypt. She slipped out as close as she dared to the iron barrier and peered in either direction, finding the street thankfully bare.

Fujita came forward with Darla by the hand. "We should start with me and her so that we can help the children over. It also occurred to me that with the broom burnt and broken in the Winchell's cellar, we have no means of covering our tracks now."

"We can only hope that at this point, our tracks will look odd, but otherwise innocuous," Syrie resolved. "Only Winchell, his bootleggers, the bribed guardsmen, and the gardener should even know that a secret passage lies under Winchell's family mausoleum, anyhow."

Fujita nodded and bolted over the fence. "Fair enough, I just wanted you to be made aware of the situation."

"Duly noted," Syrie gave back to him. "Darla, put your foot in my hands and I'll help boost you over the fence."

Darla did as asked and went over the barrier and into the waiting and helpful hands of Fujita. Next was Nareen, bearing the basket of kittens that was quickly passed off to Darla and laid aside gently.

Once the lone Palomb daughter was safely over the fence, it was Dorian's turn, who was relieved to have not had to contend with any spectres that he believed to be calling the cemetery home. He and Nareen quickly went to the kittens, who had resumed their crying from within their wicker confines.

N'ailla was called on, with the purpose of scouting the streets ahead, and went over in one fluid jump. In a flash, she was gone, leaving Syrie and Jorette as the last to leave the field of the fallen.

With a little assistance to Jorette, all parties apart from N'ailla were soon reunited in quick form on the street. Syrie bid for them to walk north down the road in an upright and casual manner and in whatever order they wanted, so long as an agent was out in front.

Within mere minutes, they managed to find N'ailla, who had taken to concealing herself against a brick wall on the opposite side of the street.

"How does it look?" Syrie asked when she was within whispering distance.

The answer that N'ailla gave came with a frustrated tone. "It looks like at least a few of the guards were not pulled to investigate the fireworks. There's a pair just down the road, having turned south along the street that runs parallel to the east side of Greffold Hills."

"That's problematic," Syrie registered, taking a glance toward Fujita, who had come to stand beside them.

"Those guards are going to want to investigate three masked people dressed in black in the middle of the night," he mused. "What are the odds that we can bribe two different guard patrols in one outing?"

"They would not be good," Jorette stated from behind them. "However, I might be able to help in the event that we are stopped. You will all have to remove your masks, though. I can present you as my personal guards that way, and I can tell the patrol that you are out of uniform at my request."

"We have two women, one of which is black, and the lone male is a white-haired Drakian. That guard detail would be highly suspect, I would think," N'ailla pointed out.

"If it is the only option..." Jorette had begun to say, trailing off dejectedly.

Syrie began to push the others into motion. "We'll cross that bridge if we have to. Time is wasting away while we stand around."

Down the road they went, somehow falling back into the same pattern that they had been forming since the escape began. At the intersection pointed out by N'ailla, they drew to a halt, and all three agents took turns peering around the side of the brick building situated at that corner of the intersection.

"The patrol appears to have gone on," Fujita observed as the last one to look. "Shall we just head forward?"

"Carefully, aye," Syrie agreed. "The other female agent will go first with the girl and the basket. Once they are over, the male agent will take the boy. You four should waste no time and head for Bryten Field. I will cross last with the lady and the nanny, and we three will meet up with you somewhere between Bryten Field and Ravenell Street. Everything understood?"

When no questions were raised, Syrie sent N'ailla and Nareen on their way, the latter carrying the basket of kittens to hand. Fujita and Dorian went next, and like the females before them, they disappeared into the shadow of Greffold Hills.

By the time that Syrie brought both Jorette and Darla across, there was no sign of the others, and Syrie had to assume that they had all done as she commanded.

They encountered N'ailla within only a few dozen steps, crouched low and with her crossbow at the ready. "I thought that I might be of use if that patrol happened to catch you," she explained while slinging the crossbow over her back again.

"The children must have ventured on ahead with the Drakian, I assume?" Jorette asked N'ailla with a hint of concern.

"Aye, he led them to Bryten Field through the wooded area up ahead," N'ailla confirmed, setting Jorette at ease. "The young ones said they knew of a path."

"They know this area well, those two," Jorette confirmed with a tinge of amusement in her voice. "I will be only glad when they will have a little more freedom."

Syrie felt poorly for Jorette and the children, for she now knew that despite the extravagant trappings of their lives, they lived under a stubborn pall that made anything more than merely existing nearly impossible. Nareen and Dorian seemed to manage thus far, creating their own enjoyment from the small things in life, such as raising a litter of kittens. Yet, as the two of them aged, such pleasures were surely fleeting. As the lone daughter, Nareen was doubtlessly a valuable token as far as the elite class were concerned. Eamon would barter her hand in marriage to a family who would offer the most in return. Dorian was but the babe of the family, but he would be expected to eventually fall into line with his brothers and serve the family interests.

The payment was but one benefit of doing this job. Jorette and her children needed rescuing just as much as any other client that I have sprung from bondage.

Walking the forested, northern outer edge of Bryten Field is where they found Fujita, Nareen, and Dorian. It was a surprise to Syrie that they caught up to them at all, but what truly shocked her was to see Fujita carrying the wicker basket and its feline contents.

"What is this?" Syrie asked as she got up on the three of them.

Fujita could not bring himself to look upon Syrie, and gave a sigh as he explained, "The boy kept tripping with the basket and it was slowing us down. I warned both children that if a threat were to appear, that I might have to quickly drop the basket, they still opted to let me carry it."

"He took it from my hand, I did not ask," Dorian corrected him.

"But you were beginning to stumble over yourself, and I did warn you both when I took the basket, and as I recall, neither of you objected," Fujita countered in annoyance.

N'ailla was looking across the field during the conversation, her eyes focused on one thing. "The ladder, I should go grab it while we have the chance."

"Leave it, there's no time," Fujita warned while continuing at his hurried pace. "From the moment the gardener met us under that tree out there it's been one delay after another. My distractions were mistimed as a result, and we were harangued by one patrol while just slipping past another. All of that has left us with but a precious hour or two remaining before both the cover of darkness is gone and our deeds are discovered. Leave the damn ladder, I implore you."

"If I can collect the ladder, it will be one less clue for the guards assigned to figuring out what happened here," N'ailla argued.

Syrie grabbed N'ailla by the shoulders. "If you go for that ladder, we can't wait for you. Are you aware of that?"

"Yes, very much so," N'ailla answered squarely.

She released her grip. "Then go, and may fortune be with you."

"You could well be signing her death certificate, agent-in-command," Fujita scolded Syrie.

"I take responsibility for that," Syrie shot back at him, slipping her mask back on over her face as she did and giving the laces some sort of rudimentary tying. "I admit that she raised a fair point towards retrieving the ladder, and I admire her determination."

Fujita snorted derisively. "And she cannot cover her tracks. Any guard worth a damn will be scouring the field for clues, and those tracks will undoubtedly lead them back to the forest."

Syrie had a retort to make on that front. "The tracks that you and I made on our way to the tree and then to where the ladder was might likely draw suspicion too. What's one more set, but no ladder to tell them exactly how we got in?"

"She has to get back here undetected with it, first," Fujita reluctantly acquiesced, his last point having been undermined by his concessional tone.

"You go on with the family to the stables," Syrie was in the process of telling Fujita, when he shoved the basket of kittens into her arms.

"No, you go with them. I'll stay and wait for the other agent," Fujita said in defiance of Syrie's order.

With neither the time nor energy to argue, Syrie left him to it. The four rescues had stopped in their tracks and were all looking to Syrie for guidance, and she took a deep breath and gave a wave. "Alright, come on then. We have a forest to navigate."

The trail, or rather what constituted such, was a ruddy hare's path that barely allowed room for one person to pass. The narrow clearing, combined with the thick, old growth all around them, ensured that the trees and brambles would make a claw at anyone daring to walk through. The three rescued females in particular had difficulty, their skirts catching on just about every stick and twig that extended into their space. All of the catching and hooking made for a racket as the wooden limbs gave up their fight against the people pushing through, and Syrie kept close attention for anyone that might be drawn toward the noise.

At the end of the path, the party emerged on a darkened, damp, alley filled with slushy snow, discarded boxes, night soil, and further rubbish. While nowhere near as unpleasant as the passage beneath the Winchell Mausoleum, their present locale was far from a pleasant sight.

Syrie glanced to Jorette, Nareen, Darla, and Dorian, and found the former two looking about in various states of disgust, and the thought occurred to Syrie that she ought to say something. "I apologise for the grimy alley, but I promise that it's not much-"

A pair of distant gunfire blasts rang through the night, and the direction that they came from made Syrie's words freeze in her mouth and her heart plummet.

Please, no. Don't let those sounds be what I think they are.

She quite nearly leapt back into the woods, but the reminder of the four standing in front of Syrie kept her from taking more than a step.

"Your friends are in danger, are they not?" Jorette asked, her eyes going in the same direction that Syrie heard the gunshots coming from.

"They might be…" Syrie managed to say, the words trailing off to nothing.

Jorette approached Syrie, taking the basket from her with one hand while putting the other against her back, shoving her gently. "Just point us towards the stable, we'll hold up there until you get back."

"No, we can't delay now, they both knew that," Syrie answered while resisting the shove. "They understood the risks. I have to get you all to safety before dawn. The stables are this way, if you please."

"We cannot abandon them, Ma'am," Dorian protested in pleading fashion.

Syrie would not allow herself to be further hindered, and as much as it pained her, there was nothing she could do for Fujita and N'ailla with the precious hour of predawn that remained.

I am so sorry, my friends. Please forgive me.

A back door to the decrepit stable sat partially open, propped into such a position by an upturned crate sitting in the jamb. Syrie approached silently and looked through the gap, finding nothing alarming to delay entry.

"Wait here until I say otherwise," she whispered to the four, giving no time for either response or queries. In an effort to leave the door unmoved, Syrie slid sideways through the available space.

The stable was lit by a single bulb in a far corner, dangling over the heads of two horses situated in the only stalls clean and kempt enough to house them. In the centre of the floor sat a long wagon designed for hauling various cargos of the League, left behind from their recent departure from Hercalest. She checked around the wagon, under it, and inside it as much as the nearly useless bulb allowed, and was satisfied that everything was in order, undisturbed, and the room vacant save for her and the beasts.

Syrie opened her mouth to beckon the family and their nanny in, when they all came barrelling through the door unprompted. Jorette and Darla were both pushing the young ones over the threshold in a near panic, the latter pulling the door closed behind them.

"Outside, Ma'am, there's something going on outside," Jorette managed to stutter out in a whisper.

"What is it?" Syrie asked, crossing the floor to go see for herself.

"It's your friend, the man, he's out there and he's not alone," Darla explained while rushing Nareen and Dorian away from the entrance.

Syrie cracked the door open a shade, and saw Fujita on his knees, breathing heavily as his left hand clutched at his ribs. Looming over Fujita and with his back to Syrie was a single guard.

"Your friend abandoned you to die, it seems," the guard taunted Fujita.

"I guess so," he said between laboured gasps.

The guard took a step closer to Fujita and kicked him hard where his hand was pressed, sending him over onto his back with a pained grunt. "That must hurt. I bet that if I got you to a clinic, we could save you from bleeding out. Tell me where the woman went, and I will see to that straight away."

"You might as well just kill me now, save us all some time," Fujita muttered from where he lay on his back.

Syrie looked back to the others and waved for them to get down low. Her knife was pulled from the sheath, and she slipped through the door effortlessly.

"Is this how you want to die, Knave?" the guard laughed. "Bleeding out in some dump of an alley and surrounded by refuse? There's no need for all of that. You could live to see another day."

Fujita began to chortle in a bewildering sort of manner. "You think an offer to let me live long enough to be hanged or sent to Biddenhurst is going to get me to give up my friend? You really are as dumb as you look, you witless cur."

"You know what? I have had a change of heart," the guard told Fujita in a sickeningly sweet voice. "I'll let you die now amongst the rubbish that you are."

Syrie had begun to advance on the guard, her knife raised, when the bluecoat attempted to bring his leather boot down across the windpipe of Fujita.

As the boot came in close, Fujita managed to ensnare it with both hands and pull the man toward him by rolling his own body over. The action took the guard off his balance, sending him sprawling down onto his face on the filthy, muddy ground.

Bolting to his feet, the guard turned about and was on his way to retaliate against Fujita when his eyes fell on Syrie, now standing where the guard was but a second before.

"So the Drakian led me right to you after all," he snarled at Syrie through gritted teeth. "You're not so fearsome without that crossbow."

He thinks I'm N'ailla, Syrie realised.

"What do I need that for against someone as pathetic as you?" Syrie answered mockingly.

The guard cocked his head to the side at the sound of Syrie's voice, and stared hard into her eyes. His mouth curled up at one corner, he reached to his side and brought forth the standard issue sabre carried by most guards. "I'm not entirely sure what's going on here, but it doesn't matter, neither of you are making it out of this alley."

Syrie's instincts told her to go on the defensive, but the guard's actions did not match. She stepped back in the same breath that the guard aimed his sword at Fujita on the ground. As he went for a downward stab, Syrie let the blade of the knife slip between her thumb and forefinger, cocked her arm back, and stepped into her throw.

The blade stuck into the guard's chest and elicited a startled gasp from him. He released his sabre and reached for the hilt of the knife while staggering backward and away from her.

Syrie took a running start and jumped at the guard with a thrust kick, sending him onto his back awkwardly atop a rotting box. The old lumber splintered beneath him and he cried out in agony, but only briefly.

Straddling his frame as it settled on the ground, Syrie yanked her knife from where it had dug into the breastbone and plunged it deep into his heart. As quickly as she did for the guard, she withdrew the knife, wiped it on his coat, and stuffed it into the sheath.

Fujita, having managed to get his knees beneath him again, had evidently witnessed the whole thing. "Impressive...I guess that really does make three for you in Hercalest now, doesn't it?"

"I guess so," she uttered nonchalantly, mimicking Fujita's earlier use of the phrase. "Come on, let's get you into the wagon, and move on out of here. We'll ride straight to the new base, no delay. The doctor should be able to fix you up if we get there quickly enough."

"No, just go on. I'll find some hole to crawl into and die," Fujita muttered while feebly pulling away from her

"Not an option," she told Fujita plainly while putting him across her shoulders and lifting from her knees. "You're coming with me, supposing I have to drag you the whole way myself, and that is an order from your agent-in-command."

Though Fujita had let out a stifled, pain-filled groan when being lifted off his feet, Syrie got no further protest out of him, and she made for the stable.

The back door swung open, and Darla stepped clear with the knob in hand, allowing Syrie to enter with her heavy load.

"Someone get the wagon door," Syrie called to the family, with Nareen obliging by turning the lever and flinging the door open hard, causing it to bang off the side of the wagon itself.

Syrie rolled Fujita in through the doorframe and climbed in behind him, dragging him under the arms until he was well and hidden in the rear of the wagon.

"Stay here," she commanded firmly, following up by getting the attention of both Palomb children standing beside the wagon door, their basket resting on the floor beside them. "Make sure he stays there. Don't worry, he can't mount much of a resistance at this point."

Outside the wagon were Darla and Jorette, the former having pulled the rear stable door shut. "Do either of you know how to hitch horses to a wagon?" Syrie asked to either of them.

"I do," Darla said while raising her hand.

"I can help too," Nareen piped in while leaping into action. "I've watched the stablehands at the palace do it hundreds of times."

The large draft horses, one black, the other in brown and white pinto, were led from their stalls with little fuss, and backed into place at the wagon poles. The three of them, with assistance from Jorette, had the two animals buckled into place and readied far quicker than Syrie would have thought. She realised, once finished, that it was due in no small part to Nareen, who had been doing the brunt of the physical work and directing what did not directly involve her.

"Everyone climb into the back of the wagon," Syrie ordered once they were finished.

The shingle-roofed wagon itself was roomier than most would think when empty, though this particular vehicle was stuffed with crates of food and supplies, or at least that was how it looked.

Syrie knelt before a particular flat panelled crate labelled 'Wheat' and undid a hidden latch that allowed a whole side wall of the crate to swing open. "Climb in here and keep going until you hit the wall. These are false crates, and are actually all one unit cleverly pieced together to look separate. There should be just enough room in this one for the wife and the children to squeeze in comfortably. Once you are in, I will close it up. The guards at the gate never look deep enough under all the crates and sacks to look at the crates buried deep in the corners, so you should all be safe enough."

Jorette grabbed Dorian and sent him in first, shoving the basket of kittens behind him. Nareen followed next, pushing the wicker container as she went, leaving Jorette to crawl in behind them.

Syrie's gaze went next to Darla. "There is a second crate, but it's only big enough for one, and my friend needs it. I have extra outfits here for me, him, and our other agent so that we might have posed as regular folk operating the cart. Given that we have one injured and the other gone missing, it's down to me alone for that part. With all of that in mind, and if you're up to the task, I'll get you to change into the second woman's clothes and lend me a hand up front. Savvy?"

"Aye, of course, I can do that," Darla said without a moment's hesitation. "Just point me to where the clothes are and then tell me what to do once I am changed."

"It's greatly appreciated, Ma'am. I'm glad for the help," Syrie thanked her.

With little other option left to her with the brief time left to spare, Syrie quickly removed her mask again and began pulling trousers and outerwear on over her existing attire. By the end of the change, she was garbed in a flannel coat, denim bib overalls, and a woollen combination of a hat, scarf, and mittens. Darla followed suit, attempting to stuff her skirt into the legs of the trousers intended for Fujita, with the other articles of clothing being used to hide that fact.

In their fresh garb, the two quickly went to work helping Fujita into a hiding crate of his own, and once done, they latched both hiding spots closed and further concealed them with sacks of flour, smaller crates, and canvas tarpaulins.

"That should do. Help me get the stable doors and we'll be off," Syrie told Darla once satisfied with their efforts in the wagon.

Apart from the increased guard activity, a few early-rising citizens were already making their way about, both on foot and by equine.

The city is beginning to spring to life. That should make blending in a little easier, Syrie thought to herself in the time it took for her and Darla to swing the cargo doors of the stable open.

Syrie cracked the reins and got the horses to a gentle canter, leading the wagon forth as casually as could be. Having cleared the exit, she brought the wagon to a stop and hurriedly helped Darla shut the heavy doors. The two were back in the driver's seat with haste and the ride to the gates was officially underway.

Prior to the operation beginning, it had been deemed by all in the planning stage that the exit point should be the gates on the far western side of the city. Syrie herself had led the charge on that, pointing out that the west end of Hercalest was primarily the industrial sector, and most shipping took place from there. The guards, as a result, were nowhere near as strict when it came to checking those passing through, giving cursory glances at the goods in an effort to keep the lines moving efficiently. Over the years, the League, and Syrie on her own as a liberator, had used the western gate for smuggling people and items with success. Barring a lockdown, she was optimistic that today would be no different.

"If anyone asks, your name is…" Syrie paused at that point, as she was about to use N'ailla's pseudonym, which was another Johnan name. "No, we can't use that name…Uh, let's go with Tara Cole, how's that? You can call me Davie Lorens. That last one is the name on the manifest papers. Should the question come up, we're hauling the last shipment of food supplies that the League of the Sacred Fist required for their southbound caravan. Are you savvy with all of that?"

Darla gave an affirmative hum and repeated everything that Syrie had said, missing nothing.

"Well done, you're a natural at this," Syrie complimented, hoping a confidence boost would help ease Darla's nerves. "Just stay calm when we get to the gates and let me do the talking unless you are directly spoken to. If we stick to the plan, we'll be out of the city before you know it."

At such an early hour of the morning, with the sun only now daring to rise, both pedestrian and equine traffic on their route to the western gate was light. Upon arrival, they discovered the line for those exiting the city to be predictably short, with only a few other wagons and convoys waiting ahead of them. A pair of guards, looking tired and likely at the end of a long, overnight shift, happened to be handling the tolls and admissions. That level of exhaustion scrawled plainly across the faces of the overseers making for a welcome sight.

As minutes ticked by and the sun creeped over the horizon, the line moved at a brisk pace. Before long, Syrie's wagon was the next to be served, and she looked to Darla while urging the horses ahead, affecting the deep voice of a man as she did. "Remember the plan."

"Papers, please," one of the guards asked upon a lazy approach.

Syrie presented the neatly folded documents from a pocket of the overcoat, and handed them over to the guard for inspection.

"Food for the fighters is it?" he asked while reading over the documents. "My boy quite enjoys going to the matches when they are in town. His favourite is Hann Bravado, but I think Tahru is the best. He's just simply unstoppable in the ring."

Something seemed to occur to the guard then, and he raised his head from the paperwork and looked to Syrie. "Is there any chance that you know the fighters? My boy would really like Hann Bravado's autograph."

Syrie forced herself to laugh. "I'm afraid not, Ser. Us lowly wagon operators don't really come into contact with the fighters."

"Oh well, it was worth it to ask," the guard gave with an amused, albeit weary sigh. He looked back to his comrade, who was doing a visual inspection of the wagon's exterior. "Oi, Butch, you want to have a look inside this one, or are you fine with this one?"

"Maybe just a quick peek," the guard referred to as Butch called back, not waiting for further discussion on the matter as he pulled open the side door.

The first guard offered back the papers, having signed and refolded them for Syrie. "Here you are. While Butch has a gander, that'll be six coppers for the toll."

"Oh, right," Syrie remembered, having forgotten that there would be a toll. Her feeling of forgetfulness grew into near terror as she rooted about her pouch, finding no coinage at all.

I gave the bit of copper I had to bribe the guards on the hill.

"It's in here somewhere," she told the guard with a nervous chuckle. "Just give me a moment."

"Oh my, Davie, how forgetful of me," Darla suddenly blurted out. "I have the coins for the toll here in my pocket. Here you go."

A handful of copper coins were quickly pressed into Syrie's hand, and she counted out six for the toll and two extra for the guards to split amongst themselves as a gratuity. "Sorry about that, lads. I was sure it had been in my pouch this whole time. I got little sleep after that damned racket a few hours ago. I'm not at my best this morning."

"I've been up all night tending to the gate, I know how you feel," sympathised the guard while giving the coins his own count. "How we doing back there, Butch?"

"It's all good as far as I'm concerned," he answered back contentedly. "Send 'em on their way."

The first guard patted the side of the wagon and stepped back, "Right then, you're good to go. You have a good morning, Mister Lorens."

"I bid the same to you, Sers," Syrie offered back with a wave.

Butch wandered off into the guardhouse and within seconds of his disappearing, the pair of heavy, wooden gates began to swing open on mechanised hinges. When the doors were wide enough to allow the wagon, Syrie got the horses moving and rolled on through, trying her best to contain her excitement as she did.

Neither Syrie nor Darla dared to speak for the better part of what Syrie felt to be at least ten minutes. When the silence was punctured, it was only after Syrie looked back toward the city and was certain that they were without pursuers.

"Alright, I think we're in the clear," Syrie uttered with the deepest breath she felt to have ever taken. "That was quick thinking back there to offer up your own coin."

"I was at the bottom of the ladder when you and the other agents were bargaining with the guards on the hill, remember?" Darla gently reminded Syrie. "I figured when you could not find your toll money that you had given it all away in the cellar."

Syrie nodded at the recollection of the recent memory. "Aye, you thought right."

That spurred a change of topic from Darla. "Speaking of the other agents, if I might ask: what about the other woman? Do you think she will be alright?"

"I'm more worried about the one in the wagon. I have to get him medical help as quickly as I can," Syrie said first, before segueing into answering the question as it was posed. "As for the other female agent, I have to assume that she is fine. Fujita made no mention that she was hurt, and she knew the risks of going back for that rope ladder. I should also mention that she was not going to be joining us past the city gates. Her job was to help us with this mission and take my place in the city once I left to help you folks escape. Granted, we were not going to part ways with her up until we reached my old neighbourhood with the wagon, but it could not be helped that we had to split sooner."

There was resentment building in Syrie for having left N'ailla behind, and Fujita's words from hours ago floated before her.

"The life of the agent must always be considered in our actions. We have worth too, you know."

"I do hope she is alright," Darla offered with worry of her own, "And the agent in the wagon too. Do you think he was shot?"

Syrie had not taken a close look at Fujita's wound, but the gunshots certainly led her to believe as much. "It's hard to say, but it is quite likely," Syrie gave as a reply once it occurred to her that she had stalled on answering.

Darla was looking about the rolling hills of the Hercalest countryside as they went, her eyes scanning the barns and farmhouses as the wagon rolled by them hurriedly, with Syrie having gotten the horses moving at a healthy canter. "Is our next stop at that inn you mentioned? I've never left Hercalest before. I can't tell you where anything is out here."

"Aye, *The Buttered Fork*," Syrie confirmed for Darla. "We might be able to get some basic aid for my agent there, and some food for you and the family. I got a woman from the Women's Road waiting there who knows the family quite well. She and her husband will join us for the ride south so that when we meet the caravan, the family will be ready to blend right in with the rest of us."

"She knows the lady and her children, you say?" Darla asked with mild surprise. "It might be that I met her too. What is her name?"

"I am not at liberty to tell you her real name yet, that's for her to say," Syrie began to respond. "When you meet her, you can call her Terra. You will like her, I think. She and Cole are mighty good people."

27
FREYARD

A kindly old doctor told Freyard that in time, his headaches would dull and eventually dissipate. A tincture with a glass dropper had been given to him to further help with the pain, and he was prescribed to take one drop to a teacup of warm water twice a day.

Freyard was already using thrice that much in each cup. During the worst of the pain, when Freyard thought his skull was either going to blow apart or collapse in on his brain, he desperately wished for more drops and water, and wine or rum to chase it down. The doctor was no longer in Freyard's continual presence to stop him, but still, he could not do as he so pleased.

He owed this lack of autonomy to his present caregiver, who had taken the tincture and refused to let him medicate at his leisure.

"You will have to fight me for it," she told him while slipping the tincture into the pocket of her trousers. "And I know you will not do that."

"Why won't I?" Freyard asked her playfully, gritting through the agony in his head.

"Because you told me that you love me, Freyard Archer," she would say with that cute little laugh.

Though his memories of the past few days were all a haze, there was one moment that stood true to Freyard, and that was when he had told Marigold Tullivan that he loved her. Regardless of how much pain he was in or how fragmented his recent memories might seem, Freyard could recall both telling her that, and having meant every word of it.

Marigold was not the first that Freyard had loved deeply, but she was alive, and he could not go on mourning for a memory. From the moment that Freyard had seen Marigold in the gatehouse at Daol Bay, he knew that to be true. In the private moments that he shared with Marigold both on the train and in the Tullivan manor, he felt close to her in a way that no ghost could offer. He wanted to return the affection, to love her as he felt he could. Yet, as much as he tried, the memory of Dayanna would combine with the fear of loving again, and the dual efforts of the two would convince Freyard to remain emotionally distant toward Marigold.

She is the Lady of Daol Bay, Freyard would tell himself. *And I am but a captain in her service. I cannot allow emotion to cloud my senses and my duty. I must remain at arm's length from her.*

Those lines had worked to steel Freyard for much of his tenure in Marigold's company. Yet, while Haymard Nothram's clipper ship burned and capsized beneath where Freyard's battered frame laid, and the frigid seas around the embattled vessels were threatening to swallow him completely, all Freyard could think about was that he had never told Marigold how much he loved her.

The waters had rushed in to take him, but by then Freyard had thought that he was all but dead anyway. The shock of the cold had roused him enough to thrash about in the water, though his left leg begged for mercy, and his whole torso screamed at him. In spite of the unbearable pain, the instincts of survival had taken hold against the ice attempting to course its way through his veins.

Hands had grabbed for him then, at least four, maybe more, and their owners wore no uniform. Freyard's first instinct was to push them off, for he could not see if they were friend or foe. The pain in his ribs joined up with the men trying to hold his arms, and from then onward, there had been only darkness.

Freyard awoke in a cot in the sitting room of a stranger's home with no idea of how he got there or how long he had been unconscious. A woman was tending to a roaring fireplace and addressing the concerns of three others in similar circumstances as Freyard. The identities of those men he could not ascertain, and he panicked in the thought that they might be his enemies from the battle. In his distress, Freyard had tried to rise so that he might assess the situation. The swimming state of his head sent him spiralling instead, and he had fallen back into his slumber.

His next memory, as cloudy as the previous, was in a private room with a different fireplace. The bed beneath him was large and stuffed with feathers, and daylight shone in across the floor from a lone window. Keeping his head against his pillow for support, he had turned about to take in the space around him, and that was when Freyard had seen her. She appeared hazy as his eyes adjusted to the bright wall of light behind her. The silhouette before him took on definition little by little, until he at last she appeared, bathed in the morning sun shining through the window and cradling a cup of tea.

"Mar," he had tried to say, his voice coming out as a dry croak.

At first, he was not sure that she had heard him, and tried again to speak, which led to a coughing fit that caused him enough pain to lose consciousness again.

Night had fallen when Freyard next stirred, and this time, she was sitting in a chair by the fireplace with a thick sheaf of papers in her hands that she looked to be intently studying.

"Mari..." Freyard had managed to mutter, his voice sounding stronger than before, but the breath needed to make the words were short and pained.

The papers fell to the floor and she had come running. "Freyard? Are you really awake this time?"

"Mari... Is it you?" he stammered in two short bursts.

"It's me, yes." Freyard heard her say joyfully, her eyes filling with tears.

Summoning all the strength he had to hold back the pain, Freyard gave his best attempt to tell her what he had wanted to for some time, the words coming through in one clear, unambiguous sentence, "I love you, Marigold."

Her hands wrapped around one of his, her lips kissing his fingers as she answered back, "I love you too, Freyard."

"I had... to tell... you..." Freyard sputtered out between the harried gasps.

"And I have been telling you with every hour of my waking since we found you," she uttered back between gentle kisses now pressed to his cheeks and lips.

From then on, Marigold had been spending every possible waking moment in Freyard's company during his initial recuperation. It was in this time that he learned of the extent of his injuries. First, the attending doctor was confident that Freyard had suffered a concussion. Furthermore, his left foot was broken in at least one place that the doctor could identify. If there truly was a lone break, the doctor remained confident that it was of a minor bone and would heal quickly. Lastly were his ribs, which had sustained one serious break on the left side, and likely several small fractures within the radius of worst injury. There was concern from Marigold, and wonder from visitors like Greggard Simillon, as to how Freyard both sustained the injuries and managed to survive the sinking of Nothram's clipper vessel. However, with his memory fogged as it was from the concussion, Freyard was having little luck deducing as much himself.

In his waking moments, Freyard sought information on the Sun's Rangers, and the identities of the missing and the deceased from what was becoming known as *The Battle of the Burning Ships*. The Sun's Rangers that had been available to Freyard in Daol Bay were, with the exception of one man left behind as a representative, on board *The Tidebreaker* with him. After the battle, Freyard was down to the last of those who was healthy enough to carry out business on his behalf, and poor Mack was begging to show signs of exhaustion.

According to Marigold, she and her friends aboard *The Princess of Daol* had pulled Mack from a lifeboat to their ship after he had fallen into the harbour from *The Tidebreaker*. The quick action by both the crew in the lifeboat, Marigold, and her accomplices had spared Mack from becoming hypothermic, and with a few days of rest, he was in perfect health again.

Crediting Marigold as his rescuer, and with no Sun's Rangers for him to answer to, Mack had devoted himself to Marigold's service. In that capacity, he had volunteered to take on the grim task of sorting through the wounded and the dead on her behalf.

Once Freyard was awake and lucid enough to converse for any length of time, Mack revealed how he came to find himself in a featherbed in a private room. One of Mack's early tasks had been to go door to door with the locals who had been involved in the rescue efforts to identify and document the wounded and deceased. It was during a routine visit at the home of a fisherman and his wife that

Freyard was located, with Mack having recognised his injured captain immediately.

According to Mack and others, those same residents of Pelican Harbour had played an integral part in saving soldiers from both sides of the battle. Fishermen had rushed to their vessels and encircled the distressed warships, and began pulling sailors and soldiers from the water as fast as they could splash down. Several people, Freyard was later told, even went aboard *The Tidebreaker* to search for survivors, and came back with wounded troops dressed in both teal and blue. Those who survived long enough to reach the docks and shores of the town were met by waiting townspeople and further transported by wagon when available, and by hand-carried, makeshift gurneys when not. With but only one doctor and a few nurses to serve the town, the residents decided to relocate the overflow of survivors of the battle to the homes of anyone with the ability to tend on the wounded. Among those injured soldiers had of course, been Freyard himself.

Upon finding Freyard, Mack had him immediately transported to Marigold's side, at her request. In between Mack undertaking and Freyard's recovery, Mack had amassed a nearly complete list of the crew and rangers that had been aboard *The Tidebreaker*. Freyard further discovered through Mack's detective work that of the five Sun's Ranger that had aboard *The Tidebreaker* with him, only one had perished for certain. Regardless, he still regretted that any members of his band had died.

Clem was the only child of a widowed mother. How do I tell her that she is now all alone in the world?

The death of Clemence Sylart was one that Freyard did not need to be told of by Mack, as he had witnessed it personally.

Those deceptive shitheels of Nothram's opened fire during their own surrender talks. Clem never had a chance to even draw his sword and pistol.

It was during that brutal ambush that Freyard's memories became fuzzy. Yet, one thing he could remember was that after Clem and a number of sailors were dispatched in one blow, he, his rangers, and the crew of *The Tidebreaker* returned the bloody gesture.

He could recall trying to organise his rangers into a defensive formation, using whatever cover they could find on the deck so that they could safely hide when not returning gunfire. The strategy had proved wise at first, and Freyard even recalled that his rangers were felling Nothram men left and right from where they stood on the clipper ship.

At some point, *The Tidebreaker* had been boarded by a group of enemy soldiers, and Freyard ordered his rangers to respond with melee combat. Captain Mavril used the cover provided by Freyard's rangers to send his own sailors forward to cut the lines connecting the ships, and Mavril himself went out to help in that capacity. It looked as though the rangers were going to be successful in throwing back the Nothram attackers, and the ships had begun to part, when a shot from an oversized, rail-mounted revolving gun on the clipper left *The Tidebreaker* without a captain.

Despite Freyard's calls for a first mate to take charge of the ship and the sailors, none appeared before him to claim the title, leaving Freyard to believe that the mate too, had been killed in the ensuing gunfire.

The last Nothram attacker aboard *The Tidebreaker* yielded, and as he raised his hands, the enemy rail gunner killed him too. While it was possible that the slaughter by one Nothram man of another was accidental, Freyard had to consider that it meant there would be no quarter for anyone not actively fighting for Nothram's side. In the wake of that sight, Freyard had commanded a retreat to safety of both sailors and rangers, before the powerful weapon could deal further indiscriminate death.

Freyard drew upon a memory wherein he arrived at the conclusion that the rail gun needed to be destroyed, and he was prepared to sacrifice himself to do so. Glendil was given command of the rangers, with a final order from Freyard to remain hidden, though he left Glendil with no further explanation. In the moment of confusion that Freyard created, he ran forth from hiding and leapt from *The Tidebreaker* to the clipper while the ships were still close enough to make such a thing possible.

In hindsight, he figured that the jump was what likely resulted in the broken bone in his foot. The landing had been awkward on the rolling enemy vessel, and he had fallen sideways at a peculiar angle. In the ensuing melee, he had no time to assess the damage and forced himself to run and fight enemy soldiers while in terrible pain. He reached the operator of the rail gun, and at the point of Freyard's sword, the gunner took his chances instead on the freezing sea below and jumped overboard. As Freyard looked to *The Tidebreaker*, he saw his men working furiously to extinguish a blaze of some sort on the port side of the main deck and down across the hull along the same side.

It was at that point that his memory failed, and there was nothing further for him to recall until he was lying on the deck of the then ruined clipper as it sank beneath him.

Given that his memory was at loss for anything past the point of removing the rail gun operator, Freyard had to conclude that the concussive blow was delivered shortly after. Somewhere between then and the point where he awoke on his back, his ribs had been broken, and yet somehow, on a ship full of enemies, he had managed to survive.

I will need help from other survivors besides Mack, who might have witnessed the events on the clipper, so that I can piece it all together.

Four days removed from the initial battle, Freyard was to the stage where his foot had been set in a plaster cast, and he was getting about with the use of crutches. His ribs still caused him much agony, but there was no amount of bandages and plaster that could make that feel any other way. The worst of it was that he could bear all of that pain, if not for the blinding headaches.

There is little else for me to do right now but puzzle out my own memories and worry about my men. I'm otherwise useless to Marigold and her cause in this state, he thought while sitting on the end of bed they had been sharing. The room that Freyard occupied was but one of a few that made up the house of a sympathiser to Marigold's cause. Once the flags of surrender were waving in the wind and Nothram's reign was no more, the friendly family had opened their doors to her and her entourage.

Marigold herself was still spending much of her days with Freyard, but with him on the mend and out of danger, she was willing to leave him to his rest for extended periods. Not that she was far away at any given time. The sympathiser's sitting room had become the primary meeting point for Marigold's party and anyone else that might be helping them sort through Pelican Harbour's affairs.

Though Freyard wished to be a part of the discussions, Marigold preferred to spend her time in his company decompressing from such stressors. As such, his knowledge of the aftermath of Marigold's incursion into Pelican Harbour was limited to what Mack was relaying to him.

It would seem though, that Marigold had everything well under control.

"You have a prescription note from Doctor Rothier to bring back to Daol Bay with us that is good for one refill of the tincture," Marigold explained to him for what felt like the millionth time. "The doctor assured us that we have just enough from him to last you for the sea voyage home if we leave today, which is exactly what we are doing. I am not going to give you more now and have you in total agony before we even reach Robbston."

She had a point, Freyard knew, but it did little to ease his splitting headache. "When do we leave port?" he asked for the sole purpose of changing the subject.

"We depart whenever we all board *Felixander's Dream*, my love," Marigold told him. She had taken to sitting beside him on the bed, dressed in a white, silk tunic that was long in the sleeves, a black leather bodice with trousers to match, and white stockings on her feet. Though gentle and soothing in nature, she spoke in a tone that carried concern in equal parts too. "You know, this will be the second time you have asked that this morning."

That gave Freyard pause, and he searched his memory banks for the other instance, drawing only a frustrating blank. "I will have to take your word for that," he offered in comment, his words sounding pained even to his own hearing.

Watching Marigold go about packing his things from where he sat, Freyard was, for the first time since the battle, dressed in something other than a nightgown. His wardrobe for the day was a black, button down shirt and a pair of light blue trousers that Marigold had obtained for him from sources untold. The left leg of the trousers was split at the seam from ankle to knee, allowing it to be worn over his plaster-encased leg. A new pair of boots had been bought for him to replace his waterlogged footwear from the battle, though Freyard could only wear one of them yet.

Marigold's hands slid across his face tenderly, her fingers working themselves into his shaggy head of hair while her thumbs traced soft circles on his cheeks as she spoke. "The doctor is sure that your ability to hold memories will return, and perhaps any memories you lost, too. Fret not, my darling."

"I could never fret when I am with you, love," he gave in response while trying to reach for the hand currently caressing him.

"Mack came by this morning. Do you remember his visit?" she asked. While Freyard had no doubt that she was genuine in her desire to bring up the Sun's Ranger, the tones of her voice also indicated that invoking the name of the interim ranger-in-command was a test.

"I do, yes," he answered earnestly. During one of the doctor's visits, he had tasked Freyard with making mental notes of things and people that came and went throughout the day, encouraging him to remark upon details as they happened and try to commit them to memory. To that end, he tried to remember what things he could for Marigold's exercise. "Mack was wearing a black, button-down shirt when he came by."

"It was teal, actually," Marigold corrected softly.

"Right, the shirt was teal, but his jacket was black leather, like mine," Freyard noted carefully. "He's growing a beard now, or at least making an attempt at one. Mack was never one for growing convincing facial hair."

"That's good, Freyard," Marigold said encouragingly. "The beard was something he mentioned yesterday. You retained that without problem."

A small notebook on Freyard's lap was flipped open with one hand, and just as quickly closed by Marigold. "Try to recall what he told you without looking at your notes."

He grunted at that, partly in pain, partly because the recollection was not going as well as he had hoped. "Mack has still not found Glendil. Clem was cremated last night, and Mack has the ashes in his possession so that we can bring them home with us and deliver them to Clem's mother."

"That's mostly correct," Marigold offered. She paused for but a second before giving Freyard further critique, "He told you about the cremation last night, too."

"You're probably right about that," Freyard had to acquiesce. "I suppose I just clung to that memory. It hurt a great deal to hear."

Her head lowered solemnly at the mention of it. "I'm sorry for the pain I caused you. This battle is my burden to carry for the rest of my life. I even lost a guard during the chaos on my own ship."

"Darrill," Freyard said, the man's name having suddenly popped into his head.

"You remembered," she expressed happily with a sad smile.

Freyard leaned in through the fire in his ribs and placed a kiss on her cheek. "My mind isn't totally broken. It can still remember the important things."

"We're going home with a heavy cargo of ashes, and they all came with us as men," Marigold reflected depressingly. "This was just one battle with an outlier threat. Where do I find the stomach to potentially go into a fully-fledged war with Eamon Palomb?"

Freyard took as deep a breath as he could, and prepared himself for the discomfort of speaking for a prolonged period. "One of my top lieutenants, Yarohmer the Graceful, once told me that, 'A man can go to war for many reasons, and he may feel that they are ultimately the right reasons, morally or otherwise. Yet, if he lives through the fighting, he will have to reckon with himself that no matter why he fought, he is forever woven into a gruesome, terrible tapestry.' I suppose the only part he got wrong was that women can and have had to make that same reckoning."

Marigold was looking at the floor as Freyard spoke, and raised her eyes to meet his when he finished. "This Yarohmer sounds like a wise man. At least we know that your long term memory is not impacted."

"Oh, he is," Freyard said after a long exhale. "I have relied on his counsel many times, and I trust him with taking the Sun's Rangers into the field without my oversight. As for my memory, I seem to be capable of remembering most things up until I jumped to Nothram's clipper."

"Speaking of that ship," Marigold said, veering the topic elsewhere, "I was made aware that it used to be called *The Western Pride*, but Nothram apparently changed it when he returned home after my announcement at my father's funeral."

"Oh? Might I ask what it became?" Freyard asked with as much amusement as he could muster. "Something sinister, I am guessing."

"He had renamed it to *The Palombs' Pride*, as a show of allegiance." Marigold uttered while slowly shaking her head.

"And we sent that token appreciation to a despot to the bottom of Pelican Harbour," Freyard mused. "Anyhow, I might need your help to get upright off this bed. I would like to give my thanks to the family... Remind me what their names are, if you don't mind."

Marigold stood up and extended her hands. "Just tell me what you need me to do."

"I'll need my crutches, and perhaps your shoulder to lean on," he told her while pointing at the walking aids.

With the walking aides delivered and Marigold's shoulder at the ready, Freyard found a way to get himself standing. The leg bearing the broken foot was bent at the knee to keep it off the ground, and he hobbled a few steps with the crutches to prepare himself for a walk.

"This might take some getting used to for a long distance," he admitted, feeling pathetic and pitiful in his present state. "It is one thing to limp my way to the privy, another to walk across town."

"It will not be for long," Marigold reasoned while staying practically glued to Freyard's hip with every step he took. "You will be right as rain again before you know it."

"We'll get there, darling, I know it. I might just be a little irritable along the way," He offered half-heartedly.

"I will be right there with you for every step," Marigold assured Freyard, taking the moment to put her hands to his face and draw his lips to her tenderly.

She stepped back and scooped up a suitcase belonging to herself and a satchel she had bought with new clothes and supplies for Freyard. "I shall carry these for you and get the door. We can give our thanks to the Earlesworth family on the way out."

"Right, that's their name," Freyard attempted to feign remembering.

Marigold clearly saw right through the ruse, though. "Yes that's correct, and the patriarch's name is Hoffman, which I am sure you also knew. They have three children, two of whom we displaced for this room. Make sure to give Gloria and Rosella an extra round of thanks for that. Young Robert is but a babe, and Mister Earlesworth's wife is Lenore."

Freyard sighed disappointedly. "Is it that obvious that I had no idea what I was talking about?"

"Plainly so, yes," she returned with a giggle.

"I will leave all the talking to you, then, if you have no reservations," Freyard conceded with a wan smile.

"None at all," Marigold accepted while opening the door.

Freyard had been going only between the privy and the bedroom since waking in the spacious home. The family that dwelled beneath its roof were of the lower reaches of the nobility class, and were supporters of Marigold in secret until her arrival. Now, with Haymard

Nothram deposed, the family were free to wear their allegiance on their sleeves. That much Freyard knew. Their names, and other pertinent information, were just not sticking in Freyard's head.

He limped his way through the open door and out through a dark hallway before emerging in the open foyer of the first floor of the two storied home. The aroma of baking pastries of some sort wafted from the kitchen in the back of the house. The source of the delicious smell was on his left from where he emerged from the hallway, and his gaze went in that direction first, finding the kitchen door closed and the pie regrettably out of sight. Looking to his right, which led to the front of the house and a large, open sitting room, Freyard got a glance of a large gathering waiting on him and Marigold.

Many of the faces he knew, including Mack, and most of Marigold's usual associates, but a few were foreign to him.

A fellow of about Freyard's age, who was dapperly dressed in a two-piece, dark green suit emerged first to greet Freyard and Marigold, extending a hand for the former to shake. "Ser Freyard, it is good to see you up and about. I must say that you are looking much better from when you were carried in here."

"Aye, your family and staff have been more than hospitable and accommodating during my recovery, Mister Earlesworth," Freyard managed to say. "I thank you deeply for the generosity you have shown by opening your home to us."

"Yourself and the Lady Marigold are welcome to our home and whatever else we may offer, good Ser. It is I who must thank you for your service and dedication in the face of great danger. Any easterner willing to join our side and thrust themselves into battle on our behalf must be commended for bravely standing against the gales, I should say."

Freyard tried to force another smile, but his aching body fought him. "My Sun's Rangers and I were merely doing our part for a righteous cause, Mister Earlesworth."

I believe that I am not the only easterner here, either, Freyard noted while glancing over the other occupants of the sitting room. A bearded man with a tight, short ponytail of matching light brown hair and a suit of riding leathers that were similar to the gear of the Sun's Rangers caught Freyard's eye. *Where have we met before, stranger? My gut tells me that it was back in Fort Dornett or thereabouts.*

The two maintained an odd, sustained bout of eye contact during Freyard's brief interaction with Hoffman Earlesworth, and once Marigold stepped in to do the talking, Freyard's focus on the man only grew. *I suspect that he knows me, too.*

"Freyard, there are two men here that I have yet to introduce you to," Marigold said to him once she concluded her pleasantries and thanks with the Earlesworth patriarch.

"The first is Stephen of the House of Marchford out of Robbston, maternal nephew to Sealord Miles Ferros," Marigold explained while gesturing toward a blond haired man in full military uniform, complete with a steel cuirass, cap, and greaves. "Ser Stephen was just promoted from the rank of captain to major yesterday for his commendable actions in leading our ground troops through a successful march and capture of Pelican Harbour's barracks and battlements. Major, this is Freyard Archer, captain of the Sun's Rangers and a hero of *The Battle of the Burning Ships.*"

"Well met, Captain Archer. The pleasure is mine, I assure you," the newly made Major Marchford said by way of greeting with a hearty handshake.

Freyard could feel himself blushing with that introduction. "I think *hero* might be a bit strong of a word. I scared a gunner into abandoning his post and managed to be clumsy enough that I broke a few of my own bones in the process."

"Nonsense," Marigold replied before Freyard could further rebuff the title. "Your actions saved most of the crew of *The Tidebreaker* and your own rangers from a weapon capable of dealing a frightening amount of bodily damage in short order. All reports say that your valiant deeds turned the tide of that encounter and allowed *The Tidebreaker* to sever its ties with *The Palombs' Pride*, which later sank, I might add. If *The Tidebreaker* had not been able to break away, *The Palombs' Pride* might have dragged your ship down."

What reports? Freyard wondered, keeping the thought from leaving his lips. *Best to wait until we are alone again before I ask. I want to see these reports. I want to know what happened.*

"I am only glad to have been of service to my adoptive country. I am honoured that I was chosen to do my duty for her," Freyard decided to say after giving thought to his words.

Marigold extended her hand toward the bearded man with the tiny tail of hair on the back of his head. "Allow me to introduce you to another who carries the same sentiment, Freyard. This is Wynne Nathers, the Captain of the Flying Hawks brigade. Your fellow easterner is the reason that Nothram's men signalled their surrender as quickly as they did. Of course, their efficient work came at the cost of several lives, I am sad to report. However, their sacrifice prevented the deaths of hundreds of soldiers on either side."

The bloody Wyvern, of course, Freyard noted to himself, the realisation hitting him like a brick to the face.

"My dear Lady Marigold, it may come as no surprise to you that Captain Archer and I have made one another's acquaintance before," Nathers informed her while stepping toward Freyard with his hand ready to shake.

"Is that so, Freyard?" Marigold asked in wonderment.

Freyard gave Nathers' hand as firm a shake as he could. "Why yes, Major Nathers and I have met one another over the course of our careers in the Illiastran armed forces of old on a few occasions. His Flying Hawks used my former home of Fort Dornett as a base for an operation at one time. Major Nathers here was but a lieutenant under Captain Hank Harding then."

"Your memory astounds me, Captain Archer," Nathers said, his voice sounding genuinely impressed. "My visit to Fort Dornett seems like a lifetime ago."

"People did not come or go from Fort Dornett without my knowing, Major," Freyard told him succinctly. "I made it my responsibility as the captain of the fort's rangers to stay on top of such things."

Though Freyard could not recall anything about Wynne Nathers that gave him any reason to dislike the man during their fleeting past interactions, the mere sight of him moments ago had drawn Freyard's instantaneous ire. From what he knew of the Flying Hawks, he had no doubt that the unit was capable of a clandestine attack, and Nathers was considered proficient at coordinating and directing such events. Perhaps it was the furtive nature of the Flying Hawks, or their sordid history weighing on Freyard's judgement, but whatever it was, he was left with a lingering feeling of suspicion towards the man known as the Wyvern.

I will have to give it some thought later when I have a moment and my skull does not feel like it's about to burst into a million pieces.

"Aye, Captain, your stewardship at Fort Dornett was well known amongst those in military service," Nathers told him with a smile that Freyard's foggy senses were having difficulty discerning as genuine. "I dare say that you were considered a legendary example of what it meant to be a ranger captain. I have no doubt that you exhibit those same qualities now in Lady Marigold's service."

"You're too kind, Major Nathers," Freyard said, accepting the compliments with a bow of his head. "Your own actions in recent days were no less admirable, from what Marigold has told me. I would say that your promotion was more than warranted."

Nathers looked to Marigold during Freyard's response, his expression entirely nonplussed. "Captain Archer, with all due respect, it was Marchford who was promoted to major recently. Like you, I am but a captain."

Freyard felt a wave of embarrassment rolling over him from head to toe, and his face grew flush. "I... I see... Well, my apologies go to both Captain Nathers and Major Marchford for my error."

Marigold spoke up in his defence, which did little to dissipate the discomfort that Freyard felt. "Captain Archer is simply feeling a little hazy on account of the concussion he sustained in battle recently."

"Oh no, Captain, there is no need to feel upset with yourself for such an understandable mistake, especially in your condition," Nathers offered while taking a step back from him. "It is I who should apologise for possibly agitating your injuries by keeping you standing around on crutches for so long. Please, I would be only glad to help you to a seat for some rest."

"That will be quite alright, Captain Nathers," Freyard declined in a calm voice. "Going from sitting to standing and the other way around are laborious tasks in my state. I would rather remain in this position until it is time to board the carriage that will be transporting those of us to the docks that will be going home by ship."

"By ship?" Nathers asked in surprise while looking between Freyard and Marigold. "I would think that the train would be both quicker and less arduous on the injured amongst your party."

Marigold took the lead on the question once again. "We have enemies between Pelican Harbour and Daol Bay. Both I and my entire advisory committee agree that it would be best if I travel in the protective company of what remains of my naval fleet."

"Aye, that does make sense. My apologies for even questioning it, Lady Marigold," Nathers uttered in conciliatory fashion.

During Marigold's answer to Nathers and his subsequent response, Freyard had been looking to Marigold's allies to gauge their response to Freyard's feeble display. What gazed back at him were eyes filled with sympathy and pity, and it only served to make a wounded man feel all the worse.

It seemed that Marigold was intent on continuing her conversation with both the captain and the major, leaving Freyard with an opportunity to slip out unnoticed.

"Mack," Freyard called to his ranger in a whisper, trying to get his attention through the crowd.

It took two further utterances of the ranger's name to get his attention, but once Mack heard it, he came quickly to Freyard's side. "Yes, Captain?"

"I would much like to get underway," Freyard relayed hurriedly. "It's getting cumbersome to remain standing. Could you see to getting me outside?"

"Yes, of course, Captain. I'll take care of it straight away," Mack obliged immediately, leaving Freyard's side just long enough to ensure that he had a clear path through which to hobble. "Follow me, Captain."

Upon making it to the door, he was greeted by a fair young woman in a billowy, light blue dress. "Captain Archer is everything alright?" she asked as he drew near to her.

"Yes, quite so, Madam," Freyard answered hastily. "I am just eager to take a seat in the carriage, given that I will not be expected to rise again until we are at the docks."

"Well then, allow me to get the door for you," she offered, turning the knob and pulling back the heavy, oak and glass piece. "I hope that your stay here was comfortable."

"It was, Missus Earlesworth," Freyard told her in as thankful a voice as could be expected for someone in his state. "Your hospitality is unmatched."

The wife gave half a curtsey while still holding the door. "You are too kind, Captain. Enjoy the rest of your day and have a pleasant journey home. I do hope that you heal quickly from your injuries."

The light falling across the room from the open door must have gotten the attention of the others, as he heard Marigold calling to him from within. "Freyard? Where are you going?"

He waited until firmly on the patio before answering, using the railing between the awning's posts to assist him in turning around to face her. "Nothing to worry about, my dear. I am simply making for the carriage so that I might sit without further expectation to stand for a time."

Marigold was unconcernedly still in her stocking feet when she joined Freyard on the cold patio, though in her hand was a long, heavy, teal cloak. "You went outside without the cloak that I had gotten for you. Surely you must be freezing."

"I could use the cloak, aye," he admitted as the frigid winds blew in across the harbour. "What of you? You don't even have your boots on."

That made Marigold laugh along with her reply, "And the toes on your left foot are completely exposed, if we are talking about a lack of preparedness for the elements. We could have wrapped a blanket around that leg."

"I may take you up on that, once I am seated," Freyard told her while she placed the cloak across his shoulders and fastened it in place.

"There you go," Marigold said once the task was complete. The entryway to the home was given a quick glance, and she went and closed the door for what Freyard figured to be for privacy reasons. In which case, it seemed that Marigold was fine with Mack overhearing what she intended to say. "You need not be embarrassed by your mistake, darling. It was perfectly harmless."

He shook his head and looked out across the Earlesworth's property, taking in the spacious grounds covered in dead, yellow grass, and the light dusting of snow resting atop it. "That played a factor, granted, but I really just felt the need to sit. You can go back to your company, I promise to wait patiently. I would like the time to speak with Mack, anyhow."

"Is it Wynne Nathers?" Marigold queried pointedly. "Do you and he have some bad blood in your history? You seemed quite tense when the two of you spoke."

"I have nothing personal against the Wyvern or the Flying Hawks," Freyard told Marigold truthfully before laying bare his concerns. "I am merely a little apprehensive in their company. They have a shady nature that tends to put more principled and disciplined soldiers like me on edge."

Her hand went to his arm, where she gave it rub over top of the cloak. "I understand how you feel. I admit that I had a great many reservations about the Flying Hawks too when Greggard first broached the subject of their inclusion. Yet, I must also admit that they fought with as much valour and vigour as anyone else serving our side in the battle. Captain Nathers reported to me that he lost several of his fighters in the effort to take Nothram's manor, and more again were wounded. To that end, his lone female lieutenant was not only killed, but her subordinates were so decimated that Nathers had to disband that lieutenant's group entirely.

"I went to the manor to see the aftermath for myself, and the walls, floors, and furniture are stained in awful splashes of dark red. The place is a mess, Freyard. I might just have to condemn it and have it torn down rather than try to make it habitable again. That macabre, crimson paint job was made as much by Flying Hawks blood as it was Nothram's guards. Captain Nathers and his group paid a heavy price to deliver Haymard to me."

"Nathers had a female lieutenant?" Freyard queried, genuinely impressed by the fact. "I had no idea that the Flying Hawks had become so progressive under Wyvern's leadership."

"There is another woman in his ranks, a scout I am told," Marigold went on unabated. "During the battle, her lieutenant was given the task of confronting Nothram directly, and the scout was the arresting member. Apparently, she threw Nothram to the ground and hogtied him all herself. Nathers could not wait to tell me that. I must say, it was a little satisfying to hear."

"I am willing to admit that I may well be wrong about Wynne Nathers and his Flying Hawks," Freyard sighed, equal parts deflated and contrite. "I would ask that you make but one concession for me: don't let him in too closely. A man like that, and his followers, is best kept at arm's length, both for your safety and for the sake of plausible deniability in the event that they go rogue."

Marigold stepped in and planted a kiss on Freyard's lips. "I can do that. In the meantime, I will give you and Mack some time to talk. The others inside have much they wish to discuss with me, anyhow."

She left Freyard then and returned to the Earlesworth's home, crossing the patio in a few steps, and closing the door with a last, loving look toward him.

Alone save for Mack, Freyard made for the carriage. The five steps from the patio to the stone walkway leading to the road were an awkward mess for Freyard to navigate in his state, and he hoped that no one was watching from the windows. Mack helped, in so much as one could, and once the descent was conquered, the ranger stepped back to allow Freyard the room to make his own mistakes again.

"Here, Captain, allow me to get the door to the carriage," Mack offered while walking ahead of Freyard once they were nearing the vehicle. The driver had already dismounted from his seat and was moving to do the same, yet Mack arrived first and the driver made no move to impede.

A tiny pair of steps was folded down by the driver to allow users to climb aboard the covered cart, and in that moment, Freyard became thankful that both men were there to help him. With only one foot to dedicate toward the job, Freyard was not sure that he could have done it without Mack and the driver holding and pushing on him. At the very least, they spared some of his dignity that day.

Once Freyard was within and seated, Mack climbed in behind, slinging what looked like a letter carrier's bag onto his own lap in the process.

"Now Captain, where would you like me to begin with this afternoon's briefing?" Mack inquired while getting comfortable and undoing the brass buckle on the bag.

"I would like to begin with an update on the rangers," Freyard requested without wasting any time. "How fare the wounded? Have those who are well enough for travel been notified that *Felixander's Dream* is departing for Daol Bay today? Most importantly, do you have any update on Glendil?"

Mack cleared his throat and produced a letter in a hand that was trembling slightly. "Well, Captain, if you will look here, this is a copy of the letter I sent out this morning on the train to Dayden Vernet back in Daol Bay. It is mostly just a brief overview on what happened to us in the battle. It also contains the status of our rangers in summary form, and notification to send word to our rangers still afield in the Daol Forest, so that they might be called back to Daol Bay."

Freyard took the paper to hold, but his eyes could offer no more than a cursory glance, and he looked back at his ranger analytically. "You're shaking, Mack. What are you not telling me?"

"You will be happy to know that Delliot has been cleared to return to light duty," Mack informed Freyard, though even in his pain-wracked state, he saw it for the evasive statement it was. "He'll have a scar on his face, and the laceration on his leg may need some further time to heal, but he's well on his way. I am sorry to say that Tobald is not yet well enough to travel. He lost all but his thumb and index finger on his right hand, which is his dominant hand, and most of his ear and eyelid on the same side were ripped off. The remainder of his visible wounds range from shallow cuts to lacerations across his face. Oh, and his right wrist is broken. All of the wounds took a lot of blood from Tobald, and the doctor is pressed to keep the open wounds clean. For the worry of infection, the doctor has advised Tobald to stay abed and away from others until the open wounds show signs of healing."

"While I do appreciate the updates on Delliot and Tobald, I have had enough of the dodging, Mack. Out with it," Freyard firmly intoned.

"It's about Glendil, Captain..."

"Aye, what of him? Is there any word?"

"We... We still cannot find him," Mack practically muttered under his breath. "At this point, both Marigold's forces and the Pelican Harbour folk who have been aiding the search all feel that it's become a recovery effort for his body, Captain."

Freyard had feared as much, but he had held out hope for the possibility that Glendil was lost, or in care of strangers as Freyard had briefly been. "You have searched every house in Pelican Harbour?"

"Aye, Captain," Mack confirmed sadly. "We've pored over every house but the Nothram manor itself and the few who simply denied us entry without a warrant to search. At this point, every home that had taken in wounded men from the ships has been identified and the soldiers in their care have been named. Those with only minor injuries have been discharged from care, and those in need of further treatment have been relocated either to the clinic or to other makeshift recovery facilities.

"As for the Pelican Harbour troops, well, Captain, many of them are fully cooperative with us, and they bear us no ill will. The problem is that there are a number of loyalists to Nothram and Palomb who are proving difficult with which to contend. Of course, that's not to mention the Triarchists. We have reason to believe that their local tower might be harbouring fugitives and perhaps hostages. It's difficult to determine with certainty at this point, Captain, as both parties have been hostile towards our side in every possible way outside of outright violence."

The information being given to Freyard was not surprising to him in the least, though there were things left unsaid to leave him wondering. "Does Lady Marigold know about all of this? I assume she does."

"Both her and her counsellors have been made aware, aye," Mack admitted with a deep breath. "You should hear from me as the representative of the Sun's Rangers that the Wyvern has been privy to the meetings in which this information has come up. I am given to understand that Marigold is planning to secure warrants with the local court judge so that she can open the doors of the holdout homes and the Tower of Ios."

"And she intends to use the Flying Hawks to execute those search warrants," Freyard finished the sentence for Mack.

"Yes, Captain, I am afraid so," Mack uttered with regret.

"That is certainly disconcerting," Freyard mused aloud. "Prior to this battle, Marigold was intent on showing her strength to those who thought her otherwise incapable of such. That was the point of the battle in the first place, for Aren's sake. Now, she has changed tack every bit as quickly and is willing to give agency to a group that specialises in spying and sabotage. The grave danger is becoming dependant on such a group. 'Spend too long in the darkness and you risk becoming a shadow', as the old saying goes. I fear what might come of keeping the Flying Hawks in our employ and giving them delicate assignments such as these, but I must be careful in how such matters are presented to Marigold. I suppose you have no information on the particulars of the operation, Mack?"

Mack seemed to be thinking about his response for a second, before offering it up to Freyard. "No, Captain, I am sorry to say. Marigold has drafted a sub-committee of just herself, the Field Marshal, Sealord Greggard, Captain Nathers, and the newly made Major Marchford to discuss that ongoing operation. You should know that she intends to leave not just the Flying Hawks here in Pelican

Harbour, but a sizeable force under the command of the Major as well."

"Why have you been keeping all of this from me, Mack?" Freyard asked with annoyance flaring in his voice. As the words came forth, Freyard felt that he already knew the answer, and Mack did not disappoint.

"I have been secretive because I was unsure of just how acute your senses were these days, Captain. Forgive me if you feel I have been insubordinate, but as acting ranger-in-command, I had to determine what was best for your health, and that includes your mental faculties. I apologise if you felt slighted by my actions in any way. They were done only with the best of intentions."

Freyard waved meekly, unable to lift his hand high on account of the damage to his ribs. "It is quite alright, Mack. I can understand the 'why'. You deserve thanks for stepping up without complaint to do a job that was thrust upon your shoulders without warning."

A look of ashamedness came over Mack. "I promise that there will be nothing kept from you going forward, Captain. It is clear to me that you are ready to return to your post, at least mentally. I will be your physical replacement for as long as you need me."

"I will have need of you for at least a few weeks, according to the doctor that treated me," Freyard responded with measured amiability. With a deep breath, he changed the subject. "Listen Mack, Marigold was mentioning a moment ago to Nathers that there were reports of my valour in the battle. Who issued those reports? What do you know of them? I am begging you: help me piece the battle back together."

Mack hesitated again, but rather than answer he reached inside his satchel and looked through a sheaf of handwritten papers. When he landed on what he seemed to be looking for, he extended the hand bearing the document towards Freyard. "This is the statement of witness that was given on the matter. The primary attester was Delliot. Two of Captain Mavril's sailors signed on it as supplementary witnesses... And I did too, Captain."

Freyard glimpsed toward Mack, hoping his eyes spoke of understanding. He let his gaze fall back to the paper, and began reading where Delliot's distinctively neat handwriting began.

I, Delliot Claired, Ranger 2nd Class, Born in Timber Grove of Lengly Region of Illiastra, of clear mind and conscience, do solemnly attest to the valiant actions of both Captain Freyard of the House of Archer of Collura, and Glendil, Ranger 1st Class of the House of Archer of Ravenkeep.

From there, Delliot went on to list the date he put words to paper, the date of the battle, the location, and even the time of the event, to the best of his reckoning. The account began with what Freyard knew already, and he skipped forward to the point where the rail-gunner opened fire and dispatched Captain Mavril.

With the ship's captain killed, Captain Archer drew rangers and sailors alike back to cover. One Ranger Glendil Archer was then named as interim captain of the rangers by Captain Archer. Before anyone could ask why, our captain sprang from cover. Ranger Archer and I went forth to follow, and discovered Captain Archer having leapt to the other ship. We meant to join him, but the gunner had opened fire on us, and we were forced into retreat again, leaving us with nothing else that we could do but watch from behind safe cover.

Captain Archer, though limping now, drew sword and pistol and engaged with any enemies who dared to meet him in combat. By my account, I estimate that he bested no less than five, and no more than eight enemy combatants in this manner while fighting his way toward the gunner situated on the quarterdeck.

The gunner seemed aware of Captain Archer's presence, and during that distraction, Glendil followed Captain Archer to the second ship to lend him assistance. With Captain Archer gaining ground on the offending gunner, Glendil Archer attempted to provide support, though I cannot say that Captain Archer knew that the Ranger Archer had followed him.

Upon gaining the quarterdeck of The Palombs' Pride, *Captain Archer levelled his sword at the gunner, and in response, the gunner leapt overboard. I cannot say what happened to the gunner after this. Captain Archer attempted to destroy the rail gun, and was successful in detaching it from the railing itself, where it followed its operator into the sea.*

During this, the remaining enemy soldiers had begun throwing a cache of ceramic containers and burning glass bottles filled with oil at our ship, The Tidebreaker, *and the smoke and flames quickly overwhelmed our remaining forces before we could join our comrades. Captain Archer saw the fire, and joined Ranger Archer in fighting off the saboteurs aboard* The Palombs' Pride. *At some point during this engagement, the allied ship,* Felixander's Dream, *rammed* The Palombs' Pride, *tearing the enemy ship apart at the bow and beginning the sinking process.*

It was in this period that we lost sight of both Archer men, and were forced to abandon our own ship as it became unstable from the impact of the other ships, and remained both aflame and attached to the sinking ship.

I attest that these actions of Captain Freyard and First Class Ranger Glendil Archer saved the Sun's Rangers and the crew of The Tidebreaker *from being utterly and completely destroyed by the enemy gunner. It is in my humble opinion that both men should be awarded with the highest honour that Lady Marigold Tullivan, Field Marshal Keneth Arisborough, and any other applicable parties are authorised to bestow.*

"So that's it, then," Freyard uttered despondently. "Glendil was aboard *The Palombs' Pride* with me the whole time, and I have no memory of it. Although, I still have no explanation as to how I earned a concussion and battered ribs. At this point, we can probably blame it on *Felixander's Dream* and its bloody ram. As for Glendil, it is plain to me why we could not find him after the battle. The rest of the rangers were all aboard *The Tidebreaker* and abandoned ship from her. Glendil and I were stranded on *The Palombs' Pride*, and somewhere between the ramming and my rescue, we were separated."

With a contemplative hum, Freyard began piecing a strategy together. "I was picked up by local fishermen. That much I know. We will have to ask every fisherman that attended *The Palombs' Pride* if they picked up a man in our uniform, or at least saw one. Once we rule out testimony from those who would be referring to me, such as my personal rescuers, we can go back over our work and see if any other accounts of rescued men wearing our uniform remain."

"Captain, with all due respect," Mack began in concerned response. "We do not have the time to complete such an investigation, what with us only having a few hours left before we depart from Pelican Harbour."

"No, you're right, Mack," Freyard had to allow, pausing to think of a plan. "Yet, the more I consider things, the more I realise that this is what needs to be done, for closure if nothing else, for both the Sun's Rangers and Glendil's family. Do you think that you could stay behind and carry out this investigation on my behalf? I can spare you Delliot to lend in the effort, and I am sure that Major Marchford will be accommodating. Leaving you both here will also give Tobald someone familiar to keep him company on his road to recovery. If nothing else, he might be valuable as a consultant during your investigation."

Mack seemed shocked by the request. "But what about you, Captain? You said just minutes ago that you would have need of me to act as your representative in Daol Bay."

Freyard had an answer to his earlier claim at the ready. "Dayden Vernet is already there waiting on our return, and your letter will see to it that Yarohmer and the others are back in Daol Bay before long. Leave me whatever records and reports you can spare from that satchel, and make what facsimiles of the rest that you can between now and my departure. I will have time on the journey home to pore over it all and attempt at puzzling everything together before the time we dock in Daol Bay."

"If it is discovered that Glendil is being held anywhere against his will, what would you have Delliot and I do?" Mack asked while flipping open a notebook and prepping his pencil.

"Send me written notification of any developments immediately," Freyard commanded primarily. "Given the distance that will be between us, though, I do not expect you to wait on my permission to launch rescue efforts. It will be for the best if you coordinate such operations with Major Marchford, and if need be, Captain Nathers. If he is eager to have our trust, this might well be a chance for him to earn it."

"What will you tell Lady Marigold, Captain?" Mack queried next, his hands already diving through the satchel for pertinent documents that he needed to copy.

"The truth, I suppose," Freyard told him plainly enough. "If she and I are to have a relationship, it needs to be founded on that or it will surely fail. In the meantime, give me some blank paper and a spare pencil. I will immediately get to writing a letter to Major Marchford explaining in detail just what it is I am leaving you and Delliot here to do. He will find you a place to stay amongst his men, and with any luck, will leave you be to do your work without much oversight. I trust you to carry out this operation in my stead, Mack. Find Glendil, alive or dead, and bring him home."

28
MARIGOLD

Compared to where Marigold and her entourage were returning from, Daol Bay had looked downright serene upon their entry into the harbour in the wee hours of the morning. By just before the eighth hour, *Felixander's Dream* was tying up in port and apart from daylight and a few more bodies walking about, the tranquillity of her home showed no signs of being broken.

Pelican Harbour, in the wake of Marigold's incursion, was left in uncertainty. Its leadership had been pulled out root and stem and replaced with martial law until such a time that new leadership could be duly elected. It would take time for Marigold to restore trust with Pelican Harbour, if it could be done at all. Yet, she hoped that allowing an open, uncorrupted election to name Haymard Nothram's replacement would make for a promising start.

At the time of her leaving, only Hoffman Earlesworth had entered the leadership race. While Marigold did appreciate Earlesworth and his contributions following Nothram's removal, she hoped that citizens of more humble origin would run for the vacant office of Sealord of Pelican Harbour.

To give time for both an array of candidates to come forward and the old electoral system to be cleansed, Marigold had set an election date of the first day of spring in Pelican Harbour. That generous span of time was offered with the hope that by the time Pelican Harbour's election rolled around, that they could learn from the example she was about to set in Daol Bay.

With Elbert Swylen retiring and Marswell Caveth resigning, Marigold now had two positions in her city council to fill. Those vacancies provided Marigold with the perfect opportunity to show West Illiastra just what a fair and honest election could look like.

Here is hoping that a few truly great candidates feel inclined to come forward, Marigold mused from where she stood on the quarterdeck of *Felixander's Dream.*

The elections were a rare bright spot that Marigold could focus on in otherwise bleak times. In her recent past was an intrusion that left dozens dead and a region in upheaval, and regardless of her moral motivations, Marigold was that intruder. The guilt of those deeds had been weighing heavily on Marigold's mind from the moment that the shots of the mortar cannons streaked through the skies of Pelican Harbour. Since then, and up until the moment that *Felixander's Dream* crested the waves of Daol Bay, that weight had not lightened in the slightest.

Despite that, she was facing the reality that Pelican Harbour was something that she was going to have to live with for the rest of her life. The realisation had finally struck Marigold that such decisions, and their unpleasant outcomes, were only going to increase going forward. That fact was especially true when it came to contending with those who had larger armies, more resources, and the will to act upon their terrible impulses.

Haymard Nothram is a horrible man with a terrible set of beliefs, but he and his allies and supporters had not the teeth to do more than draw but a few drops of blood with their bite. Eamon Palomb, his sons, Grenjin Howland, and the Illiastran army that remains to them are more than capable of devouring us whole in a single swallow. I have to prepare myself not just for what they might do, but what we may have to do in response.

"Lady Marigold," she heard coming from directly to her left from where she stood. With *The Princess of Daol* undergoing repairs and Captain Chet Brineholst placed on leave during an investigation into his deployment of the ram of *Felixander's Dream* in Pelican Harbour, the command of his ship had gone to the capable hands of Lorne Cayan. His familiar face looked to Marigold while his left hand gestured toward two approaching crewmembers. "The security officer and his mate are approaching. I should think that they are going to be requesting orders regarding our guests in the brig."

As expected, the two men wasted no time and headed straight for Marigold.

"Good morning, Lady Marigold," the officer greeted her, following it up with a full bow. He continued on with a row of standard pleasantries regarding the day, and concluded his conversational volley by politely asking her how she was feeling. When Marigold was done with that, she nudged their discussion toward matters of pertinence.

"Ah, yes, of course, my lady, forgive me. I have called upon you this morning to ask if you require me to arrange for a detail of sailors to escort your prisoners, or if you will be making other arrangements for such. If you are sending your own men, then I have a small amount of paperwork that will require your signature before I can turn the prisoners over to you."

Marigold let her gaze wander to the dockside, where the Tullivan's family carriage sat in wait beside a standard wagon from the city jail, the two vehicles flanked heavily by city guardsmen both on foot and on horseback. A pair of saddled, but unburdened horses stood beside the vehicles, waiting on riders. "I sent word ahead of us to have transport and a full complement of city guardsmen ready for our return. I will sign what papers you need, and when the gangway is down and secured, the guards will board, shackle the prisoners as they see fit, and remove them in their own fashion. You need do nothing but show the city guards to the brig and unlock the doors to the cells."

"All well and good, my lady. I will get the papers ready for your signature at once," the security officer complied with a second bow before returning from whence he came, his mate in tow.

"I wonder what the family carriage is doing there," Marigold asked idly to no one in particular, though she made brief eye contact with Moya standing to her right.

"I wouldn't know," Moya answered with a baffled shrug. "You've only ridden around Daol Bay on horseback since I moved here."

"It is not as though I wrote to Oire that Freyard was wounded and would need transport befitting someone of his injuries," Marigold pondered aloud.

Greggard, who had been looking about from at the far stern of the ship, seemed to overhear and approach. "I would venture to guess that there might have been developments in the war at home. There is no telling what the Triarchists in either city in Twin Bay might try if they know that you and I are away."

"I am seeing no cosmetic damage to any of the waterfront buildings, and the Tower of Ios is still standing. Those would all be good signs I would think," Marigold posited, taking a moment to pull her teal, sheepskin-lined cloak tight about her. Beneath, she wore a black bodice, matching leather trousers, a white tunic in silk, and leather boots that went to just below the knee.

"Perhaps," Greggard admitted, his own attention going to the two men stepping out of the carriage. "There is your uncle and steward now. We shall find out shortly enough, I would think."

The two approached the quayside area opposite of where the gangway was resting, waiting still and silent in their dark suits and woollen overcoats. At first, Marigold thought that Rory looked unfamiliar, until she realised that he now sported the beginnings of a full beard. The two made eye contact with her, and their shared look gave Marigold no reassurances.

"Shall we go meet them?" she asked Moya and Greggard, waiting until they moved to follow her before starting the descent from the quarterdeck. As the other two climbed down the starboard stairs, Marigold looked back to the captain, "Captain Cayan, I thank you for an exemplary show of service on this excursion. You have handled yourself on both *The Princess of Daol* and *Felixander's Dream* with the brilliance, professionalism, and diligence worthy of an Admiral of the Fleet. I shall see to it personally that your record reflects this commendable behaviour."

"The lady is too kind," Cayan gave in answer while stepping away from where he had been standing beside the wheel and approaching the railing beside the starboard steps. "I am only glad to be of service to West Illiastra and yourself, though I thank you all the same for the compliments. May fortune find you in the doubtlessly trying times ahead, Lady Marigold."

Marigold gave a bow and returned the sentiment, leaving Lorne Cayan to stand on the quarterdeck on his own.

On the main deck of *Felixander's Dream*, Marigold was joined by Elden and the injured Brandyl, her two remaining house guards that she had brought with her in the first place.

Leanne stood near to Elden, the upper left side of her face still showing signs of the bruising that occurred in proximity to where her eyebrow was cut open. She had chosen a deep brown, tailored men's suit and an open woollen overcoat in black for her attire, and stood with a smirk on her face at the sight of Marigold, bearing her stitched battle wound with grace and fearlessness.

At the hatch leading below decks was Gallin Myakys, clad wholly in black, and carefully assisting Freyard Archer in his ascent to daylight. On the journey home, Marigold noted that Freyard seemed to be making progress and both of them were feeling that he was well on his way to being able to put weight on his broken foot. Though he remained mostly within the quarters that Marigold shared with him, Freyard was doing daily exercises in the small space, and making a point to walk about with his crutch so that he could get better accustomed to it. Stairs though, would continue to be an obstacle until Freyard could put weight on the affected foot.

Near the gangway and speaking with sailors and soldiers alike was Field Marshal Keneth, issuing a complete briefing on the duties and expectations of the men aboard the ship and those attending from quayside. He looked as resplendent as always in his uniform, and although unexpected of men of his lofty rank, Keneth made a point to oversee such activities personally. Ensuring that those newly placed beneath his command could become familiar with him and develop personal respect for the man sitting atop the military hierarchy of West Illiastra.

At quayside, the sailors assembling the floating rails on the gangway seemed to be finished, and had given permission for it to be used. Rory stopped the nearest sailor and conversed with him briefly, their words lost beneath the sounds of the hempen rope fenders grinding between the ship and the quay. With a satisfied nod, Rory beckoned to Oire, and the two walked up the gangway as quickly as the gently moving stairway allowed.

In an effort to meet them halfway, Marigold beckoned her entourage to follow, and she joined her uncle and steward in close proximity to where Keneth already was. Gallin and Freyard came shortly after, missing only the shared greetings between both parties.

"I am dreadfully sorry to hear of Darrill's passing," Rory said to start the conversation, exchanging eye contact with both Marigold and Keneth. "He was a good man who took a lot of my coin in card games. Daol Bay will be a darker place in his absence."

"Somehow, amongst the chaos we were enduring, Darrill found a way to make a peaceful, dignified exit on his own terms," Keneth eulogised in memory of his subordinate. "His was a quiet, passive existence outside of duty. I must say that I felt it strangely fitting that he died as he did."

"I miss him sorely," Marigold offered in her own tribute. "Darrill was a comforting presence, and the rare sort of person who could make extended silences anything but awkward. He made me feel like it was okay to not say anything."

Oire stepped forward to speak, "I know your father felt the same way about Darrill, but I recall that with a little liquor, Darrill could become quite loquacious. It was quite a fascinating transformation, and undoubtedly, the shared imbuement was what brought your father so close to him. His absence in the manor will be deftly felt."

"And you, Ser Freyard, how do you fare?" Rory asked. He followed quickly with a further probe, "I understand that you endured losses of your own, atop the obvious injuries that you sustained."

"Thank you for your concern, Councillor," Freyard began in his reply. "My rangers had one confirmed death amongst those in attendance. Another went missing in the immediate aftermath of the battle, and I left two rangers behind to discover what came of him. A fifth man was gravely wounded, and stayed behind in Pelican Harbour under doctor's orders so that he might recuperate."

"What of yourself, Ser? You seem to be in poor shape," Oire put to Freyard while sending a glance toward the broken foot he kept bent at the knee.

Marigold had wrapped the already casted limb in a blanket from her quarters to keep it warm against the winter winds. The bright red, woollen throw blanket secured with bandages made the foot stick out sorely, though she was not going to let Freyard go out in the cold with his toes exposed.

Freyard followed Oire's line of sight and gave the limb some consideration. "As to that, I was concussed and gave my ribcage a solid beating in the process. The doctor is sure that the ribs sustained at least one major break and several smaller fractures. However, I remain optimistic that they are merely cracked. My foot, on the other hand, is definitely broken, though the doctor reported that it is only a small bone, and that it should heal in a matter of weeks."

"Surely the incident that led to those injuries must have been a harrowing ordeal," Oire commented.

"I would be inclined to agree with you, Steward Sellars," Freyard returned in a light tone. "If I could recall much of it, that is."

Keneth was called upon by a soldier, and with an affirmative flick of his wrist, the gangway began to thump and shake with the dozen or so guards boarding *Felixander's Dream*. Two men among the group bore links of chains slung over their shoulders, open shackles apparent on either end.

"Security Officer Janssen will show you to the brig," Keneth informed the closest guard before dismissing them to their task.

The house steward and Marigold's uncle continued on asking of everyone's well-being, even taking the time to include Moya and the uninjured Elden in the conversation. All had their say, and when the opportunity presented itself, Marigold dove into the subject of concern.

"What is the state of things in Twin Bay since our leaving?" she asked worriedly. "I have a feeling that relations between our supporters and the Triarchists have not improved."

Rory and Oire looked between one another, apparently trying to decide who would give answer. After a few seconds of wordless debate, Rory looked to Marigold and opened his mouth. "We regret to inform you that there has been a terrible rise in violence as of late."

"What sort of violence are we talking about?" Greggard inquired with haste.

Oire had taken to looking at his shoes, leaving Rory to continue handling the discussion. "In both Portsward and Daol Bay the Triarchists have orchestrated assaults and ambushes on city guards and town hall officials. Thus far, there have been no deaths in Portsward, but we have not been so fortunate. Two city guards were set upon by over a dozen Triarchists in one incident, and while one managed to escape, it was at the sacrifice of the other. City guards found another guard and an unidentified woman hanging from the same lamppost in another incident. Judging from the woman's attire, the general belief is that she was a... well, I suppose there is no other way to say it... she was a prostitute.

"Furthermore, anyone, man or woman, who might be possibly construed as belonging to the homosexual community are being brutally assaulted, often in broad daylight. Atop that, more and more men are disappearing from the streets, with many of them being forcibly taken by brutes in burgundy robes. We suspect that those who cannot be forcibly conscripted are being killed."

"These are far from good tidings," Marigold said in response, a tired sigh escaping her in the process.

"The bastards in burgundy are at it again," Leanne uttered through gritted teeth. "Have there been any arrests, at least?"

Oire nodded along with his answer, "There are a few Triarchists in custody in both cities, at present. However, the detained have become martyrs of a sort. The city jails are coming under attack as well, in poorly planned efforts to free those same Triarchists. The entire thing is taxing our city guards to the limit and eroding the morale of the whole city. People are starting to wonder aloud if they were better off under previous rule. They argue, both among themselves and to us that even though there was widespread oppression before, at least the streets themselves were generally safer."

Leanne scoffed loudly. "What utter tripe."

"It is easy to see their point, though, Leanne," Marigold replied while giving her friend a glance. "I have brought out the worst in the Triarchy, and they are wreaking havoc on both Portsward and Daol Bay. Most could understand that the Triarchists are the ones responsible for the bloodshed, but many would arrive at the conclusion that if not for my sudden changes, the Triarchists would not have been provoked to take such awful actions. To people in that camp, I caused upheaval and left the two cities to clean up the mess that I made while running off to Pelican Harbour. Now, it is time to focus on the war at home, and win back the people by taking the militant Triarchists out."

"The Triarchists have only grown bolder in your absence, too," Rory explained. "We suspect that they are being encouraged by House Palomb, who is promising a restoration to the old ways and plenty of favour for anyone responsible for ousting us."

"Eamon is still in Obalen then?" Gallin asked presumptively.

"From our best sources it seems that Eamon and his two sons have taken up an almost permanent residency in Minister Felton's manor,"

Oire explained in response, his voice grave. "They are… amassing an army, I regret to say."

That seemed to take none by surprise, save Moya, whose eyes looked as wide as saucers.

"That is exactly what any good strategist would counsel," Gallin commented following a loud hum. "While not detrimentally weakened, any military action would at least somewhat fatigue our units and deal us some losses. Attacking while we are any way disadvantaged plays well for the EMP. Plus, if both cities are in states of unrest due to the Triarchists, that gives the EMP an armed contingent that are already inside our walls, waiting on only the word from Eamon to spring to action. It would be hard for us to contain both an internal war and an army pounding on our gates. As far as Eamon is concerned, Twin Bay is presently ripe for the taking."

"Lady Marigold, if I may say something," Greggard spoke up once Gallin had finished. "Would there be any reason that you might immediately need me to stay in Daol Bay? By the sound of things, I am needed in Portsward and would like to book passage home as soon as possible."

Marigold gave it thought for a few seconds before offering a response. "I see no reason to stall you for too long, Sealord. However, if I could keep you for just a few hours I would be grateful. I would much like to call a meeting at the city hall featuring all available sealords, city councillors, and military officials so that we might begin formulating a strategy of our own. Can I count on you to stay for that?"

"Of course, my lady. I will be there," Greggard confirmed, though Marigold thought she heard apprehension in his voice.

"Do you have a particular time in mind in which to commence this meeting?" Oire wanted to know. "There is nothing in session in the city hall this morning, and I think I can have all the councillors gathered within an hour, if you would like."

"We will arrange to meet on the tenth hour. That should give them a little more than an hour and a prompt time at which to arrive," Marigold decided.

"Very good, my lady," Oire confirmed, jotting what she said into a notepad he produced from a pocket inside his coat. "I shall go make the arrangements at once."

"Excuse me, Steward, hold back one moment, please," a city guardsman said, having emerged in a rush from below decks.

"What is it, guardsman?" Oire asked him while coming to a stop in his tracks.

"We have high priority prisoners coming through and have a need to see them removed from the ship and secured aboard the jail wagon with urgency," the guard said while gesturing Oire gently toward Marigold and her group. "Please, stand back, good ser."

Oire backed away without objection, and cast his eyes toward the hatch, as Marigold and the others had already done.

The first man to emerge was a tall, serious fellow dressed in a mismatched, two-piece suit composed of deep blue trousers and a brown, tweed jacket. His hair was white, cut neatly and short, and his long face was cleanly shaven but for a weeks' worth of stubble. His blue eyes were cast straight ahead and looking at nothing in particular and his lips were pursed tight. The hands of the man were cuffed in front and secured to his waist by a chain, and a pair of irons clanked noisily between his ankles.

Two guards had been given the task of escorting the man, and they led him forward by an arm each, ushering him past Marigold and her retinue as quickly as the leg irons would allow.

"That is Quade Frothery," Marigold told Oire and Rory. "Who would be the former captain of Pelican Harbour's guards. It was discovered that Mister Frothery was in full knowledge and cooperation with Nothram's actions against Moya and Bess. As a man in his position, he had the authority to stop it, but instead gave in to cowardice. I had him charged with two counts of conspiring to commit murder, one count of facilitating the act of murder, one count of facilitating attempted murder, two counts of unlawful detainment, two counts of reckless endangerment, and one count of being in dereliction of duty."

"What was the last charge in relation to, if I might ask?" Rory queried from where he now stood directly beside Marigold.

"During the battle, Mister Frothery abandoned his post when Nothram's captain of the manor guards raised the white flag at their home," Marigold explained just as two more guards were emerging from the hatch with a second prisoner in tow. "Major Marchford's men found Frothery two days later while he was attempting to sneak through the city gates in civilian clothing. Unfortunately for Frothery, he was recognised by both one of our officers, and one of his guardsmen who had defected to our side."

"Did we get many Pelican Harbour guards defecting to our side?" Rory asked next, his voice echoing curiosity.

"We had a solid third of the remaining guards willing to pledge their loyalty to me," Marigold answered him, making sure to sound pleased with that number while she said it. The second prisoner was passing before her then, and Marigold inclined her head in his direction. "That one was not on that list."

A dishevelled looking man in his mid-thirties was led out. Shackled like his former senior officer, he was dressed in civilian clothing consisting of a grey, woollen sweater and tan trousers that looked a few sizes too big. On his feet were burlap wraps in lieu of footwear, and he complained bitterly of how the deck hurt him to walk on.

"You'll have to carry me down that gangway, guards," the man yelled at the two who were practically dragging him forward. "I can't walk it, not with these bags and chains on me feet. C'mon now, be good lads and give me a lift, would ya?"

"And who might he be?" Oire queried next, the look on his face showing both puzzlement and disgust toward the man being marched before him.

"That fellow is Zebbart Cooper," Marigold revealed to Rory, though she knew that the name meant nothing to him and that further elaboration was in order. "During the initial incident in Pelican Harbour, Zebbart and an accomplice referred to as 'Stanny' were the two guards assigned to the scaffolds outside the city gates. The one named 'Stanny' killed Bess, and was going to kill Moya, when Freyard and Glendil intervened and dispatched him. This one ran away at the time, though as we can see now, he did not run far enough."

"How do you know that he is the man you sought?" Rory put to her.

"Oh, I recognised that man's face immediately when I saw it," Marigold relayed to Rory. "It turns out that him and 'Stanny' were two prison guards with a known cruel streak that former captain Frothery offered to Nothram specifically for the task. After the incident, Zebbart was returned to his regular role, and when Major Marchford's men overtook the jail, they locked Zeb away with his comrades. As I said before, I knew him right away, but before I could even confirm it, he recognised Elden and me and did the job for us. As soon as he saw Elden, he could not help but call him a cuckold and other unsavoury words, and I knew he was our man. I almost felt bad for him, you know. We eventually turned most of the jailers free, and he might well have been among them if he had kept his head down, and his mouth shut. Alas, he had not the wit to do so."

"I am guessing that his charges mirror those of his captain?" Rory asked in what would be taken as an obvious manner.

"Indeed so," Marigold affirmed. With more to be said about Zeb, she powered on, "And when we left, Major Marchford's men had a few former jailers come forward with further grievances against him and 'Stanny'. Apparently, they had quite the awful reputation. Yet, it seems that Nothram had use for such depravity and kept them both employed."

"And though I ran from my past and crossed the world with my demons beside me, we three were brought down in an ambush by Death and Punishment, having been betrayed to them by the untrustworthy nature of Hubris," Rory spoke in a recitative cadence. "Naively, I believed my hunters to be in heated competition, battling one another for the right to my soul. Yet, they made it known to me before they closed my eyes, that both wanted me taken down, with no concern as to who dealt the final blow, so long as it was dealt."

Marigold gave a second of silence to the quote, before looking to Rory. "That's quite the piece, what is it from, Uncle?"

Rory's eyes closed and he took a deep breath. "It's the final passage from a classic piece of Gildraddi literature called *The Journal of a Corsair*. The book is among my absolute favourites, I can let you borrow my copy, if you would like."

"I will look in my own library first, and if I do not already own a copy, I would definitely like to read yours," Marigold told him.

"Oh, dear, that's an awfully large man," Oire exclaimed as the second-to-last prisoner was brought out by an escort of four guards.

The brute of a man emerged willingly, but the four charged with watching him were taking no chances and their hands were clamped tightly on the big man wherever they could find purchase. Standing nearly a head over most, the large fellow had a tightly cropped head of hair, a bushy beard, and a visibly crooked nose that looked to have been broken half a dozen times in different places. Unlike the other two former members of the Illiastran forces, this one actually wore his blue Illiastran uniform, though it had been noticeably stripped of all markings.

"What's that one's story?" Oire asked Marigold while moving close enough that he could whisper, as though he were in fear of the prisoner overhearing.

"That one is Raybert Moore, the lieutenant who was overseeing the gates on the morning of my arrival," Marigold told Oire and Rory. "He is but another with the power to have stopped the proceedings but thought more about his job than the suffering of two people."

"You would charge a lowly lieutenant for the crimes of his superiors?" Oire asked sceptically.

"Admittedly, I have charged him only with two counts of dereliction of duty," Marigold revealed to them, which seemed to do nothing to sate Oire's objection. "There is value in what he knows, though. Granted, he will serve some time behind bars for letting Moya and Bess suffer, but if he talks, there is a light at the end for him."

Rory's head turned sharply back toward the hatch, and he uttered in disbelief, "And there he is, in all his faded glory."

With his rattling chains heralding his arrival, Haymard Nothram emerged from the bowels of the ship for the first time since he was dragged aboard in Pelican Harbour. His round, balding head shone in the sunlight and every strand of his white wispy crown of hair seemed to be in business for itself. The suit Nothram wore was evidently the same one he had been arrested in by Wynne Nathers' Flying Hawks, and it showed. The jacket had opened at the seam of the right sleeve, his white shirt was yellowing with sweat, and dust, dirt, and various stains had accrued atop every piece of visible material.

It took only one man to hold the squat little sixty-eight year old, who nonetheless wriggled in his guard's grasp. "Unhand me. I can walk on my own. At least leave me that dignity," Nothram insisted, his head turned away from Marigold's party to face the quiet guard who gripped his elbow tightly.

"Lady Marigold's orders," the guard finally answered while pulling Nothram in tight beside him. "All prisoners are to be treated equally. Your days of privilege are over."

The head of the deposed minister swivelled sharply toward Marigold. "Is this how you treat a man of my class? Look at me, Myakys and Simillon! We are the same, you and I! If you think she will not do to you as she has done to me, you are fooling yourself."

"That is where you are wrong, Haymard," Marigold told him. "The Sealords here have nothing in common with you, beyond being former ministers from the Western Realm. Oh, and furthermore, you have no class to speak of."

Nothram bucked against the guard, who had to plant his feet to keep the prisoner in place. "Mockery, is that what you want? It's just as well, for the mockery you have all made of the Western Realm! You whimpering cuckolds that follow the Tullivan bitch and still call yourselves men are not fit to shine my shoes!"

"Why would a man who conspired to kill two women suddenly think he is worthy of having his shoes shined?" Gallin answered him back with a query of his own.

A ball of phlegm left Nothram's mouth and landed on the deck directly before Marigold. The poor guard holding Nothram scolded him for his behaviour and tried to pull him away, resulting in a struggle. Ser Keneth sprang into action, calling to two of the guards standing by the jail wagon to return to the vessel and assist. Elden stepped forward as well, putting himself between Marigold and Haymard.

"I did not kill anybody!" Nothram snarled. "One woman died, aye, but it is not on my head, and Marscal Tullivan's second-born daughter is not going to hold it over me, either!"

"You ordered our deaths," a familiar voice suddenly called out. Marigold looked to her right to see Moya having stepped away from the others to approach Nothram, her flower-patterned skirt swishing with every step. "You told your guards to put me and Bess in those ugly dresses and tie us to those poles in the freezing cold and you did that knowing that it would kill us. You said something else too though, didn't you? What was it you said? Shall I tell them?" Moya let the query hang on the air. Her firm, resolute gaze affixed Nothram, who for once looked fearful. When he made no move to respond, she went on, "Fine, if you won't, I will: 'When Marigold's bleeding heart lures her in, give the bitch a good show and let her have what she wants. Set the whores free with a big splash, lads.' I wasn't sure what that meant at the time, but your men made it horrifically clear."

Nothram began to snigger, "You must be the blonde whore."

"No, Nothram, I am not just some *blonde whore*, I am the woman that you couldn't kill," Moya said through gritted teeth with a fiery pride that Marigold did not know her friend to possess.

The two extra guards were on deck then and approaching Keneth at a jog.

"Get Nothram out of here at once," Keneth ordered firmly.

"You had better hope that House Palomb razes this city to the ground before you take the stand at my trial," Nothram snarled at her threateningly as the extra guards joined in and the three lifted him off the ground by his arms. "If I am found guilty because of you, all of West Illiastra will riot over the injustice, I promise you that! Forces greater than any of you can know are at work in every region that the second-born daughter of a third-rate warden lord thinks she holds dominion over! My people will rise to defend me, Pelican Harbour will rise to defend me, the Triarchy will rise to defend me, and every patriotic man in the Western Realm will rise to defend me! Just you watch, you little blonde whore! Your empty head will sit on a pike over the gates of Pelican Harbour before all of this is done!"

A fourth guard was sprinting over the gangway, arriving on the deck just as the other three were ready to cross to the quays. "Moya, are you alright?"

"Hello, Sydnee," Moya greeted him, her gaze still fixed on Haymard Nothram. "I am just fine, thank you."

Sydnee rushed over to where she stood and drew her into a hug. "I saw you approaching Nothram and I got worried." His eyes went to Keneth. "I apologise profusely if you feel that I abandoned my post."

"I will allow it in this instance," Keneth conceded after giving the matter brief consideration. "I believe that you know better than to make a habit of the behaviour."

"Thank you, Field Marshal," Sydnee uttered while still holding tight to Moya. "I missed you so much, Moya. The days dragged on with you gone and I worried my way through every minute of them. I am so glad to see you again, safe and sound."

Moya returned the hug and closed her eyes tight, her head burying into Sydnee's chest. "I missed you too, Sydnee. You have no idea how happy it makes me to see you."

"Uncle Ken, do you think we can spare Sydnee from guard duty for the morning?" Marigold asked, while giving him a playful side-eyed glance.

"Perhaps I can, but only if you agree to ride in the carriage where it is safest," Ken determined with a single, thoughtful nod. "Rory and Oire's dire report matches what my own guards have been telling me since we arrived. It is unwise for you to travel about openly, where any decent shot with a rifle can potentially harm you. Captain Archer will ride with you, given his injured state. Rus, Kandell, Elden, and I will escort on horseback for certain, and Ser Dayden Vernet as well, if his captain will allow it."

Freyard cleared his throat from where he had seated himself on a single, upturned barrel near to the railing. "I think Dayden will be amenable to that. I have a need to speak with him, but it can surely wait until after the morning meeting."

"There you have it, you two," Marigold told Sydnee and Moya with a wide smile. "Go enjoy your morning together and do not let us stop you."

"Shall we?" Moya asked while stepping apart from Sydnee.

Sydnee seemed unsure, and looked again to Keneth. "Are you sure it is alright, Field Marshal?"

"Yes, of course. Go on with you," Keneth said while making a shooing motion with his hand. "Let Rus know on your way out. I will give him further explanation if it is needed."

"You still have the authority to do that, Keneth?" Oire asked him curiously.

Keneth allowed himself a rare sigh, "I am still the acting Captain of the Manor Guards of House Tullivan. We are in a probationary phase with Rus, to see how he handles the job under my coaching. I did not want to merely hoist it upon his shoulders and leave for Pelican Harbour, so this seemed to be the most prudent course for the time being. However, if the EMP will soon be on the march, as your dire news would lead us to believe, I may have to force the issue at the manor. Of course, all of this might be better left to discuss at a later time."

"I could not agree more, Uncle Ken," Marigold chimed in, while inviting the others to join her. "Shall we be off? The morning is slipping away on us as we stand around here in the cold and in the way of all the sailors. Freyard, will you need help getting over the gangway?"

"If you would like, I can assist him," Elden offered jovially. "It would be no trouble, Captain Archer."

"I won't lie, the gangway worries me," Freyard conceded while he awkwardly got himself back to a standing position. "I would just need someone to stand in front of me and make sure that I don't go overboard, Ser Elden."

With Freyard's needs tended to, the entire group began the process of disembarking. Once the luggage of those returning home was unloaded and all party members safely situated at quayside, arrangements were made for transport.

Sydnee and Moya had already departed on shared horseback, with Sydnee promising that he would return to duty by no later than the lunch hour. Brandyl left on foot to walk home and see his family, being given at least a week of leave so that his injuries might properly heal. Keneth had several pressing duties to attend to as Field Marshal, as well as a brief discussion with Rus that needed to be had. Though he could not promise to be available in time for the meeting, he told Marigold that he would at the very least send Rus to represent her guards and an available high-ranking officer to do the same for the armed forces.

Having arrived in the carriage, Rory and Oire both decided that they would vacate their places in the four-person ride and hire the first available taxi wagon. The former suggesting as much primarily so that he could retrieve Leonice, who would almost certainly want to attend the impromptu meeting. Gallin opted to ride with Marigold's uncle and steward, reasoning that it would give him time to bring both men fully up to date on everything that had occurred in Pelican Harbour.

Once Elden had climbed into the saddle of his horse, he and Dayden were positioned by Ser Keneth to flank the forward corners of Marigold's carriage. That left the space inside the carriage for Marigold, Freyard, Leanne, and Greggard.

With everything settled and everyone in their proper places, the convoy left the waterfront. The jail wagon was sent out first, surrounded on either side by half of the armed guards, on both foot and horseback, with Marigold's carriage following behind with the rest. The two vehicles remained close to one another, and Marigold quickly came to regret that setup. The inelegantly constructed jail wagon seemed to bounce on every cobblestone it met, making such a racket that it made any conversation in Marigold's carriage practically impossible. Despite the fact that the noise was utterly grating on her every last nerve, Marigold was fine with the lack of discussion. Insomuch as was possible under the conditions, Marigold tried to take the moment to relax and take a few deep breaths. As she sat beside

Freyard, she slid her hand gently over onto his leg and then to the hand resting upon it, giving his fingers a gentle squeeze.

Outside the carriage window, Daol Bay was as alive as Marigold ever saw it, and people of all stripes of life were walking the sidewalks and traversing the roads by horse. Fresh fish was being offered up for sale in booths that were placed strategically close to the fishing stages that dipped out into the harbour in tight rows. Two men were selling fried meats being prepared on the spot over a shared charcoal pit, each one taking their turn to shout to the crowds for attention. At the next street, they began to pass storefronts, and every door seemed to have an 'open' sign hanging from it in some fashion.

Either the city guards are keeping dutifully ahead of the violence, or Daol Bay is not as terrible as Oire and Rory have made it out to be. At least not from what I have seen thus far.

The streets began to incline slightly, and before long, they came to the familiar intersection where Water Street joined Ser Davis' Road. The mass of soldiers and the caravan they were protecting all veered east on the road named for Marigold's ancestor, and from the corner of her eye, she saw an open carriage come from behind them and turn west.

That must be Rory, Oire, and Gallin. She had to figure.

A short roll later, they veered north. A few moments later, they crossed Mallard's Brook Bridge and the *Brookside Inn* that straddled the waterway and sat parallel to the red, brick overpass.

As they approached the bridge, Marigold could see the downtown core of the city coming into view. Every street in the core was built to either conform to the city centre or merge into it. Amidst it all was the main attraction and centrepiece of the area: a large, circular, sprouting fountain made of marble and topped with statues of the three gods, each one holding a jug that emptied into the fountain below.

To the north of the fountain, and facing Ios' statue, was the Arameida Amphitheatre one of Daol Bay's oldest structures. The open, domed building was named for Arameida Tullivan, the wife of Ser Davis' eldest son and heir. The son had built it as a way of inviting the music and pageantry of the world to the growing port that he and his father had been building. Ser Davis had been alive to see its completion, and Arameida herself had been the original proprietor for most of her life. After her death, the structure had been turned over to the city as a publically owned space, and had been caringly maintained ever since.

Eight centuries removed from the first family of Tullivan's, the amphitheatre was only used in the summer season in Marigold's lifetime. Its main tenants at present were the Daol Bay Orchestra and the local theatre troupe, who both used it primarily as a practice space when weather permitted. Once or twice during the season, an evening performance from either group could be expected, for the sake of nostalgia, if nothing else.

East of the fountain, and watched dutifully by Aren's marble representation, was Conley Park and the central headquarters for the Daol Bay City Guards. An architectural marvel in its own right, with roof peaks jutting in at least three directions, its mere presence provided a level of security that made the city core one of the safest places that people could find themselves.

Westward of the fountain and under the careful eye of Iia's likeness was the expansive complex of buildings that were the city hall and the courthouses. The house of justice of Daol Bay had only been home to the Court of the Western Realm prior to secession. In the weeks following Marigold's successful implementation of *The Declaration of Agency*, the courthouse had been rebranded to be the host site of the Supreme Court of West Illiastra. The highest circle of judges, those who stayed on in Marigold's new nation, that was, had been elevated to the position of Supreme Justices, a definite jump from their old title of Western Realm Circuit Judge.

Flanking either side of a tall, iron gateway in front of the city hall entrance to the complex were no less than five guards in teal coats. The fountain in the centre, the park, and the guard station, were under further patrol. The rows of stone benches of the amphitheatre sat empty, though a further row of guards looked out over them from upon the stage.

So many guards at every turn, Marigold thought distressingly. *The people of Daol Bay might believe me to be an iron-fisted despot based on the armed and uniformed presence alone. I might not even blame them.*

The carriage carrying Marigold's foursome pulled up to the gates of the complex. Looking through the window, Marigold watched as the jail wagon parted ways with the remainder of the convoy and turned toward the guard station. The horses pulling it were steered toward a rear entrance, where the prisoners would be quietly booked into temporary cells while awaiting to be formally charged. Once a judge issued them court dates to begin the trial process for their crimes, they would be relocated to the regional jail, located in a sparsely populated area on the northern side of the city.

The door to the Tullivan carriage was swung open by Elden once it came to a stop, and the driver worked the narrow set of steps out of their compartment beneath the door.

"Lady Marigold, and company, we have arrived," Elden announced, despite that fact being obvious.

Leanne and Greggard were the first to step out, doing so to give Freyard the space needed to manoeuvre himself into position for an exit. Against Marigold's expectations, though, he stayed put firmly.

"You should go on ahead, Mari," he advised with a wrinkling of his nose. "I shall join you just a little later."

"Why so, love? I do not want to leave you behind," Marigold gently protested.

Freyard's gaze went outward, and Marigold looked to see a gathering crowd. "They are here to see you. Go on out and greet them. Once you have gone, they should dissipate. I really do not want to be seen bumbling about with my broken foot. Please, for my sake, would you leave me be for the time being?"

Marigold leaned over and placed a kiss on his cheek. "Very well, darling, if that is your desire. I will see you inside when you are ready."

"Thank you, Mari," Freyard called to her as she departed.

As she stepped down to the street, it occurred to Marigold that the air felt different from what she had breathed at the quays. The crispness of the winter air filled her lungs and the once omnipresent salty aroma was now but barely tangible.

We are not even that far inland. I suppose that the city core has always been like that, though.

"There she is!" a woman cried out. "It's Lady Marigold!"

Where did they all come from?

All about the fountain and stretching all the way to Mallard's Brook Bridge, people appeared to have gathered in the hundreds, walking in the wake of where the carriage had rolled just moments ago. It looked to be women mostly, though at least a third of those in attendance were men. From the variety of clothing and outward appearances, there seemed to be no one class or demographic defining the crowd. They were, in that moment, people, and those people had gathered there to see Marigold, the Lady of Daol Bay.

"Well, Mari, are you not going to give the people a wave?" Leanne gently prodded with a beaming smile.

Marigold raised a hand on high, and the simple gesture elicited a roar from the crowd. From within her chest, Marigold thought that her heart was going to break through her ribcage. Her mouth went dry and fell slightly agape. Though an attempt was made to form words, she could get nothing out. Looking to Greggard and Leanne, she found them equally taken aback by the size and enthusiasm of those standing before them.

"Where did they all come from?" Marigold finally managed to stammer out, the open question not aimed at either person.

"A few among them must have noticed your arrival this morning, and the rest just snowballed with them," Leanne offered in explanation.

"I wonder what they know of our expedition south," Greggard posited to both women. "Perhaps the EMP's loyalist ministers do not have the popularity that they thought they did."

Having given one final wave from safely behind the line of teal coats that kept the crowd at bay, Marigold turned away so that she might make her way to the gates. In the process of climbing the steps, she leaned close to Leanne and Greggard in an effort to speak further with them. "Do you think it was what happened in Pelican Harbour that has excited them, or my proposed overhaul of Illiastran law?"

Leanne offered a shrug to accompany her worded response, "It might well be both. It is hard to say at this point. We will have to ask your councillors when they arrive."

At the top of the stretched, tall set of concrete steps that led to the terrace of the primary entry to city hall, Marigold, with Leanne and Greggard still beside her, turned about and faced the crowd once more. She waved again, and made a downward motion to bring the audience to silence.

"People of Daol Bay and West Illiastra, I thank you from the bottom of my heart for your show of support today," Marigold tried to say as loud as she could, her voice not carrying as well as she would have liked.

The audience roared out again, drowning her next attempt to speak and pushing perhaps a little too excitedly against the guardsmen on the street.

Marigold called for calm for a second time, though it seemed to go unheeded. From all the way over at the amphitheatre, there came the voice of a single guard, whose tones were amplified by a combination of the half-domed ceiling overhead and his cupped hands around his mouth. "Let Lady Marigold speak!"

"Thank you all again," Marigold cried out, making an effort to talk both as clearly and quickly as she dared, before the crowd could swell over her lone voice again. "With victory in Pelican Harbour, I bring to all of West Illiastra a new page in the history of our young nation. Those who would be our oppressors have been shown that West Illiastra will not be held beneath the thumb of the EMP, just as we shall not bow to the whims of the Triarchy's cruel leadership. West Illiastra is a place where the chains of slaves shall be broken, where women shall be free to pursue their full potential, where people of all races can come together, and where none will go cold and hungry.

"Give to me your trust, and I will deliver us to a place of pride on the world's stage. We will break bread with Drake, Cabathos, and the Gildraddi nations abroad, and with the elves and dwarves right here in our northerly realms. All of this we shall do by showing to those nations that we can be decent to each other and to them in turn. We will do through compassion at home and diplomacy abroad what the EMP and the Triarchy thought could only be done with fear and intimidation."

A wave of applause and cheers came bursting forth from the people again, and as Marigold looked about, she saw that the crowd had somehow grown even further during her speech.

"With your support, we will show the rest of Illiastra that the only people who would need fear us are those who would divide us with hate, control us with lies, and stomp us down with the weight of tyranny's boot."

An eruption of cheers sounded out from the town centre, sounding like nothing that Marigold had ever heard before.

"By the gods, I think they might hear this over in Portsward," Greggard noted with an enthusiastic laugh.

Leanne was waving broadly beside Marigold, "It is safe to say that you have established a core base of supporters, Mari."

With a last acknowledgement of the crowd, Marigold, Leanne, and Greggard left the foyer and approached the heavy, varnished oak doors of town hall. Inside, they were immediately encountered by the staff on duty, all having been standing at the door and peeking through at Marigold's audience and their collective ruckus.

"Good morning, Lady Marigold," one among them said with surprise in his voice.

"Good morning to you as well, Mister Davisure," Marigold greeted him with a bow. "How have things been at city hall since I left for Pelican Harbour?"

Mister Guerin Davisure was the long-serving Clerk of the Hall, having been in the position for some ten years prior. Marigold found him to be an amiable fellow, with his round, bearded face, portly frame, and grandfatherly demeanour. Having eschewed the jacket of his suit, Davisure was clad in a cream coloured, long-sleeved button-down shirt, and a pair of brown, tweed trousers that were held up by a pair of matching suspenders. "We have been as busy as bees, my lady. There has been much for all to do during your time away, what with the secession and all. Our staff members are adjusting to going from the Capital of the Western Realm to being the capital of an entire nation. As I am sure you can appreciate, there is a world of difference between the two, and a plethora of new responsibilities that come with such a distinction."

"Yes, of course, Mister Davisure, I apologise for the workload I have encumbered you all with," Marigold said with sincere concern. "Most assuredly, your efforts are greatly appreciated not just by me and those in my circle, but by all of West Illiastra. The need for calm, collected intellectuals such as yourself to oversee an efficient transition has never been more evident."

"You flatter us all, my lady," Guerin uttered with a warm smile while adjusting the circular-lensed spectacles on his face. "To what do we owe the pleasure of your visit today? I was given to understand that *The Princess of Daol* was not even in port as of this morning. The harbour master's report indicates that a fleet of six led by *Felixander's Dream* sailed into town. You must have come in with them aboard something other than *The Princess of Daol*, I would assume."

Marigold winced at the mention of the beleaguered ship. "*The Princess of Daol* is currently undergoing repairs in Pelican Harbour. It and *The Tidebreaker* both sustained damage enough that they were deemed unseaworthy. I travelled home aboard *Felixander's Dream*, which is a fine frigate in its own right. In fact, I would even go so far as to say that it will be the new flagship if *The Princess of Daol* cannot return to service and *The Tidebreaker* cannot replace it."

"Oh, dear me, Lady Marigold, I am sorry to hear that the two most prized vessels of Daol Bay's fleet were so badly damaged," Guerin replied morosely. "I do hope there was no bodily harm caused to you or yours."

Marigold bowed her head slightly. "We sustained a low number of deaths. Yet, I would say that any loss of life is a tragic waste."

"Yes it is grievous, my lady, truly grievous," Guerin said with a slow shake of his head. "Did you achieve your goal, at least?"

"I can say that we did, yes," Marigold revealed proudly. "All surviving perpetrators of the initial incident in Pelican Harbour have been successfully arrested and brought here to face justice. They are being processed at the guards' station as we speak."

A hand of Guerin's began nervously caressing his beard then. "That is quite good to hear, my lady. I am so very glad for you. The remaining recalcitrant ministers will not be so glad though, if I may say so.

"The lieutenant overseeing the repairs of the city walls was here just yesterday. He is close to completion of his task of patching ground-level holes. However, as you no doubt saw on your way here, the crumbling topsides of the walls are still a long ways from being battle-ready. I do hope that neither Nothram's friends nor House Palomb come rushing here any time soon. We may not be prepared to fend them off. Oh, but I suppose it is not my place to speak on such matters. Please, forgive me if I overstepped, my lady."

"No, it is quite alright, Mister Davisure, you are as free as any other to air your opinion," Marigold assured him, before another thought came to her. "In fact, I am glad that you brought it up. Could you send someone to summon Lieutenant Ashe here at his earliest convenience? I would much like to hear from him personally on the progress of the wall restoration project."

"Yes, of course I can, my lady. Consider the task done," he replied, still in a pensive state. "I hate to repeat myself to you, but I fear we were driven off course. Besides summoning Lieutenant Ashe, what is it that city hall can do for you today?"

"As to that, Mister Davisure," Marigold began in earnest answer. "I would like to hold a closed meeting in the private chambers with my campaign counsel. Following that, we would hold an open invitation for the public to join us in the centre chamber for announcements on our recent actions and matters of interest going forward. Can you arrange all of that on short notice?"

"I will need to confer with my secretary and chief of staff," Davisure told Marigold, waiting not for an answer from her before turning away to the two young men that had been standing with him. Their voices dropped to whispers and they merged into a huddle, leaving Marigold and her compatriots to stand around idly.

Marigold gazed about at the rounded hallway that encircled the city council's expansive and extravagant centre chamber, her eyes wandering to the large paintings of previous Warden Lords of the West. All of those visible in this part of the hall were relatives of Marigold's, having lived and ruled in the most recent centuries. The handful of non-Tullivan leaders to have held sway over Daol Bay had portraits too, buried deep in the private chamber halls at the back of city hall, with the other ancient dead.

While scanning the walls for her father's picture, Marigold heard a door open in the distance, paying it little mind until she heard footfalls drawing close.

Mister Davisure broke away from the huddle and walked off to Marigold's left, adjusting his spectacles again as he approached the people that Marigold could not see. "Sealord Gallin, Councillors Rory, Jaysen, Sybel, Lady Leonice, and Steward Oire, I presume that you six are here with Lady Marigold?"

"That we are, Guerin," Marigold heard the unmistakable voice of Leonice reply. "I assume from the throng of people still lingering outside that she is in fact here?"

A hand of Davisure lifted in Marigold's direction, and he left the three to find their way to her, returning instead to his private discussion.

Leonice was first to round the corner into the foyer where Marigold, Leanne, and Greggard were, and Marigold rushed to meet her beloved aunt for a hug. "Oh, my dear niece, it is good to see you alive and unharmed. Rory was telling me what he knew of your adventure south thus far. I was so upset to hear of dear Ser Darrill's passing. What a lovely man he was. Ser Brandyl and Captain Archer were wounded too, I was told, and one of Captain Archer's Sun's Rangers also perished. It is such a loss for all of us. At least their deaths and injuries were not in vain, darling. Rory tells me that the old fiend and his cohorts were all arrested."

"On that front we were successful, Auntie," Marigold confirmed as they separated. "How are you and the children?"

"We are fine as always," Leonice answered while turning to Greggard and Leanne. "How about you two? Leanne, there was some mention of you being hurt, yes?"

Leanne's hand grazed the afflicted eyebrow as she gave answer, "Just a scratch, Madam. I will live to fight another day."

"And there was no harm done to me or mine," Greggard stated, exchanging greetings with the others afterwards.

"Lady Marigold, if I might have your attention," Guerin Davisure spoke up, having broken away from his chief of staff and secretary.

Marigold and her growing retinue gave the trio their total focus, and Davisure patiently waited until he had it. "The private chambers are yours to use for as long as you want. It is clean, and a fire can be lit in the fireplace at a moment's notice. The problem is with the centre chamber. As I said before, we have been very busy with the transition to statehood, and the centre chamber has been undergoing renovations so that it might serve as the home of West Illiastra's parliamentary functions. I am afraid that it is not yet ready to receive you, your company, and least of all, the attending public. We will have to insist that you hold such events elsewhere for the time being."

"That is most unfortunate, Mister Davisure," Marigold responded rather flatly, unsure of how to feel. "We were planning to announce elections soon to fill the positions left vacant by former councillors Swylen and Caveth. On the day of the elections, we will need space somewhere within the common area of city hall to host the voting populace, both for them to cast their ballots and to register to even get one."

Guerin's hands began to tremble, and he stuffed them hurriedly into his trouser pockets in an effort to either conceal or stop the involuntary action. "That-That-That is indeed a problem, my lady. Per-per-perhaps there co-could be some allowance for the offices in the co-common areas to be used. I can cer-certainly check with the holders of those offices. W-when do you anticipate that you will be h-holding the election?"

"I can give you two weeks from today, Mister Davisure," Marigold told him calmly. "Do you think that will be enough time?"

"A fortnight?" he gasped incredulously while adjusting his spectacles, causing them to bumble their way out of his grip where they bounced around between his hands. "Why, goodness gracious, my lady. Just two weeks, you say? That is not much time at all. Can we make it three weeks or even the rest of the winter season?"

"I am sorry, ser," Marigold began apologetically, leading in to an explanation for her denial of Davisure's open-ended request, "But with the current state of affairs in West Illiastra, I have to fill those positions quickly. Daol Bay needs a full council in place as soon as possible, and I need to get on with both restructuring the laws of our nation and the general realities of being considered an enemy to the Elite Merchants. Atop that, with the removal of Haymard Nothram in Pelican Harbour and Leo Daltis in the Madore Isles, there will have to be subsequent elections in those regions for properly chosen representation. Those elections, as I am sure you can appreciate, will have to come sooner rather than later, as I will need every sealord or sealady that can be mustered to form a parliament. To that end, I want our election to be the blueprint by which elections in those regions and beyond will be built from."

Davisure lowered his head and produced a handkerchief from the breast pocket of his shirt to wipe his smudged spectacles. "Yes, my lady, yes, you speak sense. I shall assemble a ta-taskforce dedicated solely to this project, if-if that is suitable to you."

Marigold tried to impress a tone of calm compassion. "That will do just fine, ser. For the sake of transparency, I will have the team of yours report solely to city hall and yourself. There should be no involvement, beyond calling the election itself, from my campaign team or me in any part of the process. The candidates, and the eventual victor, should have no endorsement from me or anyone else of influence, that goes especially so for any noise being made by the EMP. The people must be given a choice free of undue, biased influence."

"How do you plan on having the vote decided?" Guerin asked next. "The EMP's own election model was to have the popular vote decide the winner, even though we both know that the results were forged."

"Obviously, no forging of the numbers will be taking place. As to the exact nature of rendering the decision, that will be discussed shortly by my counsel and me. When we have an answer, you will be the first to know it, Mister Davisure. For now, if you could see a pitcher of water and drinking glasses for all delivered, and eventually a pot of tea and appropriate porcelain to go with it, we would be ever so appreciative."

"I shall see to it at once, Lady Marigold," Davisure consented to the request, making a point to stand back and allow access for Marigold's group to the circular hallway. "In the meantime, my staff and I will wait patiently on your decision. May the gods guide your hands and heart, my lady."

"Yes, thank you, Mister Davisure," Marigold said with a smile that she knew full well was feigned. She was not about to put any measure of trust into deistical guidance.

Led by Marigold, the group made for the rear side of the circular hall. They went to the right from the foyer, taking the route that took them past Marigold's new office, and into the back of the building.

A single guard was patrolling, and passed Marigold with a combination of a bow and a salute. "Good day, Lady Marigold. Heading to the chambers, I presume?"

"Yes, ser," Marigold answered for the whole group. "Is the door locked at this hour?"

"Uh, no, my lady," the guard replied in slight puzzlement. "Your ranger captain came in through the rear and asked that we unlock it for him. He is seated inside at present."

Marigold thanked the guard and moved past him to the meeting room. Finding the door ajar, she pushed it open and stepped within.

Just as foretold by the lone guard, Freyard was indeed seated inside, having taken the position to the direct right hand side of the head of the table in one of the high-backed, cushioned, wooden chairs. His stance was rigidly straight, and his general demeanour looked discomforted, but he moved to greet them without standing all the same. "Good morning, everyone, it is a pleasure to see you all again."

"Freyard, just how did you get in here?" Marigold asked while walking around the table to take the head seat, as would be expected of her.

"That crowd outside showed no signs of dispersing," he began to explain as the others filled the seats around the table. "So, I merely asked the driver to take the carriage around to the back of the building, and he obliged. Luckily for me, the stables are on a higher elevation than the front entrance, so climbing the short set of steps there was less of a hassle. Your aunt and uncle came along just as I was reaching the landing, and they and Oire rendered some much-appreciated assistance."

A gentle stroke of Freyard's arm followed Marigold's reply. "Either way, I am glad you could join us."

"Now that we are mostly accounted for," Rory stated surprisingly while standing up, the button of his jacket flipping closed in the process. "I would like to start off the meeting with a brief discussion that will remain off the official recording of the minutes."

Marigold tried to hide the combination of shock and confusion that was playing across her face as she stared Rory down. "Just what is this referring to, Uncle Rory?"

Rory visibly braced himself with the arm of his chair and took a deep breath. "A few among your fellow campaigners and I believe that it is high time that we discuss your relations with Captain Archer, Niece. Given that we are a team involved with overseeing your successful ascension to a position of leadership over an entire nation, we need to be kept up to date on any and all changes that might occur. If for nothing else, we need to know these things so that we can alter our carefully laid out strategies so that they conform to new information."

Unsure of what to say in response to Rory's brazen opening statement, Marigold sat there wordlessly, her eyes remaining locked on the steward.

It was Oire who dared break the stunned silence that had fallen over everyone. "Well, that certainly is one way to begin our meeting."

Freyard visibly winced while moving in his chair. "I realize that from a strategic standpoint, the relationship I share with Marigold is something that her counsellors should be aware of. With that said, I do believe that awareness is where your collective involvement ends."

A knock came at the door, and Oire, as the closest to the entry, stood up to answer. The same lone guard from earlier was on the other side, and he addressed Oire, who held the door open just enough to converse. "Steward Oire, Field Marshal Keneth Arisborough, and Ser Rus of the House Tullivan Guardsman request entry."

"By all means, gentlemen, come on in," Oire invited them while standing back to allow passage.

Keneth walked in looking refreshed, in both attire and general appearance. His uniform appeared newly pressed and his face had the redness that could only come from a hot bath. "I apologise for our tardiness, Marigold. It was brought to my attention that I looked haggard, so I thought a cleaning was in order," he explained as he and Rus took their places.

"No apology needed, Uncle Ken," Marigold told him with nonchalance. "We had just barely begun ourselves."

"We were discussing the recently commenced relationship between Marigold and Captain Archer," Oire stated to Keneth with a certain level of indignation in his voice. "Have you any input on that, Keneth?"

If Rory had been expecting Keneth to show surprise, he would have been doubtlessly disappointed in Keneth's visual non-response. "You say this as though it is something that should alarm me."

"Are you not concerned, Ken?" Rory inquired incredulously.

"Over a grown woman deciding on a partner?" Keneth asked in a matching tone. "Why would I ever?"

"Freyard is of House Archer of Collura, an eastern family of only middling influence," Rory said outright, and immediately his face contorted into one of remorse. "I apologise, Captain Archer. That was poorly said of me."

Freyard took the slight well, from what Marigold could see, and he remarked on it similarly. "I accept your apology, Councillor Rory. I understand why you are concerned that Marigold has chosen me as a romantic partner, given that I was born into this world on the wrong side of an arbitrary line that divides this continent."

"It is not that, Captain, and you know it," Rory shot back hotly, his frustration evident. "Forgive me in advance, for what I must say will be quite frankly, unpleasant. We have been presenting Lady Marigold Tullivan, the household name, and one of the most beautiful women known to humans as a single woman, undefined by any man. Should she show any measure of success against the EMP, suitors from along the west coast and across the Casparian Sea will be lining up to win her hand in marriage.

"For as long as there have been kings, there has been value in the nuptials of the nobility. It is as important a bargaining chip as whole armies, and it is vital that Marigold be seen as both single and available by potential allies. If the dalliances of you two become widely known, we will be seen to have exchanged what might be arguably the highest valued asset in our inventory for no return to a man from the enemy lands. Again, this is not an ideal thing for either of you to hear."

While Marigold seethed and laughed nervously at the gall that Rory seemed to possess, Leanne and Leonice stood up simultaneously and stared Oire down in unison, with the latter being the first to find her words. "Well Rory, I never!" Leonice gasped at her husband. "I have not the slightest notion what has gotten into you all of a sudden, but you had best believe that you owe an enormous apology to both our niece and Captain Archer. Come on now, on the double."

"How dare you?" Leanne said in sheer outrage. "How dare you devalue Marigold's worth as a person to that of livestock? If for nothing else, you should have learned from this campaign that neither Marigold nor any other woman for that matter, are tokens to be bartered and sold to the highest bidder. Breaking that stigma and earning our place as equals is exactly what Marigold is fighting for, and why women like Leonice and I are in that battle beside her."

"Uncle Rory, I will grant to you one thing from your diatribe," Marigold impressed upon Rory and the whole room in a voice that was calm, yet resolute. "It is true that much of the ruling bodies of the world still see marriage as a useful trading asset. Yet, as Leanne just said, that sort of regressive attitude is exactly what I am trying to combat. I do not want the image of me that we send to the world to be based on what I can bring to a romantic relationship. What I want to present to the people of Illiastra and beyond is in my ability to lead our nation to a place of peace and prosperity as the leader of West Illiastra.

"My marital status does not, and will not ever factor into that. In lieu of an apology, for I know you are not remorseful for having said what you did, I want you to promise me that going forward you will not consider my hand in marriage as a tool at our disposal. Will you agree to these terms, Uncle?"

His head had lowered during Marigold's response, having gone in that direction following the scolding from his wife and later Leanne, but when called upon to answer, Rory did not balk. "Yes, I will abide by those terms. In addition, you are right to say that I will not apologise for what I said, for I did not say those things as any measure of my own personal beliefs. You have your own objectives, I agree with them, and want to help you see them realised, and yet, it does not change the present realities. Granted, perhaps in two or three generations you will live to see your vision come to fruition, and I sincerely hope that you do.

"For now, though, it occurs to me that nearly every nation in the known world is run by a man, who is attended by men, and has their government represented primarily by, believe it or not, more men. These are not young men like Captain Archer or Gallin Myakys either, who might be open to giving you equal measure, not as anything more than empty gestures of hypocritical respect, anyhow. The rulers of Drake, Cabathos, Tropuri, the Midlands of Gildriad, and even your mother's home country of the Kingdom of Northern Gildriad, are men of old traditions and antiquated ways. They may need time to adjust to your new method of operations, and many may not come around to you at all. Of course, I am mentioning only the most progressive countries in that list, those being the ones who will even entertain you. Most of the Crescent Isles and Manobius in the Johnan interior would likely oppose you and side with the EMP for no other reason than you are a woman."

Marigold found herself chuckling again. "There it is, Uncle Rory, from your own mouth. If I want to see change in this terrible old world, I had best be the change that I want to see. If it is to take two or three generations, then we should get started straight away, would you not agree?"

"Perhaps, yes," Rory conceded while sounding and looking quite reluctant to push the matter further. "I suppose I am an old man of old ways, myself."

"Putting all of that aside for the nonce," Leonice jumped in while knocking on the desk from where she sat beside Rory, who fell silent and averted his gaze shamefully. "We have immediate matters that need be discussed and most of you are exhausted from travel and in dire need of rest. While I have reservations in triplicate with the daft things my husband has said, I would much like to press on while I still have the patience to do so."

"My aunt is absolutely right," Marigold agreed, with an added notion, "I trust that anything mentioned prior to this was done so in the strictest of confidence. The last thing I will say about it all is that I am going to love whomever I choose, and that person is Freyard

Archer. That settles the matter, and I will not be reopening the discussion with anyone besides Freyard."

She made eye contact with Freyard, exchanging a wink with him and moving the conversation forward before anyone else could revisit the topic. "Our first order of business is to select one amongst us to record the minutes of the meeting. Can I get a volunteer?"

Sybel Mansfield raised a hand, and Marigold took him up on the offer.

Once he produced such from his briefcase and was ready to record, Marigold continued. "With that settled, there should be an exchange of full reports between those of us who went to Pelican Harbour, and those of us who remained here in Daol Bay. If it pleases everyone, I would start. Are there any objections?"

When none moved to oppose, Marigold went ahead. Starting with the first stop of the southbound fleet in Davring Harbour, and Sealord Cunningsbee's connection with the combined armed forces led by then-Captain Marchford and Wynne Nathers' Flying Hawks, Marigold left nothing out. At the point where *The Tidebreaker* was hailed by and engaged with *The Palombs' Pride*, Marigold offered the floor to Freyard, and he accepted the invitation, albeit reluctantly.

He told the room of meeting with the captain of *The Palombs' Pride*, though he could not recall the man's name. The other ship was apparently dispatched to treat directly with Lady Marigold, and they believed that she was aboard *The Tidebreaker*, given that it was first ship to enter the harbour. Freyard claimed that he and Captain Mavril both attested that she was in fact not aboard *The Tidebreaker*, but the enemy captain refused to believe them. The enemy captain's frustrations grew with Freyard and Mavril's requests for *The Palombs' Pride* to dock and accept surrender, and the belligerent seafarer continually yelled for Marigold to show herself. Once the white flags had begun to fly across town, the enemy captain ordered his men to attack *The Tidebreaker* and drag Marigold out of hiding.

Mavril, a Sun's Ranger named Clem, and several sailors aboard *The Tidebreaker* were killed in the initial melee, which had caught *The Tidebreaker*'s personnel largely by surprise. Freyard's testimony continued with his vague recollection of the early stages of the assault, and his efforts to get everyone to cover. Once his memory grew unreliable, he produced a written account that had been scribed by one of his Sun's Rangers. His part ended with his rescue from certain death aboard the sinking enemy vessel. From there, he spoke on Clemence, who was killed, Glendil, who was missing, and the three rangers that survived and their various injuries.

"Perhaps Lady Marigold or one of the others who were aboard *The Princess of Daol* would like to continue the account from here," Freyard offered while slowly setting his back against the chair, closing his eyes, and taking a deep, pained, breath.

"I would be glad to," Greggard stated while leaning forward and clearing his throat. "Before I do, though, I would like to say thank you to Captain Archer for his bravery in the line of duty and his testimony here today. I think a round of applause is in order."

The room responded in kind, and Freyard even offered a quick wave in answer, keeping his eyes shut in the process.

Greggard took the recollection from there, informing Leonice, Rory, Rus, Oire, and the councillors of the gallant efforts of both the sieging soldiers and the Flying Hawks, whose operation led to Nothram's capture. "With all respect paid to Captain Archer and his valiant Sun's Rangers, there were none among the auxiliary units who gave more to the success of this mission than the Flying Hawks. Their losses were numerous, and the injuries they collectively sustained have practically rendered the unit temporarily inactive."

A glance was given to Freyard, and Marigold found him exactly as he had been seconds before, and paying no mind to anything being said by Greggard.

"It is because of the Flying Hawks tenacious capture of Haymard Nothram's home that our mission was ultimately successful while sustaining only minimal losses amongst the infantry units of both sides. In fact, after the white flags were raised, it was only the crew of *The Palombs' Pride* that continued fighting. That quick and decisive ceasefire could only have been possible by the direct strike against Nothram's home by Wynne Nathers' unit."

Oire took a break in Greggard's rousing review of the unit he poached from the EMP and delved into more pointed matters. "Gallin had told Rory, Leonice, and I on the ride here that Haymard, the captain of the town guards, a lieutenant guard, and a single enlisted guard were arrested and brought back to Pelican Harbour. What about those latter two men warranted their arrest?"

"The lieutenant was on duty at the gates on the morning that I arrived in Pelican Harbour aboard the train." Marigold explained to the steward. "Though he was arrested and charged with crimes relating to that incident, I primarily wanted him here as a potential witness. He might be compelled to speak on the actions of the other three in exchange for leniency. The enlisted man is actually a former jailer for Nothram, and was one of two guards chosen to oversee the grotesquery that was on display that morning. The other jailer was felled by Freyard, Glendil, and Dayden as he attempted to kill Moya, having already killed another woman named Bess."

"Haymard Nothram has a wife, Jayellen, and a young daughter," Leonice pointed out, on route to a question. "Is there any word on them? I would trust that they were both traumatised by the operation carried out in their home."

Marigold looked to Greggard, then to Gallin, and neither one moved to answer, leaving it to her. "The daughter is in the care of Lloyd Hardnall, the Captain of House Nothram's guards. The girl requested him and his wife as her guardians, above all others, and Captain Hardnall has been nothing but conciliatory. From what our own men knew of him, and what we have obtained from thorough questioning of the man, is that he was once loyal to Nothram, but that loyalty faded in recent years. He claims that captaining the house guards became merely a job, and he stayed on solely to protect the wife and daughter from the wrath of Nothram. Hardnall states that Nothram was aware that his captain of the manor guards was working strictly to rule, and had removed the guard from his defence counsel some time ago. Although, I should mention that we have been unable to verify that."

"The Flying Hawks encountered Captain Hardnall during the skirmish in Nothram's home," Greggard stated, picking up the account following a permissive nod from Marigold. "One hawk in particular engaged the captain in direct combat outside of the bedroom of the Nothram daughter. Once our man had Hardnall disarmed, he gave up his liege almost immediately in exchange for guaranteeing the daughter's safety. What struck me as odd was that Nothram was holed up in his study with four standard manor guards as his chosen protectors. Meanwhile his captain was only stationed in a defensive position in the hallway. That leads me to believe that either Nothram did not trust his own captain of the guards with his life, or the captain assigned himself to protecting the girl. Either way, it does not paint a picture of loyalty. I have no problem granting Hardnall his freedom and giving him a modicum of trust."

"Jayellen Nothram, however," Marigold began grimly, "Is still missing."

A hand of Leonice's went to her mouth. "Oh no, not poor Jayellen. She is such a sweet little thing. There is not a harmful bone in her body. Please, tell me that someone knows where she is."

Marigold gave Gallin a glance, and he picked up on her meaning clearly. "Unfortunately, Lady Leonice, we have no leads on her whereabouts. She was originally from House Keeves, who are an ally of ours. A niece of Nayle's to be exact, from his second youngest sister. We have sent word to both Nayle, and her father, Ser Clyde Thatch, in hopes that she simply ran away and went to her family home in Gull Coast. We asked every member of Nothram's house staff, all the surviving house guards, any pliable friends of House Nothram that we could find, and no one has seen Jayellen since early springtime of last year. Given that time span, it means that Jayellen has been missing, without a trace and without contact, for nearly a full turn around the sun."

"How can she be gone for over a year without anyone noticing?" Oire asked in bafflement. "Surely Haymard himself would have raised alarms."

"As to that," Marigold addressed the room. "Those outside of the manor thought that Jayellen was simply isolating herself. Many more believe that she had gone back to the Gull Coast to be with her parents. There has been one man, though, who believes otherwise."

"Captain Hardnall, I presume," Oire guessed for all.

Marigold tapped her nose tellingly in Oire's direction, but gave no answer, instead leaving that to Gallin Myakys.

"I questioned Hardnall myself on the subject of Jayellen. Like you, Leonice, I rather like her, and had been worried about her during the battle. Hardnall was unforthcoming during formal, group discussions, but on the last night before we left, he sought me out and asked to meet in the dead of night, at a place of my choosing. We met in the bowels of *The Princess of Daol*, which is vacant now during repairs, but still under heavy guard by our side. It was only when Hardnall was sure that none from Nothram's side could eavesdrop that he told me he has reason to believe that Jayellen is already dead or in the custody of either the EMP or Triarchy."

"Did he say why he believes that?" Leonice inquired in a desperate tone.

Gallin was ready to tell her more. "The former captain revealed to me that Jayellen disappeared in the dead of night when he was off duty. His own guards and the night staff all stated to him the next day that she left the house of her own accord in a nightgown and stocking feet. They all told Hardnall that they tried to stop her, but she eluded their grasp, said not a word, and just walked straight off into the fog, like she was a woman possessed."

The nonplussed look on Leonice's face indicated clearly that she did not believe that explanation for a single minute. "That's their story? That seems a little farfetched."

"It is," Gallin agreed, having further to say on the matter. "Haymard was acting suspect as well, according to Hardnall, and he refused Hardnall's plea to go searching. Nothram's reason for not looking was that such a supernatural phenomenon happening to a noble woman would be scandalous, and that House Nothram could not afford to have it known that Jayellen was missing. From then on, Nothram told outsiders that Jayellen either was not well enough to receive visitors, or had gone home to visit family.

"Hardnall says that he looked into the matter privately, but at the risk of his investigation getting back to Nothram, he could do little more than look about the shores and forests for her. Of course, this search turned up nothing."

"What reason would Nothram have for getting rid of Jayellen?" Leonice wondered aloud. "She was such a demure, passive woman. Surely, she raised no trouble that would warrant death or detainment."

Gallin spoke up again, "Hardnall seems to think that Nothram had simply grown bored with Jayellen, and that he had eyes on a new wife. To bolster that claim, it would seem that as recently as last summer, Nothram was already pursuing a new lady of local noble stock, whose family had beliefs more in line with his. The relationship ultimately petered out, but by then, Jayellen was already long gone."

"No part of that is good," Leonice uttered in sheer despondence. "We need to find out what came of her. Surely, Nothram will spill his secrets if we let him stew long enough."

"I have tasked Major Marchford, who has been assigned to keeping the peace in Pelican Harbour, with launching a proper investigation into her disappearance from there," Marigold told Leonice, inflecting her voice with as much hope as she dared. "Uncle Ken gave Marchford leave to use all assets at his disposal to carry out that operation. Furthermore, we have sent orders to have Nothram, the captain of his town guards, and the former jailer kept in total isolation from both each other and the general population of inmates. While in protective custody, their personal watch will be composed of city guards specifically chosen for their backgrounds in sleuthing. These guards will be authorised to use a variety of means to extract information from Nothram and his conspirators on a few different matters. I should add that I would pre-emptively be banning the use of torture techniques. The investigators, both here, and in Pelican Harbour, will collaborate with one another to the fullest extent to ensure that both teams have all the information we need to properly solve this disappearance."

Marigold cleared her throat, giving herself a moment to collect her thoughts before she segued to the next subject. "While we are still on the topic of Haymard Nothram, I think now is the time to discuss the scheduling of the trials of his cohorts and he."

Counsellor Jaysen Rossadore, himself a prosecuting lawyer for the city, perked up at the mention of potential courtroom proceedings. "Lady Marigold, what is there to talk about? The booking and formal charging of the accused is only now taking place. I would think that we have little to discuss as of yet. The realm judges are currently being promoted to Supreme Court judges of a brand new country. A trial of such a high profile might be a long time waiting to be heard."

"I am aware of that, Councillor," Marigold acknowledged before laying out her wishes. "I was hoping that the process could be expedited somehow. Would you or anyone else be willing to take on the task of seeing to it that their trials occur sooner rather than later?"

"With all due respect, my lady, is there a reason why we would be asking for such?" Jaysen put to her gently.

"Yes, as a matter of fact," Marigold replied in an explanatory tone. "I am of the mind that as this trial gets stalled in the halls of justice, so too does the impact of Haymard Nothram's misdeeds wane. We have a chance to set a new standard in West Illiastra, one where your wealth does not buy your way clear of your crimes. I want both halves of human Illiastra, be they allies and foes alike, to see Haymard Nothram pay for those crimes as every other person in Illiastra would have to.

His stalwart kin and any other Palomb loyalists on the west coast need to be shown what I will do to those who think they can continue operating under the old rules. Can you make that happen for me in a timely manner, Councillor Jaysen?"

He swallowed hard, and began riffling through what looked like a scheduling notebook. "I can move a few things around tomorrow so that I can get a start on that, my lady. However, I should warn you that you will not make any friends in the courthouse with what they will undoubtedly see as pestering behaviour."

"That is a risk I am more than willing to take, Councillor," Marigold said with an understanding nod. "I thank you for taking this task on for me."

"Perhaps we should move on to other matters of a more pressing nature, now," Greggard suggested. "There are things we really do need to talk about and I do have a train to catch this afternoon."

Marigold found it hard to argue with Greggard's reasoning, and there was nothing further to add on either Jayellen Nothram or the trials of her husband and his conspirators for the time being. "Very well, Sealord. The next order of business is to hear from Oire, Rory, Leonice, and possibly Rus, and the councillors on the state of Daol Bay since our departure. Who would like to lead on that front?"

"I would, if the others have no objection," Oire said while standing up and closing his grey suit jacket with a single button. When the other three conceded the floor to him, Oire began by producing a series of papers from a leather-bound folder that he had been carrying. "Not long after your departure, we began receiving letters penned by both Eamon Palomb and Grenjin Howland. I submit them to you for review, my lady. The former writes on the recent news of our successful vote to secede from Illiastra. Or rather, as he calls it, 'an illegal secession'. Eamon claims that though we had a majority of ministers in the Western Realm, we were shy of what he called an 'overwhelming majority', which he believes to be the necessity for such a drastic action. He also goes on to say that seceding requires permission from both the leaders of the seceding realm, the leaders of the other two realms, and the Lord Master to be considered valid."

"Eamon is wholly wrong, Niece," Leonice chimed in confidently. "I organised a small team of trustworthy lawyers, men loyal to Tullivan interests. We sat together at my house and scoured every law book we could find and several versions of the *Illiastran Charter of Rights and*

Freedoms. What we found should silence Eamon's claims of illegalities on our part."

"What Leonice says is entirely true, my lady," Oire vouched on Leonice's behalf. "She and her team presented their findings to me and the councillors and we read every word of their documentation for further verification. As it goes, the three realms of East, West, and South have a level of autonomy that no other delineation of land in human Illiastra possesses. For instance, a city cannot claim sovereignty, nor can a region. Even clusters of regions cannot unify and break away from Illiastra. Such heavy-handed measures however, would create an opening for bad actors to win the Lord Mastership, install a Field Marshal who would do their bidding, and essentially, the rest of the country would be powerless to respond.

"The founders of Illiastra as we know it, who emerged from the ashes of the Phaleaynan Kingdom, agreed with that sentiment," Oire continued on confidently. "To protect against just such an occurrence, they included a failsafe, one that would allow the country to fracture and limit the power of potential tyrants. Of course, as we know now, with Phaleayna's decidedly mixed history with kings, and the attempted seizure of Phaleayna by the Valdarrow brood centuries ago, such measures had great precedent.

"Unfortunately," said Oire, with a tinge of uncertainty in his voice. "Being eight hundred years removed from such events has cost us that first-hand insight. In the wake of that blind spot of ignorance, men like Grenjin's father formed the EMP, and with the help of the Triarchy, staged a different sort of coup than the one Valdarrow attempted. One could even argue that despite the limited bloodshed compared to Valdarrow's campaign, the elder Howland simply built on the foundation of Valdarrow's strategy."

He let his words taper off for a second, while flipping a page among a neatly stacked sheaf before him. "During the early years of the EMP's reign nearly a century ago, we know that they entirely rewrote the *Illiastra Charter of Rights* that our great-great-grandparents had lived under. Nearly everything that had made Illiastra a beacon of the Known World was tossed away and replaced with a theocratic, regressive screed that would have made our founders weep. While we could argue that the *Charter* was altered without proper due process and ratified under suspicious circumstances, such protestations would be ignored with the EMP and the Triarchy. Instead, we have to work with what they left us, and as Leonice alluded to earlier, the EMP left the realms with their ability to fracture. We can only presume why they did that, given that they had a fist-tight grip on the nation. However, I posit that even the EMP were not so foolish as to think that absolute power was theirs forever."

Oire had been gesturing with a single hand while he spoke, letting his index finger fall in the direction of each listener in turn. "The fracture clause was not something that they felt they need fear, but was left intact as a useful tool in the event that their own authority was undermined. Remember, if they could do as much to the Illiastran government of the day, what was to stop someone else from repeating the tactic on the EMP? Their own answer to that question was to institute their patented trifecta of fear, manipulation, and control."

"Then, we came along," Oire reminded the room, while a hand of his fell in Marigold's direction. "Or more specifically, Marigold came along and upended a marriage pact and House Palomb's goal of consolidating all of the power of Illiastra to one family. She does not fear the EMP, they cannot manipulate her, and thus she is immune to their efforts to control her. Without such methods to keep her restrained, there is nothing to stop her from reaching out and making use of the one emergency tool that was left for their use only."

Leonice was standing then too, and Oire gave her the space to speak. "The laws on the matter are clear, Niece. We needed only a simple majority of the realm's leadership in order to enact a secession of the realm, and we had that. The other realms are not required for ratification, as that would defeat the purpose of the failsafe, which is to allow the nation to divide and limit the power and reach of tyrannical governments. Eamon can scramble to remove that clause from the charter, but it does nothing to change the fact that we enacted it before that right to do so could be rescinded. Our secession is lawful and binding. We can feel free to ignore Eamon's declarations to the contrary."

"We all know what Eamon is doing," Marigold stated while remaining seated. During Oire and Leonice's speech, she had briefly scanned the documents that Oire had produced for her specifically, and held them aloft once she had the floor. "He knows full well that we are within the rights of their own laws to be seceding and that his letter will do nothing to sway our position. We should consider that this piece of paper in my hand is likely but one copy of a stack that was sent out to ministers in all three realms."

Marigold let the letter tumble from her hand, where it floated to the table and slid well away from her across its surface. "Eamon is making his case to these ministers for war."

A silence fell over the room, and Marigold took the time to look to each person in turn, as her words hit home with each of them.

When it appeared that none among them wanted to speak, Marigold continued. "For as much power as Eamon believes himself to have, he knows that declaring war on another nation, even us, is something that will require a seventy five percent majority of ministers to vote in favour of. It will then have to be ratified before a jury of Supreme Court judges, and even then will still require Lord Master Howland himself to sign off on it.

"Furthermore, he has no cause to declare war on a nation that attained secession through peaceful means. To market a war to the remaining ministers of Illiastra in the east and south, he would need that much. Even the most ardent and fearful of Eamon's supporters know that war is a costly endeavour that is only afforded in the worst of circumstances. The war hawks among Eamon's ranks will vote for it, sure, but the misers outweigh the warmongers and it is not even a close race.

"Instead, Eamon is banking on making the case that our secession was not legal," she proffered to her counsel. "With a little obfuscation and omission, he can do that much with ease. If the secession is not legal, as far as the rest of Illiastra is concerned, West Illiastra is not recognised as a separate nation. That would mean that conflict with us is not a war of nations and therefore, does not need to go through the same channels to be authorised. In this instance, Eamon can pursue his war under the guise of defusing a rebellion, and West Illiastra will be seen as nothing more than a rogue state of the nation of Illiastra."

"Might I say something, Lady Marigold?" Greggard asked once she finished, waiting until permission was given before speaking further. "By denying the statehood of West Illiastra, Eamon and the EMP can further make the argument to the rest of the Known World that we, as in West Illiastra, are indeed nothing more than a rebel band squatting on land that is not ours. If they succeed in that aim to enough of the world's nations, we would effectively lose the legitimacy of any alliances we could make. Atop that, the national nature of a conflict between two realms of one nation, rather than one nation versus the other, impedes the ability of any other nations to intervene on our behalf, lest they be the ones to make it a global conflict."

Greggard allowed himself a humoured scoff. "I must admit that Eamon's move is as calculated as it is cunning. If anything, this hastens our own need to open communications with the other nations, especially the two in the far north of this continent. If we can get Gondarrius and the Elven Forest to recognise West Illiastra as a sovereign nation and an ally of theirs, it will go a long way toward convincing the rest of the Known World."

"The Elven Forest?" Rory exclaimed with bewildered laughter. "Do you hear yourself, Sealord Greggard? The elves will give us nothing but the pointy end of their arrows. We would be better off trying to secure an allegiance with a herd of elk."

Greggard appeared completely unfazed by Rory's words, and was sitting back in his chair, fingers tented and waiting calmly for him to finish. When silence was achieved, Greggard looked about as he said, "Would it surprise anyone here to know that I have connections of considerable influence in both the Elven Forest and Gondarrius?"

"Not in the slightest," Gallin replied without one second of hesitation. "I would wager that I speak for all here, too."

The remark earned a mild round of laughter from those seated at the table, Greggard included, and he went on with his point. "The dwarves in particular would be greatly interested in relations with West Illiastra. It would mean the formal opening of a border between Tusker's Cove and the Snowy Lands. With that, we could provide a means for the dwarven folk to reach thawed shores, and from there, allow them access to the global market."

The hope in Greggard's voice became evident as he spoke of West Illiastra's northerly neighbours. "Dwarves and humans once enjoyed a prosperous friendship, both before and after the Valdarrow crisis. The EMP, encouraged by the Triarchy, and their fervent belief that the dwarves, as Aren's creations, are impure and incompatible, are the reason that our alliance died.

"My dwarven contacts have indicated that the High Chieftain of Gondarrius and his Circle of Councillors are all amenable to an alliance with any Illiastran human entity that is unconnected to either the EMP or the Triarchy. Even more so, they are willing to lend financial and material aid to parties in rebellion to the EMP. You happen to be the leader of a group that fits both of those criteria, my lady. I would be happy to facilitate a summit between both nations. We might even be able to do so secretly in Tusker's Cove."

"It would be valuable to have any allies, my lady," Gallin advised with a positive tone. "Especially right here in Illiastra."

"I must admit that I am open to the idea of it," Marigold commented ponderously. "If we are going to host a secret summit, Sealord Greggard, how responsive do you think the elves would be to it? I would welcome them to the table as well."

Greggard gave the idea consideration for a moment, but his enthusiasm waned slightly in response. "The elves... That might be trickier to arrange if for no other reason than geographic inconvenience. My dwarven contacts are my primary means of conveying messages to the elves, through the far northern border that both of their countries share. It must be said too that the elves, while considered a unified nation, have a flexible form of governance that is without leaders.

"To give a brief overview for our purposes, the elves appoint a representative for each province in their country through an overwrought process that I do not have the time to explain. Those representatives then convene to form the aptly named Legion of Representatives. Based on the strengths of each representative, they are then assigned to be liaisons between the various departments of the government and the people that they represent. Apropos to this conversation, one of those representatives is chosen to be the Foreign Emissary, who is then responsible for representing the elves on the global stage. At any events featuring world leaders meeting for any purpose, the Elven Emissary is who attends on behalf of the Elven Forest and they, in turn, are as close as we see to any one leader of the elves.

"In our case, that same emissary would be the person to hear our plea. He or she would then return to the other representatives, and explain to them our situation and our requests. Each representative would then go back to their provinces and poll their populace. Once a single, unified decision has been rendered by the province's people, the representatives reconvene and reveal their poll results to one another. If the combined polls arrive at a unanimous decision, then they act on the decision."

Greggard gave a nearly exasperated sigh. "Even then, government-employed elves have the right to decide for themselves individually if they wish to participate in any government sanctioned actions. Therefore, even if the elves agreed to fight alongside us, the number of soldiers and equipment that arrives is entirely dependent on the whims of the soldiers themselves. The whole process seems tedious to us humans, but the elves have perfected their government, even if decisions take a long time to be made. To us, looking in, such an idyllic system seems impossible to implement, granted, and I marvel every time I think about it. However, I am told by my dwarven friends that elves operate on a level of logically driven intelligence that even the brightest humans and dwarves struggle to comprehend."

"What I gather from all of that," Marigold surmised doubtfully. "Is that given that our fight is one that depends wholly on expediency, we can rule an alliance with the elves out."

Greggard appeared reluctant to let hope die, though. "Not entirely, my lady. I would just need your permission to go ahead and open a dialogue immediately. In fact, the first thing I would do upon returning home would be to write letters to both nations and send them out at the first opportunity."

"Consider my approval granted," Marigold allowed without a second thought. "If for no other reason than I want to see relations restored with both dwarves and elves, no matter how long it takes. Amaroshans too, if they still refer to themselves as distinct among their elven brethren."

"The Amaroshan people residing in the Elven Forest are recognised as civilians with the same rights and freedoms as full-blooded elves, though they do retain status as a distinct people," Greggard informed the room. "In fact, in almost all aspects, they are elves. They merely have shorter lifespans and darker skin, on account of the human influence in their blood."

"Even though I was but a child during their exodus, and my father tried to help as many flee as he could, I still feel a weight of responsibility for what happened to the half-elves," Marigold found herself saying, despondence clear in her voice. "I hope that I can help mend the wounds caused by the EMP's wrongdoings towards the innocent victims of their callous, cruel actions."

A smirk crossed the face of Greggard. "I hope that my connections can prove valuable enough to allow you to do just that, my lady."

Oire had raised another letter to get Marigold's attention. "My lady, if I might steer us back to the foreground, in my hand is the letter from the Lord Master. You will find that it is quite different in tone and message to what Lord Palomb sent you."

The letter was passed from hand to hand until it reached Marigold.

As she read its contents, Oire gave explanation for it to the rest of the room, "The Lord Master speaks more personally toward Marigold. His writing style is informal, and although he does indeed say that she is a traitor to Illiastra, and he is going to try her in absentia for crimes relating to such, he asks for her forgiveness."

Brows furrowed and glances were exchanged between those who had been in Pelican Harbour when the letter arrived. All seemed to have the same question on the tip of their tongue, but it was Marigold who asked it, having barely gotten more than two sentences into the letter. "To what does Howland seek forgiveness for, Uncle Oire?"

"For allowing the marriage pact to be drafted in the first place," Oire revealed, earning more shock from those who were not privy to the letter before that moment. "It seems that Grenjin, although resigned to fate, has regrets. Marigold's rebellion and the dissection of Illiastra that resulted, Serephanie's disappearance, even Marscal's sickness, which is no one's fault, Grenjin feels himself to blame for all of it. In his own words, he wrote, 'As the Lord Master, I have failed to keep peace in my country'.

As Oire recited the passage, Marigold's eyes fell upon the words, and she continued reading.

> *The words 'West Illiastra' haunt me now and forevermore. The very name is a blemish on my life's work, a scar I must wear on the back of my hand, visible at all times and difficult to conceal.*
>
> *You should know that I do not blame you for what you have done to escape the clutches of Eamon and his sons. That terrible fate was one that I helped foist upon you and your sister, and I accept responsibility for that. I regret the stress that I caused to your father, who was a true friend whom I failed miserably. His illness, though not inflicted upon him by any one person, was certainly exacerbated by the choices I made and the things that I allowed to happen under my leadership. Marscal Tullivan truly deserved better from me.*

In a matter of weeks, they will rush a trial through at the courthouse in your name. When your guilty verdict is inevitably read in court and you are branded a traitor in an official capacity, know that I will feel myself every bit as judged as you.

For that matter, it is ultimately unfair that you will have to pay the price for my mistakes. I do not deny as much. When that day comes, I will grieve as though it were my own child going to stand before the hangman.

You may feel, as you read this, that as the Lord Master I have the power to end such events. However, I believe you understand, as I do, that our paths are irrevocably altered. I cannot change what must be done to restore Illiastra to a unified country, and I expect that you, in kind, would not allow me to do such anyhow.

To that end, I hope that you do not blame me for the things that I must do to restore Illiastra to the country that my father's party built. It is not my choice, but rather, it is the will of Ios. We will make his kingdom here, and he in return will make Illiastra into a utopia for all his children, but only if we are to make it a kingdom that he feels worthy of presiding over. I truly believe that the image he seeks is the one that my father and the Triarchy have tried so tirelessly to build. I promise you that I will beg Ios on your behalf for forgiveness. I owe you that much and I believe that you deserve the second chance that only our lord and saviour can give you.

"I do not know whether I should loathe old Howland or pity him for the simple man that he is," Marigold uttered flatly, dropping the letter to the table.

Gallin requested the parchment wordlessly, and Marigold turned it over, only glad to be rid of it.

"It is worth considering that he is remorseful at all, my lady," Rory offered carefully. "It might be a sentiment that can play in our favour. Granted, he goes on to say he will kill you if he can, and yet, his lack of willingness is in direct contrast to House Palomb's utter determination to impose their will. It is not much, I know, but it might be enough to cause conflict within the EMP's own camp."

"House Palomb will not hesitate to push Lord Master Howland out if the latter tries to hinder the former," Gallin stated casually, having finished with the letter and given it to Greggard. "Howland is only too aware of that. As the last obstacle standing between the Lord Mastership and the Palomb twins, Grenjin will not dare give House Palomb a reason to hasten his demise."

Leonice had an opinion to share as well, and waited until Gallin was finished before doing so. "I agree with my husband in that Howland's words are worth pondering. However, I feel that we should consider that his differences with the Palombs might be enough for him to entertain the idea of overthrowing their house if he feels that his side is on the verge of defeat. Remember that Grenjin claims that his goal is to unify Illiastra and make amends for what he perceives to be his mistakes. He will not live to see such if we defeat their side in battle. It should be said that though he does not say it outright, Grenjin does seem to prefer House Tullivan to House Palomb. He might consider that living to see an Illiastra united by you is better than dying with regret in his heart."

"That is an interesting insight into Grenjin's mind, Auntie," Marigold conceded contemplatively. "I do not know that I can make peace with Howland any more than I can Palomb, though. Grenjin is a pious man, and he believes in the doomsayer interpretations of the *Proclamation of Ios* as scribed by the current Triarchy. Those beliefs state, as the letter says, that Ios will return and reward those who make Illiastra in his image, and grant them a utopia here in this world to be led by Ios. Of course, what exactly that image is remains open to a variety of interpretations. However, both the current Triarchy and the EMP both believe that Ios desires a nation like the one they built. In this case, I am the antithesis of Ios' image. Grenjin will raze us to the ground to restore Illiastra to what he believes was the correct version of Illiastra. There will be no talks of peace, and if the Lord Master attempts such, we will see it for the trap that it is."

"Will you respond to this letter, Niece?" Rory asked softly, in an apparent effort to hide his own interests.

"I will not, Uncle Rory," Marigold told him quickly and clearly. "I understand your own desire to see no opportunity squandered, but I will not entertain this insulting drivel with a response."

Rory seemed to sink back in his chair then, though he was not done. "If you will permit such, I will go and speak with him on your behalf. I know that I will be able to do so unmolested. As the brother of one of Grenjin's closest friends, I did have a working relationship with the man. For the sake of Marscal, he will not deny me an audience and he will not harm me."

"Consider that request denied, Uncle," Marigold responded with an added fist pressing into the table with an audible thump. "There is nothing to talk about with Grenjin Howland. I know that he thought well of my father, but that courtesy will only extend so far for the brother of his old friend. A brother of a friend, that I might remind you, has joined the rebellion against him. You read the letter. Howland stated that he would let me be hanged. There is nothing to negotiate with a man already resigned to such an outcome, and that is the end of the discussion."

There came no further arguments from Rory, and Marigold moved the conversation forward by looking to Oire. "Uncle Oire, do continue with your report."

"Oh, um, yes, my lady, as you wish," Oire said while getting to his feet again. During the lively conversation between the three Tullivans, he had evidently sat down to rest at some point, unnoticed by Marigold. "We received correspondence from one more man in opposition to us, this time from nearby in Galdourn."

Gallin let out an audible, curious hum at that. "What could Ike Slake want? Was he not at least on his way to Weicaster Bay for Samhais Morton's meeting?"

"We have reason to believe that Mister Slake did not attend that gathering of holdout ministers," Leonice revealed slyly. "He wrote to tell us that Samhais Morton was in fact conducting a meeting in the first place."

"Why in the name of all things would Slake do that?" Freyard asked openly in total befuddlement, having mentally returned to the meeting.

"The loss of Leo Daltis and the Madore Isles leaves Galdourn as the lone holdout region between Tusker's Cove and Dillaney's Bay," Greggard surmised with a wide grin splashed across his face. "He's isolated now, with little manpower and few assets to put toward any sort of defence. Ike is invariably a coward, but he is not a stupid one. He knows that his only chance to stay in power is to play both sides of the standoff in the west."

"Given that Ike has asked for a parlay with Lady Marigold, I would say that you are entirely correct, Sealord Greggard," Oire commented with something akin to a smile creeping onto his lips.

"He may want a deal similar to what I gave to Daltis," Marigold pointed out.

"Most certainly, my lady," Oire agreed, prepping his pen, inkwell, and notepad as he did. "When should I schedule him?"

Marigold considered it for a few seconds, until a date suddenly came to her. "Tell Ike to be here for the elections. I would much like for him to witness first-hand how I intend for this country to operate. Speaking of the elections, I know that is the most important piece of new business before us, but prior to our discussion of that, I would like to hear more about the increased violence in our streets."

"The Triarchists are making both Daol Bay and Portsward dangerous places to be after dark, Niece," Rory explained grimly. "They hole up in their bloody tower and wherever else they hide during the day, and by night, they are assaulting guards and kidnapping anyone they believe to be in violation of Ios' rules. Women and men are disappearing, and many are turning up dead. Most of the deceased are women, I should add. We suspect the men are taken as unwilling conscripts into their growing, burgundy militia."

"Both cities need to dedicate guards and soldiers to specific task forces assigned to dealing with these menaces, Marigold," Freyard counselled out of nowhere with a beleaguered groan. "My Sun's Rangers would be excellent in that capacity. We have experience in sniffing out those sorts of nuisances. You would be shocked at how similar the Burgundy Order is to the raiding gangs. One group just prays a lot more than the other before they get on with their brutality."

"We would gladly accept the assistance from a squad with such insights and experience to add," Keneth relayed to Freyard.

"All well and good, Field Marshal," Freyard confirmed in monotone. "My rangers should be back in the city within days. I welcome the chance to meet with you and yours to form a response plan."

Leanne leaned forward then, resting her forearms on the table. "If Eamon Palomb is gathering an armed force in Obalen, it is imperative that we remove the threat posed by the Triarchists. Our defences, especially in Portsward, are already in a precarious state. The damage that those religious fanatics and any Palomb loyalists in Twin Bay can do from within city walls cannot be understated."

"I would caution against engaging in further clashes in the streets, Miss Mattersly," Councillor Sybel Mansfield spoke up for the first time since the meeting began. "In my district, we are already losing favour with the people on account of the existing violence perpetuated by the Triarchists. If we are to counter their violence without filling the streets with blood, we need a subtle approach to removing the Triarchists and a detailed strategy on what to do with them once they are detained."

"I concur with the Councillor," Ser Keneth said, shuffling through a stack of papers as he did. Producing a document of interest, he handed it down the table to Marigold for inspection. "This report was turned over to me this morning and is but one of many. A woman who was... Um, 'working the street' for a lack of better terms, was approached by a roaming gang of the burgundy brutes and taken against her will. Two patrolling guards heard her screams and responded, finding the brutes in the process of carrying her away. They engaged the brutes, despite being outnumbered six to two. One guard perished. The other lost his sword arm, and though he managed to survive, he was retired from the forces. Though the guards dispatched two brutes themselves, the remaining four members of the mob were able to abscond with the woman."

"According to this," Marigold said while holding up the papers Keneth had given her, "The woman's body was found hanging from a lamppost that next morning on the other side of the city. The surviving guard identified her from her death mask. Before she died, they had whipped nearly every last bit of flesh from her back. The responding guards were so horrified by what they saw of the dead woman that their commanding guard sent them both to a psychiatry doctor. I can only imagine what the civilians who discovered her first thought."

Marigold set the paper down and exhaled every bit of air in her lungs. "Against this depraved thuggery you want me to exercise caution? I should send every last armed man and woman in Twin Bay to the Towers of Ios and have the Burgundy Order dragged out."

"Therein is the difficult part though, my lady," Oire piped in from where he sat on nearly the opposite side of the long table from her. "Though you may personally have little regard for holy sites, the people of West Illiastra are, by and large, believers of the Triarchy. It would be seen as poor practice to desecrate a Tower of Ios by shedding the blood of a holy order on its grounds. We could argue all day that the Burgundy Order and the local Triarchist hierarchy have abandoned all pretences of honour, but the fact will remain that the people still mostly see them and the towers as sacred and untouchable."

"How do the people feel about dead flagellated women being displayed on city property?" Freyard asked with ire in his voice. Marigold looked toward him to find his nostrils flaring and his brows furrowed.

"They are appalled, of course," Oire had started to say.

"Well that's relieving to hear, because I was starting to wonder if the morality of people north of the Varras was as completely fucked up as you were leading me to believe," Freyard said sharply, his piercing gaze held firmly on Oire. "I had to say to myself, 'Freyard, have I been gone so long from the north side of the Varras that I am completely out of tune with the priorities of the so-called civilised world?' Because I know in the Southlands, at least, that the people down there put more value on protecting flesh and bone over bricks and mortar. Then again, when you wake up every morning worrying that the raiding gangs might come down on your town and either kill or enslave everyone you love, you tend to stop giving a shit about a building that some Patriarch splashed water on, talked at, and declared sacred. Oh, and you know what else I learned in the Southlands? A Tower of Ios burns the same as any other damn building, which gives me the sneaking suspicion that Ios doesn't give a shit about them either."

"My word, Captain Archer," Rory gasped as his mouth fell agape. "I think an apology to Steward Oire is in order."

"Not bloody likely," Freyard responded without breaking his stare. "I brought the Sun's Rangers here to save lives, not stones. The Burgundy Order is as direct and unrepentant a threat to your civilians as the raiding gangs are to the residents of the Southlands. As we sit around here fretting about what your people would think of us fighting *around* your sacred towers, those same people are dying because of the men *in* those towers. The Burgundy Order is hiding out in those buildings because they have every reason to believe that we will do exactly as we are right now. Do you not see that we are playing directly into their hands? I am prepared to have my Sun's Rangers dispel that belief. Can I count on your armed forces to reinforce their ranks?"

"Niece, are you going to reprimand Captain Archer for his uncouth behaviour?" Rory exasperatedly queried.

"No, I do not think that I am," she replied collectedly. "Freyard speaks with a boldness that, while many might find jarring, is altogether warranted on occasion. I wholly believe that this is just such an occasion. If anyone can fathom an alternate way of quickly neutering the Triarchists other than besieging the two towers of Ios located in Twin Bay, then please, speak and let your voice be heard."

An inescapable silence appeared to envelope the room at the end of Marigold's open invitation. She watched everyone besides Freyard, who had returned to his restive state, looked between one another, exchanging glances to see which one among them would be first to speak up. It occurred to Marigold that the reluctance of the others to speak was likely due, at least in part, to how brash Freyard had been to those who favoured a softer approach toward the Triarchists. She had to figure that her own unwillingness to curb his behaviour had played a factor in their collective reticence as well.

"Well, if everyone else has lost their tongues, I suppose I'll make use of mine," Leanne decided with nonchalance. "I think one of the first orders should be to decriminalise prostitution," she proffered in open suggestion. "Those participating in that field should be protected, not prosecuted. It is because of those old laws that women were putting themselves in precarious positions to advertise themselves in the first place. I further think that we should legalise brothels, and bring those establishments to the same level of regulation that Marigold's laws were intending to do for bars and taverns. If we legitimise the service, we can keep it relegated to such businesses so that it is largely off the streets, both for the sake of worker safety and for the image of housing such an occupation in a private, professional capacity.

"I recall attending a sermon as a girl where a story from *The God's Gift* of a prostitute was discussed," Leanne went on. "The Patriarch's primary concern with the activity was having young, impressionable eyes witnessing prostitutes on the street in the act of advertising themselves. If that is the problem, helping establish clean, respectable, private businesses in which to do that deed would remedy the patriarch's concern far better than imprisoning the workers. That says nothing about the vile imagery that comes with flaying the skin from their bones and hanging them to die in public purview."

"I think that is an excellent suggestion, Leanne," Gallin agreed following a polite applause. "Such an act of kindness towards an unfairly marginalised group would help build bridges of trust with them as well. It would be prudent for us to speak with that community and help address their safety in these harrowing times."

Marigold thought of something then too, "Many women in that line of work tend to find themselves seeking protection from men of unscrupulous behaviour. If we help establish businesses with reputable proprietors, we can drastically cut down on these strong-armed abusers."

Rus pushed to his feet with a hand raised. "My lady, based on the current subject, I believe I have a suggestion for dealing with the Burgundy Order, if I might."

"By all means, Captain," Marigold said, giving him the floor.

"Yes, well, thank you all," Rus stammered out quickly, before delving into his point. "If we can pass Miss Mattersly's legalisation idea through the necessary legislative bodies on an emergency basis, we might be able to establish contact with that particular workforce without them being fearful of entrapment. Not only could our guards collaborate with the workers to help protect them while bureaucracy runs its course, but the workers themselves might be useful assets for combatting the Burgundy Order in a venue outside of their towers. The workers could be set up in the late hours in places that the Burgundy Order frequent. At the same time, our guards and Captain Archer's rangers, will be guarding from a distance with a mixture of ranged and melee units waiting in the wings. As the mob of brutes step forward to nab the target, our men move in for the arrests."

"A classic trap manoeuvre," Freyard commented in consideration. "That would be an effective method for whittling the Triarchists numbers down. The only drawback is that their headquarters in the towers remains. As soon as our method becomes known, the Triarchy's leadership will simply burrow in and avoid arrest. Of course, we also have to worry about the Burgundy Order catching on to the nature of the traps. They might switch up their targets, or alter their strategy for approaching those targets."

"I would wager that the Burgundy Order has less than one hundred truly loyal men in either city," Greggard estimated carefully. "There are undoubtedly more men under forced conscription who would almost certainly disband if we gave them a path to do so. In fact, if we can catch a few of those unlucky fellows in the traps, they might be willing informants for our side."

Oire seemed to approve of Rus' idea as well. "Small operations such as that would not alarm Eamon Palomb either, I would not think. If we assault the towers, he might view that as an opening to attack our walls. Trapping a few Triarchists at a time though, that would not be considered even a minor incident."

"For the first time today, I think we have reached a consensus," Marigold uttered with cautious optimism. "I am going to go ahead and call a vote on this matter for myself and the city councillors. All in favour of passing an emergency status, city-wide decriminalisation of adult prostitution, show your hands."

Marigold was pleased to see all three attending councillors join her in rising to the occasion, and looked to each of them with a smile. "Very well, the decision passes unanimously. Uncle Ken, I will leave the duty of informing the guard stations of this change to you. See to it that anyone presently charged and awaiting trial for charges relating to the act of adult prostitution be dismissed and set free, if they are still currently jailed."

"Yes, Niece, I shall see to it as soon as this meeting adjourns," Keneth confirmed while jotting in his notebook.

"While that law has time to make the rounds of our city, I will ask that we increase the nightly guard patrols in the areas most afflicted by the Burgundy Order. Leanne, would you be interested in establishing a contact within the prostitution rings? We need a way to gather as many 'workers of the night' as we can in order to draft an effective strategy for combatting the Burgundy Order going forward."

Leanne gave a single forceful nod. "I would be proud to do so, Mari."

"Sealord Greggard, will you be calling a vote on the same measure when you return to Portsward?" Jaysen asked him with a hopeful smile.

"Oh, dear, I suppose there is no point in keeping this a secret any longer, but Portsward has not charged a prostitute for selling themselves since I succeeded my father," Greggard chuckled heartily.

A single eyebrow of Marigold's shot upward, and she was not sure that it was wholly voluntary. "And just how did you manage to do that without the auditors finding out?"

The Sealord extended his arm and gave his wrist a rotation. At the top of the spin, he snapped his fingers, and a silver coin appeared between his thumb and middle finger from origins unknown. "All it takes is a little sleight of hand, my lady. My people are exceptionally good at making those charged with petty crimes disappear."

Greggard continued his explanation while idly eyeing the coin he began rolling over his knuckles. "You see, most of the prostitutes had their charges altered to the petty crime of being an unescorted woman. For those charged under that crime, we had a system in place for dealing with those women quickly. First, we drafted a long, secret list of fake names, sorted in pairs by male and female. Then, we would book the woman under the charge of being unescorted under one of those fake names. One of my few guards in on the ruse would then forge a signature with the accompanying male name to say that the corresponding female was picked up by that non-existent guardian, and a warning issued to both parties. Then, with our paperwork in place, we would simply turn the woman loose.

"Every now and again, we would have to prosecute a woman duly charged with prostitution just to keep up appearances. Yet, even in those special cases, they would be booked, prosecuted, tried, and inevitably found guilty under yet another false identity. After sentencing, which the judges always reserved as short stays at the city jail, the woman, and her real name, would be put on a ship and sent north into the Tusker's Cove region. They picked a village, we shipped them off, and they would agree to stay there for the duration of the jail sentence. On paper, it looked like we had a prisoner charged with prostitution. In fact, they were assigned a cell in the city jail, a prisoner number, and everything else. With that elaborate ruse in place, we simply filed the papers away, for none but a bored, jaded auditor to spend a few seconds looking at.

"If they scrutinised the paperwork at all, they would figure out that even the cell that the prisoner was assigned to did not exist. Despite all of that, there has yet to be one auditor with any interest in conquering the mountain of paperwork that a city jail accumulates. I suppose the moral of the story is to never take for granted what can be accomplished when you make another person's laziness work for you."

"All of that effort just to keep a handful of prostitutes out of jail?" Sybel Mansfield asked with genuine surprise.

"Well, why make them suffer? They are grown women, or even men, in a few instances. If they choose to sell their bodies to other consenting adults, it is none of my concern. We allow people to copulate, we allow them to start a business, but as soon as they make a business out of copulation, we lock them up. Make sense of that for me, Councillor Sybel."

"You certainly make a compelling argument, Sealord," Sybel conceded with a shrug.

Marigold raised a hand to get the attention of both men. "Gentlemen, if I may, I would like to move this conversation forward. Sealord Greggard, despite your own secretive disregard of the EMP's old laws, I trust that you will put the formal legalisation of prostitution to a vote with your councillors at the first opportunity?"

Greggard flipped the coin high and somewhere in the process of catching it, made it disappear from whence it came, revealing an empty hand situated palm upward. "Yes, my lady, it will be done as soon as humanly possible."

Marigold clapped her hands together, and kept the meeting rolling onward. "Fantastic, Sealord Greggard. That brings us to the next order of business, and the final piece to be discussed for the day: the elections to fill the two vacant seats on the Daol Bay city council. I would like to have the elections held in a fortnight from today and no later."

She paused briefly, letting the information have time to settle with her council. "I am aware that this gives little opportunity for a full campaign that a typical election would warrant. Yet as it is city council seats in densely populated and geographically diminutive districts, I feel it is more than enough for such. In the first week, we will give potential candidates the time to decide on, and announce their candidacy, with a deadline of one week from today to do so. For the second week, we would make time for each of the two districts to hold perhaps two public debates each.

"The challenge will be the procurement of quality candidates on such a short notice. While I do not expressly desire for them to be of a mind with my ideals and I will legislate nothing to that effect, we need to ensure that the candidates are at least capable of discretion. To add to that, they must be of sound mind, and that is something I cannot stress enough. Women, of course, are fully permitted to seek election, and I truly hope that we can count on a few strong women to step forward. There will be no upper age limit on candidates, but I feel a lower limit that states that the candidate must be of at least eighteen years of age on the day of the election to be eligible would be appropriate.

"As for voters, anyone, be they man or woman, above of at least sixteen years of age on the day of the election can vote, though they will have to register beforehand, or on the day of the election, to do so. We will draw on the latest census to compile an initial competent voter registry.

"We have lived our lives in the shadow of rigged elections with only land-owning men permitted to vote. None of us has been party to anything different until now, so I anticipate that there will be more than a few hiccups along the way. To iron out as many of the issues as possible beforehand, I want our best and brightest overseeing this affair, and I am willing to allocate as much of the city budget as can be spared to that effort. Are there any questions or additions before we vote on my provisions?"

Gallin raised a hand to speak and with permission went ahead with what he had to say. "Lady Marigold, though I have no voting privileges of my own on your city council, I would still like to think that I may advise you."

"Of course, Sealord, you may freely give counsel," Marigold told him with an inviting wave in his direction.

"Thank you, my lady," Gallin stated appreciatively before pressing onward. "I suspect that Palomb loyalists and perhaps even the Triarchy will put forward candidates of their own, and with enough lies and manipulation they might frighten the voters into giving them seats. I propose that you vet potential candidates to weed out their ilk, for at least this election, at the very least."

"I second Sealord Gallin's suggestion," Greggard added directly after Gallin had finished. "As he said, the ban on candidates associated with the Elite Merchant Party and the Triarchy clergy need not be a permanent banishment. Yet, until such a time that West Illiastra is free from the clutches of both entities, it should be considered."

While she felt much the same way as the two Sealords, Marigold had erred on airing such concerns herself, and let the others know why. "I had worried that such a measure might seem too oppressive and could be used against me by my opponents to give the impression that I desire authoritarian rule."

"Outside of those who are intent on undermining the election to the benefit of the EMP and the Triarchy, I do not think that such a rule would be either unpopular or unexpected in Daol Bay, my lady," Oire commented thoughtfully. "In fact, I would expect to find that most, if not all of West Illiastra that has sided with you would be in favour of that decision. After all, why would we allow the same tyrants you just wrested control away from the opportunity to seize power back? There has to be a grace period in which the influence of the EMP and the Triarchy is allowed to wane, that is only reasonable."

"Very well, gentlemen, I see no further reason to withhold the amendment, if that is your counsel. Councillor Sybel, I would request that you add a temporary banishment on candidates associated with the EMP and the Triarchy to the provisions to be voted on," Marigold commanded.

He heeded the request, and Marigold reopened the floor for further discussion.

"Yes, Mari, I have something to add, though like Gallin, I have no vote in the matter, merely counsel," Leanne said abruptly, garnering the space in which to do so. "We should make a mention, however brief, of the specific locations in which the registration of candidates, and voters, and the voting offices will be. I say this in light of Mister Davisure having informed us that the council chamber is undergoing construction work."

"I had almost forgotten, Leanne. Thank you for bringing that up," Marigold said in gratitude, the issue having genuinely slipped her mind. "Mister Davisure has said that the registration and casting of ballots can be done here in the city hall, out of the offices of the clerks and other staff members. However, we need a venue large enough to allow a large audience to hear the results. I am open to ideas."

"I actually had a thought on that as well," Leanne chimed in again. "Before we made it inside, when you were giving your speech on the steps, you got quite nearly drowned out. However, one soldier on the stage of the amphitheatre managed to cut through the noise. The building is meant for carrying voices, after all, so why not just have folks gather outside in the roadway around the fountain, and we can speak from the amphitheatre?"

"Another marvellous idea," Marigold exclaimed. "It might be a little cold, but with winter on the way out, it should not be overly terrible. Councillor Sybel, I would like you to add Leanne's idea to be voted on."

When no one had anything else to offer, she commenced the voting session for the councillors. Leonice was given Sybel's writing pad so that she might both call and tally the vote on each provision, giving Sybel the opportunity to have his vote counted alongside the other councillors. One after the other, Marigold's rules for the election were called, voted on, and tallied, and by the end, not one item on the list was turned down.

During the voting process, the guard assigned to the hallway knocked on the door and alerted Rus that Sydnee was without, having arrived minutes before midday, as promised. Moya, they were informed, had remained at the manor and was resting while she waited for Marigold to return home.

It occurred to Marigold that she had skipped breakfast and that lunch was nearly upon them. She felt suddenly hungry, and knew the others were almost certainly of the same mind. With all their discussions out of the way and all the necessary councillor votes recorded, Marigold realised that there was nothing further to be said.

She stood up before all then, and called the attention of the room. "With all items on our agenda discussed and settled for the nonce, I move to adjourn this meeting. Do I have a second?"

"Aye," all hands seemed to say in unison, leaving Sybel to pick one among them at random to be represented in the minutes.

"Very well, then. On that note, I declare that this meeting to be adjourned," Marigold stated both clearly and loudly.

Applause broke out amongst those gathered and once it ebbed, Marigold let her voice carry across the room again. "Thank you to everyone who attended today. I apologise for how long I kept you all. I hope to see everyone here next week for the reveal of our candidates. If not, we shall meet again in two weeks when voting commences. Until such time, may fortune find you all."

29

MARIGOLD

The sun was shining through the heavy clouds where it could, water was running off the mounds of snow, and the air, oddly, felt warm. The winter season was far from over and there was undoubtedly more harsh weather to come, and yet, they had found what felt like a spring day in the midst of the ice and snow. It was an anomaly, to be sure, but Marigold welcomed the mild air that lifted her cloak from the southerly Aquas Current.

Marigold had begun her day somewhere around the sixth hour, and had been out of the manor by the seventh. She had rode horseback on Empress for the first time in what felt like forever, with Freyard feeling healed enough to even ride his own horse, Soldier, beside her. With a mixed armed escort of manor guards and Sun's Rangers, the two had ventured together to city hall, so they could take part in ushering forth a new era in Illiastran history. Rolling into the city square with Marigold came quite the procession of horses and carriages, and every member of Marigold's usual retinue were somewhere amongst that group, either in a saddle or a buggy.

Of course, the unintended parade on the morning of the elections drew a crowd of its own, comprised of both people walking on foot, or by whatever means of conveyance they could find. At every intersecting path and road, the line grew, and even more of the citizens seemed to be waiting on their arrival in the town square, until it looked to Marigold that the entire city had converged on the hall. At the city centre there stood a herald, calling directions for registered and non-registered voters to form separate lines outside the gates of the public property. It was there that Marigold and her counsellors and protectors diverged from the masses, making for the connecting building between the city hall and the courtroom complex, where the stables lay.

At the entrance to the stables, Marigold slid from the saddle and straightened herself out. Her black, silk, tapered vest required a little adjustment, though her white tunic and black trousers, both made of heavy cotton, seemed fine. Her chosen boots, a pair of supple, slip-ons that rode to the knee, were amongst the most comfortable footwear she owned. On her hip sat her grandfather's sword, the gems in the scabbard shining as brilliantly as the stainless steel basket hilt.

Though she had several sceptics step forward to air questions and concerns with her decision to carry the sword, none had been successful in their endeavour to separate her from the weapon. Rory and Oire both fretted about any damage that she might incur to what was considered a family relic. Her biological uncle even offered to send for a smith who could forge a new sword for Marigold, one that would be even lighter than her grandfather's rapier and made to her specifications. While she did find that the sword was just a touch weighty in her hand, she reasoned that in time, and with practice, she would develop strength enough to render the issue moot.

The lack of training was Keneth's concern, and Marigold, naturally, tasked Keneth with removing that barrier. His answer was to assign Kandell of the manor guards, a respected swordsman in his own right, to be her dedicated fencing instructor. While she had been given but a single lesson since then, Marigold was content with the arrangement.

In the meantime, there was none who could come between Marigold and the steel, for though she was never without guards; neither would she be without a last line of defence when so many wanted her dead.

Armed with a sabre and pistol of his own, Freyard promised to be her most ardent protector. He was well on his way to returning to full form, too. His foot was still tender, but a wooden orthotic heel attached to a new cast allowed him to walk without crutch or cane and with each passing day, he seemed to be putting increasing weight on the limb. The cracked ribs were still aggravating him with every breath, especially while riding, but those too were lessening in pain.

He was dressed today in a teal button-down shirt paired with a black vest and worn under his long, leather coat. Below the waist, he had donned a pair of loose black trousers that belled from the knee to the ankle, to best conceal his broken foot and keep it warm. Freyard was of the mind that the pants were ridiculous in appearance, but he could not deny that they fulfilled their purpose. Further hiding and heating the foot was an oversized, knitted black stocking.

With his Sun's Rangers having returned from their scouting trip afield, Freyard had his pick of the rangers for guard duty for the day. At present, he was being guided from his saddle by Dayden Vernet, Troygard of the Fog, and two broad young lads named Lahn and Brahn Pharsey. It was the two twins doing most of the work, having all but lifted Freyard from the stirrup to the ground with startling ease.

"It seems that getting out of the saddle was much harder than getting in," Freyard commented to no one in particular as he brushed himself off and got himself right.

"One day at a time, Cap," one of the two Pharsey's said while still holding Freyard's arm at the triceps, apparently not satisfied that Freyard was safely vertical. "Why, you did much better today than you did yesterday in our trial run, even. In a few days' time, I would imagine that you'll be running laps around us."

Freyard shrugged off the grip and moved a few steps away, "Brahn, most soldiers and guards would say that it is unwise to patronise your commanding officer."

"Oh, you know I was meaning no harm, Captain Archer," Brahn replied in a voice that sounded a little wounded.

He limped back in close to the ranger then and drew the hulking lad down to his height. "I know that, and you know that, but in public as we are, a certain level of decorum is expected. We are not in the Southlands or Fort Dornett now. I need all of my rangers to be on their best behaviour."

"Aye, Captain Archer," Brahn uttered with a grin on his face. "You have my word as a Sun's Ranger that I will do you proud."

"I have every bit of faith that you will, Ranger Brahn," Freyard concluded their talk, giving him a clap on the shoulder in the process. He turned then to Marigold, and strode as best as he could toward her. "Lady Marigold, before we go inside, I should ask if I am to your satisfaction."

Freyard paused then, gesturing over his attire with an awkward smirk. "This is, after all, the first time we will be seen in public as a couple. It would do no good for the citizenry's first impression of me to be that of some unwashed woodsman."

Marigold had broken out into a smile and chuckled along with it. "You look resplendent as always, my love. Though I must say, the barber did a wonderful job shearing away the excess wool."

Just the day before, once Freyard's men had helped him into the saddle for their trial run, he led them into town. Upon arrival, and at Freyard's behest, those with the need and the desire were treated to haircuts and shaves at the local barbershop. Freyard himself had decided it was time to return his shaggy locks to their usual short, feathered look. A straight razor had been taken to his beard, and his defined jaw was once more on display. Yet, she had to admit, he wore a beard every bit as well.

Beard or a clean face, either way was fine with me. It was the hair that I wanted cut anyway. Perhaps I am just not used to Freyard with a mane or a tail, but it did not seem right to me.

"And you, my darling, are as radiant as the sun." Freyard complimented, his words nearly being lost beneath a kiss that Marigold planted on his lips as he spoke.

Looking over Freyard's shoulder, Marigold espied what looked to be her entire following, and while most were otherwise occupied, there were a few eyes staring back directly at her and Freyard.

"Shall we make our way inside?" Marigold asked Freyard and the others alike, walking slowly beside her injured hero. At the doublewide, oaken doors leading from the stables to the rear hallways of city hall, Marigold gave a pair of knocks, waiting without for the posted serviceman to answer.

"Yes? Who goes there?" the guard asked while looking out through a door he held barely ajar. "Oh, Lady Marigold, you and your company have arrived. Please, do come in."

The guard stepped back, pulling the door fully open and holding it to hand in the process. "I shall send the next staff person I see to let Mister Davisure know that you are here. Mister Davisure, most others, and I have been here since before sunup, you should know. He has been working tirelessly through long hours to ensure that everything is ready for today."

Marigold raised a hand to stop the guard from following through with his first offering. "No need to send any staff running through the halls. My friends and escorts are all right behind me. We will let Mister Davisure know ourselves. I thank you for the suggestion, though, Guardsman."

"Yes, of course, as you wish, Lady Marigold," the guard relented while resigning to his position.

With Marigold and Freyard in the lead, the band of friends and bodyguards strode in a thundering line of footfalls toward the front of city hall. The round corridor led them through the perimeter of the building, until they came to the access way between the main antechamber of the council chambers and the veranda leading to the front steps. A pair of wooden tables had been set up by the front doors, with two men seated to either piece of furniture. Atop the tables sat stacks of papers and multiple pens and inkwells laid out neatly for the public's use.

Giving the four men directions was Guerin Davisure, dressed in a three-piece, grey tweed suit paired with a white shirt and a salmon-pink bowtie. He heard the approaching ruckus and turned to face Marigold and her retinue as they neared him. "Lady Marigold and her guests, I humbly welcome you all to city hall for this most momentous of days."

"Good day to you, Mister Davisure," Marigold said as she neared the clerk. "I heard that you have long been here preparing. Daol Bay thanks you for your service."

"Oh my, tis nothing, Lady Marigold, nothing at all," Guerin said with a dismissive wave of his wrist. "I must say, I am quite excited to be overseeing an election where the results are actually tabulated and released to the public. My great-great-uncle Clyvis was the last Davisure to have such an honour and that there is a little trivia for you, Lady Marigold."

"That is quite something. I had not known that House Davisure has such a connection with city hall," Marigold commented with an audible hum, feigning her lack of knowledge on the subject.

"Oh my, yes." Mister Davisure exclaimed, before diving deeply, without request, into his house's history. "House Davisure has been a service house to Daol Bay and the old Western Realm in general, going back to our founder. In fact, you and I are extremely distant cousins. The connection is right there in my surname, which was taken by

Charlton Tullivan, the youngest grandson of the third son of Ser Davis himself. There seems to be some confusion around the reason for the family split, but whatever the cause, it was apparently quite the rift. The name itself merges Ser Davis' name with the word 'ure', which in the ancient, dead Phaleaynan tongue, was used as a conjunctive form of the word we know as 'of', so the name translates as 'of Davis'."

Marigold found herself nodding and smiling along, the unpleasant answer to the origins of Guerin's surname coming to her mind as she did. The entire history of House Tullivan was vigorously recorded, and kept in heavy, hardcover tomes that were themselves stored in a vault in the basement of the Tullivan manor. The city librarian and a team of historians visited her home once a year just to curate the brittle, original versions of the collection and add to the newest edition. Everything that the Tullivans and their cadet branches had ever done, good or bad, was in those books. In her teenaged years, Marigold had taken the time to read them all from cover to cover.

"I would certainly love to exchange stories of our familiar families, Mister Davisure," Marigold commented on Guerin's explanation of his surname's origins. "When the events of the present settle into something resembling routine, you and I shall sit and discuss the past. What say you?"

Guerin laid a hand against his chest, closed his eyes, and exhaled, "Oh, Lady Marigold, it would be my pleasure. I believe we have much to discuss on that front, and I never pass on an opportunity to converse with a fellow history buff."

"Fantastic, it is settled then. I shall host our meeting at my manor, and perhaps we will even visit the vault where the records of our families are kept and maintained," Marigold said conclusively, a little surprised at Guerin's impassioned reply. "In the meantime, I have noticed that none of the candidates for the election are here. Are they waiting at the amphitheatre by chance? I do hope they are not, for it seems to be a little cold to be just standing around on an open-air stage all day."

"Oh my, no, no, Lady Marigold," Guerin uttered with a slight stammer in his voice. "They have been sequestered just down the road at the *Brookside Inn*. A small escort of guards is waiting to bring them to the amphitheatre for your speech. The candidates and their protectors are set to depart when they see the doors of city hall opening. Afterwards, they will be escorted back to the inn for the day so that they can wait on the results."

"All well and good, then," Marigold gave in satisfied response, moving on to her next point of order. "Before the doors are opened, I think that I would like a brief tour of the setup for the registration and voting process, if you would be so kind as to guide us."

"Why, yes, absolutely, Lady Marigold. Just give me a moment to finish instructing my clerks and I will join you and perhaps just a few of your followers there," Guerin agreed readily, leaving her company immediately after to see to the employees in his charge.

Marigold took the moment to speak with those in attendance with her and relay what was said between her and the clerk. As she approached, she found Freyard seated on a single chair beside the doorway leading to the antechamber of the city council chambers, his casted foot extending outwards as far as it could go. The chair was largely meant to be decorative, but Freyard's foot and ribs looked to be pressing the issue of practicality over aesthetics. With her attention on Freyard's new position, she at first failed to notice that Gallin Myakys was nowhere to be seen.

"Everyone, come in close to where Freyard is for a moment, I have something to say to you all," Marigold called to her protectors and friends alike, waving to help further illustrate what she wanted from them. "We seem to be missing Sealord Gallin. Does anyone know where he went?"

"The Sealord was called away by one of the city hall guards," Sydnee informed her while indicating where Gallin had gone with a glance in the direction that the group had come from in the first place. "It seemed urgent, judging from the guard's mannerisms. Since you were otherwise occupied, Sealord Gallin, as your chief of staff, went to attend to the matter."

"We have no idea what that issue was, I take it?" Marigold queried with a mixture of confusion and concern.

"Not as such, no," Dayden Vernet of the rangers gave in answer. "The guard who came looking for you was mum on the subject to all but Sealord Gallin, my lady."

Marigold pondered the implications for a second, a dozen different scenarios running through her head, and few of them good. "I see. We shall have to go on without him for now. Keneth and Rus, you two should stay here and wait for Gallin's return. You two can speak with him and determine if the issue is one of security. I will take Uncle Oire, Leanne, and Leonice with me on the tour that Mister Davisure will be offering of the registration and voting areas. Two more of the rangers can come along for protection. Perhaps the Pharsey brothers would care to take the job."

"It would be our honour, milady," Lahn answered on behalf of himself and his brother.

"I am glad to hear it, Sers," Marigold replied to the both of them. "The rest of you may mill about as you please. Avoid the central chambers, as the carpenters and masons are working busily in a dusty and potentially dangerous environment. It is best for all if we steer clear of it."

"I think I'll contain my *milling* to this chair," Freyard commented dryly with an extended exhalation. "You will know where to find me if you need me."

Though amused by Freyard's humour, Marigold felt the need to maintain a professional exterior, and could offer him little more than a pair of raised eyebrows and half of a smile. "Alright, we shall return shortly, for I do not think there will be much to see."

As Marigold suspected, there was little to the tour. Contrary to her estimation though, was Guerin Davisure's loquaciousness. While a simple show of the function of each room and introductions with those seated within at the desks and tables would have more than sufficed, Guerin insisted on giving detailed information on every moving piece and person.

One room was dedicated solely to registering those who had not done so prior to the election date, which Davisure believed to be just a little less than half of the eligible electorate. The other room, which was situated a few doors down the hall and cordoned off by a weaving maze of suspended velvet ropes, was the voting office. Within, Marigold found a team of four city hall workers situated behind desks that were further positioned before a wall of guarded, curtained booths. Each seated employee sat ready and prepared to double check the registration of voters and issue ballots.

The pair of rooms had been decorated with bunting in teal, white, and gold colours. Flags of the golden swordfish astride a teal field sat on brass posts at every feasible location. There seemed to be a story behind every decorative decision, but Marigold was so overwhelmed by all the information being thrown at her by Guerin, that she was sure to forget the vast majority of it before the day was over.

By the end of the tour, Marigold was feeling both tired and peckish. She thanked Mister Davisure for the thorough tour of exactly two rooms, and left him to return to his duties, with only minutes to spare before polls were due to open.

"Folks, let us have everyone back here beside Freyard's chair," Marigold called out to her group, finding them to be either scattered around the foyer or out of sight altogether. The rangers and guards all remained where she left them, and Freyard had done exactly as he claimed he would. The councillors, including her Uncle Rory, were nowhere to be seen, and neither was Moya. Gallin had returned to the hallway, but was now deeply engrossed in a whispered conversation with Keneth. They broke off their discussion of mutually urgent tones and turned to face Marigold at the sound of her voice.

"Before we begin to allow people inside, I would like to address the gathered from upon the amphitheatre," Marigold informed everyone once they were within earshot. "I will take all my guards and rangers for this. The city guards outside should already have barricades and passages set up to allow us easy access to the staging area, but Uncle Ken remains worried about potential dangers in the crowd. On that note, I will request that Freyard, Sealord Gallin, Moya, Leanne, Uncle Oire, the councillors, Aunt Leonice, and I all have protection. The guards and rangers may take a moment to strategize, but remember that anyone looking to harm me will register any of the others I just listed as targets of near or equal value.

"I know that what I am about to say truly bears no need of mentioning to such talented and experienced soldiers, but keep your eyes overhead as much as you do on the crowd. We cannot overlook the rooftops as locations for possible attackers. The Thieves were at home when they were up above, after all, and while I do not regard Lady Orangecloak and her ilk as enemies, our actual enemies might well have learned from their behaviour. Are there any questions? Does anyone have anything to add?"

"Um, Lady Marigold, I might have something to say," Moya uttered from where she stood quietly by Sydnee. "I think it would be best if I stayed back here. Being on a stage might be too much for me, and it will make for one less person that the rangers and guards have to worry about."

Marigold looked into the eyes of Moya, and saw anxiety looking back. It took courage for Moya to have spoken up, Marigold knew, and she would respect Moya's wishes. "Yes, Moya, of course you may remain here. Feel free to go and sit in my office if you would like somewhere quiet to relax. I can assign one of the patrolmen in the back hallway to guard the office door, if you would like."

"I would like that, thank you, Marigold," Moya said with a familiar meekness to her.

Though Marigold truly wanted to see Moya blossoming into the outgoing person that Marigold felt would best serve her friend, she had to accept that it was just not who Moya was. Undoubtedly, Moya had made significant strides in growth and personal development since being freed from the tortuous life she knew before. Ultimately, though, Marigold's goal was to ensure that Moya was given an environment where she could grow into her best self, with all the love and support she could possibly need. "Worry yourself not, Moya. I will see to just that before the rest of us depart."

"I can stay with her for company, if you would like," Freyard chimed in from where he sat, partially obscured from her sight line by those standing near him. "I would rather not be traipsing around out there where everyone can see just how lame I currently am."

"You are temporarily injured," Marigold corrected him softly. "Lame would imply that you are permanently disabled. Yet, if you would wish to remain behind, I do not fault you."

"Thank you, I appreciate that," Freyard said with a contented sigh, his fingers rapping happily on the solid, wooden arms of the chair.

"It should be said that I will hold it against none who wish to remain here," Marigold told her friends and counsel. "We will be directly out in the open, before an audience of potentially thousands. That alone makes it daunting for a number of reasons. Please, say the word and I will grant you leave to stay behind."

Oire was the first to withdraw, and Marigold had expected as much. Councillors Rossadore and Mansfield ultimately decided against the activity as well, opting to watch from the veranda of city hall. Rory was about to join the other three, but when he turned to Leonice for support, he discovered that she was excited to be out on the stage. In the face of Leonice's enthusiasm, Rory withdrew his request so that he might be with his wife.

Leanne and Gallin both decided to travel with Marigold, leaving Keneth and Rus as the lone respondents without answer. When Marigold pressed them, the former responded with the hopes that he and Rus could be excused to attend to urgent matters pertaining to their stations.

"If these matters are as pressing as you say, Uncle Ken, then I will not keep you and Rus from doing what you must. As for everyone else, form up and let us be on our way," Marigold instructed. "Lahn, Brahn, I will have you two in front. Keep enough space between you that I can be seen by the people. It will not do for me to be hiding away in fear."

Freyard whistled a low tune to get the attention of his rangers, the six of whom comprised the bulk of Marigold's current guard. As their eyes all went to Freyard, he gave them commands of his own. "Keep her safe, lads. Troygard of the Fog, you have the command of the rangers out there. Dayden, you are his second. Thorne, Westin, you are here because you are my most trusted scouts. Your skills will be of benefit today. Report anything suspicious that you see. Lastly, Lahn and Brahn, for the sake of all things, behave out there and let no one close to Marigold unless she gives her say so. Am I understood?"

"Aye, Captain," the six answered in unison.

Representing Marigold's manor guards were Sydnee, Elden, and Kandell. Brandyl, who had only recently recovered in full from his injuries, had been left behind at the manor with a compliment of city guards to watch over the home.

Following Freyard's briefing of his men, Marigold had approached his chair and leaned in for a kiss. "I will be back soon, my darling."

"And I will be waiting," Freyard replied while returning the kiss. "I love you. Stay safe."

"I love you too. Rest up," she gave in response, leaving him with a caress of his smooth jawline.

"Everybody to their positions!" Marigold called out to the entire room, entourage or otherwise. "The doors to city hall will soon be open, and voters and registrants will be piling in from now until the seventeenth hour. Here is to a new day in Daol Bay, my friends. May we soon see it spread to all of West Illiastra."

With the Pharsey twins taking their places just before the double doors of city hall, the remaining guards and rangers began to form up in pairs. By the time they finished, there remained enough space between them for Marigold and the others to line up in single file.

"Gallin, I would like you up front near me, please," Marigold requested of the sealord, and without complaint or query, he obliged. She turned her attention then to Guerin. "Mister Davisure, are you and your people prepared?"

"Just so, Lady Marigold," he called back with a high wave. "You may open the doors at your leisure."

"Make it so, Lahn," Marigold commanded with a deep breath.

The twin stepped forward wordlessly, turned the deadbolt in one of the doors, and pushed it outward with a groan of the hinges.

The racket of the door was quickly forgotten, as a great rush of applause and raucous cheering came barrelling at them from the gathered mass of citizens outside.

Though she was left in awe at the response, Marigold managed to urge the Pharsey twins forward.

On the veranda were numerous city guards in their teal uniforms, and as Marigold's group began to walk toward the steps, the contingent of city guards followed in near lockstep. At the bottom of the stairs, they were met by the Major of the City Guards, Lyson Crewe, who gave a salute as he greeted her. "Lady Marigold, I bid a good morning to you. Are you prepared to make your way to the amphitheatre?"

"Absolutely, Major Crewe," Marigold gave in answer, having to shout to be heard above the unyielding roar of the crowd. "We go when your guards are ready."

Lyson Crewe was a muscled man in his forties who looked like he had never missed a day of exercise. Beneath his taut exterior, Marigold knew him to be a man of diligence and compassion, and he had served for years as an officer in the ranks of the city guards. As Marigold took note of him, Major Crewe was issuing a clear command for his guards to usher Marigold's group to the path that they had built to the amphitheatre.

A single guard gestured for Marigold and her company to follow, and they did just that.

The major joined the group briefly, giving instruction to Marigold once he could go no further. "The path narrows along the way. You will have to walk two by two. Make sure to put your own guards on the side facing the crowd, and those of you to be defended on the side that faces city hall. May fortune find you, Lady Marigold."

"Thank you, Major Crewe. We will do exactly as you suggested," Keneth responded while reorganising the group to suit the passage.

Marigold was still in front, with Brahn ahead of her and Lahn at her side. The barricades were merely constructed of wooden beams extending well above Marigold's head, nailed together with horizontal braces, and further covered with vertically arranged slats. The thin, pine boards were spaced far enough apart that Marigold could see the gathered masses beyond, and they in turn were looking back at her.

"I can see her!" a woman declared.

"It's Marigold! Right there in the flesh!" another cried out.

The exterior façade of the city hall gave way to the side lawn, and shortly after, to the old orchestral pit of the amphitheatre. A tiny set of worn steps led into the musicians' seating, and more city guards waited to lead the group through it and to the stage.

The old, wooden platform was further guarded with riflemen standing at ease at each of the four corners, their eyes scanning the skylines on either side of the city centre. At the front of the stage stood five people divided into two groups made up of three and two, with each group protected by three more guards.

Upon joining them, Marigold stepped forward and took the time to greet and shake the hands of the members of each group. The trio was made up of two men and a woman, all of them running for election in Marswell Caveth's old district in the northwest corner of Daol Bay. The two vying for the City Core District, formerly held by the retiring Elbert Swylen, were both men, and one of those was Elbert's own son, Nelson.

Marigold stood back from the five and walked gracefully toward the front of the stage, where she remained flanked by a combination of the Pharsey twins and Freyard's scouts. The crowd became altogether deafening, and it took several minutes of Marigold gesturing for quiet before she could earn their silence in full.

Clearing her throat, Marigold let her voice ring out, her tones being carried forward across the city centre by the dome of the amphitheatre. "Ladies and Gentlemen of Daol Bay, I am beyond honoured to be the first to welcome you to the new era of West Illiastra!"

The audience responded with more hollering and clapping, and it seemed that minutes went by before Marigold could speak again. "Today, as the individual men and women of Daol Bay, you will be given the chance to have your say in the governance of our fair city. No more will it be only land-owning men. No more will votes against the grain be discounted. This is your city, and its future will be decided by you."

During the opening sentence of her speech, Marigold had begun pacing about the stage, a tactic advised of her by Freyard during their preparation talks. He insisted that by walking about, Marigold would make for a slightly more difficult target for potential assassins.

"Standing to my left this morning are five people who would each like to represent you. Over the course of the past week, each of them have been given the opportunity to tell you not just who they are, but what they intend to do as your elected city councillor. Now, their fate rests in your hands. Your ballots will decide who represents you, your neighbours, and your district for the next five years.

"Come forward, candidates, and greet your electorate," Marigold bid while waving the five of them to where she stood. Positioning the candidates on either side of her in their same pairings, Marigold began the introductions. "To my right are Leland Orentian and Nelson Swylen, and they are running for the seat in the City Core District, which is where we now stand. Nelson is the son of retiring Councillor Elbert Swylen, and the current owner and proprietor of *The Swylen Family Lumber Wholesale*, one of Daol Bay's oldest and most respected businesses. Competing against him is Leland Orentian, a tailor in the employ of *Byrne and Power Menswear*. I have no doubt that many of you before me are wearing clothes made by his steady hand. Mister Orentian and Mister Swylen are both well-known figures in their district and in the city proper, and they come before you today with the mutual desire to be the Centre City District Councillor.

"To my left, I introduce you first to Jon Horne, who most of you no doubt know as 'Skipper Jonny', the captain of the north side's fishing fleet. Beside him is Doctor Xavier Fielding of the Crowell Road Clinic. Lastly, but certainly with no less aplomb, is Leilana Cooper, a housewife with aspirations to pursue a higher education that was previously denied to women. I believe I can easily say that they are three highly eligible candidates, each of whom are worthy of your support."

While Marigold was certainly obliged to show no biases towards any of the nominees, she certainly had her own private opinions on all of them. From having attended both the registration of the candidates and the two debates that each region had held, favourites of hers had emerged.

The junior Swylen had proved in both of his debate performances that he was looking to implement tax law similar to what the EMP already had in place. Of course, he advocated for such legislation out of personal interest, as they were of substantial benefit to large corporations like the Swylen's lumber business. He argued that doing as the EMP had already done, in tandem with Marigold's more socially prudent policies, would ensure that companies like his passed their savings on to their employees. However, nearly a century of the same practice in Illiastra had produced results that contradicted what Swylen claimed. Simply put, the EMP tended to charge no taxes to the largest companies and their ownership and management. In the event that taxes were charged, the money was swiftly returned. The practice served only to funnel money away from people and services that needed them the most and put it back into the coffers of men who proved themselves to be only hoarders of currency. Marigold knew that Nelson Swylen was not so daft as to believe what he was pitching, which left her with the conclusion that he was hoping that the voters would fall for the scheme.

Debating opposite Nelson Swylen was Leland Orentian, a working class man with the belief that businesses had to pay their fair share in taxes. To begin the process of correcting the wage inequality, Leland put forth a legislative proposal in two parts. The first step would see a higher tax rate be levied on the wealthiest companies. The second part would see the institution of a legally mandated bare minimum wage, one that would be adequate enough to ensure that every worker earned enough to survive. Despite being from a family whose business interests would be doubtlessly impacted by such policy, Marigold happened to agree with ideals of the humble tailor.

In the northwest region, Marigold's preference was for either Leilana Cooper or Doctor Fielding, with a slight advantage to the housewife. Both candidates boasted a progressively robust approach to governance, and Marigold would be fine with sitting in council with either one. What tilted Marigold's preference to Leilana was that Marigold saw herself in the impoverished woman. During the first debate, which Leilana attended in a dress that was mended with miscoloured patches, Marigold came to realise how her own enriched life had afforded her the means to do what those like Leilana would never have been given a chance to do. Despite the fact that she was disadvantaged on account of being a woman, Marigold's wealth and status had allowed her to soar over barriers that she was not even aware of having passed. Leilana had been offered no such advantages, and her candidacy, and the courage she showed in stepping forward at all, reminded Marigold of just what her surname and finances provided.

Marigold was not about to deny that the doctor had no doubt worked hard for his own achievements. However, even though they towered above Leilana's comparatively meagre deeds, Doctor Fielding had the distinct advantage of being born into the Known World as a male. Where Leilana had to struggle to teach herself to read, and was prohibited from publicly exhibiting that skill, Doctor Fielding had been required to attend schooling in his youth and was encouraged to continue his education into adulthood. Doctor Fielding's own intellect and an admitted amount of hard work had opened the doors to his medical profession, and no one could take that away from him. However, the fact remained that Doctor Fielding had the privilege of knowing that those doors could be opened in the first place.

As far as Leilana was concerned, those doors were sealed shut, locked tight, and heavily guarded to keep her from so much as trying the handle. In Marigold's eyes, that determination to surpass overwhelming adversity put Leilana Cooper and her progress in the same light as Doctor Fielding's work.

Leilana could possibly become a doctor in her own right, if we can knock down the doors that have been barred to her. It will take time though, and possibly the rest of my life just to make any headway. The Thieves and Lady Orangecloak attempted a start, and I commend them for trying, but now it falls to Leilana, Leanne, Leonice, Moya, and I to pick up where they left off and continue the battle.

Those thoughts went through Marigold's mind as she glanced over Leilana, today garbed in a sleeveless cobalt blue dress trimmed with white and gold. A white blouse was worn beneath, and a plaid, hooded cloak topped both articles. To complete the ensemble was a pair of white, woollen mittens, serving to keep her hands warm as she waved to the gathered. Every part of it had been paid for anonymously by Marigold, the funds going directly to the best tailor that Marigold could find in close proximity to where Leilana lived.

Today she looks every bit as proper as the others do. I only hope that I get the chance to know her further.

Though Marigold had wanted to sit and speak with Leilana, and even Leland, every single one of her advisors counselled against it. They feared that bias and prejudices would be shown, and that such favouritism had as much a chance to harm Leilana and Leland's elections chances as it did to help them. In the name of fairness, Marigold had abstained from contact with any of the nominees over the past two weeks.

As the cheers began to subside, Marigold thanked each candidate again by name, and instructed the city guards to lead them back to the *Brookside Inn.*

Once the stage cleared, Marigold looked out across the audience once more, and raised her hands for quiet. "Ladies and Gentlemen, before we open the doors to city hall, there is but one more thing I would like to speak on. Every day I hear the voices of the many crying out in unison, as though the streets themselves are weeping. As the dawn breaks each morning, I am brought reports of violence carried out in the darkest hours. I want you to know that Field Marshal Keneth Arisborough, Major Lyson Crewe, Captain Freyard Archer of the Sun's Rangers, and all of the officers, guardsmen, soldiers, and rangers in their command have been working tirelessly to bring that wanton violence to heel.

"The Triarchy may try to plague those of us begging for a world free of their iron grip, but I assure you that their sickness will be stopped. On behalf of everyone working to win the battles on our streets against the Triarchists' terrorism, I thank you for your patience and efforts to assist us in the battle. I ask of you, our fine citizenry, that you continue to report activities related to Triarchy extremism. Together, we shall show those who would invoke terror in the name of Ios that we shall persevere!"

The response from the crowd came at Marigold like a blast, blanketing every part of her with pure sound and energy. Her eyes closed and she felt them all, women and men alike, shouting in wordless gratitude.

Marigold raised her hands and brought their collective volume down to where she might be heard again. "Before I give the order, let me ask one more thing of you all: please, be orderly and polite today. The lines will move, and so long as you are in line before the seventeenth hour, your ballot will be issued. With that said, and without further delay, I give to you, the people of Daol Bay, and West Illiastra after us, the grand opening of our first uncorrupted election in almost a century!"

From over at City Hall Marigold could see Major Crewe calling for the gates of the makeshift barricade to be pulled aside, and at once the voters began to pour through. Marigold watched from upon the stage as the lines of citizens climbing the steps of city hall emerged from the mass on the street, trickling forth like the sands of an hourglass.

"Well, my lady, I would say that was a rousing success," she heard over her shoulder, turning to find Gallin Myakys standing with his hands behind his back. "I recommend that we return to city hall ourselves, perhaps by going behind the amphitheatre and around the courthouse to the stable entrance. Trying to get through the crowds would be inadvisable."

"That sounds like the best idea, Gallin. Come, walk with me," Marigold bid him before assembling the rangers and guards all about her again.

The members of her entourage lined up to congratulate her on a fine speech, and the group then got underway as one. Behind the amphitheatre stage there sat a small wooden structure reserved as a changing and rehearsing space for actors using the outdoor stage. Walking through that building, the group came to a quiet little back road that cut through the side yard of the city hall and courtroom complex.

As they followed the tiny path, Marigold leaned in close to Gallin for as private a word as the current arrangement would allow. "Sealord Myakys, I must ask, what were you called away to attend to earlier in city hall?"

"Oh that?" Gallin asked rhetorically. "It was nothing to worry over at that moment, my lady. Ike Slake had simply arrived from his hotel accommodations and was looking to meet with you. It seems he showed up with a handful of his personal guardsmen, and I conferred with the Field Marshal to determine the best course of action for what I felt were armed men of uncertain loyalties."

"And what did you two decide?" Marigold asked him quickly.

"The Field Marshal sent the local patrols to give Mister Slake's men the choice of disarming or leaving the premises. I should add that no one informed me of a decision being made either way before we left the building. What I can tell you is that Sers Keneth and Rus had remained behind at city hall so that they might determine Slake's intentions."

The arrival of the soon-to-be former Galdourn minister had been in the back of Marigold's mind since his ship had reportedly landed at the south side quays two days past. From the moment he disembarked, Slake had holed himself up in the *Daol View Hotel* and refused to meet with Marigold. The same two scouts of Freyard's that were guarding Marigold had been assigned to watch the hotel, and patrol guards stationed in the area were ordered to report any of their own sightings as well.

What had unsettled Marigold was that the scouts and patrols came back with nothing to offer her. All hands reported that no one suspicious seemed to have entered the hotel, but neither did Ike leave it. All that Marigold knew was that he was there, with a servant and several guards in tow. There was also no sign of Ike's wife or teenaged son, just he and his party.

"I suppose that I should meet with Mister Slake first and foremost, then," Marigold decided, a slight feeling of unease coming over her. "Where did you leave him, Sealord?"

"In the private meeting chambers, my lady," Gallin revealed, his own tone taking on a measure of concern. "Both the Field Marshal and I thought that it would be the best way to contain him subtly, lest he grow aware that we were intentionally cordoning him off."

"That was probably for the best," Marigold replied, her mind racing with the possible directions that her discussion with Ike could take. "I think I will have him moved into my office, with two guards positioned directly outside the door. The Pharseys would serve best, I should say. Two identical strongmen standing watch over me should be enough to keep Slake honest."

"Would you like me to join you as well?" Gallin inquired, though he seemed to know the answer already.

"I would rather speak with Slake without any accompaniment, Sealord, though I thank you for the offer," she confirmed. A slow nod in response from Gallin indicated that it was what he expected, and Marigold went on. "If I put another man in the room, Slake will almost certainly speak solely to him and ignore me entirely. I would like to give him no such chance to undermine me."

Gallin hummed aloud thoughtfully. "I would have counselled the same, my lady. Not to worry about me, though, for with you otherwise engaged, I will be busied as your surrogate. As will Oire too. If you would not mind, might I change the subject briefly, my lady?"

Marigold was taken by surprise by the shift, and allowed it with piqued curiosity. "Yes, of course. What is on your mind, Sealord?"

She looked to Gallin, as silence fell over him, and discovered him deep in pained consideration. After a few seconds, he seemed content and began with what he had on his mind. "Our latest correspondence from Sealord Greggard indicated that he was having difficulty contending with the Triarchists in Portsward. As you well know, Portsward has only crumbling defences that would not inhibit even a bandit gang from accessing the city. I would argue that it is our obligation to assist, and though I am loath to criticise your decisions, my lady, you have yet to respond to Sealord Greggard's request. We both know that Sealord Greggard is a man of great patience and understanding, but inaction on your part might reflect poorly in the eyes of Portsward's populace."

"When our elections are over, and the new councillors have been selected, I will send soldiers and any other aid that Sealord Greggard and his people require," Marigold explained to Gallin, hoping that her voice did not sound angered in its delivery. "The events of the election required a higher presence of security forces than usual. These larger gatherings would have been prime targets for Triarchists and EMP loyalists to attempt to strike terror into Daol Bay's people. I believe fully that our extra patrols and guard stations made those extremist fringes of society think twice about attacking. Although, while saying as much, it dawned on me that it is impossible for us to know whether they would have launched an assault. You have to admit though, setting the traps for the Burgundy Order has led to a marked downturn in violence in the past week that we have been implementing the measure."

Gallin was nodding quickly in response, his words following shortly after, "Of course, my lady. We even managed to free a few conscripted members of the Burgundy Order in the process. I should also add that Miss Mattersly is to be commended for her swift unionisation of the midnight workers. That could not have come together any better."

"You should tell her as much yourself, if you have not already, Sealord," Marigold encouraged him, looking back over her shoulder at Leanne as she did.

"I have, my lady, to be sure," Gallin informed Marigold hurriedly, before she could say anything to Leanne. "I speak with Miss Mattersly often, and the subject came up on the morning after the first successful trap was sprung. I mentioned it because I feel that Leanne's role should be given recognition in our next meeting."

A slight laugh came over Marigold, and she looked up to see them rounding the opposite side of the building then, on what was considered the front entrances to the courthouse. "Yes, of course, Sealord, consider it done. I always give credit where it is due."

The street served by the courthouse was oddly quiet at that hour and Marigold saw only a scattered few people strolling along the sidewalks. As she looked in either direction of the road, there appeared just to be one horse and rider on the cobblestones as far as the eye could see. The difference from where Marigold now stood and where she had been moments ago on the other side of the complex could not have been a starker contrast. The tall maple trees looming overhead canopied the street, and though they were bare of leaves in the late winter, they still managed to make the sunlight dance on the roadway below. The air felt calm, and only traces of the sea salt could be detected. Marigold found that it was the quietude that she could not shake. It was as if the pair of conjoined structures had absorbed all the noise coming from the mass of humanity standing in the city centre, leaving the swaying trees and the snowbirds to attempt to fill the silent void.

"Hold up, lads," Marigold bid the Pharsey brothers as they came to stand before the staircase leading to the courthouse porch.

"Everyone, I would like to propose that rather than walk all the way around the complex to the stables on the east end, we should venture through the courthouse and to the overpass that links the two buildings. The courts should not be in session today, on account of the election, meaning that it should be near empty. Are there any objections?"

"None whatsoever from me, Niece," Rory answered with a sigh. "A shortcut would be most welcome."

Most of the party spoke up in similar favour of the act, with the remaining members having no opinion at all.

"Right then, follow me," Marigold beckoned to them with a wave. "Lahn, Brahn, could you go on ahead and get the doors?"

The twins obliged with a simultaneous response of, "Aye, my lady."

Inside the courthouse was a lone secretary tasked with informing people that the courts were closed and issuing a date and time in which events would resume. The young man, seated at the tall, circular desk in the middle of the foyer floor, gave Marigold's party only brief consideration, and let them pass without question or concern. With no one and nothing to take up his time beyond Marigold's party, the young fellow returned his attention to a novel he had been reading.

Marigold led the way from there, directing the Pharseys walking ahead of her on which way to turn and which doors to open. After a short series of connected hallways, the group came to the unmistakable passage that connected the courts to city hall.

Large panes of glass set in both the walls and ceiling allowed the tunnel to be strikingly well lit by the daylight. A wall of warm air even managed to greet them, the heat from whatever flickers of sun were managing to break through the clouds being held in by the glass.

They passed through quickly, walking through a wave of warmth before arriving back in the embrace of city hall. Once there, Marigold called Elden forward and sent him onward to relay to Keneth and Rus her order to relocate Ike Slake, and by proxy, Moya and Freyard.

"Uncle, Auntie, Leanne, and Gallin, I think now is a good time to break for the morning," Marigold announced to the four of them. "I encourage you all to mingle about and observe the events for me. We will all reconvene for a group lunch in the private meeting chambers at approximately the twelfth hour. Thank you all so much for joining me at the amphitheatre. This has the makings of an exciting day and I am thrilled that I get to spend it with you all."

Leanne closed the gap between her and Marigold and leaned in close. "Are you sure that you do not want me to come with, Mari? I heard you saying that Ike will disregard you if a man is present, but what is he to do with two women to answer to?"

"I think it will be best for me to deal with him alone. I do appreciate your offer though, Leanne, thank you," Marigold told her friend in regrettable declination. It was a tempting proposition, though Marigold felt that any number beyond one would be seen as handicapping Slake, who would already be neutered without his guards.

"Leonice, love, I was thinking that perhaps I would get some work done in my office down the hall," Rory suggested to his wife. "You are free to join me, though I suspect you might not be interested in watching me fill out paperwork."

"Nonsense, my dear," Leonice replied to him with a dismissive flick of her wrist. "Perhaps I can even help you file through it all quicker. Come, we will start in on the task immediately."

"Well, if there is no further need of me, then I am going to go watch the voting and registration areas for a bit to see how things are coming along," Leanne declared. With a final wave, she walked off with Rory and Leonice down the opposite side of the hallway from where the private meeting chambers and Marigold's office lay.

"I might as well go with Leanne and oversee things," Gallin said to Marigold with a shrug. "If I can be of service, do not hesitate to send for me, my lady."

Marigold gave half a bow to the sealord. "Thank you for your counsel earlier, Gallin. I will see you at luncheon."

They parted there, with Freyard's scouts and Troygard of the Fog leaving as well, so that they could offer further support to the guards at the front of city hall and watch for potential threats. The remaining defenders, comprised of Sydnee, Kandell, and the Pharsey brothers, followed in tow with Marigold as she headed for the private meeting chambers.

At the door of the chamber, they were met by Yarohmer Stylford, Freyard's second-in-command and the eldest active member of the rangers. The closing door to Yarohmer's hand gave indication to Marigold that he was in the process of leaving the room. "Lady Marigold, what a pleasure it is to see you today. How do you fare? I heard that your speech outside on the theatre stage was a rousing success."

"Good day to you, Ser Yarohmer," Marigold gave in reply. "I am glad to hear that my words were met with good reception. What is the status of things back here?"

Yarohmer was forward in his answer, "A guard just came through with orders from you to see to it that the fellow named Ike Snake was relocated to your office. I was just going to find the shy woman to let her know that the office where she is resting was needed. Would you care to join me?"

"Not to be pedantic, Ser Yarohmer, but Ike's last name is Slake, and the *'shy woman'* is Moya Starboard," Marigold corrected him with amusement in her voice. "Nevertheless, yes, I was just going that way myself. Is Mister Slake within the chambers still?"

"No, we sent him from the room a while ago and he told us that he was going to go fetch a cup of tea from the canteen room. Worry not, though, there's a city guardsman that went with him in escort, and the canteen itself is further guarded. You see, the reason we sent him out in the first place is that the reports from last night's watchmen have come in. So, the Field Marshal, Freyard, your captain of the house guards, and whoever else of us officers that were available are holding an impromptu security meeting to discuss what was found. Shall I send someone to bring Slake back?"

Marigold thought about it for a second, and turned to her manor guards. "You lads all know what Slake looks like, who among you would like to go get him for me?"

"I'll take care of it for you, my lady," Kandell offered quickly, his hand raised at the elbow.

"Very well, the task is yours, Ser Kandell," Marigold allowed, returning her gaze then to Yarohmer. "Off we go, Ser."

In a dozen or so steps, they were before the door of Marigold's office, and within Marigold found Moya, as expected. It appeared that she had pushed the cushioned, high-backed chair usually situated behind the desk over to the window and had made herself comfortable there. From what Marigold could see outside, Moya looked to be watching a large flock of starlings as they searched the bits of bare ground and grass for a meal.

"Hello, Moya. How are you faring?" Marigold asked as she stepped into the office, earning her a swift pivot in the chair from her friend.

"Oh, Marigold, I had no idea that you were back," she stated while standing up. "I saw you all walking across the lawn some time ago, but I was not sure where you went after that. How did your speech go?"

"I felt it went well, thank you for asking, Moya," Marigold said with a smile.

"Here, let me put your chair back behind the desk," Moya said while lifting the piece of furniture. "I was just birdwatching. I did not think you would mind if I used your chair."

"And certainly I do not mind, Moya," Marigold informed her reassuringly. "At the moment though, I need my office for a meeting with Mister Slake, who should be due at any moment. Are you hungry, perhaps? There should be plenty of baked goods and beverages in the cafeteria today."

"I might like some tea, yes," Moya decided while walking around the desk toward the door.

"Fantastic. Oh! Why not take Sydnee and Elden with you?" Marigold asked as an excuse for such arrived to mind. "They would just be waiting around outside the door otherwise, and the Pharsey twins will more than suffice for that job."

"Oh, well, if you can spare Syd and Elden, I would be only happy to have them for company," Moya accepted with a beaming smile from ear to ear.

Unsurprising to anyone at the Tullivan manor, Moya and Sydnee were officially in a relationship. What did surprise both Marigold and the associates of Sydnee was that he settled down at all. However, it certainly seemed that Moya was a great match for him, and they got along famously.

I suppose it is as my mother used to say, 'Love abounds in the strangest of places', Marigold reminded herself as Moya left for the company of her new beau and Elden. "I will see you at luncheon, Moya!" Marigold called down the hall to her friend, finding Kandell rapidly approaching with Slake at his side.

A notion occurred to Marigold then, and she directed it to the senior ranger in her company with a whisper. "Yarohmer, when you return to the chambers, let the others know that I am in the meeting with Slake. If I am not out by lunch, and you do not hear from me or the Pharseys, send someone to check in on us."

"Yes, of course, my lady. I was starting to wonder why I came to your office with you after all, but now I feel like the trip has a purpose," Yarohmer said while exiting. "Well, I shall leave you to it. Enjoy the rest of your morning."

"Good morning, Lady Marigold," a voice called out before she could say anything further to Yarohmer. "I must say, that was quite the performance this morning."

Marigold's eyes fell on the visage of Ike Slake, clad in a light grey suit with a matching derby hat tucked under his arm. His face was shaven clean, and his coal black hair was slicked back with pomade.

What struck her as odd was the upright, rigid posture and leanness with which Ike carried himself, and Marigold had to admit that his entire appearance was a marked upgrade from his typically weary demeanour.

"Why thank you, Minister Slake, you flatter me," Marigold greeted him. In an effort to keep from offending him, Marigold made the conscious choice to refer to him by his former title. "I bid you a good morning as well. Please, do come in and have a seat. I will have some tea and scones delivered, if you are so inclined to partake."

"While I will decline a hot beverage, having just finished a cup of tea myself," Ike began amiably enough. "I would most graciously accept a glass of red wine. Something out of the Bay of Fog, preferably, aged either ten or twelve years."

Marigold tried to smile, but feared that it might come across as disingenuous. "Why of course, Minister. Ser Kandell, would you inform the wait staff in the canteen of Minister Slake's request?"

"I can certainly see to it, my lady," Kandell acquiesced. "Will there be anything for you?"

"Perhaps a second glass," she replied politely. "I may join Minister Slake with that bottle of wine."

Kandell departed hurriedly, leaving Marigold standing in the hallway with only the Pharsey brothers. She stole a nod at one of them and retreated into the office, closing the door behind her.

Slake had already seated himself in one of the chairs before the desk, and Marigold walked around to take her usual seat.

"Well, here we are, Minister Slake," Marigold started once she was comfortable and settled. "How are Rosalind and Randall doing?"

"I assume that the wife is doing fine. She is presently visiting with her family in Longvale. I suspect that with the way things are right now, she might be staying there for an extended period. Randall is at home. He turned fifteen this year, so I am giving him a trial run at managing things in my absence. My steward stayed with him to supervise."

"I am sorry to hear that Rosalind is stranded in the east," Marigold offered in sympathy. "I hope that we can sort things out soon enough so that passage between Obalen and West Illiastra can be resumed."

"I do miss my dear Rosalind, I cannot deny it," Ike replied flatly. "I hope that a resolution between the two divided halves of Illiastra can be reached soon, so that I might see her again. In fact, it is much of the reason that I came to see you today. I do wonder if there is some role that I can play to help facilitate agreements between yourself and our old friends in the EMP."

Marigold did not want to dash his hopes entirely, but she could not envision any scenario where either country could arrive at a place of coexistence while both Marigold and the EMP held the elected offices.

As she was about to speak, there came a knock at the door.

"That must be the butler I sent for," Marigold told Slake before raising her voice. "Come on in!"

An aging little fellow in a black suit and white gloves entered the room bearing a white towel across his arm, a bottle of red wine to one hand, and a pair of long stemmed glasses held upside down by the base in the other. "I have come bearing your wine, as requested, Lady Marigold. Would you like me to serve now, or will you do so yourself later?"

"You may go ahead and serve now. Thank you, ser," Marigold allowed, sitting back in her chair so that the butler had all the space he needed in which to work.

Ike went silent during the butler's presence, and did not speak again until the man was gone, having left with the bottle and whatever remained of the wine within it.

Marigold thanked the butler before he left and offered a toast to Ike once the door closed and they were alone. "Here is to our health, and a peaceful end to the difficulties we face."

"And may fortune find us, Lady Marigold," Ike gave in response.

"Just so," Marigold said while laying the glass aside after taking her taste. "Now, Minister Slake, you proposed to help me bring peace with the EMP. Might I ask what that proposal entails."

"Yes, of course, my lady," Ike agreed, leaning forward in his chair as he did, wine glass cupped in his hand, with the stem extending between the middle and forefingers. "You might be aware that since Minister Daltis has left Galdourn and abandoned the Madore Isles, that I have been the lone minister in opposition to you in the immediate vicinity. Arturo Jennis is the next closest, and he is all the way south in Levelle. As such, there is a lot of pressure on me from Lord Eamon to help him enter the region."

"Is that so?" Marigold queried in feigned wonderment, having been already aware of such.

Ike nodded quite vigorously at that. "Oh yes, quite so. Thus far, I have rebuffed him, you should know. I told him, and I quote, 'I cannot allow you access to any part of my region, be it the capital of Galdourn or even the tiny village of Hawk's Cove where my family originated, so long as I have reason to believe that peace with Lady Marigold can be achieved.'"

It took every ounce of strength in Marigold's body to not outright laugh in Ike's face. *This coward expects me to believe that he actually grew a spine and said something like that to Eamon frigging Palomb of all people. What is he trying to accomplish here?*

"I am awed, Minister Slake. Your bravery knows no bounds," Marigold said instead, stifling her disbelief. "Might I ask if Eamon had a response to that?"

"Oh, he did indeed," Slake said gleefully. "Eamon said that, 'If you can find a way to mend our broken country, I will bestow a lordship of your choosing on you. That is how sure I am that it cannot be done. Name your portfolio, and it is yours for as long as you want it.'

"To that, I told him, 'As the minister of the neighbouring region to Daol Bay, whose grandfather was personally chosen by Marigold's grandfather to rule Galdourn, I have a close relationship with House Tullivan that almost none other in Illiastra can claim to have. I knew Marigold's father well from frequent visits to Daol Bay, and I know Marigold. You may feel at odds with her, but I know that she is a woman of reason. Please, allow me to try and demonstrate that to you.'"

The quotations by Slake only grew more ridiculous by the sentence, and Marigold felt her careful façade might crack at any moment and descend into uncontrollable laughter. "That is a fascinating story, Minister Slake. I am not quite certain that I know what else to say on the matter. What does one even make of it? Imagine a man as powerful as Eamon challenged to lay his fate in the hands of a man that he would only ever consider a backbencher. I think what you have achieved is nothing short of incredible. Now please, tell me what your plan for reunification is."

Ike squirmed uncomfortably in his chair, and Marigold noticed that he had seated himself with his suit jacket still closed, a move typically seen as a fashion gaffe. "Is everything alright, Minister Slake?"

"Yes, I am quite fine," Ike said with a smile that was betrayed by a distinct anxiousness in his eyes. "My plan was..."

Slake downed what remained of his wine and set the glass on the desk. "My lady, I... I want to know what you would do for me if I sided with you. Am I considered a traitor? Would you banish me as you did Leo Daltis?"

Marigold studied Ike, watching wordlessly as a man who so confidently put forward his grand story seconds before was seemingly falling apart in desperation before her. His breathing had quickened, and his hands began to show a tremble.

"I thought that you had a plan for unifying both halves of Illiastra, Minister?" Marigold asked in genuine surprise, temporarily overlooking the facetiousness with which Slake had presented himself thus far. "What happened to that enthusiasm?"

"My back is against the wall," Ike pleaded, his forehead touching down on his left arm that had come to rest on the desk. "You do not understand, Miss Marigold. Leo could run away, but I have no such luxury. I am all that stands between the Galdourn region and House Palomb's advances. You know as well as I that Galdourn is no place for Eamon to establish a base from which to attack you. He has not the defences to keep you out, but he will throw every westerner in his command at you to die. He would use my few soldiers and me as sacrificial cannon fodder so that he might call you a monster. I will be loyal to you, I will be true, all I ask in return is that you defend me, and defend Galdourn from Eamon. Please, I beg of you. He will not come after Galdourn if I side with you, for then I am just one region amongst a host of loyalists in that scenario."

The entire display was leaving Marigold bewildered, and she sat back as far as her chair would allow, wanting as much distance between her and Slake as the furniture allowed. "Minister Slake did you or did you not speak with Eamon Palomb? What did he ask of you or tell you to do?"

A soft, almost indecipherable knock came at the door, and Marigold called out to it, "Who is it?"

Her eyes went to the grandfather clock in the opposite corner of the office, and she saw that it was only half past the eleventh hour.

Still too early for that check-in. Who could that be?

"It is Guerin Davisure, my lady," the speaker revealed. "Might I come in? I have something urgent to discuss with you."

"Minister Slake, please pull yourself together, for we are about to have company," Marigold urged him in a frantic whisper, hoping to spare some of the man's dignity. "Yes, Mister Davisure, come right on in."

Ike sat up suddenly and ran a hand over his slightly dishevelled hair to smoothen it out as it had been. As the door opened, Ike adjusted how his open jacket sat on his shoulders and turned to face the clerk.

"Mister Davisure, what can I do for you?" Marigold asked him warmly, happy for any sort of distraction to the increasingly awkward conversation that was unfolding in her office.

Guerin saw himself in, closed the door as quietly as humanly possible, and began to cross the floor. "Well, my lady, I believe that what I have to say is for your ears only. Might I approach you so that we may speak in a more private manner?"

Marigold found the request odd, but there was a look of dread etched plainly across Guerin's face that she simply could not ignore. "Alright, Mister Davisure, you may approach."

"Wait, no. What are you doing?" Ike Slake asked while standing up and blocking Davisure's path.

"Stand back, Minister Slake, she must know," Guerin said sternly, trying to push away from Ike's approach.

"What is going on here? What must I know? Tell me, Mister Davisure," Marigold commanded, standing up so that she might be seen and heard more clearly.

"You fool!" Ike snarled through gritted teeth. "You ruined it. I was still making up my mind."

"Oh, gods!" Davisure cried out as Ike pressed himself against the old clerk. "What have you done? Take it out!"

"Now though, now you have forced my hand, you utter fucking simpleton," Slake uttered with a disturbing calmness coming over him. He yanked his arm away from Davisure, causing the older man to lurch backward and into the bookcase with a crash.

The door to the office blew open and the Pharsey brothers rushed in, one of them asking what the both of them were certainly wondering. "What is going on in here?"

Marigold looked to Mister Davisure to see him clutching at his rapidly reddening abdomen. Ike was looking at her then, a slender dagger tight in his hand and an empty sheath apparent on a shoulder holster that had been concealed by his jacket.

"This was the plan, Marigold," Ike told her with frightening melancholy while holding up the weapon. "I was not planning to go through with it, as I had hoped that you would offer me some sort of protection, but now... Now I have to do what was asked of me."

"My lady, get out of the room," Lahn ordered her in a tone that was both urgent and calm. Ike turned to face them, his bloodied dagger held out toward the twins as they unsheathed their sabres.

For a second, Marigold felt trapped by her desk, until the obvious solution to climb over it hit her. She jumped up on the desktop, wine glasses and loose papers going to the floor messily.

Brahn and Lahn slid themselves between where Marigold was going to land and where Ike stood with his eyes trained on Marigold.

"Put the blade down, mister, and no one need get hurt," Brahn ordered Ike.

"I do not think I can," Ike stammered out, his eyes moistening. "Marigold needs to die so that the Western Realm can return to the greatness it knew under the reign of the EMP."

"Go already!" Lahn shouted at Marigold again. "Go down the hall and get help!"

Marigold shook her head and jumped down off the desk.

There was a shout from Slake's direction as Marigold took off running, and she slammed the door as Lahn and Brahn roared back at him. From within the office, Marigold could hear an eruption of crashing and banging.

Freyard and the others are in the private chambers, Marigold reminded herself, taking off running in that direction.

A guard saw her dashing his way and approached her at a jog of his own. "Is everything alright, Miss Marigold?" he asked as they drew near to one another.

Marigold was about to answer, when she took a good look at his face. *I do not know that guard and I cannot say that I have ever seen him before.*

"I am fine," Marigold tried to tell him, her words falling short as she watched him pull a dagger from his belt. Terror ran through her veins at the sight of the steel, and her voice came out in a shout. "Someone help!"

"What is going on?" a gruff voice asked as light filtered into the hallway through the open door of the private chambers.

Marigold took the moment to run down the hallway and past the distracted guard. As she looked back, she caught sight of Yarohmer tackling the imposter straight into the wall behind him.

"Get out here, lads! We're under attack!"

Down the rounded hallway she ran, until the sight of two more men in teal uniforms came into sight, identical daggers to those carried by Ike and the first imposter already to their hands. "Come here, Miss Marigold, we'll protect you!" one among them called out to her.

She turned back the way she came, and saw the first imposter having escaped Yarohmer's clutches and advancing on her quickly.

Behind her was the exit to the stables, and with no alternative, Marigold bolted through it. She slammed the door hard behind herself and kept running, not stopping until she was halfway down the middle aisle of the rows of stalls.

She turned herself around to face the building's exit, grabbing her sword from its scabbard as she did. *I cannot run, what was I thinking? I left everyone else back there to fight for me.*

"Is everything alright?" she heard over her shoulder, turning to see a single man standing at the far end of the aisle. His clear and proper voice sounded vaguely familiar to Marigold, but his face was hidden beneath a dark blue cloak. "Oh, what am I saying? you are standing out here with a sword in hand and breathing heavily. Something must definitely be amiss."

"What?" Marigold asked incredulously. "Who are you?"

"Tsk, tsk, Miss Marigold, I had figured that you would recognise little old me, given that it was not that long ago since last we spoke."

Marigold looked closer at the man, spotting a pair of charcoal grey cotton trousers, a white, silk fencing shirt, and a pair of black leather gloves to complete his outfit. Nothing stood out as anything she should recognise, and her gaze returned to his face. There was a long, clean chin and jaw, but the upper half of his features remained hidden by the cloak, leaving Marigold unable to identify him based on what she could see.

"I ask again, who are you? Reveal yourself at once," she demanded of the stranger.

"Or what?" he chortled in reply. "Your sword arm is already trembling. I suppose all of your guards might come bursting out of there within the next minute. But the truth is that I do not need that long."

A rapier was drawn forth in lightning fast fashion, and the stranger rushed at Marigold.

She swung her own rapier at the slender blade, batting it aside as she attempted to retreat backwards toward the doorway to city hall. "Get back!"

"You must die, Marigold," the assassin shouted during his press. "It is the only choice you have left us."

"No!" Marigold cried out while trying to evade the other sword as its owner creeped ever closer by the step. "I will not die without a fight!"

The door behind her opened inward just as she neared it, and she made the mistake of looking over her shoulder. She felt something pierce deep into her side, passing through leather, silk, and flesh alike. The feeling returned twice more in hurried fashion as she screamed and recoiled.

"You bastard!" a man's voice called out.

"Someone is trying to kill Lady Marigold!" another shouted after him.

Marigold fell forward and to the ground with the pull of the rapier as it retracted from where it last pricked her, and her own sword went tumbling away.

With one hand holding her left side, she tried to crawl out of the stables and away from her attacker. Scrambling on her knees and free left hand, Marigold made for the daylight ahead, trying to find her way through the cursing voices and clashing steel that rang in her ears.

Someone tripped over Marigold's feet and landed with their full weight on her, jamming her face into the concrete floor. She laid there on the ground, groaning in pain while trying to push upward so that she might roll the body off her.

"Get him off of Lady Marigold!" a different voice cried out.

The body was lifted and thrown aside and Marigold saw plainly the uncovered face of Leo Daltis lying beside her, his rapier gone and both Sydnee and Elden fighting to restrain him.

"Marigold!" she heard Freyard's unmistakable voice roar out through the stable. "No! Oh, please no!"

Freyard came sprawling in beside her, where she was pulled into his arms tightly. "Marigold, are you alright? You're bleeding everywhere. Oh, fuck. Please, hold on, my love, I am going to get you to a doctor."

She was lifted off the ground then, a deep cry of pain escaping Freyard's lungs as he took her into his arms in complete disregard of his own injuries. "Stay with me, Mari. Just stay with me. Focus on me, and stay awake."

"Freyard... I love you," Marigold managed to gasp, as everything turned hazy and distant.

"I love you too, my darling," Freyard called back to her. "Just stay with me, please. I'm going to get you some help."

For a moment, it appeared as though the world turned bright, and she tried to shield her eyes from the glare.

"I need help over here!" Freyard shouted. "Lady Marigold needs a doctor! Somebody, please help!"

"This way! There's a doctor at the inn just one block over! Follow me!" a strange voice called out.

"Where is she?" a man with the same accent as Gallin's seemed to ask. "Oh, gods! What happened?"

"She's been stabbed, Gallin," Freyard yelled back to him. "Help me get her to the *Brookside*. The doctor running in the election is there."

"Give her to me, I can move faster," Gallin demanded.

"No, just stay ahead of me and help the guards clear a path up ahead. I will not let her go," Freyard shot back, his voice sounding beleaguered.

An attempt by Marigold to answer came out garbled and strange, as though her own tongue was getting in her way. She looked up at Freyard in her confusion, and found his face blurry. Her hand gripped his shirt tightly, and he finally looked down at her.

"Stay with me, Marigold. Please, darling, you have to stay awake, we're almost to the doctor," she heard him beg of her.

But what if I cannot stay awake, Freyard?

She blinked, and her eyes fought to rise again.

"Get that door and get out of the way!" Freyard shouted out, as the light above dimmed. "I need a doctor! I have Lady Marigold here and she is severely wounded!"

I am sorry, Freyard. I can keep my eyes open no longer.

"My word, she looks to have lost a great deal of blood," some man's voice said. "Get her in the back room, quickly!"

I tried, I really did. Please know that, my love.

"Lay her on that table," the same man demanded. "We have to stop the bleeding. Just hold on, Lady Marigold."

She was lying flat then, staring at a white ceiling above. Doctor Fielding was looking down at her, flanked on either side by Gallin and Freyard.

"Freyard, I love you," she managed to stammer.

"I love you too, Marigold. Please, darling, save your strength," Freyard cooed back softly, taking her bloodied right hand to hold.

"I'm sorry, Lady Marigold, but this is going to hurt. Just bear with us, please," Doctor Fielding told her softly while approaching with a mound of cloth in his hand.

Blinding pain went through her like lightning from her side, and the room began to spin.

"Freyard!" Marigold managed to cry out, as her world descended to black.

EPILOGUE I
ELLARIE

One thing that could be said for Ellarie's current confines was that she had a splendid view of abject misery.

Her new cell contained a single window, made thick in its frame by double panes of glass situated side by side and overlaid with generously spaced iron bars. Of course, for how high above the ground she was and the fact that outside the window there was no purchase or outcroppings from the thick bricks and mortar, Ellarie had to wonder if bars were necessary to begin with. Regardless, the view afforded her the ability to see clear across the entire western side of the city-turned-prison that was known as Biddenhurst. Those sights, such as they were, stretched for what felt like a mile, and only came to a stop at the imposingly tall, guarded walls of the massive institution.

Apart from the top of the Tower of Ios that served the town outside of Biddenhurst, there was nothing that could be discerned of the world beyond the prison. In between the window and the outer fortifications, she could see nearly all that this half of the city afforded, which, as she previously realised, was nothing more than abject misery.

Broken, crumbling stone roads that once represented a city regarded as *The Jewel of the East* led to the ruined homes and cold, rudimentary brick structures. Every window was barred, and every door was made of steel or at least reinforced with such. The walls of the city and its buildings knew only the various shades of grey, and no other colour seemed capable of penetrating its chokehold on the spectrum.

The guards, in their black uniforms trimmed in gold, stood out pointedly against their drab background. With nothing else but time on her hands, Ellarie had taken to watching every guard she saw, scrutinising their routes and patrols, noting details from each one, and assigning them placeholder names like Merion was known to do. In this way she kept sane, imagining that such minutiae could one day be used to her advantage in some grand plot to escape the waking nightmare in which she now lived.

The entry gates in the western wall received her focus as well. She knew exactly when they would open on any given day of the week, and what was coming through in each routine pass. From this, Ellarie had come to know only three variations of traffic in and out of the city. The first, and most common, were the jail wagons ferrying prisoners to their futile, farcical parole hearings at the courthouse outside the prison. Next in frequency were the supply wagons. Those carriers either delivered outside food and goods to appropriate venues or came to take the fruits of the labours of the indentured prisoners in the two factories that operated inside the walls. Lastly, there was Mackhol Taves himself, who rode into the city every morning in an ornate carriage, coming there from a spacious manor located somewhere on the other side. He often stayed late within Biddenhurst, and sometimes never went home in the evening at all.

That much I know because I see the boorish prick almost every day.

Despite the ugly brick trappings of her cell and the locked steel door, Ellarie lived in relative comfort. She had an actual bed made of soft straw, a small sitting table for her meals, a tiny shelf of books, an enclosed privy in one corner, and a full wardrobe. There was even a pair of paintings on the walls. Her favourite of the two was a still life portrait of a bowl of mixed fruit done in watercolours that hung above her bed. With little else to do, she found herself frequently taking it off the wall to study closely, analysing the brush strokes, sometimes down to even the tiniest details of each bristle.

The other painting shared a wall with her cell door. It was a large, scenic oil painting depicting a waterfall and its beautiful summertime surroundings. That particular piece was mounted in a frame so thick that it stuck out in a noticeable and unnatural way. Despite the visual allure of the scenic painting, Ellarie refused to so much as look at it, let alone touch it or take it down for closer examination.

The books, as much as she enjoyed reading, were left untouched. There was little among them of interest, at any rate. Both *The God's Gift* and *The Proclamation of Ios* were in the collection, as well as the memoirs of Grenjin Howland's father. There was a recipe book on the shelf too, the placement of which seemed like some sort of twisted joke to Ellarie, given how useless it was to someone in her situation. Finally, there was the most random of titles: *Waterfowl and Where to Find Them*. From what Ellarie could discern, it was a field guide on the subject, and perhaps the lone book that she was even remotely curious to look through. However, she made a point to touch none of the tomes, fearing that they were there as a test to see whether she was literate. Women that knew how to read, outside of the married ladies of the upper echelon, were seen as threats to Illiastra and Ellarie was trying to keep herself to a low profile. The less that Ellarie's captors thought of her, the more advantages she had. With that thought running constantly through her mind, Ellarie was not willing to risk anyone becoming wise to her literacy over some documentation about ducks.

At morning, noon, and dusk, the prisoners in Ellarie's new housing unit were given a proper meal, complete with hot beverages, and oftentimes slices of cake or pie for dessert. To go from scraps of bread and tepid, foul water to meals of actual sustenance at first had made Ellarie ill, and she was certain that she was being poisoned.

The Matron, who was one of the few people that Ellarie saw in the course of a day, had cleared up any doubts of pending death. The kindly, motherly woman in her late fifties explained to Ellarie that the retching was something she herself had endured when she was in Ellarie's position. There was no poisoning of any kind, Ellarie was told. In fact, her nausea was not even drug induced, if the Matron was to be believed. The truth was that having been on what was apparently known as 'the prisoner's diet' for so long, Ellarie's stomach became temporarily unable to tolerate flavour of any kind.

"Old bread and dirty water are definitely an acquired taste," the Matron had told Ellarie upon the first time she witnessed the vomiting. *"However, once the human stomach gets used to that and only that for so long, it does not know what to do with the first bit of food*

that is even slightly better. Give it time, and small bites, and you will adjust before long, honey."

'Honey' was evidently the Matron's name for every woman in her charge, and if the Matron was being truthful, Ellarie was but one of a dozen locked away in the tall tower in the centre of the prison city.

Like Ellarie, all were kept in a life of relative luxury, but none of it was for their enjoyment, at least not directly. The collected prisoners that were of the Matron's concern were known as Mackhol's Girls, and Ellarie, under Bernadine's name, was the newest addition to the terrible club.

The primary purpose of Taves' female company in the tower was to be his concubines, unsurprisingly. There was one notable exception to the rule, and that was the Matron herself. The duty of the Matron was to ensure that Ellarie and the other women were clothed, fed, and presentable during all waking hours that Mackhol Taves happened to be present in the tower. From her time in her new cell, Ellarie had come to learn that Taves was in his office at the top of the tower at almost all times. At least, that was what both he and the Matron told Ellarie.

Personally, Ellarie found it hard to fathom that Taves would spend more time within Biddenhurst than he absolutely needed to. If she were in his place, Ellarie figured that she would spend not one minute longer than necessary in the wretched, run down hole. It was said that Taves had a fabulous mansion, a wife, and two daughters outside Biddenhurst's walls, and more friends and acquaintances than one man could know what to do with. Other than the women he kept locked away, Ellarie had to think that there was nothing further in the tower that Taves could possibly want.

Of the other eleven women supposedly sharing space with her, Ellarie knew nothing. Two joined the Matron daily, lugging a bathtub and hot water from cell to cell. Unlike their overseer, their faces were covered with scarves and they were expressly forbidden from speaking. Instead, the Matron did all of the talking, leaving her two followers to merely comply with her orders and stare at Ellarie with the most forlorn eyes she could ever recall seeing. Of course, it was not as though the attending women would have had many opportunities to get a word in edgewise. The Matron was overly loquacious, and seemed to fill every moment she spent with Ellarie with news and gossip from around the miserable city. While the information was nothing that pertained to Ellarie with any relevancy, it did serve to give her a more complete image of the inner workings of the prison.

A second advantage to the prattling of the Matron was its ability to distract Ellarie from the frustration she felt during the visits. The presence of the silent women bothered Ellarie a great deal, both for the fact that she desperately wanted to talk with them, and that they refused to utter a single word to her. The feeling was only compounded by the general inaction and weak will of the woman charged with watching over the lot of them.

The Matron is the one person in this tower who is as much a prisoner as the rest of us with the means to do something about it, and she steadfastly refuses.

Ellarie had not asked for such outright, but she had made hints that she was willing to make a move against the overseers of the city. The nervousness of the Matron's responses indicated that she knew what Ellarie was trying to tell her, though the dismissive and fearful phrasing of the Matron's responses snuffed Ellarie's hopes.

It was not as though Ellarie's presumption of assistance was without precedent. When the Matron had initially chosen Ellarie to go with her, the Matron spent their entire walk from the gallows cells to the tower telling Ellarie how she would protect her. Specifically, Ellarie recalled the Matron telling her that she was now one of "my girls", and she never let anything happen to "my girls".

All of it was bullshit, every bit of it, Ellarie thought bitterly. *I don't know why I ever believed her.*

The unwillingness of the Matron to contemplate freedom had left Ellarie upset with the Matron, and after coming to terms with this revelation, Ellarie decided to tolerate the Matron only insomuch as her situation required. Then on, any plans that Ellarie was concocting were not going to involve the odd woman, and she considered her an enemy as much as Taves and the prison guards under his command. However, as the days went on, and Ellarie took the time to get to know the Matron a little more, her stance softened. Though it remained indisputable that the Matron had deceived Ellarie into thinking more of her than she actually was, Ellarie had come to change her belief of why the Matron had initially misled her.

It occurred to Ellarie that the Matron was as trusted as she was by Taves and the guards not for her desire to rise to a position of trust, but because she was completely and utterly delusional. From what Ellarie could discern of the Matron's past, she had been in Biddenhurst for about fifteen years, and somewhere along the way, had resigned herself to the awful world into which she was made to reside. The Matron's life before Biddenhurst was unspoken of, but simply discovering how long the Matron had been inside the prison told Ellarie something of her old life on the outside.

Inmates in Biddenhurst came in two primary varieties: those who could serve a purpose, and those who were deemed worthless. The latter were simply fodder, to be sent into situations that would result in certain death or outright hanged from Taves' massive scaffolds. That the Matron still lived told Ellarie that she was clearly lumped into the first category.

Those with a function in Taves' morbid machine could be classified under one of several headings. In the case of Ellarie, Joyce, Merion, Lazlo, and their friends, they were political prisoners. Granted, they were ultimately destined for the gallows, but they had value, even if only temporarily, to the EMP. Until such a time that their inherent value expired, Ellarie and her Thieves were to be spared from execution.

Next were those who could be enslaved with little effort. Those who possessed talent and skill in jobs pertaining to the industries that employed slave labour were cast into that category, or even those who simply had the physical ability to toil and labour. The only further requirement for worker prisoners was that they possess a docile and passive enough nature to allow themselves to be mentally broken of their will to be free.

All a person here has to do is abandon hope, and a life of labour for someone else's exclusive benefit can be theirs.

It was the only way for a prisoner of Biddenhurst to see outside its walls again, Ellarie was told. For some, like Ellarie's fellow concubines, their purpose was fornication, even if that was contradictory to the Triarchist beliefs that Taves and his contemporaries claimed to hold.

The aggressive and violent inmates had a use to Mackhol as well, even if they did make for poor slave material. As Ellarie had come to understand, many buildings were dedicated to holding those possessing the most brutal of abilities and tendencies. In many cases, such men were made to battle one another in the fighting pits for the amusement and gambling purposes of the guards. The best of them might even be chosen to fight in combat tournaments outside of Biddenhurst.

There were even a few select psychopaths who were employed as torturers, their amorality and sadism put to use against other prisoners. As Ellarie had learned from the floggings of Lazlo, Joyce, and Jorgia, the guards had no qualms when it came to harming the prisoners. However, according to the Matron, there were whispers to be heard of acts of unconscionable depravity occurring within Biddenhurst's walls. It was these deeds, among the very worst that humanity could conjure, that the guards preferred to be carried out by those whose heinous behaviour had landed them in Biddenhurst in the first place. Though Ellarie thought of herself as imaginative, she refused to let her mind even contemplate what occurred in those darkest corners of the prison.

For all she knew, there was a possibility that those horrors were being inflicted on her sister, Joyce, Lazlo, and the others. Their safety was the one thing that Ellarie dared ask about anymore, and the Matron's answer was always, "They are alive."

In this place, 'alive' tells me nothing. That's if the Matron is being honest with me to begin with.

In the Matron's case, Ellarie concluded that she was a useful prisoner due to both her talent for managing others and her own capitulation to her jailers. Yet, she was still in Biddenhurst. Such a worker would be worth a fortune to the right buyer, and Taves was known for his love of money. That Taves kept such a valuable inmate to himself was more than suspicious to Ellarie.

That the Matron remained a resident of the prison city led Ellarie to arrive at two possible conclusions. The first of those being that the Matron was not the model prisoner she showed herself to be at present. Despite making herself into a valued commodity for Taves, her value to buyers from outside the prison might have plummeted due to initial bad behaviour. This seemed an unlikely scenario at best to Ellarie, as Taves would have simply labelled the Matron as useless and sent her to the gallows without a second thought. If one thing was certain in Biddenhurst, it was that there were no second chances for anyone.

The other option that Ellarie considered, and the one she was leaning towards was that the Matron had obtained some measure of fame prior to her arrest. That the Matron was unwilling to speak of her past life, or even give her real name, lent credence to Ellarie's theory. In an effort to solve the mystery and determine if the Matron was even trustworthy, Ellarie spent hours searching her memory for any woman who might have possibly raised enough infamy and attention to warrant her arrest. Unfortunately, the search of her memories prior to the beginning of the Matron's incarceration period came up unsurprisingly blank.

I was but a ten-year-old girl back then. My concerns were taking care of my younger siblings and keeping out of trouble. I was hardly going to remember anything about a famous woman being arrested and sent to Biddenhurst.

Unlike the eleven other women, Ellarie had no designs on being a concubine, and if she was going to escape, the Matron was her best chance at doing so.

I would rather die trying to get myself and the other Thieves out of here than live as some plaything for Taves.

Unlike the Matron, Ellarie would not be broken. She steeled herself daily against the constant barrage of depression and anguish, and worked diligently to keep herself from sinking into the pit of despair that awaited all who lived inside Biddenhurst's walls.

Merion, Joyce, Lazlo, Bernadine, Alia, Etcher, Donnis, Jorgia, and Coramae were doing the same as Ellarie, and she knew it as plainly as she knew the hands folded neatly atop the skirt of her dress.

We won't give up to this place, not one of us. We're not like the other women in here, or the Matron, or even that washerwoman substituting for Nia. We won't let this place win. We won't become this. If for nothing else but the sake of the other Thieves, I won't become this.

Those four words had become Ellarie's mantra, and she repeated them almost hourly to herself. Usually the words were not said aloud, but on occasion, when she felt comfortably alone, she would whisper them to herself. With dinner, and the Matron, fast approaching, Ellarie took the waning seconds to say them to the windowpane in front of her.

"I won't become this."

It was mere minutes later that the barrage of footsteps could be heard coming down the hallway. One pair of heavy, standard issue boots seemed to lead the pack, followed by at least three pairs of soft slippers slapping behind them. Ellarie stood up and stretched, smoothing out her dress as she readied for her guests.

It sounds like dinner is right on schedule.

A ring of keys jingled outside the door, and one found its way into the lock, turning rather clumsily.

Taves' nephew is on duty again today by the sounds of that key being clanked around that lock. That's six days now without a rest. He'll be sluggish and mopey at best.

Ellarie often fantasised about beating Wendell Taves to a bloody pulp. His surname alone made Ellarie want to rain down pain upon him. However, it was that someone she regarded as utterly pathetic literally held the keys to her freedom that was enough to make her wholly endorse her violent desires towards him.

I could overwhelm him so easily, and he would never have the wherewithal to get the better of me. Then what, though? I need a concrete plan before I can lay a finger on Wendell. Knocking him down might get me out of this cell, but I need to get out of this city.

The steel door swung outward, and Wendell stood there holding the handle, the same look of utter surprise on his face that he seemed to wear every time he looked upon Ellarie. The two dutiful attendants of the Matron walked around him, with her following behind them.

And she is the one that I must convince to aid me so that I can draft a proper plan. Before I can physically escape this prison, I must first cut the bonds that keep her mentally imprisoned.

"Good evening, Miss Voyer," the Matron greeted warmly as the skirts of a faded and patched yellow dress swished around her. "How has your afternoon been, honey?"

"Good evening to you too, Matron," Ellarie replied in monotone with the exact statement that she knew the Matron wanted to hear. "My afternoon was quiet and contemplative. Thank you for asking."

The attendants came with a tray each in their hands, and Wendell retreated from the cell, slamming the door shut behind him.

The first woman brought the dinner on a covered platter. To her, Ellarie had assigned the sobriquet Sorrow. The haunting, piercing gaze emanating from the green eyes beneath the scarf covering her face had led to that name. It was only tragedy that could leave a person with such a hard, spirit-cleaving stare, and tragedy was as much a component of Biddenhurst as the mortar in the walls.

Ellarie had once seen the bare hands of the other woman, and noticed that they were covered in fine strands of filigree tattoos, like those commonly seen among the Cabathosi folk. Based on that, Ellarie named her Vine. On the tray in her inked hands at this hour were toiletries and cosmetics so that Ellarie might freshen herself up before the inevitable visit of Mackhol Taves.

The Matron had been nodding and smiling during Ellarie's greeting, though her expression changed to one of concern by the end. "Did you by chance make time for prayer?"

"Yes, Matron," Ellarie lied easily. "I said the prayer of mercy and the prayer of justice fifteen times each, just like you advised me to do this morning."

"That is good, Miss Voyer," the Matron said with relief. "Prayers are often the only thing a prisoner has to offer. Ios listens to all, even the damned, like you and I."

"We give thanks to Ios for shining his light on sinners like us," Ellarie forced herself to say, much to her own chagrin.

The Matron gave Ellarie the gentlest of pats on the arm. "Very good, dear, be sure to keep that up. Now, come and eat your dinner while it is still warm. You have a nice slice of mincemeat pie tonight, and preserved apricots for dessert. Doesn't that sound like a treat?"

"Yes, Matron, that sounds just lovely," Ellarie answered while following her to the little sitting table where her meal waited.

"While you eat, the girls will fix you up all nice for Lord Mackhol. You are among those that he has chosen to visit with again tonight," The Matron explained, as Ellarie expected that she would.

Ellarie opted to give no response to that statement, and instead focused on her mincemeat pie. With it came a canteen of clean, cool water, and a tiny pot of lukewarm green tea. Even though Ellarie and the other women were given several different luxuries not afforded to any other in Biddenhurst, they were still prisoners. Things like boiling hot liquids were still to be considered as potential weapons in the hands of an inmate.

As Ellarie took a drink of the water, she took notice of a slight flavouring that was not there before. "The water tastes different. Has something been added to it, Matron?"

"Why, yes, as a matter of fact there has," the Matron said excitedly. "One of my girls gave me the idea to add the unused cucumber slices from yesterday's salads. She said that she used to drink it that way all the time at the brothel that she worked at."

It was unsurprising for Ellarie to hear that at least one of her new compatriots was a former courtesan. Many women in Biddenhurst were there on such charges, and in a twist that was as ironic as it was hypocritical, most of them wound up being used to provide that same service in the labour camps that bought them.

The Matron sounds awfully proud of herself for acting on someone else's idea to put a few slices of cucumber in our water.

"It's a welcome addition. Please, tell her that I said, 'thank you' when next you speak to her, Matron," Ellarie offered instead of the sarcastic retort that came to her mind.

Making no further remark on the water, the Matron circled back around to the previous subject. "Are you going to present yourself well for Lord Mackhol this evening? He is a patient man, but even his patience has limits. I understand your reservations with opening yourself to a stranger, especially given how long you have been led to see him as your enemy."

"I don't know the answer to that yet, Matron," Ellarie replied with her continued flat tone. Though she was already certain she would refuse Taves, Ellarie felt it in her best interest if she was not so forthright with the Matron.

"Lord Taves is kind enough to give you the choice, Bernadine. However, if you continue to say 'no', he will not keep you here," the Matron explained in a condescending voice, gesturing to the other two girls afterwards. "They would tell you the same. We have twelve rooms here for Lord Mackhol's girls, but that does not mean that there have only ever been twelve girls, if you understand my meaning. Once a girl has worn out their welcome, there is no coming back, and where they go, the offer to refuse does not go with them. I do not want to lose another girl, Bernadine. I need you to work with me on this so as to prevent such a tragedy from happening again."

A question came to Ellarie based on that answer. She took a second to consider it and the implications that it carried, and ultimately decided to let it air. "Have girls been kicked out for reasons other than saying 'no' to Lord Mackhol?"

The Matron stared blankly at the wall, her lips curling, but otherwise giving no response.

A glance from Ellarie to the other girls earned a cutting stare from Vine, and she took it to be as much of an answer as the Matron's silence.

"It's understandable if you choose not to answer me," Ellarie offered in conciliation. "The subject is sensitive, I admit, and it might not have been my place to ask."

"Sometimes he loses interest, no matter how much they or I plead to the contrary," the Matron blurted out hastily in a low voice from at the window where she now stood, staring out across the yard. Her volume increased suddenly then. "My, that is a nice view you have. You can see the beautiful new Tower of Ios in the town outside the walls. This used to be a Tower of Ios too, you know. It was deconsecrated when Lord Mackhol deemed the prison too dangerous for the people outside the wall to travel to for tower services."

Ellarie caught what the suddenly frightened looking woman was telling her, and gave a reply that she hoped conveyed her own message plainly enough. "I did not know that this was once a tower, but that is quite the interesting piece of trivia, Matron. Thank you for sharing that with me."

Perhaps the Matron is not the impenetrable fortress of ignorance that she presents herself to be.

"You are quite welcome, Bernadine," the Matron said quickly in answer while striding back across the room. "I am only glad to share my knowledge on this place and its vast history. Lord Mackhol is a walking encyclopaedia when it comes to this region, and he shares much of that with me."

Once more, Ellarie had no response to offer, and she dug her fork into the next bit of pie that she wanted to eat. She raised her fork and looked to the Matron. "This pie is quite good. My regards go to the chef."

The Matron seemed to ignore the compliment, and Ellarie looked to find that the Matron had gone to stand before the scenic painting that Ellarie hated so much. "Lord Mackhol still insists that you be manacled to the wall for his visits. I tried to make him see what I see, that you are a good girl and that you are just a little bit headstrong. Nevertheless, Lord Mackhol insists that because you are a member of the Thieves, you are not to be trusted. It is not my place to second guess the men, I suppose."

"I see..." Ellarie managed to mutter as the bile began to rise in her throat. Her fork was held tight in her hand, though she could do nothing to cut into the remainder of her pie.

"Keep eating, honey," the Matron encouraged her while walking slowly toward the cell door. "Whatever you do not finish will be taken away, and you will need your strength. Be sure to try the apricots, they are quite nice," she knocked softly on the door then, and it was unlocked from the outside.

The head of Taves' lazy nephew poked inside and looked about. "Yes, Matron? What is it?"

"You might as well get the manacles ready," the Matron told him. "It will not be long now before your uncle is here."

Ellarie's eyes studied the steel cutlery still in her hand, and she wondered how deep she could sink it into Wendell's neck.

Not deep enough, I would wager. He has a thick, protective layer of flesh.

"Yes, ma'am," Wendell replied with despondence. "I'll see to it straight away."

His key ring was jingling in his shaking hands again, and he kept missing the keyhole so often that Ellarie thought he might be trying to make a new one.

I will not be upset if he never finds the damn lock.

"Girls, you might as well start polishing Bernadine up, since it seems that she is not going to finish her food," the Matron commanded, her voice sounding sincerely melancholic for what she had ordered them to do. As they went about their work, the Matron went to the nightstand beside Ellarie's bed and turned the switch on the dim electric lamp affixed to the wall above it in an iron cage.

Sorrow, in her long-sleeved, formless grey dress approached with the hairbrush, and motioned with it to show Ellarie what she was about to do to the dark hair that fell just past her ears.

"Get on with it," Ellarie grumbled before sticking the next piece of her pie into her mouth.

Wendell grunted and lifted the heavy frame of the painting away from the wall, revealing an ugly wooden plaque beneath and two iron manacles moored to it on folded lengths of chain. The dimming evening light almost left the restraints in darkness, but Ellarie could still make them out, and the sight nearly sent her dinner back to the surface.

"There we are," Wendell said in a low, off-key singsong voice, his eyes staring at his own two feet. "Do you want me to go wait outside, Matron?"

"No, Wendell, Bernadine is almost done eating," the Matron told him, stealing a glance at Ellarie as she did. "You should try the tea, dear, even if it is cold by now."

The Matron's insistence on drinking the tea made Ellarie leery of it at best, but she did make a show of pouring a cup and putting the mildly warm liquid to her lips. As it clattered gently back to its saucer, Ellarie offered commented, "That's quite nice, Matron."

"Isn't it? I shall have a fresh pot brewed for you in the morning," The Matron added happily, before returning to her line of preparatory questions. "Do you need to use the privy before Lord Mackhol arrives? I think that dress should suit you fine, but if you want to change, shall I pick out something clean for you?"

"No, on both accounts, Matron," Ellarie answered as politely as she felt possible in her current circumstances. While Ellarie was never one for wearing dresses, she felt equally disinclined to be constantly changing in and out of them. Her current sleeveless, cotton gown in the blue of the Elite Merchants was one of the few garments that had a bodice sewn into it. As such, it did not require a separate, unbearably tight corset, and that above all made it one of the better choices in Ellarie's new wardrobe. Its sole drawback was that it had an ungainly amount of skirts that made a racket whenever she moved anywhere, though she felt that the positives far outweighed the negatives.

"Very well, dear," the Matron relented with a shrug. "Make sure to eat your apricots too. As the saying goes, 'a wasteful eater robs everyone of food'."

Then just leave them for me to eat later. It is not as though I will have anything else to do once Taves leaves.

Though she desperately wanted to shout her sarcastic thought aloud, she instead replied with, "Yes, Matron, I will eat them right away."

The helpers of the Matron concluded their primping of Ellarie and stepped back as a signal to their overseer. The Matron moved in, looked all about Ellarie, and nodded in approval. "That is a job well done, my darlings. Be proud of yourselves. I think Lord Mackhol will be pleased as well."

"Thank you for your help, ladies," Ellarie offered in reply, her eyes on the nearly empty food platter.

The Matron waved one hand over the tray while waving the other at Sorrow. "Take this away, now. All that's left is the cold tea." She pointed to Vine next. "Take the rest of our things. The both of you can go stand in the hallway with your backs to the wall outside this cell. Go on now."

The women left without further delay, leaving Ellarie alone with the guard and the Matron.

A soft hand of the Matron slid in under Ellarie's elbow and tenderly encouraged her to stand. "Let's go, Bernadine. I like this no more than you do, but it is Lord Mackhol's orders, and you do not want to know what happens to those who disobey his orders. Believe me when I tell you that."

The motion caused Ellarie's arm to lift, and she looked at the bruising already present on her wrists from the frequent shackling. The sight of her purpled flesh and the nearby iron cuffs that caused it made her hand curl into a fist.

"Don't do that, young lady," the Matron requested softly. "Get up. You would do well to remember that this is going to happen regardless of your protests. The only choice you have is in the difficulty."

Ellarie sighed and pushed to her feet, much to the tangible relief of both the Matron and Wendell, who was still standing by the opened manacles.

"That's a good girl, now go on over to where Wendell is and he will help you."

If he wanted to help me, he would give me his keys, sword, dagger, and pistol and get out of my way.

The Matron had one hand on Ellarie's back, the other still gripping her right forearm. "Go ahead, Wendell. Get it over with."

"Yes, Matron, as you wish," he mumbled in response.

With the Matron holding one arm of Ellarie's with both hands, Wendell slipped the horrible, iron manacle around her wrist and locked it into place. The other hand followed next, and as with every other occurrence before it, Ellarie felt herself die a little inside.

In her mind's eye, she saw Orangecloak, her hand pointing at Ellarie, Merion, Joyce, and bunch of other new recruits. "Whatever you do, never let yourself be tied up. Fight back. Kick and scream if you have to. Make the pricks work for it. The second they have you bound, you are the enemy's to do with as they please. You cannot let it get to that point without resistance."

Have I failed you, Orangecloak?

Her thoughts went back to the ambush in Argesse that felt like a lifetime ago. When they had come for Ellarie's unit, they had fought back and resisted their arrests, every one of them.

Except Merion, she gave up to spare Joyce's life, Ellarie remembered, the sight of her sister throwing down her spear before the flames of the burning farmhouse flashing before her.

I didn't let the pricks take me without a fight, just as you asked, Orangecloak. Should I still be fighting back now that I only seem to live to go from one shackling to the next?

"I hate this, Bernadine, I really do," the Matron uttered while still standing before Ellarie with watery eyes. "They did this to me too, you know, back when I first arrived in the tower. This though..." The Matron's words trailed off and she turned away to dab at her eyes. "This hurts worse than when it was done to me. I know you may not believe it, considering I helped Wendell put you there. But it does."

Ellarie wanted to believe the Matron, truly, and though she was the one chained to the wall, Ellarie even felt pity for her. A dozen different responses flashed in Ellarie's mind, each one more biting and sarcastic than the last, but she instead settled on the kindest sentiment she could think of. "I believe you, Matron. We will get through this together."

A smile blinked across the Matron's face, and in that moment, Ellarie thought she saw something akin to understanding in the middle-aged woman's expression. "Yes... Let's go, Wendell."

The two began to walk towards the door, with nothing for Ellarie to do but watch them from where she remained affixed to the wall. As Wendell reached a hand to the door, it opened away from him, and he gasped as he got only air and fell forward.

"Watch where you're going, you bumbling oaf," a raspy voice croaked from without. "You nearly barrelled straight into me."

"Ser Royen, to what do we owe the pleasure?" the Matron asked with noted consternation.

The Matron stepped back into Ellarie's sight to allow the thuggish lieutenant of Taves' to enter the cell. His face was ruddy and red, and he was still dressed in a black outer coat and leather gloves, indicating that he had come from somewhere outside the tower. "I just rode in with Lord Mackhol from the town. He's coming to see this one when he's done cleaning himself up in his chambers. I was told to come have a look at her and make sure that she's presentable for his lordship's viewing."

"I can assure you that she is, Lieutenant," the Matron said while gesturing to Ellarie with an open hand. "You can see for yourself."

From what Ellarie had learned, Royen was Taves' lieutenant charged with overseeing the tower guards. Judging by what the Matron said, he seemed to hate his underlings as much as he hated the prisoners. The men he had dominion over were all weaklings by Royen's standards, and to his credit, they were mostly the sons of local nobility. Ellarie could not argue with Royen's assessment, for much like Wendell Taves, the guards in the tower were green, inexperienced, little lordlings who had been sent for seasoning by their wealthy fathers. Their relative daintiness also made Royen's guards targets for bullying from the harder brutes beyond the tower. The charges beneath Royen made what would normally be seen as a lofty position into a source of shame for him, as the other guards mocked and taunted him by association.

Though Royen often complained to his superiors of the lacklustre performances of his guards, Taves was already well aware of the natures of those who watched his tower. To hear the Matron tell it, that was exactly why the noblemen's sons were there in the first place. Taves could give out the easiest jobs to the young, soft lads to please their parents, while protecting those same guards from the jeering of their peers, and have the most harmless members of his staff watching over his most prized chattel.

The only odd piece of that puzzle was merciless Ser Royen Stannerly of Kylisport. That a westerner of middling birth was a lieutenant of Biddenhurst said nothing good to Ellarie, and his evident bloodlust and inherent cruelty more than backed up Ellarie's hypothesis.

Most guards in Biddenhurst have eastern accents and dialects, with the vast number of those being local to the region. This one came from far away, meaning he either was attracted to the place, or was selected for specific traits that Taves felt made him uniquely qualified to be a guard in the most miserable place in the world. Half of me is genuinely curious as to why he's here, but the other half of me is telling the first half that I might be better off not knowing.

"There's Queen Bitch the Second," Royen greeted her with a deep guttural laugh. "I know I say this frequently these days, but I really do like how you look in the new bracelets that Lord Mackhol got you. They really match that dress, and I think that they bring out the sparkle in your eyes."

Royen was leaning in close enough that Ellarie could feel his breath on her face. While Ellarie seemed immobilised due to her hands being chained to the wall, her legs were free, and it took every bit of willpower in her body to keep herself from kicking him square between the legs.

The sound of her chains rattling began to ring in Ellarie's ears, and she tried to steady her rage. As much as she wanted to spit on Royen and tell him what he could do to himself, she swallowed her words and gave him silence instead.

He wants an answer. He wants an excuse to hurt me. Well, you can go fuck yourself, Royen. You're not getting it from me, not today, and not while I'm manacled to a wall and unable to fight back.

"You know, if I didn't know any better, I would think that you don't like me very much, Queen Bitch the Second," Royen mocked Ellarie, the foul odour of the tobacco chew on his breath wafting over her. "You never seem to want to talk to me, and you're always scowling in my face when we meet."

If you took your face away from mine, you wouldn't have to worry about the scowling.

His hands pressed slowly against the wall on either side of her head. "Maybe you will want to be my friend if I can give you something? I have news that you might like to hear about your little chums waiting in the Gallows Hotel. If you say, 'Hello, Ser Royen, how are you today?' I just might tell you what I know. That's all you need to do. Just say hello to me."

Ellarie gave the briefest of sideways glances to the Matron, and found her staring at the floor, her face a mixture of sadness and terror.

She can order Wendell and his friends around without worry, but she's petrified of Royen, even with Taves in the building to come between them.

Her eyes returned to Royen, and she looked into the emptiness behind them, finding only antipathy and callous disregard staring back.

Even if he should lie to me, there might be something useful to glean from him.

"Hello, Ser Royen, how are you today?" Ellarie asked him with feigned sincerity.

A deep snickering laugh came forth from him then, and he grabbed Ellarie by the cheeks with one hand, causing Orangecloak's thoughts on allowing oneself to be bound to come rushing back to Ellarie for the second time that day.

"You think you're cute, don't you?" he snarled at her.

"Ser Royen, please," the Matron suddenly cried out. "Don't harm Miss Voyer. Lord Mackhol will be here shortly and he'll see what you did. You don't want him getting cross with you, I am sure."

Royen let Ellarie go with dramatic flair and took a step back from her, his gaze going sideways. "No, I suppose you're right, Matron," his sights went back to Ellarie. "She really fancies herself a little mother hen, you know. She loves you girls because she can't love her own daughters from in here. Isn't that right, Matron?"

"Mock me all you want, I can take it," the Matron said with a visible flinch. "She did as you asked, Ser Royen. Can you please just get on with whatever it is you were going to tell her?"

"Oh! I almost forgot about that," Royen exclaimed with an odious smile. "I was in to see your friends today because I had some good news to share with the little faerie lieutenant of the Thieves that fancies himself a swordsman. You might like this as much as he did: Taves said he is considering letting the faggot fight to the death against me in the pits. Isn't that just delightful news? Might be that Mackhol will let you watch, too. That's if you're a good girl and do as you're told between now and then."

From out of the corner of her eye Ellarie saw Wendell stick his head in through the door during Royen's revelation and whisper to the Matron.

"Wendell says that Lord Mackhol is coming, Ser Royen," the Matron told him as fast as Wendell could relay it to her. "You should leave now before he sees you harassing one of his girls."

"Fine by me, I've said my piece," Royen said with a derisive scoff as she stepped away from Ellarie. He stopped before the Matron for a silent second, and as she moved to speak, Royen spat a gob of black tobacco onto the floor at her feet.

The Matron refused to look at either Royen or his mess, but he pointed to where it had come to rest before her. "Make sure to clean that up before Taves gets here, Matron."

Outside in the hallway Ellarie could hear footfalls on a stairwell, drawing closer, and Royen ducked out of the room in a hurry and just as quickly turned from a snarling beast to an obedient soldier. "Lord Mackhol, Ser, I have inspected the lady, and am happy to report that she is fit to be seen, Ser."

"Thank you, Lieutenant," Ellarie could hear Mackhol offering in return. "You are dismissed for now. Please, go enjoy your dinner."

The Matron was on her knees with a handkerchief to hand while the two men had spoken. She tucked the piece of cloth, now soiled by the disgusting by-product of an already filthy habit, into her bodice and stood up quickly. With the second remaining to her, the Matron hurried in close to Ellarie, making last second adjustments to her hair and dress. "Are you alright, Bernadine? I am so sorry that he did that to you. Try to pay him no mind, and be sure to look sharp for Lord Mackhol, honey. That's a good girl."

She looks more rattled than I am.

"Thank you, Matron. Please, be strong, we will get through this," Ellarie was entirely unsure where the second sentence she said came from, but it seemed to give some comfort to the Matron. For once, she did not begrudge the Matron that, given the hurtful statement of Royen's from just minutes ago.

"Thank you, Bernadine," she muttered through stifled tears. "I'll come back later to check on you, alright?"

"Ah, Matron, there you are," Mackhol Taves said to her as he strode into the cell. "Splendid work in getting Miss Voyer prepared to see me. You are dismissed for now to go put your two other girls back in their cells for the night. Wendell will give you his key with which to do so, as he has orders to remain outside this door until I call for him. Once your girls are put away, you may return Wendell's key and wait with him until I am done here."

Ellarie looked the spiteful man over as he briefed the Matron. Tonight he wore a three-piece, cream coloured suit with a derby hat to match and a black tie.

"Yes, my lord, it will be as you so wish," the Matron managed to get out while slowly vacating the cell. With a final glance to Ellarie through teary eyes, the Matron was gone, leaving her alone with Taves.

I have wished for a scenario like this since I first joined the Thieves and heard the man's name. Of course, I envisioned a sword in my hand

and no chains to hold me back, but otherwise, it is quite similar to what I had in mind.

Taves took his time looking over Ellarie without a word spoken while he waited for the door of the cell to close. Once the sound of the steel door meeting its frame rang through the room, Taves removed his hat and tossed it upside-down onto the foot of the bed. As it thudded softly onto the eiderdown, he set himself upon the side of the bed so that he was facing Ellarie.

"Hello, Miss Voyer. How are you doing today?" Lord Taves said to her in a voice that was sickly sweet.

"I am well, milord," Ellarie said with her usual emotionless inflection. "The Matron has been treating me very well."

He nodded slowly as she spoke, his fingers rapping in a slow, rhythmic canter on his legs, "I am most glad to hear that, Miss Voyer."

She swallowed hard and forced herself to look at him again. "How are you, milord?"

"Oh, I am doing fine," he told her with a dismissive flourish of the same hand. "It has been a most eventful season in Illiastra, and I am finding myself growing tired from trying to keep ahead of it all. Did you know that Warden Lord Marscal Tullivan passed away?"

"I did not, milord," Ellarie replied. Her voice was monotone, though her interest had genuinely piqued to hear of the demise of a high-ranking member of the EMP. "I offer my condolences to you on the loss of your friend."

"Marscal Tullivan as a friend of mine?" Taves offered rhetorically with noted incredulity. "No, my dear, he was but an acquaintance, though I thank you anyhow. He and I rarely agreed on anything, but I did respect his dedication to defending the west. It will not be long before Lord Eamon and his sons will own all of that now, though. I think that troublesome second daughter of Lord Marscal might cause problems, but they will be temporary with my Lord Eamon tending to the matter, I can assure you."

"I see," Ellarie offered in barely a whisper. Though she was slightly interested in the Tullivan daughter that had the ability to cause Eamon Palomb problems, the information was hardly enough to let Ellarie forget her current predicament.

Mackhol gave his legs a slap and laughed at seemingly himself. "Listen to me chattering. You're positively bored by all this talk, and it really does not concern you, anyhow. However, I will say that it is nice to speak to a person without a horse in the race and just have someone listen to me. I am talked at all the time and I have to give an unending stream of orders myself, but no one ever takes the time to sit and listen to one another anymore. Would you not agree?"

"I suppose that might be true, milord," Ellarie sighed, her eyes going to the ceiling briefly for respite.

"Oh well, enough of that," Taves yielded on the matter while standing up abruptly. "You know why I am here, don't you, Miss Voyer?"

Ellarie closed her eyes for a second, and opened them to look straight into the face of Mackhol, so that she might face him proper. "Aye, milord, I know why you are here."

He approached her, and began to caress her face with his right hand, while the left began to slide along the side of her bodice until it found her skirts. "Alright then, Miss Voyer, then I will not mince words. Will you have me tonight?"

"I will not, milord," she told him, as certain in her decision as she had been every other night since arriving in his tower.

"You disappoint me yet again, young lady," he said with a click of his teeth as he released his hold on her and moved back a few paces. Like with every other night, he became a different man than the one who had entered the cell. In as quickly as one might snap their fingers, Taves' stance stiffened, his face wrinkled in disgust, and any semblance of amiability fled from voice. "You know I will not engage without your permission, and still you continue to take advantage of my gentlemanly ways. However, I tell you again as I have told you before that I shall not keep a woman here who has no interest in me. Your time is running out, Miss Voyer, and that is truly a shame, because you are quite fetching, and I have always wanted to have a member of the Thieves. Nevertheless, while it will pain me to see you go, I will not hesitate to do as much, as I would rather give this room to a woman who will appreciate the things I can give her."

"I understand, milord," Ellarie said through lips that fought against curling upward in repugnance. "I cannot bring myself to embrace a man who trusts me so little that he has to chain me to the wall by my hands just to be in the same room as me."

Taves found something in what she said amusing, and his cackling laugh filled the room. "Yes, and if I let you free, you will garrotte me at the first opportunity. If you want to earn my trust, you have to give me yours first. That is how this relationship will work. All of my girls have been precisely where you are, and not one of them has gotten special treatment before now. I am hardly going to make an exception for one of Orangecloak's brainwashed little cultists. You had best get over yourself and any notions that you are more special than anyone else in here is just because Orangecloak, Yassira, and the Dollen sisters let you into their club of postulant rebels. You were born a no one in Layn, and you will die a no one in Biddenhurst. That's the truth, as plain as the nose on my face. You might think that the choice you are making is only whether or not you and I fornicate, but it is more than that. With every refusal of me that you make, you are deciding how you spend the short time that remains of your life."

Taves made a motion with his hands as though they were the plates of a scale, holding the first one up high for her to see. "You can live here with me in as much comfort as a prisoner of any country can reasonably expect to have." His other hand sank as low as it could go without him bending at the knees. "Or you can be sent back down to the Gallows Hotel. At least, you will return there eventually. The guards might escort you through a long, arduous route to get there once I turn you over to them. I will tell you one thing: they are not the gentleman that I am, that's for sure. You will not get the luxury of telling them which road to take to the Gallows Hotel, if you understand what I am saying."

Though he stared directly at Ellarie, she made no move to give comment to anything that Taves was saying, and he threw his hands in the air. "Do you know what saddens me, Miss Voyer? The Matron had such high hopes for you when she picked you from Orangecloak's riffraff. Yet, I must say, that I am just not seeing the same things that she saw in you. In fact, all I am seeing is one great disappointment."

He left her there, and began to make for the door, stepping from his route only long enough to grab his hat from atop the bed. "I can afford you no more of my time today. I have needs that must be sated and the midnight hour is fast approaching us." A last look was sent her way, to see if Ellarie might change her mind. When she dared not to even return the glance, he straightened his suit and knocked on the cell door for Wendell.

As the key began to turn in the lock, Mackhol opened his mouth once more. "The sands in your hourglass are slipping away, Miss

Voyer, and it is only I that can turn it over. You would be wise to remember that."

"All finished for the night, Uncle?" Wendell asked as Mackhol pushed his way past his nephew and into the hallway. "No, you nitwit. Go in there, switch off her lamp, and then go get number five from her cell and deliver her to my chambers at once."

"Wait, my lord!" Ellarie heard the Matron calling after him. There were hurried, soft footsteps then and the two began a low conversation that Ellarie could not discern. It lasted for mere minutes, and ended in the Matron audibly pleading with Taves.

"Let go of me, Matron, I will not tell you again," Taves shouted at her roughly.

His feet began to climb the staircase in a huff, and the noise of his shoes stomping on the stones grew faint in a hurry.

Within seconds of Taves' temperamental departure, both Wendell and the Matron were back in Ellarie's cell. The former of the two began shuffling his way in front of her, making for the light switch that controlled the little lamp in the cage. "I'm sorry, Miss Voyer. I am just following Uncle Mackhol's orders. Please, don't be cross with me for what I am about to do."

"What is it that you are about to do, Wendell?" she asked him, though he deigned to answer.

The Matron strode up to Ellarie and put her hands on either side of her jaw. "Why could you not do as you were told, Bernadine?"

"I am sorry, Matron. I can't lay with him. I can't bring myself to do it. I have failed you, and I fully accept that. Yet, I cannot bring myself to allow him to touch me so long as the choice is mine to make."

"Your time is running out, Bernadine. What do you not understand about that?" she relayed in frustration at Ellarie. "Lord Mackhol is running out of patience with you, and has now resorted to punishments. Most girls don't get more than a few days after that. As it is, he has ordered Wendell to leave you in your manacles for the next three hours in the dark. You should use that time to think about your decisions. I will be back with a guard as soon as that time is up to help you get ready for bed, because believe me, honey: your arms won't work to let you do it yourself. Oh, you best keep from making any noise in that span. Lord Mackhol's chambers are right above you, and he tolerates no rackets."

"It's time to go, Matron," Wendell said as he turned out the lamp. "Follow me out, please."

The two departed quickly, and the cell door slammed shut shortly after, leaving Ellarie in total darkness with nothing to do and nowhere to even move.

She stood there, and despite the fact that she was still restrained, Ellarie allowed herself to take a few deep breaths to help her relax. There in the darkness, with only the soft clinking of her chains and her thoughts to keep her company, Ellarie rolled the events of the past few minutes over in her mind.

Above everything else, it was Royen's voice she heard the clearest, his dire news regarding Lazlo raising a lump in her throat.

If Royen told me true about Lazlo, then it means that Lazlo will almost certainly die in those fighting pits. Royen will not fight fair, and Lazlo will likely not even have a weapon with which to fight back. I may not be able to do much, but I must try something to get out of this place. If not for myself, then I must do it for Lazlo and the others. I can't stop fighting, not now. I cannot allow myself to become this.

EPILOGUE II
ORANGECLOAK

It was while walking through the dense brush of the Daol Forest, with the soft forest floor beneath her, and the fresh air in her lungs, that Orangecloak felt that she was a free woman again. The events in Atrebell had taken that feeling from her, and though she was spared from the horrors of Grenjin Howland's dungeon, she was then sprung into confines of a different sort. Tryst Reine, her rescuer, had insisted on taking her through the open northern wilds of Illiastra on a trek that ultimately brought them to Portsward. Though she was in the further company of Tyrendil Wildheart and Fletchard Miller, an elf and a man as eager to flee as she was, Orangecloak had still felt as bound to their path as a train on its track.

The course set by the man known as the Master of Blades had led them to the manor of Lord Greggard Simillon. It was there that Simillon and his city councillor, Maurice Kett, attempted to court Orangecloak and the Thieves into the service of a group known as the Musicians. Their secretive network of political figures and wealthy philanthropists were intent on financially supporting the Thieves on a mission to be the face of the Illiastran revolution.

She had listened to their pitch, and even agreed in part to certain terms of it. Yet, what Orangecloak would call her crowning achievements in Portsward was the drafting of her own plan, and the formation of a new band of ready recruits. With them at her side,

Orangecloak found herself in the Daol Forest, on a path of her own choosing.

Greggard, Maurice, and the Musicians might have a plan in mind for the Thieves and me, but I am not theirs to order about. I am indebted to the Musicians for saving me and helping me back on my feet, to that I do not argue. However, that does not make me theirs. I listened to their offer, and even agreed to an alliance of sorts, but I am under no obligation to place the Thieves and myself under the authority of the Musicians. If Greggard and his friends feel that I am to repay a debt to them, I will figure out some alternate arrangement to servitude.

One of Orangecloak's new acquisitions was scouting ahead of the group, and every now and then, Orangecloak would catch sight of her slipping through the trees as silently as a shadow. Much like Tyrendil before her, Yahmina Windleaf was an elf from their forest nation in the northeast reaches of Illiastra, and that is where their similarities ended. Ren, as he liked to be called, was an academic. Specifically, he was a tenured engineering professor employed by the Midlands University of Gildriad, which was itself a human institution in the westerly country of the same name.

Much the opposite of Ren, the female elf presently slipping through the Daol Forest ahead of Orangecloak's party was an expert of the blade and bow. Yahmina had gone abroad to advance her studies, and had earned her distinctive title from the University of Combative Arts in the Fuwachita Mountains of Drake, alongside Tryst Reine.

It could be said that Greggard gave her to me. Yet I ask, what human can say that they have dominion over an elf? She joined up with the Thieves freely and of her own volition.

Directly behind Orangecloak walked a neophyte field agent named Amyla Spade, who had pledged herself to the Thieves in tandem with the fully-fledged nurse, Athelbert Fauster, who was himself the former lover of Amyla's late brother. The two of them had fled Obalen to avoid a similar fate as Amyla's murdered sibling and had sought to join up with the cause in Portsward.

The last additions to Orangecloak's new band were the two fresh faces picked up by Tryst during his brief recruitment into the forces of West Illiastra during the Battle of Pelican Harbour. The pair was apparently the remnants of a subgroup of the vaunted and shady company referred to as the Flying Hawks, whom Tryst had been contracted to fight for during the battle. The duo consisted of a swordsman and a squire. The first was a shaggy-haired, hulking man who preferred to be called Yak. Apart from Tryst, whose inclusion was only temporary, Yak was the lone surviving combatant of the decimated foursome. With Yak came Merith Tailor, a teenaged member of the Hawks who had previously held the nickname of Cob during her time with them. Both former Flying Hawks had joined the Thieves readily, hoping to find a purpose and a place that they had lost with the death of their friend Vix, who had been the leader of their subgroup.

I found the first two with help from none but Yahmina and my west coast recruiter, Charl. Tryst brought the second pair to our fold. The Thieves never needed the musicians to attract members before, and everything that we earned since Marros' days was done through the blood, sweat, and tears of my friends and me. That is how it will continue to be done.

If it should be that the goals of Greggard and the Musicians align with those of the Thieves, then that is perfectly fine. I would have no reason to be adversarial towards Simillon and his ilk. However, I am not going to send the Thieves into the Southlands to be proxies for the Musicians in any conflict that might arise there. If we fight, it will be on our terms, for our reasons, and against our foes.

Tryst, Yak, and Cob's arrival in Portsward was only a train ride separated from the Battle of Pelican Harbour, which the two men had been directly involved in. Though the skirmish in Nothram's manor had shed a great deal of the Flying Hawks blood, their company was the ones responsible for capturing Haymard Nothram and earning the surrender of his forces. In fact, so quickly did events unfold that Tryst and Yak claimed that the Flying Hawks had taken to calling it *The Battle over Breakfast.*

Nothram deserves everything that Marigold Tullivan might have coming to him. Like Mackhol Taves out of Biddenhurst, Nothram had made cruelty into his personal brand.

From both her own visits to Pelican Harbour and the testimonies of other members of the Thieves, Orangecloak knew Nothram to be gleefully antipathetic. A number of sources told Orangecloak how excited and downright joyous Nothram would look during occasions when his local government were sanctioned to carry out corporal punishments. From those accounts alone, even the description of

Nothram's mannerisms was enough to make Orangecloak sick to her stomach.

If another person's suffering brings Nothram that much happiness, then his depravity knows no bounds. I have to wonder if he will show that same excitement at his own execution.

According to Tryst, it seemed that the only outcome for Nothram was to be found through the loop of a noose. Usually, a man of Nothram's wealth and station could expect to skate free from justice with little more than a glancing blow to both his wrist and coin purse. However, the latest news that was relayed to them in Portsward from Daol Bay was that Marigold was ensuring that Nothram was granted no such protections. Given that Nothram was facing charges of murder and attempted murder atop a plethora of further crimes, Orangecloak could imagine no other way that Nothram would pay for those transgressions but with his own life.

I will not weep for him any more than Marigold will.

As she heard it from Greggard and Tryst, the Tullivan woman was someone that Orangecloak would enjoy meeting, and she suspected that they might be at least partially correct. Certainly, Orangecloak did appreciate how quickly Marigold made use of the power given to her so that she might rebel against the EMP and, in effect, the Triarchy too.

Marigold thus far has given me no reason to believe that she will not continue to prop up the class system that holds so many down to the benefit of so few. We share an enemy, and the goal of deposing that enemy, but if we both remain standing when the fog of that war lifts, we might still be in opposition to one another.

Perhaps that is why Greggard is so eager to influence the Thieves and me. He would like to take advantage of our mutual desires while curbing the parts of the Thieves' campaign that do not benefit him. The newly styled Sealord will find himself wanting then, if that is indeed the case.

Orangecloak had consulted with her newest recruits on the matter, hoping to gain insight into the mind of Greggard from Tryst and Yahmina. Much to her consternation, all that either the man or the elf could offer was vague guesswork.

"Greggard would have known of your opposition to the class system, Orangecloak," Tryst had said on the matter with a nonchalant shrug. *"I cannot imagine that he would offer shelter, resources, and financing if he was not aware of the risk you posed to his life of luxury."*

Yahmina was similarly unhelpful. *"Lord Greggard seems none too concerned with the scenarios that await him as a result of aiding you. I would have to think that he has explored all options and arrived at the conclusion that the benefits far outweigh the detriments. To that end, I would be led to believe that he not only considered the metrics from his own personal vantage point, but from the perspective of Illiastra's greater good, too."*

How hypocritical would I be to tear the EMP down to its foundation only to allow the houses of Tullivan and Simillon to continue to be propped up by its constructs? The people would rightfully lose all measure of respect for me. There would be no reason for any to listen to what I had to say after that, knowing that I could be bent and moulded to the whims of the highest bidders.

I cannot allow Greggard to reshape me, not after all what the Thieves and I have done to get this far. If that sows mistrust between he and I, then I will be the first to apologise for it.

While Orangecloak had been lost in her thoughts, the day had begun to creep into the mid-afternoon. The food supplies given to Marigold by Greggard's staff were beginning to dwindle, leaving her party with little other option than to hunt and gather for nourishment. Such a requirement forced them to set camp earlier in the day than Orangecloak would have liked, but hunting took time, and rest was required when such an arduous task was done.

"Keep an eye out for a body of water," Orangecloak called to the others. "We should make our camp for the night at the next pond or stream we come across."

"Aye, my lady, it'll be as you want," Yak answered her from where he was at the rear of the pack.

Since starting their trek, Orangecloak had been working to strip the 'lady' part of her name from the collective lexicon of the group. Tryst was famous for referring to her as 'my lady' or 'Lady Orangecloak', and she thought that he, above the others, would have the most difficult time adhering to the request. Much to Orangecloak's surprise, he was among the first to adapt to the idea.

"I am used to being called Lady Orangecloak, and have referred to myself as such from time to time, I admit." Orangecloak had explained to her followers at the onset of their trek. *"However, it must be said that I expect nothing of the sort from you all. Ellarie and Merion Dollen have never called me 'my lady', nor did Myles or Coquarro. You, like*

they, are my friends, and friends just call me Orangecloak. It is outsiders and elites that use the 'lady' part, and that is fine, for the sake of formality. You all have no need to do so, though."

Yahmina had made the switch effortlessly, which is how the elves seemed to accomplish most things. Even the two from Obalen, Amyla and Athel, had been coming along quite nicely on that front. It was Yak and Merith that were not adjusting, and Orangecloak had to suspect that their militaristic training was playing a large factor in that.

Everything that either former member of the Flying Hawks had to say seemed to be either prefaced or concluded with 'ser' and 'lady' unless they were talking to one another. Orangecloak was at the point of simply giving up and accepting the behaviour as an unavoidable quirk of their personalities.

It was when the seven-person party had left Portsward four days prior that Orangecloak had begun that process. Their trek had begun on the Daol Plains, and the crossing of the rolling grasslands had been a fearsome ordeal to undertake. Knowing that House Palomb might soon be marching an army in their direction at any time and without warning, the group had been on constant edge. Every day was spent with all hands scanning the horizons, their legs moving as quickly as they could to put as much of the snowy ground behind them. By night, they were huddled behind one of the many rock formations to be found or burrowing down in thickets and bushes as they came across them, wishing for the warmth and comfort of a fire on every occasion. On the last night, they even found a small crop of forest, and for the first time, they had made a proper camp.

Now in the comforting embrace of the mixed-growth Daol Forest, Orangecloak and her friends had allowed themselves the space to relax and enjoy the journey.

Orangecloak glanced around to see if she could spot Yahmina, but the elven woman either was concealed amongst the trees or gone too far ahead to be visible.

"Can someone track down Yahmina and let her know of our intentions?" Orangecloak asked openly.

"I will take care of it, milady," Merith replied gaily.

"The task is all yours," Orangecloak allowed, holding out her hand as she said as much. "Here, leave your things with us so that you are not so burdened. Yahmina will not be easy to catch."

Orangecloak had grown fond of the teenaged squire since their meeting. The willingness of the young recruit to take on any task presented to her was a trait that Orangecloak admired, and her training with the Flying Hawks was thus far lending itself well to the Thieves.

"Here, allow me to help, La- Uh, Orangecloak," Amyla offered while taking the heavy pack straight out of the squire's hands. The weight of the oversized canvas knapsack became apparent in the transfer, and Orangecloak had to marvel at the strength of Merith for having carried it for so long.

Once unencumbered, Merith made a stretch of her limbs and took a deep breath. With a last nod to Orangecloak and Amyla, the youngest member of the party took off at a dash through the forest of firs and pines.

"Do you think that Merith will find Yahmina?" Amyla asked while adjusting the added baggage now slung across her back and shoulders.

"More likely that Yahmina will find Merith first," Orangecloak answered with a smile and a short laugh.

Upon resuming their hike, Orangecloak slowed her pace down to a casual stride, her eyes scanning the landscape of mid-winter snows dotted with fallen fir needles and crunching, browned leaves. The sun had begun to lower itself through the branches of the distant trees, flitting streaks of gold through the green.

"Had enough for one day, Orangecloak?" she heard Tryst ask as he, Yak, and Athel closed the gap between her and Amyla.

"Aye, the day is beginning to wane and I felt a short hunt was in order, while we could still see enough to do so," Orangecloak explained to the three men.

"Well, I cannot argue with that one," Tryst said while looking all about. "Have you happened to spot a water source nearby?"

Orangecloak focused on climbing a short embankment ahead of her while she offered an answer. "Not yet. First viable wet spot we see though, we are setting up camp beside."

"All well and good by me," Yak said with a sigh and a roll of his thick shoulders. "We surely must have put a few kilometres on our boots today."

Athel was pulling himself over the embankment then, huffing as he went. Upon his back there rested a large, veritable cabinet of medical supplies. Though it looked as though his burden was about to threaten to topple him backward, Athel managed to get in a comment of his own through the struggle. "I can feel the muscles in my legs growing, or at least growling at me, with every step. The sooner we stop, the happier I will be."

"You're in luck then, for I was planning on leaving yourself and Merith to set up our camp," Orangecloak told him while reaching for his hand so that she could pull him up to the top of the bank.

Tryst was scanning the ground on the other side of the climb, humming thoughtfully as he did. "Looks like a shallow, sloping valley here. With any luck, we might find a brook or a stream nearby."

"Here's hoping," Orangecloak added to the thought.

The descent into the valley went in a deliberate, careful manner, given that each of them was carrying a fair amount of additional weight that could send either one of them tumbling. None among them was particularly interested in taking a roll amongst the trees and the rocks half hidden in the snow, and so the five took their time. In the lowest point of the tiny valley they gathered, walking through the depths until the bank on the opposite side looked low enough to scale without much effort.

Tryst and Orangecloak were the first to top the second hill, and they extended their hands to help their more burdened comrades climb.

"I must say, Tryst," Orangecloak began while pulling Amyla towards herself. "You would think that we would have found the deeply trodden paths and broken camps of that army you travelled to Pelican Harbour with."

"We are too far deep into the forest for that," Tryst explained with a heave as he drew Yak upward. "The Flying Hawks did not know the Daol Forest as well as they had claimed, and were barely a few hundred feet from the border of the western grasslands at any given time. If it was not winter, and hunters and rangers were more plentiful, our marching army would have been spotted and reported to the western holdout ministers easily."

"Aye, I should think we were poorly hidden, considering that you found us easily enough, Lynx," Yak chided with a deep chuckle, a slap on Tryst's back following the jape.

As Orangecloak was given to understand, Lynx had been Tryst's codename during his brief stint with the Flying Hawks. Just as with his own sobriquet, Yak seemed to prefer it to any other name Tryst claimed.

"But of course, Yak," Tryst joked in response. "How could I miss a big brute like you hollering and busting your way through the trees like a moose in heat?"

Yak had a parry for Tryst's verbal jab at the ready. "Call me a moose all you want, but I didn't have to run like a startled deer all the way to Pelican Harbour. For that matter, I don't recall you complaining too much when you got to ride in the saddle at the back of the Hawks alongside me when the opportunity presented itself."

"I did enjoy that luxury when it came up," Tryst admitted with a shake of his head. "That was well met, Yak."

Orangecloak had found herself amused at the brief exchange, and was soon laughing along at it.

Despite his own recent tragedy in Pelican Harbour, Yak was quick with a joke and unafraid to poke fun at himself, or at Tryst, for that matter. The two had developed a definite rapport in their brief time together, and it showed itself plainly when the two traded friendly barbs.

The other Flying Hawk was comparatively reserved, though she seemed to be in competition with Amyla for Orangecloak's approval. As much as Orangecloak tried to dispel the notion that either girl held preference with her, Merith thus far seemed intent on besting Amyla at whatever game she imagined they were playing.

Merith is a little immature, but she is also a teenager, and the two things are not quite mutually exclusive. She just has a little ways left to grow up to get there.

On the other hand, Amyla was coming along in leaps and bounds in every way that a member of the Thieves might be expected to. Orangecloak's concern with Amyla's progress stemmed from her fear that the Obalen woman's lone motivation was the revenge she sought for her deceased brother.

I don't know that I can temper her lust for vengeance, or even if it is my place to do so. What I do know is that such quests rarely end in a satisfying conclusion, and I would rather she not rest her ambitions solely on avenging her brother. Those goals tend to invariably end in one of three ways: she dies in the attempt, the targets slip away out of her reach through escape or an alternative demise, or she actually succeeds and kills the responsible parties. Even in the lattermost and best scenario, Amyla will be left staring at an empty void where her drive and determination once were. No one ever knows what to do after they achieve their revenge.

Perhaps once she meets the other Thieves in Rillis Vale she will let the personal hate ebb into a pursuit of justice for all, as I did before her.

Orangecloak remembered herself as being no different from Amyla when she was the same age as Merith, and it was not until she reached Amyla's age that she realised the error of it. Back then, there were people in Orangecloak's mind that needed to pay dearly at her hands for the wrongs dealt to those she loved in her youth, or so she had believed. Good leadership and better friends had worked to reshape her outlook, and Orangecloak knew in hindsight that she was better off for it.

"I have discovered a tiny pond not far ahead," Orangecloak heard from a little ways off. The overly proper speech told Orangecloak that the speaker was the elven woman. "It is but a little thing, and mostly obscured by trees, but the water is of good quality. In addition, the youngling also informs me that you are calling a stop to the hike for the day. Am I to presume that we are doing so at such an early hour so that we might proceed with a hunt?"

"That would be correct, Yahmina," Orangecloak called back to the elf, turning to make eye contact with her in the process. "You will want to hunt alone, no doubt?"

Yahmina gave a nod for an answer. "That would be best, yes."

"I will not keep you, then," Orangecloak responded with a nod of her own. "Before you go, where did you last see Merith?"

With the raising of her left arm, Yahmina pointed further down the valley, toward a place that was evidently unseen due to a rise in the forest floor. "She is sitting at the water's edge trying to catch her breath. The poor thing ran herself ragged trying to catch up to me."

"Fair enough," Orangecloak commented while making a visual note of the direction that Yahmina was pointing in. "We will find her and set up camp at the pond. Which way do you intend to go for your hunt?"

The elf turned about, appearing to observe her surroundings with her ears and nose as much as her eyes. "South, I should think... But I sense that I will not need to go too far."

"Right, we will leave you to it," Orangecloak added, leaving the elf to part from their company as they made for the pond that Yahmina had pointed out to them.

If Orangecloak had not met Tyrendil Wildheart, an elf who was Yahmina's opposite in nearly every way, she would have been led to believe that all elves were like her new friend. Indeed, every known representation of the reclusive peoples, whether fictional or factual, displayed traits similar to Yahmina's in that they were given to be logical, brilliant, and stunningly beautiful paragons of physical fitness who were uncannily attuned to nature. Of course, Ren did possess many of those traits, but he did not come across as seemingly perfect as Yahmina. He had faults that one might expect to find in a human, such as his less-than-stellar marksmanship. He also seemed emotionally warmer than Yahmina, and carried himself in a relaxed state, whereas she appeared to be constantly on alert. Granted, those differences could easily be attributed to their upbringings and vocations, with one being an academic, and the other a mercenary archer and swordswoman.

All of Orangecloak's thoughts of Ren, and the inevitable comparisons to Yahmina had led Orangecloak to two conclusions. Firstly, Orangecloak could say with certainty that elves could not be disseminated down to a single set of traits and characteristics. They were each a unique individual, genetically similar, but wholly their own person. No different from humans or dwarves in that regard, no matter how determined some humans were to shoulder the other races with misleading stereotypes. The second conclusion, and the one that played on Orangecloak's mind the most, was that she found herself truly missing Ren. Though their time together was rather brief, she had rather enjoyed his presence.

I am going to find him again, if I am alive when all of this is over.

Rounding the snowy knoll, the band caught sight of the pond and Merith, who was seated on a rock before it. She looked up at them on approach and gave a weary wave.

"Yahmina tells us that you had quite the time trying to catch up to her," Orangecloak said in greeting as they descended a gentle hill to reach Merith.

"She is so very quick," Merith noted between deep breaths. "Every time I thought I was closing in on Yahmina, it seemed that she was only getting further away. I think she knew that I was following her the whole time, too. Those elves can sense that sort of thing. I think she was toying with me."

"Have you scouted a site for our camp yet?" Orangecloak asked the squire while looking at all sides of the pond. Where Merith was already seated seemed like the best place, given that it had a mostly level space protected from the north and west sides due to the embankment that the party had just navigated around moments before. The east side and the peaks of the embankment were tree covered, and the south side approached the little pond at a gentle, easily accessible shoreline.

"Oh, uh, right here should do, I think," Merith answered quickly, gesturing about with a hand. "Do you want me to come with you today for the hunt?"

"I would rather that you set up the camp, if it is alright with you, Merith," Orangecloak requested, nodding her head towards Athel in the process. "I think Athel will want to stay back and do the same. Between the two of you, it should take you no time, and then you can both relax while the rest of us go see about procuring dinner."

"You will get no complaint from me on the matter," Athel said with an exhaustive sigh while plopping his heavy pack down on the ground.

Merith looked as though she were about to protest the decision, but relented and turned her face away from Orangecloak and the others. "I will do as you request, Lady Orangecloak."

"Thank you for that," Orangecloak told her before looking to the remaining three. "Tryst and Yak, you two seem to do well as a group and I would not want to end your streak. Amyla, you and I will go east and see if we cannot find something worth eating."

"Alright, Yak and I will venture west," Tryst decided for the two in a light-hearted tone. As he spoke, Tryst shed all of the equipment on his back save for his bow and quiver. "Seems like the easiest way to go out of the remaining options. With or without food, we will be back before sundown. If we are not, send a search party."

A laugh escaped Orangecloak at the gentle joke, and Tryst winked at her during his and Yak's departure from the campsite. Orangecloak found herself intrigued by Tryst Reine, even attracted to him physically, though she felt unsure of how to proceed with a courtship, or even if it was a wise idea. He seemed ready for it, and clearly had romantic feelings towards her, yet when it came to love, Orangecloak felt broken inside.

She had kissed him once, in a half-drunken haze during their stay at the Dupoire Hotel on the edge of the Dwarven Lands in the far north. There were even times since then, in the private moments together, that Orangecloak honestly felt like there might be a spark between them. Despite that, Orangecloak could not bring herself to take things forward.

Why would Tryst even want me, anyway? He could have practically any woman his heart desires, and he deserves better than what I can give him.

"Alright, Amyla," Orangecloak said after laying down her excess gear. "Let us be off, while the daylight remains to us."

Across Orangecloak's back and strapped atop her black, bearskin-lined cloak and the namesake orange cloak was a velvet satchel that emitted a distinct wooden rattle as they walked. The noise was more apparent now that it was only the two of them, and Amyla had taken notice of it immediately.

"We're not going for a hunt, are we?" she asked with a sly grin.

"Not today," Orangecloak confirmed with a sideways glance at her new friend. "Between Tryst, Yak, and Yahmina, one of them will find some game. If you are feeling up to it, you and I are going to do some training."

Since Yahmina had opted to join the Thieves, Orangecloak and Amyla had been taking advantage of her extensive knowledge on the art of combat. Under the watchful eye of the certified instructor from the Combat University of Drake, both women had been honing their own skills. To Orangecloak's credit, she had been trained to use a recurve bow and to handle a blade when she was first initiated into the Thieves some years ago. While she maintained her efficiency with the bow through hunting and a general interest in archery, her skill in melee combat had grown considerably rusted.

While Orangecloak's skillset had waned from disuse, Amyla had the opposite issue. Having come to the Thieves from a domesticated life of being an unpaid maid to Minister Newell Felton in Obalen, Amyla had no training as a combatant whatsoever. Together, they made for apt sparring partners, with both of them having to start from the beginning beneath Yahmina's instruction.

Anything Orangecloak thought she knew when it came to fighting under the tutelage of the Thieves was quickly determined to be of little use when learning beneath Yahmina. The combined disciplines of the elven warriors and the combat university made for a structured system with which Orangecloak's basic fighting training could not compare. Among the major differences was that the approach of the Thieves to melee fighting was to use it as a means to survive an encounter. To the students of the Combat University, the goal was the defeat of the opponent.

Orangecloak had grown used to a life of running and escaping from potential encounters, living to 'fight another day', as the saying went. Yahmina, on the other hand, was teaching Orangecloak and Amyla not just to engage an enemy, but also to remain in that combative state until the fight reached a decisive end.

It was a completely new mentality for Orangecloak to adapt to, and the thought of fighting for victory over bare survival left her with a measure of anxiety. Of course, Orangecloak was no stranger to seeing death at work. From the time of her tumultuous teenage years, it seemed that the icy tendrils of the ever after were as present in her life as the orange cloak on her back. She knew death could be gentle and merciful, having seen it ushering the elderly and ill to the beyond. Yet, in that same vein, she had also witnessed death in its most cruel and visceral form. However, the thought of dispatching another human being into the insatiable arms of death was not something that Orangecloak could consider herself capable of doing.

Yet, it is what I am told I must be party to. Whether I am dealing the killing blow personally, commanding that the act be carried out by my Thieves, or ordering those same people to wager their own lives on my behalf. Though so many believe that I am the sort of person to attempt courting death for such purposes, the idea of even approaching him makes my stomach wretch.

Orangecloak and Amyla searched for an appropriate location to train, their eyes scanning for any sort of field or clearing that would allow them the space to spar. After what felt to Orangecloak like twenty minutes of walking and looking, Amyla jabbed a finger towards a spacious stretch of wild grass that was basking in the afternoon sun and attempting to shed its melting snow. It shone like a beacon before the two, and they rushed over to the open area take advantage of the remaining daylight.

The velvet bag across Orangecloak's back was slung to the ground hurriedly, where its string was pulled open and the contents dumped onto the ground with a clatter. At their feet sat a pair of two-tined claws wrapped in a leather thong, two single-handed short swords, and a hatchet, all of it made of fine yew wood and weighted with lead.

"Shall we go with swords or our primary weapons today, Amyla?" Orangecloak asked while sweeping a hand over the practice weaponry, leaving the choice to her friend.

"I feel like we should practice with swords for a change," Amyla decided with a humming noise, removing a water canteen hanging from her neck and laying it with the practice tools. "Yahmina said it was important for us to know how to use a sword, and we continually neglect practicing with them for the claws and hatchet. So, I figure why not today?"

"Admit it, Amyla. You just don't want to have to remove your claw gloves," Orangecloak chided lightly while pointing at the fingerless gloves on Amyla's hands. They were worn with a pair of buckles on the wrist of each leather glove to keep them from moving, and with good reason. Along the knuckles of either hand was a ridge of steel slotted in several places. The added steel served as both an enhancement to her punching ability and as the setting plate for a pair of steel claws currently resting in holsters on Amyla's hips.

"Well, aye, that is part of it," the former maid admitted with a smile. "The damn wooden claws can't be worn over these gloves, the steel gets in the way. Anyway, you let me pick, and I said swords."

"That I did. Swords it is, then," Orangecloak relented while scooping up one of the two long, wooden weapons.

Amyla grabbed the other and gave it twirling flourish, an altogether useless talent that Yahmina would scold upon sight.

"Now, now, Amyla, 'Swords are deadly weapons and not to be used for dancing', you know," Orangecloak said in paraphrased quotation of their instructor.

Extending her sword outward in Orangecloak's direction, Amyla gave a click of her teeth. "Aye, but Yahmina is not here right now and I don't ask much. Let me have a little fun with our wooden replicas."

"All that gallivanting won't keep me from getting inside your guard," Orangecloak warned Amyla while quickly advancing on her.

"Whoa, now!" Amyla exclaimed while dodging backward on her heels. "We have not even set the rules. Let's go light touch today. I'm still sore from that crack on the elbow you gave me yesterday."

"That's fair," Orangecloak said in acceptance of the request. "Three slashes or stabs to non-vital areas or one to the vitals ends a match.

We keep our cloaks and real weaponry on our persons. Yahmina says we should get used to fighting with them, anyhow. Does all of that sound all right with you?"

Amyla had put about two to three metres between her and Orangecloak, her sword lying across her shoulder during the Field Commander's reply. By the time Orangecloak finished, she had a response of her own, "Aye, that all sounds well and good. Now, come at me."

A look of fierceness overtook Amyla's eyes, and she began to close the distance between her and Orangecloak. It was an even match, as always it was. From their comparable height and size, to their skill levels and even their similarly tailored leather armouring, it would be difficult for an outsider to predict a winner between the two.

At the sound of Orangecloak's command, the women began circling one another, their weapons raised to chest height.

Every soft footfall that either woman made was carefully laid, one after the other. Each one appeared ready to strike at the first sign of a misstep and until such a time, it looked as though neither one was willing to give as much as an inch. Based on past sparring matches, Orangecloak knew that Amyla had limited patience, and would eventually deliver herself into Orangecloak's range to create an opening, rather than wait for one to appear.

On that premise, Orangecloak had no qualms with waiting, and Amyla did not disappoint.

"I don't have all day for this," Amyla muttered before suddenly rushing forward.

A grunt surged forth from Amyla as she pushed into Orangecloak's guard, leaving Orangecloak to evade the thrust and respond with a check to Amyla's sword to keep it away. Amyla kept the pressure up, and levelled stab after stab at Orangecloak, and she soon found herself struggling to repel the blows.

Their swords locked in a stalemate, and their faces came within millimetres of one another.

"Come on now, is that all you can do?" Amyla taunted before breaking away.

"Not at all," Orangecloak answered as she went on an attack of her own. She drove Amyla all around the little field, keeping the woman and her brown head of curls bobbing all over to keep Orangecloak's sword from touching her.

Amyla parried a thrust aimed at her thigh and on the return slash was able to make contact with Orangecloak's shoulder. "There's a kill."

"Don't you think that a shoulder mark would only count as a non-vital area?" Orangecloak queried during a brief rest.

"If it is your dominant arm, you should at least have to switch hands," Amyla asked with her tongue in her cheek. "I would like to see you keep fighting with a hole in your sword shoulder."

"Just watch me," Orangecloak replied while flipping her sword to her left hand.

Despite Orangecloak's confidence, the loss of the dominant arm proved fatal for the fictional surrogate of herself, and Amyla finished her off in seconds with a tap just below the breastbone on the left side.

"If you weren't dead before, that did the job," Amyla declared, her sword returning to its place of rest on her shoulder. "How about we have a drink of water and then go for round two?"

Orangecloak let a nod serve as an answer and the two made for the edge of the field where they left their things.

They gulped down some water and stood in the silence for a moment, listening to the gentle breeze rustle through the trees. A lone maple tree waved its empty branches from the other side of the field, and somewhere in the distance, they could hear what sounded like forest life on the move.

"What sort of animals do you think that was?" Orangecloak asked as she narrowed her eyes in the direction that she felt the sounds came from.

"A couple of squirrels or chipmunks chasing one another, perhaps," Amyla answered with a nonchalant shrug. "Or maybe a hare. Something small like that, I should think. Are you ready?"

"Aye, let's go," Orangecloak affirmed while handing back the canteen. She had walked back to the field and was adjusting her grip on the sword by the time Amyla joined her.

Orangecloak raised the blunted weapon at Amyla and beckoned with her empty hand. "Alright, come at me."

The two returned to their clash, jabbing and slashing at one another while the sun started to dip beyond the horizon. The second contest went to Orangecloak, who scored a decisive stab to the abdomen. The third and fourth matches both went to Amyla, the first on points, the other by tripping Orangecloak and levelling the sword at her exposed neck.

"What do you say to one more before we head back?" Orangecloak asked while brushing the snow and dirt from herself. "I think we have the daylight for it."

"Trying to get a last win on me before we have to stop, are ya?" Amyla questioned jokingly, her eyebrows quirked for added effect.

Orangecloak heard herself laugh at the jape. "I might be. Are you up for it or not?"

Amyla threw her free hand up. "Aye, why not? Might as well get the extra practice in. Although, if I keep beating you like this, I may start to feel bad about it."

A feigned and exaggerated "Hah!" was all that Orangecloak gave in response, and she lifted her tiring sword arm. "Don't go getting all full of yourself, Amyla. A cocksure bodyguard is not much good to me."

"And clearly you need the protection, if that is how you fight."

She tried to mask the fact that Amyla's offhand comment brought a painful memory to mind, though judging from Amyla's immediate remorse, Orangecloak realised that she failed on that front.

"I'm so sorry, I didn't mean any harm. I hope I did not upset you," Amyla gasped in immediate contrition.

"No, no, it's alright," Orangecloak said after a deep breath. "Sometimes the past just creeps up on me like that. Come on then, let's have one more go before dusk."

Amyla looked about to ask further, but Orangecloak's raised sword served as answer enough, and they began their circling.

Both were reluctant to be the first to swing, as per usual, and they went around in their slow dance several times. On what felt like the third lap, Orangecloak thought that she saw movement in the trees from the direction that would have been behind her when they began.

"Wait," she said softly to Amyla.

"I won't fall for that," Amyla responded with a direct thrust in Orangecloak's direction.

"Dammit, I said wait," Orangecloak instructed her firmly, following it up with their safety word. "Tulip."

Amyla noticed Orangecloak's fixed attention and looked over her own shoulder in the same direction.

The foliage continued to shake where Orangecloak was looking, with the undeniably large source of the movement drawing closer by the second.

Orangecloak let the wooden sword thump to the grass and went for the hollow-headed, steel hatchet resting on her hip. As she pulled it forth, Amyla took notice and threw down the practice weapon, her hands balling into fists as they attempted to arm the steel claws.

"By the order of Lord Master Grenjin Howland, I command thee to drop your weapons, raise yours hands where we can see them, and not move a muscle!" a man's voice yelled out to the two of them.

"What in Iia's name is going on?" Amyla whispered to Orangecloak through gritted teeth.

Orangecloak's eyes scanned the treeline for the owner of the voice, until a humanoid shape holding a long, wooden object began to emerge through the trees.

Too late to run.

Holding the rifle was a soldier, and following him were two more armed in a similar fashion.

They're all bluecoats.

"I said drop the weapon!" the leading rifleman barked again.

Knowing that there were at least three in sight, potentially more situated further back in the trees, and that she and Amyla were in clear sight, Orangecloak knew it was futile to simply attack. Her right hand splayed open, and the hatchet fell into the yellowed grass.

A glance to Amyla found her hands bare, the claws having not been equipped at all. Panic was rapt across her face, and she glanced back to Orangecloak for guidance.

"Raise your hands, Amyla," Orangecloak instructed her with measured calmness in her voice. "Everything will be fine, I promise you. Just do as I say, and we will get through this."

"Let's see those hands, ladies. Touch the sky," the same soldier shouted. The trio was standing within a few metres of the two of them then. "Who are you and what are you doing so deep in the Daol Forest? Where are your guardians? Are you fugitives?"

"Oh fuck, Piotr, I think that's Orangecloak," one of the other soldiers called to the man in front.

So much for concealing my identity.

"Not every ginger-haired woman we come across is Orangecloak," the front soldier replied without so much as a glimpse at his comrades. "Her cloak is black, for one thing."

"Look beneath the black cloak when the wind hits it," the second soldier instructed the one referred to as Piotr.

The third one lowered his rifle just slightly and squinted at Orangecloak and Amyla. "Wait now, isn't she dead?"

"No, stupid," Piotr spat back at the speaker. "That's just what the Lord Master wants people to believe. Why'd you think the EMP ordered us to hunt down the supposed imposter that the Master of Blades is parading about?"

"Very well, there's an easy way to sort this all out," the squinting guard said. "Hey you, redhead, are you Orangecloak?"

Orangecloak stood there silently, contemplating her options, when the one called Piotr turned toward his comrade. "You really are as dumb as you look, Higgins. If she was Orangecloak, do you think she would just say that she is Orangecloak?"

"I am indeed the one known as Orangecloak," she informed them as a plan began to form in her mind.

"Aye, sure thing, and I'm Ios reborn," Piotr scoffed humorously. "You're just some madwoman with fiery hair, more like."

Amyla was glancing between Orangecloak and the men fearfully, but Orangecloak retained her composure. "Your friend there already saw the namesake cloak. You know it's true that I am who I say I am."

"Then where is Tryst Reine?" Piotr said while renewing his grip on his rifle, drawing a fresh bead on Orangecloak in the process. "Where is the Master of Blades?"

"Now that's a name I haven't heard since I got out of Atrebell," Orangecloak told them with her own humorous inflection. "I suppose by now he's already mounted the heads of Grenjin Howland and Eamon Palomb and his sons on the gates of the Atrebell manor. He was awfully intent on finishing them off."

"What?" the second soldier exclaimed. "That can't be true."

"Oh, but it is," Orangecloak insisted vociferously. "The war is already over. Long live Lady Master Marigold Tullivan."

"She's lying, you fool," Piotr said in exasperation. "About being Orangecloak and that shit about the Lord Master being dead. Higgins, go bind their hands. We'll take them with us to camp and let the captain sort out her horseshit. I'm not paid enough to listen to the rantings of a lunatic."

"Wait one minute," Orangecloak commanded as the third guard began to lower his rifle and approach. "I am not lying. You know I am Orangecloak as sure as you are standing there. What reason do I have to lie about that? You have to admit that pretending to be the most wanted woman in Illiastra serves me literally no benefit unless I am feeling particularly suicidal."

"Then why in the name of Ios would you admit that you are Orangecloak?" Piotr asked incredulously.

"Because I want to make you a deal, and I can only do that if you know who I am and the weight my name carries," Orangecloak calmly told them.

All three soldiers broke out in laughter then, and the second one spoke for the group. "What kind of deal do you think that you could possibly make?"

Orangecloak cleared her throat and levelled her offer. "You can have me, with neither quarrel nor complaint, to take back to your captain, where you will almost assuredly be recognised as heroes of what remains of Illiastra. All I ask in return is that you let my friend go. She is no one, just a housewife from Argesse who was sickened by the bloodshed of the Biddenhurst brute squad on her doorstep. You would get nothing of use from her, and she has nothing to offer but trauma from what she witnessed."

"Why would we not just take the both of you anyway?" Piotr asked with a chortle. "You two have no weapons and we three have rifles, there is no reason for us to table any deal."

"No, what each of you have is a single shot," Orangecloak pointed out to them in frank and certain terms. "Spend that, and you'll be left with bayonets on the end of weighty, unwieldy sticks. I will grant you that we are close enough that you might well kill the both of us, but if you don't, one or the both of us will kill you all stone dead. Is that a risk that you're willing to take?"

"We've got sabres, too, you know," the second, unnamed soldier reminded Orangecloak.

"Oh don't worry, I see them," Orangecloak pointed out with a slight gesture of her head. "Again though, you had better hope that you hit the both of us with the steel balls in those rifles, because I know that my hatchet will do for you three before one of you can throw down your rifle and draw a sabre. You can avoid all that bloodshed and death though, and all you have to do is let my friend go. She's done nothing wrong in any of this."

"We could kill you right now and save ourselves all that trouble," Piotr reasoned as he trained his rifle squarely on Orangecloak's face.

"You could, but I'm worth far less dead than alive," she posited to the soldiers. "Especially if I don't have a face left for identification. Remember, what's left of the EMP will want my head, and they won't be too pleased if they think that some grunts took it instead."

"The brunette's just some waif," Higgins argued in favour of Orangecloak's proposition. "She is not worth potentially being killed over. I say we let her go. The captain doesn't even need to know that she existed."

Piotr spun about to face the other soldier. "Have you lost your bloody mind? What makes you think two women could even kill one of us? We're soldiers of Illiastra, Higgins. We're the envy of the military world. How would we manage to die against two women?"

"You have a point," Orangecloak called to him, causing him to pivot back to look at her. "Maybe you won't all perish against us. However, if you don't let my friend go, I will personally ensure that you die, Piotr."

"And then whatever is left of us will kill you, and present your head to the EMP," Piotr countered bitingly.

Orangecloak allowed herself a slim smile, her eyes going skyward. "Aye, but you will not be one of the presenters of my prized skull. You'll be here with the rest of me, lying in this field, and the two of us will feed the maggots together. You won't get to celebrate at the big feast, taste a drop of celebratory ale, or feel the tender touch of the camp followers that will swarm around the other two. All you will know is eternal darkness, and for what? Just to capture some nameless nobody who ran away from home. Is arresting her worth dying for when you could have me, free and clear?"

"Stop talking like that, I won't leave you," Amyla said with a wide-eyed face, her mouth agape at the audacity of what Orangecloak was suggesting.

"You will," Orangecloak informed Amyla with a sideways glance. "Because it is exactly what I will command if these men agree to the terms of our deal. You will not defy the order of your Field Commander, I know you won't."

"But..." Amyla began to counter, until Orangecloak gazed into her eyes. "Very well, if it is what you want..."

I hope that she has caught my meaning.

"Do we have a deal, gentlemen?" Orangecloak asked the soldiers. "Her freedom for my peaceful arrest, I believe that to be more than a fair trade."

The second guard, who still had no name that Orangecloak was aware of, took on a look of frustration and began lifting his rifle in Amyla's direction. "For the sake of the gods, just go already."

"I did not agree to the deal by so-called 'Orangecloak'," Piotr exclaimed with a sneer. "Don't you go anywhere, miss."

"I agree to it," the second guard snapped back at Piotr. "I'm sure Higgins will too."

"This true, Higgins?" Piotr asked him flatly.

"It is, Piotr," Higgins replied quickly, with a sudden inflection of bravery. "You don't outrank us, but we outvote you. The other girl goes and we take Orangecloak."

Piotr looked at the ground in growing disgust, his expression remaining unchanged as he met Orangecloak's unwavering gaze. "Fine, you have to the count of ten or I change my mind."

"Are you sure about this?" Amyla asked Orangecloak plainly.

"Yes, now do as he says," Orangecloak responded rather firmly, holding Amyla's eyes with a stare that tried to convey her intentions.

Amyla took off running without another word, and Orangecloak listened to her darting through the trees, waiting until she could hear nothing else before returning her attention to the soldiers.

"I thank you for that mercy, gentlemen," Orangecloak managed to say before Piotr cut her off.

"Oh, shut up already," he snapped as he turned his rifle vertically and held it out toward Higgins. "Here, hold this while I tie her up. What do we got to bind her hands with?"

The second guard lowered his rifle enough to reach to his hip, where he produced a small coil of hempen rope that he held out to Piotr. "We're all required to have at least five feet of rope on us when in the wild. Where's your length?"

"Fuck off with the lecturing and give that here," Piotr said as he yanked the rope from the soldier's hand. "Keep your rifle trained on her, you bloody imbecile."

Piotr approached at a quick stride, keeping that pace until he was within a metre of Orangecloak. He slowed suddenly, and a sickly strange look came over his face. "I just had an idea, lads."

"No one gives a shit about any cockamamie ideas you have. Just tie her up, already," Higgins moaned while lifting the rifles and driving the butts into the ground in an angry, simultaneous stomp.

A laugh escaped Piotr and he turned to face his comrades. "Hear me out, here, lads. This is a once in a lifetime opportunity that we have been presented with. If this here really is Orangecloak, and you both seem to think that she is…"

"What are you on about?" the second guard asked warily.

"If this fine creature is indeed Orangecloak," Piotr said while gesturing up and down her frame. "Then she's the most infamous woman in Illiastra, and we three have her all to ourselves in the middle of the Daol Forest, with no one to see."

"Oh, come on, I'm not doing that," Higgins protested loudly.

"Fine then, that's more of her for me," Piotr snickered, jabbing a finger at the unnamed man. "What about you? You have to be hard up for a bit. Weren't you telling us that you haven't seen your wife since winter started?"

"You said it yourself: I'm married," the second guard resisted. "I'm having no part in another woman."

Piotr shrugged uncaringly and turned back to Orangecloak. "Suit yourself, but I think I'm gonna get me a little taste of ginger before we turn her over."

It turns out that Piotr is entirely irredeemable after all. That puts my mind at ease.

Piotr turned back to Orangecloak, and for the first time, she took notice of his features.

Tall, dark of hair, with about a week's worth of unshaven stubble. That sure is a bulbous nose, and those teeth are surprisingly white, except for that missing one, of course. His face needs a thorough washing to get rid of those pimples. I suppose that if he still has so many of them he's likely not very old, at least not older than I am.

Piotr reached out and touched a gloved hand against Orangecloak's face, brushing away a loose strand of her red hair that had fallen there. "I'll be gentle… At first."

That's quite enough of that.

With Piotr's body to serve as a screen between her and the one soldier with a raised rifle, Orangecloak knew that this moment was her one chance to turn the tide.

The fingers on his right hand slid down her face along her jawline, until they came to a stop at her chin. His body drew in tight, and the left hand began to run along her right arm, encouraging her to lower it. "There you go," he whispered as he leaned in close, "You can have a little fun too. After all, I hear you Southlands girls love it rough."

Orangecloak let her right hand continue to drop, until it was at her side. She bent inward and reached for the small of her back, feeling the thong on the short scabbard resting there pop open at her tug.

As her hand returned before her, Orangecloak pressed the live steel against Piotr's manhood, but outside of a tangible flinch, he otherwise remained unmoving. "Wait now, what's that?"

"That is a blacksteel dwarven dagger that can cut through flesh like hot butter," Orangecloak whispered in his ear, her left hand working its way up his arm until it could wrap about his right wrist. "If you yell, I make a single slice and you bleed out in seconds like the pig you are."

"What do you want me to do, then?" he asked desperately.

"Just keep talking, but make no sudden movements," she told him reassuringly. "You're doing fine. Just keep talking like that and I'll be gentle...At first."

He let out what sounded like a snarl in her ear and Orangecloak continued talking. "It doesn't feel so good when the balance of power tilts the other way, does it? I bet I am not the first you have tried to hold sway over. This is how it feels for them, you know. Utterly powerless and at the mercy of a stranger that you already know wants to do terribly by you. Can you think of a worse feeling? Anyone else that you have done this to probably couldn't."

"What are you two getting on with over there?" Higgins asked in a whine. "Either do what you're going to do or tie her up already. We're losing daylight and none of us know these woods all that well."

"Tell him that you are 'working up to it' and throw in a vulgarity or two for authenticity," Orangecloak instructed Piotr.

"I'm working up to it, you blithering idiot," he called back to Higgins.

From behind Piotr, there came what sounded to Orangecloak like someone punching a burlap sack of flour, followed by the unnamed man gasping in pain.

"What was that?" Higgins shouted, and Orangecloak could see him throwing Piotr's rifle down so that he could lift his own. "Oh gods, he's been shot with an arrow, he's bleeding everywhere."

"Help me! Please, help me!" the soldier on the ground cried out.

"Oh gods, oh gods, stay calm, mate," Higgins replied frantically. "Who's that coming through the woods? Identify yourselves at once."

Piotr tried to jerk in Orangecloak's grip, but she held him tight and refreshed the positioning of the dagger to remind him of it, warning him as she did as much. "Just stay perfectly still."

"You lying bitch, it was never just you and the other girl, was it?" Piotr scowled in her ear.

"You never asked if it was," Orangecloak reminded him, allowing a sly tone to edge its way into her voice. "Now is not the time for that, though. You need to remember what I *did* tell you. If you so recall, most recently I told you not to move."

Orangecloak relayed her information while pulling down on the arm that she held tightly, digging her fingers into the veins and brittle bones around the limb. He went with the pain, as she hoped he would, until his face was at a level with hers. "Just stay calm, look at me, and all will be fine."

She lowered the dagger from where it sat against his thigh, and brought it up and away from his body, until she was sure that he could no longer feel the blade anywhere on him.

Higgins screamed in the background, but neither Orangecloak nor Piotr dared move from their ugly embrace.

There will be no turning back from this, Orangecloak realised as she raised the blade to a level with his throat.

She slashed from left to right and Piotr let out a stifled grunt, followed by a gurgling noise. Though his mouth opened, his words stalled in his throat and he gagged on a bloody stream.

As Piotr's weight began to fall atop her, Orangecloak rolled him sideways, and fell atop him as he came to land on his back in the grass and snow. She held tight to her blade, and grabbed his hands as best as she could to keep them from thrashing at her.

"It will all be over soon and all will be fine, I promise," Orangecloak cooed gently, her hands growing slick and wet as they struggled to restrain his flailing limbs. His throat oozed red, and what could not squeeze through the gash she created with the dagger came bubbling out of his mouth. Little by little, his strength began to ebb, until there was no struggle left in him.

Orangecloak climbed off Piotr and spun about, looking for the other two bluecoats. She turned and nearly collided with Tryst, who had come rushing in her direction.

"Are you alright, Orangecloak? You're covered in blood," Tryst asked her worriedly. "Athel is coming, if you need medical attention."

"This is not my blood, I assure you," she said with a sigh. "I think I am fine, physically. Where are the other two bluecoats?"

Tryst turned away from her and gestured with an open hand to where the unnamed one was lying as still as Piotr on the ground. As Orangecloak looked at him in the dying light of the day, she saw his hands wrapped tightly around an arrow shaft protruding from the left side of his chest.

"Please, I yield, I yield!" Higgins bawled nearby from where he wriggled on the ground beneath the massive frame of Yak. "Lady Orangecloak, please, call off your demon! I beg you!"

"That's no demon, just an awfully large man who will end you if I ask him to," Orangecloak corrected him, her eyes being drawn to the forms of Yahmina, Amyla, Merith, and Athel emerging from the trees. "Thank you, Amyla. That was excellently done of you."

Though she was out of breath, Amyla tried to explain herself, "I came across Yahmina on the way back to camp and told her what was happening. The others were already there when I got back, and we all came running to help."

"Are you hurt?" Athel asked as he drew close to her.

Orangecloak shook her head. "I am fine physically, as they did no damage, and this is not my blood. But I would like to wash it off straight away."

"What do you want me to do with this one, Orangecloak?" Yak asked while still holding Higgins down.

"Tie his hands and we'll bring him with us," Orangecloak decided on a whim. "They had a small coil of rope with them that should do fine. Merith, Amyla, help Yak bind our new friend Higgins."

She looked to Yahmina, holding her bow at her waist with a fresh arrow nocked and ready. "I owe you a great deal of thanks. I was not sure how much longer I could have held out there. The other two soldiers were getting nervous with the position I had their friend in, and I was sure they were going to find out what had transpired."

"What did transpire?" Yahmina asked in her usual, monotone manner. "I came upon you to see one soldier standing in tight over you with his two friends keeping watch."

"I'll explain later," Orangecloak said while wiping clean and sheathing her knife. "Let's gather our things and get going right away. I'm calling a march through the night. We need to be well away from here and quickly. With all the racket that those three made, more soldiers will come looking, and once they find the bodies of those two, this forest will be crawling with reinforcements. Come on, everyone, we have to hurry."

Tryst was in next to Orangecloak then, drawing her away for a side conversation while the others went to work. "Orangecloak, did you do to that soldier what I think you did?"

It hit her for the first time just what had happened and she felt herself recoil at the thought of it. "I suppose so."

"How do you feel?" he asked while rubbing her arm gently.

"Terrible," she answered him in a word. "He was terrible too, but I feel the same for what I did to him."

"That's good, Orangecloak. It's perfectly normal to feel that way," Tryst explained in a soothing voice. "I'm right here if you need to talk about it, alright? You're not alone, but you already know that. You're in the company of Yak, Yahmina, and me now."

Yahmina had put her bow away and had gone to a knee so that she could pull the arrow from the chest of the soldier she felled. Their eyes met, and Orangecloak saw the elven woman give her a nod in the dimming light of the evening.

Orangecloak glanced to where Piotr's body lay on the ground. His throat, face, hands, and the ground around him had become a crimson mess. A wave of revulsion came over her and she staggered as everything began to spin. The contents of her stomach came hurtling forth, and her knees buckled beneath her as the realisation hit her.

I just killed someone.

Introducing *The Gold & Steel Saga* Team

Editing Staff:

Kyra Shields
Stacey Smith
Erin Vance (early chapters)

Beta Readers:

Nathan Baker
Catherine Dowden
Stephanie Spurrell

Art Department:

Christina Hamlyn – Cover layout
Rebecca of atrtinkcovers.com – Cover artwork
Sarah O'Rourke-Whelan – Map artwork

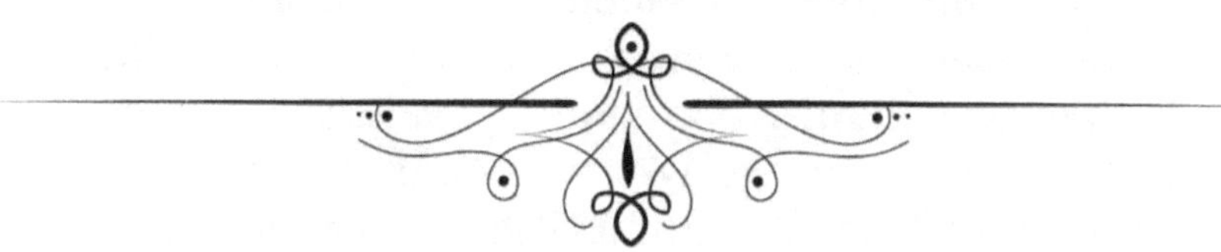

There is more yet to come in ***The Gold & Steel Saga***.

For book seller listings and to stay up to date on all things
Gold & Steel, head on over to:
www.thegoldandsteelsaga.com.

Check the site regularly to ensure that you will be the first to know
when volume III,
The Strength of Steel, will be available.

For more **Gold & Steel** adventures, look for
Legends & Tales, Christopher Walsh's short story collections.

To my readers,

Between *As Fierce as Steel* and *The Worth of Gold* you might have noticed that Marigold appeared infrequently in the first, while Serephanie appeared only in name. Meanwhile in volume II, both Orangecloak and Ellarie received only epilogue chapters and Tryst, while appearing in Orangecloak's chapter, had no chapters from his perspective at all. Initially, there was a reason for this.

From the time of *As Fierce as Steel*'s initial plotting until the first publication, it had been my intent to keep certain characters split between instalments as we have seen in the past two titles. Ellarie, Orangecloak, and Tryst were the characters whose perspectives were to be told in the books with Steel in the title. Conversely, Marigold, Freyard, Serephanie, and Syrie were to have their stories shown in books with Gold in the title. Thus, both sides were to bring together the overall *Gold & Steel Saga* in their two separate parts.

It was after publishing the first book and embarking on writing the second that I realised just how much real time could potentially lapse between such large volumes. For context, I released *As Fierce as Steel* in late March of 2016 and *The Worth of Gold* is only now seeing the light of day in early August of 2020. That's over four years between books. Between these books, I was not a full time writer. Perhaps before the series ends I will be, and I truly hope I am. However, based on present realities, it seems that three to four years might be the most reasonable timeframe for me to release each of the remaining five instalments. With that in mind, I decided that it was not reasonable to expect readers to have to wait potentially six to eight years for only half of the point-of-view characters' stories at a time. By now, you've probably guessed where I'm going with this, and yes, it means that as of *The Strength of Steel*, all the point-of-view characters will be appearing side-by-side in each instalment.

On behalf of the *Gold & Steel* team,
Thank you for reading and supporting *Gold & Steel*,
Christopher Walsh

About the Author

Christopher Walsh hails from the Southern Shore on the Avalon Peninsula of Newfoundland and Labrador, Canada, where he lives with the love of his life, Kyra. After spending several years travelling and living across Canada, he returned home to Newfoundland in 2011 and began creating the world of *Gold & Steel*. *As Fierce as Steel*, the inaugural entry in the series, was also his first foray into the published literary world.